I0766987

THE WORLD BELOW

VIVIENNE LEE FRASER

*I want to dedicate this entire series to the people who ignited the story
spark by sharing the characters they'd like to be in a fantasy story.
To Sandy, for the kick-ass girl hero who likes designer clothes;
Selina, for the sneak thief; and Serene, for the witch in the woods.
From those initial characters, a fantasy world grew
that kept me entertained for years.
Thank you for this amazing gift.*

**A special thank you to Leanne T.
Without your support, this special edition
would not have been possible.**

Vivienne Lee Fraser
www.viviennelfraser.com.au

Cataloguing-in-Publication details are available
from the National Library of Australia
www.trove.nla.gov.au
ISBN: 978-1-7637672-4-9 (paperback)
ISBN: 978-1-7637672-6-3 (hardcover)

Formatting and cover design by Kim Last, KILA Designs.

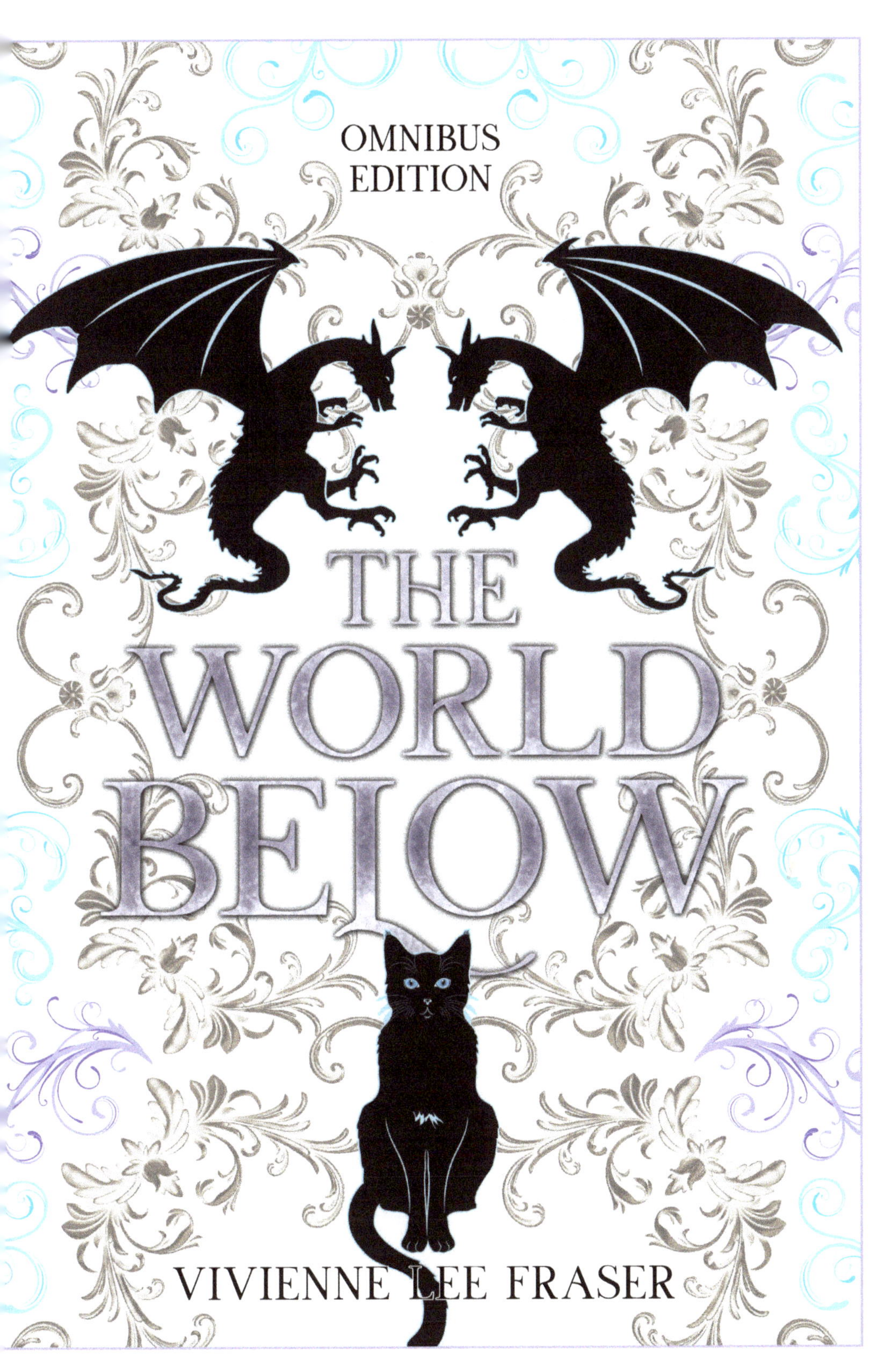

OMNIBUS
EDITION
THE
WORLD
BELOW
VIVIENNE LEE FRASER

World Above

Fairy Glen

Bodmin Moor

Lydford

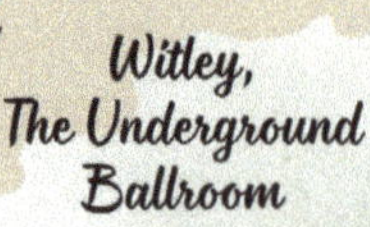

Witley,
The Underground
Ballroom

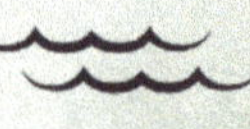

Skye
Loch Nessn
Inverness
The Unseelie Cour
London
Mawnan

World Below

World Between
Wyld Woods
Wizard Council
Melliores
Essendore
The Capitol
Avondale

BOOK
ONE
THE
WORLD
BELOW

THE WORLD BELOW

SHADOWS DARKEN THE dappled sunlight warming my body. I lazily roll onto my back and stretch, moving out of the boy's shadow to recapture the sun. My eyes droop closed, only to flick open as a bee gently lands on the flower by my nose. Ears twitching, I swipe and miss, scaring the annoying buzzy thing into going on its way.

I close my eyes and imagine I am on my sun-soaked cushion on the window seat. Buzzing by my ear ruins the illusion, and I am back in the noisy, busy street with the boy my mistress sent me to watch. I had argued with her, of course, but it didn't work. It never does. I replay the argument, wondering if would I still be here had I done something differently.

'All I want you to do is follow the boy, Snake, and report back to me each evening.'

'Must I?' I ask, not even bothering to open an eye.

'It is only for a couple of days. I promised his mother I would look out for him.'

Why don't you go do it, then? The thought pops into my mind, but I do not speak the words. Instead, I studiously lick my paw and rub it over my head, hoping she will take the hint.

'Come, my friend. I think you have become too comfortable by that fire.'

I ignore her.

'Please. I ask so little of you, and this is such a small thing.' Her fingers scratch behind my ear and I lean into her hand.

When the pleasure gets to be too much, I stand and stretch my back into an arch. 'Will I be home in time for dinner?'

'Perhaps.' She flicks her hand as if sweeping me outside, and I instantly find

myself on the front doorstep. 'Thank you,' I hear her voice say in my head.

After a couple of false starts, I had found the boy waiting outside a school—Edgington Elite Academy for Girls. He has been standing across the road, half hidden by a tree, for hours. We have been here for so long, I am beginning to wonder if his mother wanted him watched because he was likely to do something unseemly to one of the girls.

I lift a paw and check for dirt. I turn it this way and that, cleaning it with swift flicks of my tongue. Out of the corner of my eye, I see the boy tense. I pause and follow his gaze. He is interested in a group of girls chatting outside the gates. I can tell which one he is here for. Her essence shines so bright I cannot bear to look directly at her.

Her power is like a magnet attracting all my attention, and the boy is halfway down the street before I realise he's even moved. I rise to my feet, take one last swipe at the bee before creeping through the bushes lining the path as I follow the boy who follows the girl.

'COME ON, P. It's only afternoon tea to celebrate the end of school. You'll regret it if you don't come,' Agatha's voice rises above the others as I turn to head home.

'I've gotta go. Mum will make my life a misery if I miss tennis, especially as this is my last lesson.' I fling the words back over my shoulder as I keep walking, hating having to say them, hating that my parents have never allowed me the same freedoms my friends enjoy.

'You're eighteen, P—time to cut the apron strings,' Jeanna says with a sneer. She is one person I will not miss seeing after this week.

Still, she is right. I *am* eighteen, and after the summer holidays, I will begin university. I should be able to do what I want now, but a deal is a deal, and I did promise my parents I would toe the line until after our family holiday in a couple of weeks' time.

The early summer sun warms my arms through my blazer. I want to take it off, but there are still three more days of the school year—three more days I need to wear this horrid, old-fashioned uniform. Then one more week away with my parents—which adds up to ten more days until I can begin making my own decisions.

As I walk along the main road, traffic crawls past me, and I chant, 'No more tennis, no more karate, no more French, no more piano.' Okay, maybe I would still do karate, but piano was definitely going.

THE WORLD BELOW

I am so engrossed in my personal end-of-school celebration that I don't notice the hairs stand up on the back of my neck until a cold shiver down my spine finally gets my attention. I pause outside a bookshop, stretching out my awareness, trying to identify what is different.

I am used to watching out for attacks. I mean, I live in London, so it is part of keeping yourself safe in a large city. And this would not be the first time someone has followed me home.

Using the window, I search for the source of my unease. All I find is a black cat across the road. It idly flicks its tail before darting under a rose bush.

The hairs on my neck still warn me that danger is close by. It is not just my parents' constant reminders about the level of violence making me hyperaware. Someone is definitely following me. I glance over my shoulder as I straighten my straw boater, but I still see nothing out of the ordinary.

I warily continue on my journey, and when I am waiting at the crossing, I spot him. A male in jeans, a black Led Zeppelin T-shirt, and a hoodie has stopped at the bookshop. He appears normal enough, but there is something about him I can't quite place my finger on. When he glances surreptitiously in my direction, our eyes meet briefly and my nerves go on high alert; if I had hackles, they would be raised.

As the signal changes, I walk briskly across the road; no Edgington Academy girl would ever run in public. I take the first left and rush the half block to the right turn that will take me into my street.

I risk a quick glance behind. The man is just turning the corner. Now I run. I reach up to hold my hat in place, causing my backpack to bounce awkwardly against my back. I run until I reach the steps leading to my house.

As I climb I let go of my hat and reach round, fumbling in the pocket of my backpack to pull out my keys. My fingers behave like they belong to someone else. The keys slip from them and clatter to the ground. Bending to pick them up, I find myself staring into two green cat eyes.

Keeping the cat in my line of sight, I slowly straighten up. At the last minute, I break the connection and shove the key firmly into the lock just as my pursuer reaches the steps next door. The lock snicks, and I yank at the knob.

I fling the door closed, and it slams behind me with a bang. Leaning my back against the solid wood, I sag with relief. Then I tense. Mum hates the door being slammed. I wait for her to shout from wherever she is inside. The house is silent. That's odd.

I slip my school bag off my shoulder, and it drops to the floor. I pick it up again. Untidiness is frowned upon too. I drag myself up the stairs, listening to the sounds of the house so I can work out where Mum is.

Everything is eerily quiet. No one is home. Not even Susan, my used-to-be nanny, now sort-of housekeeper.

I drop my bag on the bedroom floor and throw my straw boater on the bed. Chewing my bottom lip, I try to remember when I last saw my parents. They had left for work before I got up for breakfast today, but that is normal. In the weeks leading up to a holiday, they often work longer hours.

Yesterday? No. I had gone round to Tanya's after school. By the time I got home, they were out somewhere, and I ate dinner with Susan and went up to bed.

Monday? Yes, I saw them early Monday morning. When I pulled the curtains, I had seen Mum opening the passenger door of the car, and watched as Dad leaned over to say something to her as she got in.

I wander along the hall to their bedroom and opened the door, scanning the room for anything that would tell me why Mum is not here. I skim my gaze over the huge bed to the right, past the two wingback chairs on either side of the window, and round to the doors of their dressing room and ensuite.

Their bedroom is immaculate, but then, it always is. As a child I wondered if they just kept this room for show, and they actually slept somewhere else. I had spent hours looking for their secret hideout, but had never found it.

Today I go left, open the door to the closet, and walk in. Mum never leaves home for any length of time without taking at least one case, and her luggage is sitting in its usual place. My brow draws into a frown. Only one pair of shoes is missing from the colour-coded shoe wall—the pair she had on when she left for work on Monday.

It is Wednesday today. Mum is always here on Wednesday to take me to my tennis lesson. I am capable of getting there myself, but Mum says she would never miss our mother-daughter time. I often tease her, saying she only comes because she fancies my coach.

I have no talent for tennis at all, but it is fun, and it is better than some of the other edifying things my parents have signed me up for over the years out of guilt because I am an only child and because they travel so often for work.

A quick check of my father's closet, with its rows of suits, shirts, and shoes, shows nothing that would indicate he has been called away either.

As I wonder what is going on here, a loud bang jolts my mind back to the present. It is the noise made when somebody forgets to hold onto the doorknob and it swings into the table behind.

'I shut the door,' I mutter as I speed along the hallway, stopping just before the landing. If I closed the door, then it would have locked automatically....

THE WORLD BELOW

I peek around the corner and check down the stairs. The front door is wide open, revealing a view of the terraced houses across the street.

It slammed shut. I heard it. How can it be open now?

On silent tiptoes I rush down the stairs and into the living room before screeching to a halt. Standing in the middle of the room is the man who followed me home. Up close he is younger than I had first thought, perhaps only around my own age.

I eye him warily. Standing more than a head taller than me, he is lean, but his loose hoodie makes him appear bulkier. As he takes a step towards me, his hand outstretched, I automatically begin assessing his weaknesses as I move into ready stance. I have learnt from experience that good looks and a friendly smile are no guarantee he will not attack me.

'Don't move. I'm a black belt in karate.' Okay, I'm almost a black belt, but he doesn't know that.

Standing still, he flicks shaggy brown hair out of sea green eyes and laughs as he raises his hands in the universal sign of surrender. 'Don't hurt me. I come in peace.'

'Who are you? Why are you following me? What are you doing in my house? Wait a minute…. How did you even get inside?' I add the last question as I remember the fancy burglar-proof lock on the door Dad is so proud of.

The guy's grin widens. 'Which one of those do you want me to answer first?'

Glaring at him, I'm opening my mouth to give him a piece of my mind when he says, 'Snake Fieth, at your service.' He lowers a hand towards me as if he wants me to shake it, but my hands turn in to fists, and he returns it to its original position.

'What sort of a name is Snake?' I snort.

'A better one than Priscilla Crown.'

He has me there. If there is a name worse than Priscilla, I would love to hear it.

'You may call me Pris.' The response is automatic.

'I thought your friends called you Princess P.'

Hold on. He knows my name and my nickname? Who is this guy? 'You're not a friend,' I spit at him.

He takes a step back and starts to lower his arms. 'Look, I don't have time for long introductions or—'

'Why? You got somewhere better to be?'

His eyes widen as if he is surprised by my question. 'Yes, of course.'

'Then why did you follow me? Why did you break into my house?' I narrow my eyes at him and try to look tougher than I feel. Blood is pounding in my ears, making it difficult to hear his answer.

'Because I thought your parents might be here, or that you could at least lead me to them.'

'Sorry? What? My Parents?' My eyes narrow even more. Does he know my parents aren't here? I eye him warily. 'Why do you want them?'

He ignores my questions, runs his hand through his hair, and glances around the room. There is something kind of desperate about him. 'They're not here, are they? I'm too late.'

My stomach tenses, and I frown, hoping the expression disguises the fear racing through my veins. 'What makes you think that?'

'Are they home?' His voice is barely more than a whisper.

'They're at work, but they should be home soon,' I bluster, but my voice is uncertain even to my own ears.

His arms drop all the way down and his shoulders slump. 'Really? I don't think they will be.'

He raises his head, and his green eyes rake over me as if they can somehow drag the truth from me. Finally, he says, 'I am too late. I had hoped because they were last on the list....'

'List? What list? What's going on here?' I take a step forward. What game is this guy playing?

'Your parents were taken by the…. You are not going to believe this… but there is no other way to say it. They were taken by the Bad Fairies.'

'Bad fairies?' I scoff. 'You mean bad fairies of the "it was the bad fairies" fame?'

He stares blankly at me.

'You know, like when you trip over something and your mum says, "That must have been the bad fairies."'

As I speak, my mind is whirring. I have a right one here. A real lunatic, and I'm alone in the house with him. I plot my escape route in case things get tricky, but I still think I can take him, unless he is on drugs or something—which is a definite possibility given the way he is acting.

Snake glares at me. 'No, not those ones. Well, yes, sort of those ones. They are like the police for creatures like us.' He chuckles, 'I guess they would more correctly be named Fairies for the Bad.'

He is speaking gibberish. This is worse than I thought.

I toss my plait over my shoulder and attempt to placate him. 'Creatures? That's not a nice way to speak of anyone. Do you need one of my parents to help you with something?'

My mother is a human rights lawyer, and my father is the Chief Exec of Homeless London. They deal with some troublesome clients, they talk about them all the time, but this is the first one who has come to our home.

Snake shakes his head, and those lovely eyes look at me with disbelief. He turns and picks a backpack up off the floor.

'Wait, where are you going?'

I can't let him leave if he needs help—that is not what our family does. Besides, he might be crazy as all hell, but he worked out that my parents aren't home, and he believes they have been taken somewhere. And whether I like to admit it or not, I'm worried—quite worried.

I mean, I can go days without seeing my parents when they are on a work trip. But they usually tell me where they are going and when they will be back. And their wardrobes appear not to have been touched since Monday.

He stops but doesn't turn around. 'I thought you knew,' he whispers, and I am not quite certain I hear him correctly. 'I can't be doing this,' he says, louder this time.

'Doing what?'

He turns to face me. 'I can't be teaching you about our world. I need to focus on stopping this nightmare'

'I am sure my parents can help, if you would just wait until—'

'They… are… not… coming… home.' He forces the words through gritted teeth. 'If you want to see them again, you need to come with me.'

The more the intruder talks, the more my stomach churns, and I begin to wonder if something really has happened to Mum and Dad. I am now torn between not letting on that I know my parents won't walk through the door any moment now and asking him what he knows about where they are.

In less than a blink of an eye, he is by my side, grabbing my arm and pulling me towards the door.

I don't think. I just react. I twist my arm to break his grip and sweep my leg to throw him off balance. Next thing he is on the floor, and I am on top of him, my knees pinning his biceps.

I LOOK UP into piercing blue eyes that are common in her kind but are all the more startling with her olive skin. She is quick—quicker than I expected—and that is saying something because I am no stranger to creatures with enhanced speed. Through half-closed eyes, I assess her, wondering what abilities she has and how they might help us.

'Don't look at me like that,' she hisses.

I start, then frown. 'Like what?'

'Like you've just been served a delicious dessert.'

I grin. I can't help it. I know it will only make her angrier, but she just described the trickle of sensation forming in the recesses of my mind. It is buried beneath the fear and worry that have been my constant companions for the last couple of days, but it is there all the same.

My smile fades as she presses her boney knees more firmly into my arms. I gasp and grimace. I can probably push her off me, but I just broke into her house, and I want her help. So if this is what it takes for her to be comfortable around me, I'm okay with that. Besides, if she feels any more threatened, she may break something, and I need everything in working order for what is to come.

When she has my attention, she speaks slowly and clearly. 'My parents aren't lost. They are away for a couple of days, and will be back on the weekend.'

I study her face for telltale signs of a lie. Their names were on the list. I saw them when I snuck it out of the fairy's pocket.

Had they disappeared to evade capture? It was possible. Still, they will not be returning. The Bad Fairies always get their creature.

Calling on the voice I use to make a good impression on adults, I say, 'I think you'll find that if they have not been taken yet, they soon will be. Once they are, I can help you find them.'

Her lips press firmly together. I have not managed to convince her… yet.

My hands are starting to go numb. I wiggle my fingers and say, 'If we can just go and sit down—' I nod towards the sofa, hoping she will take the hint. '—perhaps we can talk this out.'

'Who *are* you? And why do you believe my parents are lost?' She leans forward, pinning me with an intense gaze. 'And why are you so sure you can help me find them?'

I need to try something different or I could lose my hand. 'When did you last speak to your parents?'

Her eyebrows twist into a frown, and she appears a little less certain. 'I remember seeing them on Monday morning…. What's it to you?'

'Two days ago?' I'm surprised. 'They were taken that early?'

Her head tilts to the side as she peers at me, making her appear a little less threatening. Perhaps I should push her a bit harder now. 'I think I may be able to find them, but it would be better if one of your kind is with me.'

She instantly tenses, and I lose any ground I made with her. 'What do you mean one of my kind? How does being Black make a difference?'

I can't help it—a laugh escapes, and I try to swallow it, but I can't. I splutter, 'Not being Black—being an elf. Having an elf with me will open doors I can't even knock on.'

That look she had before comes back over her face, the one that tells me she thinks I'm stark raving mad.

The pressure on my arms increases. 'Can I call someone for you? Someone you trust who can come and pick you up?'

Then it dawns on me. 'You have no idea what I'm talking about, do you?' Confusion takes over her face for a moment before she schools it back in to reflect professional concern.

'How can it be possible that you don't know who you are?' This is going to be way harder than I thought if she doesn't even know she has elf blood running through her veins.

She takes a deep breath. 'You clearly believe what you are saying—that I'm an elf, and that. So, what does that make you?'

From the tone of her voice, I sense she is placating me. Still, I tell her the truth. 'I'm a gnome.'

'A gnome?' She laughs, and it comes from deep in her belly. 'I thought gnomes were short and round, and elves were tall and graceful. You're taller than me, and where are my pointy ears?'

She must have had training on how to handle the crazy. She is pointing out what she believes to be the flaws in my logic, hoping to bring me back to reality. If only she knew. I sigh. I can't help it. Why am I the one telling her what all creatures learn before they can walk?

'Every creature knows that in the human world we take human form. It is only when we are in the World Below that we can be who we truly are.'

'Is that some sort of law or something?' She sneers at me.

'Yes, actually, it is. Before 1832, when we withdrew from the World Above almost completely, many of our kind would appear as we are, but equally as many took on human form. Then, when we began setting up ministries in the 1890s to ensure balance was maintained between the worlds, we appeared as humans to disguise our presence. It has been that way ever since.'

'You make it sound so plausible, almost like a history lesson,' she says, easing the pressure on my arms a little.

I open my mouth to tell her that it is history, our history, but she carries on before I can even form the first word. 'Okay. If you're a gnome, can you do magic?'

I snort. 'Of course. How do you think I opened your door?'

She glares. 'You must have picked the locks.'

'Too hard to pick. Easier to persuade them to open for me,' I tell her, and I can't help but smirk as I answer. I actually did pick them because I am not meant to use magic except on official business.

Her face is still set in disbelief mode. I lie still and resist the urge to say anything. She doesn't speak for a while, and I think perhaps she's processing. My blood begins to flow again and my fingers prickle with pins and needles.

She gnaws on her lip as she contemplates me a bit longer. 'All right. Let's say I believe you, that we are both mystical creatures. Why were you following me, and why are you so certain someone took my parents?'

Ah, finally, a step in the right direction. I put on my most charming smile as I answer. 'I've been following you because I was unable to find your parents at work. I thought you might be able to lead me to them.'

She nods a couple of times. 'And what made you think my parents would be taken by these… um… Bad Fairies?' She says the words as if she cannot believe they are coming out of her mouth.

'As I said, I snuck a look at the list the Bad Fairy who took my mother had in his pocket. Your parents' names were on it. In fact, they were the only other names.'

She froze. 'Your mother's been taken?'

Okay, not quite the response I was expecting, but maybe telling her about Mum will convince her I'm not a lunatic.

'Yes, on Monday afternoon. Fortunately, I was home to see what happened. I tried to talk the Bad Fairies out of taking her. When I couldn't, I distracted one of the officers, lifted the warrant from his pocket, and discovered that your parents' names were there as well. I hoped with their being more powerful, they might be able to help my mother.'

The expression on her face is more quizzical than worried, and she is no longer glaring at me. I can tell she is not convinced the fairies took her parents, but she seems more open to what I'm saying now and less defensive.

'I believe my parents are missing. I'm not saying I buy into your Harry Potter worldview, but if we put that aside, where would you suggest we start looking for them… and your mother?'

'We need to go visit the Witch in the Woods. She helps London creatures who are in trouble.'

Pris's face freezes, and I wish I could take my words back.

'You almost had me believing you—'

'Look, you don't need to believe she is a witch or anything. But she is a friend of my mother's, and she will probably know where our parents are… or at least be able to tell us where to start searching for them.'

She gnaws on her lip again. I can't tell whether she is assessing me or considering her options. 'Okay. Where do we find this woman?'

'In Wimbledon. We can take the tube and be back here by dinnertime.'

Pris runs a hand over her hair. Dare I hope she is actually considering going with me?

'What will you lose if you come along? An evening of your time?' I encourage her. 'And it's not like you're in any physical danger. You've already proven you can take me down if you want to.'

I CAN'T BELIEVE I'm actually considering going to Wimbledon with this lunatic. I glance down at him. He's very relaxed even though his arms must be aching. A brief flicker of fear in his dark green eyes is quickly hidden, telling me his confidence is a mask. Is he afraid of me? Or afraid I won't help him?

I narrow my eyes as I study his face, but I quickly school my features, not wanting to let him know what is going on inside my head. I'm obviously not going to tennis lessons today—no great loss. And then there is the undeniable fact that something odd is going on with my parents.

I don't believe in his magic malarkey, but on the off chance his friend in Wimbledon might be able to give me some information about where my parents are, I should go with him. Besides, if he is in trouble and he believes I can help, it would be the right thing to do.

My right thigh begins to cramp, and I ease the pressure off Snake's arms. As I move, a thought pops into my head.

'If someone took our parents, we should go to the police.'

Snake snorts, and I mean actually snorts! And not for the first time. Who does that?

'You're kidding, right? We're going to go to the police and tell them our parents have been taken by creatures from another world—creatures from fairy tales.'

A wave of anger washes through me. 'If you truly want to rescue your mother, surely you're prepared to drop this charade for long enough to talk to the police.' I dig my right knee in a little for extra emphasis.

Snake closes his eyes. Maybe I really hurt his feelings this time. He takes a deep breath and expels the air slowly before opening them and looking back up at me. 'There's a reason why we're not allowed to show ourselves.'

'Why?' I ask, barely keeping the contempt from my voice.

'Because people no longer believe in us. They banished creatures to the realm of fairy stories a long time ago. Even if we wanted to come clean, no one would listen. I mean, you're one of us and you don't believe me.'

He's right; I don't believe him. But he's obviously invested in this alternate world. Perhaps it's his way of dealing with the loss of his mum, or stress, or something.

'Besides, humans can't go where our parents have been taken. Not without being invited.'

His voice is calm, and he sounds rational. He makes me want to believe him, but he is talking utter rubbish. I decide to test his commitment to this other world idea.

'Won't we need to "pay a cost" as well?' I ask, remembering the tales I read as a child which always told of magical creatures demanding payment.

'Perhaps, but I am sure we will be more than up to the challenge.'

I can't stop the frown this time. 'Do you actually have a plan for our parents' rescue?'

He smiles a crooked smile. He's quite good-looking when he's not acting crazy. I am suddenly very aware of the fact that I am straddling him, and parts of my body are thinking some very inconvenient thoughts. I should move, but I am reluctant to give up my advantage until I am certain of him.

'Not a plan as such.' His shoulders shift in something of a shrug. 'I guess we could always beg.'

My astonishment must be written on my face, because he bursts out laughing, and I knew I had been got.

'Actually, I thought that once we talk to the Witch of the Woods, we will be in a better position to plan our next move.'

Sounds logical, I think, but I am still skeptical. 'How can you be so sure this… woman will help us?'

'She's helped Mum in the past, and I'm hoping she still thinks kindly of her in spite of what has happened.'

Those alarm bells go off in my head again. 'What exactly did your mother do, Snake?' I silently add, *She didn't murder someone, did she?*

Snake lowers his eyes. 'She and your parents have been accused of the heinous crime of profiting from magic in The World Above.'

I can't have heard him properly. 'Profiting from magic?'

A blush creeps up from Snake's neck and over to his cheeks. 'Creatures who live in the human realm are here to help the people of the World Above, and to maintain the balance between worlds. We agree to live as humans do and must only use our special abilities when assigned a task.'

I nod for him to go on, hoping that amidst the mystical explanation, I will be able to figure out exactly what his mother, and therefore my parents, are actually accused of.

'We gnomes are—'

'Good at digging underground?' I offer, *Lord of the Rings* springing into my mind. 'Or are you more like garden gnomes?'

Snake snorts again. 'Garden centres have a lot to answer for, and it's dwarves who dig underground in Tolkien's book,' he says under his breath. Then carries on as if I hadn't said anything at all.

'We gnomes are skilled at finding and taking things. My family was tasked with tracking misplaced magical items and returning them to their true owners. In particular, my parents retrieved magic artefacts so they could be returned to the World Below.'

'Is your explanation going to take long?' I ask. I'm tired of all the magic nonsense, and my leg is cramping again.

'You could let me up and we could finish this in comfort,' he offers.

I chew my bottom lip.

'I promise you on my mother's life, I will do you no harm.'

His voice is encouraging and sincere. I hate to admit it, but I am no longer afraid of him. Besides, as he pointed out, I've already proved I can deal with him if he gets out of line.

I rock back on my heels, stand, and stretch. I then sit back on the floor, cross my legs, and face him.

Snake looks at me questioningly. I nod, and he sits up, crossing his own legs to mirror me, arms resting loosely on his knees.

'When my father returned below, my mother was unable to take on some of the bigger jobs, so our income was barely enough to pay the bills.' Snake glanced around the ostentatious living room, and I imagine he is thinking I have never experienced what it is like to live hand-to-mouth, and he is right, but I can imagine.

'That must have been hard,' I say, urging him on.

'I tried to help out, but with school I could only work on the weekends. There just never seemed to be enough to make ends meet. Mum began stealing food and little things that I needed for school. None of it amounted to much, but, apart from it being illegal here, it's a big no-no using our powers to steal for our own benefit in the human world.'

Snake colours again, as if he is ashamed of what his mother did. I say nothing, hoping he will tell me more. My patience is rewarded.

'It is one of the unbreakable rules we all agree to follow when we live here. It was a long time ago, though, and she paid for her transgression. I don't understand why this is being brought up again now.'

'Why didn't you and your mother return to the other world with your father?'

The boy frowns. 'Why do you want to know that?'

I almost blurt out, 'I want to make sure you're not completely crazy,' but I don't want to make him angry.

'I just want to… know why your father isn't helping your mother now.'

He nods slowly, as if he can now understand my curiosity. 'Mum didn't share all the details with me. All I know is, Dad just disappeared without a word, and I suspect her pride kept her from running after him.'

His voice cracks a little as he says this, and a niggle of guilt for doubting him tugs at me. I'm also angry. His father should not be let off the hook that easily.

'Didn't your father have to look after you? Like here in the human world where fathers pay towards the keep of their children?'

'Of course, but we don't need anything from him. I have been able to help out more recently, so I thought we were doing better, but maybe we weren't. If she did do something wrong again, she did it for me, and… I can't let her be punished for it.'

A tear slides down Snake's face, and I catch my hand reaching out towards him. I snatch it back before he notices.

'Surely your gnome friends in the human world know what's going on and will help your mother,' I suggest.

'As if! They might decide not to help at all because if my mother is found guilty of breaking this law, my father's family will be brought into disrepute. They will have to tread carefully to ensure this doesn't happen. So, it's up to me to rescue my mother, and I will do whatever it takes—whether you're with me or not.'

His expression hardens and all signs of vulnerability are gone. His support of his mother touches me more than anything else he has said, and I want to help him find her.

More importantly, though, Snake's concern has raised my anxiety levels. If his mother has done something wrong and my parents are somehow tangled up in it, they could be in serious trouble too.

I stand. 'Wait here. I'm going to change.'

'You mean right here?' he asks cheekily.

I smirk, and my cheeks warm. 'No, you can wait in the hall or take a seat. I won't be long.'

I take the stairs two at a time and rush into my bedroom, almost tripping over my bag. I walk to my closet and stop. What do you wear when going to visit a witch? Something similar to what Snake is wearing? No, I can't do the scruffy look. I grab a denim jacket, my favourite white T-shirt with the stylised cat on the front, and my purple skinny jeans.

I look down at my feet. High-tops? No. I pick up my white Mollini trainers with the leopard trim—perfect. Once I'm dressed, I pull my unruly hair into a messy ponytail and run some lip gloss over my lips, then rub it off; it's not like this is a date or anything.

Grabbing my wallet, I check to make sure my Oyster card and my platinum Visa—only to be used in emergencies—are safely inside. I shove it, along with my phone and keys, into my favourite Coach shoulder bag. I am ready to face anything.

When I return, Snake is sitting on the second step from the bottom, elbows on his knees, shoulders slumped, head resting in his hands. For all his confidence before, he actually looks lost, almost forlorn.

He needs help. I tell myself I am doing the right thing. Plastering a smile on my face, I say, 'Come on. If we're going to do this, we'd better hurry. I must be home in time for dinner.'

THE WITCH OF WIMBLEDON

I MANAGE TO hide myself away from prying eyes under a bush. I wait patiently in the garden across the road from the house the boy broke into. He has some skills—I will give him that. The afternoon sun warms me, and I'd like nothing better than to sleep, but I must remain vigilant.

He went inside a while ago. Perhaps he is not planning to come back out. Should I go home and report? No, my mistress will want me to find out what his next move is. I glare at the house. I suppose I could make it up to a windowsill. I might be able to find out what is going on if I choose the right room.

A bird twitters nearby, and I rest my head on my paws. It is so warm here. Maybe I will wait a little longer, until the sun goes down.

Just as I settle in for a long wait, the boy emerges with the girl following close behind. She closes the door and puts the keys in her bag before heading off along the street.

Sighing, I stretch. I have no option but to follow. My stomach grumbles as I creep through the bushes conveniently placed in front of the houses. I hope they won't be long. I want to return to my place by the fire and let my mistress reward me with some tasty morsels of food.

Keeping to the shadows, I trail along the street behind them, hoping to overhear their plans. Then maybe I can simply meet them at their destination. They tell me nothing, and I endure listening to that girl ask *the* most stupid questions. How can one who shines so brightly be so ignorant?

'If you're a gnome, and you're not like the garden variety, where do you fit in, say, compared to me?' she asks.

The boy answers her more patiently than I would. I mean, she is clearly an elf, perhaps from the Unseelie court in the north. She should know all about this stuff. I flick my tail in frustration.

'Gnomes are quick of hand and of mind. We love puzzles. In general, we are bound in service to elves, but some of us, like my family, become…. Well, I guess you could call us detectives.'

I mean, honestly, everyone knows gnomes are simply lesser elves—well everyone who matters.

'If there are others like you in London, how can you tell if someone is one of them?'

I groan out loud, and she turns at the noise as I dart behind a car. I must be more careful.

'Our magic causes a glow if we do not know how to contain it. If you watch people carefully, occasionally you can see a shimmer that will tell you who they really are,' Snake explains.

The elf starts to stare intently at people passing by. When someone mutters, 'How Rude,' her gaze drops to the pavement.

'Perhaps you should be a little more subtle,' Snake chuckles.

Honestly, how can he put up with her? Mercifully, I am able to fall behind when increased foot traffic means I have to duck behind a fence, and I no longer have to listen to her inane prattle.

I finally find out what their plan is when we are almost in front of an underground station. They stop by the map outside and discuss their options.

'We're here, at Ladbroke Grove. If we head to Hammersmith and change to the District Line going to Earl's Court, then we can take a train to Wimbledon from there,' the girl says, and the boy nods his agreement.

Oh no, this is going to take a lot of energy. My tummy rumbles again. And on an empty stomach too!

I cast my spell and follow them through the tube station entrance, confident that now no one will see a black cat.

As I enter the nondescript Victorian brick building, I brush past a woman in a floral summer dress. She squeals and stumbles into a tall gentleman carrying a briefcase.

'Excuse me,' she says, turning bright pink.

'Not at all, my dear. These things happen in a busy station,' the man responds and almost steps on me. I jump out of the way. I do so dislike travelling like this.

I keep my eye on the boy and girl as they wend their way through the bustling station, heading for the turnstiles. I rush to catch them up.

A train pulls into the station as I reach the platform. I spot them just as the blips sound. Slipping into the carriage just as the doors close and quickly raising my tail to make sure it doesn't get caught, I find an out-of-the-way spot under a seat and sit down.

I stick close to the humans I'm following so that I know when to change trains. Finally, they find two seats together and sit. I don't let go of my spell though. It wouldn't do to let people see a cat travelling with them. Imagine the chaos!

Just as I am getting comfortable, the driver calls our stop, and we are on the move again. I sigh with relief when we leave the Underground and it is again all right for me to be seen.

I LOATHE TAKING commuter trains. They are always packed, you never find a seat, and the carriages reek of stale sweat. When we finally get out at Wimbledon, I heave a sigh of relief as I gulp in the fresh air.

As I follow Snake through the meandering paths of Wimbledon Common, I sneak a sideways glance at him. He hasn't spoken a word since we entered the Underground. His jaw is tense and though his hands are now shoved deep into his pockets, during the train trip they had fiddled incessantly with the cord of his hoodie.

He catches me looking at him and I turn away, suddenly interested in a group of dog walkers standing around chatting. I am so intent on avoiding looking at Snake, I forget to check my surroundings. Normally when I find myself in a new place, I scan the area for potential hiding places for attackers. This evening I am so off balance, I completely forget my father's training.

We are almost at the edge of the common when I realise my mistake. I catch a movement in the bushes, and I don't react immediately. This small hesitation is a mistake. I jump and am almost pulled off balance as a hand roughly grabs my arm, and moments later, I am held tight against my attacker's chest.

A sharp point sticks me around kidney height. I gulp back a gag as I am engulfed in the scent of cheap beer and cigarettes clinging to the fabric encasing the arm around my neck. I struggle briefly before muscle memory takes over.

I allow my body to go limp. A smile curls his lips, the only bit of his face I can make out under his hoodie, and I catch a glimpse of the knife as he raises it to strike. This is my cue to act. I twist out of his grasp, then use my momentum to swing back around and punch him in the jaw.

I don't stay to see the effects of my handiwork. Grabbing a hold of Snake's sweatshirt, I pull him into a run. Moments later, we are off the common and in relative safety on North View.

'What the hell was that?' he gasps when we finally slow to a walk.

'It's Wimbledon Common, so I guess it was a mugger,' I respond as I check behind to make sure we are not being followed.

He stops, and a few steps later I do too, turning to see what is delaying him. I find Snake staring at me as if I have gone bonkers.

'What?' I ask.

'A mugging? In broad daylight? When you are walking with someone?'

'Of course.' I shrug. 'What else could it be?'

His eyebrows shoot up. 'Does this happen to you often?'

'Probably only as often as it happens to other Londoners,' I respond.

'You don't think it has anything to do with who you are?' he asks, his brows forming a frown.

Who I am? I'm no longer exactly sure. Wanting to change the subject, I say, 'Where does the witch live? These houses must cost a bomb. I can't believe the residents are happy about a witch living on the common…. It's so close to their homes.'

Snake's frown deepens, and he doesn't answer for a moment. I am sure he is going to say something more about the attack, but then he relaxes, and I hope he has decided to let our previous conversation go. 'She doesn't live *on* the common.'

He begins walking again, checking off house numbers before turning into the drive of a three-story, semi-detached house. Taking the steps two at a time, he knocks firmly on the door.

I remain on the driveway, not wishing to waste energy climbing the six steps only to be turned away.

A boy of about four or five years old with a mop of curly black hair opens the door. He looks like he's stepped out of a Gap Kids catalogue, further confirmation that Snake must be out of his mind. Witches do not live in Victorian mansions on the edge of Wimbledon Common or dress their kids like that.

'Yes?' the boy asks as a black cat slips through the opening. The boy's eyes follow the animal as it disappears down the dimly lit corridor. 'Nan, someone is at the door for you,' he yells after it.

He leaves the door open and returns to whatever he was doing before we interrupted him. My mouth drops open in shock. Who leaves their door wide open with strangers on the doorstep in the middle of London?

Snake catches my eye and, as if he has read my mind, he says, 'I don't think anyone would dare enter this house without an invitation.'

I close my mouth and join Snake, trying to brush off the ominous undertone of his words. Moments later, a woman appears in the doorway. She is tall and graceful with long black hair caught in an untidy bun. She is obviously related to the boy, as they have the same piercing blue eyes.

I grab Snake's arm, an apology for disturbing the family this close to dinner ready on my lips. I pause when the woman's face breaks into a smile as she catches sight of Snake.

'Snake, finally,' she says pulling the door open wider. 'Come on in.'

She leads Snake along the hallway to the back of the house. As I follow, I catch glimpses of a dwelling tastefully decorated with what I assume are all original Victorian features. The woman raises her hand, and I jump at a bang behind me, and I half turn to find the door has closed by itself. A shiver runs up my spine. Was that magic or the wind?

The kitchen at the back of the house is bright and modern, and as I enter, the woman moves in behind a butcher block and begins chopping carrots.

'I expected you earlier, young Snake. You know you are always welcome here. Although, now that I see who you are with, I can understand why you delayed your visit. Having an elf on your side will make things a little easier for you.'

I stand in the doorway. This whole thing is surreal, and I can't quite get my head around it. 'You're a grandmother?' The thought pops into my head and out of my mouth before I can stop it.

The woman who Snake claims is the Witch of Wimbledon smiles at me. 'Yes, my dear—many times over. Carlos is just the youngest. He stays with me while his mum works in the health food shop on the High Street.'

She turns her attention back to Snake. 'You know you are welcome to stay here through this troubling time, but I sense you want something else from me.'

Snake shuffles his feet a bit, as if he is trying to make up his mind what to say. 'Ma'am, I was hoping your friendship with my mother means you might help me rescue her from The Court—and of course, Pris's parents too.'

The last bit about Mum and Dad was definitely an afterthought. I try not to mind too much. I mean, it is not as if I believe in any of this.

'I am sure that the last time we met, I told you to call me Eleanora.' Her piercing gaze swings round to me. 'They took your parents too. I can't say I'm surprised.'

I nod, unwilling to speak because I am not sure I've bought into all this other world stuff yet. Still, this woman is talking as if she knows my parents. Perhaps she is a part of whatever my parents are involved in, and she might be able to tell us where they have gone.

Eleanora cocks her head to the side and stares at me for a long moment before turning her attention back to Snake. I get the feeling I have been assessed and found wanting. I stiffen as anger at being so readily dismissed threatens to make me lose my cool.

'I expected you to come and ask for my help when I found out your mother was taken,' Eleanora says to Snake.

'Does that mean you will help us?' Snake's voice is so eager, it almost breaks my heart. Not waiting for an answer, he rushes on. 'I believe there are ways to wrangle an invite to The Court, I just don't know how. If you could set us on the right path, I'll do whatever it takes to attend and plead my mother's case.'

My jaw drops. I know I must look like a moron, but I can't help it. Snake is talking to this woman as if the subworld he talked about is real. At best, this urbane woman will laugh at his flight of fancy, and at worst she will throw us out. This last would be bad because she did offer to take Snake in, and he could do with somewhere to stay and get his head straight.

'And what about you, Priscilla?' I flinch at the use of my full name. 'Will you do whatever it takes to help your parents? Even if it means suspending your current beliefs and committing to attend spring court in the World Below?'

'I…. But surely….' I don't know what to say. She sounds like she believes this nonsense is real. Perhaps it's code for some sort of nefarious activity. Is someone listening in on our conversation? What are my parents mixed up in?

The woman's mouth curls with amusement. 'Yes, my dear, I do believe in all this stuff. I am a witch, as I am sure Snake already told you. He and his mother are indeed gnomes, and you are an elf.'

'But—'

'Perhaps if your parents spent more time with our community, they would not be appearing before The Court now. Then again, I must thank them because now Snake has a high-status elf to help him on the journey he must undertake.'

I am speechless, and that is something that doesn't happen often. The whole world has gone mad. The anger I have been holding in check bubbles inside of me, and flashes of red distort my vision. I glare at the elegant woman Snake told me would help us, annoyed I have wasted my time.

'You seriously expect me to believe my parents were abducted because they used magic for profit?' I sweep my hand around the room. 'Apart from the fact the very idea is absurd, we are no wealthier than you. Why weren't you taken too?'

Ice-cold blue eyes stare at me, and for a moment, I wonder if I have gone too far. All warmth has gone from Eleanora's voice as she says, 'My family and I have been working on the surface for centuries. One of my ancestors fell in love with and married a human. He left this house to her when he passed. We never, ever use our skills to gain from humankind, and it is the greatest insult for you to even hint at it.'

Eleanora's eyes pierce my soul, driving home her words. Even though my stomach is curdling, I meet her gaze unflinchingly.

GREAT. THE ONE person who can help us get to The Court and Pris has pissed her off. I must have been out of my mind to bring her here. I mean, sure, her elf blood will open doors, and she has as much of a stake in this as I do. On the other hand, she has shown she knows nothing about our world, and she just demonstrated how much of a liability that can be.

I insert myself between the two women, holding up my hands, palm outwards, and saying, 'I am sure Pris didn't mean any offence.'

Pris's sharp intake of breath makes me pause—just for a second though. Clearly, she doesn't like anyone speaking for her, but at the moment, her injured pride is the least of my worries.

'She doesn't know much about our ways, but she shouldn't be punished for her parents failing to teach her,' I finish.

Eleanora's shoulders relax a little. 'The Queen should never have let her parents choose this path,' she says, followed by, 'If it were not for Petunia….' She returns to chopping her vegetables, although the aggressive way her knife rises and falls has me wondering if she has actually let go of her anger.

From behind, I hear Pris mutter, 'Who's Petunia, and what has she got to do with this?'

I ignore her. 'I would appreciate your help getting to the Midnight Court,' I say, hoping to distract Eleanora and gain her support at the same time.

She vigorously chops a few more carrots. Her ferocity makes me think she is imagining Pris on the chopping board. Finally, the knife pauses, and she places it on the worktop. Wiping her hands on a towel, she says, 'All right. I guess I do not get to choose who comes to me for help or how they behave when they get here.'

Pris shuffles behind me, and I sense her moving to the side. I take a step, keeping myself between her and Eleanora. She does not realise the massive insult our hostess is choosing to overlook.

'A creature who is not a member can attend the Seelie Court if they receive an invitation from the Queen or if your attendance is endorsed by four senior members of The Court. Above ground, that means you must approach the senior creatures of four races and ask them to approve your attendance.'

It sounds too easy. There must be a catch. 'So, if you endorse us, then we only need to find three more,' I say, feeling Eleanora out.

She laughs. 'You of all creatures should know that nothing in our world is ever that easy. I may be a member of the Seelie court, but I am a minor representative. If you want the witches to endorse your entry, you must speak to the most senior of our kind in England. Only she can grant what you desire.'

'You're saying it can't be just any court member, but the most senior of each kind living in the human world?' I ask.

Eleanora nods, then adds, 'And they must be approached formally at the source of their power in the World Above.'

Damn it, this makes things more difficult. Instead of being able to approach their representatives in London, we must travel to find the creatures we need to speak with.

'Can you give us an idea of who is most likely to support our petition?' I ask, hoping to save some time by only calling on those most likely to help.

'I am sorry, Snake, but the witches gave me leave only to tell you how you might gain entry to The Court. If I help you directly, you may not be allowed in.'

'Can you at least tell me where and when The Court will be held?'

Sighing, Eleanora again wipes her hand on the towel and reaches into her pocket. Her hand emerges, clasping a piece of paper. 'You must solve this riddle to find The Court and to gain entry.'

I take the piece of paper and open it. I read the words and splutter, 'You're joking, aren't you? How are we supposed to decipher this?'

Pris moves behind me, and I turn so she can see the paper.

"When the old man's face looks down on earth, and two hands meet in the dead of night, the underwater ball begins.

"Pass the gatekeeper the token and the gold, heads up tails down, before speaking the word for that which needs our breath but cannot breathe to prove your worth."

'Two hands meet in the dead of night. That must be midnight. And the old man's face. That's what my dad calls a full moon,' she says.

I look to Eleanora to confirm Pris's guess, and although she is trying to remain impassive, a smile tugs at the corner of her mouth.

'That's amazing,' I tell Pris. 'If only the rest were that easy.'

'I'm sure that with a little time, we can work out the rest of the riddle,' Pris says.

My stomach clenches. 'If you're correct about the when bit, then there isn't much time for us to figure the rest out—the full moon is in seven days.'

I point at the calendar hanging on the fridge, then look at Eleanora. 'Is that right? We only have seven days to get four endorsements, solve the riddle, and make our way to wherever they are holding The Court?'

Sadness clouds Eleanora's eyes as she answers. 'As that is part of the riddle, I cannot answer your question. All I can say is, your knowledge of our law will help you.'

My knowledge of the law? My mind is spinning as I look at the paper again. Nothing is coming to me.

Fingers gently squeeze my arm, and a hand takes the riddle from me. 'We don't need to work this all out now. Why don't I put this somewhere safe, and we can figure it out later?'

I allow Pris to fold the paper and put it in her bag. I'm numb. In my mind, the Protector of London was going to invite us to The Court as her guest and all we would have to do is count down the days. This wild goose chase is completely unexpected. Then again, it was obvious if I stopped to think about it—nothing to do with the Seelie Court is ever that easy.

'I have done all I am able. With so little time for you to complete your quest, you had best be getting started.'

I slowly shake my head to clear my thoughts. Eleanora has done the best she can to help us under the circumstances. Remembering my manners, I say, 'Thank you, Eleanora. You have been a great help. And yes, we must get going now.'

Pris opens her mouth, and the cross set of her face tells me she is not thankful at all. I grab her shoulders and turn her around, bundling her through the door before she can say anything to anger Eleanora further. She may only be a second-tier member of the Seelie Court, but she is a powerful witch.

'Good luck to you both, and I hope to meet you again when The Court convenes,' Eleanora calls after us.

The door opens as we reach it, and I push Pris through before she can say what is on her mind.

As we walk back across the common, Pris turns angrily. 'How can you be so polite to her? She gave us a riddle and told us to seek out endorsements, which means she gave us very little.'

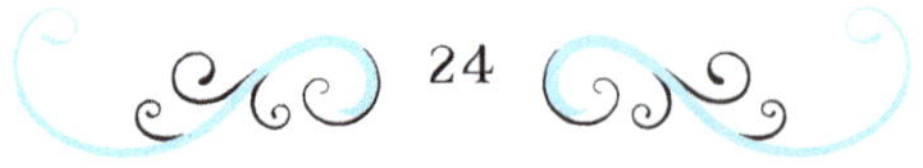

I stop and stare at the ground, wondering again why I had thought bringing Pris along was a good idea. Sure, as an elf she can go places I can't, but how helpful will she actually be if she doesn't know a thing about our world? I raise my head, ready to tell her I will continue on my own and do what I can to help her parents as well as my mother.

I can't say the words. My gaze follows the line of tears trailing down her cheeks, and I find my own fears and worries reflected in her face. She roughly brushes the tears away as I realise I can't leave her like this.

'Lesson one about the Seelie Court. Invitations are issued by the Elven Queen. Only those with invitations or a royal appointment can attend, and in some instances, they can invite another creature. I had hoped Eleanor might have made arrangements for me at least to attend with her.'

Pris opens her mouth to respond, but before she can say anything, I rush on. 'For some reason Eleanora was not given leave to invite us. Instead, she found a way for us to enter by ourselves… and that means she must have called in a lot of favours.'

Springs of black hair blow across her face. She pushes them away distractedly as she processes my words. Her anger slides away as quickly as it came, and a blush colours her cheeks.

'Oh my goodness, did she really go out on a limb for us? And I was so rude to her….'

I grin at her. 'Yes, you were. I would not be asking any favours of her for a while if I were you. And next time when you are talking to her, try and remember she could turn you into a toad with a thought.'

Laughter dances in her eyes as her smile lightens my heart. 'Okay, I'll try.' Her eyes suddenly go dark, and she says, 'All this is new to me, Snake—this other world you talk about. I am not sure I quite believe in it yet, and I certainly don't understand it.' She draws her bottom lip between her teeth. 'But I am trying, really, because I want to find my mum and dad.'

STANDING ON THE doorstep with my mistress, we watch Snake and the elf talking. In spite of her rudeness, I am still attracted to the girl's shining magic. Then again, that is always the way with elves. They are rude and entitled, but everyone is drawn to them.

'He has his hands full with that one,' my mistress says. 'And I am not sure whether she will be more of a hinderance or a help.'

Something moves in the bushes beside them, and my mistress stops speaking. I catch the flash of a knife, and my mistress mumbles something and points. There is a tingle of magic in the air, and the figure falls to the ground with the barest rustle of leaves.

'They are safe. He will sleep for a long, long while,' my mistress says before turning her attention back to the two figures. 'I wonder if they know the full extent of what they are up against.'

My stomach is full, and all I want to do is to go back into the lounge room and curl up in my basket over the radiator and sleep off my meal. I fear it will be a long time before I am allowed such luxury, as I can guess what is coming next.

My mistress pulls in some magic and casts a spell so we can speak.

'I promised Ginth that should anything happen to her, I would take care of Snake.'

'You have. You gave him a way to rescue his mother.'

She considers my words for a moment, and I allow a small flicker of hope to warm my gut. Then The Witch of Wimbledon sighs, extinguishing that flame.

'It is not enough, my lovely. Other forces are at play here. Someone wants to make sure the Crowns are no longer a part of The Court, and that someone must be powerful if they are prepared to take on royalty, however distant they are from the throne.'

'I thought we were helping Snake.' My tone is petulant, but I can't help it. I just want to go inside.

'Ginth being taken is obviously meant to sow seeds of disorder in the higher echelons of gnomes. Her husband's family are as close to the royal line as their kind can get.'

I say nothing. I don't think I am expected to. Eleanora is merely processing her thoughts out loud.

'What I cannot work out is whether someone is making a play for dominance here in the human world, or are they making a power play in the World Below. I fear these two young creatures may be in more danger than they realise.'

With her words my fate is sealed.

'My lovely, I hate to ask this of you, but I need you to stay with them and report any unusual activity to me.'

'What can I do if someone comes for them?' I ask, still hoping beyond hope she will relent and let me stay.

'Maybe nothing, but there may also be something.'

'If it is your wish, then I will go.'

I pause a moment in case she changes her mind. No, nothing. I stretch and start down the steps.

'I will contact you on the tenth hour each night.' I throw the comment over my shoulder.

I reach the bottom step as she says, 'Percival.' I pause. 'Please be careful.'

I am grumpy, but it is hard to stay that way when she sends such love and gratitude with her words. I glance back, but she is already inside.

Dodging the evening traffic, I reach my travelling companions in time to catch the elf girl saying, 'I'm tired, and we need to figure out where we go from here. Let's go home and see what Susan is making for dinner.'

She slips her arm through Snake's and leads him towards the tube station. Instead of following them, I close my eyes, and cast one of my favourite spells.

When I reach my destination, I creep around the side of the house and jump up onto the window ledge. Peering in to a large open-plan kitchen and dining room, I find them empty. I thought the Susan person was supposed to be making dinner.

Not my problem, I think. My problem is that I will be seen if I remain here. I find a hiding place under the garden furniture and nap while I wait for the others to join me.

THERE ARE ELVES.
AND THEN THERE ARE ELVES

THE TRAIN CARRIAGE rocks gently back and forth as it makes its way back to central London. Dusk is settling, and I catch Snake's and my reflections in the window across from us. His hands are shoved into his pockets and his face reads as despondent.

I study my own reflection. Do I look different after the revelation that other life-forms share the world with us? Hold on—not *us*. If Snake is to be believed, and I am starting to believe he should be, I am not human. I am an elf.

I don't look any different. Same corkscrew hair and copper brown skin as my father, and the ice blue eyes I got from my mother. The face staring back at me is mine, and it shows nothing of the inner turmoil finding out about my origins is causing.

Moving my gaze to the other people in the carriage, I try to find the 'glow' Snake spoke of before. There is nothing. Part of me hoped to see a small sliver just to confirm I am not going mad. My eyes slide sideways to Snake; surely, he must have it. I think I almost catch a glimpse of… something, then it slips away as he raises his head to look at me.

'You can stay in our spare room tonight. We can eat and decide what to do next,' I say to him, and perhaps I can take some more time to get my head around all this.

He turns his head slightly so his eyes meet mine in the window opposite. 'Or we could go to Mayfair and meet with the Regises.'

'Who?'

'Giles and Amandine Regis—the most senior fey in the upper world. If we visit them tonight, and if you convince them to endorse us, then we will only need to find three more races to help.'

My stomach roils. The inner turmoil I had begun to tame by planning our evening rears its head again. 'Oh, so we just knock on their door and ask them to give us an invite? It's as easy as that, is it?'

'I didn't say it would be easy.' Snake turns in his seat so he can look directly at me. I want to meet his gaze, but I concentrate on the houses rushing by out the window. 'None of this will be easy,' Snake says. 'But if we can convince the Regises to endorse us, then that will hold some sway with the others.'

'How about you go, and I head home and let Susan know we will have a guest tonight.' I cross my arms over my chest.

Snake snorts. 'You think they would let the likes of me inside their home?'

My head pivots round. 'Why wouldn't they?'

'Because they are fey, because they have royal blood, and because I'm a gnome. They won't even speak with me without you.'

This time I turn round to face him. 'And what makes you think they will speak with me?'

'This is so strange, me teaching you about this,' he mutters.

I blush, suddenly ashamed of my lack of knowledge of this other world I am a part of. All those years I accepted Mum and Dad's tales of how they both had no family and so we had to be there for one another. What if even that is a lie?

I want to be angry at them, but I am too worried about where they might have been taken. Then a thought hits me—what if the reason they kept everything secret is because something bad happened in the past?

Snake takes my hand, sending a tingle of electricity up my arm. I look up in surprise. I did not expect that. I mean, he's cute and all, but we only just met. Besides, this other world thing he has introduced me to is just plain weird, and I don't quite know what to make of him. His next words tell me Snake obviously did not feel the same frisson.

'I'm sorry, Pris. Getting your head around everything must be difficult.'

I draw a deep breath and try to concentrate on the task at hand. 'Okay, explain exactly why you need me to go with you.'

'The Regises will at least listen to you because you are an elf—one of the fey. They are obligated to ask you in and offer you hospitality by the rules of our society. Also, the rules that operate in the World Above make them responsible for those of their kind who work here.'

His tone is patient and his explanation is logical, but it does nothing to make the situation less surreal. How can people I have never met be obliged to offer me hospitality? It's too strange, like something out of Greek history. I'm not sure I can face any more strange people.

'I just want to go home. I feel… overwhelmed. I'm not at my best, and I don't want to be with strangers who know more about who I am than I do.'

My words are cross and sharp, and Snake flinches, but he keeps hold of my hand.

'This is hard, but it will be harder if you are left up here alone, trying to deal with the disappearance of your parents. Don't you want to do everything you can to find them?'

Harsh, I think. Before I lash out, returning the favour, I stop myself. Although he must be worried about his mother's disappearance, there is genuine concern for me in his eyes. And, frustratingly, he is right—I want to find my parents.

'Perhaps,' I say, buying some time to process my swirling emotions.

Knowing my parents have lied to me my entire life makes me simultaneously want to hit something and hide under my duvet and forget this ever happened. Unfortunately, self-indulgence is not a luxury I can afford. With only seven days until the solstice, I need to put on my big-girl pants and do something to save them.

Snake must have read my change of heart from my face because he lets go of my hand to pull his phone from his hoodie pocket. 'Okay, if we get off at Bond Street it's a short walk to Grosvenor Square. If we change onto the Circle Line—'

'Hold on…. How do you know where the senior elves live? I mean, is there some sort of online directory, or an app?'

He laughs so loud, the elderly couple down the other end of the carriage turn and stare at us. Their glare sobers Snake up, and his laughter subsides to a chuckle.

'Our kind are not that tech savvy, and besides, they would be worried the information would fall into the wrong hands. A lot of our rules about living in the world above are to ensure our presence remains a secret.'

This is like talking to a politician—I ask one question and he answers a completely different one. 'You still haven't said how you know this,' I point out impatiently.

He looks sheepish. 'Sorry, I didn't want to rub your nose in something else all creatures know.'

I forgive him instantly. After all, it isn't his fault my parents didn't teach me these things. 'So…,' I prompt him.

'Yeah, well, because the senior members of each race of creatures are responsible for their kind in the World Above, there is a designated place for us to contact them. Sometimes it's where their kind come and go from this world, sometimes it's their base of operations. All creatures learn these contact points much like human children learn the address and phone number of family they can call on.'

'And you're telling me that the contact point for elves is in Grosvenor Square?'

'Yeeesss.'

The word is drawn out, almost like he can sense what is coming.

'So, I am guessing in this instance the elves actually live there?'

'I believe so. In Blackburn Mews.'

My temper explodes again, although, recognising I am in a public place, I spit my next question out in a whisper. 'How is it my parents are accused of using magic for profit when the senior members of our race live in one of the most expensive, exclusive squares in London? How can they do that without using magic?'

Snake answers in the same tone teachers use when dealing with recalcitrant children. 'They don't own the house as such. Well, on paper they do but only because humans would become suspicious if they didn't. But it's perhaps best to think of the house as an Elven Embassy. When the current family are recalled, ownership will be transferred to the next inhabitant. It has been this way for generations, since long before Grosvenor Square became a sought-after address in London.'

My head is spinning. I have gone from thinking Snake insane talking about elves and fairies and gnomes, to beginning to think it may all be true, to finding out they built up a whole infrastructure aimed at keeping their identity secret during their hundreds of years of residing in England.

Snake takes my hand in his again, and I find his touch strangely calming.

'You know, it wasn't always like this. Once our people mingled with humans, coming and going as they pleased.'

'What changed?' I ask, intrigued. History has always been one of my passions.

'Religion changed. When Henry the Eighth started the Catholic-Protestant divide, both religions became more dogmatic. You were one or the other; there was no room for a third category. Those of us who wanted to remain in the upper world changed themselves to appear more human to fit in.'

'And that is why we take human form now?' I guess.

'We?' Snake raises an eyebrow.

My cheeks warm. When had I started to think of myself as one of Snake's creatures? I'm not sure, but somehow, I have.

'Yes, that is why we take human form. But soon even appearing human wasn't enough. In Oliver Cromwell's time, the border between worlds in England was closed to preserve our kind. A few chose to stay above ground, but most creatures returned to the World Below.'

Snake falls silent as the doors open, and a young couple enters. He scowls at them, and they react as you would expect most Londoners to. They immediately head down the other end of the carriage, distancing themselves from potential danger.

'I'm sensing a "but" here,' I encourage once we are alone again.

'That was when we found out that the World Below and the World Above were linked. I guess if the two realms were people, you could say they are linked by a common aura.'

'Only if you believe in that sort of thing,' I say under my breath.

Snake frowns at me. 'Magic and auras and world energies may be a leap of faith for you, but they are as real to our kind as air and water are to humans.'

He pauses as if waiting for me to make another facetious remark. I bite my tongue, wanting to hear the rest of what he has to say.

'Anyway, when things are in turmoil up here, there is turmoil below. You get the idea?'

I nod. I may not believe it all, but I do understand what he's saying.

'In 1690, the Seelie Court called a full council and decided to open the border and allow a few of our kind to come here and keep the humans on the right track. Rules of interaction were drawn up to keep our secret, rules we still follow today.'

I appreciate how this potted version of his history fits with English history as I know it, but it still feels a little like Snake is telling a story. Notting Hill Gate is announced. We jump off and head to the Circle Line platform.

As we travel the three stops to Bond Street, I feel Snake's eyes on me, as if he's making sure this new info dump hasn't broken me. I want to reassure him that I am fine, but I'm not. When I think about this new world I am a part of, everything keeping me anchored to who I am slips from my grasp, my head spins, and I no longer know who I am.

My hands shake and I clasp them together. I take a shuddering breath as I make a decision. The only way I can cope with my parents' disappearance at the moment is to deal with this other world stuff and who I really am later. If I want to find my parents, I need to focus on the task in front of me, and hopefully it will take me one step closer to my goal.

AS WE EXIT Bond Street tube station, Pris is still distant. She has disappeared somewhere inside her head. When I found out she knew nothing about who she is, I didn't want to take on the responsibility of bringing her up to speed. Now I'm worried I have broken her.

She walks beside me, hands stuffed in pockets, shoulders hunched and head down, dejected and alone. All I want to do is hug her and tell her it will be all right, that we will get through this together. Not in a romantic way… Not that she isn't attractive…. I mean, I could get lost in those eyes, but she is a bit buttoned down for my tastes.

Still, when she sat on me before… No, I don't want to imagine running my hands up her legs and kissing that mocking mouth. She is an elf, and they are all about the purity of their race. Even my offering her physical comfort would be frowned upon and, this close to the elven stronghold, I don't want to take the risk of being seen.

Damn it. *Focus,* I tell myself. *The objective here is to get all of your parents back, and you can't do that if she is a total mess.*

With my actions suitably justified, I take her hand and give it a squeeze. Okay, it isn't a hug, but I think she needs to know someone is here for her. And the warmth spreading through my body at the contact is totally beside the point.

She smiles wanly at me, and my stomach does a somersault. My body obviously doesn't know what my head does. We turn around the corner into Blackburn Mews and a shiver runs down my spine. Someone is watching us.

I pull Pris to a stop and check out the area. I can't see anything obvious—no shimmers from invisible fairies and no creatures in human form loitering in doorways. Perhaps the attack on Wimbledon Common has set me on edge.

'What is it?' Pris asks.

She is already overwhelmed, so there is no need to burden her with my overactive imagination. 'Just stopping for a quick briefing,' I improvise. In fact, that's not such a bad idea. Things will go more smoothly if she knows what she's letting herself in for.

'You'll need to do all the talking once we're inside,' I carry on. 'I'm only able to speak if the Regises ask me a direct question.'

Her eyes focus on my face, and she frowns. 'You're kidding, right? That sounds so servile and, well, medieval.'

My cheeks warm, and I look at the ground, attempting to hide my embarrassment. This is one piece of creature law I had hoped to avoid for a while.

'Snake, what is it?' She tugs at my hand and I let go.

If I distance myself from her, I won't feel so bad when she realises what gnomes really are, and she no longer wants to have anything to do with me.

Deciding to own who I am, I raise my head and look her in the eye. 'Gnomes are lesser elves. We are those with elven blood who perform the menial tasks true blood elves do not want to lower themselves to do.' There. Finally, it's out in the open.

Pris laughs. 'You're kidding, right? You're not kidding?' She shakes her head. 'You mean other elves treat you like servants…. No, worse than servants—like indentured labourers?'

I say nothing, but I am surprised as her cheeks redden. At first, I think she is embarrassed by being seen with me. I couldn't have been further from the mark.

'That is barbaric, and wrong on so many levels. I…. I….' Her words are angry and a lot louder than they were moments ago.

I can't let her go where she wants to with this. Although it warms my heart that she doesn't buy into the whole lesser creature thing, I need her calm and collected and acting like the elven highborn she is when she meets the Regises.

'Calm down,' I say and immediately regret it when I see a flicker of fire in her eyes.

'Doesn't it make you angry? I mean, in this day and age, to treat someone as if they are little better than a slave—you can't tell me it doesn't bother you.'

I shove my hands in my pockets. 'Of course it bothers me, but I'm not going to be able to change that in the next few minutes. We have to work with what we have, so, for the moment, that means you must behave like other elves.'

She stares at me blankly, as if she can't believe what I'm saying. I don't back down. My mother's life may depend on what happens in the next few minutes, and I will not risk her life to salve my ego. Perhaps Pris's thoughts are running in a similar direction. Her jaw loosens and she takes a deep breath.

'Okay. Tell me what you need me to do.'

'You are elven royalty, but so are the Regises. The only thing we have over them is that you are closer to the throne than they are, since Giles and Amandine are, at best, cousins—distant cousins.'

'I'm royalty? For real?'

'Um… yes?'

She throws her head back and laughs, then stops suddenly. 'Hold on, how royal?'

I shrug. 'I'm not sure exactly. Your mum's a princess, so I guess—'

Pris squeals. 'I'm some sort of a princess.'

Passersby are giving us strange looks, and that's never a good thing in London—especially not in this swanky neighbourhood.

'Calm it down, will you? People'll think you're nuts,' I say.

Pris sobers up but can't wipe the grin off her face. 'I always thought Dad calling me Princess P was a family joke. Do you think I'm actually, like, Princess Anne royalty, or more like Princess Beatrice? No… don't answer that.' Pris chews her bottom lip. 'Whatever this means in the other world, it means nothing here—I am still just me.'

'But—'

'But it matters to them, doesn't it? That's why you told me.'

I nod.

'You want me to play the princess demanding her right to be heard—to be given their endorsement?'

'Exactly.' I grin, happy I don't need to explain the details.

'And what about Plan B?'

'No. What? Why would we need that?' I am confused.

'Because it is my experience that people who love wielding power are not so keen when others use their authority against them.'

That stops me in my tracks. I have never been in a position of power. Can this really be how it works?

'My experience of bullies is that when someone bigger and stronger fronts up to them, they back down,' I argue.

She nods. 'True, but they will always find a way to hit back. I wonder if we might get a little more from them if we try stroking a few egos?'

'But—'

'How about we try it my way first? If it doesn't work, I can go all imperious.'

Argh, she's good at this. And, of course, she makes a fair point. After you demanded something and get nowhere, it is difficult to back down and then ask politely.

'All right, we'll do it your way.'

She starts down the street. 'Which house?' she asks.

I point to the white five-story affair. As she turns to ascend the steps, I grab her arm. 'Don't forget to tell them I am your bodyguard.'

'My what?'

'Bodyguard. If you don't, they'll make me wait outside.'

'This is madness,' she sighs, 'but I guess you know best.'

She starts climbing, and I follow one step behind. As we reach the door, voices and music drift out into the night. Through the window in the room to the left, I can see figures moving around, mingling in groups, chatting and laughing.

'Sounds like they are having a party of some sort,' Pris says, sending a questioning glance my way before dropping the knocker.

I fold my arms across my chest, standing firm.

'What if they're… you know… a little tipsy? We might not get a fair hearing,' she presses.

I relax a little. 'I guess we could come back tomorrow, although alcohol may—'

'Make them a little more relaxed,' Pris finishes as the thump of the knocker rings out.

Almost immediately, the door is opened, and a petite blonde woman glittering with sequins and diamonds smiles in welcome. Her face soon changes to a frown. 'You're a little… underdressed. Ahh, you're not here for the party, are you?'

'No, we're not. I was wondering if I can speak with—'

The door is wrenched open wider, and another woman appears and gives us the once-over. She is an older, taller, thinner, blonder version of the first woman, and she looks down her nose at us as Pris starts again.

'I am Priscilla—'

'I know who you are. You had best come in. Elodie, could you be a dear and go ask Giles to meet me in the library.'

'Of course,' the younger woman says but doesn't move. She is assessing us, clearly wanting to know why we are here.

'Now!' It's a command, and the younger woman reluctantly departs.

The older woman turns her ice-blue gaze to Pris and says, 'Follow me.'

Pris does as she is bid, and I follow her.

'Not him. He waits outside.'

Pris's eyebrows rise, and I realise she didn't completely believe me when I said I wouldn't be granted entry. *Please just do as I asked*, I plead with her inside my head.

'He's my bodyguard, and he goes where I go,' Pris says. Her tone is firm and authoritative. A smile tugs at the corner of my mouth. She has obviously taken to being a princess like a duck to water.

The woman doesn't even bother to answer. I close the door behind me and heave a sigh of relief at having passed the first hurdle. Squaring my shoulders, I follow Pris down the hallway into the… library?

The room may well have been a library once, and certainly one wall is filled with bookshelves, but there isn't a single book in sight. The shelves are filled with filing boxes. In front of them sits an oak desk with a closed laptop placed in the centre. A sofa and a few chairs are set on a Turkish rug in front of a fire, and this is where Amandine leads Pris.

'Please, take a seat,' the woman directs. 'My husband will be here any minute.'

Amandine Regis is very, well, very elven—cool, aloof, and entitled. All I know about her is her reputation for enforcing the rules of our kind to the very letter, and usually to her advantage.

I take up a position just inside the door and stand to attention, hands behind my back, trying to look like I would know what to do if Pris were attacked. In reality, as she had already demonstrated today, she would have more chance defending herself than waiting for me to save her.

Pris sits in the furthest armchair, where she can see me and whoever comes through the door. Amandine remains standing, silent and imposing.

We do not wait for long. Moments after Pris is seated, an elegant, tawny-haired man enters the room with what most would take as a welcoming smile plastered on his face, only there is no warmth in his eyes. I pray Pris is not taken in, because if rumours are correct, this man makes his wife look like a pussycat.

'Ah, Priscilla, so wonderful to finally meet you. No, don't get up. I am afraid it is my daughter's birthday, and she has friends over, so this won't take long.'

Pris raises an eyebrow at Giles Regis's approach and his lack of introduction. *Stick it to him*, I will her. *Deflate that ego. Go on! Do it!*

'I assume you are Giles Regis, and this is your wife Amandine. So pleased to meet you too.' Without rising, Pris holds out her hand and Giles is forced to shake it.

She looks every bit the princess greeting her subjects, and the slight drawing together of Giles's brows tells me he has noticed this too. A flicker of doubt crosses his face, but it is gone so quickly, I am not totally sure I didn't imagine it.

'I apologise for gatecrashing your daughter's birthday, but it is unavoidable under the circumstances. I learnt today that you are the only person who can help me find out what has happened to my parents, and so I came here immediately to request your help.'

Neither of the Regises moves.

'You do know my parents were taken to the World Below, don't you?'

The Regises share a quick glance before Giles takes a step forward. 'Ah—'

'Oh, but of course you know. You are the most senior elves in the human world. I am sure nothing goes on up here amongst our kind without you hearing of it,' Pris continues.

'Of course, my dear. Tragic for you. But I am not sure how we can help,' Giles says. 'If we had been able to do anything, we would have prevented the arrest itself.'

Giles presents his hands palms up as if to show he has nothing to hide. I'm immediately suspicious and want to find out what Giles knows but isn't telling us. Pris's face shows no reaction at all.

'Obviously, my parents' situation has hit you hard—'

'And if we can do anything to help you while they are gone, we will, of course, for you are still one of our charges,' Amandine interrupts, the chill in her voice making a mockery of her words.

'So kind of you to offer, and so timely, given that I found out today that if you endorse my bodyguard and I, we can go to the next sitting of The Court and help my parents.' Pris presents this as a done deal, almost daring them to refuse. Well played. I suppress a grin.

The smiles freeze on the Regises' faces. They had not expected this.

Giles looks at his wife and says, 'Well, Priscilla, of course—'

'What Giles is trying to say is, there would be no point. You would still need three other endorsements to gain entry, and as you have never been part of our world, you are unlikely to get any more, and—'

'And it would be cruel of us to give you false hope,' Giles finishes for his wife. 'What we can offer you is our guidance on how to deal with the authorities. Help you with the paperwork pertaining to your parents' disappearance and such. We must ensure no one asks any questions that might shine an unwelcome light on us.'

From my position by the door, I can see Pris stand, drawing herself up to her full height, which isn't very tall at all, ready to put Plan B into action.

'Mother, Father, how could you?'

I jump. The voice comes from right beside me, and I hadn't even heard the girl enter. She is almost an exact duplicate of the woman who had opened the door, except her face openly shows distress.

'If you were taken somewhere I would expect all the elves up above to do anything in their power to help me find you.'

'Verona, you do not understand all the forces at play here.' Amandine strokes her daughter's arm as if to soothe her. It doesn't work.

'Would you be breaking any laws if you gave her your endorsement?'

Giles shakes his head. 'No, but—'

'Then give it to her and come back to the party,' the girl pleads.

'It may be the only one she gets,' Giles says again. 'What good will one do her?'

'What good? Why, it will show her that at least her own kind are prepared to help her,' Verona says. 'Come on, Daddy. It's my birthday.' She takes her father's hand and smiles up at him. 'It would ruin my party if you refused her.' She pouts prettily at him. This girl knows how to get her own way. It's very impressive.

Giles catches Amandine's eye above his daughter's head and sighs. 'What harm can it do?' he asks.

His wife scowls. Clearly, she doesn't agree. When Giles does not respond, she purses her lips. 'I must go and attend to our guests.' She turns on her heel and leaves the room.

'It seems it is your lucky day, Priscilla,' Giles says as he moves to the desk and opens a drawer.

As he reaches inside, Pris mouths, 'Thank you,' to Verona, and the elf smiles in return.

Pulling out a shiny black box, Giles carries it over to Pris. Sitting on the chair beside hers, he opens it. I am so engrossed watching the two, I have forgotten Verona. When her hushed voice sounds from right beside me, I can't help but jump. Perhaps bodyguarding is not really my thing. Maybe next time I should masquerade as a servant.

'Be careful, gnome. Dark forces are at work here. I have done what I can to help you. It may still not be enough. Good luck.'

Before I can turn my head to respond, she is gone, and Priscilla is walking to the door, escorted by Giles. 'You will each need to gather three other pieces to complete the endorsement—that is, if you want to take your bodyguard with you.'

'Thank you so much, Giles. I will not forget our meeting,' Pris says as he opens the front door to escort us out.

I KEEP MY back straight and my head high as I walk past Giles and leave the Regis house. Our host's face is impassive and his body tense. He hadn't wanted to give me the token of his endorsement. As he passed the two quarter coins to me, his eyes flicked to where his daughter had stood. Seeing her gone, he had hissed under his breath, 'You and your family are no true elves. You are no better than that gnome by the door. Don't ever come back here. You are not welcome.'

I was shocked by the hatred in his voice, but I kept my expression blank and considered how to respond. Remembering Snake's words about our relative stations, as I stood to leave, I said, 'Is that how you speak to someone of high blood? Perhaps my extended family will be interested to learn of this insult.'

The words sounded childish to my ears. The threat was hollow, as I had no idea who my family was. Giles clearly did, though, as he blanched and went all stiff and formal on me. Who were my family that wielding their name could put someone as high up as Giles in their place?

The door closes behind me and my body relaxes, but only a little. We have what we came for, and we are one step closer to finding our parents. I should feel satisfaction, or at the very least relief, but my stomach is churning as my world continues to spin off its axis.

Snake places his hand on my arm. 'Are you all right?'

His voice comes from far away. I lift my head, and it takes a moment for his face to come in to focus.

'He hates me.' My voice is barely above a whisper. 'I only just met him, yet he despises me.'

I don't know why this upsets me so much, but it does. I want to know why a complete stranger bears me such animosity, but at the same time, I want to go home, curl up under the duvet, and forget this strange new world exists. Unfortunately, that will not help me find my parents.

Snake gives my arm a gentle squeeze. 'Hey, you did well. You got us our first endorsements.'

I shake my head. 'No, *I* didn't. Verona did. If she hadn't intervened, Giles would have sent us away empty-handed. I wonder why she cared?'

Snake leads me down the steps, then helps me thread my way through the people crowding the streets. I look around me, suddenly aware that while my life is in crisis, the world still goes on. Londoners are heading home from work or are on their way out to enjoy an evening's entertainment.

As we turn towards the tube station, I'm suddenly hungry and weary to the core. I can't face the crowded trains. I think this may be time for my trusty emergency Visa to make an appearance.

When we reach Grosvenor Square, I hail a taxi. I give the driver my address, he closes the partition, and I finally relax.

Turning my head slightly, I find Snake resting his head back against the seat, his eyes closed. He has been doing this for two days already, and the tension doesn't totally leave his face. As if he senses me watching him, his eyes open to meet mine.

'Verona gave me a warning, you know. She said other forces are at play, and we should be careful.'

My stomach clenches. Why would she do that? Especially as her parents clearly did not want anything to do with us. 'Snake, do you trust her? I mean, she had no reason to help us.'

His startled expression tells me he wasn't expecting the question. 'I don't know if she is trustworthy. Rumour has it, she was sent below for a while because she was drawing too much attention to herself. I mean, she was in the society pages almost every week. It might have something to do with that. Perhaps she is hitting back at her parents—or perhaps she has her own agenda.'

'Maybe.' But Verona's skillful manipulation of her father seemed like more than childish rebellion to me. My brain is too fried for me to put this into words, so I stare out the window as familiar streets flash by.

The seat moves as Snake sits forward a little. 'The more important question is, what did she mean? Up until now, I believed Mum was taken as part of a cleanup of above world practices—that's what the Fairy Guard said. Now, I'm not so sure. But I can't think of any other reason why she might have been taken.'

On top of everything else today, this is too much for me to even start to contemplate. My phone vibrates in my pocket, and I am relieved to have something to do that is not associated with this madness.

The text is from Susan. I swipe my passcode and read, 'Sorry Pris, emergency at home. Dinner in fridge. CU tomorrow.'

I stare at the screen, trying to make sense of the words. Susan always lets my parents know her whereabouts, and then they tell me. So why is Susan texting me herself today? Then it hits me—she already knows Mum and Dad aren't coming home. Is she part of this other world too?

'Snake, do you know if Susan, our au pair, is an elf, or someone from, you know, below?'

'What makes you ask that?'

I show him Susan's text. 'She knows Mum and Dad are missing. That's why she sent the text to me.'

Snake looks up from the phone and smiles. 'Pris, remember what I said about elves. No self-respecting elf would take a position as a servant. She may be a gnome, but I can't say for sure.'

My heart starts to pound in my chest, and I can't breathe. And just like that, my brain shuts down. I can't go on like this. Not if I am going to find my parents.

'Snake, I can't do this.' My voice waivers.

Beside me his body stiffens. 'Find our parents?' His voice is tired, uncertain, fearful.

I reach across the seat and entwine my fingers in his. The warmth of his touch gives me the courage to speak.

'No, I want to do that. But I can't deal with all this other world stuff. There is too much I don't know, and the enormity of it is paralysing me. I need to ignore that side of things, otherwise I am going to be no help at all.'

Snake's laugh is hollow. 'How are we going to do that when we must track down three different races of creatures?'

All right, my plan is not foolproof. I draw my bottom lip between my teeth as I think.

'I guess we can't ignore it completely. How about we treat this as a normal human search, and you limit your lessons to what I need to know to get my parents back. Everything else I can sort out later... with them.'

Snake thinks about this a bit. 'Aren't you and I a bit old to play pretend?''

'Perhaps, but I guess even adults can be a little childish sometimes,' I tell him, certain that this is the way to go for me to retain my sanity. My head is already spinning less.

'You do know you must face who you are and where you come from at some stage, don't you?' His voice is gentle as his fingers curl around mine.

'Yes, but I can't deal with being someone else... something else, and focus on finding our parents at the same time. It's too much. Every time I think about being a... you know... elf'—I lean in and whisper the last word in case the driver can overhear—'all I want to do is hide in my bed. I'm afraid if I don't ignore that fact for the moment, I will fall apart.'

Snake keeps his own voice low as he replies, 'I believe you are stronger than that, but it is totally up to you. We can play at being humans for now, concentrate on finding the endorsements, and deal with the rest later... if you're sure that's what you want?'

'It is,' I say as the taxi pulls up in front of my home.

After paying the driver, I resist the urge to rush inside, away from the turmoil of the day. As I open the door to let Snake in, I realise that without my parents waiting for me, this is no longer my safe haven—the place where I can escape the world; either world.

THE GRAND PLAN

ONCE INSIDE, THE uncertain girl from moments before is gone, and Pris is all business, giving me the impression that she goes into organising mode when she is stressed. Leading me upstairs, she shows me to a guest room that would take up half of Mum's and my entire flat.

'The bed should be made up, and your bathroom is through there.' She waves a hand towards a door to the right.

I drop my backpack on the bed, take a look at the pristine white duvet cover, and move it to the floor. I pull off my hoodie, fold it up, and place it on the chair beside the bed. My T-shirt is a little wrinkled, but there isn't much I can do about it because I'm sure whatever's in my pack is little better.

What I can do something about is the fug of stale sweat reaching my nostrils. I poke around in the front pocket of my bag, then reach under my shirt, spraying my armpits before returning the canister to its hiding place. I pass the bathroom sadly as I head downstairs—I'd love to hide under the soothing water of a shower, but there isn't time.

Sounds of movement from the back of the house draw me along the corridor. I enter the kitchen in time to catch Pris sticking her head inside the most enormous fridge I have ever seen. Pulling out a large dish covered in cling-film, she asks, 'Lasagne all right for dinner?'

My mouth waters. My last meal was a hasty breakfast before I left home this morning, and I'm suddenly ravenous.

I politely answer, 'That would be great, thanks.' Mum would be proud of me. My stomach voices its approval, and the effect is lost.

Pris chuckles. 'I'll get this sorted quick smart, then.'

I watch her as she moves around the kitchen, feeling somewhat like a spare wheel. I need to be doing something… anything. 'Can I help?'

She stops unwrapping the meal and tilts her head to the side. 'I've got this covered. But… um… I put my laptop in the dining room. I thought we could eat and work in there. The office is next door. Could you grab us some supplies?'

I raise my eyebrows. 'And the dining room is where?'

She laughs. 'Next door. And the office is the next one along.'

I head back down the corridor to the second door and open it tentatively. I can't help feeling like a burglar as I turn on the light and survey the room.

The only window is a thin strip of glass above the bookshelves in front of me. To the left, an antique wooden desk takes up most of the space, and to the right is a comfortable chair by a faux wooden filing cabinet.

On the shelves opposite the door, I spy a world atlas. As I reach out a hand, I find tucked in beside it an old, dog-eared atlas of England and take that instead. From the shelf closest to the desk, I grab one of the legal pads from a neat pile before pulling a couple of pens from the holder on the desktop. I turn off the light and pull the door closed behind me.

Pris is already seated at the dining room table when I enter, shovelling salad into her mouth with her right hand and logging on to a laptop with her left. I drop my supplies beside a second bowl of salad.

'I'm so hungry, I thought this would do as a starter while the lasagne heats up.'

'Thanks,' I say, sitting down at right angles to her, my back to the door. The salad barely touches the sides as I wolf it down.

'So, how do we do this?' Pris asks.

On the trip back from Wimbledon, I'd been thinking about how to approach the other races, especially as we only have a short amount of time.

'Creature strongholds are dotted all over England. I think we would make best use of our limited time if we decide on a region with a creature cluster, so to speak.'

Pris stops, her fork dripping leaves halfway to her mouth. She places the potential mouthful back in the bowl and stares at me.

'Why don't we just head straight to the gnomes. I mean, if it's good enough for me to go to the elves, why don't we go to them next?'

My stomach lurches, and the salad threatens to reappear. That we would get to this point was inevitable, but I didn't think it would be so soon. I like Pris, in fact I more than like her, if I'm being honest. Still, I'm not sure I'm ready to trust her with something this important—this personal.

'It's complicated,' is all I say.

'So was my going to the elves,' she presses.

How can I put her off this idea without telling her the truth? 'It's political, and you just told me you don't want to know about that sort of thing.'

I hate using her fears against her, but I'm just not ready to talk about my relationship with the gnomes yet. Her eyes narrow, and I can tell she is trying to decide whether or not to press her point. *Let it go,* I will her, hoping my fear doesn't show on my face.

Pris studies me for a moment longer, then says, 'Just out of interest, if we had no other option but to ask for the gnome's endorsement, where are they based?'

I've been let off the hook, or so I think. I catch a glint in her eyes, alerting me to the fact that a plan is formulating in that head of hers. Although I don't want to, I must tell her the truth because this may prove to be important later. Besides, I think I can work out where she's going with this.

We don't want to travel too far away from Cornwall, where the gnomes are, to gather the other tokens because if I am forced to throw myself on the mercy of our leader in the upper world, then we don't want to have to travel days to meet with him.

'Cornwall,' I say.

'And if we were to head towards that part of the country, is there a chance we would find some other creature strongholds on the way?'

Taking a deep breath, I open the atlas and flick to the map of South West England. I study the area, searching for some place names I memorised as a child.

Finding the elves was easy because they're London based, but they are the only race whose stronghold is situated in England's capital.

Although I know the names of the creature strongholds, I've never actually visited them, and my knowledge of England is limited. I'm embarrassed to admit Mum and I never leave London—not even to go to visit the gnomes in Cornwall. Whenever we met with other gnomes, we did so on neutral ground close to our home.

I scan the map and am relieved to find three names I recognise on the way to Cornwall. We can complete our endorsements without having to resort to the gnomes. Phew. I'm reaching for the pad to write down the locations when my eyes are drawn to another name.

'Hey, Pris, do you have the riddle handy?'

'I can get it.'

Her chair scrapes across the floor, and she leaves to return a moment later with the piece of paper. She opens it and places it in front of me. Then she leans over and looks at where my finger is marking a place near Godalming.

'What's that? It looks like some sort of park with a lake.'

'The Underground Ballroom,' I say.

'Underground Ballroom?'

'Yes, I remember overhearing my father talking about attending court.' I think back to the conversation they had while Dad helped me build some Lego. It is one of the few happy memories I have of my father. It hurts to dwell on it, but if it will help Mum, I will put aside my personal feelings. 'He was telling Mum about the amazing ballroom underwater. And see, here in the riddle, it says "under water ball."'

Pris grins 'So we know where and when we have to roll up for The Court.'

And we have our first endorsement, I mentally add. After two days of treading water, today I finally achieved something that could lead to freeing my mother.

I RETURN TO my laptop and search for the place Snake believes The Court will be held. I don't want to dash his hopes, but he must have it wrong. The Underground Ballroom is an abandoned folly under a lake?

'The Underground Ballroom hardly looks big enough to host the Seelie—is that the right word?—Court,' I start in gently, 'and it's….' I search for the right word. I want to say derelict, but I go for abandoned.

Snake's shoulders rise and fall in a somewhat unconcerned shrug. 'The World Below is hidden from humans, so things aren't always what they seem.'

'But it's in the middle of a lake that's part of a conference centre. If magical creatures were using it, I am sure someone would have noticed by now—and there's nothing on the internet,' I press on with my objections.

Snake's jaw takes on a stubborn set. 'You didn't know another world existed under your very nose, and now you're an expert?'

Ouch. That hit home. For a moment, I consider hitting back, but we have more pressing matters. 'We can argue where the ball is later, once we wrangle our endorsements from the other three races.' I change the subject. 'So, do any of these places on the way to Cornwall ring a bell for you?'

'Yes. Bodmin Moor in Cornwall is the home of the sprites. Wistman's Woods in Devon is the goblin stronghold. And here, the White Lady Waterfall in the Lydford Gorge is the witch's source of power in England.'

Ignoring the surreal vibe in the room as we discuss witches, goblins, and gnomes in the same way we might talk about people from other countries, I chew the end of my pen. I reach for the legal pad Snake scribbled on.

'That makes four potential sources for endorsements. Should we visit them in any particular order? I mean, we don't want to offend anyone,' I say.

Snake shakes his head. 'The elven token means no one will object to supporting us on political grounds for fear of upsetting them. So, we should be able to do what works best for us, time wise.'

Part of me wants to ask what were the other grounds they might object on, but the minute I think of that, my head starts swimming with possibilities. I need to focus on something more tangible.

The timer on the oven pings, rescuing me. I hurry out of the room and immerse myself in the normalcy of serving dinner. I dish the lasagne onto the two plates, then take them into the dining room. By the time I return, I have regained control of my thoughts.

In my absence Snake has been flicking through the book of maps. As I place food in front of him, he says, 'I hope all these guys are happy to support us, because the next closest race stronghold is the fairies' in North Wales.'

I push my laptop out of the way to make a space to eat. 'I thought fairies and sprites were the same thing,' I say before chomping down on a large forkful of food. I can hear my mother groaning over my table manners, and my cheeks heat at the thought.

'Don't ever say that to a sprite or a nixie,' Snake laughs. 'Think of them as cousins. Fairies get all the good press. Nixies and sprites are sort of the black sheep.'

'So, are you saying I should ignore everything I ever read about magical creatures?' I ask, still trying to find some sort of order in the chaos of this new world.

'Yes and no,' Snake says between mouthfuls.

'Not helpful.' I respond.

My voice sounds tart to my own ears, so I am not surprised when Snake freezes.

'Sorry,' he mumbles. 'The stories you heard were once true. Over the years, humans distorted them, turning the tales into fantasies to explain away things their minds couldn't comprehend—'

'Which means there is always a little truth to the tales,' I finish for him.

He nods and carries on eating. That makes sense in a way. I push the plate away. My meal is only half eaten, but I no longer have any appetite.

'If the different races can be approached in any order, I suggest we start at the closest and make our way down to Cornwall last.'

I start tapping keys, bringing up train times and making notes on of potential routes. Where I cannot find a train going to where we need to be, I search for local bus routes. My planning stops at Bodmin. I can do no more until Snake tells me exactly where to find the gnomes.

I shut the lid of my laptop before ripping the pages off the pad. On a fresh sheet, I write our schedule and push it across to Snake. While he reads it, I take our dishes into the kitchen and start cleaning up.

I bend to start the dishwasher, and when I stand back up, I find myself face-to-face with a set of green eyes staring through the kitchen window. I bite back an involuntary scream as I twist to look for a knife to defend myself. When I turn back, carving knife in hand, the eyes have gone.

A nervous laugh escapes. This has been a strange day. I must have been imagining things.

'Pris, are you okay?'

I turn at the sound of Snake's voice, wondering what he is on about. I follow the line of his gaze and my eyes land on the knife clenched in my hand.

I smile, suddenly feeling rather foolish. 'Yeah, some animal outside startled me, that's all. Do you want some coffee or tea?' I ask, placing the knife back in the block on the bench.

'Do you have hot chocolate?' Snake asks. 'I might need a little something to help me sleep after tension the last couple of days. Not to mention, your schedule is pretty hectic. I will need all the rest I can get tonight before tackling that.'

I grin. Our train tomorrow leaves Paddington at 6:30 in the morning, so perhaps hot chocolate is in order—the good kind. I grab milk from the fridge, decant some into a jug, and put it in the microwave to heat.

From the cupboard above Dad's super-deluxe coffee machine, I extract two chocolate balls wrapped in cellophane and two mugs. I pour the warm milk over the balls and stir each cup slowly with a spoon before sprinkling some baby marshmallows on top.

Snake picks up the cups, and I finish putting everything away, then follow him back into the dining room. The chocolate moustache over his upper lip tells me he's already sampled his drink.

'This is heaven in a cup,' he says, taking another mouthful.

I have my first sip and I have to agree. 'This is my mother's patented down-in-the-dumps drink,' I tell him. 'She says things are always better after drinking chocolate.'

A wave of sadness engulfs me as I think of the times my mother's made this drink to cheer me up. Memories of curling up on the sofa together and watching girlie movies threaten to overwhelm me.

Snake reaches out and places his hand over mine. 'We will find them and bring them home,' he says.

He sounds so sure we will succeed, but I'm not, so there is little comfort to be found in his words. Still, I am grateful he tried, and his touch helps me feel a little less alone.

I take another couple of sips of my drink as I scan my notes to see if I missed anything. My gaze is drawn to the list of creatures we are to visit, and something occurs to me.

'Snake, in fairy stories you have to give something up to get something from magical creatures. Is this one of those things that has been exaggerated over the years, or is it true?'

Snake is focused on getting the last of his chocolate from the bottom of his cup with a spoon. He suddenly looks much younger than I thought he was, and it occurs to me I am relying on him to lead us on the quest to find our parents when I know nothing about him, not even how old he is.

This thought disturbs me as I reflect on the few "more-than-a-friend" feelings I had for him today. What if he is still a kid? Or do gnomes age differently? Is he actually much older than me?

Unaware of my inner turmoil, Snake continues to scoop melted chocolate from his cup as he answers. 'I'm not sure. I mean, you didn't give anything up for the elven token.'

'Perhaps I didn't need to because Verona asked for it as a birthday gift.'

Snake raises his head, a smirk twisting his lips. 'I wondered if you had realised that. Look, we will have to give something to them, but we have no way of knowing what until we face each creature. So, there is no use worrying about it until we need to.'

I want to ask more, but he is right. You can't plan for the unknown. Which now takes me back to my new problem: finding out a little more about my travelling companion.

My phone vibrates, and I glance at the text. It's from my friend Amalie. It says, 'Do you want to meet for breakfast before school tomorrow?'

School. I forgot about school. I finished my A-Levels last week but had returned to school as part of a community outreach programme supporting potential scholarship kids through the selection process. I enjoyed working with the candidates, and it was especially close to my heart as my best friend Amalie was a scholarship student.

My screen flashes with another text. 'Pris, you home?'

I picked up my phone, reluctant to answer. We only have one more week of school, then Amalie will be working all summer before heading off to Edinburgh University. I, in turn, would have been off on a family holiday and then interning for my mother in the remaining weeks before taking up my place in Cambridge.

I was throwing away my last few days with the person who had been like a sister to me, and I would be damned if I would lie to her about it.

'No can do,' I text. 'Heading off on family trip early. Call u when I am back.'

Okay, not full the truth, but close. This *was* a trip, and it really was for my family.

I scroll through my contact list, find the number I am looking for, then head next door to the office. Using the landline, I dial and, using my best impersonation of my mother honed over years of practice, leave a message for the school, giving the same reason I gave Amalie to excuse my absence for the rest of the term.

My phone beeps. 'Bummer. Why now?'

'Family crisis or something.'

'Cu when ur back.'

I text a thumbs-up as I return to the dining room.

Snake is leaning back in his chair, feet stretched out in front of him. 'Problem?'

'No, well, sort of. I was catching up with my friend before school tomorrow, and it reminded me I needed to tell them I won't be round for the rest of term.'

His eyes narrow as he assess me. 'I don't know why, but I sort of had the idea you were like me, finished A-Levels and finished with school. But that was stupid, of course, since I found you at school today.'

Chuckling at his confusion, I say, 'I am finished. I was just helping out for a couple of weeks until the end of term. They are sticklers for uniform, even if you are technically no longer a student.'

'Good, because this could have gotten tricky if we had to explain to the authorities why you weren't turning up to classes.'

I nod, aware for the first time that I really am free of school and all the constraints being a child placed on me. I no longer have to answer to anyone. Thump! From the heady heights of freedom, I drop back to reality. The people I usually answer to are no longer here to question my choices.

As if sensing the change in mood, Snake stands and stretches.

'It's late. We should sleep. Let me tidy up while you head to bed.'

He places his hands on my shoulders and steers me out of the room. My feet do the rest, taking me to my bedroom of their own accord. As I reach for the handle, I glance towards my parents' suite, wishing I could simply walk down the corridor, open the door, and find them safely inside.

THE WORLD BELOW

I LEARN FROM my mistakes. This time, I wait until the lights are out downstairs before making my way back to the house. I tell you, that girl took away one of my lives, appearing in the window like that. One moment the room was clear, then she popped up out of nowhere.

I should have used a 'don't see me' spell, but I could not help it, I froze. Fortunately, she turned away for a minute, and I was able to escape into the shadows, hiding under the patio furniture again.

Once my heart stops pounding, I begin considering my options. I must find out what Snake and the girl are planning so I can report back to my mistress. I stretch as I ponder, then freeze. There is another presence in the garden, and a tingle in the air tells me they are using magic to cancel themselves.

Fortunately, cat sight has its advantages. In the gloom, I find something crouched in the corner of the stone wall, watching and waiting.

The lights on the ground floor blink out, and the other creature moves ever so quickly. The presence disappears for a moment, reappears, then is completely gone.

I wonder if they found what they were looking for. Regardless, I need to know what they wanted. Keeping to the shadows, I pad to the door, incant a simple spell in my mind, and the lock clicks open as I reach it. I slip in through the smallest of gaps and sniff the air, trying to get a sense of the place.

Snake and the elf did not spend much time in the kitchen. I follow their scents to the dining room. Papers are spread over the table. I jump up, sending a pen clattering to the floor. Freezing, I wait for the sounds from upstairs telling me I have been found out. All is silent.

I walk over the papers, and they move under my paws, no matter how light-footed I am. Then I see it: the faint glow of magic where the other visitor touched the pad just for a moment.

I peer down and read what appears to be travel plans. Ah, they are going after endorsements in the West Country. Smart move. The density of magical creatures in the area should give them ample opportunity to complete their tokens.

I take note of where they are going, ready to relay the details back to my mistress. She will do what she can to help from her end.

For a moment, I think of my bed by the radiator and sigh. I will not be home for some time. My mistress is right; some other force is interested in what Snake and his friend are up to, and I will need to stay close to them if we are to find out who is behind this.

I return to the kitchen, jump onto the bench, and flick on the cold water tap for a quick drink before dropping down and heading to the fridge. I leap up and grab hold of the handle, hanging off it until the door opens.

I jump back onto the bench, and I survey the contents. On the top shelf are two sausages covered in cling film. One of them will do nicely. I leap across and hang from the shelf. It wobbles a bit, unable to hold my weight for long. My back feet find purchase on the door of the freezer.

I make sure I am stable before reaching up to slice the cling film with a nail. I hook a sausage and fling it towards the door before letting myself drop gracefully to all four paws.

Finally, I leap and push the fridge door closed. I take the sausage and leave, using magic to shut the door to the garden behind me. Of course, I could have used a spell to steal the sausage, but it is so much more satisfying going old school.

Back under the patio furniture, I finish my meal before lying down and clearing my mind so I can report to my mistress

THE HAG IN THE BOG

IT IS STILL pitch black when Imagine Dragons blare out "Radioactive" in my ear. Reaching under the pillow, I grab the phone to turn off the alarm. Still half asleep, I stumble to the ensuite and use the shower to fully wake up. After changing into my one clean set of clothes, I fold the dirty stuff into a plastic bag before stuffing it into my pack, followed by my phone and e-reader.

After making the bed and ensuring the room is left as I found it, I can't help but smile. Mum would be proud. My eyes tear up at the thought of her and how far away she is. Swallowing the lump in my throat, I pick up my hoodie and backpack and head downstairs.

Early though I am, Pris is even earlier. She is scraping scrambled eggs from a pan onto a plate, frowning as they tumble onto buttered toast.

'What's up?' I ask.

'I could have sworn there were two sausages in the fridge last night, but when I went to get them to add to the scrambled eggs, I only found one.' She looks at me, eyebrow raised.

I hold my hands out in front of me, palms facing outwards. 'Hey, it wasn't me. I was stuffed after all that chocolate and lasagne.'

Pris rinses out the pan and places it on the draining board, the frown deepening as she tries to work out what happened to the missing food.

'Look, eggs by themselves are fine,' I tell her. 'In fact, they're more than fine. I have eaten better since meeting you than I have for days.'

The smile she gives me sends heat rising up my neck. *Get a grip*, I tell myself. Spying the large pack by the backdoor, I opt for a change of subject.

'Good, you found some camping gear. Hopefully, you packed a tent?' Pris plonks a plate down on the counter in front of me.

'You're kidding. That's my clothes.'

Clothes? How many clothes do you need for a week? Fortunately, I didn't let that thought out. 'Oh, okay.' I eat some of my eggs. 'Do you have a tent? I'm happy to carry it.'

'A tent? What for?'

Man, this is like wading through treacle. 'Where do you think we're going to be sleeping this week?'

Pris doesn't miss a beat. 'Motels, hotels, B&Bs.'

I stop eating as I think of the small amount in my bank account. As it is, I will have to work every free hour to pay for uni next year, I probably won't be able to go if I use all my money now. I shake my head. What am I saying? Of course I will use every penny if it means getting Mum back. Still, I may not have enough to pay for accommodation and food for an entire week. 'They cost money, Pris—money I can't afford,' I reluctantly admit.

Pris studies me for a moment before saying, 'My parents gave me an emergency credit card, and I would say this is an emergency.'

'Still, it will have to be paid back.' I am embarrassed at her offering to pay for me, while at the same time a little relieved most of my savings will still be there once this is over.

'Think of it this way: my parents will be happy to cover the costs if we rescue them. And if we don't….' My heart clenches as tears well in her eyes. It nearly breaks when she brushes them away almost angrily. 'If we don't, it will be my money to dispose of anyway.'

This is the first time I allow the possibility of failure to enter my head, and the thought turns the food in my mouth to sand. I put the fork down and take my plate to the bin. Scraping the leftovers into the rubbish, I refuse to think about not getting Mum back. I can't leave her down there alone in the World Below.

Pris grabs my plate, rinses it, and puts it in the dishwasher. I bag up the rubbish and take it to the bin out back. I'm not sure, but I think there is a shadow under the patio furniture. A fox or a cat, perhaps? It is watching me as I return to the kitchen, and the hairs on the back of my neck stand on end at the thought.

Pris is standing with hands on hips, looking at my backpack. Oh my goodness, what is she wearing? The jeans and designer sweatshirt are fine, but the Converse high-tops are not going to be any good for hiking.

'Don't you have any walking boots… something more suitable for rough terrain?' I ask.

She frowns and stares at me like I'm speaking a foreign language. 'I was just about to ask if that is all you brought for the next seven days. We're going to be together a lot, and I don't want to put up with… you know… unwashed boy odours.'

'This is all I need: one set to wash and one to wear. I was hoping to find laundromats along the way.'

'We won't have time to…'

I don't catch the rest because Pris takes off down the corridor. Footsteps thump up the stairs before fading into nothing. I check the time on my phone. We have to move, or we will miss our train.

I pick up our packs and head to the hallway, meeting Pris at the foot of the stairs. She is carrying some walking boots, an identical pack to the one her gear is stowed in, and an assortment of clothes. She dumps it all on the floor before sitting down and unlacing her trainers.

'These are Mum's boots—they should fit. The clothes and pack are for you. Some of Dad's things. They might be a little big, so I grabbed a belt. You can also use his pack. Come on. We have to hurry.'

Still in a daze, I shove the stuff from my pack into the larger one before holding up one of the two pairs of jeans from the pile on the floor. Right length, but Pris is correct, they are at least a size bigger than I would buy. I roll them up, along with a couple of plain black t-shirts, a red-and-black checked shirt, and a zip-up hoodie.

Three packages are left on the floor. Two contain new underwear, and one is an unopened three-pack of socks—all from M&S. I look at them as if they are alien.

'Dad always keeps a few new packs around for when he travels,' Pris explains. 'He won't notice any of this is missing.'

I shove them inside the larger pack and put my own backpack on the top, thinking it might come in handy. As I transfer my phone and wallet to the outside pockets, I can't help thinking how the other half lives. The clothes I am borrowing cost more than my entire wardrobe, and Pris has virtually given them away without a second thought.

Pris shoves her high-tops into the top of her pack and hauls it over her shoulder. Picking up her keys from a bowl beside the door, she looks at me. 'Are you ready? The taxi should be here now.'

'Taxi?'

'Of course. There's no way I am missing the train because of delays on the tube.'

She opens the door and bundles me out towards the black cab idling by the curb.

'Damn it,' Pris says from behind. 'I won't be a mo.'

I head down the steps and say, 'Hi,' to the driver before opening the door into what must be the oldest London cab still in action. The driver obviously isn't a morning person as he doesn't even acknowledge me.

I have just hauled my pack over to make way for Pris, when she jumps into the cab, waving sheets of paper in a plastic document wallet. 'I almost forgot these,' she says. 'Won't get far without our itinerary. And I left a quick note for Susan saying I will be staying at Amalie's for a few days, just in case she isn't, you know, one of us.'

As she shoves the wallet into the front pocket of her pack, she pulls out a D&G cap, pulls it down firmly on her head, and tells the driver, 'Paddington Station, please.'

I SLUMP INTO my seat as the train lurches away from the platform. Snake dumps his pack across from me and settles down beside it. I take a moment to catch my breath as he leans forward, arms resting on the table between us.

'I was sure we were going to miss it,' he says, panting.

'Who would have thought traffic would be so busy this early in the morning,' I grumble. 'Still, we were lucky the train was running a few minutes late.'

As we pull out from the station, I relax a little, and Snake sits back in his seat. The trip to Lydford will be over four hours, giving us plenty of time to plan our attack.

Snake reaches into his bag and pulls out his phone and some earbuds. He slips them in, rests his head against the window, and closes his eyes. Clearly, we won't be doing any planning together on the trip.

I, on the other hand, am too keyed up to sleep, and I always perform better when I am prepared for whatever life throws at me. I pull a book from my bag. I found it in Dad's office when I went to look for a plastic folder for our itinerary. The title, *Magical Places of Great Britain*, caught my eye. It was exactly what I needed for this adventure. I put it on the table and search for my earbuds.

As I slip them in place, I look up and find Snake eyeing the cover, his lips forming a smirk. I snatch the book off the table and hold it in front of me, aware I am being overly defensive. Snake double taps his right ear.

'I see you brought some research. Just don't take everything you read as gospel. Things aren't always what they appear to be in the human world.' He taps his ear again and closes his eyes.

I find my pen pal Ausgirl04's playlist she made to introduce me to her kind of music on my phone. I settle down and open the book. As Bic Runga's sultry tones form the lyrics to "Drive", I search the index for White Lady Waterfall, Lydford, flick to the page, and begin reading.

I'm so engrossed I do not realise Snake has moved until he touches my shoulder. I pause my music and look up at him.

'Would you like a tea or coffee?'

'Tea with milk, please,' I say, reaching for my wallet.

He smiles wryly. 'I can run to a couple of drinks.'

My cheeks warm, and I'm grateful my dark complexion is likely hiding my embarrassment.

He disappears down the carriage, and I glance at my phone. How long have I been reading for? Two hours? My eyes slip to Snake's e-reader, which he left still running on the table. I read the upside-down title *Where Science and Magic Meet*. My eyes widen. From what I can gather from the text, this is proper science.

'Just getting in some pre-uni reading,' a voice says from behind me as Snake reaches over and places a cup for life on the table. 'I'm going to need a lot of these over the next few days, so I did the right thing—save the planet and all that.'

Funny, he appeared to be more embarrassed about caring for the environment than reading a science book for fun.

'Thanks for the tea,' I say. As he sits, I ask, 'So you're going to uni? What are you studying?'

'Physics,' he answers before taking a sip from his cup. 'Ahh, coffee. I can't function until I've had my first cup. What?' he asks when he realises I haven't moved. 'Don't tell me you have never met a coffee addict before?'

I'm suddenly conscious that I am staring at him. 'Physics?'

Okay, so words have escaped me. To my eyes, Snake looks like your average guy. If I am honest, a little bit better than average with those twinkling green eyes and the floppy brown fringe he keeps flicking out of the way. And I sat on the guy. He is all muscles and sinew. He is not your regular geek.

'Is there something wrong with that? My background gives me a unique perspective on the energies powering our world, don't you think?'

'You don't seem the type,' I say, floundering out of my depth.

He grins at me. 'No glasses and nerdy clothes, you mean. Things have moved on since the eighties.'

Caught out stereotyping, I resist the urge to look away and am searching for something cutting to say when I stop—suddenly aware he's right; I'm out of touch with the world.

I've had most of the same friends since primary school. I spend my leisure time with them, except when we go on family holidays, always overseas and always somewhere educational. I've had very little experience of the world at large, and not even London at large.

'Sorry, not many sciency people in my social group,' I say to cover my confusion.

'No magical people, no science people. You're missing out on making some great friends.' Snake grins and picks up his book. 'We're just the same as everyone else, you know. We eat the same food, listen to the same music, watch the same movies.'

He focuses on his book, occasionally taking sips from his mug. I turn my music back on and close my eyes, wondering if he was talking about magical people, science people, or simply people who do not live in my exclusive world.

LYDFORD STATION IS exactly what I expected from a country stop. The wooden building stands on one of the two concrete platforms separated by two railway lines—one for each direction. I am surprised to find it staffed, and by one of the most helpful station workers I've ever met. Then again, as I am well aware, my experiences of living in London have not prepared me for the way the rest of England works.

George, as he asks us to call him, is happy to store our packs in a locked room, so long as we pick them up before 5:50 p.m. when his shift ends. We assure him we're only going to walk the Lydford Gorge, and we should be back in plenty of time. Snake pulls his daypack out before leaning his bag up against mine.

'So, you're trekking the gorge,' George says as he locks the door to the storeroom. Walking a few paces to the ticket counter, he then reaches over and scrabbles for something. Moments later he hands Snake a pamphlet. 'This is the path to the gorge car park and a map of the track.'

'Thank you,' Snake says, shoving the pamphlet in his pocket.

'It is a good two-to-three-hour walk, so you might want to nip across the road to the cafe. Myrtle does a lunch pack for hikers such as yourselves. Reasonably priced too.'

'What a great idea,' I say. 'Thank you so much for your help.'

'My pleasure,' George responds, opening the door to his office, mind already on his next task.

I walk, or more accurately float, out of the station, marvelling at how someone taking a little time to help us out has made my day.

Snake insists on buying lunch, and I let him, realising that this was his way of contributing to our search. He has no idea that his very presence is giving me the courage to travel round the country, so far out of my comfort zone, and that is more than worth any amount of charges on my parents' credit card.

While I wait, I study my surroundings. Lydford is my idea of a typical English village: a mixture of ancient stone houses and modern new builds trying to blend in. Apart from the pub, which doubles as a B&B, I find a post office, the cafe Snake entered, and a local restaurant slash takeaway, which strangely does both fish and chips and Indian meals. I half expect a Miss Marple type figure to pop out of one of the doorways.

As Snake emerges from the cafe, shoving water bottles, sandwiches, and fruit into his pack, I smile at a middle-aged woman jogging by who says, 'Hello' as our eyes meet. It's odd being spoken to by a total stranger, but I feel compelled to acknowledge her friendly greeting.

'Let's get going,' I say as Snake joins me.

'Not quite Kensington High Street, is it?' he says, accurately guessing at my discomfort as he hauls his pack over his shoulder.

'Everyone is so nice and friendly,' I say under my breath as Snake consults the pamphlet.

'Odd, isn't it. It's so quiet, and the people are so chatty,' he says, then points down the street, away from the station. 'The track is this way.'

By the time we reach the carpark, I'm over walking. We take a drink break before we start on the hike, and I ask how much further to the falls.

Snake laughs. 'I would say about an hour or so from here.'

I think he is teasing me until I read the signs at the beginning of the track. The journey here had clearly not been part of the stationmaster's calculations.

As we walk the track through the gorge, I lose myself in nature. Everything is so green and beautiful, and everything smells… fresh. It's the only way I can describe it. Most of the track is boardwalks interspersed with some gravelled sections. As I slip for the third time on the wet wood, I appreciate Snake suggesting a change of footwear this morning.

'If you haven't been out of London much, how did you know about the shoes?' I ask when we stop at a viewing platform for yet another drink break.

'My father used to go and visit some of the other races, and he always kitted himself out like this.' He looks down at his clothes, and shrugs. 'So, I thought it might be a good idea to be prepared.'

Snake turns away and gazes down into the gorge, and the silence is uncomfortable. The way he looked at his feet makes me wonder if his shoes, like mine, were borrowed from a parent. I want to ask him about his father. I also want to ask my parents if their weekend hiking trips were to meet with representatives of the other races.

I can do none of this. Instead, I pop my bottle back into the side pocket of Snake's pack and say, 'Come on, not long until the top now,' and carry on walking before my body decides it's had enough and refuses to go on.

Near the top we meet an elderly couple who do not look nearly as knackered as we do, and I say an embarrassed 'Hello' as our eyes meet.

'You're almost at the falls, love. Keep it up,' the woman, who must be seventy if she's a day, says as she passes.

I mumble thanks, and not for the first time, I think I really should fit some more cardio into my life. The woman is right though. As I climb, the roar of the rushing waters of the White Lady Falls fills my ears.

I catch Snake up. He clearly spends more time walking than I do, even if he isn't used to country treks. When we arrive at the top of the trail, I pause and take in the view.

The falls are like nothing I have ever seen in real life. I could stand here and watch the water all day, following it as it froths and gushes over rocks and finally calming when it reaches the pool below. The frantic movement of the falls is a counterpoint to the serene greenery surrounding it.

'Up here or down there?' I ask, still almost too out of breath to form a full sentence.

'Down, I think.' Snake leans forward slightly over the railing to get a better look.

'Of course,' I say, glaring at the steps down to the pool at the bottom of the waterfall. I sigh and take a sip of water as I peer down the shadowy path again.

I could have sworn I saw a black cat descending—well, the tail of one at least. When I look again, it has gone. Oxygen deprivation is obviously playing tricks with my mind. I place my foot on the first step—the sooner we get to the bottom, the sooner we leave, and the sooner I can be done with all this walking.

I PAUSE BEFORE following Pris down the path beside the waterfall. For the whole morning, I have successfully put off thinking about approaching the White Lady, the most senior of witches above ground. Although I made light of it to Pris, I am worried what toll she will exact from us in exchange for her endorsement.

Will she ask too much? Will we have to turn her down? Will she even come when called? What if she turns up but won't endorse us?

'Snake, are you coming?' Pris calls up.

Standing here worrying won't get the job done. I urge my body down the stairs. When I arrive at the viewing platform at the bottom, I find Pris already there, staring into the water.

'Are you sure this is the right place?' she asks, glancing around.

I follow her gaze upwards to the top of the falls, which now dwarf us, and I nod, surprised she can't sense the magic swirling around us.

'What now?'

I tear my eyes away from the mesmerising flow of water. 'We call the witch.'

Pris turns to me. 'What, just say something like "White Witch, we want to speak with you?"'

'Pretty much,' I answer, and I can't help but laugh as she raises an eyebrow.

'You're kidding.'

'I don't exactly do this every day,' I tell her. 'I'm sort of winging it.'

I wait for a group of school kids and their teacher to head past before lowering my pack to the ground and facing the waterfall. I close my mind and let the magic in the air wash over me until the medallion on the leather strip around my neck warms, signalling that I am at one with the energies of this place.

'I, Snake Fieth, request an audience with the White Lady.'

My voice is loud and clear, and it rings around the gorge. Giggles drift down from the group of kids on the path by the waterfall, and I can't help but be a little embarrassed.

'Nothing's happening,' Pris points out.

'Be patient. She doesn't actually live here,' I tell her, more confidently than I feel.

We wait another five minutes, and still nothing.

'Did I hear you call The White Lady?'

I start at the voice so close behind. Swinging around, I come face-to-face—well, not exactly face-to-face, more like face-to-top-of-hat—with an elderly lady dressed like an advertisement for a walking magazine.

'No, of course not.' Pris colours as she answers, then drops her gaze.

'It's all right, no need to be embarrassed. Many come here to call her, but she doesn't speak to them all.' She waves as she heads back to the track. 'Must be on my way, things to do, people to see. Good luck with whatever you want her for.'

Pris waits until she has disappeared before saying, 'Should we call for her again? Maybe make contact with the water when we do?'

My medallion is still warm, so the magical connection is still active.

'No, I think we should just wait. Perhaps we should eat our lunch.' My stomach rumbles as I lower myself to the ground.

Pris hesitates, starts to say something, then joins me. 'If you're sure.'

I'm not sure exactly. Mum normally handled contacting the elders of our race and any inter-creature communications. Whenever she did, the medallion given to me by my father's family at my birth always heated up.

We eat our lunch in silence, facing the waterfall. The crusty ham-and-cheese roll is fresh and crunchy, just the way I like it. I'm finishing off my apple when I notice the waterfall begin to ripple. The air around us thrums as I nudge Pris and haul her to her feet just as a face appears in the water.

At first it is a shimmery outline, but in moments it forms into a 3D head protruding from the flowing water, like some CGI thing from a movie.

'I was expecting someone more like the Witch of Wimbledon, not a hag like in the fairy stories,' Pris leans in and whispers into my ear. She is trying to sound casual, but she can't keep the excitement from her voice.

'We don't use the term hag,' a melodic voice says. 'Hag is what men threatened by our power call women like us as they burned my kind at the stake. Some of them even had the temerity to call me the Hag in the Bog—as if this place could ever be a bog.'

'I'm sorry, I meant no offence,' Pris quickly stammers as the image changes to one of a beautiful woman.

'You prefer me like this?' the voice asks. 'Is physical beauty easier to deal with than a visage showing age and wisdom?'

'Is this some sort of test?' Pris asks. Her words are brave, but her voice is uncertain, and her hands are tightly clasped in front of her.

'No, child; merely a comment on what society now values.'

'This is going well,' I say under my breath before taking a step forward. 'Greetings, Eugenia, White Woman of Lydford and Earth Mother of England. Thank you for coming to meet with us.'

'It is a pleasure to meet you again, Snake. You have grown a little since you and your mother returned my ancestor's grimoire.'

'That was a few years ago now.' I smile, remembering how generous she had been with her thanks. Real diamond earrings for Mum, which had long since gone to pay some bill or other. For me, she brought my first guitar. She told me my family were gifted musicians and she was sure my talent for slight-of-hand was not the only gift I had inherited.

'You summoned me to this place. What can I do for you today?'

So, we were moving right on to the formalities. I had hoped for a bit more time on the catch-up, reminding Eugenia of our shared past before we got down to business.

'This is Priscilla Crown—'

'I know who Priscilla is. I was one of the three of my kind who attended her christening, welcoming the new princess to the royal line.'

'You know me?' Pris splutters, and I place a hand on her arm. I cannot allow a repeat of our audience with Eleanora. For a moment, she tenses, then puts her other hand over mine. I let out the breath I was holding, relieved she will let me handle the audience.

'We are here today to request your endorsement so we might attend the Spring Court to speak up for our parents at their trial.'

'As I already suspected. Eleanora sent her friend to speak on your behalf, and I am inclined to support you both. However, we must follow the correct forms before you receive the tokens.'

'See, I told you we would have to give something up,' Pris whispers, worry creeping into her voice.

'Not give something up, child, but give something of yourselves. I want to be sure you are honest and trustworthy and are prepared to fight for your parents' freedom.'

'What must we give to gain our tokens?' I ask, suddenly wary. Personal information is common currency in the World Below, but one that can have unforeseen repercussions if you aren't careful.

'I want you to tell me what you most fear at this very moment.'

'That's easy,' Pris says, stepping forward to answer. I again grab her arm before she can say anything more.

'Our fears can be used against us. I want your promise that once you assess our commitment, you will forget you ever heard them.'

Pris turns angrily to me, wrenching her arm out of my grip. 'What are you doing? You don't bargain with someone you are asking a favour of.'

'No, child, the boy is correct. Knowing someone's fear is a weapon beyond price, and Snake is right to ensure it cannot be used against you. As it is not my intention to ever use this knowledge beyond today, I agree to your terms. I will wipe my memory of whatever you tell me.'

I move out of Pris's way so she can answer Eugenia.

She states her fear simply and directly. 'I am afraid I will not be able to free my parents.'

The White Lady's lips form a smile. 'Of course you are, but that is not the root of your fear, is it?'

The tension around Pris's eyes tells me Eugenia is right, and my stomach knots —we will not be let off the hook by offering up any old fear. She wants to see into our very core. I begin formulating an answer that will satisfy her without giving too much away, but I am distracted by Pris's next words.

'All right,' Pris almost hisses. 'I am afraid all this nonsense about magic and creatures and the World Below is real, which means my parents haven't prepared me for who I need to be to rescue them. That scares me, but it also makes me angry.' She folds her arms across her chest and glares at the image in the waterfall.

Eugenia glares back, not giving Pris an inch.

Pris's shoulders slump, and she says, almost in a whisper, 'I am afraid I don't know who I am anymore.'

I reach out and place a hand on Pris's shoulder, but she doesn't appear to even notice my clumsy attempt to console her. My hand drops back to my side as the witch finally speaks.

'You are right to fear you have not been prepared well enough to complete your quest, but you are stronger than you think. If you work with Snake, you will do well enough. In the meantime, you might do well to remember that what you are is different to who you are.'

Pris actually humphs as she drops back to the ground. She does not understand that in return for her honesty, Eugenia gave her some useful advice.

'Now, Snake, what is your greatest fear?'

My stomach somersaults. I have been so engrossed in the exchange between Pris and Eugenia, I have not fully prepared my answer.

'I am worried I will not be able to save my mother and I will be left alone in the World Above.' The words tumble out, and before I am even finished speaking, I realise it will not be enough.

'Partially true, but you can do better.'

I gaze into the water roiling at the base of the falls as I consider what to say next. Can I actually say the words that will unlock the fear that built inside me over the last eight years? I worry that if I do, my heart will break and I will be of no use to anyone.

I gulp in air, suddenly unable to breathe.

'Come on, Snake. You can say it. If you don't, it will fester inside you and may prevent you from succeeding in freeing your mother.'

Eugenia's musical voice is gentle, and I can't be sure she hasn't put some magic behind it, because I find myself saying, 'I am afraid I am more like my father than I would like to be, and that I will let my family down when they most need me.'

Freeing my fear is like pulling out a rotting tooth: equal measures of pain and relief. Eugenia's watery figure produces a hand that reaches out to me, as if to offer comfort in the same way I had to Pris moments ago.

I wipe the tears from my eyes. Anger and sadness war inside of me as my head drops and I shove my hands in my pockets.

'There is more to that story than you know, young man,' the White Lady says, her voice compassionate but controlled. 'What happened with your family eight years ago is very likely linked to what is happening now. Do not close your mind or your heart in the coming days or you may fail this mission.'

I worry the coins in my pocket as I consider her words, and I come across some new odd-shaped ones. Drawing them out, I find the witches' tokens.

Pris reaches into my pack and pulls out the two we got from the elves. Taking one of her pieces, I give her one of mine. I then hold my two tokens together, and Pris's eyes widen as they snick into place, forming a half coin. She follows my example and laughs as her pieces do the same.

'Thank you,' I say to Eugenia. I elbow Pris.

'Yes, thank you. We appreciate your help.'

'It is my pleasure. I just hope our support is enough. I fear darker forces are at work here. Good luck on your quest.'

As Eugenia's face merges with the waterfall again, I catch sight of a form behind the water. Is that a cat? I open my mouth to ask if Pris can see it too, just as the image disappears.

As I bend to pick up my pack, Pris asks, 'What does she actually look like, the White Witch? Crone or White Lady?'

'Whatever she wants to,' I reply. 'Witches are amongst the longest lived of creatures in human years, and they use their magic to shape shift into whoever humans will accept.'

'Cool!' Pris says, clearly impressed.

I check my phone. 'Oh no, this has taken far longer than we anticipated. We're going to have to leg it to get back to the station in time.'

All thoughts of our quest leave my mind as we rush to rescue our luggage.

A LITTLE BIT OF GLAMOUR

FROM MY PERCH above the waterfall, I wait while Snake and the elf leave the clearing. A hand strokes my head, and I arch my back as it moves down my body. Eugenia tickles my ear, and I purr my pleasure.

'Did you like my water show?' she asks, and I shake my head. I think it was showy and unnecessary, as she had to also hold a vision of the waterfall as normal for other passersby. She would pay for that later.

'What else was I to do when they did not recognise me in the flesh?' She gestures to her elderly form encased in walking gear. 'I blame the *Harry Potter* movies. Ever since they came out, everyone expects magic to look like something special effects technicians dreamed up.'

I say nothing, but I think she enjoyed the show she put on rather too much.

'Well, we can't hang around here. I mean, I can, but you still have work to do. If the figure you saw last night was sent by the person behind this, then the goblins may already be considering not supporting Snake and Priscilla. You must go and persuade them otherwise.'

I want to argue that I can do that just as well in the morning. That I will do better on a full stomach and after a good night's sleep, but we have had this argument already. She will remain in Lydford tonight with Snake and that elf, and I will go talk with the goblins.

Nasty creatures, goblins. They are rude and do not respect their betters, so they will have little patience with me, even if I go as Eugenia's representative.

Eugenia reaches into her pocket and pulls out a handful of cat kibble and places it on the ground. Not my favourite food, but I tuck in hungrily.

'I can't let you go on an empty stomach. Come visit me once you speak with the goblins, and I will give you a proper meal.'

I finish the food as she walks away. Before I depart, I clean my face and stretch. I consider a five-minute nap in the last of the sun, but voices drift along the track and I am gone before the walkers turn the corner.

GEORGE IS PULLING the station door closed as we rush down the road.

'Wait, please wait,' I yell as I put on a burst of speed.

George grins when he finally catches sight of us. 'Cutting it fine, you two. Another minute and I would be gone.' He nods towards the car idling at the side of the road and raises his index finger to the middle-aged woman driver, indicating he will only be a minute.

'Thank you for doing this,' I say, following him into the station.

We retrieve our packs and hurry out, not wanting to delay the kindly man any longer.

'Next train out of here isn't for an hour or so, so if you want a meal, the bistro at the pub is pretty good,' George says as he locks up.

'We were sort of hoping to stay here tonight,' I say, and he raises an eyebrow.

'Only B&B is at the pub, and they're a bit old-fashioned. They won't take kindly to two young people like yourselves staying without parents. Maybe better to head to a bigger place where they don't mind such things.'

I am about to tell him I am over eighteen and don't need a guardian, but he is already heading towards the car.

With no outlet for my anger, I turn to Snake. 'We need to stay here because this is the best place for us to head out from tomorrow. I can't believe they won't let us rent a room without a guardian. I mean, it's not like we're going to share a bed or….'

Snake smirks and I stop mid flow. 'You didn't think we were sharing a room, did you?'

'It would be one way to save money,' he says.

My heart skips a little at the thought of him that close to me. *Stop it.* We're just… what? Almost friends? The look in Snake's eyes suggests he would not be averse to being something a little more. I haul my pack onto my shoulder. I am not going to go there. 'Two rooms, but it's moot if they won't let us stay.'

Snake shrugs, almost as if to say you can't blame a boy for trying. 'You could just glamour them,' he says, and I actually choke on air.

'Sorry? What?'

'You know, elves have magical abilities. With not knowing you're a creature, chances are no one has helped you discover your unique talents. It doesn't matter, though, because the one thing all elves can do is glamour humans.'

Is he mad? 'You think I can persuade someone to do something against their will?'

'Well, yes. You can't tell me you haven't done it before.'

I turn to face him. He is serious about this. 'Of course I have changed people's minds before, but I did it by persuading them, and eventually they come round to my way of thinking.' Why is he making such a big thing out of this?

His head tilts to the side as he asks, 'And how often does this happen? I mean, do you win most "arguments"?'

He actually air quotes the word argument with his fingers. Really, who does that anymore?

'On average, I win more than I lose, but I am good at building a convincing case,' I tell him.

'Okay, when is the last time you lost an argument against anyone but your parents when it was something you honestly wanted?'

'Just last….' I trail off. I actually can't recall the last time I was not able to persuade someone to do something I believed was right, something I was passionate about. 'You mean, I'm not great at turning people round to my way of thinking?'

My world is starting to shift again as another thing I was so sure about myself turns out to be a lie.

As if sensing my unease, Snake rubs my arm. 'You probably are good at it. I also imagine that when you are passionate about something, you can push a little persuasion behind your words. Maybe you never actually glamoured anyone as such….'

'Oh.' I'm relieved but also somewhat disappointed. I really thought I could use magic. 'If I haven't done it before, how will I be able to do it now?'

Snake frowns and runs his hands through his hair. 'I was taught to use my magic, so I can show you. I am not sure whether it will be the same for you, but it's worth a try.'

I am distracted for a moment by how cute he looks with his hair all messed up. *Focus.*

'When you want to win an argument, do you do anything differently to when you don't care?'

I chew my lip. *Do* I do anything differently? Mum once told me when she was helping me with debate prep that it's important to look a person directly in the eye when you are trying to convince them of something they might be opposed to. My hands tremble a little as I remember her words, and a wave of loneliness washes through me.

I clasp my hands together as I try to concentrate on what she actually said. Ah, that's right—she gave me some speech about people being able to tell if you are genuine or not, and Dad had teased her about being too intense. Now, looking at things in a different light, I wonder if maybe Mum was surreptitiously teaching me to glamour.

'I have an idea,' I tell Snake.

'No harm in trying, if you're game?'

I grin, excitement over the possibility of being able to do magic warring with my fear that this might all not be quite real. 'Sure, why not. Hold on.' My conversation with the Witch of Wimbledon comes back to me. 'I thought we were not allowed to use our magic for personal gain.'

Snake shakes his head. 'Personal gain would be getting the room for free, not talking them into giving us the rooms in the first place. Or, if there was a legal reason for us not to stay, then it would be wrong to persuade them otherwise.'

Nodding to show that I understand the distinction, I force my weary limbs to move along the road towards the pub. It was a typical whitewashed Ye Olde English building, with a B&B sign out the front. As we walk, I notice Snake looking around, checking alleys and scanning the rooftops.

'Is everything okay?' I ask.

'Yes…. Um… I'm not sure. I thought I felt someone watching us,' he says as he leans round me and pushes open the door. 'But I must have been imagining things.'

Although I am old enough to legally drink, my social life has been limited to cafes and clubs. This is my first ever time in an actual pub, and I am not impressed. The fusty smell of stale beer wafts over me as I enter, overpowering the supposed homeliness of the bright patterned carpet and the heavy wooden furniture. My overall impression is of walking back into a bad eighties sitcom.

It is still early, but two of the tables are occupied by couples, and three men sit at stools in front of the bar, half-drunk pints of ale in front of them. Everyone turns as we walk in. A barman appears from nowhere and starts to ask, 'What can I get…. Sorry, guys, I will have to see some ID before I can serve you.'

Fumbling in my backpack for my driver's license, I offer it to the barman. Snake, one step behind me, does the same. Having checked our ages, the bartender continues, 'Now, what will it be?'

'Actually,' I say, 'we would like a couple of rooms for the night.'

The man freezes. 'You must be twenty-one to book a room.' His tone is terse and dismissive.

'Is that a legal requirement?' I ask.

'House rules,' he says, refilling the pint of the man sitting closest to him.

'Why?' I press.

'Just the way it is, missy.'

'We can pay in advance, if you're worried we will skip out. And you can keep my credit card number and charge any damage we do to the rooms.'

He concentrates on wiping the bar, making it difficult for me to catch his eye. 'Everyone pays in advance. And you don't look like the room-trashing types.'

'We're not,' I agree, perplexed as to why he won't let us stay if we're so respectable. 'We can vote, join the army and fight for our country, and you would serve us at the bar, but you won't let us sleep here?'

Sighing, he raises his head, and I use the opportunity to capture his gaze. 'I can't be responsible for you,' he says, a tinge of sadness in his voice. 'I am the only one here most nights, and I don't have time to check up on children.'

'We are more than capable of looking after ourselves,' I say, but I get the impression there is more to this. 'What is it you are really worried about?' I ask.

Nothing,' he mumbles.

'Tell me,' I say, willing him to speak with all my strength. I feel a little foolish, staring intently at him and trying to push my will through my eyes.

I'm about to break away when he says, 'What if something happens during the night, a fire or the like? I might not be able to save you.'

What an odd thing to say. I search his face and find a real fear in his eyes. 'Has that happened before?'

He nods. 'A young lad stayed here once, and there was a gas leak. The boy almost didn't make it.'

Still holding the man's gaze, I place my hand on his. 'It's all right. We can look after ourselves just as well as any adult staying here. We can get ourselves out if there is a fire, or if something else happens.'

He pulls against my hand as if he wants to wrench away, but I refuse to let him. Throwing all my weight behind the words, I say, 'If you rent rooms to us, everything will be all right, I promise.'

Neither of us moves. It's as if we are frozen in time. I am about to break away, feeling foolish at having even tried this, when the barman relaxes.

'Yes, you're right. Everything will most probably be fine if you stay tonight.'

I bite back a smile and ready myself for one last push. 'So, you will allow us to stay.'

The room is silent and the air around me seems electric as the barman nods slowly. 'Of course. You had best come through.'

It worked. It actually worked! I want to dance and sing as we follow the barman through the door into the hallway, but I contain myself, aware every eye in the bar is on us.

As we pass by the public toilets and a door with a sign saying, "Office", I wonder if the real power of the elves is not to confuse or befuddle people into agreeing with them, but in finding the real reason for their resistance and offering a way out.

I suddenly realise that the barman is speaking to me. 'Sorry, what?' I look around in confusion.

Snake is leaning against a counter, signing his name in a register. 'He said he has given us the two rooms at the end of the corridor, closest to the shared bathroom. Breakfast starts at six, and there is room in the bistro if we want to eat here tonight,' he says as he reaches out a hand for the keys.

'You'll need to sign in.' The barman pushes the register towards me. I add my details below Snake's and hand over my credit card.

'Tap all right?' he asks, and I nod, still a little distracted, trying to work out how my glamour worked.

'Right, top of the stairs and keep going. Bistro is already open if you want to eat.' He slips back through to the bar and asks, 'Who's next?'

The rooms continue the theme of bad eighties decor, but they are clean, when I sit on it, the bed is comfortable. My weary body wants to lay down and sleep, but Snake is already in the doorway.

'Shall we eat?'

I want to tell him all I need is a bath and bed, but he's right, we should put food in our stomachs. Tomorrow will be another long day of walking, and we need to make sure we fuel up.

After eating a surprisingly good meal downstairs of homemade pumpkin soup and fresh bread, I wait while Snake finishes off his steak, eggs, and chips. We head back upstairs, and he offers me first use of the bathroom. I don't argue.

I'm disappointed that there is no bath to stretch out in, but the shower is hot and strong, and as the water washes over me, my aching muscles begin to relax.

After standing in the steam, my hair's turned into a frizzy mess of corkscrew curls. I don't have the energy to deal with it, so I comb through some leave-in conditioner and bundle it into a loose ponytail before slipping into my favourite oversized Minnie Mouse T-shirt and some cotton sleeping shorts. On the way back to my room, I knock on Snake's door.

'Bathroom's free.'

He mutters something, and I take that as thanks and head back to my room.

Knowing I should not sleep so close to eating, I put my phone and earbuds on to charge and grab my laptop from the bag. The B&B has Wi-Fi, but my laptop is set up to use my phone data, and I don't like the thought of using a public connection.

I bring up a web browser and begin researching the Underground Ballroom, looking for anything that might link it to the magical world. Dad's book didn't mention it, and I want to confirm whether or not Snake is right about it being where The Court will meet.

The first page I open tells me it was built by Victorian industrialist Whitaker Wright on his estate in Surrey. It was once impressive but fell into disrepair after his death.

'He was a dwarf, still is in fact, but he moved back underground. He couldn't take the shame of being forced to lose his fortune; he was drawing too much attention to himself, and The Court decided he should disappear.'

How on earth had Snake opened the door and made it to my bed without my noticing? I had been engrossed in what I was reading, but still…. And I wish he would put some clothes on.

Snake is standing right beside my bed, a none-too-large towel wrapped round his waist. He is all lean muscle, and *omg, get a grip, girl.*

He pulls a T-shirt over his head, and I manage to force my eyes away from the muscles rippling across his stomach and back to the screen. 'A dwarf?' I choke the words out.

'Yep, they are attracted to gold and precious metals. They often became captains of industry in the nineteenth and twentieth centuries. Nowadays, they're mostly merchant bankers, although some of their kind will do almost anything for money, not all of it strictly legal.'

The heat from his body is making it difficult to concentrate. 'You said he had to give up his fortune?'

'Yep. It wasn't the personal gain thing because he used to give a lot away to charity, but he was getting too well-known. Humans think he committed suicide, but he moved back below. Rumour has it, he's a bit of a recluse.'

'So, why don't people, humans, use the ballroom now?' I ask. Snake leans over to get a better look at the screen. As his arm brushes against mine, tingles shoot all over my body and heat rises up my neck. It is all I can do to bring up the next page.

'The ballroom was built on what was once a door between the two worlds.

I guess technically it still is, although it's closed most of the time. Whit asked the Queen to place a glamour on it so no one would demolish it or use what he believed was his crowning glory.'

An awkward silence follows his announcement as the tension in the room almost overwhelms me. I'm about to ask why he is here when he clears his throat and says, 'Just popped in to suggest we head down for breakfast at six. I'm not a morning person, so I need to set an alarm if you want an early start.'

I glance up, and there is a twinkle in his eyes, as if he is aware of how his presence is affecting me.

'Six will be fine,' I say, turning back to my screen. 'Sleep well.'

Then he is gone. An hour or so later, my hormones have settled down enough for me to feel drowsy, if a little lonely.

GOBLINS OF WISTMAN'S WOOD

THE SOUND OF "Love Music, Pt.2" by Ren blasts in my ear through the pillow. I grab for the phone. I struggle to find it, and my fingers fumble as I try to turn off the alarm before it wakes the entire village. Love the song, but it's a bit full-on for first thing in the morning—I guess that's why it works so well as an alarm.

I force my legs from under the warm covers. My body is heavy and still half asleep. I could do with another couple of hours kip, especially because I couldn't sleep last night.

I would love to say my restlessness was due to worry about Mum, but it was nothing that altruistic. No, my mind kept replaying the scene in Pris's bedroom, and try as I might, I couldn't help but wonder what would have happened if I had kissed her like I wanted to when I leaned over to read what was on her laptop.

She looked so cute with her hair all messed and wearing that Mickey Mouse tee…. I almost forgot why I was in her room. I had to force myself to leave before the effect she was having on me became obvious.

Any other girl, and I might have made a move. Not that I'm any sort of ladies' man, but I do all right. And it's not that I don't like Pris—I do. And there is definitely a physical attraction—very definitely. But she is beyond my reach, both in this world and the other. Especially the other. The powers that be will never allow such a match between the races.

I sigh and dress in the clothes I laid out last night. Before I leave my room, I make sure everything is in my pack, ready to go. I turn from locking the door and almost bowl Pris over.

I suppress a smile. The only thing country walk about her is her shoes. Her denim jacket is lined with a purple-and-black-checked fleece that matches her purple jeans and black D&G t-shirt. Her hair is tucked under a slouchy black beanie.

'Love the hat,' I say to cover my chuckle.

'You know, people have no idea how difficult this type of hair is,' she grumbles as she leads the way down the hall. 'Taming it will take time—time we need for walking.'

'Hey, I loved the look last night, so don't hide it on my account.' The words tumble out before I can stop them.

She half turns to check I'm not taking the mick, then her lips curl into a smile. I follow her downstairs. At the counter, she pulls a pamphlet from the display box as we pass. I catch a quick glimpse of the title: *The Lych Way*.

'We might need this,' she says as she leads us through the bar to the bistro on the other side. The smell of breakfast has my mouth watering.

The only other occupant of the dining room is an elderly lady. She looks familiar, and I realise she was the woman we spoke to on the walk yesterday. And is that a cat under her table? The animal shifts into the shadows as a harried middle-aged woman bustles through the kitchen doors.

'Full English for you two?' she asks.

I nod enthusiastically, and Pris says, 'Yes, please.'

After placing a full plate in front of the other guest, the woman bustles back into the kitchen, and we take a seat.

'Good morning,' our breakfast companion says as she reaches for the pepper shaker. 'Nice day for a walk.'

'Yes,' I respond as Pris opens the pamphlet so we can both study the map.

'According to my book, the Lych Way is also called the Way of the Dead,' Pris says as a pot of tea and two mugs are plonked on the table between us.

'Nice,' I say reaching to pour.

'So, this map confirms what I thought. It's about five hours to Two Bridges, and the route passes through Wistman's Wood. Then it's about another hour and a half from Two Bridges to Postbridge, where we need to catch the bus to Yelverton at 2:30.'

My muscles groan at the thought of another walk today, especially such a punishing one, but I ignore them.

'Is the bus from Yelverton to Plymouth the only option that keeps us on track?' I ask, sipping my tea.

'No, probably not, but time spent replanning is time lost for our walk, and if we are to walk to Two Bridges today…,' Pris says, leaving me to make the connection.

I take her word for it. She is very organised, and I'm sure she has plotted the optimal route.

'I am sorry, but I could not help but overhear.' I start at the voice so close by and turn to find the woman at the next table leaning towards us.

'I am driving over to visit a cousin in Postbridge after lunch and would be happy to swing by Two Bridges to pick you up. Do you think you could be at the end of the walk by about one thirty?'

I am taken aback by the offer. 'That is very kind of you—'

'Hope you don't mind cats, as mine will be with me, but there should be plenty of room for you and your gear for a short trip.'

'It would help us out…,' Pris says, turning a questioning gaze to me. 'And I for one would appreciate not having to walk the extra miles.'

I am still reluctant to say yes. Growing up in the world of creatures, where nothing is ever given for free, tends to make you suspicious of kindness.

As if sensing my reluctance, the woman says, 'You are right to be suspicious of strangers, young man, but I assure you my offer is genuine, and I am not an axe murderer or anything. Just ask Mable here.'

I turn to find myself face-to-face with a plate piled high with bacon, sausages, mushrooms, tomatoes, and scrambled eggs, topped with a slice of fried bread. My stomach grumbles in appreciation as I take the food and settle it in front of me.

'Ask me what?' Mable asks as she puts Pris's plate down.

'Whether or not I am trustworthy.'

Mable laughs. 'Mrs Wilson has been a regular here for as long as I can remember. She is as honest as they come, even if she does insist on sneaking the odd animal into the dining room.'

'See,' Pris says around an enormous mouthful of mushrooms. 'We can trust her.'

I can't stand the pleading in her eyes. Besides, it would be nice to not have to walk the extra miles.

'Can we pay you for petrol, perhaps?' I offer, still not completely comfortable with accepting help.

'Nonsense, young man. My offer is made without obligation.'

The words she speaks are the formal release from a potential bond, and I start, knocking my teacup. Is this woman more than she appears to be? Is she from my world? Mrs Wilson seems ignorant of my scrutiny as she slips some sausage under the table to her cat. Pris kicks my shin and I jostle the table.

Realising I had better answer before anything else happens to breakfast, I say, 'All right. Thank you, we would be grateful for a lift. I am Snake, by the way, and this is Pris.'

'I am pleased to meet you both and happy you accepted my offer.' Mrs Wilson stands. 'Well, I have things to do this morning. I will see you at the Two Bridges entrance to the Lych Way around one-thirty.'

'We will be there, and thank you again, Mrs Wilson,' Pris says.

I say nothing as the woman leaves, cat close at her heels. Something about both the cat and the woman niggle at me, but I can't place what it is.

'Are you going to eat your mushrooms?' Pris asks, bringing me back to reality.

'Yes, I am,' I say as I fork a mushroom, shoving it straight into my mouth. 'Delicious.' She rolls her eyes at me, and I smile, digging into my meal.

Talk is limited as we stock up on fuel for the walk ahead. I leave Pris to settle the bill and buy some bottled water and nuts for our trek as I head upstairs to retrieve our packs.

At just after seven, we arrive at the Lychford green and find the start of the Lych Way. As we follow the meandering path, I fully appreciate why it is known as the Way of the Dead. In spite of the warm early spring morning, the air is heavy with morning mist stifling any noise and creating a sombre tone. Pris says the name comes from times past when locals took this route to bury their dead, but I wonder if there is more to the name.

Still, it is a beautiful walk over the moor, and I wonder why Mum and I never came here. She has always been friends with the witches above ground, and a few gnome kin live down this way. Maybe when she is back, we can spend some more time out of London.

The thought is bittersweet and brings with it a nagging doubt about my ability to rescue her from a court I have never attended. I try not to wonder if cutting myself off from my father's family might play against me now. Instead, I concentrate on putting one foot in front of the other—and on getting the next endorsement.

TREES FORM MISTY shadows in the distance as morning dew paints the grass intense shades of greens and browns and reds. The picture is framed by slate grey fences. It is difficult not to be distracted by the beauty of the moor.

Every muscle groans. After yesterday's efforts I suspect they were wanting

a rest. The pack on my back is way too heavy, but even as my body protests, I find myself enjoying the experience of walking in the fresh morning air.

When we stop for a drink break, I take off my jacket and tie it around my waist before pulling my pack back into place. By the second stop, I am so hot, I take off my beanie. I grimace as I tidy my hair into a loose braid in an attempt to tame its wildness.

Snake has been silent the entire time and, unusually for me, I don't feel much like talking either. It's almost as though being somewhere less frantic is allowing my brain to slow down and relax, to appreciate the silence rather than feeling a need to fill it.

Three hours into the walk, I check the map. We will soon be at Wistman's Wood, the goblin stronghold. At the very thought of the place, any sense of peace vanishes. I am all too aware that I don't know what to expect and, even worse, I have no idea how to behave. I have spent my life learning what is expected of me in every possible social situation, so this realisation is mortifying.

'What are goblins like?' I ask, breaking the silence. 'I mean, I always imagine them a little like Dobby from *Harry Potter*.'

Snake barks out a laugh. 'You'd best keep that thought to yourself when you meet them.'

'So, what *are* they like? And why is their stronghold so close to the witches'?'

I hate not knowing this stuff, and I really hate relying on Snake so much. But I do want to rescue my parents, and I can't do that if I don't learn more about the creatures we will be meeting.

'Human storybooks got some things right about goblins. They are fast and mischievous. Mostly, though, they are game players. Like gnomes, they are not as well thought of as elves and witches. Even though they aren't a lesser race, they often feel the need to ally themselves with the powerful,' Snake says.

The snarky tone of his voice tells me he doesn't like goblins very much. Which is interesting because he would rather go and ask for a token from them than his own people. I file that away to consider later while wondering what had happened that was so bad, he wouldn't ask his own race for help.

'Actually,' Snake continues, 'we can use that to our advantage. They like flattery, although not obvious flattery. In this instance, because of who you are, you should speak with them.'

I frown, trying to catch up. 'Because I am an elf and you are a gnome?'

'Exactly. And because your family is from the royal bloodline.'

'Does it really matter that much?' I ask.

He stops in the middle of the path and his eyes pin me in place. 'Ever been somewhere in the human world where people speak to your friends but not to you? Where they won't even meet your eyes?'

I'm about to tell him not to be ridiculous, people don't behave like that in civilised society. But I bite my tongue. He is right, much as I hate to admit it. There are enough people who judge me not worthy simply because of the colour of my skin that I know what it feels like. Dad says things are better than when he was a kid, but that doesn't mean racism has disappeared. It's more that most people hide it better.

'And in the World Below, you are treated like that?'

Snake nods. 'Pretty much. Not by the lesser creatures so much, but by the others. And to be fair, most goblins are treated that way too. The only difference is, they are always playing power games, trying to trade into better positions. That earns them respect from some, fear from others, and vilification from most.'

'That's so sad.' I'm liking the World Below less and less. From my current perspective, it makes medieval times sound progressive. Perhaps Mum and Dad had good reasons for keeping me away.

'Is positioning their stronghold close to the witches' a sign of a political alliance? Is that why you think coming here is a good idea?'

'You're catching on.' He turns and starts walking. 'Come on. I think that's Wistman's Wood over there.' He points to the edge of a copse of trees.

My muscles twinge and complain as I force myself to move. I keep fit with karate and tennis, but this walking lark is a whole new ball game. It takes about another half an hour for us to reach our destination.

As we move under the shelter of the trees, I am taken aback by how dark and weird and twisted and tortured they look. I mean, these are right out of every creepy forest in every horror movie, and I can almost hear their cries of pain as we brush past them. The air is cool, and at the same time, oppressive.

Goosebumps prick my skin as I ask, 'Do we need to go right in?' I'm hoping the answer is no.

'A little further, I think,' Snake says.

I try to suppress a shudder. 'How do you know when we're at the right place?'

He takes a few more steps under the trees, stops, shuts his eyes, then slips his backpack from his shoulders.

'Close your eyes,' he tells me.

My natural instinct is to snap at him to stop ordering me around, but I do as he says, trusting he has a good reason for being so bossy.

'What are your senses telling you?'

I peek through a single eye, thinking he can't be serious. His face shows no sign that this is a joke, so I squeeze my eyes shut and describe everything I am sensing. 'I smell damp earth. It is cool here. A breeze is blowing hair across my face. The rustle of leaves sounds so loud.'

'Good. Now hold on to those feelings, listen to the trees, and block everything else from your mind.'

This sounds very new agey, and I cringe as I do as he says. Moments later, the noise in the clearing changes. The rustling is louder, and the air feels almost as though it is charged with something. The ring on the middle finger of my left hand starts to warm up, and the sensation pushes everything else out of my mind.

'Ouch!'

'What is it?'

The worry on Snake's face is the first thing I see as my eyes fly open. I glance down at my ring, then look up. 'It was…'

'Warm?' he asks, an excited smile forming on his lips.

'Ah, yes. How did you know?'

He reaches up to the neck of his T-shirt and pulls out a medallion on a leather thong. 'We are all given a token when we're young. It's a tool to help us learn to use magic. When your body senses or draws magic, it will warm up to show you're doing it right.'

I stare at the ring. I felt magic? For a moment, I'm not sure how I feel about that. Actually, that's not quite right. My head is not sure, but my body is singing.

'Here is okay then?' I say, dumping my pack beside his and turning away to cover my confusion.

Snake steps up beside me, his green eyes dark with concern as he flicks his fringe out of the way. 'Here should do fine.'

I take a deep, shuddering breath, surprised to find I'm more nervous than I was when sitting my exams. *You can do this,* I tell myself as I turn to face Snake.

'What do I do? Do I just call the goblin like you called the White Witch?' I try to ignore the tingle of magic I now sense all around me and focus on the task at hand.

'You will need to use magic to contact him. Are you okay with that?' he asks, unable to keep the worry from his voice. I glance away, not wanting to see it written on his face.

'I am fine with it,' I say, my voice flat and even—controlled. My stomach, on the other hand, is churning like a washing machine on spin cycle.

'If you're sure….'

His tone telegraphs his doubt, and this ignites my anger. Good. Anger is better than a fear of failure.

'What is his name?' My voice is harsher than I mean it to be.

'Grossman Green.'

Laughter bubbles its way up from the pit of my belly and rushes out. Once it escapes, I can't stop it.

'Please, don't say anything,' Snake says. 'He may be listening to us.' There is laughter in his voice as well, but he is doing a better job at holding it in than I am.

It takes a while, but finally, I am able to calm down. I close my eyes like Snake had me do before and reach out, letting the magic tingle over my skin. The ring on my finger warms up, and I start to call for the goblin, but then break down again.

I'm laughing so much, I can't stand. Dropping onto the log behind me, I draw in some deep breaths. I don't know why I find the name so hilarious—I just do.

'Are you going to be able to do this?' Snake asks. 'I mean, without cracking up?'

His face is so stern, laughter bubbles out again. I look away and nod, unable to speak.

'Sometime today?'

My shoulders shake. Then I can hold it in no longer. It feels good to laugh, and it is like all that tension that's been building over the last couple of days drains out of me. Wiping the tears from my eyes, I turn to Snake. 'Yes, today.'

He raises a single eyebrow, but the twinkle in his eye shows me he also appreciated the joke.

I gulp in some air. Giggle. Then take a few more calming breaths. I remind myself of what is at stake, and the urge to laugh disappears.

'I'm ready now,' I tell Snake as I close my eyes and allow the magic to flow through me again. 'I, Priscilla Crown, request an audience with Grossman Green.'

I slowly release my magic and open my eyes, prepared to wait, only to find a suited man standing beside Snake looking very out of place in the woods. Something in my face must have alerted my companion to the other man's presence, as he turns, stumbles over a root and face plants.

The suited man sneers at Snake, as if his actions are to be expected from one such as him. Looking down his nose, he turns to me and performs a sketchy bow. 'Princess Priscilla, I am here at your request.'

Without the supercilious twist of his lips, Grossman Green would be a moderately handsome man in his late thirties, perhaps early forties. He is dressed in a smart pinstripe suit that could be found in offices all over London but is completely out of place in the middle of a forest.

I watch Snake haul himself off the ground and move to stand behind me. Dusting leaves and forest debris from his clothes, he takes a position behind my right shoulder. The waves of distaste swirling around him are every bit as real as the magic in the air.

'Mr Green.' Too formal? The way Grossman stands a little straighter tells me I hit just the right note. 'I would like for myself and my bodyguard to attend The Court Below this week, and I was hoping you would do me the honour of endorsing us so we may do so.'

My eyes widen a little. Is he actually preening? Could it be this easy?

He clears his throat and says, 'I must respectfully decline.'

I do a double take. 'I am sorry. You decline? You are refusing me, a member of the royal line?' I try to sound as haughty as possible, which is actually quite haughty, but it has no effect.

'With respect, you may be a princess, and of royal blood, even, but there is nothing you can give me that would persuade me to endorse you. Not even your pet witch's familiar could do that.'

Pet witch? Familiar? What is he talking about?

'I came out of courtesy when you called, but now I must go. I was in the middle of a merger meeting.'

Before I can utter a word, Grossman Green blinks out of existence. I turn to find Snake with his jaw hanging open, as confused as me.

I had just walked almost five hours to spend less than five minutes with a goblin who never had any intention of helping us. Confusion is quickly replaced with anger, and my fingers curl into fists.

'What just happened here?' I ask.

Snake shakes his head, as if he can't believe what he has seen either.

'I'm not sure. The Greens always ally with the witches, who are second only to elves in the creature hierarchy. For him to have turned your request down can only mean one thing—a powerful elf got to him first.'

I frown, trying to work out what elf might want to stop me from going to the World Below. 'You mean, someone like Giles Regis?'

Snake's laugh is tinged with bitterness. 'No, someone way more powerful than him.'

'But he called me a princess. I am of the royal line. Who is more powerful than that?'

'Exactly.' Snake moves to pass me, running his hands through his hair. 'I am starting to wonder if there actually is more going on here than our parents being taken before The Court to answer mundane charges.' He pauses. 'This isn't right. Something else is going on here, Pris.'

Snake is clearly upset, and with my lack of knowledge of the creature world, I have no idea what would rattle him this much. 'Like what?'

Snake's jaw tenses. 'I don't know. Come on. If we want to catch that lift, we had better get a wriggle on.'

I don't move. Is he really going to drop a bomb like that and then leave? He turns away from me, and I realise that is exactly what he is going to do. No way am I going to let that happen.

I move to follow him and trip, grabbing hold of a tree to stop myself from falling. What the…? I stare down at my feet—well, down at the vines covering my feet and winding up my ankles.

Anger is replaced by confusion. 'Snake? What's happening?'

I look over to find my friend struggling with his own problems. The tree behind him has reached out and wrapped its limbs around Snake, who is frantically wrestling, trying to get free.

'Green. GREEN. Get back here,' Snake growls as the branches grip him more tightly.

Nothing happens other than the forest pulling us in further to its clutches.

'Mr Green, please,' I beg.

The goblin appears, his face a mask of concern, but the hard look in his eyes tells me he knew this would happen.

'Oh dear. I do apologise. This is Wistman's Wood, and I thought you knew that no one leaves without sacrificing something.' He smirks. 'Oh, I see you didn't know. How remiss of you not to do your research. The forest needs something of yours—any trinket will do.'

I smile sweetly at him, and my voice is sugary as I say, 'I have nothing on me, and we are unable to get to our packs.'

'I guess I could pay the price for you, but that would mean each of you will owe me a favour.'

Grossman Green's smile is oily, and my stomach heaves in revulsion at the thought of owing this creature anything. I want to howl in frustration, but I am aware the vines have reached my thighs and Snake is turning a strange shade of grey. He wants to negotiate. All right, I can do that.

My minds starts ticking over what I can offer him in the real world, Nothing, I suspect, because whoever is pulling his strings is likely in the World Below.

'Time is ticking,' he reminds me.

I don't know much about the creature world, but Giles Regis's reaction to my threat gives me an idea; I may have something he wants or might need.

'Here is my proposal. If we get to the World Below, and the plot against our parents fails, I will put in a good word with the Queen for you—tell her how you helped me out of a bind.'

Grossman Green smiles, and I think I have misjudged the situation. Then, as the grin widens, I start to wonder if I have offered him more than he could have imagined.

He reaches into his pocket, takes out a couple of pound coins, and tosses them in the air. 'Deal,' he says before they land, and disappears.

Snake falls to the ground as the trees release him, and it takes a moment for him to start breathing normally. The vines slowly leave my body, taking their time, almost caressing me as if they are reluctant to let me go.

I shudder as I am finally freed, then rush to Snake and help him to his feet. As he brushes himself off, I say, 'I feel like I gave away the house when he only wanted a room.'

He shakes his head. 'No, the bargain was fair, though it was more than the sneaky bastard deserved.' He picks up his pack, slings it over his shoulder, and adds, 'Come on. We were already late for our lift before this.'

He strides off, not even waiting to see if I'm following. I grab my pack and take a more sedate pace, wondering if he is annoyed at me or at Grossman.

I am well out of the oppressive air of the woods when I realise what Snake probably already had the moment Green turned us down—we're one step closer to needing to visit the gnomes if we want to attend court.

WHAT NOW?

PUTTING ONE FOOT in front of the other, I ignore my bruised ribs and the pain stabbing my chest each time I draw a breath. I can't believe how that smug prat played us. It wasn't enough to turn us down; he had to profit from our visit as well.

Targeting my anger at Green allows me to hide from the one thing I don't want to think about. If I allow my mind to go there I might fall apart, and I can't do that…. Not yet anyway.

With each step I take, my heartbeat slows, and my anger slowly drains away until I can think clearly again. I mull over our options and realise that the goblin's refusal to help doesn't necessarily mean we will end up in Mawnan. I'm sure there's time to go to Bodmin and then up to Conway to the fairies.

As I begin to relax and breathe normally, something slowly dawns on me. Only a highborn elf would have enough pull to lure the goblins away from the witches. So, why is a high elf trying to prevent us from rescuing our parents from the World Below?

Gathering endorsements will be difficult enough without someone actively working against us. Do we even still have a chance?

Our next visit is to the sprites. Would they give in to a high elf's request to refuse us? They are mercurial creatures, so it is difficult to predict their reaction.

Gnomes will never side with elves against me, a voice inside my head whispers. I shut it out. I'm not ready to go there yet.

The fairies in Conway also have no allegiance to any particular higher race, and…. It hits me like a sledgehammer. I swing round to find Pris is a long way behind me, and my face colours in shame. We are supposed to be in this together, and I took off without her. I stop and wait for her to catch me up.

When she finally joins me, I know I should apologise for my bad manners, but I can't find the words. Instead, I say, 'Pris, did you take our itinerary to bed with you the night before last, or did you leave it in the dining room?'

For a moment, I think she is so annoyed with me she isn't going to answer, but then her eyes widen. 'You're wondering how whoever is working against us knew to apply pressure to the goblins. Do you think they broke into my home?'

'Yes, I do. And maybe my thinking someone has been watching us isn't too far off the mark.'

Pris twists the ring on her finger as she says, 'This is not good.'

'No, it isn't,' I agree. 'I am now wondering if continuing with our current plan is such a great idea.'

Her shoulders drop, and I see how weary she is. 'Sorry. I'm so tired I can't think straight. Let's just make it to the train station in Plymouth. We'll have time to talk then.'

She's right. We're in the middle of nowhere. Once we are at a train station, we will have options. I nod. 'Okay.'

This time when I start off, I make sure I am walking at a pace Pris can manage. I am still in no mood to talk, and I get the impression Pris is none too happy with me, because she is unusually silent. The air around us is so tense that I am somewhat relieved when we arrive at Two Bridges to find a car waiting for us.

'I am pleased you made good time,' Mrs Wilson says as she opens the boot for our packs. Pris's fits inside, but she tells me to squish mine into the back seat.

I stick my head inside and find Mrs Wilson's black cat stretched out on a rug, taking up half the space. He looks up laconically and makes no attempt to move. Sighing, I wonder how much worse this day can get.

As I push my pack into the well behind the driver's seat, the cat narrows his eyes. I try to ignore him and concentrate on bending my frame into the small hatchback, folding my legs into the least uncomfortable position before I do up the seatbelt.

'Right, are we all in? Goodness, this is a bit of a squish. Fortunately, Portsbridge is only about twenty minutes away. Was your walk productive?'

What an odd way to phrase that question, I think as Pris starts chatting away. I pull out my phone and start doing some checking. We can definitely make it up to Conway and back to Godalming and still fit in Bodmin. The only problem is, if the sprites decide not to help us, we will have to go to the gnomes in Mawnan. I put my phone back in my pocket as the car slows down.

'The bus to Plymouth goes from just over there,' Mrs Wilson is saying. 'And if you need something to eat, the cafe inside does amazing toasted sandwiches. And a pretty good coffee, too, as I remember.'

'Thank you so much, Mrs Wilson. You are a godsend. I am not sure I could have walked all that way to here,' Pris gushes.

I mumble my thanks and earn a frown from my travelling companion. I hide my embarrassment by hauling my pack out over the seat, taking care not to disturb the cat. He glowers at me anyway.

'Thank you for the lift, Mrs Wilson. It was a really nice thing for you to do,' I say, pulling my pack over my shoulder. After all, she was being kind, and it's not her fault my day has turned to crap.

'You are most welcome, young man. Oh, look, that is your bus heading this way. You had best hurry, or you will miss it. Happy travels.' Mrs Wilson slips back into the car, and I shut the door as she pulls back into traffic.

'I'll sort our tickets if you can buy us a couple of toasted sandwiches and coffees,' Pris orders as we cross at the lights.

We manage to make it to the National Express terminal just as the bus pulls in. Pris does not wait for me to agree. She heads straight for the ticket office without even telling me how she takes her coffee.

Mercifully, the line is so short, I barely have time to scan the menu before a cheery voice asks what I will have. I freeze.

'Two ham-and-cheese toasties, please. And two cappuccinos.'

'Any sugar with those?' the girl asks as I hand over my card.

'Um, no, thanks,' I respond, hoping Pris takes her coffee the same way she takes her tea.

I arrive beside the bus in time to load my pack underneath before slipping into the aisle seat beside Pris. She takes her meal without saying a word. I guess she's still not happy with me.

The bus eases into traffic, and I place my food and drink on the pull-down table and grab my earbuds. Staring at the screen of my phone, I flick through my playlists until I find Mum's. I feel less alone listening to some of her favourite songs while I eat.

Tears form in my eyes as Stevie Nicks sings the lyrics to "Dreams", and I remember Mum singing along to it as she cooked dinner just a few days ago. My appetite is gone, and I wrap the remains of my sandwich back into the bag before grabbing our rubbish and heading down the aisle to place it in the bin.

By the time I return, the song has changed, but I am still wrapped in sadness. I close my eyes, shut out the world, and pretend to sleep for the rest of the trip.

When the bus pulls into Plymouth train station almost an hour later, my mood has not lightened. I am pulled between wanting to rescue my mother and not wanting to ask my family for help.

My body protests as I stand and make my way off the bus. It protests even more as I grab our packs from underneath as Pris goes to buy our train tickets. She is so quiet as we walk to the platform, my guilt gets the better of me. I mean, I was a little, well, childish, taking off before, and I have been Mr Grumpy ever since.

'I am sorry I walked away from you at the woods,' I offer as I lean our packs up against the edge of a bench on the platform.

Her blue eyes search my face, as if looking for something. I turn away and stare at the opposite platform.

'Are you ready to talk about why?' she asks.

My stomach clenches and I shake my head. 'No. I'm still processing.'

'That's what I figured.'

I slump onto the seat.

'Do you want a tea or something?' she asks.

'Another coffee would be great.' I fumble in my pack and pass her my clean mug for life.

Just like that, things are back to normal between us. We still sip our drinks in silence, but it is more companionable this time. I stand and stretch out my back before taking our mugs to the drinking fountain to rinse them out.

As I amble back to our seats, I catch a movement from the corner of my eye, and all of a sudden, I am running, but I am too late. A woman in a black hoodie, jeans, and Doc Martens is already striking at Pris, her wicked-looking hunting knife glinting in the evening sun.

Pris moves so fast, my brain takes a while to process what is going on. The result is clear though. The knife clatters to the ground, and Pris kicks it off the platform and then turns on the woman, who jumps to her feet and takes off through a startled crowd.

The woman turns as she reaches the stairs, says something and waves her hand, and immediately, it is like she was never there. People stop staring at her and Pris and return to what they were doing. I reach Pris seconds later.

'What was that?' I ask. Then think to add, 'Are you all right?'

'I'm fine. I guess muggers venture out of London as well.' She shrugs.

I search her face for any sign she is hiding her real feelings, but she actually appears to think this sort of attack is normal. First the mugging in Wimbledon, now this, and she is not even a little concerned. I sit and put our mugs back in my pack.

'Pris, how often does this sort of thing happen to you?' I ask.

'I don't know, about once or twice a month, depending on how often I am out alone.' She carries on flicking through her phone.

'And why do you think that woman chose you to attack out of all the people here?' I gesture to the busy platform.

She shrugs again. 'Perhaps because I look like I have money, or I guess I am just unlucky….'

As her voice trails off, I can see her mind working as she slowly looks around at the busy platform. When it hits her, her eyes widen in surprise. 'Do you think that had something to do with us and all… well, this?'

'Maybe…. Or—'

She tilts her head to the side and studies me. 'Dad always calls me unlucky, says I'm in the wrong place at the wrong time. But you don't think these attacks are random, do you?'

I shake my head.

'You think this is something to do with your… our world?'

What should I tell her? I have no idea why she would be a target, but whoever just attacked her was definitely a creature. Only a creature with magic could cast a forgetting spell on humans.

She drops her head into her hands, and I can almost hear the cogs of her mind working. When she raises it, her eyes are clear and her voice decisive. 'I can't deal with this now, not with everything else going on, and not when I can't talk to my parents about it. In the meantime, solving the why won't stop these attacks from happening. I'll continue to simply face each one as it comes as I've always done.'

The stubborn set to her jaw tells me her mind is made up. I am amazed at how easily she can compartmentalise things. Still, it's her business, so who am I to challenge her? Besides, the train to Bodmin pulls in, and we are otherwise occupied finding seats.

We arrive at Bodmin Central just after six. I'm so tired, I can barely walk, and Pris is not much better. We must look like a couple of old codgers as we leave the station.

She leads us to a motel across way, and manages to arrange adjoining ground-floor rooms for us for the next two nights. As I fumble with my key, Pris asks, 'Do you mind if we do room service for dinner? I can't bear the thought of going out, or doing the restaurant here.'

I wonder if this is because she doesn't want to risk any more attacks, but I don't bring the subject up. Instead, I say, 'I'm fine with that.'

Very fine, in fact. I would go as far as to say I am relieved not to have to face anyone else tonight. Listening to Mum's music has left me a little down, and we will be talking about where to go next. That is best done away from strange eyes.

'All right. I shall order it for about seven-thirty in my room. Do you want to take a quick look at the menu and tell me what you want?'

'Nah,' I say. 'Just order me a burger and chips and a ginger beer, or sparkling water if they don't have any.'

She slips inside, so I don't catch her answer. My room is serviceable and looks like commuter hotels on TV and in the movies. I sit on the bed to take off my boots. The bed is a bit soft for my liking, but I'm so tired, it probably won't matter.

The shower, though—the shower is perfect. As hot jets of water soothe my aching body, I groan out loud. I would stay here all night, but of course I can't. At some stage, I will have to face Pris. Besides, I am more than hungry.

I drape myself in a towel and use the sink to wash out some clothes before dressing. I resist the urge to lie on the bed for a while because once I do, I won't be getting up until tomorrow. Instead, I walk stiffly to the door between our rooms and lean my forehead against the cool surface.

There is a lot for us to talk about if we are to move forward from here, some of which will not be easy for me to say. Still, Pris deserves the truth. She has come this far with me on trust, so the least I can do is tell her why I can't go to Mawnan. I knock on the wood—time to face the music.

SWINGING OPEN THE door, I let Snake in. He seems clean and refreshed, but the haunted look in his eyes that appeared when the goblin turned us down is still there.

I return to my bed and the laptop that is already open. Snake swings the armchair around, sits down, and puts his bare feet on the end of the bed before resting his head against the chairback and closing his eyes.

'There is some time before the food arrives,' I say. 'Shall we do some planning?'

He shakes his head, and I swallow my frustration. Then he surprises me with a compromise. 'After we eat dinner. I'm too tired to even think now.'

I have a Plan B. I always have a Plan B.

'All right, I've been looking at the second part of the riddle, and I'm pretty sure the golden token is supposed to be a golden coin.'

Snake doesn't even open his eyes. 'I think so too. Only it can't be gold coloured, like a pound coin. It must contain actual gold.'

A smile tugs at my lips as he confirms my thoughts. Perhaps I am not so useless at this World Below stuff after all. However, I keep my voice even as I say, 'That's what I thought. A pound coin would be too easy. I searched online for places we might buy gold ones, and there are a few coin dealers in Southampton. We need to factor in a stop there on the way back. That is, unless the coins should be something special.'

Snake's chest rises and falls a couple of times before he answers in a heavy voice. 'No, I think from my knowledge of creature law, they just need to be actual gold coins.'

'And you're sure you can't just turn a normal coin into gold?' The comment is intended to illicit a reaction, to lighten the sense of gloom he has brought into the room.

Snake bites. His eyes fly open, and he snaps, 'Do you think my mother and I would live like we do if I could make gold?'

I try not to smile, but I can't help it.

A sheepish grin replaces Snake's sullen look. 'You're joking, aren't you?'

I'm saved from answering by a knock on the door. The waiter puts the food on the dresser by the television. As I let him out, Snake takes the covers off the dishes. I return to find him looking at the two chocolate brownies with ice cream I ordered for dessert.

'After that walk today, I think we deserve a treat,' I say.

He grins for the first time since we left Wistman's Wood. 'I'm not complaining.'

We eat in companionable silence. Well, I eat. Snake inhales his burger and chips, then decides to make a hot drink while I finish my main course.

He takes my plate and hands me dessert before placing a tea on the bedside table. With his drink on the floor, he settles back into the chair and starts playing with his brownie.

'The senior gnome, he's my dad's best friend, and he's family,' he says before shovelling a spoonful of brownie and ice cream into his mouth.

'But that's good, isn't it? I mean, he is unlikely to refuse to endorse us if he's a relation.' I am struggling to work out what the problem might be. Is it because of Snake's mother?

'He would never refuse us even if we weren't related…. He is one of the good guys,' Snake admits.

Instead of looking happy at this thought, his eyes are more haunted than ever.

'Still sounding good to me,' I prompt, worried he might leave it there.

Snake takes a deep breath, then places the rest of his brownie on the floor. I tense. What could make Snake upset enough to put him off his food?

'It's what he will ask in return that worries me.'

He sounds so bleak, I want to wrap my arms around him and tell him it will be okay, that we don't have to go to Mawnan. But he is no fool, and we both know we might well have no option but to go there if we want to rescue our parents.

So, I remain where I am and force myself to ask, 'And what would that be?'

Snake does not answer immediately. I am about to repeat the question when he says, 'He'll want me to speak with my father.'

The words come out in a rush, and I glance up from my food, sure I could not have heard correctly. Snake won't look at me as he continues.

'It's what he always wants. Every time he's met with Mum and me since Dad left, he's begged me to speak with him. He will use this as an excuse to force me to do it.'

'You're telling me that the last time you spoke to your father was eight years ago?'

I can't imagine going a week without speaking with my dad. I mean, he's often distant, and quite strict, but he loves me. The thought of not speaking with him for years is unthinkable. Then I realise that may be exactly what will happen if I don't make it to the World Below and free my parents. The thought takes my breath away.

Snake stares out the window and says nothing.

'What does your mum think?' I prod.

'She says I shouldn't let what happened between the two of them get between us, that I have a family below….' His voice tails off.

When I realise he isn't going to add anything else, I ask, 'Wouldn't you do it if it meant rescuing your mother?'

A tear forms in the corner of his eye, but he says nothing. I am dying to know the rest, but I don't want to push him. It was obviously difficult for him to tell me this much. He will tell me the rest when he is ready.

I take a mouthful of brownie and chew thoughtfully before flicking the screen on my laptop to my notes. 'If the sprites endorse us tomorrow, we can go to Conway, then come back to Southampton to get the coins before going to Godalming.'

Snake doesn't move.

'Snake, are you listening?'

He turns around slowly and nods. 'Yes, I am.'

'Do you also realise that if the sprites turn us down, we will have no option but to go to the gnomes? If we go to Cornwall, we will still make it back in time if we rent a car and drive through the night. It will be tight though.'

'If you can drive, why have we been taking trains?'

Really? That is what Snake takes from this conversation?

I suppress the urge to shake him. 'Because what I would have to pay for insurance would be horrendous. Besides, I haven't ever driven outside of London. A car is a last-resort option.'

He nods. 'Oh, right.'

'Does that mean all right about the car, or all right we will visit the gnomes if we don't get the sprites onside tomorrow?'

'Both, I guess. I did the calculations as well. This is how it has to be.' He still will not meet my gaze.

Snake's sadness fills the room, and I decide we can plan the rest tomorrow, after we visit the moor. I change the subject. 'Shall we go back to the last bit of the riddle?' I ask.

'Sorry, I'm tired. I can't do this now.' Snake stands abruptly and strides to the door. 'Goodnight,' he says as he closes it behind him.

Funny, what strikes me is not his abrupt departure, but the fact my usually almost compulsively tidy travelling companion has left his half-eaten dessert on the floor.

I scooch off the bed, grab his plate, and add it along with mine to the tray before placing the remnants of our dinner outside. I walk across to the window. I pull the curtain aside and take a surprised step back as I come face-to-face with a black cat sitting on the rubbish bin outside.

What is it about black cats on this trip? I seem to be seeing them everywhere. I draw the curtains, still a little unsettled. I'm not sure whether it's by the appearance of the cat or by Snake's behaviour. I decide it is the latter. What did Snake's father do that was so bad, he would not talk to him for eight years?

The room is less welcoming without Snake's presence. In fact, if I'm honest, I have felt alone since he began withdrawing this afternoon. Alone and, for the first time, scared.

Until this afternoon, this whole adventure was like some sort of treasure hunt. I had managed to push the fact that my parents are being held somewhere, probably against their will, to the back of my mind and concentrate on our plan.

Until now, everything had gone according to that plan, and it lulled me into a false sense of security. Then the goblin turned us down, the forest captured us, and Snake withdrew to balance his fear of facing his father against the need to rescue his mother. Suddenly this was all very real.

When Snake pointed out that it is not normal for someone to be attacked so frequently, it almost undid me. Of course, I had thought about this before, but Dad had always smoothed things over, and I had no real basis for thinking I was different to anyone else…. Well… apart from the colour of my skin. Now? Now I knew there was more to this. My parents have plenty to answer for when I free them—*if* I free them from The Court.

Is the black cat I keep seeing an omen? Is it telling me we are doomed to fail? No, I refuse to think like that. We still have time, and we still have options. We will bring our parents back from the World Below.

I wander back to the bed, close down my browser, and click on the Netflix app. It automatically goes to the next episode of a fantasy series I've been watching. I can't face others failing in their quests tonight. I scroll through and stumble on a rom-com. Just what I need: bubblegum TV to take my mind off everything.

I JUMP DOWN from the rubbish bin and join Eleanora and Eugenie in the car.

'How are they doing? Have they decided to go to Mawnan yet?' my mistress asks.

I shake my head.

'We cannot interfere anymore, Eleanora. Percival could not persuade the goblin, not in your name or mine. I cannot believe my longtime ally, Goodman Green, would do this.'

'I know, Eugenie. Remember, your connection with the goblins is the only reason we could talk to him without it getting back to the council. I am afraid they are on their own with the sprites. At least *they* will not be persuaded or scared in this matter by any of the higher races.'

Pesky sprites, I think as I curl up on my rug on the back seat. They respect no one, not even their betters. At least I won't be sent to deal with them. Perhaps now I can return home to my rightful place.

'Have you found out any more about who is pulling strings behind the scenes?' Eugenie asks.

'I visited Giles Regis, but he was tight-lipped. His wife, now, she was a different matter. Her ambitions have long outweighed her abilities, and I got the impression she is in this up to her neck.'

'Amandine? I am not surprised. She married above her station when she wed Giles. Who would she work with to raise her husband's status? Her family has some unsavoury connections….'

'Whatever is going on here is not criminal or related to the upper world. This started below, sister, and we need to find out what is going on.'

'Did I tell you my invitation to the next court came from Elias, not the Queen?' Eugenie asks.

'Elias standing in for the Queen? Now, that is interesting. I wonder what has happened to Bernais. Isn't he her First Minister?' Eleanora muses and shifts position in the front seat. 'That seals it. We really do need to find out what is going on in the World Below.'

I hide my face under my paw so she will not be able to see me.

'Maybe we should send Percival there to do some digging?' Eleanora muses.

I stay very still. If I don't move, they might forget I am here.

'Who will keep an eye on our friends?' Eugenie asks.

'I can stay here for a couple of nights, just to make sure no one interferes directly with them. Well, not me, but Annie can.'

A strange energy fills the car, and I risk raising my head. My mistress is now a slip of a girl with long blonde hair and large brown eyes. She is dressed in jeans and a sweatshirt displaying the University of Portsmouth insignia.

I am shocked into sitting up. It is so long since my mistress has changed appearance, I had almost forgotten she was capable.

'Annie is here to study The Tor on Bodmin Moor for her thesis. She is around their age, and they will not suspect her.' My mistress smiles at her sister before turning back to me.

'In the meantime, Percival, go visit the sprites and ask if they will let you below. We need to find out what is going on there and why someone is interested in the Crown and the Fieth families.'

The door beside me clicks open, and I stare at it before glaring at my mistress.

'Yes, now. I need you back tomorrow afternoon. I will pick you up from the Tor.'

I stretch, arching my back. With one last accusatory glare at my mistress, I jump down and take a couple of steps from the car before casting a transportation spell to Bodmin Tor.

THE PHANTOM CAT
OF BODMIN MOOR

SHUFFLING INTO THE lobby after an early wake-up call, my mind is still replaying last night's conversation for about the hundredth time. I slept very little last night. Fear and worry over whether or not we will be forced to visit the gnomes still gnaws at my stomach. For Pris's sake, though, I try to put on a bright face.

I mean, her parents are being held too. And she has every right to force me to ask the gnomes for their endorsement. The fact that she didn't endears her to me more than her willingness to launch herself into a strange, unknown world ever did. I appreciate the fact she didn't push me to make a decision last night, that she gave me space. It isn't her fault that I wasn't able to sleep as I tired to convince myself it would be okay to go to Cornwall.

Watching her at the desk, organising our transport to the moor, brings a smile to my lips. Part of me understands that controlling the small things helps keep her mind off the bigger issues, but she is just so good at it. *A future Prime Minister*, I think to myself, *or a drill sergeant.*

Pris hands over her credit card, and it is returned with a pamphlet and some tickets. She thanks the woman behind the counter and turns. Upon seeing me, she smiles. 'Good morning, sleepyhead. Everything is sorted. The bus arrives in an hour, and I ordered walkers' packed lunches. They'll bring them to our table after breakfast.'

'You have been busy,' I say, leading the way down the corridor to the dining room, her energy making me feel all the more tired.

We load our plates from the buffet and find a table in the corner, away from the other early risers so no one can overhear our conversation. A waiter fills my cup with coffee and Pris's with tea. I tuck in to my bacon and eggs, and I half expect Pris to bring up last night's conversation once we are alone.

Surprisingly, her first words are, 'Tell me about the sprites.'

'Political or in general?' I ask, not sure how much detail she wants.

'I guess I need to hear it all,' she responds, resignation laying heavy in her words.

A twinge of guilt twists my gut. She is being so brave. If only I could do the same when it comes to my family. Pushing that thought down, I try to formulate an answer that won't freak her out.

'Sprites are part of the fairy class of creatures. Like all fairies, they're considered lesser beings, although don't ever say that to their faces, as they are fiercely independent and have never bought into the whole class system.'

Pris grins. 'I like them already.'

She seems quite excited, and I find myself lifted by her mood. 'I thought you might. They have a reputation for being mischievous, but they aren't, not really. They use tricks and scare tactics to keep people and other races at bay. Our biggest problem today may be getting them to even appear at all.'

'So, we can't call them with magic?' she asks before taking a sip of tea.

'We can try, but they're not compelled to answer in the same way other creatures are. I mean, they will respond to any of their own who call, but they don't recognise any obligation to other creatures.'

The waiter approaches to refill our drinks, and we are silent until he leaves.

'Yesterday I read about the Phantom Cat of Bodmin Moor. Is that anything to do with the sprites?'

She has been doing her research. If she ever becomes a lawyer like her mother, I pity anyone who comes up against her.

'People have lots of theories about the cat. There are even some who believe it's an escaped puma from a private zoo, but I am pretty sure it is the sprites' way of keeping people away from Bodmin Tor, which is their gateway to the upper world.'

Pris nods and is about to ask something else when a figure appears beside our table.

'Two packed lunches?'

'Ah, yes, thank you.' Pris takes the two bags and hands them to me.

I stow them in my small backpack as Pris checks her phone.

'Just enough time for a quick toilet stop before we are expected in the lobby,' she says, gulping down the last of her tea.

I look sadly at my half-finished meal, then at her empty plate. How had she managed to talk and eat at the same time? I shovel a couple of quick mouthfuls down, drain my coffee cup, then follow Pris back to the lobby. After a quick trip to the men's room, I wait by the check-in desk while she goes to the ladies'.

A slim, attractive girl is standing nearby. She turns as I approach, and I see she is wearing a Uni of Portsmouth sweatshirt, and her long blonde ponytail is threaded through the back of a university cap. She smiles tentatively as I approach.

'Are you taking the tourist bus to the moor?' she asks.

I nod.

'Me too. I'm doing a study of the rock formations around the Tor for my thesis.'

I nod again, but I don't say anything else. She is very friendly, and normally I would be happy to chat, but my mind is on our meeting with the sprites and the consequences should we not be successful today.

'Oh, hello,' the girl says again.

I turn to find Pris approaching.

'Are you two together?' she asks. 'I was just telling your boyfriend I'm going to the moor too.'

An intense heat rises to my cheeks, and I open my mouth to tell her Pris and I are just friends when Pris says, 'That's nice. Are you walking anywhere in particular?'

I zone out from their chatter. Pris didn't correct the girl. I sneak a look at her. She is totally comfortable with us being seen as a couple. I don't really do the boyfriend/girlfriend thing but, if I'm completely honest, the thought isn't totally repellant to me.

Pris and the girl, who introduces herself as Annie, talk the whole way to Bodmin Moor. My input is not required, so I stare out the window at the bleak scenery. I understand now why so many horror movies and books are set here. Although the sky is bright blue, a wind sweeps across the almost barren terrain. Only occasional small copses of trees or outcropping of rocks break up the monotonous vista.

Finally, the bus comes to a stop, and we tumble out. Annie and Pris are still talking, and I wonder how we're going to extract ourselves from the girl. I mean, we can't go calling magical beings with a human tagging along.

I need not have worried. As the bus pulls out and Pris says, 'Are you sure you're okay waiting here alone for your guide? We can stay with you, if you like.'

I frown at her. *No, we can't.* Then we would have to find a way to ditch two humans.

'He shouldn't be long. You guys head off and enjoy yourselves.'

'If you're sure….' Pris chews her bottom lip.

'I'll be fine. See you back here at three for the pickup.' Annie shoos us away with a flick of her hand.

I entwine my fingers through Pris's and tug her towards the path. She glances reluctantly over her shoulder. 'Do you think she'll be all right?' she asks. 'I mean, it *is* quite isolated, and there are horror stories about the moor.'

'If she wanted us to stay, she would have said,' I say to soothe her, but a part of me is wondering whether we should leave her by herself. I don't want to hear of her disappearance on the news tonight.

Now I'm torn. Is there anything I can do? I reach out and find a faint tingle of magic. Under my breath I say, 'Local guardians, please look out for Annie until her friend comes.'

'What was that?' Pris asks, twisting her ring.

Suddenly embarrassed, I say, 'Nothing. Come on. It's a bit of a walk, and we don't want to miss our pickup.'

Pris tugs at my arm, stopping me in my tracks. 'No, you did something. I felt a tingle in the air and my ring warmed up. Tell me!'

Heat rises to my cheeks, and I mumble, 'I… um…. I asked the local guardians to protect Annie.' The words tumble out, and I quickly walk away before she can see the blush that is surely colouring my face.

Pris soon catches me up and says, 'Why, Snake, I didn't know you were so sweet.'

My face heats even more as I stride ahead. Annoyingly, Pris keeps pace.

'You have to teach me how to do that,' she says, the words breathless as she pushes herself to keep up.

I slow down, and she falls into step beside me. 'Will you?' she asks.

I shrug. 'Sure, if we get a chance.'

We make good time to the Tor. Although my body is tired from yesterday, it isn't too sore, and I'm invigorated by the fresh air. I'm also grateful for Pris's fathers' jacket, which helps considerably with the wind.

Pris herself is dressed more for walking today. Her purple tie-dyed fleece comes halfway down the thighs of her black-and-purple animal-print leggings. She is snuggled into a down parka and is wearing her beanie again, but today I suspect it's more to combat the wind than to hide a hair disaster.

Finally, the Tor appears on the horizon, a fact I am pleased about because Pris says we should wait until we get there before breaking for lunch, and I am starving. As we approach, my medallion warms, which is odd because I am not reaching for any magic. Pris glances at me and fiddles with the ring on her finger. She must be feeling it too.

'Ouch,' Pris says, reaching a hand around to rub the back of her neck. Something pulls at my hair, and I turn my head just as something pinches my earlobe. Damn sprites! I resist reacting because a reaction is what they want.

'Ignore them,' I say, and carry on towards the Tor.

The closer we get, the harder the pinches become, and I begin to make out small figures in the air. Finally, the torment stops, and the figures buzz and coalesce into an enormous black cat. No, it's a panther. I break into a grin as I realise this is the mysterious panther of Bodmin Moor.

'Cool,' Pris says and pulls out her phone to take a picture.

I laugh as she frowns at the screen. Leaning over, I see exactly what I expect—rocks and grass and sky, but no cat.

'You can only photograph a creature if they want to be seen,' I explain.

'What do you want here, gnome?' the cat says.

'Wow, mega cool,' Pris says. She is clearly too starstruck to take the lead here, so I step forward.

'I am Snake Fieth, and my friend is Priscilla Crown.' Pris flinches at the use of her full name, and my lips twitch upwards.

'Yes?' The panther's voice reverberates.

'Our parents were taken to stand before The Court Below, and we would like to attend to help free them. We were hoping you would endorse an invitation for us so we can be admitted to the realm.'

The panther flicks its tail. 'We don't care for The Court and rarely attend.'

'You don't need to attend. We want to go so we can save our parents from an unjust punishment,' Pris says.

The panther turns and pins Pris with its gaze. 'I hope you are not suggesting our brothers and sisters took your parents under false pretenses.'

'They think you just accused the Bad Fairies of unfairly taking our mums and your dad,' I whisper. 'Can you let me handle this so we don't insult them even more?

Pris ignores me. 'No, you have it all wrong. I think your brothers and sisters did what they were asked to do. But maybe the charges against our parents are not quite what they seem.'

I groan at Pris's attempts to smooth the situation over, but I know there is no stopping her.

'If the Bad Fairies took them below, they must have done something really bad,' the panther insists.

Pris balls her hands by her sides, ready to defend her parents. My stomach sinks as I realise we will now have no option but to head to Mawnan, and I brace myself for Pris's outburst. However, when she speaks, her voice is controlled. 'We believe the charges might have been overstated, but that is not the point. They are our family, and we want to be there for them when they face The Court.'

The panther drops his head to the side and stares at Pris as if seeing her for the first time. 'Family is important.'

Buzzing fills the air. The panther comes apart and reforms into a human.

'I thought all creatures take human form while in the world above,' Pris whispers.

'They do, but for some reason, sprites and fairies do not feel compelled to follow the rules, and no one has ever had the guts to force them to.'

'If you are truly here to support your family, we think that admirable, but some of us are not sure of your intent,' the form bellows.

'Tell us how to prove ourselves, and we will do it,' Pris says.

I groan again. Has she still not grasped the idea that you never make such an open bargain with creatures?

'What she means is, I am sure we can come to an agreement about how we can prove our intent to you,' I amend, trying to put some limits on what she has signed us up for.

Pris frowns at me, clearly not liking being corrected, but I don't waiver. She has no idea what the sprites might ask for, and I am definitely not committing to some of the things my imagination conjures.

'Here is our offer. You will each let one of our kind walk inside you to assess your intentions.'

Pris blanches and I chuckle. I bet she is pleased I intervened now.

'Possession is illegal,' I counter. 'Find another way.'

'There isn't, one that fits within your timescale. Possession for a limited time in cases of emergency is allowed.'

'So, what is your full proposal?' I ask, trying hard to keep the fear from my voice.

'One of us sits inside your head, looks through your eyes, and thinks and hears what you do until you arrive at the road of men. They will then either grant you our endorsement, or not. Either way, you will leave our lands.'

I want to reject the idea. Every fibre of my being wants to run from anything getting inside my head.

'We will consider your offer,' Pris says, taking my hand and leading me over to the rocks.

'What?' I say as I stumble after her. 'Have you gone completely mad?'

'We need to weigh up our options,' Pris says in her don't-argue-with-me voice. 'Let's eat some lunch. Perhaps you will be less grumpy when your stomach stops rumbling.'

I still owe her for being so understanding last night, so I can let her have this. We sit, and I pull out our lunches. The sprite figure also sits, cross-legged, watching us but giving us space to talk.

My appetite deserts me, but I eat anyway because my body needs energy. The ham sandwich tastes like cardboard, and the crisps are too dry for me to swallow. Pris finishes off my bag as well as her own. I wash the meal down with water, and zone out while she finishes eating.

'Aren't you freaked out by the thought of someone being inside your head?' I finally ask.

'A little, but I can't see another way around this. The alternative is that we give up on the sprites, and that makes our job all the harder.'

'Mmm,' I respond noncommittally.

'Besides, the way I see it, I genuinely want to help my parents. I have no ulterior motive. I'm sure that for the short trip back to the road, I can concentrate on the scenery and not let them into any of my juicy inner thoughts.'

I dwell for a moment on what her juicy inner thoughts might be and whether they include me before pulling my mind out of the gutter and back onto the task at hand, and my real concern over why having a sprite in my head for even a little while would not be a good idea.

All day I have been debating over whether or not to go to Mawnan and the gnomes. Can I concentrate on something else for the couple of hours back to the road? Perhaps I can if it means we won't need to go visit my uncle.

'All right,' I say, sweeping our rubbish into a single bag and putting it back in my pack. 'Let's do this.'

Pris's lips break into a grin, and she almost claps with excitement. Even while my stomach knots with worry over being possessed by a sprite, her obvious enthusiasm brings a smile to my face.

She stands and takes a step towards the sprites. Two lights break away from the human form and flit around her head, and a look of pure joy crosses her face as she says, 'We agree to your terms.'

Seconds later, something that feels like a cool knife slices into my scalp. I shiver, repulsed by the thought of anything being in my mind. I concentrate on the scenery and Pris, and my stomach settles. The sprite presence is still there, but it is more like a stray thought. If I ignore it, I don't even notice it—well, not too much.

The other sprites disperse as I stand and pull on my pack. If I concentrate, I can block the slightly odd sensation in my head, and I head back to the bus pickup point with a little more confidence.

As we walk, the silence between us is peaceful. When my mind starts to wander, I replay the story line of Daphne du Maurier's *Rebecca*, thinking of how this windswept moor fitted the tone.

About halfway back, we pass Annie. I am relieved to find her all right. Then I stop walking, seeing that she is alone. As I open my mouth to ask her where her companion is, she yells, 'My guide couldn't make it today. We rearranged for tomorrow. I'm just getting a quick look at the Tor from a distance before the bus comes.' She rushes by us at a jog, and we continue on.

A little while later, I catch a glimpse of the road. This is almost over. I relax and a pressure pushes its way to the front of my mind.

'Your love for your mother is true, and your desire to help her is very real. For that I must endorse you.' I almost sag with relief before being overwhelmed by a sharp pain, and I fall to the ground. 'Yet, you will not go to your family for help, not even to save her. For that I must penalise you.'

The presence is gone, and cold seeps through my clothing. By my nose I make out a quarter coin, the sprite's endorsement. I reach out and grab it. As I do, the world goes black as pain engulfs me.

I roll over to my side, keeping my leg as still as possible. Pris drops to her knee, her face a picture of worry.

'Ankle?' she asks, and I nod.

'How did it happen?'

I almost tell her the truth, but I am too embarrassed at being outed by a sprite that I only tell her part of it. 'I tripped as the sprite left me.'

I slip the pack from my back and put the endorsement in my pocket before trying to stand. It takes a couple of attempts, and Pris's help, before I make it to my feet.

Once I am upright, I wait for the wave of pain to pass. I test my weight on my ankle and attempt to hide the agony I am in. Come what may, I must make it back to the bus. The road that looked so close only moments ago now looks unreachable.

'Did you get your token?' I ask, trying to keep my mind off the pain.

'Yes,' Pris tells me.

'I thought you would be happier about that,' I say, sensing a little anger in her tone.

'I'm pleased, yes… but the sprite said I was true to my family, even though they weren't always true to me.'

When she doesn't continue, I ask, 'Are you angry at the sprite because of what they said, or because they're right?'

'Humph. Let's just get to the road.'

I don't say anything else. If she can give me space to deal with my family issues, the least I can do is repay the favour. I hobble on, leaning on Pris and concentrating on not passing out.

'So, did you get your endorsement?' Pris prompts.

'Aw, that doesn't look good,' Annie says, bouncing up beside us. 'Oh, here's the bus. Hold on.'

She rushes ahead while we wait. I sense Pris looking at me, waiting for an answer, but it is all I can do to stay upright. Moments later, the bus driver is beside me, helping me to the bliss of a seat inside the safety of the vehicle. Toasty warm, with my foot raised and throbbing, the motion of the bus rocks me to sleep.

Back at the hotel, Pris orders me to my room while she sorts everything out. I use the wall for support as I make my way down the corridor. By the time I arrive at my door, I'm in a lather of sweat and shaking all over.

I resist dropping onto the bed and make my way to the bathroom. After showering and dressing in pyjama bottoms and a T-shirt, I collapse onto the bed. Curling up the duvet to make a bolster, I close my eyes, exhausted… defeated.

'ARE YOU DECENT?' I ask as I knock on the door. A mumble comes from within, and I take it to mean yes.

Snake is lying on the bed, almost as white as the sheet. At least he has had the sense to raise his foot up. It's already beginning to swell, but there is no bruising yet. Experience tells me that is not a good sign. The longer the bruising takes to come out, the longer the recovery, unless gnomes are blessed with some sort of super-healing powers.

I want to ask Snake the question that's been preying on my mind since I asked it on the moor, but it can wait. I head to the minibar and remove a bottle of water before taking my bag of goodies to the bed. I hand the water to Snake and pop a couple of ibuprofen with extra paracetamol out for him.

While he downs the painkillers, I reach into the bag and pull out a box of ice packs. Opening one, I crack it, and when it turns cold, I place it on Snake's ankle. He winches. I head to the bathroom, grab a clean towel, then use it to hold the pack in place.

'You're pretty good at this,' Snake says.

'I play tennis. I'm forever doing my ankles,' I tell him, trying to hide my worry. 'Are you comfortable?'

He shrugs and winches again.

'Perhaps we should take you to the hospital. It might be broken.'

'I can move my foot and place a little weight on it, so it's probably just a bad sprain,' he says.

I want to insist, but I can't force him to go. My concern must have shown on my face because Snake places his hand over mine and says, 'If it's no better in the morning, we'll get it seen to.'

'All right.'

His touch is comforting, and I reluctantly withdraw my hand so I can finish getting him settled. From the closet, I grab a couple more pillows. One I put under his ankle and the other I use to prop him a little higher on the bed.

'The painkillers will kick in soon,' I reassure him.

'Yep.'

'If you're all right for a bit, I wouldn't mind a shower.'

'I should be fine, if you could just pass me the remote.'

I do as he asks and then head for the door. As I reach it, he says, 'Thanks, Pris, for all this.'

I grin, then turn away, hoping he hasn't seen how stupidly pleased I am at his praise. I leave the door open in case Snake needs anything.

The shower is magic and, in spite of Snake's mishap, I'm feeling pretty good when I return to his room with my laptop and my coin, the three quarters now joined.

Snake is dosing with the TV on in the background. I settle into the armchair and rest my feet on the end of the bed. Snake's eyes flicker open and focus on me. I breathe more easily; there's a little more colour in his cheeks.

'Are you up for some planning?' I ask, then mentally kick myself. Why can't I ask how he is? Does his foot still hurt? Does he need anything else? I'm clearly not a natural carer.

'In a minute. My jeans are in the bathroom. Could you please get my endorsement? It was hard won, and I want to put it with the rest before I lose it.'

Well, that answers my first question, I think as I ask, 'Can you lose it? I mean it's magical, so I kind of assumed it would stick with me.'

'That's a good question. I'm not sure, but I am not going to risk it.'

I retrieve his quarter from the bathroom and hand it to him. He leans over to the bedside table and opens his e-reader. He picks up the half coin and joins it with the new piece before shutting the cover and putting it back.

Turning back to me, he says, 'Thank you. I feel better now it's all together.' He blows out a breath and says, 'And thank you again for all this. Without your help, I think I would have wallowed in self-pity, but you have me feeling better already.'

'You're welcome,' I say as I walk back around to the chair, allowing my hair to fall forward to cover my smile.

'So, where do you want to start?' he asks.

'Can you tell me where to find the fairies in Conway so I can plot a new route?'

'Easy. The Fairy Glen is reached by a walk from Betws-y-Coed station along the Afon river.'

I pull up a map of Wales and the route planner. Flicking through our options, I say, 'That's definitely doable. If we travel to Birmingham tomorrow, we can find a coin dealer there. Then the day after, we could drive to Betws-y-Coed.'

I pause and do some calculations in my head. 'Can we do the walk in one day and head back to Birmingham? If we can, we can still make it to Godalming the following day in time for midnight.'

Snake sighs. 'Normally, we'd be able to do it in a day. But I checked the walk last night, and the trek to the Fairy Glen is two and a half hours. I can't walk it like this.'

I won't be defeated. 'You would be travelling most of tomorrow, and you can rest up in a hotel while I buy the coins.'

'Lovely idea, but this is quite bad, and gnomes don't have super healing or anything.'

Damn, there goes that idea. Potential super healing aside, why is Snake being so negative?

'Don't you want to go to the fairies?' I ask, trying to keep the exasperation out of my voice. I clearly don't succeed, because Snake jerks like he's been slapped.

'No. I mean, yes.' He runs a hand through his hair. 'I don't know what I mean.'

He looks up at the ceiling, then back at me. I wait for him to speak.

'I think the sprites gave me this handicap for a reason—'

'Hold on—I thought you said you tripped.'

Snake blushes but still holds my gaze. 'I wasn't sure at the time, but there was pain, and the sprite told me this was because I wasn't trusting my family.'

My jaw drops, and I stare at him. Then I close my mouth and swallow my exasperation. 'Why didn't you tell me before?'

The tension around his mouth signals his anger before I hear it in his voice. 'Perhaps because I was in a world of pain, and it was all I could do to get back to the bus.'

I don't back down. 'Or perhaps it was because you didn't want to think too much about it.'

He glares at me, then his face relaxes into a wry smile. 'Perhaps that too. Anyway, because Earth, the head gnome, is family, I think my ankle injury is supposed to force me to go to Mawnan and face my fears.'

Snake lies back and closes his eyes. I sit statue still. He takes a deep breath, as though setting his resolve, and says, 'Tomorrow, we go to Mawnan.'

I don't respond yet. This is hard for Snake, and I want to give him time to come to terms with his decision. Secretly, though, I'm pleased. We'll definitely get an endorsement from the gnomes because by Snake's agreeing to meet with them, he is also agreeing to do whatever it takes to get that piece of coin.

As I tap queries into the browser, some show's theme music plays in the background, followed by ads.

'Okay, it's two trains and two buses, but not much walking, and we can be set down outside the Red Lion in Mawnan within a couple of hours of leaving here. Is where we are going too far from the pub?'

'I've never been there, but I looked at a map last night. It's about five minutes' walk. Or ten, in this state,' he laughs.

'Sooo, we can stay the night in Truro, then make it to Southampton in time for some coin shopping before heading to Godalming.'

'Then that's the plan. I hope I'm up to the walking.'

'I also bought an ankle brace. If you're careful, you should be all right.' I frown, suddenly worried. 'Are you sure you didn't break it?'

'Pretty sure, and besides I don't think the sprite wanted to hurt me, just force me to face the gnomes.'

'Family counselling,' I say, trying to lighten the mood, and Snake smiles ruefully.

'Yes, I guess so.'

'And you're okay with it?' The question rushes out before I can stop it, and I immediately wish I could take it back when Snake stops smiling and his eyes darken with pain.

Impulsively, I lean forward and squeeze his hand. 'We don't need to do this. We can find another way.'

His smile is back. 'The pain of facing Earth won't be as bad as facing the walk to the Fairy Glen. Besides, it's past time I faced him.'

'If you're sure....'

'I am. Now, I must ask one more thing.'

'Sure.'

'Are you okay to do room service again tonight? I think I am beyond going to the restaurant.'

I laugh, perhaps a little too much for the weak joke. But I feel like a burden has been lifted from my shoulders and I am giddy with the lightness. The end is in sight, and I will see my parents soon.

'Anything in particular?' I ask.

'I saw they had a butter chicken on the menu. That would be nice. And… I didn't get to finish dessert last night.'

I order two curries and two brownies and curl up in the chair to wait. Snake flicks through the channels until he finds a binge session of a crime show. We pause it for food, then lose ourselves back in the plot again. With both of us mentally and physically exhausted, it's nice to switch off for a bit.

Snake falls asleep at around nine. I take the plates out and find a blanket in the closet to cover Snake. I reach out to push his fringe from his face, and I quickly withdraw my hand. We may have pretended to be a couple today, but we aren't. I head through to my room, leaving the door open in case Snake needs anything in the night.

As I slip between the cool sheets, I listen to Snake's even breathing, and relax. Tonight I don't feel so alone.

I CURL UP on the end of my mistress's bed. It is not home, but it is warm, and my belly is full. And at least I am no longer confined in that smelly bag she put me in when she picked me up on the moor.

Now that we are relaxed, Eleanora closes her eyes and casts the spell that will allow her to understand my language so I can report.

'It is chaos, mistress. The Queen has not been seen in public for some time, and Elias is organising the spring court, just as your sister said.'

'What happened to Bernais?' Eleanora asks.

'None of our friends know. He was beside the Queen one day, and the next he was banished from her home. Not long after, the Queen retreated from public life.'

Eleanora strokes my fur as she digests my words.

'I wonder how this relates to what is going on with Snake and Priscilla,' she muses.

I am reluctant to offer my opinion. It has been so long since I have been a part of creature politics, and I am not sure I want to become embroiled again. Finally, the silence forces me to speak. 'Perhaps it has to do with the past? With all that trouble when we fought the blight, and the backlash after?'

'That was centuries ago. Besides, Pris's and Snake's parents weren't involved.' My mistress runs her fingers through my fur, and I can almost sense the thoughts rushing through her head. 'Though their families were affected by the outcome, I suppose.'

I sigh. I must tell her all I learned, even though I know it will drag up unpleasant memories. 'There is a rumour that Snake's family are to be elevated to elven status at The Court.'

My mistress's sharp intake of breath tells me she understands why this is important. 'Bernais and his family would be livid. They would do almost anything to stop that from happening.' She pauses. 'And… if he is behind this… then perhaps it is to do with the past. Pris's family have never been fond of Bernais and his ilk.'

I wait. I can almost hear the cogs turning. 'If the Fieth clan become elves, there will be one more family supporting the Queen. If they are discredited because of the actions of Ginth, Snake's mother, then that is one less family to oppose Bernais.'

I lean my head into my mistress's hand so she can better scratch behind my ears.

'And if he discredits the Crown family…. I wonder…. I think perhaps Bernais Regis is making a bid for the throne.'

'I do not believe he is strong enough to do that yet, mistress.'

Her petting stops at the use of the word mistress. She does so hate it when I use that word. 'What makes you say that, Percival?'

My mistress runs her fingers around my ears. The pleasure is so intense, I forget the question for a moment. It is too much. I move away and shake my head. The question comes back to me. 'If he were strong enough, he would not have had Ginth and the Crowns arrested. He would not have needed to neutralise their threat,' I explain.

'Of course, Percival. There is that.'

I watch Eleanora pace around the room, turning everything over in her mind. I leave her to it. Creature politics is no longer my concern, and I have given enough tonight. I close my eyes, hoping that we are done and I can get some sleep.

'Why try and stop Pris and Snake from going below?' I open an eye, hoping the question is rhetorical. Unfortunately, it is not. Eleanora is looking directly at me, expecting an answer.

'I do not know, and there was no talk about them while I was below.'

'All they can do is plea for clemency for their parents… and if they don't make it to The Court, then that is one less risk. Mmm…. I believe Bernais might have overplayed his hand and moved too soon. He does not have these trials sewn up as tightly as he would wish.'

There is more coming. I feel it in my bones, and I am not going to like it.

'We must do what we can to see Pris and Snake get below. Once they are there we will see how Bernais reacts.'

And there it is. My chance of going home vanishes, because by 'we' she surely means me. I sigh as Eleanora carries on with her planning.

'With his sprained ankle, I believe Snake will now be forced to go to Mawnan. Quite handy, that little trick of the sprites.'

'Mistress, is that why you did not fix Snake's ankle? Because he would have no option but to go visit his uncle?

'Partially, and partially because it would have been rude to mess with the sprite's lesson, especially as it is one I agree with completely. It is past time Snake Fieth faced up to his family.'

'Still, could you not heal it a little for him?'

My mistress carries on as if I had not even spoken. It is so frustrating when she does that.

'They will be safe from pursuit in Mawnan. The only other place Bernais may try to stop them is on the way to the meeting place. You must stick with them, my lovely, and thwart any attack.'

'What can I do against a greater being?' I ask grumpily. Surely, she cannot expect me to do more?

'Come now, Percival. Bernais will not send a greater being to do them harm. That would be too obvious. No. He will send a lesser creature who owes him a debt.'

'I am sure Snake can handle a lesser creature's magic.'

'Now, Percival, you know some of the smaller creatures can be quite creative with their tricks, and Snake might not even realise he is being hoodwinked. And as for Priscilla, she is as defenseless as a newborn babe.'

I sigh. She is right, even though I don't want to admit it.

'But you can stay with me in the warm tonight, little one.'

I curl into the heat of her leg, grateful for this respite. I sleep, dreaming of my bed by the fire and fish—lots of fish.

THE OWL OF MAWNAN

I LEAN MY backpack against the whitewashed wall of the Red Lion as the bus pulls away. It's a shame we can't stop for lunch in the picturesque thatch-roofed pub, but we're on a tight schedule.

Beside me, Snake takes care to make sure he is braced before hauling his pack into place. Even though I took some of the heavier items from him, he grunts with the effort of standing with the extra weight.

He glances at me, and I avert my face, hoping he didn't catch my worried frown. Even with the strapping I helped him put on this morning, and dosed up with painkillers, walking is a struggle for him. His foot should be propped up, but we don't have the luxury of time.

Snake pulls his phone from a pocket and checks his map of Mawnan.

'This way,' he says, hobbling along at what is really a snail's pace.

A little ways in front of him is a signpost indicating we're heading to the local church. I easily catch Snake up. He is walking so slowly, there is time to turn and take a photo of the pub and send a snapchat to my friend Amalie.

As I swing round to continue, I pull up quickly before I bowl Snake over. He has stopped walking and is watching me, raising a single eyebrow in query.

'I told my friend I was visiting family. She'll think it's strange if I don't send her anything, and she would love this pub.'

He shrugs and carries on, and I realise I haven't seen him contact anyone this whole time. I want to ask him about it, but given what he is preparing to face today, I don't want to upset the apple cart.

'My friends are all living it up in France. They won't be back for a couple of weeks,' he says out of the blue.

'You didn't go?' I ask.

He shakes his head. 'I was going to work the holidays before starting uni.'

As I think about his friends, I wonder if he has a girlfriend. Or boyfriend? I sneak a glance at Snake as I put my phone in my back pocket. His lips are pressed together as he concentrates on putting one foot in front of the other—or more accurately, one foot forward then shuffling the other to meet it.

The thought of Snake having someone he is that close to tugs uncomfortably at my heart. I do a mental eye roll. It was one thing to pretend we were together with Annie yesterday, but I need to remember it isn't real.

We make slow progress along the quiet country lane, and there isn't even anything to look at, as the hedges are so high I can't see over them. Then Snake stops abruptly, and I pull up beside him. Is his ankle bothering him? I follow the direction of his gaze.

A man has exited a thatched cottage opposite. He walks to the car parked in the driveway, gathers some grocery bags from the boot, then heads back towards the door. It is surreal, like I am looking at Snake in thirty years' time.

As if he senses he is being watched, the man turns his head and stares. The bags drop from his hands, and I hope he hasn't any eggs inside because they are surely scrambled now. He ignores the spill of groceries as he literally runs towards us. One moment he is in his garden, and the next he has enveloped Snake in a hug.

'My goodness, Snake, you've grown so much, it took a moment…. I am so happy you came. Glisth and I have been looking for you since we heard about your mother. Oh my, what am I doing, standing here blathering for? Come inside. Tell me where you have—'

I watch Snake as the man wraps his arm companionably over my new friend's shoulders. His expression goes from embarrassed to sheepish to sad all in a few microseconds. Tears glisten in his eyes as his shoulders relax.

As if this is some sort of cue, the man stops midsentence and turns his head to look at me, as if he suddenly realises I am there. 'Oh, excuse me. My manners, I don't know where they disappeared to. I am Earth Fieth, Snake's uncle. Well, his father's uncle really, but we grew up together, more like brothers. And you are?'

I paste on my best polite smile and offer my hand. 'I am Priscilla Crown.'

Earth blushes from the tips of his ears. 'My goodness, Snake, why didn't you warn me you were travelling with royalty? I am so embarrassed.'

'If you had let me get a word in—'

Earth's arm drops from Snake's shoulders, and he turns to me, then back to Snake, and then he gestures to the house, his hands shaking. 'You must both come inside. Glisth is making tomato soup for lunch.' He frowns and shuffles a little, then adds, 'You will join us, won't you?'

He manages to bundle both of us towards the cottage, and I catch Snake sending a fond smile his uncle's way as he hobbles forward.

'Oh goodness, look what I did,' Earth says, spying the grocery bags laying on the ground. 'I will never hear the end of it if I have broken anything.'

He bends to gather the items back into the bags, and in his excitement drops almost as much as he manages to get in. I slip off my pack and join him.

'Oh no, Princess Priscilla, I can't allow—'

'I don't mind,' I say, unable to stop myself grinning at the flustered man who looks so much like Snake but is so different.

'Oh, if you insist, then thank you very much.'

I pick up a couple of the bags and follow Earth into the cottage. Snake follows us in and props our packs by the door. The door leads directly into a flagstone entrance. To the left is a living room, and to the right there is a table down the end of a short hallway. The smells drifting towards me tell me this is likely the kitchen.

Earth heads along the corridor. I wait for Snake to take the lead, and as he passes me, I ask, 'Is he always that… effusive?'

Snake's chuckle comes from deep inside. 'This might be hard to believe, but he is one of the finest political minds in the World Below. So don't be fooled by that bumbling exterior.'

'Don't tell me he is faking it?'

He shakes his head as his gaze slips past me to his uncle. A tender smile curls his lips. 'No, we have thrown him off his game, and he really is that pleased to see me. Come and meet his wife. You'll find they love nothing more than having family to fuss over.'

The flagstone floor continues on into the most perfect country cottage kitchen. Earth takes the shopping bags from me, and I hang back by the doorway as Snake hobbles over to the petite dark woman busy putting bake-in-the-oven rolls onto a tray. She pauses when Snake approaches, and the joy on her face lights the room as he hugs her.

'You naughty boy. Why didn't you at least ring? Earth was so worried. When we heard about your mother….'

'I am sorry, Glisth. It was a little thoughtless of me, But—'

The woman holds Snake at arm's length and frowns. 'You don't think we had anything to do with your mother being taken, do you? Your uncle has been working night and day for her return.'

Snake takes her hand in his. 'Of course not. I know I have been… distant… but I never doubted you and Earth were there for us.'

'Good. Now tell me, who is your friend?' Glisth turns her beaming smile my way, and I bask in its welcoming glow.

It is Earth who steps round Snake and introduces me to his wife. 'Oh my. Glisth fo Dnat, may I formally introduce Princess Priscilla Crown.'

I can't believe my eyes when Glisth actually curtsies. 'Welcome to our humble home, Princess.'

Snake is choking on his laughter and wiping tears from his eyes as my face heats with embarrassment. I'm so shocked, I don't know what to say. I mean, what is the protocol when you are introduced as royalty in someone's home? Hearing creatures tell me I am of the royal bloodline is one thing, but being called Princess not as a joke is a whole other level.

'Um, please call me Pris,' I fumble, wondering how I might tell them to treat me just like anyone else.

Snake comes to my rescue. 'Guys, Pris is travelling incognito. So, a little less of the royal treatment would be great.'

He winks at me, and my bones melt. I must have overdone the walking the last two days for him to affect me that way.

'Well, if that is what you wish, then it shall be our command,' Earth says.

'It is my wish,' I confirm, relieved not to be feted as apparently befits my royal heritage.

'You will stay to lunch?' Glisth insists. 'I always make plenty.' She wipes her hands on a dishcloth and appears nervous as she adds, 'It isn't anything fancy, though, just plain old soup.'

My stomach rumbles at the thought of a homemade meal. 'Soup would be perfect, thank you,' I say.

Earth seats us at the table and makes hot drinks while Glisth puts the rolls in the oven.

'These are the people you were afraid to visit?' I whisper.

'Don't get me wrong, I love them to bits. They have not yet been blessed with a child of their own, and when I was younger, they treated me like a son. To be honest, I've missed them terribly…. Catching up with them is not what I am afraid of.'

I wait for him to continue, but we are interrupted as Earth sets the table before joining us.

'I am sorry about your mother, Snake. I have been doing what I can for her. She is being held in a state room, not a cell, and is allowed time outside. But I am blocked at every turn when I try to argue for her release.'

Snake sits forward and covers the man's hand in his. 'That is why we are here, Earth. We need your help so we can help her.'

Before Earth can answer, Glisth takes a seat. 'Eating first, business later. Surely you have not forgotten the house rules,' she admonishes, and both Snake and Earth mumble apologies.

The meal is relaxed as Earth quizzes Snake about how he did in his exams, what his plans are for university, and how his band is going.

I look at Snake in a new light. 'You didn't tell me you're in a band,' I say.

'Oh yes, and they are very good. Snake sings and plays guitar,' Earth says.

'Are you musical?' Glisth asks.

I grimace as I think of my piano lessons. I enjoy music, but musical talent bypassed this body. 'Not in the slightest.'

Glisth pats my hand. 'Me neither. But my Earth, he can sing the birds out of the trees. That was how he stole my heart and lived up to his name.'

She winks at me, like she is sharing a secret. As I eat my soup, I roll her words around in my head. Stole my heart and lived up to his name. Earth? And anagram Heart. Fieth? Hold on. His name is Heart Thief.

I smile to myself. That means Snake's name is… 'Sneak Thief.' The words pop out, and Snake claps a hand over my mouth. 'We don't say our true names out loud. It's bad luck.'

Great. Another faux pas. I wonder how badly I transgressed this time. My gaze meets Snake's, and he is clearly amused, perhaps because it took me this long to figure out gnomic naming conventions.

'We are with family, Snake, no harm done,' Earth says, smoothing over the situation.

Snake removes his hand. 'Sorry, Pris. I'm just not used to hearing anyone but my mum call me that.'

I touch his hand as it rests on the table. 'No, Snake. I'm the one who's sorry. There's so much Mum and Dad haven't taught me….'

'I grew up with your mother, you know, and I met your father once. His brother is surely one of the great leaders of our age,' Earth interrupts, his tone solemn as if he is speaking about someone famous.

I look at Snake, who appears as surprised by this revelation as I am. Glisth stands and starts picking up dishes.

'It seems it is time for business. I will clear away while you all go into the lounge.'

'Can I—'

'No, dear. You have things to discuss, and I prefer to keep out of the business side of Earth's life.'

I follow Snake along the corridor and into the cosy lounge room. The walls are covered in shelves of books, and there is no television. This room is designed to shut out the world.

Earth crouches by the fireplace and points at the logs as he whispers something. I eagerly lean forward, watching him use a spell to light the fire. I have to restrain myself from clapping my hands—this is real magic, like something from the movies. The gnome mutters a few other words, and the fire is blazing.

Earth takes an armchair on one side of the fireplace, and I join Snake on the couch opposite. As we sit, I whisper to Snake, 'Can I do that?'

He grins. 'We can all do that.'

My excitement simmers down as the fire settles. Watching the dancing flames, I remember the question that had formed in my mind as we entered the living room. I lean in and ask, 'Snake, who is my uncle?'

He shrugs. 'I've no idea. All I know is, your mother is one of the Queen's cousins, but I don't know anything about your father's family.'

I mull this snippet of information over as Earth relaxes back in his chair and places his hands in his lap. 'So, what can I do for you?'

'Who is my uncle?' The words are out of my mouth before I even realise I have spoken.

Earth freezes for the merest second, then recovers with the smile of a consummate diplomat. 'My dear, I am sorry, but I don't really feel comfortable being the one to provide you with that information. Perhaps that question is best asked of your parents.'

'Is he some sort of criminal? Is that why you won't say anything?' I blurt out.

Our host blinks a couple of times, as if my question startles him. 'No… no… Quite the contrary. Oh dear. I fear I have made matters worse.' Earth wrings his hands. 'Yes, I think it would be all right for me to say that he is not well thought of by many in the World Below, but to many others, he is a hero. You should ask your father for his story.'

He turns to Snake, and I get the impression he has said all he is going to. 'Now, is there something I can help *you* with?'

A little bubble of anger is forming inside me as Earth glibly moves on. I was so close to learning something more about who I am. Shutting my eyes for a moment, I remind myself that this is an important meeting for Snake, and not everything is about me. I turn to Snake.

'Are you okay?' he asks.

I shrug. 'I guess.' I nudge him, signalling that it's up to him now. We need to focus on getting our final endorsement.

'I would like you to endorse us so we can attend the Spring Court,' Snake says.

'Straight to the point, as usual.' Earth smiles. 'And why does a princess need an invitation to attend court?'

Snake takes my hand, and Earth's eyes fixate on our entwined fingers. He seems disturbed by the action. Sooo, it's okay for us to be friends, but nothing more than that? I decide to ignore the look.

'Because my parents were taken to stand trial with Snake's mother,' I say. 'I was not invited to attend The Court, so I must go through the same process as Snake to speak for them.'

'Interesting. I expected Snake's request, but not yours.' He taps a finger against his lip. 'I guess it doesn't make any difference. I will clearly support you, but it is creature law that I cannot do so without exacting a price.'

I squeeze Snake's fingers, knowing this is the bit he has been dreading.

'I will give you my endorsement after you spend a night in the church.'

'What?' Snake says. 'Is that it? Then we ag—'

'Wait a moment.' I turn to Snake. 'If we stay here the night it is going to give us less time in Southampton tomorrow. We need to at least get back to Truro today.'

'If time is the only thing stopping you, I am sure it is not against any rules for me to take you to the nearest form of transport in Truro tomorrow morning. You will be at the station in time for the first train, the one you would be taking anyway.'

I can think of no further reasons to object, except that my gut is saying Earth's task is more than it seems. Snake's eyes meet mine, almost begging me to agree. He is totally relaxed for the first time today. How can I refuse him? I nod.

'Agreed,' he says.

EARTH SLOTS A large antique key into the opening, and it turns smoothly in the lock. The door is heavy as he pushes it, but it opens silently.

'How do you have a key to the—?' I start.

'My human job is caretaker and tour guide of the church,' Earth says with a smile. 'St Mawnan and St Stephan's church has a long history and a long association with our kind.'

Inside, the late afternoon sun streams in through the lead-light windows. For a moment, Pris is caught in the coloured light, and she glows—luminescent.

My heart reaches out of my chest for her, like she is a missing piece of me.

I turn away to find Earth watching me thoughtfully. Heat prickles my skin. I know exactly what he is thinking—elves and gnomes do not mix. It doesn't matter what my heart might want; my head is calling the shots.

'What do we need to do?' I ask, getting down to business.

'Just stay here the night.' He hands me a couple of quilts. 'It can get a little cold. Behind the altar are some candles and matches if you want some light later on.'

'And that's it?' I can't help feeling there is more to this, but Earth is being cagey.

'Yep. That simple. I will lock the door, though, just to be sure you keep to our bargain.'

Definitely something else going on. Even so, I nod my agreement. Earth hugs me, which is a little odd given we are just staying here for one night. Rather than comforting me, the action feeds my fear. I'm still searching for the catch when Earth lets me go.

Hobbling to the closest pew, I drop down with a thud. The door bangs shut as my uncle leaves us alone. Moments later, Pris slips into the pew behind me with her phone in her hand.

'Do you think our staying the night here has something to do with this?' she asks, handing the device to me.

Her browser displays references to the Owl Man of Mawnan. I flick through some of them.

'Sounds like this was some sort of local legend, perhaps even some of my ancestors playing tricks to keep people away from something they didn't want them to see.' I hand the phone back.

'Are you sure? I'm not great with anything reeking of horror. Movies with jump scares are a complete no-no.' She laughs, but it sounds hollow and nervous in the empty church.

In light of the frequent attacks she endures, I am sure she doesn't need any more scares in the rest of her life.

'I can't be totally sure it won't appear, but I am here to protect you if anything scary happens.' I laugh to show her I'm not serious.

'My hero.' Her chuckle this time is genuine, dispelling the tension in the room. I can barely walk, and she's some sort of karate super ninja. I'm well aware of who would be protecting whom should anything nasty appear.

'We may as well make ourselves comfortable,' I say as I hand her one of the duvets.

She makes a nest on the floor between the pews, using her backpack as a pillow. Having made her bed, Pris heads to the altar and grabs four candles.

She sets them on holders at the end of the two pews we are using, ready to be lit when it turns dark.

Having organised us, she lies down and picks up the book she bought at the train station this morning and opens it. She's already halfway through. Glancing up, she catches my eye and asks, 'E-reader?'

I nod, and she reaches into one of her pockets and pulls out my device. I prop my ankle up on my backpack and roll my duvet to make a back rest before opening an old favourite, the *Dune* trilogy. I am halfway through book two and am soon lost in a faraway world.

As the sun sets, Pris rises to light the candles. She passes me one of the packages of food Glisth had given her, and I open it to find a roast beef sandwich in a crusty roll. I salivate as I take my first bite, devouring the pickles and cheese along with the thick slices of roast beef.

'There are worse ways to spend a night,' I say to Pris as I tidy the crumbs and open my book again.

'Apart from the floor being a little hard, this is better than I expected,' she agrees.

She smiles a sleepy smile up at me, and I briefly wonder what it would be like to curl up beside her. The moment is lost when she rolls over to carry on reading. I sigh. Well, back to *Dune* it is, then.

Some time later, the candles flicker, flames catching in a draft as the wind whips up outside. I look around to make sure Pris isn't freaking out to find her sound asleep. I glance around the room, which is shrouded in darkness outside our little pool of light.

Shifting a little in the seat, I make myself more comfortable, not in the least bit tired. My eyes flick back down to my book, only to swiftly rise again as the sound of scratching reaches my ears.

'Just the trees against the windows,' I say out loud, as if speaking the words makes the idea more real.

The flames dance in unfelt eddies of air, and the scratching becomes more persistent. The hairs on the back of my neck stand on end.

I place the book on the pew beside me and slip around for a better view of the back of the church. Waiting for my sight to adjust to the darkness, my gaze roves the shadows. Nothing there. I drop my foot to the floor and turn slowly back to the front. My heart freezes and my mouth opens, but no scream escapes, even though it is rising in my throat.

Looming over the altar is the silhouette of the largest owl I have ever seen, and it is growing. I swing my head back and forth, trying to identify what is casting the shadow. I can't find anything.

The air is freezing, and my stomach clenches as a deep voice booms. 'If you want to leave here tonight, you must feed the Owl Man. You must feed him your fear.'

'What?' My voice is thin and reedy in the cavernous space compared to the deep timbre of the Owl Man's.

'If you want to live through the night, you must tell me your greatest fear. If it satisfies my appetite, you may leave.'

Really? That is it? This is almost the same question Eugenia asked. My heart slows down and my ears are no longer filled with its pounding. I have got this.

Pushing myself into a standing position, I shuffle away from the pew. As I straighten my shoulders, I reel off my answer. 'My biggest fear is being like my father and letting my family down when they need me most.'

'Oh.'

The response sounds choked, and the Owl Man begins to shrink, then crumples to nothing. The church is silent and still for a moment, and I wonder whether or not I have passed the test. Then the sound of footsteps comes from the front of the church.

'Hello?' I say, and the word echoes in the night air.

The shadows behind the altar shimmer, and a figure emerges into the light, forming into a man.

'Oh, Snake, what did I do to you?'

My jaw drops. I take a step back and collapse into the pew.

'Dad?' I whisper.

Silence hangs in the air between us as we both regard each other. He is just the same as he is in my memories. I peer a little closer. No, there are more lines on his forehead, and he looks… sad.

Part of me longs to run to him, to have him wrap his arms around me like he used to when I was little. The more rational part of me wants to rail at him, ask him why he left me, and why he has come back now.

I do none of these things. Instead, I say, 'It was too easy. I should have known Earth would do something like this.'

Surprise flickers across my father's face before it settles into resignation. 'Don't blame Earth. When I heard rumours of what you were doing, I hoped you would come to him for help. So, I arranged this meeting as the price for your endorsement. I am selfish. I wanted to see you. And I wanted to help you help your mother.'

So many emotions chase each other through my head, I can't settle on one. For a moment, I can't respond. Finally, anger wins the battle and I spit, 'What do you care about me or Mum? You abandoned us years ago.'

'Oh, Snake.' My father takes a step towards me, and I hold up a hand before he can take another.

'Stay where you are.'

Surprisingly, he does as I command.

'Your mother—'

'If you're going to say my mother poisoned my mind, you're wrong. All she ever said about you is that you did what you had to. My contempt for you is of my own making, born from abandonment. We barely survive up here, and you didn't even care enough to check in or support us.'

Years of anger and bitterness fill my heart, and it is all I can do to stop myself from rushing at the man in front of me and pummelling him to a pulp. I expect him to defend himself, but all he does is stare at me, tears streaming down his face.

'You are right. I deserted you and your mother. We argued. She thrived above ground, and you were happy there too. I had too much time on my hands. My jobs were few and far between, and I was restless and wanted glory. I wasn't a good husband. Rather than support Ginth, I tried to make her return below, knowing she would not be valued there.'

'I don't want to hear your excuses,' I say.

'Please, I am not trying to excuse my actions. I was proud, and young, and arrogant. After one particularly bad argument, I returned home without leave from our elders. It was stupid. I got caught and was sentenced to ten years below without any contact above.'

'So, you're telling me you couldn't even get a message to Mum? I don't believe that.'

'Earth acted as go-between. What those messages contained is between your mother and me. If she chose not to share the contents with you, then I will not betray her trust any more than I already have.'

For a moment, I don't know what to say. Mum and Dad had been speaking all this time? Although I know that changes things, I am not ready to let go of my anger.

'So, how come you're here now? According to your story, there is still a year and a bit to go.'

'I bargained an hour with you for another five years banishment from the World Above.'

What? My jaw drops again.

'You would not come to me no matter how often Earth or your mother asked on my behalf. So, I had to find a way to get to you. I am not asking you to trust me or forgive me. All I am asking from you is to let me help you help Ginth. She was taken below because she married me. I cannot let that act cause her any more pain than it already has.'

'Pris and I have that in hand. Earth will give us the last endorsement we need. We don't need your help.'

'What about the rest of the riddle? Have you solved it all?'

'Yes, we worked out we need to pay a gold coin for entry. Pris has a plan for that.'

'That reminds me.' My father reaches into his pocket and holds out his hand. 'Your grandfather asked me to give you a gift.'

I stare at two gold coins but make no move to take them.

'Are you allowed to do that? Isn't it against some sort of rule? Shouldn't we find everything ourselves?'

'There is no rule against a grandfather giving a gift to a family member. It is up to you how you choose to use them.'

I still don't move. My father spins the coins in the air and directs them to the pew beside me, where they settle next to my e-reader with a slight clink.

'Did you work out where the Spring Court is being held?'

'Yep, in the Underground Ballroom the night after tomorrow,' I say to prove I do not need his help.

My father shakes his head. 'The Court is held from midnight tomorrow night until midnight the following night. It is how it has always been. Those twenty-four hours above ground are the equivalent of one month in The World Below. One month twice a year when those above ground and those below congregate to make new laws, settle disputes, and confer thanks.'

My eyes widen. 'Are you sure?'

'Of course I am. I am to attend on behalf of the family, so I should know.'

My stomach lurches. We will be cutting it fine, but if we don't need to stop to find coins, we should make it. My mouth goes dry as I think about how we were so close to missing our chance to save our parents. Bending, I scoop the coins into my hand. Beggars can't be choosers.

'What about the word?'

I frown, trying to remember the riddle. A rustle from behind causes me to start as a hand pops over the back of the pew, waving the note. I wonder how long Pris has been listening. I'm not sure how I feel about her overhearing my reunion with my father. Then again, I'm not sure how I feel about anything at the moment.

'Thanks,' I mutter as I take the paper from her.

I read the rhyme: 'Speak the word to create that which needs our breath but cannot breathe.'

It still means no more to me than it did the other dozen or so times I've read it.

'I cannot tell you the answer, but I can tell you that those who enter The Court from the World Above for the first time must prove they are from the magical realm,' my father explains.

'I am so stupid.' I slap my palm to my forehead. It refers to the first spell we all learn, and one of the few spells all races can perform. In fact, Earth used it earlier today right in front of me. I hold out my palm and say, 'Lasair.' A small flame appears a centimetre or so above my palm.

'Perfect. You are set. What about you, young lady? Can you produce a flame?'

'What, me?' The pew wobbles as Pris bangs into it just before her head appears. 'Can't Snake just do it for the both of us?'

My father laughs. I'd forgotten how infectious his laughter is, and it takes my breath away.

'No, you must produce it yourself to show you are truly from the World Below.'

Pris uses the pew to push herself to her feet. 'I've never done any magic.'

'Yes, you have,' I tell her. 'You called a goblin, and you used your glamour.'

Her eyes lock with mine, her uncertainty and fear warring in their bright blue depths.

'You can do this,' I tell her, placing my hand over hers. 'Open your other hand. Now reach for magic like I showed you.'

Pris closes her eyes, and the ring under my fingers warms up.

'Good. Now imagine a flame on your palm.' She nods, eyes still closed. 'Now push your magic into the flame and say the word lasair.'

'Lasair,' Pris says.

A small light flickers over her palm, then fizzes out.

'Not bad for a first attempt,' I say. 'Maybe this time, you could do it with your eyes open.'

Pris's eyes flick open. 'Should it be hot? And does it matter what colour I imagine the flame to be?'

'You're overthinking this.'

I start at the voice, and Pris draws her hand back, as if suddenly aware of my father's presence.

'You almost had it, but you doubted yourself. Try again,' my father directs.

Pris stands up straighter, concentrates on her hand, and says, 'Lasair.'

Again, a little flicker of light, then the flame dies.

'I can't do this.'

'Yes, you can,' Dad and I say together.

'If you can start a flame, you can finish it,' I tell her. 'You just need practice.'

'And you also need to believe you can do it. But you will never be able to do that until you admit to yourself who you truly are.'

I swing round to tell my father he doesn't know what he's talking about, but I stop short. He is watching Pris with such compassion that I realise he understands completely.

His gaze lifts to meet mine, and I am blown away by the strength of the love his look conveys. The angry shell I have built around my heart to keep my father out cracks a little; not completely, but enough for me to recognise there will be more to our story when this is over.

'I appreciate your help and what it cost you to deliver it.' Okay, it's not forgiveness, but it is a start.

Tears leak from his eyes. 'I know it is too little too late as far as you are concerned. But I will do all I can to save Ginth fo Drefin, and not just because she is your mother, but because she does not deserve this.'

He draws in a breath and says, 'Just seeing you for this short time… I would have given much more.'

I lurch forward and hug him. 'I have not forgiven you, but thank you.'

From far away, a bell tinkles. Dad holds me tight, as if he doesn't want to let me go.

'This has not been nearly enough time,' he says as he releases me. 'I will be there to support you when you make it below.'

Then he is gone. My heart is breaking into pieces, just like it did the first time he left me, and I want to curl into a ball and cry.

Pris's voice fills the room as she says, 'Well, that was all completely unexpected.'

I whip around to tell her exactly how hurtful and unsupportive her comment is, to find she is right behind me. A moment later, she gathers me into a hug.

I want to collapse into her arms, but I remain stiff, trying to maintain my facade of nonchalance. Then I can be strong no longer, and it all comes out in a rush. I turn into a howling baby. She rubs my back and croons something by my ear. I am not sure how long we remain like that, me releasing years of hurt and her letting me. Finally, the tears stop, and I raise my head.

'Better?'

I nod, unable to speak.

'Uhm.' The voice comes from the doorway. 'There are comfy beds next door if you would rather spend the rest of the night inside.'

I want to yell at Earth. To tell him he is a sneaky no good… whatever he is. I cannot think of the word. My mouth opens to do just that, only to find all my rage has disappeared. Suddenly I am weary and drained.

Earth looks past me at Pris. 'Take him inside. Glisth has hot chocolates with marshmallows ready for you. It should help with the shock. I'll bring your gear.'

I am sitting in front of the fire, allowing the sweetness of the drink to do its work, half listening to Glisth give Pris tips on how to produce her flame when Earth sits beside me.

'You all right?' he asks, placing his hand on my knee.

'I will be,' I say as warmth radiates down my leg. It reaches my ankle, and I tense as the pain lessens. 'Did you just—'

He chuckles. 'If you hadn't avoided me all these years, I could have taught you a thing or two about what we gnomes can actually do.'

'But that's an elven power,' I hiss under my breath.

'So many believe.' Earth's lips curl into a half smile

There is more to this conversation, and I sense Earth willing me to ask the questions forming in my head. But I am emotionally drained, and my mind will not take any more in.

My gaze wanders to Pris, and I have a new respect for how she has dealt with the upheaval I brought into her life.

THE FINAL LEG

THE COLD MORNING air clings like a limpet, and I pull my jacket more firmly around my body. I am grateful for the beanie Glisth insisted I take, as it helps keep the warmth in.

Earth leads me to the car, and I dump my pack in the boot. Although my ankle twinges a little as I walk, it is way better than yesterday. After this is over, I must return so I can learn about how gnomes can heal. I can hardly believe that two days ago I was reluctant to come here. Now I don't want to leave.

As I take my place in the front seat, I breathe in the smell of the straight-from-the-oven cinnamon scrolls Glisth handed to Pris as we left. We did not have time for breakfast, but the ever-thoughtful Glisth made some for us while we showered and changed. I had forgotten how kind and loving she is, and tears had formed in my eyes as I hugged her goodbye.

Before we back out of the driveway, Earth turns on Radio 2, and I close my eyes to the sound of the golden oldies I remember my father listening to. The simple thought of him no longer tugs at my heart, or causes resentment to well inside of me. I have not forgiven him, but I guess I realise now that there is more to my parents' story than I had previously thought.

In my mind, it had been all about an upper-class gnome falling for a common girl. They married, moved to the human world, and he could not take the loss of status. He begged her to return, and she wouldn't go with him because here she was valued for who she was, not where she came from. Taking matters into his own hands, he abandoned his family, never to be heard of again.

As if guessing the train of my thoughts, Earth says, 'I am so happy you spoke with your father. Now I am free to talk of things I was bound by your parents never to discuss.'

'Parents?' I raise an eyebrow.

'Yes, I am afraid neither of them have been very fair to you while they sorted out their marital issues, but it is not my place to say more than that about them.'

'What things?' I prompt.

'Things? Oh, we can talk about that when this is over.'

Sometimes Earth can be exceedingly frustrating to deal with.

'After I drop you off, I will be returning to the World Below to see what I can do to help your mother. It may not be much, I am afraid, because the family is treading a very dodgy political path at the moment, which I suspect is why your mother is facing these charges.'

'We thought something else was going on,' I admit to Earth. 'Are you able to tell me anything more about what it is?'

Earth does not take his eyes off the road as he shakes his head. 'I am sorry, but I think in this instance, you will be more effective freeing your mother if you stay well away from the politics. Creatures are more likely to be persuaded by you if they think you have nothing more to gain than your mother's freedom.'

When it comes to creature politics, there is none better than Earth for forging a path without setting off any major explosions. I heed his advice and don't ask any more questions.

The sun is just peeking over top of the Victorian brick frontage of Truro station when we pull up. He takes off to buy us tickets for the 6:40 to Reading while I sort out our packs. Leaning them against the building, I turn to wait for Earth, only to find him standing in front of me, two steaming mugs of coffee in his hands. 'Glisth made me promise to set you on your way with a proper breakfast.'

Emotion clogs my throat again over my aunt's kindness as I take the cups. With such a strong family standing with me, how can I help but rescue my mother? Pris appears by my side, taking her cup so I can hug Earth.

'We will meet again at court, my friends,' he says through the window as he drives off.

We make our cumbersome way to the platform and wait patiently for the train, which seems not to want to appear. I check my phone. It's ten minutes late. I stand up and look down the track, then sit again.

'Chill. Trains run from Reading to Guildford every twenty minutes or so,' Pris tells me calmly. 'And there are plenty of trains from Guildford heading down to Godalming.'

I try and relax, but I can't. 'I thought we had more time,' I say. 'Dad pointing out that The Court starts on midnight the day of the full moon rather than the evening… well… I just thought we had more time to prepare.'

Pris chucks her empty coffee cup into the bin beside her and shrugs. 'We would have spent most of today getting our golden coins, so we really are no worse off,' she says, ever the practical one. Then she mumbles under her breath, 'And at least you don't need to learn how to cast a spell before midnight tonight.'

I open my mouth to reassure Pris, but the train chooses that moment to finally arrive, and we are distracted with making our way through commuters and finding spaces to sit. Because we spend time putting our backpacks in the luggage racks by the doors, we are the last to find seats, and there are no two together.

At Exeter the woman beside me leaves, and I shuffle over to make room for Pris. Her face is pale, and she is unusually fidgety. I sense she wants to talk, but the packed train carriage is not the place to discuss magic.

Finally, she says in hushed tones, 'If I can't do it, will you speak for my parents as well?'

I want to tell her this is unnecessary, that she'll be able to make a flame. The fear I read in her eyes stops the words in my throat. 'Of course I will,' I say instead. 'But we will have time for you to practice once we are at the conference centre. We should be able to find somewhere to rest and to perfect your flame.'

'It may still not be enough,' she says.

This is unlike her. She is normally so positive, or at least focused on a way she can achieve her goals. Is she really that worried about calling fire? About actually admitting she is a creature? Or is something else going on? I smile in what I hope is an encouraging fashion, hoping to talk some more about it.

She doesn't smile back. Opening her book, she mumbles, 'Okay.' Her eyes drop to the page in front of her and the discussion is over.

I study her profile for a while, wondering how I can help her. Over the last few days, she has been so supportive of me, and I'm pretty sure I wouldn't have had the courage to face my family alone. Now she is troubled, and I want to offer the same to her.

She can make the beginnings of a flame, which means she can use magic. Is my father right? Does she need to accept who she is before she can use her powers? And if he is, how do I help her accept her elven heritage in half a day?

I pull my earbuds out of my pack and click on my classical playlist before immersing myself in a piano version of Satie's "Gnossiennes" on continuous loop, hoping for divine inspiration.

TRAINS ARE SUCH dirty, smelly things. Humans jam themselves in like fish in a can, and it makes the smell even worse. I wrinkle my nose and slip back under the luggage rack to avoid trampling feet.

From my hidey hole, I can protect Snake and that elf. They are fully endorsed, and I can smell the gold they carry. And they are travelling in the right direction to attend The Court. Why are they not happier? Have they had an argument? Surely, I did not miss that.

All right, I did delay a little in Glisth's kitchen. It was warm, and she made me a very special breakfast. Even so, I made it to the station just as they did and have been tailing them ever since.

No, there is something else going on. I slip forwards a little and check the carriage. There is nothing obvious, but an air of doubt hangs heavy, and it is centred around Snake and her.

Whoever is doing this is well hidden, and I cannot cast a spell to seek them out without drawing attention to myself. I settle back down. I will bide my time.

The next station is announced, and the girl and Snake make their way towards me. I ensure I am well hidden before they arrive to gather their bags. They stand by the luggage rack, waiting for the train to stop.

At first, they don't say anything, then the elf says, 'Glisth told me last night that most creatures cast their flame spells almost before they can walk. I think she meant to demonstrate how easy it is, but it isn't easy for me. I start out okay, but I can't make it form completely. I can't do this.'

Stupid elf. I can make a flame. Even most humans could make one if they slowed down for long enough to sense magic in the air.

'You can do this, Pris. We will practice this afternoon.' Snake glances around. 'When we are alone.'

He is far too nice to her. The elf girl sighs, and I resist the urge to swipe her with my claws. She is a *princess,* for goodness' sake. She should start acting like one!

The doors open, and my quarry disappear amongst the commuters. I wind my way through legs and dodge feet to catch them up. There they are, heading for another platform. Seriously, someone should tell them they *can* use other forms of transport.

They reach the platform just as a train slips away. Shoulders slumped, they take a seat to wait for the next train to their destination. I take up a post beside a dispensing machine and scan the area. No obvious creatures here, but there are three people who were also in the carriage on the other train. It could be any one of them.

I hunker out of the wind and fight off a sudden urge to pop home. Whoever is doing this is throwing everything at Snake and the elf. Snake is giving the girl a pep talk. He fumbles in his pack, and his hand comes out with two mugs. He stands up and heads to the kiosk. The girl looks around forlornly, twisting the ring on her finger, and I realise she is on the verge of leaving.

Snake is nowhere to be seen. I don't like elf girl, but Eleanora will be displeased if I let her get away.

I force myself to my feet and out into the cold, blustery wind sweeping the platform. No one gives me a second glance as I pad over to her and rub against her legs. Immediately, I am swamped with self-doubt. How can I, a lesser creature, ever believe I can help a princess of the crown?

As Pris leans down and rubs a hand through my fur, I feel the heat in her ring. There is a spell, and it is directed at Pris. That was why she was twisting it.

It cannot completely dispel whatever the other creature is doing, but as the princess continues to pat me, I cast a spell of lightness and well-being. As I do, I sense the elf girl relax.

'Oh, aren't you a handsome fellow,' she says as her fingers find the sweet spot behind my ears, and I lean into her. Perhaps she isn't so bad after all.

Familiar trainers enter my line of vision, and I slip under the seat and away before he catches sight of me. The air is a little clearer after my spell, but it won't be so easy to thwart the creature once we are in the confined space of a carriage.

The elf girl leads us on to yet another train, then one more after that. During each leg of the journey, she sinks more and more into herself, and I worry. I fear she will not make it to The Court tonight if this carries on. The only small ray of sunshine is that Snake is so intent on keeping elf girl's spirits up, he does not appear to be as affected by the spell, but it does worry me that he has not sensed what is going on.

By the third train, I have narrowed the culprit down to two men. One is wearing a business suit, and the other is clearly a tradesman of some description. It is obviously the suit—never trust anyone in a suit.

Snake stands up. We are clearly changing trains again. I wait until everyone departs, then dash out before the doors close. Turning my head this way and that, I cannot find Snake or elf girl. Finally, I spy them on the other side of the barrier.

He and the elf are arguing about something. I walk by them. Are they really fighting about clothes? I slip in behind a fence and survey the area. Suit man and tradesman are both waiting by the station entrance. Are they in this together?

While I keep an eye on Bernais's henchmen, I fail to notice Snake and the elf begin walking into town, meaning I have to rush to catch up with them. Then I almost get caught by Snake as he turns to glare at a garden. His figure blurs, and the elf turns, her eyes widening in surprise.

I am close enough to catch the girl's words when she says, 'What did you do?'

'If people persist in thinking gnomes look like those abominations, they deserve all they get.'

'So, the urban legend of garden gnomes moving by themselves is true?' The elf girl's laugh must be infectious because Snake's face loses its grouch, and he grins.

'You could say that. Come on. If we really must buy suitable clothes for tonight, let's get it over and done with.'

As they walk off, I jump lightly up onto the stone wall to survey Snake's handiwork. I am shocked, to say the least. Snake had been very inventive with the poses he had placed the gnomes in—inventive enough that I am surely blushing under my fur.

I find Snake and elf girl wandering the high street. Snake is pulled into a clothing shop, and I park myself in a doorway to wait for them.

The spot I chose is cold and dank, and it smells faintly of human functions that should not be done in such a public place. Some people have no shame! My nose wrinkles and I shuffle forward to get some fresh air, and then I spot him, the tradesman, two doors down, leaning against a store window.

Peeking around the doorway, I check the rest of the street. Suit man is nowhere to be seen. I have my culprit. Leaving my post, I walk past the man, giving him a sniff as I pass by.

'Leave off, you eejit.' A foot kicks out at me, and I dash away to save myself from injury.

I sniff again. Leprechaun. Really, have they no imagination? He could have disguised himself as anything—a tradesman is way too stereotypical. And Bernais, of all the low tricks, sending a leprechaun to do your dirty work. They should not even be above ground in England, let alone allowed to practice magic here.

I double back and return to my hiding place. Even the smell of urine is preferable to being near a leprechaun. They are tricksters and make sprites and fairies seem like amateurs.

Moments later, Snake and elf girl reappear, carrying bags. I slip in behind them as we head away from the leprechaun. Raising a shield of air to dispel any spell sent our way, I am confident in the knowledge that the henchman could not call enough power to break through it, not this far from his native land.

A few doors on, the girl heads into a food shop, returns a couple of minutes later with some extra bags, and they carry on down the road. Snake checks his phone, and they turn a corner and stop outside a small, nondescript building. He waits outside with the bags while elf girl enters. Before she returns, a car pulls up and a man jumps out.

'You the party for Whitley?'

'We are,' the girl says as she reappears behind Snake.

Their bags are loaded into the back, and in less time than it takes me to lower the shield protecting them from evil thoughts, they are gone.

'Bloody hell, I'm for it now.' The voice comes from behind me, followed by a rush of air, and the leprechaun is gone.

My job is done. Time to wait for the ballroom to open so I can join Eleanora.

THE TAXI PULLS up outside the gates of the conference centre, the nose of the car pointing directly at a sign telling us it is closed for a private function.

'Are you sure this is the right place?' the driver asks, not moving to open the boot.

'I am,' Snake says from beside me. 'We are part of the function.'

In the rear vision mirror, I see the man raise bushy grey eyebrows.

'I mean, we're here to help with the catering,' Snake explains, realising we are not the type of people normally attending private functions here.

'Okay, then.'

The boot lock clicks, and I open the door beside me. The man doesn't even leave his seat to help with the bags. Given the exorbitant amount I prepaid for this trip, I'm about to give him a piece of my mind. Snake places a hand on my arm, and I turn to find him shaking his head.

'It's not worth it,' he says as he slams down the boot.

He's right, it isn't worth worrying about given the task ahead of us. My stomach sinks at the thought. All day I've had this overwhelming feeling of futility, wondering why I am even trying to get into the ball.

When we were at Guildford, I had almost told Snake to go on alone. I was heading for the platform to Waterloo when Snake grabbed my arm and virtually dragged me to the Portsmouth Platform as if he had read my mind.

Nagging doubts about my magical abilities still eat at my stomach, but I'm resolved to at least try and see this through.

'Hey, what about my tip?' the driver leans out of the door and yells, bringing me back to the present.

'Here's one for you: next time get out and help,' Snake says before turning and walking up the path.

'Bloody kids today.' The response follows Snake and me up the driveway.

'Shouldn't we be hiding, or at least be careful no one sees us?' I ask as I catch him up.

His shoulders rise in a shrug. 'Earth said court entrances are owned by creatures. They will be expecting a number of our kind to be arriving today, so they won't be worried.'

'This early?'

'Probably not, but there doesn't appear to be anyone about. Come on. Let's go round the back. Maybe I can find a window or door to let us inside.'

'I'm not sure about this, Snake. I mean, not only will we be breaking and entering, but isn't using your magic for personal gain wrong?'

Snake turns the corner, and we're faced with a series of French doors opening into various conference rooms. Reaching into his pocket, he pulls out two long pick-like things, and moments later, the door swings open.

'Firstly, I don't propose to use magic, and secondly, I never break anything.'

I hesitate in the doorway.

'Come on. We won't be damaging anything, and we will leave it as we found it. We just need somewhere to eat, and rest, and for you to practice your magic in private.'

And there it is, the real reason why I don't want to go in. I remain where I am, not yet ready to face the fact I can't even produce a simple flame, something children can do.

I take in a gulp of air. This person who is afraid to even try is not who I am. Besides, I have come too far to turn back now.

Snake has arranged the deli food I bought on the table, and is busy piling some onto a plate. That boy's capacity to stuff food down his face no matter what is going on around us is amazing. I am surprised he isn't the size of a house. He catches me watching him, and grins. 'It's good food. Aren't you eating?'

I close the door and join him on the other side of the room. The food does look good. I drop my pack and bags to the ground before loading my plate with a pork pie, some coleslaw, and potato salad. Taking a seat opposite Snake, I dig in.

'These pies are the best,' he says, leaning over to add another to his plate.

I open an iced tea and take a gulp before sitting back in my chair, unable to eat anything more. Wearily, I close my eyes. We have been on the go for a week, and, more than anything, I would love to spend the evening curled up on the couch at home watching crap TV before hauling my tired body upstairs and sleeping in my own bed.

I must have dosed for a bit, because when I open my eyes, the table is clear, and Snake is standing before me with a steaming mug of tea.

'How?' I ask.

'I assumed conference centres must be able to provide refreshments, and I was right. I found a bar outside with a fancy coffee machine and a great selection of teas.'

I wrap my hands around the mug and take a sip. Tea soothes the soul, my mother always says, and it does exactly that for me. Snake takes a seat on the floor and pats the carpet in front of him. I sigh. I can't put this off any longer. Sitting cross-legged in front of him, I take another sip of tea before putting the mug down beside me.

'Do you do any breathing exercises when you do karate?' he asks.

I frown at him. 'Yes, but what's that got to do with my making a flame?'

'You're as stiff as a board. This is never going to work when you are so tense.'

My head tips to the side as I consider his words. 'When you learned to make a flame, did you do any drills or anything beforehand?'

'Of course. I was given my medallion, and I had to practice reaching for magic until I could sense it and hold it without having to think too much.'

I rise to my feet. I think I need to relax and allow magic to flow through me as if it is a part of me. Taking up a position in the middle of the U of tables, I begin running through my karate kata. At the same time, I reach out and touch the magic in the air.

The first time, there is no flow to my movements because I am concentrating too much on feeling the magic. By my third run through, I am moving from memory, and the magic, which began as a slight tingle, flows through my body almost as if it has always been there. I am ready.

Snake is leaning back against his pack. His eyes are closed, but I had sensed him watching me as I practiced.

'Ready?' he asks, moving his body to sit up and opening his eyes as I join him.

I nod. Holding out my hand, I do not need to call magic this time, as it is pulsing through me in time to my beating heart. The flame forms easily, but I still cannot grow it or hold it. It simply slips away.

'What do you think of when you lose it?' Snake asks, after my tenth attempt.

'I don't know.' I chew on my lip while I start over, concentrating more on when the flame disappears. 'I see the flame form, and I…. It's like I can't believe it is me making it.'

'Like something inside of you is blocking your magic?'

'No,' I snap. 'I can't describe what happens. It's like I can't believe *I* am making the flame.'

'But it is you,' he says, stating the obvious.

'I know,' I shoot back, frustration bubbling over. I rise to my feet and pace, too agitated to try again.

'Maybe what you can do will be enough,' Snake says. 'We have a few hours before we need to get ready. Perhaps we should rest for a bit. It might be a long night.'

I humph, aware that Snake is being amazingly supportive and I'm acting like a spoilt brat. While Snake pulls a jumper on, I continue to pace. He lies down and drops a cap over his eyes to block out the light.

I place my pack down beside his, pull out my denim jacket, and use it as a blanket as I rest my head on my bag. My mind is buzzing with pent-up energy and frustration. Too restless to sleep, I roll on my side and stare out the windows. Snake is snoring gently, and this only frustrates me more. I'm not going to be able to sleep like this.

Being as silent as I can, I put my jacket on and let myself outside. Pulling my phone from my pocket, I slip in my earbuds before scrolling through my playlist. I start listening to "She Speeds" by Straightjacket Fits, but quickly change it. It may be one of my current favourites, but it doesn't suit my mood. Then I spot "Mascara" by Killing Heidi. The kick-ass female anthem is exactly what I need.

As I sing along to the chorus, I think of the number of times Mum has told me you can put lipstick on a pig, it is still a pig. Killing Heidi and Mum have hit the nail on the head. Deep down I'm afraid calling myself an elf doesn't make me one.

I walk over to the lake in front of the manor house and stare at the dome of the Underwater Ballroom. As the sun begins to set, I find a seat nearby and skim a few pebbles across the water before sitting down.

I remove my earbuds and put them and my phone back in my pocket, happy to sit here and listen to nature and the faint rumble of cars in the distance. Snake's father said I need to accept who I am if I'm to make a flame. But how can I do that when I don't know anything about being an elf?

'I'm an elf,' I say out loud, as if the words will somehow make it more real. Instead, I just feel stupid. I swing my legs, admiring my purple Converse high-tops before dropping my feet to the ground and scuffing the gravel.

What more can I do? What if my beginning of a flame is not enough? What if they won't let me into The Court? I can't let Snake face this without me. He said he will speak for my parents, but we started this together, and we should finish it the same way.

I kick out again, and a spray of gravel spatters into the water, causing droplets to disturb a cat sleeping in the last of the sun. It turns its head accusingly towards me.

'Sorry, puss—my bad.'

It lazily stands and moves until it is directly in front of me. I reach down to pet it, wondering what it is about black cats and this trip. The cat avoids my touch and pads towards the water. Halfway there, it pauses and glances over its shoulder. In international cat language, I am pretty sure this means 'Follow me.'

Rising to my feet, a smile tugs at my lips. If attempting magic is not bad enough, now I am following a cat. How strange my life has become in less than a week.

My feline friend stops at the water's edge and looks down, as if staring at its own reflection. I drop to my knees on the grass beside him and lean over so I can see what he is staring at. In the water is an image of me… and the cat, of course.

My face reflects how weary I am. I run a hand over my eyes, and as it drops back to my side, the image shifts and ripples, like someone dropped a stone in the water. When it settles again, the person staring back at me still has my blue eyes, but my face is longer and thinner, my hair is silver-white, and… oh my god, my ears are pointed! I reach up to check, but the tips of my ears feel as round as they ever were.

I turn to the cat, and it meets my gaze. I swear his look says, 'See, this is who you are.'

Thinking I must have dreamed it, I drop my gaze back to the water. The silver-haired me is still staring back. Is this the real me, this strange, alien creature? In this moment, my world completely shatters, and yet, somewhere inside, I know this person in the reflection is more me than I have ever been.

For a moment, the image shimmers, and then my usual face is back. The cat nudges me.

'What now?' I ask, still reeling from the undeniable truth that I really am an elf.

It sits in front of me like Snake had, waiting patiently.

'Oh, I get it,' I say, holding out my hand. It's time to make a flame.

I take a deep breath and let the magic flow through me. Before I form the flame, I give myself a pep talk. 'Right, elf girl. If you are going to do this, you are going to do it Pris style.'

In my mind, I envisage *my* flame. 'Lasair,' I whisper. A glow starts to form on my hand, then I allow it to take shape. The flame grows, flickers, and almost splutters out. 'Not this time,' I tell it. 'You are mine,' I say, forcing it to appear as it did in my mind. It holds for one… two… three seconds before it disappears.

'I did it,' I tell the cat, and it simply stares at me, as if it knew I could do it all along, before standing, flicking his tail, and sauntering over to the bushes.

'Thank you,' I yell after him, not worrying how crazy I sound talking to a cat.

Standing up, I do a little happy dance. I just cast my first honest-to-god spell Harry Potter style, and it was incredible!

Once I calm down and return to the conference centre, I walk as if I'm floating on air, with a stupid grin plastered on my face. I did it. I cast a spell and—I pause midstep—I am a freaking *elf princess.*

THE UNDERGROUND BALLROOM

PRIS SNORES. I would like to say it's a delicate sound befitting someone of royal stature but, quite honestly, a freight train is what comes to mind. I force myself to my feet and stretch out the kinks. The room is all shadow and moonlight. It is late, but my alarm hasn't gone off, so I still have a bit of time.

I creep out into the reception area to make some coffee to wake me up, then have a better idea. I wonder if this big old building has somewhere to shower.

The toilets off the reception area are just that. I wander along the corridor and spot what I'm looking for: a sign for a gym. It is in an annex, and I find showers in the changing rooms, along with a good supply of large, fluffy towels.

Standing under the steaming hot water, all the knots and strains leave my body. I am fresher and more awake, and I smell pretty damn good as well, all pine and sandalwood. I wrap myself in one of the complimentary robes, roll my dirty clothes into a ball, and head back to the conference room.

By the time I get there, Pris is awake and rubbing sleep from her eyes.

'Your alarm went off and I couldn't stop it.' Her tone is accusatory, and I grin at her.

'Not a morning person?' I ask.

She glares back and snaps, 'This is not morning.' Her eyes widen as she takes in my attire. 'What are you wearing?'

'Would your evening start a little better if I tell you I found showers?' I tease.

She rises gracefully to her feet and says, 'I would kill for a shower, and I will kill you if you don't give up their location immediately.'

I grin as she gathers her toilet bag and clothes, and I point her in the right direction. Once she leaves, I go about dressing. The moon provides enough light to pull my clothes on, but I use the bathroom mirror to shave and tidy my hair.

I stare at my reflection in frustration. The black open-necked shirt with a subtle purple stripe is perfect for an evening function, and I definitely look ready, except for my damn hair. No matter what I do, it keeps flopping over my forehead. My mother would have something that would sort it for the evening. My heart wrenches at the thought of her.

'I'm coming, Mum,' I say to my reflection as I flick my hair out of my eyes. I sigh. It will have to do.

Returning to the conference room, I tidy up and look around for somewhere to secure our packs. The only place to leave them out of sight is behind the coffee bar next door. I remove my token before I haul mine around the back, leaving Pris's behind, not sure if she is finished with it yet.

As I check to make sure no one can see my bag from the reception side of the bar, a noise from behind startles me and I turn, ready to confront the intruder. I stop dead in my tracks. My jaw drops, and I close my mouth again quickly, not wanting to appear like an idiot.

I have dated girls, and have even taken them to some swanky places. But I swear none of them have ever taken my breath away as Pris does now.

She wears a simple shift dress with purple and blue flowers growing up it from the bottom, leaving the bodice white. Her hair is pulled back into a loose plait, but she has left tendrils hanging down around her face, and they dance with some fine silver earrings she has threaded through holes in her ears I didn't even know she had. She must also have done some sort of makeup thing because her blue eyes almost leap from her face, and her lips glisten as she smiles shyly.

'Do I look okay?' she asks as she pulls a midnight-blue shawl from a shopping bag.

I want to tell her she has almost stopped my heart, she is so beautiful. 'You…. Um… yes.' Not my best work, but quite honestly, I can't think straight, let alone form a complete sentence.

'I'm still a bit worried. I mean, we look pretty good, but this is a ball. I'm pretty sure we will be underdressed.'

I shrug. 'We were not able to buy tuxes and ball gowns in Godalming. Besides, I think we did pretty well to remember not to turn up in jeans and tees.' I run my hand through my hair, pushing my fringe out of my eyes again. Pris frowns.

'Here, let me sort that,' she says as she pops the bag containing her old clothes onto the floor. Rummaging in a toilet bag the size of my day pack, she pulls out a container. Before I am able to tell her I'm fine, she is in front of me, rubbing something on her hands. Reaching up, she runs her fingers through my hair.

My senses overload. I smell roses and spring air, and the touch of her fingers on my scalp sends a shiver down my spine. I close my eyes and lose myself in the sensation. If my night ended now, I would be in heaven.

Looking down, I find two startling blue eyes staring up at me. I give myself over to the moment and lower my head, pressing my lips to hers. They are soft and taste faintly of strawberries. As I deepen the kiss, Pris responds, and I wrap my arms around her, pulling her body against mine.

Electricity runs through me, and the touch of her hands down my back increases the sensation. I shift so I can fit her closer to me. I run my tongue along her lips, and she sighs, leaning into me. Everything except for the taste, the smell, and the touch of her is driven from my mind. Have we time before the….

I freeze. The Midnight Ball. I take a step back. This is not just Pris, my friend. This is Princess Priscilla, cousin to the Elven Queen. Could there be a more forbidden fruit?

With swollen lips, Pris looks up at me, confusion written on her face. Every fibre of my being wants to pull her back into my arms, but I take another step away.

'Um… we'll be late if we….'

She does not move, her eyes searching for an answer to the unasked question hanging between us—why did you stop?

She has no idea what other creatures would say about my being friends with her, let alone… this. I have so much to say, but I can't find the words to smooth this over.

Turning on her heel, she gathers her gear and leaves me standing alone. I stand there a while longer as I wait for the aftereffects of our kiss to become less noticeable. Taking deep breaths, I remind myself that this is not a date. We are here to rescue our parents, and that is the only reason an elf would go anywhere with a gnome like me.

I follow her into the conference room. The air is charged and awkward. I watch her for a moment, both wishing our kiss had not happened and perversely wanting it to happen again. As she goes to pull her backpack over her shoulder, I move to her side.

'Let me,' I say, taking it from her hand before she can refuse.

By the time I return, her feet are encased in some strappy blue sandals, her shawl is around her shoulders, and there is a small blue drawstring bag hooked over her wrist.

I hold out my arm and ask in what I hope is a dashing way, 'Are you ready, Princess?'

Her nose wrinkles, and I'm not sure whether it is because she doesn't like the formality or isn't comfortable with my escorting her as though this is a date, especially after the last few minutes. The moment passes, and she slips her arm through mine. I'm careful to not hold her too close as we take the short walk to the lake's edge. Even this small contact threatens to weaken my resolve.

When we find the round entrance to the Underground Ballroom, I blow out a breath, not realising how worried I still was about making it here. The door is open, and I lead Pris through.

The narrow stairway is not wide enough for two people, so I let go of her arm and allow her to descend the circular wrought-iron staircase ahead of me. I take it again as we reach the bottom.

In front of us is a corridor which must go under the lake. At the end is a… the only way to describe it is a shimmer. It isn't a door, but we can't see anything through the throbbing, thickened air.

'What do we do now?' Pris asks.

'I don't know. Perhaps—'

The sound of footsteps above stops me midsentence, and we duck into the shadows under the stairs. In silence, we watch a short, dark-haired man in a tuxedo and two women in glittering ball gowns sweep along the corridor and disappear from view.

'Should we…?' Pris's voice drifts off as more people arrive and follow the others through the entranceway.

'Right, let's do this,' I say once they have gone.

Pris slips her hand through the crook of my arm, and we walk along the underwater path and confidently step… into a wall.

'OUCH!' Pris exclaims, hopping on one foot as she rubs the toe of the other.

'Excuse me,' a voice says from behind, and I help Pris out of the way to allow two besuited men past.

'Is it because we don't pass the dress code, do you think?' Pris frowns as another group of spectacularly dressed people are admitted through the barrier. 'Or maybe we're doing something wrong,' she says. 'Perhaps there's a lever, or a magical word they say—'

The rest of her words are drowned out as a bell tolls, filling the space with its vibrations. As the sound dies away, a tall man dressed in red livery, complete with a white wig straight out of Eighteenth Century England, walks through the barrier and stands, holding out his hand.

I look at Pris and she pushes me forward. Great, I love being a guinea pig.

I slip my fingers into my pocket and pull out my endorsement, then I place it in the white-gloved hand. The man takes it between two fingers, turns it from side to side, then presses his fingers together, and I stare open-mouthed as my hard-won coin turns to dust and disappears.

The footman extends his hand again, and I place the gold coin on his palm. He doesn't even look at it. He simply slips it into his pocket. His hands drop to his sides, and he tilts his head as if waiting for something. I pause a moment, at a loss, then I remember. Holding out my palm, I speak the word, and a flame appears.

The footman takes a step aside, extends an arm, and ushers me inside. I step forward and my foot easily passes through the barrier. Rather than stepping all the way through, I turn to wait for Pris.

To my surprise, she confidently steps up, hands over her coins, then extends her hand and says, 'Lasair.'

On her palm appears a small, perfectly formed purple flame. I hide my surprise as she raises her eyes and grins at me before closing her fingers and extinguishing the light. The footman moves aside, and Pris steps forward and clasps my hand.

'How did you manage that?' I ask.

She winks at me. 'A girl's gotta have her secrets.' Then she pulls me through the icy cold barrier into the World Below.

The Underground Ballroom is a circular dome of windows rising above us. It is already crowded with bedazzled creatures standing around, chatting and eating canapés. The amazing array of otherworldly creatures is jaw-dropping, and I attempt to guide Pris around the edge of the assembled crowd without staring like a shell-shocked tourist.

When we are a couple of metres from the door, I turn to see if Pris is as stunned as I am at the spectacle, and for the second time today, my heart stops. Pris had been beautiful before, but in her elf form, she is breathtaking.

Moments ago, she had been as tall as my shoulder, but now her piercing blue eyes stare directly into mine. While her skin is still a warm brown, her hair is silver-white, framing an elongated face with slightly tilted eyes. And she glows. I mean, there is a shimmer of power around her, forming a glowing aura. In spite of her transformation, she nervously scans the room.

'You look every bit the Elven Princess you are,' I reassure her, offering her my arm.

SNAKE EXTENDS HIS arm, and I clutch at it, feeling disoriented. I knew the World Below would be different, but it is like we walked into a movie set where the makeup and special effects team have been having a field day. Snake is my only constant, and I cling to him like a lifebuoy.

I lean into his shoulder. His warmth and strength steady me. I'm pleased he hasn't turned into a garden gnome. In fact, he has hardly changed at all. No, that isn't quite true. Here he is more—more of everything.

His eyes are greener, his skin is more olive than it was, and he emits a definite calming energy. Above ground, he was good-looking enough in a boy-next-door sort of way, but down here, he is supermodel good-looking. Other than that, he is reassuringly the same.

'What?' he asks.

I must have been staring. Trying to ignore the heat rising from my belly, I say, 'It's just, you look surprisingly normal. You've hardly changed at all.'

He turns to catch a glimpse of himself in the window, and I stifle a giggle as he does a double take.

'Dang, that's an improvement,' he chuckles.

Tearing my eyes from him, I remind myself that I'm still annoyed with how he treated me earlier. I allow the hurt and rejection I buried for the sake of tonight to resurface, and it makes Snake instantly less appealing. I turn away to survey the ballroom and its surreal occupants.

It is difficult to fathom that this circular room is actually underwater. In the dead of night, the windows are ink black, so the effect is kinda lost. If the place is disappointing, the inhabitants are not.

There are tall, angular creatures whose ears come to a point. Their clothing is understated but still dazzling to the eye. There are equally tall, but not quite so lean, creatures whose clothes are a bit more sparkly, as if to make up for not being so gaunt. Their groups stand close together but slightly apart.

Every creature here is light skinned and almost human in appearance. There are no hags, or sprites darting round, or anyone with green skin, or gold skin, or dark skin like mine. I glance at Snake and notice him taking in the crowd.

'Is this it?' I ask. 'I mean, this could simply be a dress-up party in the World Above.'

Snake continues to study the assembled creatures. 'There are a smattering of goblins, and obviously a lot of elves.' He pauses. 'There are the gnomes.

They're never far away from the elves, just in case one of their betters might ask them for something.' Bitterness laces his voice.

'Are you sure they're not enslaved?' I ask, the note of disgust clear in my voice.

He shakes his head. 'Quite sure, but our families are bound by history. And there are many gnomes who crave to be elevated to the same status as elves.'

'Can that actually happen?' I am not sure whether or not he is joking.

'Not often, but yes.'

Laughing, I say, 'So, what do they do, make your ears more pointy, or something?'

'Well, yes, sort of.'

I turn to check he isn't pulling my leg. A ghost of a smile tugs at his lips, and he cannot contain it any longer. 'Centuries ago, gnomes rebelled against elves. As a punishment, their power was bound and they were bonded to elven families until they proved their loyalty. When a gnome family is elevated, their bonds are removed, and I believe there are cases where their ears regrew after.'

He is too serious. This must be a joke.

'You're kidding, right? Snake?'

My partner is no longer listening. He is peering over my shoulder, and I turn around to find a tall dark-haired woman walking towards us. Her emerald-green velvet dress clings to her body like a second skin, emphasising her curves as she saunters over. At first, I think Snake is leering, but the smile he sends is open and full of welcome as he mutters to me, 'And there are witches too. So, all the higher creatures are here.'

I raise my gaze to the woman's face and realise she is the Witch of Wimbledon.

'Princess, Master Fieth, welcome to the World Below. So pleased you were able to join us,' she purrs.

How had I not noticed how stunning she was when I first met her? The moment my mind flicks back to that first meeting, heat rises up my neck and I am sure I must be blushing. I am glad of my dark complexion as I hope no one notices.

'Good evening, um… Eleanora? Is that the correct title to use?'

Her lips curl into a smile. 'Ah, you have found your manners, little Princess. You may address me by my name, but here I am called the Protector of London.'

I duck my head, shame over my behaviour in Wimbledon curdling my lunch. She was gracious and helpful, and I was a spoilt brat. Now, finding she is more than a grandmother and a witch, that she has rank and status within the creature community, I feel unworthy of her kindness.

There is an awkward silence, which Snake ends. 'We wouldn't be here without you, Eleanora. We owe you our thanks.'

It is as if his voice releases something in me, and my words rush out. 'Yes, thank you. You set us onto the right path, and we owe you our heartfelt thanks.' I stop, trying to find the right words, then realise that sometimes the simplest words are the best. 'And I'm sorry I was so rude to you before.'

One of Eleanora's eyebrows arches elegantly. 'You *have* had a change of heart, Princess Priscilla. You will need it if you are to help your parents.'

'Excuse me, mistress. They have arrived.'

I was so taken up with the presence of Eleanora, I had not noticed her companion. The man was barely five feet tall with slicked back black hair and the most amazing green, catlike eyes. As if he realises he is being scrutinised, his head swings around. I could swear I've met him before, he seems so familiar, but my mind is blank. I can't place him anywhere, and he isn't someone you would easily forget.

'Snake, Princess, this is my right hand and my oldest friend, Percival,' Eleanora says as her gaze sweeps past me and fixes on someone across the room. She frowns slightly.

Before I can find the source of her unease, I feel a hand on my elbow, and I shift to find myself face to face with… 'Earth,' I exclaim, pleased to see a familiar, friendly face.

He is handsome in a formal tuxedo with his World Below glow. He stands straighter and appears more in control than he had earlier today.

'Welcome,' he says, leaning around me to include Snake in his greeting. 'It is not long until the formalities start, and I am sure the two of you would like to spend a little time with your parents.'

My heart rate speeds up with the mention of seeing Mum and Dad, but I hesitate. So much has happened since I saw them last. What will I say?

Eleanora steps aside to allow us to pass. 'I will see you both later.'

I follow Earth across the room, trying not to stare at the variety of other races who have entered in the last few minutes: tiny delicate, ethereal beings, individuals who look almost human except for elongated fingers and ears, and square-looking people with almost black eyes. One thing they all have in common is the glitter of their clothing and jewellery. The other thing is, they are all white. It hits me that I am the only person in the room with dark skin.

My gaze slides over the array of creatures and rests on the man and woman on either side of the corridor directly in front of us. They are my height, dressed in severe black suits, their long dark hair pulled back into ponytails which emphasise their delicate faces. There is nothing delicate about their bodies though. They obviously spend a lot of time at the gym. My eyes almost pop out of my head when I spot gossamer wings rising above their shoulders.

They move to block the doorway as we approach. Earth shows them a piece of paper, and they move aside to allow us passage.

'Bad Fairies?' I whisper to Snake.

'Yep, they are the World Below's police.'

I can't help but chuckle. 'They aren't bad. They deal with the bad.'

Snake stops and stares at me. 'Isn't that what I've been saying?' he asks.

I realise that it is, but while he meant one thing, I read into it something completely different. This misunderstanding reminds me how little I still know about my homeland.

Earth stops in front of a door. 'Your mother is inside, Snake. I am afraid that because I am a member of The Court, I cannot join you for your reunion.'

Snake hesitates outside.

'Go on,' I urge. 'She'll be waiting for you.'

He smiles at me, and mouths, 'Good luck' before he disappears inside.

Earth leads me towards a room further down the corridor. We are stopped outside by a tall, incredibly handsome man, an elf by the shape of his ears, and an older one if the grey hair over those ears is anything to go by. He grabs one of my hands between both of his.

'Priscilla, I am so pleased you are here. I am Elias, your mother's cousin. I can only allow you a small amount of time with your parents because we are about to start proceedings, but you can speak more later. And when this is over, I hope we can talk, as it is past time for us to discuss your royal role.'

I am stunned. Royal role? I don't know what to say. It seems I am not expected to say anything, because he smiles a politician's shark smile that is all teeth and no substance, lets go of my hand, and heads down the corridor towards the ball.

Pushing the odd conversation aside, I turn to the door and go to knock, then pause. I understand now why Snake was reluctant to enter his mother's room. We worked so hard to get here—I can't believe I am actually about to see Mum and Dad.

'Go on. They are waiting.' Earth's hand is gentle on my back, giving me comfort and support, and a little nudge.

I take in a big breath, turn the handle, open the door, and enter. My gaze goes directly to the two figures standing in the middle of the room. They turn to me as one, and I stop dead in my tracks. These are not my parents, and yet, they are.

I take in the changes in their bodies, my father's silver hair and my mother's now auburn tresses. Then I look into their faces, and something clicks into place; I rush towards them, sinking into their embrace. I am home.

Strong arms hold me close, and teardrops dampen my hair as my father lays his cheek on top of my head. I find myself gripping my parents tight, reluctant to let them go.

Finally, my mother pulls away and leads us to the table at the back of the room. We sit, but I can't let go of their hands. I can't believe I am with them, and I am not sure they won't just disappear.

I blink a couple of times, as if to clear my vision. 'It's so strange, seeing you look like this,' I say. Everything about them is elongated, giving them a regal appearance, in spite of the fact they are still wearing casual human clothes.

Dad is in chinos and a white open-necked shirt, and Mum is wearing capri pants and a floral top. This was not what they were wearing when I last saw them, and their clothes look clean. Do people here wear similar clothes to people in the World Above, or are my parents trying to make some kind of a statement?

'For you to be here, in your true form, it's something we were never sure we would see.' My father's teeth flash white against his dark skin.

'Why didn't you tell me?' I blurt out. 'Why didn't you prepare me for… for… this?'

Neither of them speaks. Their eyes meet, and I imagine some sort of wordless communication passing between them. My mother brushes a stray strand of hair from her forehead and pins me with eyes that are mirror images of my own.

'It was not an easy decision, Pris, and we don't have much time to go into the ins and outs of it, but we felt your life was in danger, so we decided to distance you from our families,' she said, squeezing my hand.

I frown, thinking of the number of times in my life I had to deal with muggings and attacks. My parents' decision for me to train in karate so I would be safer. Snake forcing me to admit it is not normal to be attacked a couple of times a month and hinting at another reason.

My head swings from one parent to the other. 'Are you telling me the random attacks I have faced my entire life are not bad luck, but creatures wishing me ill?'

My father nods. 'We always believed so.'

My jaw tenses. 'But you didn't think you should tell me?'

How could they believe I was better off not knowing I was being personally attacked? Why had they believed not accessing my magic was a good idea, or that not helping me to understand my abilities was for the better? They had forced me to fight with one hand behind my back.

A knock at the door jolts me. My father grabs my hand again; when had I let go of him and Mum?

'There is not much time left, and we can explain everything to you later. What is more important at the moment is that you believe the charges against us are false. They've been trumped up as part of some political machinations down here. We are fighting them as best we can. If you want to help, you can try appealing to everyone's sense of fairness and decency. The vote is close, and a plea from you may just sway some in our favour.'

'How?' I ask. 'What should I say?'

Mum laces her fingers through mine. 'Use all those skills you learned from debating. Listen to the arguments and use what you know to refute them.'

'We believe in you,' my father adds.

My stomach clenches. His eyes are bright with fear, and my father is never afraid of anything.

'What will happen if you are found guilty?' I ask.

I understand now that feathering your own nests while working above ground is frowned upon, but it isn't murder or anything. How bad could this be?

Dad runs his thumb over the back of my hand. 'Best case, we will be banned from returning above ground for a time.'

'It is time we treated her like an adult, Malachi. Pris, there is a chance we will be banned from returning above ground—ever.'

The door opens, and one of the Bad Fairies who has been guarding the hallway enters. 'It is time,' she says. And just like that, with the threat of never being able to return to our old life hanging over my head, our reunion is cut short.

SPRING COURT

WALKING BEHIND THE Bad Fairy, I resist the urge to touch the wings gently swaying in front of me. My hand reaches out as if of its own accord, only to be grasped by my father's large brown one.

'Don't. Touching them is a very intimate act.'

My hand drops down, and I am sure my face turns beetroot red. Before I have time to compose myself, we are led back into the ballroom.

Is it just my imagination, or has the room grown larger in my absence? On my right, a dais has appeared, and most of the creatures gathered in the rest of the room are turned towards it. On the stage itself are three chairs, only one of which is occupied—by a woman in a bright, loose-fitting dress with brown wavy hair tumbling free down her back. Her dark brown eyes are fixed on someone in the crowd. I follow her gaze and find Snake standing beside Earth and his father.

Dad folds me into a hug as my mum's hand cups my face. 'Here goes,' he says as he lets me go. 'Time to face the music.' My gaze trails after them, wanting to follow, but I know I can't.

'Good luck, I love you,' I whisper, then make my way across the room, slipping between creatures as I head towards Snake. Whispers follow my progress, and heads turn to stare at me.

By the time I make it to Snake's side, I'm sure the whole room is talking about me. I sweep my gaze around the gathered creatures, holding my head high and taking them all in. Snake's fingers entwine with mine, and at his touch, the confidence I am displaying becomes real.

As we wait for proceedings to begin, a group of severely dressed muscle-bound creatures enters the ballroom. They are similar to the square creatures I noticed before, but in amongst the glitter and dazzle, they alone stand out as drab. My eyes follow them as they span out around the edges of the crowd.

'Who are they?' I ask.

'Dwarves,' Earth says, his brows drawing together in a frown. 'Few of them ever attend court. Too busy amassing their fortunes and disdaining decent folks.'

Snake leans into me, and his breath tickles my cheek as he says in a low voice, 'Dwarves will do anything for gold or jewels. I wonder who here is paying them?'

My senses reel at his being so close, and my eyes are drawn to his lips as I remember our kiss. I close my eyes to shut out the distraction and consider his words. When I open them again, I find myself scanning the crowd, trying to work out who might be behind this display of force.

My gaze finally settles on my parents as they take their seats on the dais. As they settle, the man from the corridor steps in front of them and waits for the room to fall silent before speaking.

'Elias, the Queen's Prime Minister,' Earth tells us, just as a hush falls over the crowd.

'On behalf of Queen Anastasia, welcome to the Spring Court. The Queen is a little indisposed and will join us for some of the later events. In the meantime, I will be chairing this evening's proceedings.'

The crowd murmurs. Someone behind me says, 'When was the last time anyone saw her?' And another adds, 'I doubt she will be here tonight or any other night.'

'Our first order of business is to deal with some terrible accusations levelled at three members of our community who carry out work for us in the World Above. They are charged with using their magic for personal gain.'

The room gasps collectively.

'It isn't like they didn't already know. They have been talking of nothing else for the last couple of days,' Snake's father says through gritted teeth.

'I am sure many of them thought the charges would be dropped before it was taken to full court,' Earth said.

'How can you impartially oversee this trial when one of the accused is your beloved cousin?' a voice shouts from the floor.

Elias squares his shoulders and stares down his nose at the man in the crowd.

'I will refrain from getting into an argument about *our* cousin, Bernais.

As always, if you are not happy about how I carry out my duties, you are within your rights to appeal to the Queen. Now, if we are ready.'

I crane my neck, trying to catch a glimpse of the man speaking from the floor. He is almost an exact match for Elias on the dais, except his hair is lighter, and more auburn like my mother's. Looking from one to the other, I see the family resemblance. *So, this is what having family is like*, I think as I wonder if I might have been better off not knowing.

'Many of us would prefer this matter to go before the Queen herself. We are prepared to wait,' Bernais says.

The crowd shuffles restlessly, and I can't tell whether it is because they support this man, Bernais, or whether they are annoyed that he is causing a scene. Whatever the reason, the air thrums with tension. I catch movement out of the corner of my eye as some Bad Fairies move to place themselves in front of the dais.

Bernais opens his mouth to continue his argument, a few more Bad Fairies appear, and he steps back. When everyone settles down, Elias carries on.

'Now that is settled, I call upon Ginth fo Drefin's accuser to present their case.'

As the crowd parts, I quickly shuffle the letters of Snake's mother's name. 'Finder of Things,' I mouth and smile as Grossman Green moves to the middle of the dais. My smile freezes.

'What's that slimy creature doing here?' I mutter, sneering at the goblin.

'I've no idea, but it can't be anything good,' Snake answers.

One of the creatures in front half turns and shushes us. I am about to give them a piece of my mind, but then Grossman starts speaking, and I find I have bigger things to worry about.

'I, Grossman Green, Senior Goblin in the World Above, accuse Ginth fo Drefin of profiting from her skills while living amongst humans. I have received reports from our kind who have seen her using her gifts to steal from shops and pick pockets.'

There is a collective gasp from the room.

'Her own kind turn a blind eye to her transgressions, and this must stop. She must face up to the consequences of her actions.'

'Bloody goblins. They have always resented us.' Snake hisses.

'Why?' Pris asks.

'Because we are close to the elves, closer to the power they desire,' Earth says.

'You have evidence to back your claims?' Elias is asking as Pris's attention returns to the front.

'Not specific evidence—'

'You mentioned reports?'

'Um… they were verbal.'

'But you can produce witnesses,' Elias prompts.

'Of course, given a little time.'

'Give him enough time, and I am sure he can bribe as many witnesses as it takes to convict my mother,' Snake mutters.

Not put off by Elias's requests for proof, Grossman carries on. 'I can work out what she earns from her work for us, and I cannot believe she can afford to live in London without helping herself to things she shouldn't,' Grossman says, searching the crowd for support.

'Okay.' Elias draws the word out. 'In that case, will anyone speak on Ginth fo Drefin's behalf?'

There is movement beside Snake as Earth steps forward. He is beaten to the dais by Eleanora.

'I would like to speak for Gin. Since her husband has been unfairly held in the World Below, I have given comfort and support to Gin in my role as Protector of London. Ofttimes, I provide food and money when the powers that be below stop family funds from reaching her. Other times, I give her and her son little gifts and luxuries to make life more bearable. Perhaps it is these items Goodman Green is referring to.'

Elias smiles. 'Thank you, Eleanora, and thank you for the work you do for our people above ground. I know many would not be able to cope without your generosity.'

The witch lowers her head as she accepts Elias's thanks and steps back. As she does so, Earth makes his way to the front of the gathering.

'I, Earth Fieth, speak as the Senior Gnome in the World Above. My nephew's disappearance left Ginth struggling, and she was initially too proud to ask for help. A few years ago, she was caught stealing food for herself and her son. We brought this matter before our own council and agreed that as she only took what she needed to survive, making this a minor transgression. We placed Gin on probation, and since then, to the best of our knowledge, she has not strayed again.'

'Thank you, Earth. If this is all, then I propose we drop the charges against Ginth fo Drefin as already dealt with by the Gnome Council,' Elias says.

Grossman Green moves as if to step down from the dais. I watch in stunned silence as he catches Bernais's eyes and stops. Bernais shakes his head, and Grossman lets out a sigh. So, it is this elf, Bernais, pulling Grossman's strings.

Grossman clears his throat, then says, 'The original accusations were never brought before the full court. How do we know Earth is telling the truth and the charges were dealt with fairly—after all, Ginth is married to his nephew.'

Grossman is clutching at straws. It is written on the faces of the crowd around me, and even I can sense most creatures have no appetite to uphold the claim. Unfortunately, it appears he has struck a chord with Elias.

'I will need to check the fine print of the laws governing lesser council's dealings with offences under their remit. In the meantime, we will suspend Ginth fo Drefin's trial.'

Grossman steps down from the dais, and before Elias can release Snake's mum and announce the details of the next case, Giles Regis leaps onto the platform. He is followed more sedately by his wife, Amandine. The pair stare expectantly at Elias.

'Oh, um… I guess you are here to present the case against Princess Cecily and Malachi Crown.' Elias appears to be a little flustered by the influx of elves, but he soon regains his composure. 'Princess Cecily and Malachi Crown are accused of using their position and skills above ground, specifically their glamour, to benefit themselves at the expense of humans. Giles Regis, if you would like to state the case against them.'

Amandine virtually pushes Giles into centre stage, leaving no doubt about who is behind these accusations.

'Hm. Although the Crowns hold prestigious positions, their income from those roles does not explain how they can afford their house, private school fees for their daughter, regular overseas trips, designer clothes, high-end cars….' His voice drifts off, as if he has run out of steam.

'How can Amandine Regis stand there, dressed in something so obviously not off-the-rack, and accuse my parents?' I fume.

Snake's fingers reach for mine, and I gratefully grab hold of his hand.

'Our time will come before the vote. Just keep it together until then.' His breath tickles my ear as he leans in to whisper. He moves closer, and I lean into him for support.

'Have you specific evidence, or just suspicions?' Elias asks.

'You only have to look at what they own,' Amandine spits.

'Says the woman who lives in Grosvenor Square,' I murmur.

'All right, who will speak on behalf of Princess Cecily and Malachi?'

My father stands up to respond, and a voice from the crowd yells, 'Outsiders cannot speak in the court.'

'What the?' I ask, thrown by the vehemence of the accusation.

Snake turns wide eyes towards me. 'I have no idea.'

My mother rises gracefully. She may not be decked out in designer clothes, she may not glitter, but she is every bit a princess as she takes centre stage.

'That was a mistake,' I say. 'They obviously have not seen my mother in court.'

Mum clasps her hands in front of her and gazes around the room, meeting the eyes of all those judging her.

'Many of you know me. You grew up with me, or you oversaw my education. I would love to believe that was enough for you to judge my honesty, but there is something else going on here, and I am forced to open my life to your scrutiny to meet some political objective.'

A wave of whispers goes round the room. Some creatures shuffle uncomfortably, others cannot not meet her gaze, but quite a number stare openly at her. I cannot tell if that is because they are offering support or because they are revelling in her embarrassment.

'It is a matter of public record that my husband's family has amassed great wealth in the World Above over the centuries through legitimate means. Prince Malachi's brother offered us the use of one of his London properties while we live in the city. When our daughter began experiencing frequent attacks on her life, he also offered to pay for her to attend a private school. This was discussed in the Elven Court, and it was agreed that we would accept the offer. Everything was open and above board.'

Now the muggings have grown into full blown attacks on my life? What is going on here? My parents have a lot of explaining to do when this is over.

Snake squeezes my hand. 'We can sort this later,' he whispers, his words mirroring my own thoughts.

'Our frequent overseas trips are for work purposes. We do sometimes add on a holiday at the end, paid for by ourselves. The rest of our luxury items are bought with our salaries. We work long hours, often at the expense of family life, in jobs that help the world become a better place. Do you begrudge us these small pleasures?'

The crowd falls silent as Mum's gaze roams the room and finally falls on Bernais. I shiver at the intensity of it, but she doesn't say anything as she turns and takes her seat.

'What? Is that it?' I ask. 'Why doesn't she mention the fact that she had Dad make large donations in cash and give time to many charities, and that they make me work half of my holidays volunteering for various organisations?'

'Perhaps that will sound better coming from you when you make your plea to The Court,' Snake offers.

The room is humming with low conversations as Giles and Amandine step down to rejoin Bernais and Goodman Green. That man is at the centre of this, I am sure. But what has he to gain from all of this? He turns, as if he senses I am watching him. His eyes meet mine and he smirks. Fury wells up inside me.

'Before we vote, is anyone here to make a plea on behalf of the accused?' Elias asks, raising his voice to be heard over the crowd.

Snake and I go to step forward, but I find myself taken in a gorilla grasp from behind as a hand clasps over my mouth. Turning my head, I find Snake in a similar position. Where are Earth and Snake's dad? I try to catch a glimpse of them through the dwarves, who have made a tight circle around us. I just make out someone hauling Earth to the back of the room. There will be no help from that quarter.

I am turned so I can watch Bernais step onto the podium and shove Giles out of the way. 'Let us vote and get this trial over and done with.'

The anger that has been slowly boiling inside me since this farce began threatens to explode. I struggle against the strong arms, but my efforts are futile. My captor tightens his grip, and I almost suffocate as the hand extends over my nose.

That is it! I did not spend all those hours training in karate to escape this very sort of situation for nothing. Sensei's voice sounds in my head. 'Channel that anger, use it to sharpen your attack.'

I close my eyes and assess the situation just as she taught me. My attacker is taller and wider than I am, and his centre of gravity is lower. I will not be able to take him off his feet. What I can do is attack his weak points.

Shifting my weight slightly so I can breathe, I force my teeth to clamp down on his hand. He grunts and his grip slackens imperceptibly. Reacting immediately, I stomp down on his toes, making full use of the sharp point of my heel and, at the same time, swing back with my elbow, taking him by surprise.

He lets me go, and instead of moving away like he expects me to, I turn and bring my left knee into his groin with all my force before stepping back and punching him in the jaw.

I am in ready stance, breathing heavily, waiting for him to retaliate, when a Bad Fairy slips in between us. I'm not sure whether he is protecting me or the dwarf. I don't relax yet because I am not sure what is happening. The room has divided into two, with a small clearing around Snake, the two goons who held us captive, and the Bad Fairy.

I swing my head around, taking in the shocked expressions on everyone's faces. Then I find what I am searching for. My parents are standing on the dais, restrained by fairies, but the pride on their faces makes me stand taller and hold my space, meeting the glare of the dwarf over the shoulder of the fairy.

'That was awesome,' Snake says from beside me. 'Is it bad that I found you taking down a dwarf superhot?'

Laughter bubbles out, and the last of the tension leaves my body. I lean into Snake, and he wraps an arm around my waist in support. When I have composed myself, he asks, 'Are you okay now?'

'Yes,' I say.

'Are you ready to fight for our parents?'

I nod. He releases me and takes hold of my hand. We turn and face the stage.

'We would like to speak on behalf of our parents before any vote,' he says, his confident voice filling the room.

PRIS AND I stand together in the middle of a sea of creatures. I feel their stares, but I focus on my mother. A smile curves her lips as her gaze drifts to mine and Pris's hands. My collar is tight around my neck as I realise everyone can see us together. I resist the urge to let go of her hand, but I am reluctant to show any weakness.

Pris was awesome as she took out that dwarf goon. If she can fight someone twice her size, surely I can stand in front of the whole court and show that Pris and I are here to free our parents—together.

You want more than that though, a sneaky voice in my head says. I want to shut it down, but it speaks the truth. At the moment, though, as much as I want to be with Pris, my focus is only on getting our parents back and away from whatever force is manipulating this court and using our parents for their own ends.

'All right,' the Prime Minister says. 'But you do realise, young man, that if we vote on your mother's case before I have the chance to check our laws, the verdict will stand?'

I look at my mother, and she nods. We had so little time together before the court began, but she had told me she trusted me, and to follow my gut. Now she is reminding me of her parting words—that she will support me whatever I choose to do this evening.

'I do,' I say.

'Which one of you wants to go first?' Elias asks.

'Wait!'

I had forgotten the other man on the dais, the one who had stood with Grossman and the Regises.

'Our laws allow for another way to resolve this… ah… situation.'

'They do?' Elias appears skeptical, and I trust him more than I trust the man who stood with my mother's accuser.

'Our laws allow for anyone to undertake a trial. If they succeed, then they may ask anything of the court.'

'How does that help us?' I ask, not able to understand why he had brought this up, but sensing a trap.

The creature's head pivots around, and he glares at me. I straighten my shoulders. I will not be bullied by this elf, not when my mother's freedom is at stake. His mouth pulls into a sneer.

'Why, gnome, if you were successful in your quest, you would be able to petition for the charges against your mother to be dropped. Surely that is better than a guilty verdict.'

His superior tone rubs me up the wrong way, and I bristle at the implication that my mother is likely to be found guilty. What is he seeing that I am not?

'Is this true?' I direct the question at the Prime Minister.

'Well, it is not what the trials were designed for, but I guess it is possible. Yes, indeed, it could work the way Bernais says.'

'What would it entail?' I ask.

'If you choose to go down that path, the Queen's advisors would meet tonight and set you a task to complete. If you accomplish what is asked of you, you may ask for your parents to be released.'

It could not be that easy. Nothing is ever that easy.

'Can you give me an idea of some potential tasks?'

Giles frowns, and my stomach clenches. Why is he so worried?

'The rules forbid me from giving you details, but I can tell you that many of our great sagas tell of past trials and quests.'

I stare at my feet, trying to remember the details of the stories my mother used to read to me as a child. All that comes to mind are half-formed images of rescuing treasure from dragons or fighting sea monsters. I'm no hero to be taking on such things.

'Thanks, but I will take my chances with the vote,' I say, and my mother smiles her support.

I expect Bernais to argue, but he simply shakes his head sadly. 'Of course, The Court might find for your mother on this charge. But ask yourself if this is truly the worst she… or you… can be accused of?'

Fear roils in my stomach as I catch my mother's stricken face. She searches for and finds my father, and the look that passes between the two of them feeds that fear. What is it that I don't know? What can be worse than this?

I raise my head and glance around the room, hoping to find Earth or someone else to tell me what is going on. While we have been talking, the room has divided.

On one side stands the dwarves, Grossman and his cronies, the Regises, and a number of other creatures. Their faces are fierce, and determined, and scornful. They are looking at my mother as if she is… trash. What exactly have they all banded together to fight against?

On the other, standing behind a line of Bad Fairies, were my family, Eleanora and her sister, and the rest of the creatures. They stand tall and proud, facing down their opponents across the room.

Then there is a third faction. Some of their faces show concern, some curiosity, and some are enjoying this battle. Can I convince enough of these creatures to back me? And if I do, what does Bernais have up his sleeve? It will definitely be worse than this. And will they still support Mum and me after that?

I swore to myself I would do whatever it takes to save my mother. Sucking in a deep breath, then slowly expelling the air, I make up my mind. 'All right, I choose to take on a quest.'

The room erupts before I complete the sentence.

'Silence. SILENCE!' Elias's voice booms, obviously boosted by magic. When the noise reduces to a few whispers, he speaks again. 'Are you—'

'They have chosen to undertake a trial,' Bernais declares. 'This court is over.'

'Hold on a moment! Wait!' Pris is saying beside me, but I think I am the only one who hears her as the noise level rises.

'I SAID SILENCE. WE ARE NOT DONE HERE.' The Prime Minister's voice shakes the room.

My father's face is stricken as he looks through a gap in the line of Bad Fairies. He tries to push through towards me. Others in his group are also trying to get free, and a scuffle breaks out. Suddenly, the fairies are pushed out of the way, and chaos erupts around us as both sides turn their frustrations into pushes and shoves and threats.

The sound of thundering hooves fills the room, followed by hushed whispers racing around. Finally, everyone is silent. You can hear a pin drop. I stand on tiptoe to see what could possibly make these enraged creatures pull back.

Centaurs. Unbelievable. Honest-to-god centaurs. In my head, I knew the Queen had chosen a troop for her personal guard, but I never expected to actually see one. Glancing at Pris, I wonder if my face mirrors the amazement and awe on hers. Two guards joined Elias on the dais, surveying the crowd, looking for any further signs of trouble.

'Please escort Princess Cecily, Prince Malachi, and Ginth fo Drefin to their accommodations and make sure they are comfortable. They are to remain there, safe, until the trial is complete,' Elias commands, breaking the spell.

My mother finds me in the crowd and mouths, 'I love you,' as she leaves the dais. Once a fairy guard has escorted them from the room, Elias continues, 'In light of that outburst, the rest of tonight's court proceedings will be delayed until after the trial.'

Grumbles and mumbles run round the room. I'm a little disappointed because Mum had told me my father's clan was due to be elevated to elven status this evening in recognition of their service to the crown. Then again, with my mother not completely cleared of charges, that may have sparked another outburst.

One of the centaurs moves restlessly on the stage, and the room immediately falls silent.

Elias turns his gaze to Pris and me. 'I invoke trial rules. You two will meet here at ninth bell tomorrow to receive your instructions from the council. Appropriate food and equipment will be provided. Until that time, you are free to enjoy the ball and the hospitality of your families.'

'Hold on,' Pris says, but people are already moving. She stamps her foot, and I hold back a smile. 'I said, wait.' Someone shoves past us, and I realise no one is going to listen to her.

Pris grabs hold of my hand and drags me through the crowd until we are face to face with Elias.

'I did not say I would do this,' Pris says. 'In fact, why would I? I'm sure my parents would have been cleared.'

Bernais sidles up beside the Prime Minister, and his smile is oily as he says, 'I am sorry, Princess. I thought the gnome spoke for you both.'

My fists clench. I really want to punch that smirk off his face. One look in his eyes tells me he would enjoy that, as well as the punishment I would receive as a result. This stokes the fire of my anger, and it is all I can do to not react.

'No one speaks for me. I want to speak on behalf of my parents and let the people decide their fate.'

'I am afraid our Prime Minister, who is speaking for our Queen, has already invoked the rules of trial. It is too late.'

Again, that smirk. Seriously, I want to punch him so badly.

'I think we can make an exception,' Elias says. 'After all, she did not specifically agree to participate. We have enough witnesses to that affect to make the change.'

I freeze, and then turn to Pris. I was prepared to do this alone, but I will admit I was pleased when I believed she would be coming with me. As Pris's eyes meet mine, I sense her internal conflict.

She leans closer and whispers, 'What made you choose to go on a quest rather than speak for your mother?'

Bernais is straining to catch our words. I shift my shoulder around to block him out.

'Bernais led me to believe that if I didn't do this something worse would happen to my mum, and my family. Besides, I did a quick count up of numbers, and I wasn't convinced we could win a vote. And with all the tension in the room, I was worried that if we voted tonight, we would start a riot. I wanted to buy some time. I didn't mean for you to be included, I mean, I said—'

'I heard what you said.' She leans in closer. 'I'm wondering if this was Bernais's plan from the beginning.' Pris scans the room and must see what I saw moments ago. Tensions have everyone on edge, and anything could spark another outburst. This was never going to end the way we wanted it to.

Keeping hold of my hand, she straightens up and faces the two men. 'Cousin Elias, I have changed my mind. Snake and I will undertake this quest together.'

I blow out a breath I didn't know I had been holding. Before either of the men can respond, Pris turns on her heel and leads me back through the crowd towards my family.

A DEAL IS STRUCK

AS THE TENSION in the room disperses, I follow Eleanora and her sister. Near the door our dear friend Gin left through, they stop the Prime Minister.

'That didn't go well, Elias,' Eugenia says. 'We are left in limbo, and Bernais bought time to consolidate his position.'

'I am sure that is exactly what Bernais thinks as well.' Elias's smile raises my hackles. I am sure he planned this whole evening and is exceedingly happy with the result.

My mistress taps her lips thoughtfully with her index finger. 'I get the feeling you are not completely surprised by what happened tonight.'

A smile plays around his mouth. 'I'm not sure what you mean, Ellie.'

'So, Fairburn and his centaur guards just happened to be passing by the ballroom…. What are you up to, Elias?'

'I am not without eyes in Bernais's camp, and I had some inkling of his plan. It could have gone one of two ways tonight, and I believe I had both bases covered.'

Eugenie huffs. 'You are playing with fire… or at the very least, two young creatures' lives. I fail to see how this outcome works in their favour, or in yours.'

'I have been talking with some councillors who are as concerned as I am over Bernais's plotting. We have some ideas on how this trial might work to our advantage…. With a little nudge in the right direction and a little bit of planning, Bernais will be sorry he ever pushed for this.'

Elias's smile is almost sinister, which is unnerving, because the man has a good heart and is one of the nicest creatures I know. When he was appointed by the Queen to replace Bernais as Prime Minister, many thought he would not be up to the job because he is too laid back.

Eleanora, though, said it was the quiet ones you had to watch, and that Elias plays a long game. She should know, since she was close to him once. Even now she is studying his face, trying to work out what is going on.

Chuckling, Eleanora asks, 'Tell me, Elias, did you actually ask the Chief Centaur to wait in the corridor just in case things went bad?'

'The centaurs are only interested in protecting the Queen's interests. They bow to no one,' Elias replies, quite serious.

'So, this has something to do with the Queen?'

'Eleanora, you know I cannot discuss state affairs with you.'

Eugenia smiles. 'You didn't answer her question, Elias, but no matter. If you do have a plan, what do you need from Eleanora and me?'

'Just for you to support my proposal in the council.'

'Of course,' Eugenia says, 'but that support might be more full-bodied if we knew what you have up your sleeve.'

'I cannot tell you yet, except perhaps that you are not going to like it because it will put the Princess and young Snake in harm's way.'

'I am not sure about this.' Eleanora frowns at Elias. 'I promised Gin I would look after Snake.'

Elias's eyes are troubled as he speaks. 'And I would not put Cecily's child in danger if I had a choice. Unfortunately, Bernais and his cronies will not agree to a token quest. It must be real. Please trust me, and trust my plan.'

'You will really be placing these young creatures' lives in danger as part of a political manoeuvre?' Eugenia asks.

Is that a flicker of uncertainty I see cross Elias's face? Or is it sadness? It is gone so fast, I cannot be sure exactly what I saw.

'Yes, I suppose I am, but I also believe they might be in danger already. Besides, after hearing reports of their recent activity, I believe Pricilla and Snake will come through this… perhaps not completely unharmed, but alive.'

Eleanora and Eugenia share a look, and the buzz in the air tells me they are speaking. My senses prickle. What are they talking about that they don't want me to know?

Eugenia nods, and Eleanora returns her gaze to Elias. 'We will support you on one condition: that you find a way to allow Percival to go with them.'

What? Hold on. Me? No. Definitely not!

I move around my mistress to catch Elias's attention so that I can object. I clear my throat, but the noise is lost as the Prime Minister speaks.

'I think that can be arranged. Both Priscilla and Snake are new to the World Below, and it would only be fitting to provide them with a guide, and one whose powers are not strong enough to materially assist them should be acceptable to Bernais.'

My head swings from the minister to my mistress. Have I just been insulted and hung out to dry all in the same sentence?

'But, Ellie….'

Eleanora reaches out and cups my face in her hand. 'Percival, I promised you could return home when this was done, but I cannot let the children go on a dangerous quest alone. They would benefit from your wisdom and knowledge.'

And I would benefit from time in front of a roaring fire and some tasty morsels of chicken. My sigh is deep. When she looks at me in that way, like I am the only one she can trust, I can deny her nothing.

'As you wish,' I say, all the while thinking, *This is not over yet*. The council might not agree to my going.

I follow Eleanor out of the ballroom towards the council chambers, wishing I could do more than hope for a council vote in my favour to release me from this commitment.

THE MIDNIGHT BALL

PEOPLE STARE AT us as we walk through the crowd. All I want is to hide away and think through what just happened, but I'm stuck here. I don't even know where I'll spend the night. I stop walking, suddenly unsure about where to go. Can we leave? Stay the night at the conference centre? Or would that muck up the time difference thing?

Snake's hand cups my elbow, and he steers me towards his father, who is deep in conversation with a group of gnomes. I am shaking, and I pull my shawl around myself. Snake drapes an arm over my shoulder and pulls me close.

'Are you okay?' he asks.

I nod, but I am not, not really. Sensing this, he pulls me in closer, and I allow the warmth of his body to calm me. Snake's father and Earth draw away from their friends and join us.

'Agret and I are lining up votes on the council to stop this farce from going any further. We will present the paperwork absolving your mother, and that will be that,' Earth says, and I marvel at how businesslike the gregarious man appears now.

'No.' Snake shakes his head. 'If you succeed, Pris would be left facing this alone, and that is not right.'

'Son, we can clearly see that Bernais railroaded her inclusion, and so could everyone else. We want this whole thing to be called off.'

Again, Snake shakes his head. 'Something is going on in The Court. It is not of our making, but someone is using our families to make a point for some reason. At least at the moment, we are in control of what's happening. If we stop this, then we will be looking over our shoulders, waiting for the next strike.'

I feel in my bones that Snake is right. The tension in the room has lessened, as this was perhaps the only outcome that would not end in bloodshed tonight. I move closer to Snake, his presence calming me and boosting my confidence. We must face this quest head-on and end this nonsense. It is what my parents would do. They would never give in to bullies, and they raised me the same way.

'We agreed to do this, so please don't waste your political capital for us. I fear you would lose anyway. For some reason, Bernais, and many of his friends, want Snake and me out of the way.' I stand a little straighter as I voice my opinion.

Agret grunts. 'It was a long shot, anyway, but I felt we had to try. I cannot just stand by and allow the two of you be sent on some useless quest that could get you killed.'

I wiggle out from Snake's comforting arm, refreshed and ready to face whatever this was. 'You won't be standing idly by. While we are away, you'll be working to find out why Bernais wants us gone, what he wants with our parents, and what is really going on in the World Below. And you can start by telling me why my father is not considered part of this court.'

Agret looks at Earth, who shakes his head. 'But she deserves—'

'For reasons of their own, your parents did not tell you about their past. I believe you have a right to know, but this is their story to tell.' Earth reaches out and takes my hand. 'What I can tell you is, I know them. As I have already told you, I met your uncle once. He is a kind and wise man, as is your father. You can trust their intentions were good when they decided to keep their history from you.'

I roughly withdraw my hand. 'I suppose you cannot tell me why people keep attacking me either.'

Earth shakes his head. 'That would be part of the same story, I am guessing.'

This skirting around the subject of my past is getting beyond a joke. My fists clench as my temper threatens to take hold, but I am suddenly overtaken by a deep weariness. It will do no good to rant and rave. If outright questioning will not gain me answers, then I will have to be more subtle… but not tonight.

Tonight, I'm exhausted and overwhelmed. To my shock, tears form in my eyes, and I resist the urge to brush them away. I am a mess. I want to appear strong, but at the moment, I have never been more lost and alone in my life.

'I worked out I am related to Elias, and I guess to Bernais too, but I don't want to stay with either of them. Do I have any more family here? I mean, I need to find somewhere to stay the night.' I know I sound forlorn, but I don't have any energy left to hide that that is exactly how I am feeling.

Earth again grabs my hand, and I see that underneath his facade, he is still the kind and generous creature I met in Cornwall. 'Of course, you will be staying with us. Agret already sent word for rooms to be made up.'

I sag with relief. 'Perhaps if we leave now, you can tell us something about what to expect on this quest.'

Again, Earth looks at his nephew, and a wry smile forms on Agret's mouth. 'We might have boasted about going on quests when we were youngsters, but truth be told, no one has been on one in generations.'

My stomach clenches. If I had not realised what a big deal this was before, it was made clear to me now.

'All we know is that it is likely to be dangerous, and you will need your wits about you to succeed,' Earth adds.

I am stunned into silence. Fortunately, Snake is not. 'Can someone go and fetch our packs from the conference centre behind the refreshment bar in the lobby? We may need some of our stuff for tomorrow.'

'Of course, I will arrange it now.' Earth departs so hastily, I believe he is relieved to be away from us.

Agret smiles at his son. 'I will look after your mother while you are gone. I will make sure nothing happens to her.'

'I trust you to honour that promise,' Snake says before turning to me.

'If we are to be sent to our doom tomorrow, we should enjoy a little of tonight. I believe we have earned it,' he says, grinning crookedly, a glint in his green eyes. He holds out his hand. 'Would you like to dance?'

I look around in amazement at the people swaying around us. I had been so deep into our conversation and my own misery, I had not even noticed the band take the stage, and they are singing music from home.

'Don't they have their own music?' I ask.

Snake smiles. 'They do, but the first night of the ball is always a mixture of songs from both worlds to celebrate people from the World Above coming home.'

As the band finishes off Fleetwood Mac's "The Chain" and the first notes of Chris Isaak's "Wicked Game" drift out, Snake takes my hand and leads me to the dance floor. He draws me into his arms and says, 'For a while, let's pretend we're just two normal people at a dance.'

SWAYING TO THE music with Pris in my arms feels right, more right than anything has since the Bad Fairies took my mother. The music changes to Coldplay's "Trouble", and I can't help but chuckle as I start singing along under my breath.

'This should be our theme song,' I say. 'You've had nothing but trouble since I stumbled across your doorstep.'

She pulls away from me just far enough so I can look into her eyes.

'If you hadn't tracked me down, I would never have known what happened to my parents, and goodness knows where I would be now.' She smiles softly at me, her eyes warm, inviting me to move closer, and I oblige.

She is so beautiful, and I want nothing more than to lean forwards and brush my lips against hers. In her eyes, I see that she would not object if I did. I hesitate, and the moment is gone when, over Pris's shoulder, I catch sight of Bernais glaring at us.

He may not like Pris, but he would never stand for a mere gnome taking advantage of an elf, let alone an elven princess. My eyes flick around the room, and I realise he is not the only one.

Pris's face is now a picture of confusion, and the hurt I glimpse stabs me like a knife. I pull her back into the circle of my arms. She is not for me, not in the long-term, but we can have tonight, can't we?

'What's up?' Pris asks, her breath tickling my ear as she speaks.

Should I explain the social norms of the World Below to her?

'Is it because they are all staring at us?' she presses.

'Partially.'

'And they are doing that because gnomes and elves….'

I wait for her to finish, but she doesn't.

'Yes, because gnomes and elves don't mix,' I confirm.

'I deal with people treating me differently because of my skin colour all the time. You must know all that doesn't matter to me.'

She doesn't go so far as to say she likes me, but I hear the unspoken words, and a grin forms on my lips. I pull her even closer and rest my cheek against hers.

I finally admit what I have been trying to ignore for the last week. I want to be with her so much it aches, but this is all I will have. We might be able to overcome the race thing, but she is elven royalty, and I am a not-quite elf. We will never be able to overcome our different social statuses.

'If they won't accept us down here, we will be fine when we return home,' she says, snuggling closer.

I stop moving. She is so positive we will succeed. That we will go home and everything will be normal.

'Snake?'

'Sorry, got lost for a moment there,' I say.

I will not be the one to tell her nothing will ever be the same for us after this. Battle lines have been drawn in the World Below. If we survive our quest, the ripples of this war brewing around us will permeate into the World Above, changing the world as we know it.

The song changes to The Fray's "How to Save a Life", and I croon along softly as we sway to the beat. I close my eyes, blocking out the room, wishing we could stay like this forever.

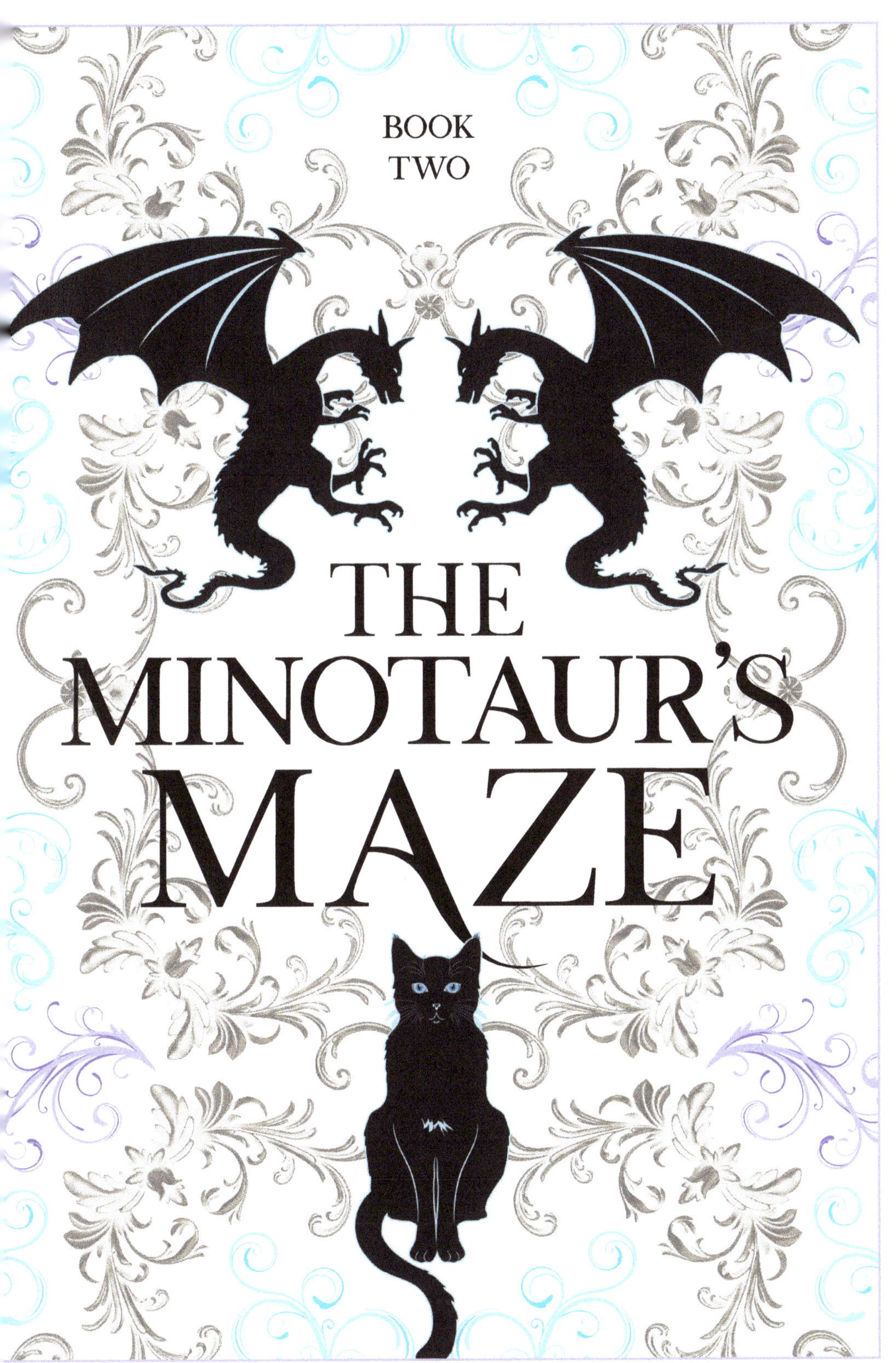
BOOK TWO
THE MINOTAUR'S MAZE

THE MORNING AFTER
THE NIGHT BEFORE

EARLY MORNING SUN casts a giant shadow over the common of the ancient oak resting at its centre. It is a brother to the two magnificent specimens that wizards encouraged to entwine their limbs to frame the entrance to the council chambers millennia ago. The tree sings his song to me as I shelter under his branches, waiting for Eleanora to appear.

I will his song to soothe me, but I remain agitated. I could lie to myself. Tell myself that my unease is because this is my last chance to escape back to my bed beside the fire in the World Above. Honesty forces me to admit that is only part of it.

Unease creeps through my bones because of this place and the memories it brings of a time in my life of great misery and change. No, I will not go there. Better to focus on the present. Better to work out how to avoid joining Snake and that blasted elf in their foolish quest to save their parents from being banished.

If only they'd had the skill to sidestep Bernais's machinations last night. If only they allowed their parents to go through the judgement process, all would have been well.

No, I am lying to myself again. All would have been well for the elf's parents. Their connections would ensure that. Snake's mother, however, being only a gnome, and with Bernais intent on her downfall… who can say what will happen to her.

I pace a little under the arms of my friend the tree, and I only stop when two council members enter the great hall. It is almost time. I take a steadying breath. Ginth fo Drefin, Snake's mother, is still in captivity, albeit in the castle under guard. Through no fault of her own, she is caught up in some political scheme beyond my understanding. If I can do anything to help her, I should just do it and stop dithering.

I release a frustrated sigh. That elf, Priscilla, is so very ill-equipped to help her parents. They kept who she was from her, so she really has no idea how to even be an elf, let alone how to live in a magical realm. I should not hold who she is against her. I should be the better creature and support her more.

My resolve wavers as I catch Bernais, one of the Queen's cousins, and his cronies entering the common area through one of the surrounding archways. There is something of his father about him, and it sends shafts of fear to the very pit of my stomach. Once I had not believed him to be as evil and bitter as his father, but the events of the last few days have caused me to change my mind—the acorn has not fallen far from the tree.

'Ah, there you are, Percival. Shall we go in?'

Eleanora's voice comes from behind me, and I wait until she and her sister, Eugenia, join me before saying my hellos. Elias Crown is with them, as are two wizards I have not met before. I can only assume they are the rest of witchkind's representatives on the Great Council.

I suspect this group spent last night plotting and scheming for some particular outcome today. It is, after all, what the greater creatures do whether they are forced into it like this group, or by choice like Bernais and his followers.

Elias smiles at my greeting. 'Are you ready to do this, Percival? The Queen will consider it a great service, and—'

'Yes, I am ready,' I say, cutting him short. I do not want him to voice what such a debt of gratitude may mean for me, or what I may or may not request from the Queen for helping out. I have a nice life now, and I am no longer sure I am ready to start down that path again.

Besides, that is not why I will help the two children from the World Above. I will help them because I should, and also because Bernais is up to something. He may call himself Crown, but he is a Baarenson through and through. And, like his father, his plans will no doubt end up causing harm to others, and I will do everything in my power to prevent that from happening.

As if summoned by my thoughts, Bernais walks close by as he enters the hall. I am positive this is so we will overhear his words.

'This charade of Elias ruling our kind stops here and now, and I will return to my rightful place at the Queen's side.'

'She must name you heir soon. I am surprised she hasn't already,' a superior-looking elf turns to say.

They are too far away from me to make out Bernais's response, but from the corner of my eye, I catch Elias stiffen.

With all thoughts of my warm bed at home driven from my mind, I wonder why the Queen does not just attend the Seelie Court and put an end to this infighting.

As I walk beside Eleanora into the chambers, I straighten my shoulders, determined to thwart Bernais's schemes at any cost. The song of my friend the oak follows me in, strengthening my resolve.

THE GENTLE PRESS of his lips on mine melts my legs, and I lean my body against his as I reach up to twine my fingers through his hair. My heart beats a tempo in time with his, and he draws me closer as he murmurs, 'Pris.' His voice is deep with longing. I part my lips and…

Crash!

The covers fall to the ground as I sit bolt upright in bed, staring at the open door bouncing against the wall.

'Oops. Ever so sorry, Your Highness.' A young girl—a gnome, judging by the rounding of her ears—colours a deep shade of crimson as she makes her way across the room and places a tray on the table by the window.

'No worries,' I say. 'I was awake anyway.'

My hope that the small lie will make the girl more comfortable as well as cover my own embarrassment at having been woken from such a dream fall on deaf ears. She mumbles something unintelligible and rushes from the room, slamming the door behind her as she leaves.

'Good one, Pris,' I mumble. 'How to make friends and influence people.'

I reach my arms above my head and stretch, a yawn escaping my lips, then rub the sleep from my eyes. It is hard to believe only a little over a week ago, all I had to worry about was how to fill the time between finishing my A-Levels and starting university. In the short time since then, my parents were kidnapped and I had been persuaded by a guy who thought he was a gnome to go on a wild goose chase to rescue them—only to find he really is a gnome, and I am an elf; and not just any old elf, but a goddamn elven princess.

Now I am in a magical world, about to go on some sort of quest, and the only person I have spoken to rushed from my room like a banshee was chasing her. Hold on, are banshees even real? I should ask Snake.

At the mention of Snake, my thoughts rush back to the dream, and my heart starts to race all over again. Unfortunately, the dance at the World Below's Midnight Ball had not gone quite like the scene in my head.

Most of the night had been spent watching our parent's trial, falling into a trap set by one of my newly found cousins, and ended with us committing to a quest to ensure our parents' freedom. Hardly the perfect build up to a romantic kiss.

Only after all of that had we danced. And Snake had indeed lowered his head as if to kiss me—something I would have more than welcomed—only to stop when he became aware people were staring at us.

If the covers had still been on the bed, I would have thrown them off in agitation. All right, people were watching us, but he knows I do not hold with the stupid notion that creature races should not intermingle. If Snake cared for me even a little, he wouldn't worry so much about it either.

I wander across the room to pour some tea. Catching sight of myself in the mirror, I do a double-take. My white corkscrew hair is a fright, making a fizzy halo around my head, which manages to accentuate my now pointed ears—just one of the changes my body underwent when I entered the portal into the World Below last night.

Frowning, I spend a moment trying to calm my hair, then give up in disgust before really studying the strange reflection staring back at me. It's a little alien, but I guess it is still me. I mean, I don't think I'll ever get used to seeing my hair white instead of its usual brownish black. Although my blue eyes are a little more almond shaped, they're definitely mine. And my skin is still its normal light brown.

Mmm, that was something else that bothered me last night. Dad and I were the only elves in the room with dark skin, which made us both stand out in the crowd. I'm used to being in a minority because of my colour, but there's something more to it than that, I'm sure. What's more, I suspect that something is why people won't tell me about my family history.

When I ask questions, they act cagey. At best, they'd tell me it's something for my parents to explain. It is more than frustrating and means I still know very little about where I fit in down here.

I shake my head and move to the table and pour myself a cup of tea. There are so many questions my parents need to answer, I barely know where to begin. Then again, they can't say much while they are locked up, accused of profiting from their work in the World Above.

THE MINOTAUR'S MAZE

So, I guess finding out who I am and why they kept our magical origins from me will have to wait. In the meantime, I need to concentrate on figuring out why that elf Bernais was so intent on railroading Snake and me into going on a fantastical quest—the first one to be undertaken in hundreds of years.

He wants me and Snake out of the way for some reason, I'm sure of that. I wish I knew why. And I don't trust him to wait for us to return before he makes another move against my parents or Snake's mother. If I want them to be safe, this quest needs to be wrapped up in a few days, giving him little time to plot anything new.

I take a sip of tea and glance towards my backpack sitting by the door. Should I get dressed? Will my clothes even fit me? When I walked through the portal, I didn't just get pointy ears, I grew about half a foot. Fortunately, my dress grew with me or that would have been embarrassing. But what about my other clothes?

An unknown someone had placed the pack in the carriage as we left the ball last night. I was so excited to be riding in a horse-drawn carriage and then to arrive at a gnome house, I had not even checked the contents.

Because it was late, I hadn't been able to see much of the World Below last night, but now…. I spring to my feet and fling the window open. I'm instantly disappointed. This is one time when expectation does not meet reality. My window opens onto a walled garden that can be found in almost any English village.

Sighing my disappointment, I sit back down and content myself with an in-depth study of my room. By candlelight last night, it was all shadows. Perhaps in daylight I will find something different in the magical realm. The bedding and furniture are all made of wood and natural fibres, but they look and feel very little different from anything in the World Above. My study of the bedding is interrupted by a knock at the door.

'Come in,' I say before looking down at the ankle-length embroidered white cotton nightgown left on my bed last night, wondering if it was the done thing to invite people in when still in my nightclothes.

All worry about my attire disappears as a familiar figure enters the room. I jump from my chair and rush over to Snake's aunt. 'Glisth, I am so happy to see you again,' I say as she envelopes me in a one-armed hug.

'And I you, my dear Princess.'

I slip from her embrace, a little embarrassed by the intimacy, as we had only met the day before.

'Glisth, please, I have already asked that you call me Pris.'

The gnome nods almost shyly. 'As you wish, Pr… Pris. I hope you slept well.'

Smiling, I respond, 'Like a log. I was just about to get dressed, but I'm not sure….' I gesture to my pack.

'My visit is timely, then. I have brought you some clothing.' She holds out one of her arms which is draped in cloth.

I make no move to take the clothing. 'I have my clothes here, and I think I would feel better in my own things.'

Glisth places the clothes on the bed before returning to the hallway to retrieve a pair of boots.

'I know, but where you are going, anything not of this world may not be admitted.'

'What would happen if I wore my own things? I won't find myself naked, will I?' I laugh at the thought.

Glisth frowns as if actually considering this as a possibility. 'Well, I am not quite sure, I must say. I think… um….'

She is saved from providing an answer by a girl entering with a bowl of warm water and towels. Glisth uses the interruption as an opportunity to place the boots by the bed and change the subject. 'I am sorry there is no time to visit the baths.' She waits until the girl leaves before adding, 'I will wait outside while you wash and dress. Then I will take you down to meet the family.'

The water is a perfect temperature, and I let out a sigh as I scoop up the warm water and splash my face. After washing the sleep from my eyes and taking a quick bowl bath, I pull on the fine cotton underthings. Why had I ever thought man-made fibres were so luxurious?

I hold up the green, almost black, moleskin trousers and laugh. Surely they can't mean me to wear these. A twelve-year-old would have trouble fitting into them. Still, they must mean them for me.

I sit on the bed and try to force a foot down one leg. The material is slightly stretchy, and they behave more like leggings than trousers, and they expand to fit—perfectly. I stare down in wonder. Is that a result of the material, or is the clothing here magical?

The knee-length black leather boots I pull on over top are also a perfect fit, reinforcing my theory about magical clothing. The boots would be quite stylish except that there is no dainty heel. The soles are flat and ridged, suitable for walking long distances, but not for setting off an outfit.

Finally, I pull on a loose white linen shirt before taming my hair into a plait, using the linen ribbon provided to tie the end. Washed and dressed, I am ready to face anything.

Glisth nods approvingly as I enter the hall before turning on her heel and leading the way through a maze of corridors. The house's internal walls appear to be made from a whole tree, and I resist the urge to reach out and feel if it is real.

Finally, we emerge onto a landing encircling a large room. I can see at least three other entrances at our level as well as a beautiful carved wooden staircase circling down to the living area below.

My eyes are drawn to the roaring fire surrounded by an array of armchairs and couches, but a quick scan of the area below also reveals the largest wooden table I have ever seen. As someone is already seated there, I am pretty sure I will be denied a relaxing breakfast by the flames.

As we descend, Glisth explains the dwelling houses of the extended Fieth family. She tells me that each branch has their own quarters for relaxing and sleeping. However, in a gnomen dwelling, mealtime is generally a communal affair, and this room is where everyone congregates to eat.

'Most of the family broke their fast an hour or so ago and are gone about their business. We thought it best to let you sleep so as not to overwhelm you with their questions,' Glisth says with a chuckle. 'They can be a bit much when they are all together.'

Sitting at the head of the table is a male who, if he was human, would be about sixty or seventy years old. He is definitely related to Glisth's husband, Earth, as he has the same round face and bright eyes. There the resemblance stops. His eyes hold merriment, and there is no sign of welcome as gaze meets mine.

'Good morning,' I say in my politest voice. 'I'm—'

My words are drowned out when a woman around the same age as the man bustles through a swing door, carrying two plates piled high with bacon, eggs, sausages, mushrooms, and tomatoes.

I don't realise I am hungry until the smell of food wafts by. My stomach grumbles. Loudly.

'Excuse me,' I say, colouring a little in embarrassment.

'You should never apologise for a healthy appetite, my dear,' the older woman says, indicating a chair at the table. 'Come. Sit. Eat. I will get some coffee. I understand my grandson prefers it with his breakfast.' The woman heads back into what I suspect is the kitchen.

As she disappears behind the swing door, I shuffle awkwardly towards the table, conscious of the scrutiny of the man seated at the table.

'Come on, then, lass. Let's be having yeh. Don't let the food go cold or Chríona will not be pleased. Where is that boy?' His voice is gruff, but not unkind.

I pull out a chair as Glisth says, 'Fieth, may I introduce you to Princess Priscilla Crown. Pris, this is Fieth, the head of our clan.'

'I am pleased to meet you, sir. And, please, call me Pris.'

The man guffaws in response. Not quite what I was expecting.

The door behind me bangs, followed by an admonishing voice. 'Fieth, do not be so rude, staring at our guest like that. It is not like elven royalty are strangers to our home. Leave the girl alone and let her eat.'

She pats me on the arm. 'Don't mind him. He is not at his best in the mornings. I am Máthair Chríona, but you can call me Chríona. Everyone does.'

The woman, who must be Snake's grandmother, pours coffee for everyone before sitting down and saying something quietly to Glisth. Under instructions to leave his guest alone, Fieth joins their conversation, allowing me to enjoy my meal.

Although the food is amazing, I am so tense, I can't force much of it down. Finally, I admit defeat and take a mouthful of coffee before asking, 'Where are Earth and Snake this morning?'

'That young lad is still in bed. No doubt my son will bring him along soon. Earth is due at the council any time now, so I expect he is getting ready.'

'The council?' I repeated.

'Yes, the council are meeting this morning to finalise plans for your little adventure.' Fieth smirks.

My appetite disappears completely at the reminder that this is not some pleasant visit to the Fieth house, but simply a night's stay before Snake and I must undertake some sort of epic, and very probably life threatening, quest to free our parents.

'COME ON, YOUNG Sneak Thief. My father awaits us downstairs, and I must head away to the final council meeting soon.'

It takes me a moment to realise Uncle Earth is speaking to me. I'm not accustomed to anyone but my mother calling me by my secret name, but we're in the family stronghold, so of course they would not call me Snake.

'You go on. I'll be ready soon,' I say as I finish making my bed.

I slept last night in the room given to me as a baby before we left the World Below. Someone at least updated the decor to be age-appropriate. The centre of the room is taken up with a double-sized four-poster bed, yet there is still room for a couple of chairs around the fire, a desk in one corner, and a heavy oak wardrobe in the other.

In between the fire and the desk is a window, and I stare out it now while I finish doing up the buttons of a dark green linen shirt. The street below would not be out of place in a Jane Austen novel. The English village scene, however quaint, is a reminder that I know so little about my family home—I'm as much a stranger here as Pris.

There is a brief knock at the door, and my father enters. A young boy follows him in. The boy is wide-eyed and can't take his eyes off me. I smile, but the boy ducks behind my father before daring to peek out again. Behind him, Earth moves into the doorway and taps his foot impatiently.

'See, I told you your cousin was here.' Agret, my father, ruffles the boy's hair. 'Go say hello. He won't bite.'

'You are the son of the Oidhre?' the boy squeaks, not moving an inch from his hiding place.

'What?' The word escapes before I can stop it.

'Oidhre—the heir,' Agret explains.

My mind whirrs. 'I… I thought as grandfather's brother, Earth would be….'

'When my father leaves this land, which I do not believe will be any time soon, as his eldest son I shall be The Fieth. He named me his successor at a family gathering last month.'

'But…. What…?' My mind freezes, unable to process this news. What will that mean for Mum? And for me? Will we be able to return aboveground once dad is outed as heir?

My father places a hand on my shoulder. 'It has not been formalised yet because I am still under censure, so no one outside the family knows.'

I turn to stare out the window, mulling things over. Will my father ever rejoin Mum and me in the World Above? Just when I'm getting over his having abandoned us in the first place, will we lose him again? 'So, this means you won't come back with us to the World Above?'

There are footsteps as my father follows me. 'Your grandfather is still young, and none of the details are set in stone.'

Still, I don't move because another thought has crept into my head. Dad is the heir because he is the oldest son. I am my father's only son, so is there an expectation that someday I will become the head of our family?

As if my father senses the change in my thoughts, he leans in closer and whispers, 'As I said, nothing is set in stone, and there is plenty of time to worry about the future later.' So the rest of the room can hear, he says, 'Come, it is time for you to pay your respects to the head of our clan. He is waiting.'

I nod and turn in time to see Earth leave, taking the awestruck cousin with him. Agret waits while I tuck the shirt into black moleskin trousers and pull on the black leather boots someone left by the bed. They, like the clothes, are a perfect fit.

I am in no hurry to meet the rest of the family. Knowing how uneasy Mum felt in their company makes me wary. Still, I can't put it off any longer. Following my father through what appear to be corridors made from the trunk of a tree, I smile as I realise all those traditional English cottages I saw through the window were likely built around a tree like this one.

I keep an eye out for Pris. I know she stayed in Earth's dwelling last night, but I had thought she would meet me for breakfast.

A smile pulls at my mouth when I remember how beautiful she was, dressed for the Midnight Ball. So beautiful that she sent my senses into a frenzy. So beautiful that as I had bent my head to kiss her, I'd almost forgotten who was watching us.

I might have had a memory lapse, but the disapproving gazes focussed on us reminded me that most of the creature races in the World Below don't allow mixed relationships. So, while Pris might be okay with us being together, there are many here who are not. I had drawn back at the last minute, aware that, at the very least, we should not flaunt our attachment.

'Snake, are you all right?'

Dad's voice brings me out of my reverie.

'What?'

'For a moment there, you looked all… well, all gooey-eyed.'

'I didn't,' I reply, automatically defending myself. 'I was just thinking.' My relationship with my father is still too new for me to share my feelings about Pris. For a starter, I have no idea if he would approve.

Seconds later we arrive at the central family room, and my heart races. I remember this. But surely I can't really. I was only three when we left. My eyes fix on Pris, who is picking at the food on her plate and looking decidedly uneasy.

She glances up, and her eyes meet mine. There is uncertainty there, but also defiance, and—is that worry? Is all that directed at me?

Okay. We haven't had a chance to talk since last night. So we haven't spoken about the almost kiss, or the fact that Bernais's cronies were watching us like hawks. Which means I haven't explained that I hadn't wanted to make our situation worse by such a public declaration of our friendship—especially when I had no idea how the laws currently stand on mixed race liaisons. Hell—I don't even know how my family would feel about it.

When we reach the bottom of the stairs, I move to sit beside Pris, but my father places his hands firmly on the chair back. I am left standing awkwardly by the table. The move does not go unnoticed by the older woman sitting beside my aunt, Earth's wife—Glisth. I get the impression that maybe my grandparents are amongst those who would not appreciate a close friendship between a gnome and an elf.

My father formally introduces me. 'Fieth, Chríona, may I present my son, your grandson, Snake Fieth—Sneak Thief.'

There is silence for a moment, and my stomach clenches into a knot. Finally, my grandmother stands up and rushes towards me.

'Welcome home, youngling. It has been too long.' She pulls me into a hug. I hide my embarrassment at being embraced by a stranger by bending down to allow her to better wrap her arms around me.

When my grandmother finally lets go, she stares up at me almost as if she can't believe I am here as tears trail down her cheeks.

'You have grown into a fine gnome, as I knew you would. You do your mother credit. Although it is grand to see you, you should have returned to us way before now.'

She turns to her son and opens her mouth as if to say something. Agret starts to speak, but the old man at the end of the table holds up his hand.

'We know, son. You had a disagreement with the lad's mother, one you should have sorted out years ago, but they were always welcome here. You could have made yourself scarce while they visited.'

'Ginth never felt right about…'

'We know,' Chriona said. 'She lived with us, grew up with you all, and she always thought your love story was trite: the wealthy son falling for the ward. She never could believe it was real.'

Chriona's gnarled fingers clasp mine. 'Your mother was not a child of my body, but Ginth is a child of my heart. It was I who discovered her talent for finding lost things, and I who trained her and gave her a family name.' She lets go of my hand, pulls out a handkerchief, and dabs at the tears on her cheeks. 'I do so miss my girl.'

My father looks at his feet, shuffles a little, and sits before gratefully accepting the coffee cup Glisth pushes his way. The words he speaks next are flat and lifeless. 'I did not treat her well, Chríona. I was young and foolish. I never saw her as a person, only as my love and my wife. I never made her feel valued for who she is.'

This is the second time my father has admitted his responsibility for the split in our family, and it's one of the reasons why I let him back into my life years after he deserted Mum and me.

'Yes, there is much for you to atone for, Agret. And now, because of something you caught us all up in, she is suffering again. She is being held prisoner, and your son must go on a quest to free her.' My grandmother shakes her head. 'Here, Snake, sit down. Eat before it gets cold.'

As I sit, Pris turns to look at my father. 'What does Chríona mean? Were our parents… are we about to go on this stupid quest because of something you are caught up in?' she demands.

My father stares into his coffee cup.

'Why didn't you say something when we met with you in Mawnan, or even last night?' Pris presses him.

'Ah… um….' My father cannot seem to find the words to answer.

'What is going on is that the men of this family are a part of something. Political business, Chríona means,' my grandfather starts to explain.

My father sits taller in his chair. 'No, Father, let me. Snake has a right to hear it from *his* father.'

I pick at the eggs and toast in front of me, waiting for Dad to explain.

'For a long time, our family has been friends with Elias Crown, especially my uncle, Drow. Since my return to the World Below, I have been working for Elias. Not just to get this spurious sentence commuted, but also because something odd was going on at the palace. The Queen was worried, and he felt our family's particular skills might be useful.'

Why is my father working with the Queen's people?

'What is going on with the Queen?' Pris demands before I can gather my thoughts into a question.

Agret doesn't respond. The silence lengthens, and I realise this is a good time to add my piece. I raise my head and ask, 'I thought Grandfather was the Queen's right-hand man? Why did Elias need you in the castle?'

Did my father's eyes just widen? Is he impressed I know this much about our family alliance with the crown?

Fieth's hand crashes down on the table, causing the dishes to clatter. I twist in my seat and find obsidian eyes glaring at me. 'We do not speak of palace business out here where anyone can scry our conversation.'

While my mind contemplates the possibility of someone spying on us in the family home, Pris clenches her fists.

'If you didn't want us to know about any of this, why did you bring it up?' Her words are clipped, a tell-tale sign she is reining in her anger.

The Fieth half stands and leans his own fists on the table, making an imposing figure. 'Being of royal blood will buy you much, but it does not allow you to question me in my own house. I said it has to do with why Snake is here. Your reason for being pulled into this is something very different.'

'You know what—'

'Enough, Princess. Eat your food and let Agret finish.'

Pris locks eyes with my grandfather, and for a moment, I think she is going to challenge him. I don't remember much about Grandfather, but what I do remember is that he doesn't like to be crossed. She holds his gaze for a moment, then folds her hands in her lap. Her voice is contrite as she says, 'My apologies. I know so little about your world. I did not mean to offend you.'

'Our world. This is your world too, my dear,' Chríona said. 'Fieth, sit down and stop frightening the girl. You men are making a real hash of this, aren't you just.'

Under the stern gaze of his wife, the head of the clan sits down, snorting his displeasure, but not daring to disobey. In the royal castle, he might be a man to be reckoned with, but here there is no doubt who is in charge.

Satisfied everyone is calmer, Chríona continues. 'What Agret and Fieth are trying to tell you is, something has been going on at the palace for some time now. Bernais is obviously involved. Elias has been trying to figure things out and protect the Queen's interests. Great Thief—Agret—has been using his skills to help out.'

'We noticed they were involved in some sort of power struggle last night,' I tell them.

'It is more than just a simple power struggle,' my grandmother says. 'None of us common folk have seen the Queen for some time, and many fear she is ill. Bernais has been making the most of the power vacuum to shore up his position.'

'Hush, you talk too much, Chríona,' Fieth interrupts.

'It is no more than they would hear in the markets,' Glisth says, defending her sister-in-law.

Agret wraps his hands round his mug and does not meet Grandfather's eyes as he speaks in support of his mother. 'She is right, Father. It is no secret. Nor is it a secret that Bernais has taken the opportunity her absence provides to sideline everyone else of royal blood—all except Elias, who was appointed Chancellor and so sits above him on the council.'

'Are you suggesting my parents are caught up in all of this because my mother has royal blood?' Pris asks, glancing round the table.

Fieth nods, and Pris's fingers drum a beat on the polished wood. I can almost hear the cogs of her mind moving.

'But why attack my mother? We live in the World Above. My parents distanced themselves from everything to do with your world,' Pris ponders as her fingers continue moving.

'And what do Mum and I have to do with any of this?' I ask. 'We were also far away from The Court. Can it be as simple as Bernais not wanting the Fieths to be elevated to Elvenkind?'

I found out last night that Elias petitioned the Council on the Fieth clan's behalf to have them raised to the status of elves. He believes we have paid our debt to society by faithfully serving the crown for hundreds of years.

'Not that I can fully understand why the gnomes rebelled centuries ago, nor why they had their powers limited and were indentured to elves, but your mother being charged with benefitting from her work in the World Above would not wipe out all those years of good deeds,' Pris points out.

'Oh, Fieth, there is so much these younglings should know before they head off today. So many strands of the past are coming into play, pulling their lives this way and that. Can we not delay their departure by even a single day?' Chríona asks.

Fieth opens his mouth to speak, but my father speaks first. 'I am afraid not, Mother.' Dad takes Chríona's hand across the table. 'I would hold no hope of convincing the majority of the members to delay their departure for anything that may help them in their quest. In fact, the time for these two to meet the council is almost upon us.'

My mouth is suddenly dry. It can't be time already. I am not ready to find out what Pris and I let ourselves in for when we agreed to go on a quest last night. I stand on unsteady legs and allow myself to be hugged by everyone.

Pris moves to my side, and I try to meet her eyes over my grandmother's head, but her eyes are glazed over as if her mind is elsewhere. She is only brought back to us by Glisth wrapping her arms around her and wishing her all the best.

Finally, the goodbyes are done. Dad leads us towards the door, and Glisth follows. My stomach grinds, and I take some deep breaths to settle myself. My family reunion has left me more unsettled than I have been for some time. With all the revelations, and hints about World Below politics, I have more questions than answers. And I still need to talk to Pris about what happened last night and try to make things right with her.

As Dad opens the door, Pris asks, 'Where are our packs?'

'Remember, dear, I told you that where you're going, you can only take things from this world.' Glisth squeezes her hand.

There is such a forlorn air to Pris as we step through the door. I drop in behind my father and slip my arm through hers. If I'm feeling so out of place here, it must be even worse for her. A week ago, she didn't even know this world existed. Now to be told she can't have anything familiar with her on this quest to provide comfort…. The least I can do is remind her I am still here.

'Come on.' I grin at her in what I hope comes across as encouragement. 'Chin up. I mean, what is the worse that could happen?'

'SNAKE, WHY WOULD you tempt fate like that?' I ask, unable to stop myself from smiling as a horse-drawn carriage pulls up and Agret helps me inside. I take a moment to marvel at the fact I am going to be riding in a carriage, like the Queen does through the streets of London.

Snake grins back as he sits beside me. 'Do you think it would be odd if we did a royal wave?' he asks.

The knot in my stomach loosens a little as I chuckle. Relaxing back into the bench seat, I finally admit to myself that the conversation during breakfast disturbed me more than a little. All the talk about political machinations and how Snake and I were being used—well, anyone with half a brain could have guessed that. It was everything they weren't telling us that bothered me.

Agret takes the seat opposite and pulls down the blinds. Closing his eyes as if to doze, I realise he is attempting to give Snake and me a little privacy.

Snake leans closer me, and I notice the tension around his eyes and mouth. 'I said it because I'm scared out of my mind, but I don't want anyone to know. I'm worried they might do something foolish if they find out.'

His breath ruffles my hair as he speaks, and butterflies do a little dance in my stomach. This morning's dream is still forefront in my mind. I am moments away from one of the scariest meetings of my life, and my body reacts like this? Really? And after he wouldn't kiss me last night?

My eyes close for just a moment, and I draw in a calming breath to get a grip on my emotions and my traitorous body. I turn to Snake. 'I'm scared too, but I can't believe they'll send us to do something that will place our lives in danger. I mean, they're not barbarians.'

Agret clears his throat. 'I could not help but overhear, and… um… while the council will not do anything like throw you into an exploding volcano, much as Bernais might want to, this quest must be a real test of both mind and body for it to be meaningful.' He shrugs, a rueful smile crossing his face. 'I am afraid it will not be some easy task they set you.'

Snake's laugh is hollow. 'Thanks, Dad. We were trying to calm our nerves, not stoke our fears.'

Agret's eyes widen, and his tone is stricken as he splutters, 'Oh, um. Sorry, I didn't….'

'It's okay, Mr Fieth. I don't think there's anything you could say to make me feel worse than I already do this morning,' I assure him, and his embarrassment and discomfort appear to ease a little.

Before any of us can say anything to make the morning more awkward, the carriage pulls up. Too full of nervous energy to wait for someone to open the door, I jump out and stumble as I try to find my footing on the cobbled road.

Having steadied myself, I turn around to take in my surroundings. If I didn't know I was in the World Below, I would believe myself to be in a hall at Cambridge University, only on a grander scale. There are four several-storied buildings with a green-grassed common at the centre. Along the longer two sides of the green stand ancient oak trees. An arched stone entrance stands opposite us, cut into the first storey of a building topped with a clock tower. A smaller, older dwelling can just be made out through the other side.

Our transport pulls away, revealing an imposing entranceway made entirely of the entwined branches of two massive oak trees. My jaw drops. The space between the enormous tree trunks is easily two stories high and, surprisingly, has no door.

I peer into the shadows, and my jaw almost unhinges when a centaur makes his way down the stone steps towards us. He appears as if conjured by magic and, as he comes closer, I realise he is the creature who enforced peace at the ball last night.

The head of the Queen's Guard, Captain Fairburn, is a tall, imposing creature with the most amazing muscled torso I ever seen. The lightly bronzed skin of his abs ripples as he moves, and it is difficult to pull my gaze away. I force my eyes upwards as he draws to a stop in front of us. The sardonic smile he throws my way tells me he is well aware of the reaction he causes.

'Well, don't I just feel inadequate,' Snake says from close by, and my cheeks burn.

'Fairburn,' Agret acknowledges the Guard Captain.

'Good morning, Agret,' Fairburn responds, his smile changing to one of welcome, and I actually swoon. I mean, the creature must be older than my mother, but when he smiles, something happens to my insides… something I can't control.

Agret leans down. 'It's perfectly normal, Princess. Something about the centaur's magic means few can resist their charms.'

The words don't help much. I hate not being in control. It is hard enough trying to sort out things with Snake without a magical creature playing havoc with my hormones.

'Princess, Snake. I would welcome you to our council chambers, but I am sure that for you two, this does not feel like a social occasion. Agret, I am afraid we must leave you here.' Fairburn gestures to the carriage now waiting on the other side of the common.

'But….'

'Some of our friends are inside, Agret, and you know we will do our best by the younglings.' He gives Agret a reassuring smile, and my belly does that swoony thing again. I really need to work on that.

I resent being called young by this creature who stirs such a physical response in me, even if he is probably hundreds of years old. Unfortunately, I am too nervous to think of a suitable quip, so I make do with sending a glare his way.

Agret hugs Snake and tells us both to take care of each other. As Fairburn ushers us in through the entrance, I am sure I catch Snake's father wiping a tear from his eye, and my stomach tightens in response.

Standing under the branches of the magnificent oaks, Fairburn asks us to wait a moment. 'We may not get a chance to speak again. This is a brave thing you two undertake, and I must say, I regret having ever been a part of it.'

I catch Snake's eye, and the look he sends me tells me he is also unsettled by this admission. For a moment I consider ignoring the remark—after all, we have more to worry about than the centaur's conscience. That moment soon passes, and my pent-up emotions flow forth.

I dislike being forced into anything, and I am tired of creatures telling me how sorry they are that Snake and I were manoeuvred into doing this, yet they've done nothing to prevent it.

'If you're so unhappy, why didn't you stop that farce of a trial last night? Why didn't you stop Bernais from railroading us into this?'

After letting the first words out, I can't stop the rest from following. 'You're all sorry we're paying for something you did or failed to do, yet none of you will explain what's going on. And none of you will tell us why you involved Snake and me.'

Snake's arm drops around my shoulders, and he pulls me close as he too addresses the centaur. 'If anyone can stop this madness, then it is you or the Queen's cousin, Elias. Can't you speak to the Queen and ask her to intercede—to put a stop to this?'

Fairburn's eyes cloud with some emotion I can't name. It looks like fear, but that can't be right. What could he possibly be afraid of?

He takes a deep breath and shakes his head. 'Rest assured, Princess, we have done all we can for you. Now it is up to you to show those who wish to belittle you and your families and yourselves how brave and resolute you are—to show them you will not be cowed by their petty games.'

As far as pep talks go, it isn't a bad one. Then he goes and spoils it when he adds, 'Use your heads as well as your brawn. Trust in who you are. You are more special than both of you believe, and for different reasons. We have put our faith in you. Don't let us down.'

I tense as my anger threatens to bubble over again. I did not ask for this. I don't care about their faith. I just want my parents back and to get as far away from their stupid games as I can. Snake gives me a squeeze, and I remember this is not just about me. I force my anger to a slow simmer.

'Fairburn, I think you need to understand that Pris and I are doing this for her parents and my mother, not for some greater good.' In that calm manner he has, Snake articulates my thoughts exactly.

'Don't get me wrong. Bringing Bernais down a peg or two would be nice, but it's only the icing on the cake,' I add, unable to stop myself from smirking.

The centaur sighs, and I almost lose my focus as his muscles ripple. 'I have had my say. You can do with my words what you will.'

I close my eyes to clear my head. When I am again centred, I turn to Snake and square my shoulders. 'Are you ready?'

He nods, and I face the centaur. 'Captain Fairburn, please lead the way.'

He doesn't move. He stares pointedly at Snake's arm still draped over my shoulders. I glare back defiantly.

Snake removes the offending limb, although he doesn't move away. 'No use aggravating them more than we need to,' he whispers.

'They do not appear to be concerned about how we see them, so I don't see why we should extend them that courtesy.'

Snake stares straight ahead. It is almost as if he hasn't heard me. I seethe. I have dealt with racism all my life, and if you don't stand up to it, other people's expectations will limit your choices. At some point, Snake will need to choose to stand up to them, or he will lose me.

Unfortunately, now is not the time to have that discussion, as there is too much else we must deal with today. Still, I find it hard to let go of my disappointment as we walk in to meet our fate.

THE TRIAL OF THE MINOTAUR

THE BUTTERFLIES IN my stomach multiply exponentially as we enter the council chambers. I instinctively reach for Pris's hand. Our fingers lightly brush, and I quickly draw back, then check myself. Her words in the entranceway struck a nerve, even if I did not want to show it.

My butterflies settle as I entwine my fingers through hers. We may not be able to be together as a couple, but that doesn't mean we can't face our fate as friends. In spite of my resolve, my stomach does a somersault when Bernais emerges from the shadows. The scowl on his face intended just for me deepens when he catches sight of our clasped hands.

I have no idea why he hates me. He glares pointedly at our hands, and I resist the urge to let go. Instead, I raise my chin and defiantly meet his eyes. I or my mother will pay for that later, but I enjoy a brief moment of triumph.

My glory is short-lived. Elias walks to the centre of the room, and his movement draws my attention to the other creatures already there. Seated in a semi-circle in front of us, all the higher creatures are represented: elves, witches, wizards, gnomes, and dwarves. The glow around them tells me they are powerful magical practitioners, each and every one of them.

Their display of magical ability reminds me that Pris and I are starting out on our quest relying solely on my meagre magic. Pris only recently learned to create a flame, and she hasn't even had a chance to explore what she is capable of. Will that be a problem? I can't help but think it will be. Mum always talked of how commonplace using magic is in the World Below, so I am sure we will have to cast spells at some stage.

Still, Pris can fight. I mean, I can throw a punch, but she can really fight. She is almost unstoppable when she goes all ninja. That has to be to our advantage—maybe Pris offers more on this quest than I do.

I mean, I've studied the theory of magic and physics, but I've only used my talent to pick a few locks. Living in the World Above, we tend to avoid magical displays in case people notice.

Apart from knowing about magic, there is little else to recommend me. I can fight in a pub brawl and probably survive. I play a pretty mean guitar, but I really don't think that is something that will help us out of the situations we will face.

By the time Elias speaks, I'm breaking out in a cold sweat, and I know I made a mistake committing to do this stupid quest.

'Princess Priscilla, Snake Fieth, welcome to the Creature Council.' Elias's formal words of welcome stop me from bolting from the hall and halt my dwelling on how unprepared I am for what lies ahead. Pris gives my hand a brief squeeze, and I stand straighter. For better or worse, we are here, and we pledged to this quest to save our parents. Whatever my failings, I will give it my best… for my mother's sake.

Elias continues, ignorant of the fact that I'm spinning through a range of emotions and trying to talk myself back into this game.

'Ginth fo Drefin, Princess Cecily, and Prince Malachi—'

'That upstart is not—'

Elias stops the other elf short. 'Whether you like it or not, Bernais, Malachi is entitled to be called Prince.'

I barely have time to wonder why the interchange between the cousins seems so significant before Elias starts again.

'Ginth fo Drefin, Princess Cecily, and Prince Malachi have all been charged with personally profiting from their magic in the World Above. This crime is punishable by banishment from that place. In the most severe cases, the convicted are also banished from the World Below.'

Elias stops and waits for the import of his pronouncement to sink in. Beside me, Pris stiffens, almost as if she had not realised the severity of the crimes her parents were charged with.

'Although it appeared that these cases would be successfully defended—'

'I must object here,' Bernais interrupts. 'I do not believe we can definitively say anything of the sort.'

Elias closes his eyes for a moment, whether because Bernais is stretching his patience or to gather his thoughts, I have no way of knowing for sure. I suspect the former.

THE MINOTAUR'S MAZE

After taking yet another deep breath, the Chancellor carries on. 'Although there seemed to be a good chance that the defendants may have been judged not guilty, Snake and Priscilla have decided to undertake a quest so that they could petition the Queen to absolve their parents of all charges.'

Pausing again, Elias makes sure there are no objections to this statement before continuing.

'Last night and early this morning, the council sat and agreed upon the details of the quest.' Elias pauses for effect.

I bite back a sigh. This guy should have become an actor. He really knows how to milk the moment. Unfortunately, at this rate, we'll be starting out tomorrow, not today. I wish he would speed things up and get it over and done with. Not just because my nerves have my stomach doing somersaults, but also because each minute spent here is a minute more my mother has to spend in captivity.

'Because neither Priscilla nor Snake has spent much time, if any, in our world, the council agreed to send a guide with them in the form of a creature of limited magical ability. Percival, please step forward.'

A funny-looking man about the size of a ten-year-old child steps out of the shadows. It takes a minute for me to place him. Then I recognise him—he was Eleanora's companion at the ball last night. Today he is dressed totally in black. His pencil moustache and slicked-back black hair are groomed immaculately. In his pale face, his catlike emerald eyes are disconcerting as they flick over us disdainfully. Dismissing us, he turns his attention to Elias.

Again, like I did last night, I can't help thinking I know him from somewhere, but I don't know where. I also can't figure out which creature race he belongs to. What I can see is that he is not at all happy to be going with us.

'Percival's role is to help the two of you understand the limits of what you can and cannot do while in the World Below. He can explain our customs and practices and let you know whether something you want to do will break any of our laws,' Elias explains.

Pris leans around me and smiles cheerfully at Percival. 'Welcome to the team.'

He glares back. 'I am not, nor will I ever be, part of your team.' He manages to make the word 'team' sound like something nasty he trod in.

'Well, this is going to be fun,' she adds, winking at me.

She is trying for levity, but my stomach is clenching, and I'm regretting the small amount of breakfast I ate. The longer this audience drags out, the more my sense of dread increases. It's almost like they are putting off telling us about the quest. Why don't they just get on with it and put us out of our misery?

Then, as if Elias reads my mind, he takes a deep breath and announces, 'Your quest is to retrieve what is at the centre of the minotaur's maze.'

My jaw drops, and the buzzing in my ears blocks everything out. Sometimes you should be careful what you wish for. We're going to face a minotaur! This is way worse than anything I could ever have imagined.

I SHAKE MY head, trying to clear my ears, because I am sure I did not correctly hear what Elias said. A minotaur. He can't be serious! I look over at Snake for support, but he gives me nothing. His face is sort of blank, and he's staring straight ahead like he's gone into shock.

'But minotaurs are mythical creatures,' I blurt, my mouth moving into action before my brain kicks in.

Elias's smile is condescending, which sets my teeth on edge. 'Many myths are based in truth. The minotaur has lived in our world for millennia. He is a solitary beast, and only those who can successfully traverse the maze are deemed worthy to enter his domain.'

Beside me, Snake relaxes. 'Oh, so you don't want us to fight him, then?' He tenses. 'Or do you?' It seems saying what comes into your head before thinking it through is catching.

Again, Elias smiles. 'I cannot say either way, Snake. Whether or not you must fight him to gain entry to the centre of the maze will depend entirely on how your quest progresses.'

I'm numb. I've read myths and legends in the same way all school kids do, but I'm a realist. All those fanciful tales weren't my thing, so I paid very little attention. If I'd known that at some time in the future, I would face something from those legends, I would have studied harder—prepared better.

I realise I am gripping Snake's hand tightly when he reaches over and pries his fingers loose before shaking his hand to revive his circulation. My eyes slip sideways, trying to work out how Snake is taking Elias's revelation. I'm concentrating so hard on him, it takes a moment for me to register that Eleanora, the Witch of Wimbledon, is speaking to us.

'…so you would be fools to concentrate on the end of the quest,' she finishes up.

'Sorry, what was that again?' I ask.

Bernais sneers and I ignore him. I like that man a little less every time I meet him.

Eleanora catches my eye and offers me a patient, sad smile. 'I was saying you would be fools to concentrate on what happens when you reach the centre of the maze, when the maze itself will pose its own challenges,' she repeats.

I stare at the glamorous woman, allowing her words to sink in. She's warning us that this quest will be dangerous from the moment we begin. I'm speechless. I mean, part of me realised I had committed to going on a quest with Snake. Part of me also realised it would be no stroll in the park. Still, traversing a dangerous maze to confront a half man, half beast to retrieve what he is guarding—that is next-level crazy.

'Is there another option?' I ask.

Everyone, and I mean everyone, including Snake, stares at me in amazement. I resist the urge to squirm under their scrutiny. I want to tell them all that I refuse to go. This is madness. We're in the twenty-first century, and these sorts of barbaric practices went out of favour years ago. The set of the faces around me tells me this is not an option. Eleanora's next words simply confirm my guess.

'I am sorry, my dear. You committed to the quest last night. Since then, the council has formulated the most appropriate challenge for you two to undertake. There is no turning back now.'

My mind is racing, and it's hard to grasp hold of any one thought. Her words replay in my head. I stop them and play them through once more, probing for a hidden meaning. I believe she chose her words carefully—very carefully. I think she might be trying to tell us that some of them have worked out a way to try and help us through this ordeal.

No. I mustn't think that way. To rely on anything but ourselves will be too dangerous. My martial arts training taught me to assess each situation as it presents itself, identify the dangers, and act accordingly. That training is what will get me through this, not waiting to be helped by complete strangers.

I turn to Snake. His face is a little pale, and there is a sheen of sweat on his brow. I don't think he expected anything this dangerous either. I give his hand a squeeze and smile at him in what I hope is an encouraging way. 'We got here by ourselves. We can do this too,' I assure him with perhaps more conviction than I actually feel.

His face is blank with not even a hint of a smile. 'This is a whole new level of hard,' he whispers.

'But I have a whole new body with an even greater reach,' I say with a laugh, but it comes out a little strangled.

Snake turns a stricken face to me. 'I never thought of that. Will your, um different, er… dimensions affect your ability to fight?'

It's like he just threw a bucket of cold water over me. 'You know, I haven't even considered that possibility.'

My heart beats a little faster as my mind identifies this as a real cause for concern and starts to turn it into a worry. I gnaw my lip and catch Bernais smirking as if he has overheard our conversation and finds our fear amusing.

I will not let him see I am anything other than confident. I will not give that slimy elf the satisfaction of knowing I am scared. So my body is a bit bigger. So our guide doesn't want to be with us. So Snake is freaking out. I *will* find a way around all of this—for my parents' sake.

Two servants carrying packs enter the room, and a third enters hidden behind a towering array of weapons. Fairburn appears from nowhere and ambles over to them. How does a cloven-hooved creature move that quietly?

'Each of these packs contains a jacket, wet weather gear, a sleeping roll, and travel food,' he tells us.

I look in horror. 'What about a change of clothes?' I ask. On top of everything else, I am not going to be able to change my clothes for goodness knows how long. It's a step too far.

The centaur frowns. 'Why would you need to change your clothes in the middle of a dangerous quest? Surely there will be more important things to worry about.'

'Ah, I guess,' I mumble, embarrassed I hadn't considered that. Then again, it's not like I go out on dangerous missions every day. If I am going to be in these clothes indefinitely, then that means there are unlikely to be any bathrooms…. Hold on. What about toilet paper? Was that on the list of things we're carrying?

I open my mouth to ask, and Fairburn grins. Can he read my mind?

'Everything else you need can be found in the forest, Princess. Moss especially can be quite useful, I think you will find.' I am immediately grateful to the rather forbidding-looking head of the Queen's Guard for pointing out this piece of information.

I take my pack, and Fairburn waits until it is in place before saying, 'Now you will need to choose your weapons.' He motions the weapon carriers forward.

'What?' Snake looks doubtful. 'I think giving us weapons may put us more in danger than it will any enemies we might come across.'

Fairburn frowns. 'Of course, you missed out on military training…. Still, you cannot go completely unarmed.'

He rummages through the metallic array. 'Here, each of you should carry a decent knife.' He hands over two sheathed blades about the size of a decent kitchen knife and two leather belts. 'Carry these at all times. You never know what they might come in handy for.'

As we attach the sheaths to the belts and secure them around our hips, Fairburn studies the remaining weapons. He hands a bow and arrow to Snake, saying, 'I seem to remember Percival being a decent shot. If you get time, perhaps he can teach you to use it.'

Behind me, Percival snorts, and I resist sending him a glare. If he isn't going to be helpful, the least he can do is be quiet.

'Take the rest of these away,' Fairburn orders the servants before retreating to the back of the room.

Eleanora takes his place behind us as Elias says, 'We are all set, then. The council appointed Eleanora as adjudicator of this quest, and she will take you to the start point. We wish you good luck in your endeavours.'

Before I can say anything in response, my stomach lurches, and the room spins around me.

THE MAZE ENTRANCE

THE WIND WHIPS around us, chilling me to the bone. I had forgotten how cold the mountain air can be—then again, it's been a while since I have been this high in the mountains. I distance myself from Pris and Snake as I turn slowly to survey the scene below.

A central tower peaks above stone walls that are so tall, they block out the ground on the other side, even from our elevated vantage point—the home of the legendary minotaur.

My stomach clenches, but not because the minotaur or the maze are so imposing, but because of where it is situated. Reluctantly, I walk past Eleanor to stare at the source of my unease. Below us, on the other side of the mountain, is a hamlet almost encircled by a great forest—the Wyld Woods—my home.

Eleanora's hand rests on my shoulder. She is the only one who understands what being so close to home means to me and why I rarely ever return. A heavy sigh escapes my lips. Wishing for what might never be is a waste of time. I must focus on the job in front of me—of us.

'Are you ready?' she asks quietly.

I nod and we turn back to the maze. I join Snake and the elf while Eleanora moves to our left.

'Below, you should be able to make out the door you must go through to enter the maze. Once you are beyond the walls, the quest begins. The minotaur only allows those who are worthy into the inner sanctum to face him. Whatever tests you face while traversing his realm are designed by him, and they are unique to each individual or team.'

Snake and the princess tell her they understand. I am sure they think they do, but they are woefully unprepared for the games our minotaur likes to play with those who enter his domain.

'As Elias said, Percival is here to support you and help you understand the laws of the World Below. He may not assist you directly or he will become part of the quest.'

'I don't understand what this means,' the princess says, her brows drawing together. 'Can he help us or not?'

'He can give you information. He can answer a question or tell you how things behave differently here than in the World Above. The moment he physically or magically helps you to complete a task, he will be a part of the quest, not a helper. Is that clear?' Eleanora finishes and waits for a response.

Snake nods, but the princess shakes her head. 'Surely by choosing what information we need and when, he will be helping us.'

Eleanora catches my eye. *This one is going to be trouble,* her look tells me. She rubs her forehead. She has been up all night, and no doubt the princess's questions are taxing her, especially as she still has so much to do to make sure this quest turns out as they have planned. She squares her shoulders and says, 'He will tell you when he is unable to do something.'

'Oh, okay.' The princess's shoulders relax fractionally, and guilt twists my stomach as I realise that I am not the only one nervous about what the next few days will bring.

Eleanora's voice jolts me from my thoughts before I become lost in them. 'Right, moving on. If you decide you no longer wish to proceed with the quest, simply say 'soars' and you will be brought back to this point.'

'Will you meet us here?' At least Snake is asking practical questions—questions that will not lead me back into my head.

'Yes. I will await your return in the village below and will come and meet you should you decide to give up. Are there any further questions?'

Yes, why am I here? I think but do not say because I am distracted, and also because I am actually asking myself, not Eleanora. I may behave like I am merely following Eleanora's direction as a true familiar should. However, all I would have to do is voice my fears and tell her I do not want to do this, and she would find another helper.

Why do I not say the words? It would be so easy. After all these years and even from this distance, I sense the trees and plants of my home calling to me. I can no longer commune with them as I once did, so their song brings melancholy, not joy. To be so close yet so far away from them is a kind of torture.

I could go back to the village with Eleanora. But would that really be easier? My family is down there. They would welcome me, but they would also have so many questions, and I still have no answers… even after all this time.

I shake my head, as if that will dislodge the fears and memories that have haunted me all these years and force my attention back to the others. The princess is saying, 'What happens to our parents should we decide we cannot continue?'

'A good question. Their fate will be in the hands of the council. Given its current makeup….'

'I'm guessing that would not be a good thing,' the princess finishes.

'Is there any advice you can give us?' Snake takes a step forward as he speaks and now stands beside the princess. In spite of last night's closeness, they are so far apart today, as if they now dance to different songs. The mean part of me, the part that cannot abide elves, says thank goodness Snake has come to his senses.

Unfortunately, I suspect the closeness the two developed getting to the World Below will be needed in their quest to retrieve the item from the centre of the maze. I arch my back to release my tension. This is not so effective when I am standing upright. I adjust my clothes and make sure I am presentable.

'I would suggest we try not to get killed,' I say, hoping to alleviate the tension.

The princess blanches, which serves to make her dark skin almost as pale as the other elves in the World Below.

Eleanora frowns at me. 'I suggest you keep an open mind, use your brains, and play to your strengths. Now, we can put this off no longer. It is time to go.'

She points to a path on the right that winds down to the valley below. Snake adjusts his pack and heads off.

As he leaves, Pris gestures at me. 'Where is *your* pack?'

I glare at her. 'I am able to access everything I need.'

'Percival keeps all he needs in his pockets.' Eleanor lips turn up playfully as she adds, 'He would never let his appearance be marred by something as inelegant as a backpack.'

Pris glares at her own pack with distaste. The one thing she and I have in common is our attention to appearance, and I feel some sympathy for her having to carry that monstrosity.

Eleanora smiles. 'I understand.' She waves her hand, and Pris's pack turns her favourite colour—purple. 'No need for everything to blend in on this quest.'

Pris smiles, a hint of a tear glistening in her eyes. 'Thank you. That was very kind.'

She walks past me and waits at the top of the path while I say my goodbyes.

'Take care of them, Percival.' Eleanora bends to hug me, and for that moment, she ceases to be the Witch of Wimbledon and becomes my friend Ellie. 'Take care of yourself as well. I am aware being this close to the forest will test you, but perhaps you may decide to do a little more than give advice, and gain something more than the Queen's gratitude for yourself for taking part in this nonsense.'

'Such as being granted peace to sit by the fire at last?' This is not what she means, but I am trying to deflect. My emotions are still too raw to bear discussion.

Her smile is sad. 'You know what I mean, Percival.'

I do know, only too well. While I gave up hope of that a long time ago, tired of the hurt that longing brought, my friend, Ellie, still dreams it is possible.

FEAR AND ANGER give wings to my feet, and I am almost running as the mountain begins to flatten out. I keep expecting to hear footsteps behind me, but I am surrounded by silence.

What is Pris up to? Why hasn't she caught up? Neither of us want to do this, but putting it off isn't going to achieve anything. The sooner we start this, the sooner it will be over and our parents will be safe.

I keep repeating, '*Will be safe*' in my head in time with my steps. I picture my mum sitting on the stage in the Underground Ballroom last night, her eyes expressing trust that I would do the right thing. A vision of Bernais sneering as the others do his dirty work eclipses it. My stomach flips, threatening to dislodge my breakfast as I remember the moment I realised he would do whatever it took to convict my mother. Remembering it also recalled the moment when I studied the faces in the room and saw that everyone hated my mother and wished to do her harm.

The path is twisty, and I almost wrench my ankle on one of the numerous rocks jutting out from the dirt. I stop and suck in gulps of air. I need to calm down. It will not do me any good to dwell on last night—to wonder what my mother could have done for so many creatures to hate her so much. I need to keep a calm head.

No matter how much I tell myself to stop replaying last night, I can't help it. The vision of Pris dressed and ready for the ball and bemoaning how plain her dress was makes me smile and softens my anger. I couldn't understand her concern, as she was easily the most beautiful creature I had ever seen.

I fast forward to her fixing my hair, then to our kiss and the way it lit a fire inside me. Then later, when we danced, how she fitted so perfectly in my arms as we moved in time with the music. We were so in tune that everything was perfect, then I bent my head and almost kissed her.

The visions disappear, and all I am left with is my regret at not finishing the second kiss. Not just because it would have been amazing—because it would have been—but mostly because of the hurt on her face when I drew back.

Pris is against racism in any form, but withholding my kiss was not just a reaction to the class and race lines my mother drilled into me as a child. It was the pure hate Bernais and others displayed towards my mother and towards me that made me reconsider my actions. The set of their faces as I danced with Pris was not common old prejudice. There was more to it, and whatever that is still chills me to the bone.

What frustrates me about this is that I can't work out why they are that way. Although I know a lot more than Pris about the culture and history of the World Below, I know little more about my family than she does her own.

My mother never talked about them, or why she was brought up a part of the Fieth clan, or why she always felt less than them. Apart from Earth and Glisth, the Fieth clan are strangers to me, even my own father.

If I put that together with all the things hinted at this morning but not said, I am more confused and feeling more alone than I was when I arrived.

I walk a while longer, wrapped in my thoughts, trying to unpick what my grandfather and father's work at the palace has to do with why I am here today. I'm sure it's something more than a preoccupation with our clan being returned to the status of elves. There is a bigger mystery behind what is going on.

As I reach the bottom of the path, a rock clatters behind me, and I slow a little for the others to catch up. I expected the walk would clear my head, but I am more agitated than I was when I started off, and it is mixed with guilt at taking off alone when we should be working together.

Percival appears first. Who is he? Who does he remind me of? *A cat.* The thought pops into my head, and I almost laugh out loud. It's absurd, but he really does remind me of the cat who is always sitting in front of Eleanora's fire in the World Above. His eyes and his mannerisms… they're just so… feline.

Pris follows close to Percival, and soon our small group is standing silently in front of the wooden gates that break up the stone wall. From here the wall is so high, I can't see the top. The gates themselves appear to be made of a single massive plank of wood. There is no opening, no hinges, and no lock. There isn't even a knocker to summon a gatekeeper.

I take a step closer, studying the ancient wooden surface, hoping to find a spark of inspiration. I had thought getting us through the doors would be something I could contribute, but there actually has to be a lock for me to pick or manipulate before I can be of any use. I'm stumped.

'Over here.' I wander over to where Pris is tracing some writing carved into the stone with an index finger.

'Do you know what it says?' she asks.

I shake my head. 'No, I can't even guess.'

We both turn to Percival. He sighs heavily, as if we're asking him to do some impossible task. He ambles over, reads the words, and translates for us. 'Questers Must Force Entry.'

'What? Are you sure you are translating it correctly?' I snap.

Until that moment I would not have believed anyone so short could look down their nose at someone my height, but that is exactly what Percival did.

I resist the urge to take a step away from him. 'Okay, if that is what it says, what does it mean?'

He shrugs. 'That is for you to work out.' He turns, finds a rock close by in the shade, and sits.

I turn to Pris. 'Any ideas?'

She frowns, and for a moment I think she is puzzling an answer. Then I realise she is frowning *at me*.

I am immediately defensive. 'What?'

'So *now* you want to work together?'

Heat flushes my cheeks. I know she deserves an apology for my taking off, but it is actually difficult to form the right words. I mean, the almost kiss from last night is forming a wall between us I can't seem to get past—I can't explain to her the hatred in the creatures' eyes. And I can't explain my need to rescue Mum from their clutches as quickly as I can.

'This morning's been strange. I just needed a little time to myself to get my head in order,' I tell her.

'This situation is hard for all of us,' she points out, rather unnecessarily, I think.

There's another long silence, and still the right words don't come. If I simply say I'm sorry, what am I apologising for? Walking ahead? Not kissing her? For not knowing enough about what is going on to plot a way through this? For dragging her into this in the first place?

In the end it is easier not to speak at all, so I shrug. 'Well, we're here now; we had best get on with it.'

Her sigh is a touch overdramatic. 'I guess so.'

Silence falls again as we hold each other's gaze. So many unspoken words hang between us, and I can almost feel Pris willing me to explain what is going on in my head. I am first to break away. 'Let's see if we can find something that might help us.'

I follow the line of the gate while Pris walks in the opposite direction, checking the stones. I examine every part of the door, every crack in the stones at the edges. I even use my toes to dig a little around the base. There's nothing. Frustration gets the better of me, and I bang my fists on the wood. The door creaks, and I freeze. Am I imagining things, or did it shift a little? I plant my feet and push as hard as I can. Next thing I know, I am standing in the open and the gate is behind me. Was it really that easy all along?

'Hey, guys. You just need to push really hard, and the door will open,' I yell.

My voice echoes around me. Did my voice carry over the wall? I turn and press on the wood, meaning to go back through and tell them what I found. Nothing happens.

I'm sorting through possible options for a way to communicate with the others when Pris and Percival stumble through the gate, almost falling at my feet. Relief washes over me as I steady Pris. Her smile at working out the solution fades as she meets my eyes.

'Did you hear me call?' I ask, surprised at how hopeful I sound.

'No.' Pris's response is terse. 'Fortunately, Percival saw how you managed to get through.'

'Oh, that's good,' I say, fully aware of her subtext—that I shouldn't have gone all the way through without making sure we all knew what was happening. I want to tell her that hindsight is a wonderful thing, but I'm sensing now is not the time to be flippant. Besides, she has stepped away and is looking at something imbedded in the wall.

I walk a few short paces to her side. 'What's that?'

'Some sort of stone marker.' She moves to allow me to get a better look, then gestures at the scene in front of us. 'It shows the destination of the potential paths we can take through the maze.'

I follow her gaze and see five paths leading into darkness, showing five possible ways we can go.

'What are our options?' I ask, leaning over her shoulder to read with her. I'm distracted by the faint smell of lavender that still lingers in her hair, but I force myself to concentrate on the words, which are fortunately in English.

Engraved inside each of the arrows pointing to the paths are the following options: Heart's Desire, A Desirable End, Heart of the Matter, Journey's End, and Centre of Life.

'Could they be more oblique?' I mutter.

'Perhaps we're meant to choose what resonates most with why we are on this quest.' Pris's voice wavers as if she is a little uncertain.

It's so obvious these are quest choices when she puts it like that. I stare at them, trying to work out which one will get us to the centre of the maze and back to our parents the quickest.

'We are here because we desire to set our parents free, so we should follow the arrow of Heart's Desire,' Pris says as I am still thinking.

'If only I could,' I say under my breath.

Pris cocks her head to the side. 'What was that?'

I can't tell her I am unable to follow my heart, because it will not lead to our parents, but to her, and that is not why we are here.

SNAKE IS STARING at me in confusion. Then his face hardens as if something has hit him, and he doesn't like it. I wait impatiently for him to speak.

'We need to get to the centre of the maze as quickly as possible. The longer we're out of the picture, the more scheming Bernais and his cronies can do. That means taking the most direct route, so I think we should follow the Centre of Life path.'

Now it is my turn to stare, and I hope my annoyance is clear to Snake. On top of his being distant since we almost kissed again last night, he is now arguing about why we are here; arguing about which statement resonates with us. And why can't he see his path will not lead to the centre of the maze?

The maze isn't life, the maze is a test. What does the Centre of Life mean anyway? Air could be the centre of life. It could also be water, family, love. It's too airy fairy and is clearly the wrong path—both for our quest and if we want to move as quickly as possible.

'Why not the Journey's End, then?' I counter.

'What if the end is the other side of the maze, the way out, instead of the centre?' Snake asks. 'Then we wouldn't be able to retrieve the object, and we would fail. We are looking for something with centre in it.'

'Oh.' So he is actually thinking this through. I didn't consider what end we might be led to. 'What is wrong with following your heart? I believe it would take us to the centre of the maze too, given that is where we want to go.'

'It's an emotional response, and both Eleanora and Fairburn counselled

us to use our heads,' he states matter-of-factly.

Okay, he has a point, but my gut tells me he is approaching this the wrong way. We both chose to be here because we love our families.

I place my hands on my hips, ready to challenge him. 'So we should just disregard our feelings?'

He nods. 'For the duration of this quest, yes, I believe so.'

I get the impression he is talking about more than choosing our path. Although my heart sinks a little at the thought, I am not ready to let this go yet.

I keep my voice controlled as I point out, 'Wasn't it love for your mother that sent you to find my parents? It was love for my parents that helped me overcome the shock of finding out magical creatures were real. I don't think following our hearts again will do us any harm.'

Snake will not meet my gaze. What is going on with him? Why is he being so obstinate?

'Getting to the World Below was a piece of cake compared to this.' He sweeps his hand out, indicating the five paths in front of us. 'And when we're finished here, Bernais will still be waiting for us, ready to cause more havoc. I'm just saying that although our hearts brought us this far, perhaps it is time to start using our heads.'

Okay, that is hard to disagree with. There is definitely something bigger than the both of us going on here, but surely trusting your heart is the best way to move forward when there aren't enough facts to base a decision on. I am about to suggest this when a voice comes from behind us. Percival. I had forgotten he was there.

'Can you not compromise?'

I consider this for a moment before asking, 'Which path would you choose?'

He shakes his head. 'It is not for me to decide. I simply observe you are at an impasse, and if we want to move on from here before it gets dark, you need to work together to find a third way.'

I resist the urge to throttle the smug look from his face. But he is right.

'Do you like any of the other options?' I ask Snake, ready to compromise if he will.

Snake shuffles his feet and stares at the pattern they make on the ground. 'I still think we should go with the Centre of Life.'

Is he not even prepared to try and meet me halfway?

'Can you at least take some time to consider one of the other options? What about A Desirable End. Surely that would also take us to the centre of the maze given that is where we want to go?'

Snake continues to look at the ground. My anger is beginning to bubble. He's not even trying to work together. 'Look at me,' I demand. When he doesn't, I decide I've had enough of all this beating around the bush. 'What's going on with you? Can't you even consider an option with heart or desire in the wording?'

He raises his head, and his green eyes are blazing. I have never seen Snake angry before, and the sight shocks me into silence.

'My heart leads me to you. My desires lead me to you. As I can't be with you in this world or the other, I can't trust my heart, and I can't have what I desire. I am left with trusting my head, and it is telling me to go to the centre.'

As he holds my gaze, challenging me to respond, his fists clench and unclench. Anger and frustration radiate from him.

I'm so stunned by the ferocity of his emotion, I can barely breathe. The depth of his feelings blows me away. I mean, I knew something was growing between us, and I for one want to see where it goes…. But hold on—is he saying we are not worth fighting for? Even after all we've been through together?

'We can work something out—' I start to say, but his look of stony resolve silences me.

He shakes his head. 'Haven't you seen the looks on the faces of the greater creatures when they see us together? They would rather see me dead than with you.'

He is so certain of the animosity directed towards us. Did I miss something last night? I start to doubt myself. I shake my head, certain I would notice that type of disapproval. I always have done in the past.

'Your father, Earth, and Elias are friends,' I say. 'Maybe things aren't as impossible as you make out.'

'Whatever their friendship is, my family are servants to the crown, and we always will be, whether we are called gnome or elf. But this is more than that. Surely you saw something?' Snake begs me to confirm his assessment of the situation, but I can't.

I'm sure Snake isn't lying, but perhaps his own upbringing and heightened emotions are affecting his perception. I turn to Percival to inject some sanity into the situation.

'Percival, tell him he is mistaken, that we can be friends… close friends.'

'There are many forms of friendship, Princess. What type are you referring to?'

Ooh, I want to shake him. 'For instance, would anyone object if I were to date Snake?' I almost spit the words out.

'Date?' Percival rolls the word around in his mouth, and I clench my fists in frustration. 'I am not sure the concept has an equal here. Would you be able to court him? No, given who you are and who he is, it would not be acceptable.'

I am so shocked, my mouth falls open. He speaks so matter-of-factly with no concept that this is not acceptable in a modern world. I straighten my spine and glare down at him. I have fought racism all my life, and I will fight this—but only if Snake wants to as well.

I lift my chin. 'I will not accept this.'

Snake's shoulders droop. 'I don't think it is up to us.' It's almost as if Percival's confirmation of his fears has dispelled his anger and left him defeated.

His acceptance of the situation irks me more than his despair. 'Are you just going to give—'

I stop mid-sentence as Snake hoists his pack over his shoulder and strides off down the path leading towards the Centre of Life.

A PATH ONCE CHOSEN

THE CRUNCH OF gravel under my feet fills the late morning air as my boots briskly pound the path heading towards the Centre of Life. I resist the urge to turn and make sure Pris and Percival are following me, not wanting to confirm what my heart already knows—that they are not there… yet.

My stomach churns as I contemplate the enormity of choosing our path through the maze without getting Pris to agree. I am pulled between wanting to help my mother, becoming a part of my family below, and sorting out some way of keeping Pris in my life without losing the other two things.

I'm a mass of worry and fears, and I am fighting to keep my head in amongst the emotional confusion clouding my senses.

Can't she see it's not that I don't care, but that I care too much? All this talk about fighting to be together is tearing me apart inside. I'm fighting my attraction to her with every fibre of my being, then one whiff of the shampoo in her hair almost does me in.

I stomp on, keeping an ear out for the sound of footsteps telling me Pris is following. As time passes, I have to admit she has chosen her own path to the centre of the maze. I am alone, with no one to blame but myself. I've pushed her so far away, she would rather not be with me. She will probably be better off without me anyway.

My plodding feet eat up the miles as I fight the urge to turn back and reunite with Pris. I follow the twists and turn of the hedge-lined path leading me through the shadows until they spit me out through a gateway into a clearing.

This isn't how a maze is supposed to work. This isn't the centre of anything.

In fact, it looks like the beginning of a path through a forest. I turn to find I am now in the shadow of the hedge, and the opening I came through is nowhere to be found. There is no way back. I am on my own.

At around midday, I stop by a stream to eat some trail bread and drink some water. I fill the water skin I find in my pack, then lean back against a tree and close my eyes for a moment. The bubbling of the stream as it flows over rocks takes me back to when Pris and I went to the White Lady Falls to meet the White Witch.

I miss her jokes and how she teased me as we walked. Hell, I even miss her quirky clothes. I wonder which path she took? Is she okay? At least she has Percival with her. I will do perfectly well by myself, but the magical world is new to her, and she hasn't fully gotten used to her powers.

Deciding I can't stop here all day, I pick up my pack and carry on walking. The path winds through the woods, and just when I think I will turn a corner and arrive at my destination, I find more trees lining more paths. I have long since stopped wondering about which route to take because each choice leads me exactly nowhere.

I continue to walk on until the sun begins its descent. My limbs are weary and I'm sick of trees and rutted paths and, most off all, I'm sick and tired of walking. I wish I had someone to complain to. I really miss Pris.

Venting my frustration, I kick a loose rock, sending it flying. It bounces off a tree trunk and back onto the path. Why did I have to go and fall for the one person I can never have? A bitter laugh escapes my lips.

'Okay, I am falling in love with her, and I can't do anything about it.' My voice echoes.

Let it go. Concentrate on freeing your mother, and worry about the rest later.

My peptalk lifts a weight from my shoulders. I am certain Pris and I will meet up at some point and get through this—together. With a lighter heart and renewed determination, I follow the path through towering green trees.

Appreciating walking through such a beautiful forest, I start to hum a tune, and my fingers make the chord forms as if they were playing guitar. The song I write in my head is melancholy—a love song of sorts for a love that can never be. It is one of my best yet, and I wish I had some paper to write to it down. Instead, I repeat it over and over so it will stay in my head.

So intent on remembering the tune, I let myself get lost in the melody. I don't notice the forest thinning until I turn a corner to find the path carries on through some fields towards a village. The hamlet is close to the forest edge and nestled by a stream—probably the same stream I drank from earlier.

THE MINOTAUR'S MAZE

To the other side of the village are fields and a smattering of farm buildings. I make out more trees on the horizon. There is only one way for me to go, and that is through the village. I pick up the pace. Perhaps I can camp the night in a field on the other side, then start out early in the morning.

Shrugging my pack more squarely in place, I continue on, humming under my breath. As I draw closer to the dwellings, I begin to pass creatures. Most of them have rounded ears peeking through their hair, telling me this is a predominantly gnome village; although some of the inhabitants are squarer in shape, indicating some dwarf heritage too. Most of them ignore me, but some raise their eyes from their work to follow my progress.

As I enter the market square, I am surprised when many of the stall holders stop what they are doing and stare at me. My skin prickles with discomfort. Perhaps they don't get many travellers through here.

Murmurs follow my progress, and I walk a little faster, sensing I am not welcome here. I catch the words of one female when she speaks more loudly than the others. 'It's Breaker of Hearts returned to us.'

I frown. I don't know who they think I am, but I'm certainly no heartbreaker. I almost laugh at the thought, considering the state of my love life.

A small crowd is gathering outside one of the shops on the edge of the marketplace, and I slow as I approach, wondering if they will allow me to pass. They make way for an elderly gnome who steps directly into my path, halting my progress.

The gnome looks me up and down before leaning on his stick. 'Well, you have the look of him, but your eyes are green, and you are slighter in build. The tune your mind is holding on to could be one of his, but you are the age he was when he left—he would be much older now.'

What the…? I sense everyone is waiting for some sort of response, but what do you say to that?

Nonetheless, the words spill out. 'I'm sorry? Who would be older? And where did he leave? I mean, where am I exactly?'

The gnome chuckles. 'This is Elder Grove, in the Western Edge of the Wyld Woods.'

I frown. That can't be right. The Wyld Woods? Weren't they on the other side of the mountain Eleanora took us to?

'But I'm meant to be in the maze.'

Everyone laughs.

'The maze can send you anywhere it wills, and you were sent here,' the gnome explains.

'Why would the minotaur want that?' I ponder out loud.

'My guess is your quest is to find that out.' The gnome's tone tells me he is quite serious.

More people are joining the group, and I shuffle in discomfort. Why am I here? Because I remind the locals of someone? There is only one way to find out.

'Who is this, um, Breaker of Hearts you think I resemble?'

'He is my son.'

Okay. What else might I need to know?

'Why did he leave?'

The gnome closes his eyes, but not quickly enough to hide his pain. When he opens them, he answers in a steady voice. 'He was tempted away by an elven princess to join her court when he was about your age. We have not seen him since.'

His pain permeates the air as the gnome beside him places a comforting hand on his arm. My next question sticks in my throat as his words tug at my heart. I was going to ask if they know any of the Fieth clan, but now I wonder if the minotaur sent me in the wrong direction. Pris is the only elven princess I have met. Perhaps the minotaur has mixed up our quests.

'I answered your questions, now I have one for you,' the gnome continues, oblivious to my inner turmoil. 'Did you bring an instrument with you? I am sure we would all enjoy listening to your song.'

I didn't expect that. I shake my head, operating on autopilot. 'I didn't think I would need one in the maze.'

The man nods. 'Quite sensible. If I loan you one, will you play your song for us? I sense its beauty, and I would be grateful if you would share it.'

'Do you have a guitar?' I ask

The gnome stares blankly at me.

'It's a stringed instrument. You strum it,' I explain.

He nods. 'A lute might work. How many strings do you need?'

'Six,' I answer, still trying to get my head around the bizarre turn this encounter has taken.

He disappears inside the shop and returns with an honest-to-god lute, like something out of a history book, and hands it to me. People move aside, revealing a bench outside the store. I sit on the seat, placing my pack at my feet.

I run my fingers over the strings, turning the pegs to tune it as close to a guitar as I can. Strumming produces an unusual sound, but with finger picking, the sound is closer to what is in my head.

It takes me a little while to get the tune exactly right, and I hum along to the notes as the song comes together. A little while later, I am adding the lyrics I played with as I walked. When I stop, a loud applause echoes through the crowd.

Feeling like myself for the first time today, I pick out some Irish ballads from my childhood. When I run out of them, I play Ed Sheeran's "Galway Girl," which gets everyone's feet tapping. As I finish up, the elderly gnome steps forward.

'The lad must be tired.' I start to object, but the gnome shakes his head. 'It is almost dark. That is enough for now.'

The crowd grumbles, but starts to disperse, muttering their thanks as they depart.

Handing me a supple leather case for the lute, the gnome helps me put it away. I hold the lute out, but the gnome waves his hand as if to brush it away. 'No, lad—that instrument has claimed you. It would be a sin for me to take it back.'

It is a beautiful instrument, but I can't take it. 'I haven't any money…. I can't—'

'Please—your performance was thanks enough. We have not had music of that quality in the village for quite some time. Now, my wife will flay me alive if I do not offer you a meal and a bed for the night.'

Now I'm even more embarrassed. 'You're too kind, I really—'

'Should accept. You may sleep under the stars for many nights before the maze has done with you. Sleep in a bed while you can.'

I believe my host will be quite upset if I refuse and, to be honest, I would prefer to eat a hot meal and sleep in a bed. So I agree to stay. I follow the gnome into his shop and wait while he closes up, resisting the urge to touch the amazing instruments on display. He then leads me through a workroom and into a dwelling at the back.

As I step through the door into a large family room, the smell of food cooking hits me, and my stomach grumbles. I chuckle as I spy a well-used wooden table set for three. Seems like my host would have been in trouble had I decided not to join him.

I resist the urge to drop into one of the armchairs placed either side of the roaring fire as the elderly gnome shuts the door behind us. 'I am so sorry, my manners escaped me. I must introduce myself. I am Mender of Hearts.'

I gasp. He used his true named even though we are all but strangers. To offer such intimacy on first meeting is not common. Not comfortable with returning the favour, I introduce myself using my public name. 'Pleased to meet you, Mender. I am Snake Fieth.'

The gnome's expression freezes when he hears my name, then he catches himself so quickly, I wonder if I imagined it. 'Ah, a city gnome. I thought as much. In our hamlet, the new fashion of using formal and informal names has been slow to catch on.'

I bite back a snort. The convention of public and private names has been around since the rebellion, which was hundreds of years ago.

Unsure what to do now, I wait for the gnome to give me some direction. He stares at me long and hard with a face that is difficult to read. The silence is becoming awkward, and I feel the urge to blurt out something to break the tension. Before I can make a fool of myself, an elderly female gnome enters from what can only be a kitchen, carrying a steaming bowl of stew.

'Ah, Snake Fieth, please allow me to introduce my wife, Keeper of Hearts.'

'Pleased to meet you, ma'am.' I hold out my hand, and she beams as she shakes it firmly.

'Put your things over by the door and come and eat,' she orders. 'I stayed a while listening to you, so I am running a little late. I will just fetch the bread from the oven.'

I lean my pack against the wall by the back door where she indicated, and as I straighten, my eyes linger on the portrait of a full-grown gnome and a female gnome about my own age. The girl looks familiar. I look closer, but her name doesn't spring to mind.

'That is Breaker of Hearts and his daughter. Her mother died in childbirth, and her father moved to the World Above soon after,' Mender tells me when he finds me in front of the picture.

I get the sense he is waiting for me to comment or react in some way. I'm starting to find this all a little odd, but the moment is gone when he says, 'Come, we do not want the food to go cold.'

I TAKE A seat at the table where I can sneak another look at the portrait while we eat. I'm sure I know that girl. I wonder if she is one of the gnomes I met in the World Above.

The meal is delicious, and the conversation mostly revolves around music. They enjoyed my songs from the World Above, and Mender is interested to hear about the instruments we use. He explains that he makes and sells a wide variety of instruments, and as we speak, I'm sure he is working out how he could produce something new.

At his request, I draw a rough sketch of a guitar, and I swear if Keeper had not sent a warning look his way, he would have headed into his workshop right away to begin making one of his own. Trying to distract him, I ask

Mender if he himself plays at all.

He smiles shyly. 'My gift is for making instruments, not playing them.'

'You play the pipe for dances,' his wife interjects, 'and a very pretty sound you make too.'

Mender demurs. 'The true musical talent in the family went to our son, Breaker. Much like you, he plays the lute and sings. He could draw deep emotions from even the coldest of hearts.'

'You obviously miss him a great deal,' I say. 'You said he's in the World Above?' A small touch of guilt flashes through me because I am only encouraging him to talk about his son in the hopes of finding out who the girl in the picture is.

'Yes, he is, or I hope he still is. It was an odd business for sure. Princess Petunia, heard him play and invited him to join her household. He was not ready to leave home, but then he saw the princess's companion, and we lost him,' Mender reminisces.

'More than taken with,' Keeper adds. 'It was love at first sight for both of them.'

The elderly couple's eyes meet across the table as they share the memory.

'So, Breaker joined the princess's household and moved to the Capitol. He made many friends and gathered quite a following of fans of his music. I could say he got in with the wrong crowd, but—'

'His friends were right thinking, and you know it,' Keeper of Hearts says. She turns to me. 'You will not remember the time of the blight when all the passages to the World Above were closed. Now we all understand that keeping the two worlds apart caused disease in our land, but back then, it was considered to be blasphemy to speak of such things.'

I knew about the blight. My mother had spoken of it a few times, but in the same way she spoke of any other period of history. It is obvious that for these gnomes, the events were very real. I want to ask them more.

'What Keeper is trying to explain is, our son was part of the group trying to convince the Creature Council to open the gates and allow movement between the worlds as a way to cure the blight. His Patron, Princess Petunia, was the group's leader.'

'He must have been very brave to support such an idea,' I say simply because there was a pause in the conversation, and I was sure they expected me to say something. They nod, and I am relieved I hit the right note with my praise.

'He was also perhaps a little foolish.' Mender said. 'The group was full of creatures from all races, and they mingled without considering how much they challenged the established way of doing things.'

My stomach tenses as my comfort levels drop. Breaker's story is turning out to be somewhat similar to my own. In the maze, that can't be a coincidence.

'He and his loved one married, and they had a daughter,' Keeper says, carrying on the story. 'His wife never recovered after the birth. We begged him to come home, but he had work in the Capitol, and he was proud of his position. Besides, the wife of one of his friends was willing to help with the raising of our granddaughter, Pure of Heart.'

'It wasn't until a few years later, once the doors were opened and things returned to normal, that the council got their revenge for being shown up by Princess Petunia's set,' Mender continued, his tone turning bitter. 'There was a backlash against the openness in her court after she was named heir.'

The mood in the room has turned sombre. The couple's pain is heavy in the air, causing me to feel a little awkward when I am forced to ask, 'Princess Petunia is Queen Ariana's sister, isn't she?'

Mender nods. 'When Queen Ariana's husband died, she vowed never to marry again. With Princess Petunia next in line for the throne, she declared her as successor. the council decided that was the time to exact retribution and issued the princess with an ultimatum—she could denounce her friends and remain heir or stand with them and be banished.'

Although I had heard about the heir's banishment, as we all did when we learned our history, this personal version of events brings the tale to life.

'Of course, the princess chose banishment to the World Above along with all of her friends who were married to creatures not of their race. We had hoped that because Breaker's wife was dead, he would be excused, but he was not.'

'So your family is stuck in the World Above?' I ask, tears forming in my eyes.

'Oh no,' Keeper says. 'Breaker wanted his daughter to grow up in the World Below. He had contacted us to see if we would take her in, but it all happened so quickly, and Pure of Heart was left with Breaker's friends. They formally fostered her, and she is part of their family now.'

It is like a blow to the stomach. I suddenly know who the girl in the portrait is and why she seems so familiar. Mender's next words confirm it.

'By the time we realised Breaker had been physically exiled, Pure had been living so long with the family, there was no thought of sending her back to us. We had never met her and, without our son to make the introductions, we would have been strangers to her. Some time later, she was fully adopted into the family, accepting a new name and a new identity.'

My heart is racing, and my hands are shaking so much, I need to place my cutlery on the table. Their metallic clatter fills the now silent room. The woman in the portrait is my mother—well, at least I think she is. These people I am eating dinner with are my great-grandparents. I keep my head down, processing everything I've just learnt about my family, wondering what to do about it.

'Fair, our grandchild, used to send us letters, but I from what I understand, she moved to the World Above herself to create a new life, and the letters stopped coming.'

I need to confirm my suspicions, and I want to find out if they invited me to dinner because they suspect who I am.

'Do you know anything more about her?' I ask.

Was that too obvious? Too late to take it back now.

Keeper sighs. 'We got the sense from her new family that she wanted to hide her true identity. Life was not easy for her—because of her true parents. We allowed her to slip away from us because we thought it was what she wanted... what she needed.'

'That is so sad,' I say, and I really mean it.

'It is, but we are not alone. Our daughter and her family live in the next hamlet. No doubt when we grow too old to run the shop anymore, we will move closer to her.' Keeper takes her husband's hand.

I have cousins. A smile tugs at my lips. I so want to tell them who I am and be welcomed into the family. I check myself. Is it fair to do that to them?

They let go of their son and granddaughter a long time ago and are content with their lives. Do I have a right to disturb their peace of mind, knowing their granddaughter is in disgrace and that I must leave tomorrow to try and save her? Would they appreciate that?

As these thoughts race through my mind and I attempt to force them into some sort of action, I am conscious of Keeper standing and clearing the table. As if on automatic pilot, I rise to my feet. 'Please, let me help you with the dishes.'

'No, no young man, all is good.' She pats my hand. 'Perhaps Mender can show you to your room. You must be tired, and you set out on your quest again tomorrow. The maze waits for no one.'

I thank her for the meal before following Mender up the stairs and into a small bedroom with a single bed. A blue rag rug is the only floor covering, and a window in the ceiling frames the night sky, providing light.

'It isn't much,' he says as he pulls a comforter and sheets from the cupboard. 'It was our son's, and our grandson uses it when he comes to stay.

'It's perfect,' I assure him. And I mean it. I was going to spend the night sleeping in a field, and now I will be sleeping in my grandfather's old bedroom. 'Let me,' I say, taking the linen from him, and proceed to make the bed.

'Yes, well…'

I sense he wants to say something to me, and I will him to say the words I want to hear, making my decision for me.

'Well, goodnight, then.'

'Goodnight,' I say as the door shuts behind him.

I am left alone, wondering if I should have said something, and now it is too late.

I SNUGGLE UNDER the down comforter, and even though my body is exhausted, I can't sleep. My thoughts chase each other in my head, not slowing for long enough for me to focus on anything.

Tonight I met my mother's family and found out that they're rather notorious compared to the straight-laced Fieth clan. When I think of my grandfather and everything he lost, I am hit by a sudden understanding. I know why my mother hid her roots all these years. I also know why Bernais treats her with such disdain—she's half elf, half gnome.

Her being charged with the crime of benefitting from her magic is not only to discredit the Fieth clan, it is also to reinforce the belief that any issue of a mixed union cannot help but be a vile, untrustworthy creature.

My journey through the maze took me to the Centre of Life all right—the centre of my own life. Pris was right to be wary about where this path would lead. It was never going to take me to the centre of the maze, but rather to a place where I could understand more about myself.

I sit up and lean back against the wall, all thoughts of sleep gone. I twist my newfound knowledge this way and that, probing my thoughts, wondering how this changes me.

My mother buried who she was so far inside, she never spoke of it, yet she carried feelings of inadequacy with her for her whole life. I now understand why she did not want to return below. In the World Above, people are more accepting of difference. Returning here would put her in the firing line of Bernais and other creatures who think like him.

Oh, and that is why Bernais is so against Pris and me being close. He's thinking, *like grandfather, like grandson.* Or is it that he doesn't want the royal line tainted with *my* mixed blood?

Funny thing—I'm more upset about my mother's treatment than the way Bernais and his friends have been treating me. It angers me beyond words that people think of her as an abomination.

I bite back a self-deprecating chuckle. This is a night of revelations. It is now clear to me why Pris insists on standing up to racism whenever she encounters it. If I accept other creature's views on Pris and me being together, then I am all but saying I agree with how they treat my mother.

I see my actions as Pris must, and shame eats at me. My stomach churns, and I worry I am about to lose my dinner. I want nothing more than to find her and tell her how sorry I am from the bottom of my heart. I can only hope I haven't lost her forever because of my own stupidity.

My mind is calming down. I crawl back under the covers as my eyelids close and sleep finally beckons. I'm just dozing off when footsteps on the stairs wake me. I roll over, but I cannot settle because of the voices coming from the room next door.

Mender and Keeper have lived so long alone, they mustn't realise how every word they say is booming its way through the thin walls. I try not to listen, but the conversation is too clear to block out. Besides, they're talking about me.

'If he did not recognise his own story in the telling of it, I am not sure we should tell him who he is to us. It would not be fair to him if his mother went to the trouble of concealing who she is, and we undo it all for nothing other than our selfish need to claim a great-grandson.'

'But Mender, we cannot let him leave without telling him.'

'Keeper, are you wanting to tell him for his benefit, or for ours? What good can it do for him to find out who we are when he is called to a quest in the maze? He cannot waste his energy, worrying about a new family when he will need all his wits about him if he is to succeed.'

'But it cannot be by chance that the maze brought him here. For some reason it wanted him to meet us. Perhaps we are meant to tell him who he is.'

'You know that is unlikely, Keeper. If the maze brought him here as part of his quest, then we can tell him nothing. He must find out for himself.'

'Ooh, you are such an infuriating gnome.'

They are silent for a while, then Keeper asks, 'Mender, do you think this is all still to do with Bernais Baarenson's campaign against his cousin, Petunia? He has never been the same since the Queen announced her as heir, then refused to retract it even when she left.'

'She is banished and can no longer take up the throne. Surely he cannot hold a grudge that long?'

'But husband, the Queen will not name another successor, and she is yet to produce any offspring.'

'True. Both the Crown cousins, Bernais and Elias, are high in her esteem. It will surely be one of them.'

'Which is why I think Snake's being here must be part of one of Bernais's schemes,' Keeper muses. 'Perhaps he wants to use Snake to remind everyone of how close Elias was to Petunia.'

'That is all so far away, Keeper, and knowing this will not help young Snake when he leaves here tomorrow.'

But it might help me when I get back to the Capitol.

My great-grandparents fall silent, and soon the sound of not-so-gentle snoring fills the air. Sleep now eludes me completely. I was given so many puzzle pieces to help me work out why I am here tonight, but they won't fit together. My head aches as I move them around, trying to make a coherent picture.

Eventually, I give up. All I can do is deal with what is in front of me and hope I will soon be able to gather enough pieces to make out the whole image.

As I doze, I'm still trying to decide whether or not I should introduce myself to my great-grandparents before I leave tomorrow. I mean, they know who I am, I know who they are—what can it hurt? Right?

I CAN DO THIS ON MY OWN

THE MINUTE SNAKE disappears from sight, Pris picks up her pack and stalks off down Journey's End. I trail after her, not mentioning I do not think it a good idea to split up. I am pleased I kept my mouth shut when she spits, 'If he thinks I will follow him again, he is mistaken.'

A few minutes later she turns on her heel and heads in the opposite direction. She passes me, then moments later I hear her footsteps behind me.

'What the?'

She runs past me, then disappears only to be returned to her starting place once again. When her footsteps approach a third time, I put out a hand to restrain her.

'The maze does not work that way, Princess. You chose a path, and you must follow it to the end—there are no do overs.'

Her face crumples, but before I can reassure her it will be all right, she rearranges it into a look of fierce determination.

'We don't need him, do we, Percival?' she says, but there is a slight tremor in her voice.

I want to say we would be better off if he was here, but I sense that is not the right thing to say. 'We will be fine without him,' I tell her.

We walk in silence for some time, then the elf appears to recover herself and starts prattling. At first I try to block it out, but it becomes harder and harder. Finally, I can bear it no longer.

If I hear her say one more time that she doesn't need Snake and she has no idea what she ever saw in him, I am going to leave her to her own devices and join him. I would rather be with him than here with her anyway. She is an elf, after all, and elves are not my favourite creatures.

We started out all right. She was so certain she had chosen the right path. Then she decided to turn back and follow him because it would be better if they were together, but she found she could not.

'I mean, he is not really much use in a fight…'

I tune out her voice.

You had to go with her, I remind myself for perhaps the hundredth time. She is a princess, and of royal blood. If something happens to her because she understands so little about our ways, I will never be forgiven.

Something in the trees lining the path catches my eye. I pause for a moment but am unable to see anything. Mind you, if it was a sprite, they could easily hide from me. Especially as I can no longer sense them the way I used to.

I sigh. Being back here reminds me I am odd, fitting in nowhere. No longer a sprite, but not quite anything else either. And being in the forest reinforces that fact for me, especially as I am so close to my home. I cannot imagine how much more horrendous my life will be when I visit the World Below if I let a princess down, and creatures have one more thing to vilify me for.

I do wish she would shut up though. It is difficult enough resisting the pull of the tree's song without her whinging in my ear as well. I mean, it is not as if I can do what the trees ask and join them—not anymore.

We are in a dense part of the forest, surrounded by woodlands as we follow a winding path. This is an ancient woodland, and the sage trees sense I want to be with them. If only they had taken away the song as well all those years ago, today would be much easier on me.

'He really should have waited. I mean, he needs me more than I need him…,' Princess Priscilla drones on.

My hackles begin to rise, not that I have hackles in this form. Really, this self-absorption is too much for me to bear. I stop walking, place my hands on my hips, and stamp my foot to gain the princess's attention.

'Oh for goodness sake, will you listen to yourself. Have some self-respect,' I hiss. 'So you got on well. So you came here together. So you are doing this partially for him. You chose not to go with him. Now own your decision, grow a backbone, and let us get moving.'

The princess stares at me, eyes widening in shock, and I brace myself for her reaction; she is known for her temper, after all. Then, after a moment's pause, she laughs. Not a small, ladylike giggle, but a loud burst of laughter. It's quite shocking. I stand tall and glare at her. Is she laughing at me? She carries on for a while. I spy some dust on my shirt and flick it off. She still hasn't stopped. Have I broken her?

She finally wipes the tears from her eyes and takes a couple of deep breaths.

'You're right, Percival. I'm acting like a lovesick teenager. I've never needed a boy before, and I don't need one now. Besides, you're with me, and you are much more valuable.'

Her brows draw together. 'Actually, I want to ask, why did you decide to come with me and not with him? I mean, I get the impression you don't even like me.'

I pause, wondering how much to tell her. In the end, I ignore the obvious invitation to deny that I dislike her and say, 'I came with you because you need me more, and saving you is more likely to gain me a better reward.'

Her head cocks to the side as she considers my answer. 'Self-interest is the only reason you came this way?' She nods. 'I can respect that. Well, I'm glad you are with me, whatever the reason.'

I resist the urge to preen. Elves are all silver-tongued, and they don't mean half of what they say. I will not fall for her words, as they are obviously intended to make me think kindlier of her. Instead, I say, 'If you are finished with your—what do human girls call it?—your pity party, there is a village not far up the road. I suggest we head there and get our bearings.'

Priscilla laughs again, and this time it's more controlled and a lot less alarming. 'It's a good thing you know where you are going, because I'm completely lost.'

Oops, I inadvertently took the lead. Perhaps not. I only made a suggestion. I must watch myself, as I do not mean to become part of this quest. What is done is done, but I will have to be more careful in the future.

'You know,' the princess is saying, 'I expected this to be a maze more like the one at Hampton Court. I expected hedgerows, twists and turns and dead ends, with the prize in the middle. All this open space leading to a forest feels more like an adventure.'

'Mazes can be different,' I say, not sure how much I can tell her in my role as observer.

'I get that, but once we were through the initial gates, it turned out to be more like a country stroll. Not that I'm complaining. Walking around the edge of the forest is lovely. The trees provide shade, and the bird song is so pleasant. Still… this can't be all there is. This is a quest, after all.'

Will the girl never cease talking? How I long to be able to return to Wimbledon and curl up by the fire in peace. All right, I will be in cat form when I do, but at least I will have some quiet.

The path wends its way through the forest. The trees now grow more tightly together, and we are deep in the shade. I could have sworn we were close to a village. The princess's chatter continues as my anxiety grows.

'I can almost imagine us walking through a forest in a fairy tale. You know, a path meandering through ancient trees… the deeper we go, the darker the path. I almost expect something to leap out at us.'

'Honestly, child, have you no common sense? Do you want to bring ill down on us?'

She stops walking and turns, her eyes growing wide with fear. Guilt pricks at my conscience. Just a little, mind you—she is still an elf, after all.

Her voice is uncertain when she speaks, and there is a tinge of fear mingled there. 'Can that actually happen?'

What do I say? Do I soothe her fears and tell her no. Or do I go with the truth, and say that of course it could, but it is unlikely.

She waits earnestly for my answer, and I realise I misread her. She is not angry at losing Snake. She is scared because she is in a strange world, and he is not here. *She should have thought about that before she decided to follow her own path*, I think rather uncharitably. Then I mentally kick myself. I remember what it is like being a stranger in a strange place. It is not her fault she is an elf, or that she knows nothing about her heritage.

'Come on. The sooner we are out of the woods, the better.' I am not confident it will be better for her, but it will be better for me because I will be further from my family, and the tree's song will no longer thrum through my veins.

MY MOUTH IS running non-stop. It's irritating Percival, but I keep going, unable to control my tongue. If only I hadn't been so pigheaded about getting my own way, we would still be with Snake now. I'm sure Percival would rather be with him than me too, even if just to get a moment's peace.

Although my mouth has been telling the world how I don't need Snake, my head has been mentally shaking me. I am always so certain I am right. Why didn't I just listen to him?

Now I am stuck in a world full of magic, and I know virtually nothing about it, or what creatures I might encounter. I'm only just realising how much I relied on his knowledge of this strange world I only found out existed last week.

Funny, in spite of his wealth of knowledge, I was quick to pooh-pooh his concerns about how our being friends, more than friends, would be viewed.

I decided I knew best.

Perhaps I was lulled by a false sense of security with the Fieth family and the dance at the ball last night. It all seemed so normal, I had almost forgotten this is a different world, and we were to sent out on a dangerous quest.

Then Percival asked me if I was tempting fate by talking about things coming crashing out of the woods, and suddenly, I am now all too aware that I'm in a foreign land where I know none of the rules. For the first time in my life, I feel inadequate to face the challenge.

'Are you all right?' Percival asks me, his face contorted into what might pass for a worried frown.

I realise I have been silent, lost in my thoughts, and given my constant chatter up until now, he is worried.

'I'm okay,' I tell him, but I am not. Talking prevented me from thinking too much about… well, about everything. As we walk along in silence with only the rustle of the leaves and the twitter of birds punctuating our footsteps, I am forced to confront the demons lurking in my head.

Will I be able to find the middle of the minotaur's maze without Snake? If I can't, then my parents will be convicted. The farcical trial at the ball last night was enough to tell me the charges were trumped up, but that does not make them any less real. It will not make the punishment any less real either—Bernais will see to that!

The very same Bernais who railroaded me into this quest with Snake— perhaps to get me out of the way. Or does he have something more sinister in mind? Is he hoping I won't return?

'Bring it on,' I say under my breath, checking Percival didn't hear me. He is oblivious. He appears to be having another of his 'moments.' Ever since we entered the forest, he has been zoning out every now and then. At first I thought he was just blocking me out, but I think it might be something more than that.

'Bring it on!' I say a little more strongly, drawing strength from the words. In the World Above, muggers targeted me all the time. Some of those attacks were quite violent, and I am still here. I will survive this too.

I instantly feel better, in control again. Okay, it was Snake who pointed out my muggings were unlikely to be random attacks, but I was the one who fought them off. Snake is not here to educate me on the World Below, but so what! I have Percival, and Percival seems to know more about this world than he does.

Ah, Percival is my guide in the World Below. I wonder if he could tell me more about who I am? After all, it might help me understand why I'm in this mess.

'Percival? Can I ask you something?'

There is no response.

I try again. 'Percival, are you able to tell me something more about my family, like how I'm related to Bernais and Elias?'

I may as well be talking to one of the trees.

While I am waiting for him to come out of his funk, I decide to go over what I already know. I am a Princess of Royal Blood—whatever that means. I also know that since arriving in the Seelie Court of the World Below, I'm the only elf I've seen with dark skin—apart from my father, that is. And I also know that many in the World Below believe my father is not part of the court.

Wind sweeps some strands of hair across my face, and I tuck them into my loose plait as I walk. I want to know about Bernais and Elias, but I also want to know why my father seems to be an outcast, and does that have anything to do with why my parents never told me about my heritage?

Percival is still lost in thought, but around midday we stop by a clear blue stream to get a drink and fill our water skins. He appears to be a little more aware, so now is as good a time as any to question him.

'Percival, you're here to help me understand this world, and I think it might be helpful for me to know a little more about my family, especially how I am related to Bernais and Elias in particular.'

Percival stretches in an almost feline way before pulling a comb from his pocket and tiding his already immaculate hair. When he is satisfied with his appearance, he answers.

'I am here to help with the quest only, but… as those two are part of why you are undertaking this particular folly, I think it might be all right to answer you. Can we walk as we talk? I would like to be out of these woods as soon as possible.'

He has not looked comfortable since we started walking under the trees. I would say he looks pale, but I am not sure whether that's his normal colour or not.

'Are you all right? You seem… um… unsettled. Is there something I can do to help?' I ask.

He pauses, his comb halfway back in his pocket, and regards me as if he is seeing me for the first time. I don't think he expected me to notice his unease. He slowly shakes his head. 'You cannot help me. It is just the woods. I will be better when I am out of here.'

He slips the comb fully into his pocket and we start out again.

'They are not your close relatives,' he starts. 'Bernais and Elias, I mean. Their mothers are cousins to Queen Ariana.'

He walks ahead a little. Is that all he is going to say? I catch him up.

'That still doesn't explain why Bernais appears so set against me, while Elias isn't,' I point out.

He humphs. I mean, literally humphs. Who does that?

'Elias was always sweet on Princess Petunia, the second daughter of Queen Althea. She chose to marry another, and he left the Capitol soon after. He was only recently recalled by Queen Ariana to take up the role of Chancellor. His absence from the political arena for all those years left him rusty. He is still finding his feet. If he remained at court, maybe he would have been better placed to keep you out of things.'

Well, that's an interesting tidbit, but it doesn't explain Bernais. 'And Bernais? Why does he hate me?'

Percival shrugs. 'I suspect he does not hate you personally, but rather, he is set against those of the old Queen's bloodline. You see, Queen Althea did not have Ariana until late in life, so her niece, Bernais's mother, was named heir.'

I can see a pattern here. 'So, when Althea had a child that changed?'

'Yes, and Bernais was not happy about his loss of status. Then, some years later, when Princess Petunia, Ariana's younger sister, was born, Bernais was no longer considered to be of Royal Blood. Bitterness at his loss of station has taken over his life since then.'

'I think I heard someone say Princess Petunia is the current heir, is that correct?' I ask.

'Not exactly. There was some… well… some horridness about who her friends were, and she was banished. Queen Ariana has no children, and did not remarry after her husband died, so….'

'So events created a power vacuum, and Bernais sees himself filling it?'

Percival nods. 'Precisely, although I am sure there is more to his machinations than that.'

'Of course there is,' I mutter. Percival has given me quite the history lesson, but at least listening to him is better than listening to the demons in my head. 'Carry on,' I urge as I almost trip over Percival.

He has stopped in his tracks, as if frozen in place. I step forward to see what happened to him, only to be encased in some sticky substance that prevents me from moving. I can't even open my mouth to voice my frustration. My heart is pounding and fear washes through me. Give me an opponent to fight and I'm fine, but being trapped like this… it's mind-numbingly scary.

We stay locked in place for goodness knows how long. My fear builds and my mind imagines all kinds of bloody and murderous ends for us. The air is turning cold when a woman appears on the path.

Wrinkled beyond imagining, wearing a long skirt and blouse of good quality but well-worn fabric, she cackles like a witch as she moves closer. My heart pounds in my head. This is it. This is how it ends, and I can't even use my get-out-of-the-maze-free option.

'In a bit of a bind, are we?' She laughs at her own joke.

My fear turns to anger. I would say something smart back, but I can't move my mouth. I can't even clench my fists to release my frustration.

'Ah, Percival, it is a long time since you visited these parts.' She steps past him and stands in front of me. 'And this must be Princess Priscilla. Such a pleasure to meet you.'

The woman snaps her fingers, and my eyelids begin to droop. If my life is about to end, I want to face it front on. As I try to fight what is happening to me, my head starts to swim and my vision clouds. Try as I might, I cannot keep my eyes open, and I am soon sinking into an inky blackness.

MY BRAIN SENDS a message to my eyelids to open, but they are still heavy with sleep and magic and refuse the command. Listening to my surroundings, I try to sense whether or not I am in any immediate danger. I try to move my arms and legs, but they are heavy, like a weight is pressing down on them. I freeze in panic. Am I still bound by the spell?

Keeping my rising fear at bay, I force myself to concentrate to try and work out where I am. Apart from crackling, which I assume to be a fire, everything is quiet, I can't even hear birds singing. Wherever I am, I think I am alone.

I roll over and manage to half open one of my eyes to find I am lying on a bed in a simply furnished room. Opposite me, a fire warms the cosy space with comfy chairs sitting on either side of the hearth. In the centre of the room is a well-worn wooden table with a chair at each side. To my right is a door, and to my left is a bench under a window.

I wait for my head to clear before I open both eyes, swing my still heavy legs around, and place my feet on the ground. Pushing myself up, my legs are stiff but I'm able to stand. I'm not woozy, so I'm pretty sure the crone didn't drug me.

I make my way across the room, and then I fling open the door. Instead of the expected escape route, I find a wooden bench with a hole in it. I lean over and peer down. The depth of the hole and the smell tell me this is what passes for a toilet.

THE MINOTAUR'S MAZE

Back in the room with the door securely closed, I frantically search for another way out. I rush to the window, pulling and pushing against the frame, but it doesn't open. There's no other door to be seen. I am trapped unless I want to smash the window.

'Please do not break my window.' The voice comes from all around me, and soon after, the woman from the forest appears in one of the chairs by the fire.

She waves her hand, and a pitcher of water appears on the bench, and a bowl of apples and pears materialises on the table. With a click of her fingers, a cast-iron pot places itself over the flames of the fire, filling the room with a juicy, meaty aroma.

'Come sit, child.' The woman gestures with a hand to the chair opposite her.

I eye her warily. What does she want with me? The tale of Hansel and Gretel floods my mind. I was terrified of that story as a child, and my knees tremble now. As I am trapped in this cottage in the centre of a strange wood. Has she brought me here to end my quest?

'I'm okay,' I say.

She smiles as if I amuse her. Perhaps she read my mind. 'Please, you will be more comfortable if you sit while we talk. Besides, if I meant to harm you, why would I go to the trouble of providing you with food?'

To fatten me up before eating me.

I consider the stew simmering over the fire. *Or maybe she intends to poison me.*

I sigh as I realise the true meaning of the food. I am going to be here for some time. I continue to stand as a sort of protest against the idea, then I reconsider. I want to leave here, and she is the only one who seems to be able to come and go, so I need her goodwill.

'Excellent,' she says when I lower myself into the seat. She folds her hands in her lap. 'Now, you can go no further in the maze until you access your powers and show you can use them. The minotaur's rules prohibit entry to the uninitiated.'

I grip the chair's arms as my wariness turns to alarm. 'What? Why didn't anyone tell me this before?'

'That is not my problem. My job is to check all those who come my way to ensure they meet the requirements of the quest and are able to proceed. You do not.'

I am frozen in place, my fuddled brain processing her words but coming up blank. The maddeningly calm creature sits in front of me, saying nothing. Is she waiting for me to speak?

'Where is Percival?' I ask, then mentally kick myself. I should be asking

exactly what they need from me so I can get out of this goddamn prison.

She shrugs. 'He is free to go on.'

Is this woman purposefully trying to irritate me? I narrow my eyes and study her closely. No. I think she is answering my questions and no more. I decide to test my theory and try a different tactic. 'Are you going to train me to access my magic?'

She emits a tinkling laugh. 'Oh, my goodness, no. I am only the gatekeeper. All you need to do is complete the training you began in the World Above, access your full powers, and you will be able to move on.'

She can't be serious. I only just found out I had my magic. I can barely produce a flame, the simplest of spells. 'What training?'

'You can make a flame, can't you?' the old woman asks, a perplexed frown drawing her brows together. 'Of course you must be able to. You got here from the World Above. To do that, you must have discipline, focus, and be able to access your magic. Someone must have at least trained you to do the latter.'

Snake helped me form my flame—well, Snake and some random cat.

'You can access your magic. You just need to be able to figure out what the source of it is so you can learn to use it. Once you do that, you will be able to leave.'

She makes it sound so simple. I am not taken in. 'So I stay here until I learn that, even if I take a week? Or a month?'

'Oh no, my dear. I cannot let you stay in my home that long. You may stay two nights, then you must be gone.'

Surely it can't be that easy. 'What? So all I need to do is wait two nights, and then you will let me out?'

'No, dear. Either you use your magic to let yourself out before your time is up, or I use mine to expel you from the maze.'

I knew it had sounded too easy. So now, not only must I work out why members of my own family hate me, but I also have to learn how to use my magic and control it enough to get out of this prison. I curse my parents for keeping me apart from my true heritage. My life would be so much easier now if they had just fessed up. As it is, I don't even know where to start to figure out the origins of my power.

'Can you at least tell me what kinds of magic elves can use?' I ask, suddenly feeling very meek.

'Well, I do not normally do that… but I cannot see how that breaks the rules. It should be all right.'

My eyebrows raise. 'There are rules to this?'

The old woman frowns again, 'Of course. Rules govern everything in the World Below.'

'Sorry. Everything here is so… so alien to me.'

'Of course it is, my dear. In the World Below, we recognise four different types of magic: earth, air, physical, and particle.'

I am no better off knowing what they are. 'Can you tell me what each of those do?'

'No.'

'Sugarcoat it, why don't you?' My tone is harsh and sarcasm taints my words. The woman flinches, and a thread of remorse trickles through me. No, I will not feel sorry for her. She has trapped me here, and getting a straight answer from her is like wading through treacle.

'Can Percival help me?' I ask.

'He cannot come in. Whether he waits for you or not is up to him. He is free to wander the maze and can come and go as he wishes.'

My head is spinning. Is there anything else I need to ask to make sure I don't find myself unceremoniously kicked out of the maze? While I marshal my thoughts, the woman decides she has said all she is going to and blinks out of sight.

'What the…?' I jump to my feet. 'I can't believe this place.' I pace in front of the fire. 'I'm supposed to figure out how my magic works while stuck in a room with no one to help.' I spin on my heel and walk the other way. 'And if I don't, this is all over, and my parents will pay the price.'

I continue pacing for a bit longer, spiralling into my anger and muttering to myself. Pausing in front of the fire, I watch the flames for a moment. Being angry isn't helping, but I can't seem to calm down. I walk to the window and stare out at the trees.

'It is not going to help you, all that ranting,' a voice says from beside me. 'You need to be calm when you use your magic, or it will get out of control.'

I swivel my head, looking for the source of the advice. Glancing down, I strain to see. The angle isn't great, but I just make out Percival, who is sat leaning against the house, reading a book. In front of him is a blazing fire in a pit. Behind that is a tent erected with a camp stretcher set up inside.

'What *are* you doing?' I ask, speaking more loudly than normal so he can hear me through the window. 'And where did all this… stuff come from?'

'I have made myself comfortable while I wait for you to find your magic and use it to release yourself,' he answers as he pushes himself to his feet, walks around the fire, and places the book on the bed. He returns and stands in front of the window so I can see him better. He doesn't explain the source of his comforts, but that is the least of my worries.

'How do I do that? Find my magic, I mean.' My voice sounds churlish even to my own ears, so I am not surprised when he glares at me.

'You will start with what you have and work hard to improve.'

My cheeks heat with shame, but I say defiantly, 'But two days is such a short time.'

Percival's gaze is unflinching. 'You had best get started, then.'

Panic bubbles up inside me. Until now I have been focussing my fear and transferring it into anger. Now Percival's call to action has stripped me bare. I cannot do this. I can barely make a flame. I will fail. And I hate to fail.

I hear my father's voice in my head. *Failure is a part of learning. And you can't learn if you don't even try.*

'Dammit, why do you have to be so inspiring,' I mumble. I take a deep breath, ignore the panic threatening to overwhelm me, and ask, 'Right, where do I start?'

Sighing, Percival moves closer to the window. 'You are an elf. Your magic is strong. You just have to learn how to use it. It should only take a small amount to release you from here.'

His gaze holds mine, and I am again reminded of the cat I met—was it only yesterday?—who showed me who I really was. Who convinced me I could make a flame.

'Percival, was that you—'

'We will start off using your flame to identify your magical abilities.'

He is deflecting, but why? If he is some sort of shapeshifter, then that is really cool. Still, if he doesn't want to talk about it. 'My flame? How?'

'We use your flame to identify the source of your magic. There are simple tests we can do that creatures have been doing for millennia.'

'All right.' What else can I say? It's not like I have many options.

'We will start with the easiest—earth magic allows you to pull the flame from heat found in the world around you.'

I take a deep breath to settle my nerves before saying, 'I understand. How will I tell if I form it using earth magic?'

He stands on tiptoe and looks into the room. 'Ah, how helpful—you have apples. Go stand close to the fruit bowl and make your flame.'

I walk to the table and take a deep breath. It takes a couple of attempts, but soon I have a small purple flame sitting over the palm of my hand. I only learnt how to do this yesterday, and I am still amazed I can draw power and make fire dance on my palm. I smile.

'Now, can you sense any heat in your flame?'

My smile disappears as I focus back on the task at hand. I stare at the licking fire, but I can't see any darker bits that might indicate heat. I pass my other hand over top. The flame is cold. I put my finger through it, waiting to feel the burn, but it is cool to the touch. I turn to Percival. 'It's cold.'

He shrugs. 'There is no point in the next step, then, which is sensing heat in the fruit, a part of its life-force, then drawing it out and using it to increase the volume of your flame.'

I try not to be disappointed. There are three other types of magic, after all. 'So I have no affinity with earth. What's next?'

'Air is the next easiest to master, but I think that is not your type of magic either.'

I frown. 'Why not?'

'Because there is no heat in your flame. Air magic moves an existing flame to you,' Percival explains.

I nod. 'You mean something like taking a flame from the fire and moving it to my hand?'

'Not quite. More like sucking the heat from the fire and using air to fan it into a flame on your palm,' he explains.

'And it would be hot because it comes from an actual fire,' I finish.

'Exactly.'

'Hold on, there was no fire nearby when I made a flame yesterday.'

Percival sneers. 'There is always heat around. What do you think is at the centre of our earth?'

I resist the urge to slap the palm of my hand to my forehead. Any pleasure I took from working out how air magic makes a flame disappears. All this talk of magic has me forgetting things I know to be true about the world. Now I see why Snake is so interested in physics and magic. My flame starts to flicker. I try to hold it, but it splutters out.

'You are tired,' Percival says. 'We shall test the other two options tomorrow.'

He turns to his tent, and I rush to the window. 'No, Percival, I am fine. I can keep going.'

He half turns back towards me. 'You need to make sure you rest. Magic takes something out of you, especially when you are learning.'

'But if I can figure out my magic, I can get out of here sooner.' I don't want to spend a night in here.

Percival shakes his head. 'You need to make sure you are well rested. Not just so you can find the source of your magic, but also so you are able to use it to get yourself out of there once you do.'

My stomach lurches. I had forgotten about that.

'Goodnight.' Percival picks up his book.

I lean my forehead against the windowpane and watch him as he lies on the camp bed and begins reading. For a few minutes, I watch the flames in his fire grow brighter as the sun sinks below the trees. I wonder where Snake is and if he is close by.

'Goodnight.' I am not sure whether I am speaking to Percival or to Snake.

I turn my back on the scene outside and begin to pull together a meal of stew and fruit. As the thick meat and gravy warms my belly, I stare forlornly around the room. I have never felt more alone.

MAYBE I CAN'T

FIXING MY EYES to the page, I sense rather than see the elven princess staring at me. I want to tell her I think her affinity is with particle magic so we can move on to getting her out. I cannot. Not just because this is the same process all the greater creatures go through, but also because I am not meant to be helping her like that.

I worry I am exceeding the terms of my agreement with the council. Having the elf skip the air test is definitely close to overstepping my bounds. From now on I have to be careful to merely point her in the right direction.

The shadow she casts disappears. I rise and move to stand under the window. A chair scrapes and is followed by the familiar sounds of someone eating. Dishes clatter, and I suspect she is clearing up. Then there is quiet. I sit down, leaning my back against the cottage, listening to her movements, waiting impatiently for the sounds that will tell me she is sleeping.

My fire dies down, and I place some more logs in the pit. Before retaking my seat, I dust down my clothes. There was a time when forest elements such as dirt would not have bothered me. Perhaps I have spent too long as a cat and now I cannot help but fuss about my appearance.

The princess tosses and turns. I count the minutes, trying not to become impatient, but she will not settle. I go to the tent and retrieve my book to pass the time until she falls asleep. When I am certain her breathing has become slow and regular, I bank the fire, close up my tent, and will myself to the maze entrance.

Eleanora is pacing when I appear.

'I only just called you,' I defend myself before she speaks.

My friend and mistress turns, hands resting on her hips. 'I have been waiting for your call to meet for hours,' she responds. 'You have no idea how worried I have been, imagining all sorts of dangerous tasks the minotaur might set for Snake and Princess Priscilla.'

'She prefers to be called Pris,' I say automatically, then clasp my hand over my mouth.

Eleanora's laugh rings in the night air. 'I thought she was "that elf", and now you are worried about what she prefers to be called,' she teases me.

I resist the urge to defend myself a second time. More worryingly, she might be right. Sometime in the course of a single day, my opinion of Princess Pricilla Crown shifted.

I humph, not ready to admit I might be warming to the elf, and change the subject by asking, 'So, do you want to know what happened today, or do you want to carry on teasing me?'

In a heartbeat, Eleanora transforms from amused to concerned. 'Percival, are you all right?'

'The minotaur decided to send us through the forests.' No other words are needed; she will understand without elaboration.

She rests a hand on my shoulder. 'Oh, Percival, no. How are you holding up?'

Her touch undoes me, and tears form in my eyes. 'Not well,' I grudgingly whisper. I cannot say more for fear I will fall apart.

'I did not think this would be a test of you as well. If I had even an inkling….'

I shake my head. 'We both knew there was a possibility of my being drawn into the quest. For a number of years, I have been considering petitioning the Queen, but our trips to the World Below are always so short, there is never any time. The minotaur may have sensed my desire and made additional plans for me. Perhaps he thinks he is doing me a favour.'

Eleanora crouches down so her eyes are level with mine. 'Is that what you want, my old friend?'

I close my eyes to gather my thoughts. I have no idea what I want. I shrug.

'If you stick to the agreement we made with the minotaur, you will still be able to choose your own path,' she reassures me, then pauses. 'Hold on, you haven't been helping out already, have you?'

Time to change the subject. 'The elf and Snake split up this morning.'

A frown draws Eleanora's brows together. 'What do you mean, they split up?'

I knew that would distract her. 'Snake wanted to go one way and the princess another. They could not agree, so they each took their own path.'

Eleanora's mouth forms a perfect 'O.' She rises to her feet and begins pacing again. 'This is not good.' A few minutes later, she follows that statement with, 'Working as a team, they stood a chance. Apart? I just don't know. But our plan still might have a chance.'

Eventually, she stands still, staring at the gate, her lip with her index finger. 'Who did you go with?'

'The princess,' I respond.

She nods. 'And where is she now?'

'Trapped by a hag who will not let her go any further without learning to use her magic. If she cannot demonstrate her control, she will be expelled from the maze the day after tomorrow.'

Eleanor is silent for such a long time, I am not sure she heard me. 'Eleanora.'

'I am thinking. If she does not make it through, our plans might all be for nothing.'

'Snake might still make it to the centre without her,' I say, feeling the need to defend the boy.

'I am sure he will, and we will need him as well, but the princess is key.'

I am aware that the greater creatures Eleanora is friends with were up long into the night, plotting and planning. They are no novices in creature politics, but it has been a number of years since they have been forced to play the game at this level.

Although I am not part of their scheme, I understand that there is more at stake than I am privy to or want to be privy to, and I should give Eleanora time to move the pieces around to their new positions and see where that leaves us.

'It appears the minotaur is testing their strength of character before he allows them into the centre of the maze. It may have been his design that separated them. There is still a chance they may win through to face the final challenge together,' she muses.

'It is possible, but not a given,' I tell her. 'They are quite annoyed at each other for some reason. I cannot see them working side by side again any time soon.'

'Perhaps this too is part of their testing,' she says.

Again, I have to disagree. 'I think this is… um… more personal.'

Eleanora's eyes crinkle with laughter. 'Ah, I understand. A lovers' tiff. I am sure they will get over it.'

'I am not so sure. Snake was very determined, and Pris…. She is quite conflicted."

'Love is a fickle thing, Percival, especially young love. They might come together again just when we fear they will always be apart.'

'And what would I know about love?' My tone is tart. My chance at love was scuttled before it was even afloat. No, I will not think on the past. I must focus on the task at hand. 'What do you want me to do, Mistress?'

A chuckle rolls from the Witch of Wimbledon's throat. 'It always comes back to that, doesn't it? You asking how you can be of help, and me being all too demanding. You can always refuse me. I will think none the less of you.'

Now I am embarrassed. I normally only refer to her as Mistress when I am teasing her. Or when I am annoyed that she has asked me to do something I dislike but will do it because I know it needs to be done. I like helping her because she stands up for all creatures like she and her sisters once stood up for me.

'Perhaps you could go and visit with your family one evening while the princess sleeps. Take some real time to figure out what you want for the future.'

I briefly consider her proposal. I would like to see my mother and brother… and Nisha too. However, I am not sure I am quite ready to decide my future. Besides, Eleanora really does need my help to see this through, even though she pretends otherwise.

'I am only suggesting you take the lead on this. I am a mere pawn in your plans,' I backtrack.

'Oh, Percival.' I sense she wants to say something more, but instead she asks, 'Are you all right to continue helping Priscilla—Pris? Being so close to the forest must be breaking your heart, and having to deal with an elf too….'

'I am fine, Eleanora,' I lie. 'I will do this for you and the others.'

'As always, my friend, our plots would not succeed without you.'

'Yes, we lesser creatures are often overlooked and therefore can do what you cannot.' It is difficult to admit that the only reason I can help is because greater creatures underestimate me.

'You had best go get some sleep, Percival. I believe tomorrow will be another long day for you.'

She hugs me briefly before disappearing into the night.

I PUNCH THE pillow into shape and pull the blanket back up before rolling over and trying to go back to sleep. Exhaustion seeps through my bones, as I only dozed off and on all night. I flop over onto my back and stare at the ceiling. It's no use. I'm awake.

I throw off the covers and stretch before padding barefoot across to the window, wanting to check whether or not Percival is an early riser. His tent is firmly closed, and the fire in front of it is nothing but embers, so I am guessing not. My breath fogs the pane as I lean my head on the cool glass.

In the predawn light, I can just make out the trees at the edge of the clearing in front of the cottage. They loom ominously, and my stomach does a little flip. Is Snake out in the woods? Is he all right? We should have stayed together. I wipe the fog away impatiently. Worrying about the past won't help me now.

I pour some water into a bowl and rinse the sleep from my eyes before washing myself as best as I can. After tidying the bed, I take my clean plate from the bench over to the table. I guess it is either apples or stew for breakfast.

When I take the lid off the pot, I am pleasantly surprised to find a porridge laced with dried fruit and nuts bubbling away. I load a good dollop into the bowl and turn to find honey and cream on the table. I do love magic, especially if it can do this. I pour a little of both over the top of my breakfast and hoe in.

The food is gone in moments, and it only takes a little longer before the living area is clean and tidy. Although the sun is not fully up, I head to the window, hoping Percival has appeared. It is still too early for him.

I pace around for a while, too restless to settle. Perhaps now would be a good time to do some exercise. Clearing a space, I start with some breathing exercises followed by a warmup before running through my kata. As always, the process centres me, and when I am finished, I am ready to face anything the World Below throws at me.

After returning the furniture to its original position, I pour myself a glass of water and gulp the liquid down. Then I make one last hopeful journey to the window. Percival has packed up his little camp and is patiently waiting for me. His face is drawn, almost as though he didn't sleep any better than I did last night.

'Good morning,' I smile. 'Have you eaten?'

He nods but says nothing.

'Are you ready to begin?' I ask.

'I awoke some time ago. I am merely waiting for you to finish whatever you were doing so we can begin.'

Someone got up on the wrong side of the bed this morning. 'I needed to clear my head before we start. I'm good to go now.'

I watch as Percival stands up and walks towards me. As he draws closer, I'm surprised to find his face is grey, and there are deep creases around glazed eyes. He has the look of someone ignoring a massive headache.

'Are you all right?' I ask. 'Perhaps you should go back to bed.' There isn't really time for him to take the morning off, but I worry he might collapse if he doesn't.

'I am fine. Nothing some tea won't fix.' The words are forced out through gritted teeth.

He clearly isn't anywhere near all right, but if he doesn't want my sympathy or help, so be it.

'Let us begin. Mind magic is what is tested for next. Magicians with this skill tend to be empathetic, and their magic allows them to heal, including healing the mind. I am pretty certain this is not where your abilities lie, but I could be wrong.'

Hold on, did he just call me unsympathetic? After I just asked him how he was?

'Are you paying attention?'

'Yes,' I answer, although I obviously wasn't.

'When those with physical magic, or mind magic as some call it, make a flame, they are actually forcing themselves and anyone close by to imagine the flame is there,' he explains.

'Like creating an illusion?' I ask.

'Exactly.'

I gnaw on my lip. 'So how do we test whether or not my flame is made this way?'

'First make your flame,' Percival instructs.

It is getting easier to create fire on my palm each time I do it. I hold up my hand and show it to Percival.

'Now, while you are holding the flame, imagine it is now a coin spinning in the air.'

'What? Are you serious?' My flame goes out as I lose concentration. 'How am I supposed to do that?'

Percival sighs, and I feel like the most incompetent creature ever. 'As I understand it, you imagine a coin near the flame. When you have control of it, you push it to where the flame is and make the fire disappear. It should convince you, and me, that the flame is now a coin if you do it quickly enough—if your magic is mind magic, that is.'

I look at him as if he is mad. He sighs again. 'Or I guess you could just try making the flame appear somewhere else.' He holds out his hand. 'See if you can make one on my hand.'

I take a deep breath and go through the process I usually do when my flame appears, only this time I try to put it on Percival's outstretched hand. Nothing.

I try twice more, but I can't see anything. I try once more, and I imagine holding the flame there.

'Can you see anything?' I ask in desperation.

'Oh, you started? I was not sure,' Percival says innocently, and I want to punch him.

'Yes,' I growl.

He shrugs and drops his hand to his side. 'I guess that only leaves us with particle magic.'

'Are you sure?' I ask. 'I mean, from my perspective, this is an odd way to test for magic that deals with the physical being. Come to think of it, all these tests are rather odd.'

'No, I'm not sure,' he snaps. 'It is not like this is something I do every day. I'm a sprite. We do not need to be tested because we all use earth magic.'

'Then how—'

'From watching greater creatures being tested,' he finishes. 'And none of them are as difficult about it as you!'

I ignore his bad temper. It's not my fault his headache is making him grumpy, and it isn't my fault I don't know much about magic. Still, he is trying to help me despite what is going on with him, so I try to keep my tone neutral as I ask, 'Is there something else we can try to test whether or not I use mind magic?'

He closes his eyes, and I wonder if I've pushed him too far. They fly open. 'Yes… perhaps. Eleanora has spoken of seeing colours around living things.'

'What, you mean like an aura?' I scoff.

He frowns. 'You asked, so no need to get snippy with me.'

'Sorry,' I say, and I am.

'I believe if you relax and attempt to absorb everything about a living object, the colour is just there,' he explains.

He isn't joking. I did ask him if there was another way, so I guess I will give it a try—even if it sounds like spiritualist mumbo jumbo.

Percival rubs his forehead. 'Perhaps you can have a go while I take my tea.'

Without waiting for an answer, he moves away and finds a tree stump close by to use as a seat. He reaches into his pocket, and a table appears, followed by steaming a teapot and a cup and saucer.

As he makes himself comfortable and pours some tea, I am dismissed. I may as well do what he said while I wait for him to finish. It's not like there is anything else to do.

I pick an apple from the bowl and drop cross-legged to the floor. Holding up the fruit, I try to take in every detail. When I peer at it more closely, I see that the skin is red, laced with flecks of a darker red. There is a slight bruise near the bottom that is turning a little brown. I smell its sweet, sharp scent before running my fingers over the silky-smooth surface. Nothing. I stare so hard at the apple, my vision blurs and the fruit shimmers. This is not working.

I rise and place the apple back in the bowl and then wander over to the window. Percival's tea things are gone, and he is cleaning his clothes with magic, then 'ironing' out the wrinkles. He pulls out a comb and tidies his hair. He is so fastidious. It makes me smile.

Glancing down at my rumpled outfit, I wonder if Percival will tidy me up when I escape from here. Or, better still, will I be able to do it for myself? Best I find my way out first.

'Ahem, Percy.'

He swings round and I feel the full force of his death stare. 'I am Percival, never Percy.'

'Um… okay…. Anyway, I don't think my magic is anything to do with nature and the physical.'

He raises and eyebrow. 'I am not surprised. You lack empathy.'

'Snippy,' I retort. I want to add, 'I don't,' but I am well aware that it is not one of my strengths.

We glare at each other. Time almost seems to stop as we face off. We can't go on wasting time like this—my deadline is looming. I break eye contact first. 'What now?'

He shrugs. 'Your magic must be particle magic.'

I almost sag to the ground with relief. We have finally moved a step closer to getting me out of this prison. 'Great. Can you teach me how to use it?'

'Hold on, let us not get ahead of ourselves. We should test it to make sure we are right.'

I tense a little, but force a smile. I mean, we tested all the other options, why are we wasting time on this?

Percival sighs. He does that a lot. 'We test to make sure we are right. And we test because that is your first lesson on how to use your magic.'

That is so logical, I can't argue with it, but it slows things down. I clench and unclench my fists, trying to let go of my anger. If I am honest though, I am also trying to calm my nerves.

My mind circles back to my learning to make a flame, which was so difficult. Now that we have found my magic, I am worried I won't be able to use it before I am kicked out of the maze.

Oblivious to my misgivings, Percival carries on talking. 'Creatures with this sort of magic often describe seeing the individual parts that make up an object. Sometimes they can even see them moving.'

A light switches on in my head, 'Ah, like they see the particles that make things, like electrons and neutrons.'

'What?' Percival says, then simply ignores my comment. 'Start with the apple again. This time when you look at the fruit, you want to try and find all the tiny pieces that make it an apple.'

'Honestly, Percival, isn't any of your advice practical?'

Dropping his head into his hands, Percival moans, 'Must you always argue? Just once can you not do what I ask without complaining?'

I glare at him through the glass. 'Perhaps I wouldn't argue so much if you were a better teacher.'

He looks up, catches my eye, and calmly reaches into his pocket and pulls out a book. Opening it to the bookmarked place, he drops his eyes and starts reading.

My temper has got the better of me, and I have overstepped. Although my anger still has a hold of me, I say, 'I'm sorry, Percival. I didn't mean it. I wouldn't have been able to come this far without you.'

He continues reading as if I haven't spoken, although maybe his posture isn't quite as rigid. I wait a moment, hoping he will relent.

'Grrrr.' Of course, he has no idea how infuriating his passive dismissal is. I have to try something else or resign myself to waiting until his mood changes. 'Tell me, do you shrink things to fit in your pocket?' I ask him.

He raises his eyes. 'Don't be ridiculous. I created a portal in my pocket that opens into the library at Eleanora's. Her daughter is home, and she is the one making sure I am fed and watered.'

My eyes go wide, and my mouth drops open. *What?*

'Get out of here! Really? That is so cool. What sort of magic allows you to do that? Will I be able to make a portal?'

He stares unblinkingly at me with his startling green eyes as if he is waiting for something.

The penny slowly drops. 'I know. I must find out what my magic is before I do anything more advanced.'

His eyes return to the words on the page in front of him. I am dismissed again.

Turning my back on the scene outside, I rake my gaze over the room. Percival is not going to help me until I try his stupid idea.

I pull out a chair and face the bowl of apples and pears. I take some deep breaths to relax, then I stare at an apple for forever. Well, at least for a couple of minutes. Nothing happens.

I resist the urge to leap to my feet and tell Percival he is wrong, that this is not my type of magic. I lean back in the chair and stare at the fire. I am so tired, all I want to do is sleep. I clear my mind and allow the flames to send me into a trance.

As I watch the fire flicker and dance in the fireplace, something seems to shift within my vision. I'm able to pick out every tiny particle that makes up each curling tendril of fire. Percival was right, they do not sit still—they move around as if full of energy.

I turn my head towards the bowl. The room swirls about me and my head spins. I narrow my focus down to the bowl of fruit. I can identify all the bits that make up the apples and the pears and the bowl and the table, plus some stray pieces in the air.

'Percival,' I call. 'I can—' My vision returns to normal.

I turn and find the sprite peering in through the window. He is smiling.

'So particle magic *is* your forte. Can you do it again?'

I am grinning, and laughter bubbles up inside me. I resist the urge to clap my hands like an excited child. Instead, I return my gaze to the bowl and try again. I clear my mind and try to relax. Nothing happens. Frustration roils inside, but I press it down. Turning to the fire, I start the process of "seeing" the particles again.

I do this three or four times and then try breaking the fruit into pieces without using the fire. After a number of attempts, I am finally able to do it.

'One more time,' I tell myself. 'I did it,' I shout when I succeed.

'Now, can you make your flame and observe as the particles create the shape?' Percival asks.

I am shaking with excitement, but I do as he bids, and I'm amazed as all the stray pieces of stuff floating around in the air come together over my hand to form a flame. I rise to my feet, knocking over the chair, and punch the air. 'I rock!'

'Yes, indeed,' Percival responds drily.

My stomach rumbles, punctuating the celebration.

'You need to eat,' he tells me.

He's right, I'm hungry and exhausted. I finish off another large serving of porridge from the pot, and as I push the plate away, a portion of apple pie with cream appears.

So the crone is watching me.

I finish the desert. 'I wish I had some coffee,' I muse, wondering if the crone will oblige.

Nothing magically appears, and I chuckle out loud. I can't believe I actually expected coffee to appear. How this world has changed me. Percival disappears from the window, then reappears moments later. A cup of coffee materialises in front of me.

A smile curls the edge of Percival's mouth. 'With Eleanora's daughter's compliments.'

Could this day get any better? I sip the hot brew and relax in my chair. I am going to savour every mouthful of this because I have earned it.

I'm not quite done when Percival's voice shatters my peace. 'Well, if you have quite finished, you still have to find a way out of there.'

'You mean, like, make enough fire to burn the place down?' I ask cheekily.

'No.' The voice comes from nowhere, sounding very much like the crone.

'This is probably her home,' Percival tells me.

I glance around the room. 'If it's her home, then wouldn't there be other rooms and a way in and out?'

'Of course.' He nods. 'She is probably concealing the rest from you.'

'So if I can't burn it down—'

'You have to think of another way of getting out,' Percival finishes for me. 'And preferably one that causes as little damage as possible—you don't want to make an enemy of a crone.'

My slice of happiness has obviously ended. Damnation, must everything in this world be so difficult? I stand and study my prison, hoping for some divine inspiration.

IT'S ALL ABOUT
FAMILY AND FRIENDS

HAVING TOSSED AND turned for quite some time last night, I awake surprisingly refreshed as the rising sun bruises the sky a deep purple. Although I believed myself to be up early, my hosts were earlier still. When I arrive downstairs, the table is already set with a selection of fruit, breads, cheeses, and meats, and the bustle in the kitchen tells me more food is coming.

'Ah, good morning, my young friend. Are you ready to be on your way?' Mender asks, coming through the door, carrying a steaming pot of tea and some mugs.

'Yes, thank you.' I am suddenly awkward. While I dressed and tidied my room, I resolved not to tell Mender I worked out who I am. I find myself undecided again as I see him in the flesh.

Telling them I believe I am their great-grandson is the type of thing you do when you can spend a few days getting to know them better. Not when you're leaving a few minutes later.

'You didn't have to go to all this trouble for me,' I say a tad awkwardly.

'Nonsense. It isn't often guests grace our home nowadays.' He places the pot and mugs on the table.

As he settles himself, my eyes are drawn to the picture on the wall.

'An interesting pair, aren't they?' Keeper says as she enters the room.

'I think…. I am…. The girl in the portrait—I think she's my mother.' The words slip out before my mind is aware I'm saying them.

A hand gently squeezes my shoulder, and I turn to meet Keeper's eyes. 'Well, of course she is, lad. You look so very much like her.'

'And why else would the minotaur send you here to us if not to find your lost family?' Mender added.

Keeper's gentle pressure on my shoulder urges me towards the table. 'Come, eat. Then perhaps you might tell us what brings you to the minotaur's maze and how we might help you finish your quest.'

I take a seat, and Keeper loads my plate with food while Mender pours the tea. Meanwhile, I gnaw my lip, wondering how much to tell them about the pickle I find myself in.

In the end, it all comes tumbling out. Not just Mum being taken to face charges of benefitting illegally from her position in the World Above, but about Pris's and my search for the tokens to admit us to the Seelie Court, and how we were duped into taking on this quest. And I don't stop there. I also tell them about how I am sure I'm falling in love with Pris, and how we can never be together, and even if we could be, I messed everything up.

I clap my hand over my mouth, my cheeks heating. I hadn't meant to say any of that last bit. Keeper and Mender chuckle, and Mender slaps me on the back.

'Ah, the path of young love never runs smooth. I am sure if she is the one for you, you will be able to make it up to her.' Mender smiles as he speaks and laughter lines crinkle around his eyes.

'Aren't you shocked that I… um… like an elf?' I ask, wondering why they decided to focus on this rather than my mother's situation.

'Son, things are a little less strict out here. There are almost as many mixed marriages as not. If you are happy, we are happy for you. I am more interested in spending our time finding out what we can do to help you help our granddaughter,' Mender says.

Keeper places her hand over mine. 'Snake, the heart wants what it wants. What I cannot understand is, why did you decide to go on this quest when you believe your mother would have been cleared?'

'It was because of something one of Bernais's supporters said to me. He told me that even if my mother got out of this, they would make sure she was charged with something even worse. I looked around me and saw that a large number of people in the court felt as he did. I needed to think of another way to rescue her from Bernais's clutches,' I tell them.

My great-grandparents nod their understanding.

I carry on. 'At the time I thought they hated her because she is not a creature of high standing, but after last night—'

'You think it is because she is half elf?' Keeper asks.

'Yes. Now, if I get through this quest, I will be able to request a boon from the Queen, but I'm not sure what to ask for. How will I keep my mother and myself safe from people with such hatred inside them?'

'Perhaps you should simply petition the Queen to keep you both safe,' Mender suggests.

Keeper places her hand over mine. 'You will always be welcome here—you and your mother. You will be far from the political intrigues of the Capitol, and they will likely forget you exist.'

'What about—'

'Your father would be welcome too,' Mender assures me, his eyes full of such love, it brings tears to my eyes.

'You have definitely given me something to think about,' I say. I wonder whether Mum and Dad would consider moving here after my quest is done— just for a while, until everything blows over.

As if sensing my concerns, Mender adds, 'Of course, you would need to discuss it with your parents first.'

'And whatever you decide, you must at the very least come back for a proper visit before you head back to the World Above.' Keeper smiles and releases my hand. 'We would love to spend more time with you, and I am sure everyone here would appreciate some more musical performances.'

There is a companionable silence while we finish our meal. Mender pours us each another cup of tea while Keeper shows me photos of the rest of the family. Through the window, I can see that the sun is well up in the sky, and I am forced to admit I can put my departure off no longer.

'I wish I could stay another night with you both and get to know you better…,' I start.

'We understand. You are on a quest, and you must be heading out, for we are not the end of the journey, just a stop on the way.' Mender's face wrinkles with his smile.

They help me adjust my pack to better carry the lute, and Keeper insists I take some home-cooked pies with me, saying, 'If you meet back up with your girl, these will surely help melt her heart.'

I kiss them both goodbye, promising to come visit properly once this is all over. I step away, then turn back and hug them both again.

'Whatever happens, I am so happy to have met you both.' I choke up as I speak.

Mender wipes a tear from his eye and gently pushes me towards the door.

'The sooner you leave, the sooner you can return,' he says gruffly, trying to hide his emotions.

Keeper follows me out, and they both stand by the doorway, watching as I head away. When I reach the edge of the forest, I turn and see that my great-grandparents are still following me with their gazes, arms around each other. I raise my hand in farewell before continuing on, and waves of love wash through me as I start out on the next part of my journey.

I stride along under the trees, more determined than ever to succeed in this quest. Perhaps I am more confident because I have more family in the World Below, and if I am forced to stay here at the end of this, it will not be such a bad place to be. Or perhaps it is because I have a better sense of who I am now.

This idea turns my thoughts to my mother. Why had she never mentioned her father's family, or who her parents were? Did she think I wouldn't understand, or did she not want me to be tainted by my mixed parentage?

Do I feel tainted? The creatures I know generally don't accept inter-creature relationships. Still, my father's family must know who I am, and probably Eleanora does too. They don't seem bothered by it. And, surprisingly, nor do I. I am still exactly the same person I was yesterday.

Ah! I palm my forehead. Pondering my parentage has given me a different perspective on Pris's behaviour and why she doesn't give in to prejudice. I get it now.

My mother is the polar opposite. She spent her life hiding who she is, even from me. Would things be different now if she had stood up for herself and been counted?

To be honest, I don't know if my mother made the right choice. Or perhaps I'm thinking about this the wrong way. She chose what was right for her at the time, but it does not have to be my choice too. I swear, here and now, I will never be ashamed of who I am, or of any of my family.

One problem down, one to go. I still have no idea what I am going to ask for if we complete our quest. Then again, maybe I should wait and see if we are successful before worrying about that.

I move further into the heart of the woods, the air cooling my skin as I'm cut off from the sun's direct heat. My feet eat up the miles. My mood is so much lighter compared to yesterday, as if a weight has been lifted from my shoulders.

I have so much to tell Pris when we meet up again. I will see her again before this is over, won't I? Suddenly, I am uncertain.

'Hey, minotaur, am I going in the right direction to get back to Pris and Percival?' I laugh as my voice is muffled by the dense vegetation.

Of course, that is not how the maze works. It probably doesn't matter which way I go. The minotaur will place me where I need to be according to his grand plan, and I will only meet with them if he wants me to.

Besides, Pris might not be that happy to see me anyway. She is probably still angry with me for storming off like a child. No doubt there will be fences for me to mend. Then we might have a chance at making up.

My mind wanders, imagining an encounter similar to the one two nights ago in the conference centre when Pris fixed my hair and I leant down and brushed my lips to hers. When she didn't pull away, I pressed a little harder, and she responded, her mouth moving against mine.

Whoa, enough of that. Not that the thought of our reunion ending in a kiss isn't pleasant—it's that it is a little too pleasant. I slow my pace as the trees open up to a slow running brook, and I bend to splash water over my face to cool down.

Starting out again, my thoughts are still filled with images of Pris, her sparkling blue eyes, her flawless bronzed skin. I have to remind myself to keep my eyes on the prize. Only now, my treacherous mind is not sure precisely what the prize is—entering the centre of the maze, or winning Pris back.

Sometime later, I stop and eat a bite of trail bread for lunch before heading off again. The trees are less closely packed together, and the sun creeps through the canopy. I am unsure of where I am going, but I hope I am heading towards Pris… and Percival, of course.

As my mind once again fills with thoughts of Pris and our reunion, I spot a cottage through the trees. The whitewashed one-story dwelling has a thatched roof and is very picturesque in the later afternoon sun. I hope this is the maze providing a place for me to sleep tonight.

As I draw closer to the clearing around the cottage, I spot Percival sitting on a tree stump, head in hand in a pose that screams despondence. My heart races as I scan the surrounding area. Where is Pris? Of their own accord, my feet start running towards Percival.

CURSING AND FOOTSTEPS drift out from the cottage again. I wriggle my bottom, finding a more comfortable position on the tree stump I am using as a seat, and try to concentrate on reading. It is my second book today.

I should not complain; it is quite pleasant sitting here in the shade. When I am in cat form, I do not read, and I am seldom home in the World Below long enough to indulge the habit.

At the end of the chapter, I reluctantly close the book and rest my head

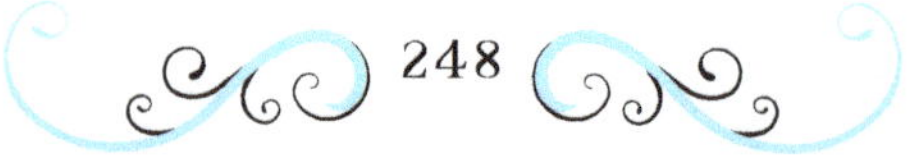

in my hand. The princess has made progress, but she is no closer to finding a way out of her prison than she was this morning. We will be here a while longer, so perhaps I had best set up camp. Standing up, I catch a shadow emerging from the tree line. Now alert, I peer into the distance, trying to discern if this figure poses any threat. My goodness, is that Snake?

My stomach unknots a little, and I allow myself a small smile of relief. At least if the elven princess is expelled because she cannot use her magic, there is someone to carry on the quest.

'Percival,' Snake says when he is almost at the clearing. He seems anxious. 'What are you doing here? And where is Pris?'

'It is good to see you, young man,' I respond. 'Unfortunately, we were caught in a crone trap. Pris is inside the cottage.'

Snake frowns as he takes in my words. I, in turn, am surprised to find the neck of a lute peeking over the gnome's shoulder. I am sure that is new.

Snake scratches the stubble on his chin and asks, 'Why are you out here while she is in there? And where is the door?'

'I am out here rather than in there because this is your quest, not mine. I am waiting for the elf to use her magic to free herself. Once she does, we can be on our way.'

A frown draws the boy's brows together. 'What do you mean, she must use her magic to free herself? She only learnt to make a flame a couple of days ago. It would take months, if not years, of training to be able to make a door.'

I grin up at him. 'She can more than make a flame now—she can turn an apple into a pear.'

His eyes widen, I like to think in surprise, but I concede it might be disbelief he is displaying.

'But… but her magic hasn't been tested. She doesn't even know what type she has. It could be dangerous for her to use her gifts without knowing their nature.'

'Particle,' I inform him, unable to keep the pride from my voice that she and I identified her magic in less than a day.

'What?'

'Her gift is based on particle magic. She can manipulate her flame using traces of the things around her. I am unable to take her any further than that; sprite magic is very different.'

Snake's mouth forms an 'O.' I cannot tell if it is because he did not realise I am a sprite, or because he is impressed we made it so far into the princess's training.

Eventually, he shuts his mouth and slips his pack and the lute off his shoulders, leaning them against a nearby tree. He walks purposefully over to the window and stares inside. I follow him, standing on tiptoes to find out what the princess is up to. She is sitting cross-legged on the floor, making her flame change colour.

'I can hear you talking out there,' she says without missing a beat.

'Pretty flame,' Snake says with a touch of humour in his voice.

Does he not realise this is no joking matter? If she does not get out of here by tomorrow morning, her quest will be over. I open my mouth to tell him this, but I am stopped by the elf's laugh. It is a musical sound and is a big improvement on her ranting.

'Shouldn't you be working out how to get out of here rather than putting on magical displays?' Snake asks.

'I would. Only I can't find a way to use what little magic I know to manipulate the particles, make a door and leave this place. So I am passing time until the witch sends me out of the maze so I can start my quest again.'

'What do you mean, sends you out?' Snake turns and glares at me.

I shrug. 'She was only given a certain amount of time to free herself. If she does not succeed, she will be cast from the maze.'

Snake's glare turns to a growl. 'How can you be so calm about this? Why aren't you using every moment left to try and find a way out of here?'

This is directed at the elf. She does not answer, but her shoulders tense. She slowly turns her head, and her eyes glitter like ice. In spite of the warmth of the early evening sun, I shiver. When her gaze meets Snake's, she begins to speak in a tone meant to cut.

'It's easy for you to turn up out of the blue and criticise. I only learnt the nature of my magic today. Is it too much of a stretch for you to understand that I might be struggling with the next steps?'

In the silence that follows her words, I think I hear her whisper, 'Of all the things to fail at, why did it have to be this?' The words and her tone tell me she is tired and defeated. This does not bode well for her chances of escape.

Beside me, Snake clenches his fists in reaction to her anger. I wait for him to explode, but instead, I watch as he takes a deep breath and forces his fingers to relax one by one. When he finally speaks, it is with compassion.

'Of course it is difficult. Nothing in life worth having comes easily. I know you can do this.'

'How can you know? I haven't shown any natural talent with magic. And I have run out of ideas. Without magic I will be of no use to you on this stupid quest, so it's best I leave.'

I bristle at her self-indulgence. I open my mouth to tell her if that is how she feels, then she should call for Eleanora, but Snake speaks before I can get a word out.

'Using magic is like using any other tool. First you identify what you want to do, then think of ways the tool might be able to help you,' he explains patiently.

I turn and stare long and hard at the young gnome. My expression must have shown my astonishment, as he grins at me.

'I'm not just a pretty face,' he says and taps his head. 'My brain cells are in full working order.'

I am still staring in disbelief. Why did I not think of this simple first step? I mean, I am supposed to be helping the two of them understand this world, and Snake just talked me out of a job.

Pris's flame snaps out, and she shuffles round, half turning towards us. There is curiosity in her eyes, but her voice is still tart. 'What do you think I've been doing? I've spent hours trying to make a portal to get out of here, but I can't even start one.'

'Hmm, perhaps that's because making portals is some really advanced stuff. Think smaller,' Snake encourages.

Pris rises to her feet in one graceful movement, and her eyes dart over the room. She paces around the small area, a sign I now know means she is thinking. Snake is smirking, and I don't think that is helping her mood. She does a circuit of the room before she stops in front of the window and glares at us, hands on hips.

'Okay, smart arse—tell me what I am so obviously missing.'

Snake's grin widens until it is almost splitting his face. 'You need a door.'

MY JAW DROPS. I don't move for a moment. I have been attempting to make a portal for hours. Snake turns up, and five minutes later, he points out the obvious. Frustrating does not cover my response, but I'm also a little annoyed at myself for not thinking of that. I force my hands from my hips and shove down a little of my frustration, 'So, Mr Know-It-All, just how do I make a door?'

Okay, so the comment is a bit snippy, especially as he came up with a great idea to help. What can I say? I'm tired and irritable, and at this point, I want nothing more to do with magic.

In spite of that, I am absurdly pleased to see he is all right. The moment I heard his voice, my heart started racing, and it is still fluttering—I'm just so relieved to see him. Even the smirk on his face doesn't bother me—well, not too much. When that cheeky smirk disappears, my heart sinks.

'Well… I….'

'Can you do it?' I ask, hoping the answer is yes, but sensing from the way his face changes, it will be a no.

Snake gnaws at his lip. 'Well… no. I mean, my talents stem from particle magic too. I open locks by moving the pieces inside to the open position with magic. I can also do small sleight-of-hand tricks, and I track artefacts from the World Below using the trail of magical dust they leave behind.' He runs his hands through his hair, and he looks so damn cute, my heart does a skip.

Then his words sink in, and my shoulders drop. 'Does that mean you can't help?'

'I can't outline the exact steps for you to make a door, but I can tell you that using particle magic is sort of like physics—you need to rearrange the pieces already there to be what you want them to be. Does that help?'

'You make it sound so easy,' I say, trying to keep the panic rising from my gut out of my voice.

'Percival told me you made a pear from an apple….' The hope in Snake's eyes almost breaks my heart. He is so sure I can do this.

'I did, and I wish I knew how I did.' I sigh. 'I was staring at the apple and wishing it was a pear because I ate the last one earlier and I really felt like another, and one appeared. I was so excited, and I tried to replicate the process, but….'

I am too embarrassed to tell him that I hadn't had the chance to enjoy eating the pear because I threw it against the wall in disgust. I relax my stance and try to shake the tension from my limbs. Most things come easy to me, and if they don't, I can work them out by studying and applying that knowledge.

Nothing magical I try works. For me, trying to use the power I can now sense inside me is like trying to grab hold of mercury. It moves and breaks and slithers away, leaving me angry and feeling useless. The fact that time is running out just adds to the pressure.

'You were doing it with the flame when you changed the colour. I'm sure you can change a small object.'

I raise my eyes to meet his, but he isn't laughing at me. He is serious.

'Why not try with the spoon there.' He nods at the bench beside me.

I pick it up and look at it. 'What now?'

'You have to visualise what you want to do with it,' Snake instructs.

'Like, turn it into a table?' I ask, raising an eyebrow.

He laughs. 'I applaud your ambition, but I can see why you're having problems. A spoon does not have enough molecules to do that because it is so much smaller than a table.'

I nod. That is so sensible and so glaringly obvious. I bite back a snarky comment, realising that I am annoyed at myself and shouldn't take it out on Snake.

Using my magic is still tied up with my parents not telling me who I am and feeling inadequate because I am just learning how to use my talents. Now the ever-present fear of failure is almost overwhelming. I take a breath, trying to rein my emotions in because they are clearly fogging my brain.

'So, maybe I should make a knife?' I suggest, and he nods.

I stare at the spoon until the moving pieces that make it up are visible. 'Okay, how would you change this into a knife?' I ask.

'The way I work is, I have a vision, then add intent and will—I guess that is the using the magic part. Have a picture in your mind, then see the particles in the shape of the new object. Once you have done that, tell them where you want them to go, but you need to do it forcefully because they will want to remain where they are.'

I nod, indicating I understand the concept. Turning around, I make sure my back is towards the window. I want to do this without an audience.

Closing my eyes, I envision a wooden knife the same length and colour as the spoon in my hand. When I have a clear picture, I open them and stare almost trancelike at the spoon until the surface appears to be moving. Focusing my mind, I will the molecules to move into the shape I want them to be in. The edges of the spoon start to move, wavering and softening. I am almost there. I mentally congratulate myself, and they spring back into place.

'Did it work?' Percival's rich tones break my concentration. I turn to find him and Snake trying to look over my shoulder.

I move backwards to block the window so they can't watch me work. I try again and again, pushing frustration and fear down between each attempt.

'I will do this,' I tell myself between gritted teeth.

Fifth time is a charm. Okay. Not a charm exactly, but it turns out sort of knife-shaped. I hold it up for inspection, expecting ridicule, and am surprised at the level of praise.

'That's great—better than I can do,' Snake says.

I grin, almost giddy with pride and relief, pleased I have achieved something today, however small.

'Good. Now it is time to make a door.' Percival's words evaporate my newfound happiness, and my stomach returns to its churning state.

Snake glares at the smaller creature. 'She should work her way up to something that big.'

'No,' I interrupt. 'I hear what you are saying, but Percival is right. I've spent one night here already, and sometime tomorrow morning, I'll be expelled if I am still inside this cottage. I don't want to leave this to the last minute.' I pull together what little confidence I have left and say, 'It's time to go big or go home.'

Snake's head tilts to the side and he studies me with intense green eyes. Finally, he sends me a soft smile. 'I know you can do this, Pris.'

The warmth in his eyes and the way he says my name draws me towards him like a magnet. His words calm me, and his confidence bolsters my spirits.

Breaking the spell, I shoo him and Percival away from the window. 'Promise me you won't look,' I tell them.

Percival tells me he won't, but Snake folds his arms across his chest. 'I can't promise that. What if you need our help?'

'That is kind of the point, I think.' Snake stares blankly at me and I feel the need to explain. 'This is some sort of test of the maze, and I believe I must pass it myself.'

What I don't say is that while I was playing with my flame before, I wondered if the minotaur somehow sensed that I have not fully accepted who I am in the World Below. This test is forcing me to face myself by making me learn to use magic. Snake must read something in my face, because his expression softens, and he offers me a sad smile.

'Funny sort of test,' Snake mutters.

You don't know the half of it, I think.

'But it is a test nonetheless,' I tell him. 'You're here, so I assume you passed your one alone. Please, Snake, let me do the same.'

Our eyes lock, and I can sense the struggle going on inside him.

'If you are thrown out—'

'If I don't succeed today, there will be time to try again in the morning,' I assure him.

He holds his hands out towards me. 'There are things I learnt… things I need to tell you… just in case….'

'You can tell me when I get out,' I say with more confidence than I'm feeling.

As if he senses my fear, he takes a step away from Percival towards me. When he is next to the window, his lips tug into an almost smile. 'Then I guess the only important thing to say now is, I'm sorry. I was an ass. I promise it won't happen again.'

I can't help the grin that splits my face. 'Yes, you were,' I tell him, then add, 'and you shouldn't make promises you can't keep.' His eyes twinkle, and I say, 'I was kind of an ass too, not as big a one as you, but still… it wasn't all on you.'

Our eyes lock, and I want nothing more than to walk through the wall and have Snake hold me and his arms. Then I want to find out what prompted his apology, but both will have to wait. Getting out of here is my only priority.

'Now, away with you.' I shoo him with my hands. 'If you ask nicely, Percival might organise you some tea or coffee from somewhere. I have work to do.'

He doesn't leave immediately, and if I'm honest, I enjoy his being there—albeit with a wall between us. Finally, he mouths, 'Good luck,' and walks over to Percival's rock, where the sprite is placing a pot of tea on a table. I watch as Snake sits beside him and accepts some of the steaming liquid.

Certain they will stay away, at least for a little while, I sit on the floor and face the wall beside the window, the obvious place for a door to be. I take a couple of deep breaths to calm my nerves before staring at the wall until the molecules move. With my will, I push them apart as if making a hole. When it is dinner-plate-sized, I can make out Snake and Percival chatting. I struggle to hold it for more than a moment, but the molecules press back in, closing the gap. I try again, but the same thing happens.

Okay, that won't work. The molecules clearly need to go somewhere. I try pushing the wall up far enough for me to slip under. It crashes back down with a *thunk*.

Of course—the wall has no support if I do that.

I attempt to make the wall into a wooden door, but nothing happens at all. I wonder if it is possible to turn something made of wattle and daub into wood. If it is, I conclude, it is probably more advanced than my basic skills can manage.

I lie back on the floor and stare at the ceiling. I am beyond exhausted—I'm completely drained. My stomach grumbles. Dragging myself to my feet, I head to the fire. I fill a bowl with stew, then I shovel a couple of spoonfuls into my mouth, and my body almost groans in pleasure. As I eat, I continue to stare at the wall.

So, I'm not strong enough to make the wall into a door. I can't make a hole large enough to get through because there is nowhere for the spare bits to go. Pushing the wall up makes the molecules denser and doesn't work because you can't defy the laws of gravity…. Perhaps Snake is right—this is too big a project for me.

No, think out of the box, Pris.

I glance down at the hard wooden table. Maybe I could turn the table into a door and move the wall particles around it. Just the thought of the mammoth effort it would take to achieve all that exhausts me.

I need to think small. Then it hits me—something small that can go up…. I place the half-empty bowl on the table and stare at the window. In my mind, I form a clear picture of how it would look if it were a sash window. Not much would need to change. I start rearranging the particles, pulling in a few extra ones to make two frames.

The window shimmers, then returns to its former shape. The steps are clear in my mind now: split the vertical frame in two between the four panes, create a horizontal break in the middle and push the top piece out a little, add some stray particles from the grooves for the sash to move up within in, and some stray particles to strengthen the two pieces. I am able to form the new window more quickly, pressing my will on the particles, forcing them to stay in place. Slowly, I let go. They hold their form, not wavering or changing from their new shape, and I breathe again.

My legs are like jelly, but there is no time to lose. I rush to the window. It is stiff and not particularly well-made, but I manage to force it open. Snake and Percival are still staring at the wall, waiting for a door, but they turn at the squeaking sound of the sash moving up, eyes wide.

I climb up and launch my body through the open window. I would have fallen to the ground, but Snake is there to catch me. I don't quite fall at his feet when he lets me go, but it's close.

'You did it! Not quite the way I expected, but well done, you!' Snake's face is warm with pride, and I take a moment to bask in my glory.

'Yes… um… well done,' Percival adds dryly.

I can't help myself. 'Go on, Percival—you didn't believe I could do it, did you?'

Colour rises from Percival's collar, and he glances at the ground before raising his eyes to meet my gaze. 'I had hoped, but no, I did not think this was possible. However, I find myself pleased you proved me wrong.'

My goodness, this is almost better than Snake's praise—almost.

I kind of expect the crone to appear and congratulate me, but she is nowhere to be seen. I am somewhat disappointed, but not enough to call her to me.

My purple pack appears at my feet, telling me my jailer is aware I am no longer inside. The cottage shimmers and expands, returning itself to its normal state. I guess that is all I will get from her.

By the time I hoist my possessions over my shoulder, Percival has cleared away his table and tea things. Snake has hauled his pack over his shoulder and is waiting for me.

'Let's get away from here,' I suggest.

The others do not need to be told twice. Although I am tired, I am floating on air as my fellow travellers continue to marvel at how I escaped from my prison using both my brains and my magic.

MENDING FENCES

FALLING INTO STEP beside Pris, I resist the urge to offer to take her pack. In spite of the fact that she can hardly walk in a straight line, she would not thank me for even hinting she can't carry it herself.

Her face is grey with exhaustion, which is only emphasised by the mass of white hair curling around her face. She turns to me, and her violet eyes are ringed with dark shadows. It is clear her first test in the maze was more physically and mentally demanding than mine.

She moves a little closer to me. 'I didn't get a chance to actually tell you I'm sorry too.' Her voice is pitched low so Percival, who is a few steps in front of us, can't hear.

'You have nothing to be sorry for,' I assure her. 'I was a selfish prat. I didn't even try to understand what you were telling me. When I thought things through later, I realised it hurt you when I put other people's opinions of us before your feelings. And, if I'm being completely honest, I never tried to understand your reasons for never accepting discrimination.'

I reach out to take her hand, but she pulls away so my fingers only brush against hers. My heart stutters in my chest. I am too late. I pushed her away with my stupidity, and it's too far for her to come back.

She continues to walk beside me though, so perhaps all hope is not lost. After a few paces, she speaks again. 'I always believed we needed to work together to successfully navigate the maze. As soon as you left, I knew it was a bad decision. I tried to follow you, but the maze wouldn't let me.'

I don't know what to say to that. I deserted her, and still she tried to follow me. I am such an ass.

She laughs, which surprises me. 'I was so angry at you for not being prepared to fight for us, and I think I nearly drove Percival crazy with my ranting.'

My lips curve in a smile as I imagine the scene.

'Buuut… I had time to think last night, and two things occurred to me. The first was that maybe we both had some things we needed to face, and maybe the maze would always have separated us.'

I consider that for a moment. 'You may be right. What was the other thing?'

She reaches out and takes my hand. 'I have had to deal with being treated as if I'm different my whole life, and I'm used to it. I should have given you more time to come to terms with people treating you differently because you're with me.'

A little flame of hope flickers in my heart, but I am almost too scared to fan it. 'Does that mean you forgive me?' I ask, sending a sideways glance her way to assess the impact of my words.

She drops my hand. The corners of her mouth move to form a smile, but it doesn't quite get there.

'I am no longer angry at you,' she concedes. 'But if you ever run off like that again….'

'I won't. I promise.' There *is* hope. I suppress the stupid grin that threatens to plaster itself over my face. At least we're back to the stage of playful banter, even if there is a touch of acid in her comment.

'Did it take you long to find us once you realised what a prat you had been?' Pris asks.

'Not really. When I set out after breakfast—well, it was almost lunchtime I guess—I had some things to think over. I walked the rest of the morning and into the afternoon, going over what I now realise was my first trial. I had a bit to deal with. Then, I was thinking about how much I miss you.' Heat rises to my face as I remember exactly what I was thinking, and I hope Pris doesn't choose this moment to turn around.

I clear my throat. 'It was almost as if thinking about you brought me to where you were. I believe the maze is able to do things like that.'

'And you arrived just in time to rescue me,' she laughs.

'I didn't rescue you, I simply gave you some advice. You did the rest. I mean really, overachieve much? Even I can't change anything larger than a piece of fruit, and you changed a whole window.'

She stops and studies me. 'Is that true, or are you trying to make me feel better?'

'True story,' I tell her. 'I change mostly small things, imitating sleight-of-hand stuff.'

Her gaze still pins me in place. 'Have you ever tried anything bigger?'

'No, I mean we gnomes don't do higher magic. Besides, in the World Above, you don't want to stand out, so you only do small magic.'

'If you have no interest in higher magic, why are you going to study physics at uni, and why were you reading that book on magic and physics when we were on the train?'

'I like it,' I offer somewhat sheepishly.

Sometimes I hate that she is so smart. Of course I'm interested in higher magic. What gnome doesn't want their magic released and to be raised to elven status again? If only we could find a way to do that ourselves without waiting until the Creature Court deems a family has served their debt for a centuries-old rebellion.

Besides, I believe there is a different sort of magic in the World Above, or there once was, and I would like to be the one who rediscovers it.

Pris smirks, then carries on walking.

'What?' I ask as I catch her up.

'You really shouldn't lie. You're no good at it.'

Busted! We walk in silence for a while with Percival still a few steps ahead of us. This is more pleasant than travelling alone.

'Snake?' Pris's voice interrupts my musings.

'Mmm.'

'What was your first test?'

'Sorry?' I was so lost in the moment, her words don't actually register.

'You haven't said anything about what you did while we were apart. And there must be a story behind how you got that lute.'

'Yes.' Percival half turns as he speaks. 'Where did you get that lute from? It is a fine specimen—made by a master craftsman, I should think.'

I was so busy processing, I hadn't thought about what to tell Pris, let alone Percival, about the visit with my great-grandparents. I need some more time to think things through before I share.

'Let's find somewhere to camp for tonight, and I will tell you everything,' I say, hoping they don't realise I'm putting them off.

They agree, and I relax a little, but just for a moment. How do you break it to people that you are a creature of mixed race when you only just found out yourself?

As the sun begins to sink below the tree line, there is a definite chill in the air. I am considering getting some warmer clothing from my pack when we find a clearing not far from a stream.

We set up camp, digging a firepit and lining it with stones before starting up a roaring blaze. I gather enough firewood to see us through the cool night, almost tripping over a fallen log in the process. Dumping the wood, I return for the log, thinking it might be useful as a seat. Meanwhile, Pris sorts through her pack, mumbling about finding some trail bread, when I stop her.

'My hosts gave me some pies for our meal tonight.' I pull them from my pack.

Pris's brows draw together. 'You had hosts who cooked for you?'

'Most thoughtful of them,' Percival says before I can answer her. 'Here, let me.'

He takes the package and mutters something under his breath. He hands the now warm pies back to me, and I share them out.

Pris continues to study me curiously as she greedily bites into a pie. 'Mmm, I think I am in love with your hosts.' She wipes some crumbs from around her mouth. 'This is the best meat pie ever, and I am not just saying that because I'm starving.'

She takes another huge bite and closes her eyes. I laugh as a look of bliss crosses her face. In the meantime, Percival has come through with a pot of tea and mugs. We place our sleeping bags around the fire and settle down to enjoy a cuppa. To be more precise, Pris and I settle down. Percival stands in front of the fire, staring into the flames, shuffling from one foot to another, his tea forgotten.

I raise my eyebrows to Pris, and she shrugs. 'Something about being in the forest bothers him,' she whispers. 'He won't talk about it.'

'Perci—'

'If you will excuse me, I have an errand.'

Before we can say anything, the sprite disappears.

'I wonder what that is about?' I ask.

Pris is frowning at the space where Percival had been seconds before. 'I've no idea, but I hope that where he is going, someone can help him with whatever is giving him the headache that is making him cranky.'

She leans back against the fallen log we dragged over earlier and sips on her tea. 'So,' she starts, 'are you going to tell me about your quest?'

I take a deep breath, wondering if there is any way I can put it off a little longer. She is so beautiful in the firelight, and all I want is to spend an evening with her without all this stuff coming between us.

As if she can sense my reluctance, she turns, and her eyes bore into mine. 'Come on, Snake. Spill.'

I sigh. Nope, no way to put it off at all. I shuffle until I am close beside

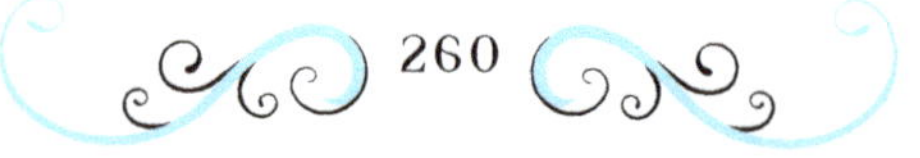

her, and then I lean back. She hands me my tea, then leans her head against my arm. I am stupidly happy she is so close, and for a moment I want to just enjoy the moment.

She nudges me. 'Your quest?'

Okay, so that moment has gone. I wish I had something stronger in my mug, then I wonder if I can use magic to make that happen. I am procrastinating again. I let out another sigh, and then I begin.

'Well… you know how my mum was adopted by my dad's family?'

I feel her head move against me, and I assume she is nodding.

'I always assumed the fact that she was not born into the Fieth clan, that she must have come from some sort of shady background, was at the root of why she felt she wasn't good enough for my father, and why we stayed in the World Above.'

Pris already knows this, but she listens patiently, as if she understands my need to lead in to what is coming. I take another sip of tea, gathering my thoughts. Then I tell her about my great-grandparents, and how I found out who my grandfather and grandmother were. When I am finished, I'm almost too scared to look at her.

'Ah, so the lute is from your great-grandfather. Ooh, and your great-grandmother made the pies. Fantastic, we can visit her after this and eat our fill of them.'

I freeze. Does she really not understand what I said? I wait for a moment to make sure before saying, 'My grandfather was a gnome and my grandmother an elf.' I say the words slowly so there can be no mistake. 'My mother and I are of mixed race.'

She leans forward and captures my eyes with hers, making sure I can see into the depth of her soul. 'I heard you the first time. I only care *who* you are, not *what* you are.'

'But—'

She leans in until all I can see is her eyes. Then closer still, and her lips press to mine, and all my objections about what people think about us being together fly out of my head. I pull her closer, and my body instantly responds to her soft form. I groan and force myself to pull away.

A frown draws her dark brows together, and her blue eyes turn stormy grey. 'Tell me you aren't going to say we shouldn't do this because of what people will think.'

I shake my head ruefully. 'I'm not going to say that, but I still don't think this is a good idea. We are on a quest, and you are….' My body stirs again, responding to the smell of her hair and the warmth of her body so close to mine. I take a deep breath in an attempt to drown the parts of me protesting at what I am about to say. '… more than distracting. I don't want to be caught out with my pants down, so to speak.'

She blushes and lowers her eyes before leaning forward and placing a gentle kiss on my lips. My resolve wavers just as she pulls back and sits beside me, leaning her head on my shoulder again.

'You're right, of course, but just so long as you promise not to talk any more nonsense about races mixing and whether or not other people are happy with us being… um… friends.'

It takes a little while for my heart to stop pounding and for my body to settle enough to answer sensibly. 'I swear,' I tell her.

We sit together for a while, finishing our tea and staring into the flames. As the temperature drops, I put some more wood on the fire, and we snuggle into sleeping bags. I pull her closer, thinking two layers of bedding plus clothing makes us safe. It doesn't, and I lie very still, waiting for the deep breathing that tells me she is asleep before I am able to relax.

I watch the firelight flicker over her face until my eyelids begin to droop. A branch cracks behind me, and I am suddenly wide awake and alert. We are in a forest on a quest, for goodness sake. Why didn't we think to stand guard?

I sit bolt upright and turn my head to search for the source of the sound, only to find myself face to face with a panther.

I STAND OUTSIDE the entrance to my home, waiting patiently, unable to enter. I do not have to wait long. As the spiritual advisor in waiting, my brother Emrys is uniquely attuned to the nuances of the Wyld Woods.

'What took you so long, brother?' he asks, holding out his hands and bidding me to enter. He always insists on greeting me when I visit.

I step into the glade, and a sense of wellbeing falls over me as the trees' song stops for the first time since I entered the woods.

'I am part of a quest, brother. My time has not exactly been my own,' I explain.

'So the trees have told us.'

'I am—'

'Babysitting some young creatures. Yet you left them to come and visit?'

If sprites had eyebrows, Emrys's would have been raised questioningly.

'I planned to visit once my duties were fulfilled, but… the trees have been calling to me. I am afraid if I do not get some relief, I will not be of any use to my young charges.'

Emrys is the only creature I can be this open with. Perhaps it is because he is my brother, or maybe it is because of his ability to connect with me on a spiritual level. Not even Eleanora is privy to the true impact that no longer fully being a sprite has on me.

'I will guard your charges while you meet with Mother. She awaits you. Will you spend some time with Nisha?'

'I… I….'

My brother hugs me, fully aware of how my need to spend time with Nisha warred with my guilt at not being able to fully be with her and tore me apart.

'Until the next time,' Emrys says as he releases me and disappears back into the forest.

I stare at the tree guarding my home, remembering the night Emrys led me through—the night I left for the Capitol. That fateful night when I became less than I was, and I realised that Nisha and I could no longer truly be as one as our bond intended. When I knew staying here would bring danger to all I loved and cared for, and I made a decision to break my newly formed bond.

I offered my decision to Nisha, knowing she would be free to mate with another sprite, but would never be able to bond again. At least she would not have to be alone. My lips twisted into a wry smile as I remember the response of my new mate.

At that moment, I learned that Nisha had a mind of her own and would not be moved once she had made it up. I could not break the bond without her, and she had decided she was not interested in such a move. She would wait until I was whole again, however long it took.

I take a deep breath and head towards the centre of the glade where the elders commune. My home is silent as I avoid the family groupings of trees nurturing sleeping sprites. Some move restlessly as I pass, on some level aware that a creature who did not quite belong was in their midst.

Tears form in my eyes as I try to harden my heart against the pain my visit inflicts on it. This is why I return so infrequently. It hurts less to stay away than to be here.

I take a step into the elder circle, and immediately step back into the shadows. My mother is not alone. My uncle, Nathanial, sits beside her amongst the roots of the Truth Tree, chatting animatedly.

'Do not hide from us, Percival.' My mother's voice rings in the thin night air. 'Emrys sensed that there is much you have to tell me, and I think it better another elder is here to listen and provide council.'

Steeling myself, I enter the moonlit clearing, then force myself to move closer, dropping to the ground to sit cross-legged, just out of the reach of the tree roots.

'Greetings, Mother, Uncle. I bring you news from the Capitol.' *And you are not going to like it,* my internal voice adds.

When I have finished my update, the clearing falls into silence. From experience I know that my mother and uncle are discussing the news, using the Truth Tree to speak mind-to-mind, and to give them clarity of vision.

'Thank you for your report, Percival. You have given the elders much to discuss,' Nathanial finally says. 'But now, I suspect you want to spend some time with your family.'

'I have to—'

'Surely you would not leave without at least saying hello,' a voice says from behind me.

I rise to my feet in a swift movement and turn, my heart thudding and a new song running through my body. My bond mate, the other half of my heart, stands less than a step away, and it is all I can do to stop myself launching myself at her.

'Nisha, I….'

'I know, my love.' She holds out her hand and leads me from the elders' clearing. 'You must leave soon, so let's make the most of what little time we have.'

As I follow her, my mother's voice rings out, 'Come and see me before you leave. I have a tonic that will help you with the tree song as you complete your quest.'

Did she say complete *my* quest? I turn to say I have not decided whether or not to become a part of this folly, but Nisha tugs on my arm, and I forget why it was important to tell my mother anything at all.

SNAKE MOVES RESTLESSLY beside me, and cold air creeps inside my sleeping bag. I snuggle down, trying to warm up, then roll over onto my other side. As I start to drift off, my face is suddenly covered by something soft and filmy.

I am instantly awake and fighting to move the offending object away so I can breathe. I gasp in fresh air into my lungs and turn to abuse Snake for almost suffocating me with his sleeping bag, only to find myself face to face with a panther. It snarls and bares its teeth, giving the distinct impression it isn't happy.

Well, I'm not in such a good mood either. I'm never great when woken in the middle of the night. I glare at the panther, and it snarls again. My heart is pounding in my ears, and a sliver of fear runs down my spine. I reach out, searching for Snake. When my fingers find his, I lace them together. I do not have to face this threat alone.

'How may we help you?' Snake's voice rings clear in the night air.

I frown. Why is he talking to an animal? Wait, do animals speak in the World Below? Then I notice a slight shimmer around the edges of the beast. With my free hand, I rub my eyes, then really focus on the predator. The panther is made up of hundreds of sprites, like the one we encountered on Bodmin Moor, only the ones forming this animal appear to be vibrating with anger, and I can make out multiple sets of bared teeth. My grip on Snake's fingers tightens.

'You speak of help when you come here unbidden, threatening our home with fire.' The voice resonates through my body, raising my anxiety levels.

I glance behind me at the firepit, which has died down to a rich orange-red glow. It isn't a threat to anyone.

'We were just trying to stay warm.' Snake's tone is calm and soothing.

'You endanger us,' the sprite-panther insists. 'We demand you pay a tithe to our people for the damage you caused, then leave the area immediately.'

I bristle at the request. This is blatant extortion. I rise to my feet, I would like to say elegantly, but it actually takes me a couple of attempts to extricate myself from my sleeping bag. Stumbling, I'm forced to use Snake's shoulder to push myself upright.

'We were careful. We built a firepit and lined it with stones, and we made sure the fire stayed within the pit, well away from any trees,' I point out from my superior height.

The panther bares its teeth again. 'You did not ask permission to come here, nor did you ask leave to make a fire.' Although the voice is less menacing, it is clear the sprite-panther is not going to let us off the hook.

Snake joins me in front of the fire as I move into ready position. If the panther wants a fight, I'm game. Snake, ever the diplomat, has other ideas.

'We apologise most sincerely for not asking your permission,' he says, moving slightly in front of me.

'Even though we didn't know we needed to,' I add under my breath, earning a frown from Snake, who clearly does not want to fight with these creatures.

'Sprites have excellent hearing,' he tells me before turning back to the panther. 'We arrived with our friend Percival, and we followed his instructions, taking care to see our fire was well away from trees and would not harm anyone. He did not tell us we required permission to camp here.'

The glade falls into silence as we wait for a response. And of course, at that exact moment, there is a crash, and sparks flare behind us as wood shifts in the firepit. Fortunately, no embers spill on the ground, otherwise who knows what might have happened next.

The panther moves imperceptibly, its muscles bunching as if it is getting ready to spring into action. The clearing vibrates with tension, but ever so slowly, the beast relaxes.

'If you are friends with Percival, where is he?'

'He left us not long after we arrived here. We expect him back any time,' Snake assures them.

The sound of whispering fills the air as the panther figure shimmers. The whispering becomes more frantic, and I tense. Are the sprites arguing over what to do about us? It's kind of disturbing to watch.

Finally, the panther's head rises, and its yellow eyes sparkle in the firelight. 'If you truly are friends of Percival, we will forgive your trespass—this time, but there is a cost.'

'Of course there is,' I mutter, but Snake sidesteps to place himself directly between me and the sprites, I guess to ensure I don't do anything stupid.

I'm tired and annoyed, and I'm convinced the opportunistic sprites are taking advantage of us and our lack of knowledge on creature etiquette. Part of me is also angry at Snake for giving in to them so easily, until he speaks, and I realise he doesn't trust them either.

'What do you mean by price?' he asks warily. 'We do not possess any gold. In fact, we have very little more than what you see here.'

The panther sneers. 'We do not want your gold or your possessions, gnome.'

'We will not tithe to you or offer our bodies for you to share—not even for a short time,' Snake insists, and I shudder as I remember the feeling of a sprite taking residence in my body as I walked on Bodmin Moor.

'We do not ask that either.' There was more whispering. 'I repeat, we do not ask that of you,' the panther says more firmly this time.

'In that case, how can we possibly repay your generous gift of letting us stay the night on your land?'

Do my ears deceive me, or is there a tinge of sarcasm in Snake's words?

The panther stares pointedly at Snake's lute.

'Ah,' Snake says, and his shoulders relax. As he half turns to me, I see laughter dancing in his green eyes. He raises a questioning eyebrow, and I shrug—a little music couldn't hurt.

He bends down and picks up the instrument before sitting on the log.

Still weary, I move our sleeping bags out of the way while he tunes the lute, then sink down beside him.

As the first notes ring out clear and true, the panther dissolves, and the trees are decorated with hundreds of winged sprites. My lips curl into a smile as the sparkling beings light up the clearing. *Now this is truly magical.* I lean my head lightly on Snake's shoulder for a moment, and he drops his head to mine as we enjoy the moment until the sprites have made themselves comfortable on branches and leaves—anywhere, in fact, they can plant their bottoms, and the warm glow of the fire is the only light around.

I slip off the log and use it as a backrest as Snake starts picking out a tune. He shifts slightly so he is half facing me, and his eyes capture mine as he starts to sing "More Than Words", and I know the Extreme song is all for me. I try not to swoon as he moves seamlessly into Tracy Chapman's "Baby Can I Hold You", but it's difficult, as his voice is rich as chocolate and is melting my insides in ways that should not happen in public.

As the last words of the song float into the night, the air in the clearing changes as the sprites twitter. I tear my eyes away from Snake and half turn to find Percival standing by the dying fire with two creatures about his size and two beings we have not come across before.

They have two arms and two legs, and a head with two almost black, liquid almond-shaped eyes in rather rounded faces. Although they are humanoid, they are not human. Their skin is the colour of trees once the bark has stripped. In fact, they resemble trees as much as they do humans.

Tree Sprites, I murmur, a smile forming on my lips.

Our audience reforms into a panther and confront the newcomers.

Here we go again, I think.

'What's happening here?' Percival demands. 'Emrys fetched me, saying the wood sprites were about to attack my friends. How is it these visitors, my guests, are not welcome in the Wyld Woods?'

I hear whispers about a spiritual leader as the panther drops its head and looks so much like a dog who has been told off that I snort back a laugh, earning a glare from Percival. No, Percival can't be their spiritual leader—one of the sprites with him must be. A rumbling voice pulls me from my musings.

'We saw the lute and just wanted some music,' the panther mumbled. 'The gnome was never in any danger, and besides, he had a warrior to protect him. We didn't think it would hurt if we encouraged the gnome to play for us.'

Percival shakes his head. 'That is not the way of our people. You embarrass us all with your thoughtless behaviour. Be gone.' He flings his hand out as if to shoo them away. 'Go ply your mischief elsewhere.'

'What the?' The words escape my lips as the panther slinks into the shadows at Percival's command.

I study Percival with new eyes as he watches the creatures leave. Who is the sprite who has been helping us? He has got to be more than Eleanora's lackey to be able to command others of his kind.

I turn to Snake and find him also contemplating Percival and the group he is with.

'Can you feel their power?' he asks, wonder lifting his tone.

I close my eyes, and to my amazement, I can.

AS THE WOOD sprites slip into the shadows, I attempt to calm my anger. I had so little time to spend with my family as it was, and they robbed me of a great portion of it.

A hand gently rests on my shoulder, and I turn my head slightly to stare into Nisha's liquid black eyes, so beautiful in her sprite-form face.

'Do not let your anger overtake the joy of our reunion. Whatever time we had together would always be too short,' she tells me. 'Be happy and rejoice in the moments we had.'

As always, her ability to enjoy life no matter what it throws at her shames me. I close my eyes and allow her touch to flow through me, just for a moment. The mate bond urges me to embrace her as I force myself to step away.

I take another step and turn to face her. When I open my mouth to speak, she leans forward and places a finger over my lips, stopping my words before they can form.

'You will ask it again, and I will answer the same way, so let us save ourselves time and heartache. I am content as I am. We will be together again the next time you visit.'

She steps back and disappears into the tree behind her. My body jerks as if an essential piece has been wrenched from inside me, as indeed it has. Before I can react and follow her, Emrys drops an arm over my shoulder. 'We will take care of her, my brother, as we take care of all our family, until you are able to return fully to us.'

'How can you—?'

'Still believe this curse will be broken? I have to believe. To do otherwise would be to allow anger and disappointment into my life, and I refuse to do that.' He opens his arms and says, 'Come, let us say farewell.'

THE MINOTAUR'S MAZE

I move into his hug. For a moment I consider returning with him, at least for the rest of the night, but Nisha is right. No amount of time with my family is ever enough. Emrys follows Nisha, and I am left with the two elders: my mother, who did not have time to change into human form, and Nathaniel.

'It must be goodbye again, for now.' Nathanial clasps my hand in his. 'Thank you for bringing us the news of what is happening in the Capitol. Visit us again soon.'

My mother clasps my other hand and slips something into it, closing my fingers around the cool glass. 'This should help with the forest song, at least for a few days.' She touches her forehead to mine. 'Be well, my son. I will pray for your return.'

There is nothing else to say that has not already been said. What Nisha left of my heart when she departed breaks as my uncle Nathanial and my mother disappear.

I take a moment to compose myself before returning to the fire and facing the gnome and elf I must accompany to the centre of the maze. Their eyes question me, but the night's events are still too raw to be discussed with strangers.

'Why don't the two of you get some sleep? I will stand guard to make sure we are not disturbed by any other woodland creatures,' I tell them as I sit on a stone across the firepit.

The princess starts to say something, but Snake touches her arm and, when he has her attention, shakes his head. She glances back at me. I let out a breath of relief when she curbs her natural instincts and nods before following Snake back to where their sleeping bags are in disarray.

'Goodnight, Percival,' she says as she wriggles into her bed.

'Wake us if you need anything,' Snake adds.

'Of course.' It is difficult to even force those two words from my lips as I struggle with the whirl of emotions threatening to overwhelm me.

I place a couple of logs on the fire, barely holding myself together as I watch and wait for my two charges to fall sleep.

My hands clasp and unclasp as I try to manage my anger towards them. They are not my family, yet it is not their fault that I am with them and not the creatures I love. Yet to be with my family and my heart mate is always a painful reminder of all I lost through my own arrogance all those years ago. If it is anyone's fault, it is my own. It will do no one any good to dwell on the past though. What I must focus on is what I am going to do now.

Being so close to the forest, my forest, these last few days has been difficult—more than difficult. Today, watching the gnome and his elf reunite brought on a longing so strong, I could not bear it. I miss my bond mate. Although I told myself I was going to the glade to ask my mother for help, in reality I could no longer resist the urge to be with Nisha.

I have lost count of the times I asked Nisha if she had changed her mind about breaking our bond after that first night. When Eleanora took up the post of the Witch of Wimbledon in the World Above and asked me to go with her, I really thought she would accept. Nisha is always unshakable. Tonight was the first time my visit had not ended with the question, and if I am honest, that was not totally because our visit was cut short.

I had not returned to the Wyld Woods for some one hundred years when I went home tonight. As a cat in the World Above, my tortured soul was laid to rest, replaced with the constant focus on food, warmth, and hygiene. I was content for the first time in years. That contentment led me to ensure my visits to the World Below were not long enough to visit my family, and I fell into apathy.

Being in the woods these last few days, having the trees call me, but knowing I could no longer enter their embrace, has woken my soul. For the first time in years, I want to be who I was meant to be before I was cursed, ironically, by the father of the very man who sent us on this journey.

The only way left for me to reverse the curse is if the Queen agrees I have been punished enough and asks the magical flow to release me. If I join the quest, I could petition her to show leniency and free me. Nisha and I had been discussing the possibility when Emrys returned, and we never finished the conversation.

I am wracked with indecision. The longing to be whole again has returned. This half-life is no longer enough for me. But what if it doesn't work? To hope and then to have my hopes dashed a second time—will I survive that? Perhaps it would be better to remain a cat in the World Above than take the risk.

I jostle the embers in the fire with a stick in an attempt to raise a little heat to combat the predawn drop in temperature. As the sky begins to lighten, I am still no closer to an answer. All I know is, I must decide who I want to be soon, the cat familiar or the sprite I was born as, before there is no longer time to choose.

WHO'S THAT
WALKING ON MY BRIDGE?

AS WE PACK up camp, taking special care to bury the fire so it can't spark a blaze, I worry about Percival. Surreptitiously observing him, it's obvious he didn't sleep last night. His pale complexion is grey, but more shockingly, his hair is ruffled. I'm sure he has been running his hands through it, and, worryingly, he's made no attempt to comb it.

Pris is chatting away, telling the sprite how we decided we will work together from now on. She leaves a gap for one of his acerbic remarks, but he doesn't stir. I doubt he even heard a word she said.

'We're ready,' Pris announces, and this brings Percival out of his daze.

The sprite reaches into his pocket to retrieve his comb and absent-mindedly neatens his hair. He then runs a hand down his clothes, using a spell to tidy himself up.

'All right, let us go.' He heads off down the path, not even checking to see if we're following.

Pris raises an eyebrow as she pulls on her pack. I shrug, as I've no idea what's up with Percival. Maybe it is something to do with the sprites he arrived with last night. By the time we catch Percival up, he is humming under his breath. He obviously does not want to talk.

Percival is completely off his game today as he deals with whatever is going on with him. I, on the other hand, have a spring in my step. After singing my heart out to Pris last night, albeit in front of hundreds of sprites, something has settled inside me. There is a promise of a future together, and I will not let anything get between us and that opportunity.

Pris slips past Percival and takes the lead. 'If anything attacks us, I think I'm better equipped to handle it,' she tells him, and Percival obligingly drops behind her, then allows me to pass him.

I wait for him to object, to say something along the lines of how he has forgotten more about these woods than she will ever learn, but he simply carries on humming. I hope he is at least aware enough to deal with anything that might sneak up on us from behind.

Fortunately, we travel most of the morning without encountering anything more dangerous than a hedgehog. I start to relax a little, but it would not pay to forget we are still in the maze and that the minotaur is still testing us.

My stomach begins to gurgle as the forest starts to thin out. Moments later we arrive in a clearing, and I am about to suggest we stop for lunch when Pris grabs my arm and points to the left. 'Snake, look.'

Raising my head, I find the path meanders through the open space for about another fifteen metres or so before turning into a rocky edge, then drops off completely. The other side of the gorge is far enough away for me to see it is deep—very deep—with the hint of a blue ribbon of a river running through it. We have somehow ended up in a mountain range.

To my left the cavernous mouth of a cave stands near a wooden swing bridge spanning the gorge. Surely that can't be the only way across? I peer more closely. There are slats missing, and those ropes holding it together look old and worn. I'm not usually bothered by heights, but the thought of crossing over on that bridge has me sweating as my anxiety level rises.

Something hits my pack from behind, causing me to stumble forward a step. I tense and swivel round, ready to take on whatever attacked me. Percival regains his feet and frowns at me, like the collision is my fault. At least walking in to my back has jolted him out of his daze. He rushes past me and looks around, distress written across his face.

'Why this?' I am pretty sure Percival isn't talking to us as he carries on asking what he did to deserve the bridge crossing. 'Why not the caves? Or the river?' He grabs at his hair again, as he tends to do when he's frustrated or stressed out. This time I'm pretty sure he's stressed. I know I am.

Pris glances questioningly at me.

'I've no idea what he's talking about,' I tell her.

Pris reaches out to the sprite, 'Percival—'

She stops as a huge, shambling creature covered in matted hair emerges from the cave by the bridge. 'Oh my goodness, is that a yeti?'

'No, how could you insult her like that? How can you be so….' Percival's shock at Pris's perceived rudeness causes him to momentarily lose his words. He recovers quickly though. 'This is a member of the ancient race of trolls.'

Pris grins like it's Christmas morning. 'For real? A troll? Like in *The Three Billy Goats Gruff*?'

Percival stares disdainfully at her. 'Please. Trolls are not only ancient, they are also noble creatures and are not to be confused with characters in some silly children's story.'

I bite back a grin. 'To be fair, Percival, *The Three Billy Goats Gruff* is based somewhat on truth. Trolls do guard bridges into magical areas.'

As I say these words out loud, I realise the troll is the next test the maze has for us. I hastily kick my brain into gear, trying to access what little troll lore I learnt as a child as a deep voice rumbles around the gorge.

'Who goes there? Who wishes to cross into the centre of the minotaur's maze?'

As she talks, the troll shuffles to stand in front of the mouth of the bridge, and the largest sword I have ever seen drags behind her, gouging a furrow in the earth. Taking a defensive position, she brings the sword up, crossing it over her chest. She cuts quite the daunting figure.

Pris stands with her jaw open, and Percival tucks himself in behind her. I sigh. I guess I'm up.

I step forward and announce with more authority than I feel, 'I, Sneak Thief, along with Princess Priscilla Crown and Percival the Wise, seek entrance to the minotaur's maze.'

'For what purpose?'

I do a double take. I don't remember that being one of the questions trolls ask. How much am I supposed to tell her? Should I spill everything? No, that wouldn't be right, as she only needs to know what we want to take from there. Well, at least I think that is all she needs.

'To retrieve what is held within.' I am rather proud of my quest-like response.

'Under whose authority?'

'What?' What is this, twenty questions?

I glance over to Pris and Percival for some help, but their postures scream 'We're leaving this up to you, mate.'

Pris does send me a smile of encouragement. I spread my hands in a beseeching 'a little help here' gesture, which she ignores. She nods towards the troll as if to indicate I should go ahead and answer her.

'Who gave you leave to enter?'

I widen my eyes at Pris, subliminally sending, 'Seriously, you're forcing me to do this?' She doesn't respond, which I guess is an answer in itself. I turn to the troll.

'Sorry, what was the question again?'

Did the troll actually sigh? 'Did the Queen invite you? Or the minotaur himself?' She annunciates each word clearly as if I am a total idiot.

I don't know how to answer because neither the Queen nor the minotaur invited us. The troll shuffles her feet, and I catch a glimpse of a thin face with a protruding nose through her matted, dirty hair.

Yep, there she goes, sighing again. I don't know what she expects. I mean, the council didn't issue us with a questing manual or anything. We're learning as we go.

'You can only enter the maze by one of three ways. You are either invited by the minotaur, or the Queen grants you entrance,' the troll repeats.

There is silence.

'You said three,' Pris prompts.

Finally, some help.

The troll crosses her arms over her chest. 'You defeat me.'

'What the…?' Okay, so most of my words have now left my brain. I glance over at Pris and do a double take. Is she honestly considering this?

Yep, she is assessing the troll, her gaze travelling over her like she is looking for any weaknesses. Percival is stepping away from her, as if he senses her madness and is distancing himself.

After a few moments, she turns to me and shrugs. 'I could probably waylay her long enough for you and Percival to cross, but it would likely result in myself and the troll getting badly hurt if she is intent on defending the bridge.'

'I will defend the bridge until my death,' the troll offers, standing taller, pride ringing through voice.

'Okay, let's leave that as our final option then,' I say, pleased my powers of speech have returned. 'What about you, Percival?

Panic crosses Percival's face before it returns to his usual blank expression. 'Me? You cannot ask me to do anything. I am only here to provide information about the realm, not help you overcome the obstacles.'

I smile. 'I meant have you any ideas from your knowledge of troll law that will help us get past her without anyone dying?' I clarify.

'Oh.' Then, 'Ooh, in my role as advisor, you mean.'

'Yes, Percival, that is what I mean,' I confirm, wondering what was going on in his head that had him thinking otherwise.

'Hmm, let me see. Trolls do not like direct sunlight. See how the bridge entrance is placed close to that cliff? I would think this side of the bridge is in shadow all day.'

'What happens if they are in the sun for too long?' Pris asks.

'Too long in direct sunlight and their body starts to close down, and they will die,' Percival says matter a factly.

Pris's eyes widen. 'We are absolutely not going to draw her out into the sunlight to kill her!'

'Thank you for that.' The troll's tone is sarcastic.

We three turn as one, suddenly aware the troll is listening to every word of our plans. Hustling everyone back to the edge of the woods, we form a close group out of her earshot and continue planning. As we chat, I observe the troll's eyes drifting to my lute.

'Can I bribe you with my lute? Or some music?' I ask.

She shakes her shaggy head, and an odour that reminds me of a rubbish dump wafts towards us. This troll could do with a bath.

'No, you cannot. However, the last troll gathering was moons ago. I don't suppose I could convince you to play a bit for me before we fight, can I?'

'I don't suppose you would let me cross in return for a song?' I counter.

'If it were up to me….' Her shoulders move in what could almost be a shrug.

Pris tugs at my arm, and I turn my attention back to our planning committee, although Percival seems more intent on glaring at the troll than helping us. For some reason he is taking this all very personally.

Pris taps her index finger on her lips. 'Have you noticed that in spite of water being close by, that troll is filthy and stinks to high heaven?'

What has that got to do with anything? 'Perhaps she can't leave her post for long enough to bathe.'

'I don't think that's the reason.' Pris frowns. 'Percival?'

The sprite continues to stare down the troll.

'Hey, Percy!' Pris tries again.

He turns around, raises himself to his full height, and glares at Pris. 'I told you never to call me—'

'Then you should be listening and not playing mind games with the troll,' Pris interrupts him. 'Is it possible trolls don't like water?'

Percival frowns at Pris, but slowly his anger leaves him, and he clasps his chin in his hand.

'You know, I do believe there are some trolls who dislike water. It will not kill them, but it causes so much discomfort, they avoid it if they can.'

I nod, then a thought occurs to me. 'Pris, with your type of magic, you should be able to move water up here, perhaps even enough of it to distract the troll long enough for us to dash across the bridge.'

I FREEZE AND a coil of panic rises from my belly. Snake must be mad. I reshape things, and only just. I can't move solid items, let alone slippery watery things.

'I haven't done anything like that with my magic,' I explain. 'I'm not sure I even can'

'Of course you can. You made a flame, which means you're able to draw particles together. Moving things around is the next step. You'll probably find pushing and pulling things easier than reforming them.'

Snake probably thinks he is being supportive and reassuring. Surely he can sense the blind panic rising inside me as he speaks. 'So, I just click my fingers and water will come to me.' Fear forces an extra dose of sarcasm into my words.

He grins a cheeky grin that would normally set my heart fluttering, but at the moment, it just adds fuel to the fire of my fear.

'No, of course not. It will take a bit of trial and error. Percival, can you help her?' he asks.

Percival's head drops to one side as he considers Snake's request. 'I can, but wouldn't you be of more help?'

'Perhaps, but I will be busy doing something else.'

Percival studies Snake, curiosity brightening his eyes. 'All right,' he finally agrees, 'but only if she promises to only ever call me Percival.'

'No can do,' I retort almost before I think.

'Pris,' Snake beseeches.

I sigh. 'All right. I promise to try to never call you Percy again.'

I shake my hands, trying to loosen up. What is wrong with me? All I want to do is needle Percival and aggravate Snake. All they are doing is staring at me like I have grown an extra head. Can't they tell I don't want to do this? *Can't* do this?

Worry and anger are clouding my mind until I have a thought that might get me out of this stupid plan. 'It might take me a while to learn how to move water. Won't the troll notice and think something is up?'

There, that will put a hole in his idea.

Snake grins again, and I have to resist the urge to slap that smile from his face.

'I've thought of that. I'll tell her you're going to fill our water skins because we've decided to eat lunch while we consider our options. I mean we can't fight on an empty stomach, can we? Then I'll play some music for her, and mention we hope it will mellow her when it comes to the fight. Hopefully that will distract her long enough for you to get some water up here.'

His smile and his posture tell me he is confident his plan will work. It isn't a bad plan, as far as plans go. If only it didn't rely on me doing the magic bit.

'I will distract her for as long as it takes for you to get control of enough water to drench her and move her out of the way of the bridge,' Snake finishes.

Percival taps his chin thoughtfully. 'It would help if you could move her closer to the stream below. Then the elf would use less energy to move the water.'

Apparently, we are doing this. When was that decided?

Snake nods approvingly. 'Good point. I'll try and do that.'

'Hold on, I didn't agree to this,' I snap. Some of my panic must have made it into my voice, because Snake stops and looks at me—I mean *really* looks at me.

'You were happy to fight the troll, but…. Ah… Pris, you can do this. I know you can.' Snake squeezes my arm.

I am disappointed that he is brushing over my concerns without truly considering them, without understanding my gut-wrenching fear that I will fail them both. At the same time, I want him to pull me into an embrace and tell me everything will be all right. How inconvenient being attracted to someone is.

I close my eyes, dig deep for the courage to be honest, then turn to Snake. 'I don't want to do this. The plan relies too much on my using magic—new magic which I can't even control yet. What if I let you down?' The last words come out almost as a whisper.

Then Snake does take me into his arms and says into my hair, 'Then at least we tried, and that is all we can ever do. No one will think any the less of you, whatever happens. I promise.'

For a moment I allow myself to lean into him, almost won over.

'But must we use magic?' I press, even though I know the answer.

'There must be a point to you learning how to use it,' he tells me, 'just as there is a reason the minotaur put me in touch with my musical heritage.'

I let out a weak laugh. 'You make it sound like he planned this.'

'Can you be so sure he didn't?'

I open my mouth to point out that he could not know we would decide to use water and music to defeat the troll, then shut it. Perhaps this is exactly what he expected when he set our first task. 'I thought he was a beast,' I say, my comment sounding weak to my own ears.

'But clearly a very thoughtful beast if his tests so far are anything to go by,' Snake says wryly.

'You seem so sure this will work,' I say, my face still pressed against his shoulder.

He chuckles and his breath tickles my ear. 'I am nowhere near confident that this will work. If you have another idea, we can go with that. Otherwise…'

I'm still for a moment, trying to come up with any option that doesn't include my magic. Percival clears his throat, reminding me of why we are here.

'What if the point of telling you about your heritage was for you to explore what it means for your magic, rather than to make you sing more?' I ask.

'That's ridicu—' Snake stops mid word, and his breath tickles my ear. 'Mmm, that is a real possibility,' he concedes.

'But not one we have time to consider now.' Percival's tart tone breaks the spell.

Reluctantly, I pull away from Snake. I don't have a better plan, and this one is worth a shot.

'Okay, let's do this,' I say, grabbing Snake's water skin from the side of his pack.

He leans forward and plants a kiss on my cheek, 'This is better than luring her into the sunlight,' he tells me.

'That can be plan B,' Percival jokes as he starts down the path to the river below. Well, I *think* he is joking.

As I follow him, my eyes drift towards the river running below. How am I ever going to move water? Hold on. 'Percival, why don't we just cross over the river?'

Percival laughs. 'The other side is a sheer cliff. If you balk at moving a little water, you would never be able to levitate all three of us to the top.'

My eyebrows rise up so high, I nearly strain a forehead muscle, 'Wait, I can levitate things?' Perhaps this magic thing will not be so bad after all.

As we walk, we hear Snake's voice drifting down, then the sounds of him tuning his lute. The lyrics of "Every Breath You Take" follow us as we make our way to the river.

When we reach the bank beside the fast-flowing water, I drop to the ground, cross my legs, and look expectantly at Percival. 'Teach me, oh master.'

Percival frowns. 'I really wish you would take this more seriously.'

I don't say anything. I mean, what should I say—'*I do take this seriously, but I am scared to death, and so I'm joking with you to relieve the tension*'?

Percival fidgets a little, and I realise he is also nervous. Finally, he says, 'Snake would be better at this than I, but I cannot sing as he does, or entertain the troll to buy us time.' He stares into space for a moment before taking a deep breath. 'Why don't you start by looking into the water and seeing if it

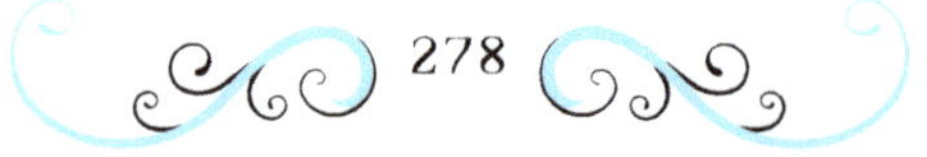

is any different to other substances?'

I stare at the water, just like I did with the fire, allowing it to calm my mind until the particles are visible. There aren't as many as there are in solid objects, and they seem more loosely bound. I play a little with the water, practicing forming little waves and bubbles.

'Ah, that bubble thing might work. Can you make it bigger?'

I form the water into a small bubble, using my hand to tell my brain what shape to impose on the water, then add a little more liquid. It works. I clap my hands in excitement, and the bubble collapses, spraying water everywhere.

In spite of the last little lapse, I beam with pride, and even the usually dour Percival is smiling.

'You might actually be able to do this,' he says in wonder.

'Gee, thanks for the vote of confidence,' I retort, although there is no anger in my voice.

Buoyed by my success, I form another ball, making it bigger until it is the size of a giant beachball before the water drops back down into the river.

I think if I stick with beachball size and move it across the water before getting it to follow me, I might be able to make this work.

After a couple of attempts I manage to move the ball and we are halfway up the path when I stumble over a root and the water balloon bursts, drenching Percival.

'I will lead you so you can concentrate on carrying the water,' Percival suggests dourly.

That will help, but will one small sphere of water be enough to distract the troll? I need a backup.

Back down at the bank, I fill the water skins and leave them open just in case. Then I return to Percival. In my absence, he has dried himself off.

His right eyebrow rises. 'Where is the water bubble?'

'I want to try something,' I tell him.

I follow him a little further along the path until we come to an outlook about two-thirds of the way up. I lean out until I can see the river, and I stretch my magic out, calling the water into a ball. It takes a lot of energy and it's draining me, making me a little weaker, but I float it upwards, imagining a string attached to my hand. The water ball floats behind me like a balloon.

'The rest of the way is flat,' I say to Percival. 'I am less likely to drop it now.'

Percival grins. 'I do believe you are getting the hang of this, Priscilla.'

Percival just used my name for the first time. Okay, it's Priscilla, and I hate that, but it's better than elf girl, or princess said with a sneer. Perhaps today will not be such a train wreck after all.

By the time we reach the clearing, my head is like mush, and it takes all my energy to float the ball of water high above the troll. Snake launches into "The Script's Rain", and I almost lose control when I bark out a laugh. Trust Snake to make a joke at a time like this.

'I do not like this song of rain.' The troll scowls at Snake. 'The others are back. Will you eat, or will we fight?'

The troll is now a little away from the bridge, but not far enough for us to slip in behind her.

Snake raises a finger in the universal 'wait a minute' sign. 'Give me a moment, please, I don't want my instrument to be damaged.' He puts the lute into its case. 'Is there somewhere safe I can put it while we fight?'

Gleaming white teeth appear in the troll's face in what I suspect is her version of a smile. 'Put it inside my cave. It will be mine when we are done anyway.'

As she speaks, the troll moves towards the entrance of her home as if to make sure Snake knows where to go. Percival and my path to the bridge is clear, but Snake is still blocked by the troll. There is no way we will all make it to the bridge from these positions. I frown, worry starting to knot my stomach. My fights are usually one on one. I'm not used to worrying about others.

Snake is almost level with the bridge's defender when he says, 'Now.'

Even though I am worried Snake won't make it, I don't hesitate. I drop the oversized water bomb and run. As I near the bridge, my ears are filled with a piercing howl of pain. Percival is ahead of me and almost at the bridge as I half turn to find the troll rolling on the ground. The vision reminds me of a dog rolling in something foul smelling. Snake is dodging her outstretched hand. Two steps later, he joins me.

'What are you waiting for?' he pants.

'Go ahead of me.' I move out of the way so he can pass.

The bridge swings and sways as the three of us move forward at a fast walk, testing each slatted wooden step as we go. A few steps in front of me, Snake grips the thick rope sides with both hands. I steady myself, holding tight to the rope with one hand as I clutch the open water skins in the other.

I almost slip a couple of times on my unsteady legs, straining to maintain my balance as the bridge swings to and fro. As I approach a gap in the slats, my mouth goes dry and my palms grow sweaty. I slow down to make sure I cross safely.

Glancing up, I see Percival is almost to the other side, and this gives me hope. Snake and I are about halfway across when the bridge undulates like a slinky, and my stomach clenches in fear—I had hoped we would be further across before the troll recovered.

'Run,' I yell at Snake.

He turns and glances over his shoulder, blanches, then increases his speed. I wouldn't quite call it running, but he pulls away from me. With the water bottles clutched to my chest, I can't match his speed, and I slip as the bridge moves under me.

Once I regain my balance, I twist my head to find the troll thundering after us, her huge body looming ever closer. One of the bridge slats cracks under her weight and I gulp, wondering if the ancient bridge will hold with all four of us on it. She may not have to fight us to prevent our getting to the other side.

I take a couple more uncertain steps and let out a relieved breath as Percival reaches solid ground. Then I concentrate on moving forward, but the bridge is less stable with the troll lumbering behind me. Silently I urge Snake to go faster, but he's finding it as difficult to move as I am as the planks ripple up and down, swaying with each movement. When he places his first foot the other side, the troll is so close behind me that her dank, musty smell fills my nostrils.

I turn, letting go of the side as I start to tip the water from the water bottles. The troll stops to watch what I am doing and bares her teeth.

'That tiny bit of water does not scare me.'

I'm grateful the lack of movement is slowing the swinging. I gather the water into another ball as the troll's eyes widen. She takes a step forward.

'It is over, little elf. Come with me now,' she coaxes, her eyes fixed on the water.

There is uncertainty in the troll's voice as I move back in time with her. Her steps are longer and surer than mine, and she is almost at arm's-length when I fling the gathered water at her and turn to run in a single movement.

The board bucks under my feet, forcing me off balance. I grab hold of one of the bridge's roped sides as something grasps my ankle. I swivel my upper body to find the troll lying flat, grinning triumphantly as she pulls at my leg. My heart is in my mouth, and I feel sick.

Pushing my fear down, I decide my quest will not end this way. My only weapon is the water skins. I am about to hit the troll's hand when, desperate and breathless, I tip the skins and dribble the last of the water out on her fingers. It isn't much, but it's enough to cause her to loosen her hold.

I pull free. The end of the bridge is still so far away, but I don't hesitate. Dropping the water skins, I grip the rope sides in both hands and half run, half pull myself forward.

The troll is crawling behind me as I try to move faster, but the bridge is moving so much, all I can do is hold on and stumble forward when the bridge swings flat. The troll doesn't seem to have the same problem. She is gaining on me. My heart is pounding so hard, the sound fills my ears.

Ahead of me Snake is calling for me to move faster. Fingers grasp at my boot and slip off. I'm not going to make it. In desperation I reach out with my magic. Gathering the last of my strength, I call the water from below.

A roar fills the air as a wall of water rises up over the bridge. Magic pulses through me, and for a moment, I am pure energy—then it overwhelms me, and I lose control. Water smashes down, and I hook my arms over the ropes, holding on for dear life until the water recedes.

Exhaustion flows through me in waves, but I can't stay here. My legs buckle beneath me as I try to move, and my wet boots slip on the soaked wood. Just as my body gives up, a hand clutches at my arm, and Snake literally drags me off the bridge to safety.

With my feet on solid ground, I turn to find the troll cowering a few steps away, clinging to the sides as if she might still fall off. A pang of guilt tugs at me. I try to tell myself we made it and the troll is uninjured, but she is shaking as if she is petrified.

Snake steadies me on my feet. 'Are you okay?'

I nod.

'You won fair and square.' The troll is so forlorn as she drags herself to her feet and shakes herself like a large hairy dog. As she returns to her side of the bridge, her shoulders are slumped in defeat.

Snake tugs at my arm, urging me away from the edge of the gorge. I am frozen in place, watching until the troll reaches the other side. Collapsing, she curls into a ball, and I can see her shaking from here. As I witness her distress, this no longer feels like a victory.

I stare down at my hands as if they are somehow responsible for what I have done to the troll. But it is not them. I have fought before and never caused this much damage to another being. It is my magic. The joy I felt using it to escape the witch's house is now replaced with horror at what it did to the troll.

Somewhere in the back of my mind, I sense Snake leading me away, but I am so wrapped up in my own thoughts that I pay no attention to where we are going. All I can do is focus on what an abomination my magic is.

ANOTHER DECISION

OUT OF SIGHT of the bridge, we find a clearing. We don't need to talk to agree we all need a break. I offer to make a fire to dry Pris out, but Percival steps forward and incants something. I stand aside as he points down the length of her body, and her dripping wet clothes dry instantly. My eyes widen.

Drying spells are commonplace for earth and air creatures, so it's not the spell that surprises me. It is more that Percival went out of his way to do something for Pris. Does this act of kindness mean he no longer dislikes her?

When he is done, Pris lets her pack slip from her shoulders, drops to the ground, and leans back against a tree trunk, her blank eyes fixating on some distant point. Her skin is pale, and she hasn't said a word since we left the bridge. I join her on the ground and start rummaging in my pack for some of the travel bread. We all need something to revive our flagging spirits.

With his head tilted slightly to one side, Percival stares thoughtfully at us both. 'I think this calls for some tea and cake,' he declares decisively.

The next moment he is pulling a collapsible table from his pocket, followed by a full tea set for three, and lastly, a two-tiered iced cake cut into eight slices.

My mouth waters and my stomach rumbles. 'Is that banana cake?' I ask as the sweet scent wafts past.

Percival smiles. 'It is. Eleanora's daughter makes them for the whole-food shop she runs. I am sure she will not miss this.'

I'm not so sure, but I'm not going to argue. I want a slice of that cake too much.

Pris still has not moved. Percival hands her a cup of milky tea and a slice of cake, and she takes them automatically. There is no cheeky remark about being civilised in the wild, or any comment about how delicious the cake is as she takes a bite.

As Pris eats and drinks, it is like watching a robot. I catch Percival's eye. 'Did she use too much magic, do you think?'

The sprite shakes his head as he dabs at the side of his mouth with a napkin. 'No. I mean there's no doubt she is tired because she is not used to using magic, but she did not deplete her reserves. The cake should restore her energy. I believe this is something more—something about *how* she used her magic.'

I finish my cake, and Percival offers me a second slice. I shouldn't, but the cake is amazing, and the cream-cheese icing is to die for. I wolf it down before taking a surreptitious sideways glance to see if the dessert has magically revived Pris. She ate every crumb, but her eyes still look haunted.

Percival begins to clear away our forest feast. We should move soon, but we can't go on with Pris like this. Reaching over, I take her hand in mine, lacing our fingers together.

'Are you all right?' I ask, then mentally kick myself. Is that the best I can come up with?

Her fingers move in my grasp as if she wants to pull away. I hold tighter.

'Tell me what's worrying you. We can work through it together,' I encourage.

She takes in a deep breath and expels the air slowly. 'There isn't really time for self-indulgence. I think maybe we should move.' She makes as if to stand, and I pull her back down.

I don't normally do the macho thing, and I know she could whip my ass if she put her mind to it, but I'm worried about her. Pris is normally so decisive. She makes a plan, enacts it, and moves on. Her almost catatonic state is out of character.

'Pris, I don't think we're going to get very far with you like this. Tell me what's wrong, and perhaps we can fix it together.'

She jerks her hand out of mine and turns to me, her face twisted in anger. 'We can't "fix" this.' Her fingers form air quotes around the word fix. 'The only way to fix it is to go back in time and change my decisions.'

There are tears in her eyes now, and as the anger drains from her body, she looks… lost… or maybe haunted. Her gaze that meets mine is full of hurt and fear and a little bit of hope.

'Or perhaps… magic can remove it?'

I want to ask her what she means, what she wants to remove, but she's in no state to answer questions, so I need to figure it out for myself. I am so not good at this emotional stuff. I don't know what she is talking about, and I don't know how to help her.

A hand drops onto my shoulder, and Percival leans in to whisper in my ear. 'I think she means her magic.' He steps away and takes a seat on a fallen log, pulls a book from his pocket, and begins to read.

Magic? She wants to lose her magic? Why? Then it hits me like the wall of water hit the bridge—she's afraid of what she can do with it.

I turn back to her and try to pull her into my arms. She resists for a moment, her frame rigid, but a little of the fight leaves her and she allows me to hug her, although her body remains stiff as a board, as if she thinks herself unworthy of comfort.

For a moment I don't know what to do other than hold her. I'm good at putting my emotions into songs, but not so great at putting them into words in this sort of situation. Still, if I don't try, how will Pris get through this? I take a deep breath and expel it slowly. Perhaps I should just start talking and the rest will come to me.

'We all go through something similar,' I say before rushing on. 'Every creature uses magic instinctively in a crisis at some point and does something that scares them. It's part of learning, or so my mother told me.'

I pause, checking Pris is listening. She shifts in my arms, and I take that as a sign to continue. 'For me, it was moving a knife through the air to chase off a bully.'

'Did you stab him?' Pris's voice is muffled by my clothes.

I shake my head at the memory. 'No, fortunately. I don't believe I intended to go that far. I did believe he was going to hurt me though, and I was scared. I only wanted to scare him away…. I'll never really know if I would have hurt him.'

'Why? What happened?'

I gulp. This is still difficult to talk about, even now. 'He stumbled backwards, tripped over a chair, and when he hit the ground, he landed on his arm.'

My heart is racing at the memory, and I take a moment before finishing the story. All these years later, the memory still makes me sick to the stomach.

'I can never forget the way his arm was twisted out of shape when a teacher helped him up. He was white as a sheet and howling in pain. I remember throwing up, and for months after, my dreams were haunted by those few minutes.'

Pris is still. I am not sure my story helped or made things worse. I'm about to offer something more, but she relaxes against me, then she shuffles around so she can speak.

'Over the years I've fought off quite a few attackers,' she starts, 'and I was scared each and every time. Those fights were different than today. When I use karate, I am in control, and my focus is on defence.'

She stops speaking, and I dare not say anything or even move. There is more to come, and she needs to get everything out.

'Even with the bubble of water today, we meant to frighten the troll, not hurt her, and I was in control. Then when I called the water…. I couldn't control…. I could have…. The fear in her eyes—that moment will haunt me forever.' She turns her face back into my body as if to hide from the sight.

I hug her to me, wanting to take away the pain—to make her feel better. But as my mother told me once, the pain and worry are there for a reason. I gently push Pris away so I can see her face—and so she knows my next words are said with love.

'Magic is a wonderful gift, but it must be respected. Next time you're scared, you will remember the face of the troll, and you will not lose control— the memory of her fear will stop you.'

Pris shakes her head, 'I will never use magic again.'

'To learn to control magic, you must practice, just like learning karate.' I want to explain that if she doesn't keep practicing, then she will then increase the chances of lashing out with her gift when she is emotional, but perhaps this isn't the time to point that out.

She shakes her head a second time. 'No, I won't use it again.'

I sigh, getting some insight into how my mother felt when we had the same conversation. 'That's a shame, because then you would be ignoring the purpose of the lesson. Magic is a tool like any other. You must learn to use it safely and not lash out. What happened today was one step in that learning.'

It feels weird hearing my mother's words come from my mouth, but I have never been more thankful for her advice than I am today.

Slowly Pris leans into me, and her lips brush my cheek with a kiss.

'Thank you for trying, and I hear your words….'

'But they will take a while to sink in. I know. I lived through this myself.' I offer her a small smile.

'If you two are finished, there is no time for canoodling. *We* must continue.'

If I had not seen the concern on Percival's face when he set up tea, I would take offence at his brusque tone. As it was, I simply laughed and said, 'The quest must go on whether we are ready or not.'

I stand up and hold out my hand to help Pris to her feet. Moments later we set out along a narrow trail leading us along the mountain ridge. As I walk behind her, I focus on the tense set of her shoulders. She is still quiet, but at least she answers direct questions now. Still, I hope we don't encounter any more challenges today, as I'm not sure she can cope with anything else.

No sooner does the thought jump into my head than we round the corner and come face to face with a stone wall across our path. The door in the centre is covered in black runes. Although I have learnt some of the language of our people, I cannot read these.

'Ah.' Percival smiles. 'Finally, the entrance to the maze.'

'I thought we were already in the maze,' Pris says, her voice still worryingly lifeless.

Percival shrugs. 'We are, sort of. Only the worthy can enter the maze proper. Everything you did over the last two days was to test your worthiness.'

Beside me, Pris tenses, and I worry that her temper is going to get the better of her. She surprises me by not ranting. Instead, she sighs and raises her eyes to the sky. 'Seriously, how many more hoops do we have to jump through before we actually meet the minotaur?'

I agree with her, but I want to lighten the mood, so I joke, 'At least we haven't had to face any fire-eating dragons.'

One of Pris's hands flies to her mouth, and her eyes widen. 'You mean, that's a possibility? Really? After all we've faced, there might be dragons?'

Lead balloons spring to mind, and my rapidly failing joke is not helped at all by Percival's next words. 'The maze isn't far from the dragon breeding grounds. I have no doubt they are called to play a part in the maze on occasion.'

Pris turns white. Time to change the subject.

'Well, this isn't a dragon,' I explain the obvious. 'It's a door. And if we don't find out how to get in, what's on the other side won't matter.'

I have seen doors like this before in creature houses in the World Above. They are our form of safes. The runes are a distraction. The real trick is in the locks down the left-hand side. They are invisible to the naked eye, but when I place my hand on the wood and reach out with my magic, I can sense them hiding.

I smile, as this should be easy. As the locks appear, I realise I have spoken too soon. Five locks emerge. The most I have ever managed to hold and open before is three.

I try not to react, but my shoulders slump. I had thought that after all Pris had been through today, I could handle this one alone. Maybe Percival can help. I glance over my shoulder to ask him for advice, only to see him disappear into thin air.

THE CALL TO return home is so strong that I am pulled away so quickly, I do not even get the chance to explain to Snake and Priscilla. Guilt tugs at my stomach. After our troll fight and coming up just now to our next challenge, Snake and Pris will need me. However, I appear directly in the glade. This alone gives me pause to worry. Emrys rushes forward, and the fear on his face chases my guilt away.

My mind instantly conjures an image of a lifeless Nisha, and I almost collapse to the ground. 'What… what is… wrong?' I manage to stammer out.

Emrys slows down and waves me forward. 'Father. He hears The Spirits calling and asked for you to be brought to him.'

When I was home the night before, my father was working away from our glade, and I had not had a chance to speak with him. In truth, I had not missed catching up with him. For the last few hundred years, he has turned ignoring my existence into an art form. His disdain is based on his warning that my friendship with a witch would be my downfall, that I was reaching above my station.

When I was cursed, he felt vindicated. Even though an elf hexed me, and it was my decision that led to the action, my father focused on the fact that I only did what I did because of Eleanora.

'You called me back for this?' I ask, anger replacing my fear for Nisha.

'Apart from the fact that this might be your last chance to mend things with Father, he says he must see you,' Emrys admonishes me.

I draw in a deep breath and expel it slowly. 'Do you really believe there is any hope of his accepting me even now… at the end?'

Emrys's eyes darken with sadness. 'I truly do not know, Percival, but can you honestly say you would not regret trying to work things out with him?'

He is right, of course. I allow him to lead me to the Mother Tree. It sits at the centre of our glade, the heart and soul of our family and the only link with our ancestors. My father has been placed within the embrace of its roots.

When I am close enough to make out my father's form, I stop moving, shocked at how wasted the body of our once vital spiritual leader is. 'Is that really him?' I ask, unable to believe the change.

Emrys nods.

'Then it is truly his time,' I whisper.

'He has not got long in this world. We have called Mother back from tending the forest. Spirits grant us that she arrives before he passes.'

I find myself unable to move. Emrys prods me in the back. 'Father called for you. You should go to him.'

'What happened to him?' I ask, putting off sitting with him for as long as possible.

'He has been spending more and more time in the trees these last months. A few weeks ago, he began babbling about a big change that will eclipse the blight, and how we will need to protect the forest,' Emrys tells me. 'He came back this afternoon and announced that the time is come—the spirit world is calling him to help with the coming storm.' Emrys's voice catches, and he wipes a tear from his cheek. 'He walked himself to the Mother Tree, lay down, and asked for me to call you back. He gave me instructions about his passing and has not spoken a word since.'

'Why speak with me, then? Surely, as you are his apprentice, he needs to spend time with you.' As I try to process the fact that my father is leaving this plane of existence, my emotions battle for dominance. I am saddened by the state I find my father in. Angry because the last time he spoke to me was hundreds of years ago. Disappointed in myself because I never quite measured up to his standards. And, amongst it all, is the love for him I packed away so many years ago, but never really stamped out.

Emrys wipes away the last of his tears. 'You had best ask him.'

I square my shoulders and force my feet to take me closer. Stopping between the tree roots, I lower myself down to sit by the creature who once told me I would never amount to much and that perhaps it was justice that I was no longer a true sprite.

My jaw tightens as I push down the bitterness at being summoned by the sire who abandoned me. I take a moment before I speak. 'Father, I came as you requested,' I say, forcing my words into a neutral tone that hides my inner turmoil.

'But you are not pleased to be here,' my father croaks, rolling onto his side to face me.

Apparently, I was not as successful as I hoped at hiding my feelings. I study my father, taking in the translucent skin and hollow cheeks. His eyes, the sign of vitality in any sprite, are almost the same colour as his skin. There is very little life-force left inside him, and an unexpected wave of sadness passes through me.

He was always such a strong force in my life. Always determined we should set an example for the other sprites.

'Ah, you still hark back to that night.' My father barks out a laugh. 'You are still not happy about your punishment.'

He refers to my curse. Or not the curse as such, but to the fact that it was not able to be reversed.

'The magical flow only allowed Princess Petunia a partial reversal because you carried blight through our lands. Our great spirits tempered the process to punish you for your actions.'

Bitterness laces the words I spit out. 'And you fully supported them.'

'Ah, what a bad father I am, holding my son responsible for his actions.'

And so it begins—the arguments and the recriminations. I do not know why I bother. As if reading my thoughts, my father says, 'In spite of your misgivings and our… past, you still sit here beside me at my end. Why?'

Sick to my stomach, the urge to stop the snarking is strong, and I attempt to appease my father as I always do. 'More than anything, I guess it's because I am surprised you called for *me*.'

'And quite rightly too,' he says. 'And you are clearly still angry at me—and at the world. Well, at least your anger shows a bit of backbone. Good… good. If what I learned these last few days comes to pass, you will need the strength that anger brings.'

My brows draw together as I try to make sense of his words. 'I don't understand,' I say, trying not to snap. Must he talk in riddles? Why can't he just say his piece and let me be on my way?

With a sigh, my father rolls back and lays flat again. 'I am not sure I do either, not completely. There is something amiss with the flow of magic in the World Below—'

'Another blight?' I ask warily, leaning in closer. Did my father just show me weakness? Or is this another of his traps?

'If you keep interrupting me, I will never tell you all I must.' My father's voice is tart and disapproving.

There is the man I am used to talking to. I tense, thinking this time I might walk away. Or at least tell him I am no longer a child to be spoken to like that. I do neither though. I wait, like a good son, for him to impart his wisdom.

His body shifts slightly, and when he has found a more comfortable position, he speaks. 'I am sorry. Time is short, and that was rude.'

My eyebrows almost leap off my forehead. What that just an apology?

'I was hard on you, not appreciating that you had a larger role to play in the world than I envisioned. The Spirits set me straight, and I know you are somehow entangled in these events. Until I join them, I will not know any more, but it is enough for me to know that your life has not been a waste of time… that my son will be a part of world changing events.'

He closes his eyes, and the glade falls silent. His chest rises and falls with uneven breaths. Has he finished with me, or has he fallen asleep? I am not sure whether I should leave, or if there more to come. I drum my fingers on the root of the tree while I wait.

'What I learned… I cannot tell you. The spirits say I must not… but I know I was wrong about you, and I wanted to tell you that.'

My fingers stop mid motion, and I am a statue beside my father. I cannot believe I am hearing words I long since gave up waiting for. He is not exactly offering an apology, but I believe this is as close as the shaman of our community will ever get to one.

'Soon you must choose between what you have and what you want, and the repercussions of that choice…. Ah… I should not speak of that either. What can I tell you?' He sighs, his brows draw together, and he sucks in a shallow breath before continuing. 'Perhaps all that is left is advice. Have faith in yourself. Trust your heart, my son.'

He reaches out a shaky hand and grasps mine. His skin is dry and almost lifeless already. He will not be with us for much longer.

'I am grateful for this farewell. Do not tarry now, for there is work for you to do.'

His eyes droop closed, and he drops my hand. I do not move. Having finally made a connection with my father after all these years, I want more. It is as though the years have been stripped away, and we are father and son again. I want to talk to him about my life, ask him whether or not I should join the quest and try to return to my natural state.

Instead, my mind keeps returning to the fact this is it. He has hours to live, and this is it for us. There are others he will want to speak with before his time comes, and I should make way for them. But I cannot leave the grove as he requests.

'I must stay for the mourning and the release,' I say, wondering how I will fit in the ten days of mourning before the body is burned to release the soul and still help Snake and Pris through the maze.

'No! You must go immediately.' His words come out with more strength than I believed he had left. 'Worry not, I am to be taken to the great Mother Tree and will live a life among the spirits. There will be no mourning and burning for me. Say your goodbyes now.' My father's voice is back to its usual commanding tone.

Every fibre of my being wants to rail against his command, but my heart knows it cannot disobey the request of a dying creature. I place my hand on top of his and say, 'Fare thee well, Father. May your spirit mingle with the Great Magic for eternity.'

The ritual words sound hollow. I have had so little time to process this awkward meeting, so to even begin to say goodbye to him is beyond me. Fortunately, we have a ritual for these types of farewells, and that must be enough.

'May you do great things and join with me one day long in the future,' my father finishes. He offers me a weak smile, the first I can recall since I was just a child. He closes his eyes, and as his face slackens, I understand his body is still here but his soul is already departing.

Emrys touches my arm and I look up. 'Come, I will send you back.'

I hesitate a moment, looking upon my father one last time, I stand up and follow my brother out of earshot. 'I cannot leave. I must stay, no matter what Father said.'

'He does not wish it, and he will not thank you.'

When I make no effort to move, Emrys says, 'Father told me the great Mother Tree will take his body when he joins our ancestors. He instructed the elders that there is to be no mourning because it is a great honour, and without a body, there is no need for release. We must respect his wishes.'

'But what if he is wrong? What if he is delusional? I cannot disrespect my father by not attending the rites, not when I am so close to home.'

My argument sounds hollow even to my own ears. My father would never disrespect the spirits by falsely declaring his heart's desire to be their wish, not even if he was losing his grip on reality. Emrys does not speak. He simply raises an eyebrow and waits. My body slumps as I give in to the reality of the situation. My brother places a hand on my shoulder.

'We will wait the full thirty days and hold the Celebration of Life meal. Perhaps by then you will be finished with this quest, and you can return for that.'

I am unable to judge whether this fits with protocol or is respectful, as the only shaman our people have had in my lifetime lies dying. Emrys is our new shaman, and I must abide by his decision.

'Have the spirits spoken to you? Do you know anything about the crisis he speaks of?' I ask, hoping for some clarity before I leave.

'The spirits will not speak of it to me, so I cannot tell you anything more.'

'Perhaps Father is overstating the importance of what is going on,' I suggest, unable to keep the relief from my words.

Emrys shakes his head. 'It might be nothing. Then again, it might just as well be something. Regardless, his words are wise. All we can do is trust in ourselves, whether we are everyday folk, or we are someone facing an extraordinary destiny.'

Sage advice, I think as I hug my brother and we share our sorrow for a moment. In thirty days, we will celebrate my father's life. Until that time, I must return to my quest.

'Spirits guide you.' My brother speeds me back to the maze before I can answer.

'DAMN, WHERE'S PERCIVAL gone?' Snake says.

'What?' I turn slowly to find the sprite has indeed disappeared. 'That shouldn't be a problem, should it? I thought lock picking was kinda your thing.'

'But—'

'Besides, Percy isn't allowed to help us—something about if he does, it becomes his quest too.'

Snake laughs. 'You're only brave enough to call him Percy because he isn't here.'

He's right, it does feel a little naughty, but honestly, the guy needs to loosen up. Snake, though, is changing the subject. What doesn't he want to tell me? I'm not fragile. I don't want his protection—I need his honesty.

'Can you pick this type of lock?' I ask.

He snorts. 'With my eyes closed.'

I'm unimpressed. 'That goes without saying, doesn't it, because isn't it all done by touch?'

He's silent. My brows draw together as I take in his slumped shoulders and the fact that he will still not meet my gaze. 'So, what *is* the problem?'

He releases the locks back into the door and turns to face me. 'I can't pull the locks out of the door, hold them in place, and pick all of them at the same time. There are too many.'

This is not good. Maybe fighting a dragon would be easier. Although my stomach is knotting, I school my face into what I hope is a look of bland curiosity. I can't let Snake know what I am thinking, as he clearly thought this would be his shining moment and is worried he will let us down.

'How would Percival help?' I ask.

'I hoped he would come up with some ideas on how I could open more locks at the same time—perhaps provide a way to boost my magic.'

I shift my focus to the locks. Did the minotaur know this would be beyond Snake's current abilities? Is he forcing Snake to dig deeper, to learn another lesson? If this is a test, then perhaps we need a different perspective.

'How many of the locks can you hold and open?' I ask.

'Three definitely, perhaps four,' Snake answers.

'Interesting that there are five locks, then.'

Snake's eyes widen as he catches my train of thought.

'Another test? Of course it is.' Snake blows out a sigh. 'We're both tired. We should take some time to think this through.'

He's right. With Percival gone and other problems facing us, now is the right time to rest and regroup.

'Let's make camp. When we've eaten and rested, you can show me how to pick the last lock.' I drop the lock picking into the plan casually, as if it is just something I should do to pass the time. Truth is, I have never picked a lock in my life. I don't know how to do it with my hands, let alone with using magic.

'Are you sure?' Snake asks. 'I mean, you defeated the troll, I sort of thought this was my thing to do. I mean, I must be on this quest for a reason.'

I was right, he wants to prove himself. Boys can be like that sometimes. I cross the couple of steps between us and force myself into his arms—a rather awkward manoeuvre with both of us wearing packs, but I hope it will take some of the sting from my words.

'You can't do this alone, and I don't think you are meant to. I might be wrong, but I think this is less about testing your lock picking abilities and more about forcing us to work together.'

Snake still holds me stiffly. I don't want to relive this morning, it's still too raw, but the one positive I have taken from it is that I would still be a quivering mess if Snake had not been there to support me. It is Snake's turn now. He must understand we're a team, and it is only as a team we will succeed.

'Look, if you hadn't distracted the troll with music, or if Percival hadn't helped me with the water thing, we would still be at the gorge. It took all three of us to get over the bridge.'

Snake does not relax his hold. I resist the urge to shake my head. Whether I want to or not, I am going to have to open up about my reaction to the water incident.

'And it was you who showed me how to deal with my… umm… angst over dousing and almost killing the troll.'

Snake's arms tighten, and this show of support warms me, but I can't let him shift the focus. 'You are not alone in this, but you do have to teach me how to pick a lock.'

It takes a moment, but Snake pulls me tight against his body. 'I'm being too macho, aren't I?' he murmurs into my hair, and there is a touch of laughter in his voice.

'Yep,' I say with a nod, then snuggle closer to him.

I want to stay where I am for a while longer. It's nice… more than nice. Unfortunately, my insides are beginning to melt, and my body is starting to get ideas that are best left until after this whole fiasco is over. I force myself to take a step back and say, 'Come on, let's find some wood and get a fire going.'

As I gather logs, I spot a stream not far from the clearing and return to gather our remaining water skin to refill. By the time we are settled round a blazing fire, Percival is still not back, and we decide to wait to eat until he has returned. Snake produces a padlock from his pack and passes it to me.

'Most locks, whether physical or magical, work the same way. The prongs from a key push pins back into a housing and keeps them there. The springs those pins lean on want to force them back into place.' He stops to make sure I am following.

'Got it,' I confirm.

He holds up two of the metal picks he has. 'This curved one is to push the pin into the housing, like a key would, and this flatter one is to hold it in place while you move on to the next pin.'

I nod.

'Okay, you have the theory, now comes time for the practice.' He hands me the picks.

At first I am all fingers and thumbs, but at least my fumbling makes Snake smile.

'Don't you have something better to do?' I snap.

He chuckles. 'No.'

Infuriated, I try to block him out and concentrate on the lock. Finally, after much practice and a few curses—okay quite a few curses—I get it.

'Yes!' I fist pump. 'I'm the master,' I crow, a grin splitting my face.

'Master?' Snake asks dryly, the twinkle in his eye taking the sting from his words.

I will not let his sarcasm ruin my triumph. Okay, this is just the first step. I still need to learn to do this with magic, but I did it!

The sun is putting on a spectacular show of reds and purples behind the mountains, and the temperature is dropping fast. Percival still has not returned, and my stomach is protesting. I put on a billy of water and search for some leaves to make a warming tea while Snake rations out the trail bread. When we have finished and tidied up, Percival is still AWOL.

'We should get some sleep,' Snake says, reaching for his sleeping roll. 'We should be well rested when we tackle this lock.'

'Mmm,' I answer, laying my roll next to his.

I place a couple of extra logs on the fire before crawling in beside him, lock clutched firmly in my hand.

'I'm sure we can do this if we work together.' I wriggle back into him, searching for additional warmth.

He wraps himself around me and I settle into his embrace, allowing the heat of his body to relax me and all thoughts of lock picking disappear as I imagine rolling over and….

'I'll take first watch,' Snake says, abruptly sitting up, pulling me back into reality by reminding me we are not yet safe enough to be distracted by… things—no matter how much I'd like to be.

I drift off to sleep and am completely out cold when he wakes me for my turn to stand guard. I prop myself up on one elbow and find Percival must have returned sometime during the night and is now asleep across on the other side of the fire.

'What happened there?' I ask, pointing at the sleeping form.

'I don't know. He reappeared a little while ago, produced a sleeping bag, and went to sleep without saying a word.'

A frown worries my brow as I consider the sprite for a while. *Nothing I can do now,* I tell myself. There will be plenty of time to sort Percival out in the morning.

I lean over and press my mouth to Snake's, losing myself for a moment in a long, lingering kiss. 'Go to sleep. We have a big day tomorrow.'

I watch the firelight flicker over his face until his breathing evens out and I'm sure he's asleep. Once I am certain, I pull the lock out and work at using my magic to open it. I easily hold the tension on the lock and push one or two pins into place, but it takes practice and a lot of concentration to force all six pins up and be able to twist the barrel to release the lock at the same time.

As the sun rises, I place the lock in my lap and take stock. I can now pick it relatively quickly, but I am certain I can only do one. If we want to make it through the door today, we might need something more. Perhaps I can help in another way.

Being careful not to disturb Snake, I make my way over to the door, press my palms to the wood, and try to sense the locks inside. I think I can make out their shapes but can't force them to come to the surface.

'It's a gnome specialty.' The voice comes from behind me, and I turn to find Snake watching me. 'Something about our magic draws the locks to the surface, like magnetic attraction.'

I run a hand over my hair and tug a little at my braid. No, there is nothing I can think of that will solve our problem. 'I can only open one lock,' I tell Snake. 'I thought I may be more help drawing the locks out, which would allow you to focus on picking them.'

Snake shakes his head. 'Not many gnomes can expose one, let alone five.'

A little bit down but not completely out, I return to the dying embers of the fire as Snake reaches into his pack and draws out some travel bread. What I wouldn't give for a full English breakfast about now. Still, the food is nourishing, and I'm hungry enough after my magical training to eat just about anything.

'So do all the locks need to be released at once for the door to open?' I ask as I chew the berry bread that is more like a muesli bar than actual bread.

Snake mumbles something, his mouth so full of food, I can't make out a single word.

'Sorry?'

He swallows and takes a sip of water. 'Yeah. The idea is to work one lock at a time, push all the pins up and hold them there until all the locks are ready. Then you turn the barrels all at once.' He makes it sound simple, but my nighttime antics have taught me it is anything but.

'Okay. That makes it a bit more difficult.' I wrack my brains for something that may give us an advantage, but I've got nothing.

'We can only give it a go,' Snake offers.

'What if we can't do it though?' The words slip out. 'I mean, our parents would then be at Bernais's mercy, and we both know that is not a good thing.'

Snake's green eyes darken as he holds my gaze. 'We have to try. We have come too far. I'm not prepared to give up. Are you?'

I am emotionally battered and bruised. My body screams with exhaustion, and I want nothing more than to soak in a hot bath and sleep in a warm bed. I allow my eyes to sweep down the length of Snake's body. Okay, there is *one* thing I want more.

My eyes return to his, and a sigh escapes from the depth of my soul.

'No,' I admit, 'I won't give up. If we are kicked out of the maze, then I want to go knowing we've given it our best shot.'

'Then let's not talk of failing before we've even tried.' Snake laughs as if he's trying to make light of everything. But the hard, stuttering sound does not come from his heart, and I think perhaps it comes from a place of fear. It dawns on me he is just as worried about our ability to enter the maze as I am.

Nibbling on my bread, I give myself a peptalk in an effort to lift my spirits and focus my energies in a positive way. I do not succeed, and my spirits fall as I finish my meal.

Snake starts clearing up and putting out the fire, taking care to cover it with earth. I sip on some water to wash the food down, then follow suit. Percival still has not moved, though I sense he is awake. I wonder what happened last night to make him more withdrawn than normal. When everything is tidy and packed up, Percival remains curled up in his bed.

I walk over to his sleeping form and announce, 'We are going to open the door.' My voice carries more conviction than I feel. 'If you want to come with us, you had better get up.'

He doesn't move, and Snake touches my arm. 'Leave him. He didn't look so great when he came back last night. I think he may have had some bad news.'

I reach out as if to comfort Percival, but I draw my hand back. The prickly sprite isn't big on physical contact, and I am not sure he would accept help from me.

'We can't just leave him,' I murmur. 'It feels wrong to go on without him. And if he is hurting, then he may need us. I mean, he has been there for me….'

Snake drapes his arm around me and pulls me close, leaning his head against mine. We stand there for a moment, indecision holding us captive.

As the minutes draw out, and Percival doesn't move, my mind attempts to balance our need to get to the centre of the maze with my unexpected desire to help him.

'Perhaps he isn't meant to come with us into the maze proper,' Snake says. The scales tip towards leaving.

'No.' The word slips out. 'We're a team.'

Snake shakes his head. 'No, we're not. Percival is not a part of this quest. He is an advisor, someone to help us learn about the World Below. Perhaps when we make it through the door, we will have shown we have outgrown our training wheels and can go on alone.'

I consider his words. Could this really be another part of the test?

I slip from Snake's embrace. 'Okay, shall we do this?' I keep my voice low but strong. Hoisting my pack onto my back, and with one last glance over my shoulder, I lead the way to the door before I change my mind.

Standing by the maze entrance, Snake runs a hand over the door. He squares his shoulders, then takes control. 'Once I expose the locks, you work on the one at the bottom. Hold the last pin until I tell you to go.'

I nod my understanding.

'Right, let's do this,' Snake says. Leaning his forehead against the wood, he takes a couple of calming breaths, then places his hands on the door.

Following suit, I kneel and put my hands close to the bottom lock. Allowing my magic to reach out, I study the mechanism. It is slightly different to the one I picked last night, but similar enough that I am able to work out how to open it. It takes me a little while until I am ready to hold the pins in place, and the effort causes beads of sweat to form on my forehead.

I concentrate on keeping the five pins open, waiting for Snake to tell me to finish the job. A headache is starting to form behind my eyes when he admits, 'I can't do it. I can move a couple of pins in the fourth lock, but can't quite get the last one…'

We can't do this alone. We need the whole team. 'Percival.' I reach out with my voice, reluctant to pull the sprite from whatever it is that has laid him so low.

There is no response. The quest is slipping away from us, and I can't let that happen. I let go of my empathy and make my voice as commanding as possible. 'Percival, we need your help. I'm sorry, but if you don't pitch in, we will fail here, Eleanora's plans will all be for nothing.'

The last words are a guess. I am sure something more than our quest is going on, and that Eleanora is involved in some way. What I can't work out is whether Percival is a party to it. I don't look over my shoulder, as it takes too much effort to hold the pins in place, but I sense his presence as he draws near.

'I am not sure…. It's not my area….' His voice holds an uncharacteristic uncertainty and a deep weariness I force myself to block out.

'You must be able to do something… anything,' I plead, the desperation coursing through me leaking into my words.

'My magic is relatively weak but… sometimes I boost my mistress.'

A shadow crosses over my face, and I see a small hand cover Snake's, the one closest to my face. Sweat drips into my eyes, and I long to brush it away, but both of my hands are on the door, holding my lock in place, and every ounce of my being is focused on that one task.

'I have one more.' Snake's voice is strained. 'Almost… there…. Now!'

Snick, snick, snick, snick, snick. With a loud thump, the locks release, and the door swings open. The momentum and wave of magical energy knocks me back onto my butt.

YET ANOTHER BIG DECISION

AIR WHOOSHES PAST me, and a thud reaches my ears as Pris hits the ground behind me.

'Ouch.'

'Are you okay?' I half turn to check she hasn't been injured and bite back a grin as she looks up with wide-eyed surprise.

'I'd help you up, but….' I jerk my head towards the door I'm holding open.

I'm so bone-crushingly tired, I want to join her, but I'm afraid the door will not stay open for long, and I'm not sure I can go through opening it again. If I'm exhausted, I can only imagine how Pris is feeling.

Sucking in a deep breath, I place my foot in between the door and the jamb and hold my hand out for Pris. Her fingers entwine with mine, and I pull, helping her to her feet. She lets go of my hand, and I hear the rustle of clothing as she dusts herself down.

I give her a moment before asking, 'Okay, guys, are we ready for this?'

I take the silence as a yes and push at the heavy door. It slowly creaks open, the noise piercing the air. Percival ducks under my arm and is the first to enter. Pris and I allow him to take the lead, and we follow him into a dark corridor.

Holding out his hand, Percival creates a ball of light, revealing that we are not in a hallway, but a long, thin room. I jump as the door thumps back into place.

Waiting for my heartbeat to settle, I take in more of our surroundings. The sides to my left and right are walls. In front of me are three doors.

'Nooo,' I groan. 'Not another decision.'

'This is a maze, so I guess the decisions are in lieu of corners and turns,' Pris muses from beside me. 'How are we supposed to choose?' She takes a step closer to the doors. 'There's nothing to show us where they lead.'

'I don't know,' I tell her, finding it difficult to rouse my interest in solving yet another puzzle. Guilt prods at me as she continues to study the doors, and I add, 'Perhaps we can find some minor difference? There must be something about them to give us a clue.' I peer closely, but our options seem maddeningly identical. 'What do you think, Percival?'

The sprite doesn't speak. In fact, he doesn't move at all, and his face is still wearing the bewildered, hurt mask it wore last night.

I crouch down until I am at eye level with him and ask, 'What is it, Percival? Are you okay? Can I… we… do anything to help?'

His green catlike eyes focus on me. 'I… um… I have had some bad news. I shall be fine in a moment.' His voice cracks as he speaks, telling me he is unlikely to be okay any time soon. With that thought comes an understanding that getting through the next set of doors is not as important as helping Percival.

I place a hand on his shoulder. 'You take all the time you need.'

'But are you sure we have time to—'

I glare at Pris, and she stops midsentence. She glances down at the sprite, and understanding softens her gaze.

'Thank you for what you did, Percival. I hope that doesn't mean you joined our quest,' I say, wondering if that is adding to his worries.

He blinks a couple of times as if he is just waking up. 'What? Umm… no…I do not know. It makes no matter for the moment.' He shakes his head as if clearing his thoughts, then stares intently at the doors.

'These doors look familiar, like a test I saw once before. It's like… Mandor?'

Who or what is Mandor?

'Hello, old friend.'

I jump back up at the sound of a voice behind me and spin around.

A tall, gaunt male creature appears in front of us. 'It has been many years since we last met, Percival.'

Apart from his piercing grey-blue eyes, he is unremarkable looking, but there is something compelling about him. It takes me a moment to realise what it is; he literally throbs with power, which may explain how he is able to just appear in front of us.

The creature does not take his eyes off Percival when he speaks again. 'You managed to work out that these doors were made by me, so perhaps you can tell these children how to activate them.'

For a few seconds, Percival's eyes rake the man, and the idea that this might be some sort of trap is just wriggling its way into my mind when Percival says, 'You need to make the instructions written on the door appear by casting a reveal spell.'

It can't be that simple, surely. I slide a look at Pris, but she is watching Percival and the newcomer. I glance back at the sprite to find he has locked eyes with the stranger. It is as though the two of them have forgotten about us.

'How is she?' the man asks, his voice softening.

'You can always visit her and find out. It is easier down here. You must be aware she is close by.' Percival's tone is flat, uninviting.

I am surprised when tears form in the stranger's eyes. 'You understand better than anyone how it hurts us to be together while knowing we must soon part.'

'Perhaps you should have thought of that before you decided to ascend,' Percival snaps.

I frown down at the sprite. I have never seen him angry, but his hands are balled into fists. The appearance of the man and his doors have upset him, perhaps even more than the news he received last night.

'You act as though the decision was mine alone—like I had a real choice in the matter. Neither of us wanted to part, but it was for the best. Still, she asked this boon of me, and I came for her.'

'What is going on here?' Pris's voice breaks the tension, startling me.

I have to admit, the drama of the situation with Percival and the stranger had drawn me in so far that I had forgotten she was here.

Percival finally breaks eye contact with the stranger and turns to us.

'Princess Priscilla, Snake Fieth, meet the wizard, Mandor—Eleanora's mate.'

'Eleanora's mate?' Pris's eyes widen, and her eyebrows nearly fly off her forehead. 'I didn't know she was even—'

'Eleanora and I were parted by… have been apart for many years. Although my heart resides with her, we both moved on a long time ago,' Mandor's tone is neutral, though his hands shake a little as he utters the words, giving the impression he has not really moved on at all.

While Pris quizzes the Wizard, I am silenced into awe. Witches are only able to access their full power if they forsake their worldly ties and join the wizard council. Most wait until later in life to ascend, but Mandor is clearly still young.

Why would Mandor go through the heart-wrenching pain of breaking with his bond mate to do something he could have put off until the end years of his life? He clearly still has feelings for her. There must be more behind this story than a desire to devote the rest of his long life to the study of magic.

My musings are interrupted by Pris's demanding tones. 'And what is your role in this?' She gestures to the doors.

'I perhaps should not….' The wizard gnaws at his lips, then shrugs. 'I guess it does not matter now. Eleanora contacted me and asked if I would… um… offer myself… for the wizard's part in this quest.'

The frown draws Pris's brows together. 'She wanted you to help us?'

Mandor laughs. 'Eleanora is aware I would never betray my responsibilities to the Wizard Council, and she would never ask me to. It was more a case of making sure no one else tampers with the proceedings by offering myself to set the Wizard's Question.'

Pris's mouth forms an 'O' as I mull over the implications of the wizard's words.

'And why are you here in person?' I ask. 'I'm sure we can figure the doors out ourselves.'

Mandor chuckles. 'Go ahead.' He gestures to the doors. 'Try it.'

I step forward, reluctant now as I sense a trap. Reveal spells are amongst the earliest learnt by creatures. I point at the doors and say, 'Noct.'

The wood glows orange as runes slowly appear. They swirl and dance, then finally fall into formation. I study each of them carefully, but they are unlike any runes I was taught. I turn a questioning gaze to Percival.

He shakes his head. 'Those are wizard runes. They are magical in themselves, and the options they offer depend on the creature asking them to appear. That is why Mandor is here, to translate for us.'

I turn to the wizard, not surprised to find the corners of his mouth tugging into a smile. 'Would you like me to read the script for you?' he offers.

I nod, not able to think of anything witty enough to recover my dignity.

'All right, then. Door number one leads to a true maze with twists and turns and traps, the type I believe everyone expects when they hear of the minotaur's maze. There is danger there, but it will take around a day or so to make it to the centre of the maze if you avoid the traps. If you succeed, you will bypass the minotaur.'

'What happens if we fall to one of the traps?' I ask, thinking it must be bad if we wouldn't have to face the minotaur. I am not disappointed.

'It depends on the trap. Consequences range from expulsion from the maze to… to…well….' He shrugs. 'Death.'

'I'm not liking the sound of that,' Pris mutters. 'Too much is left to chance.'

'Not to mention the potential death thing,' I add.

Mandor carries on as if we hadn't spoken. 'Door two opens to a garden maze. Think hedgerows and Hampton Court. It is less hazardous and normally takes about three days to traverse if you don't get lost along the way.'

'I am guessing the lost bit can go on infinitely?' Pris asks.

'Correct.'

'And the final door?' I ask before Pris can state her preference for the longer route even with the attendant risk.

'Ah, now, that takes you directly to a confrontation with the minotaur.'

Okay, I am not liking any of these options, but if I am forced to choose, I am thinking door one. We are exhausted from using our magic opening the door here, so at least if we choose that option, we only have one more day of this, and I'm confident we can overcome the traps.

'I will give you ten minutes to decide,' Mandor states before disappearing.

'First things first,' Pris says before I can put forward any suggestions. 'We must all agree to go the same way, no splitting up. We finish this together.'

'Yes,' I agree. I learnt my lesson last time.

'Percival?'

'What? Me?'

'Of course. You're part of this team,' I tell him.

'Um… I guess…. All right, I agree,' he says.

Then, before I can open my mouth to speak, Pris announces, 'I am tired of this whole game. I want to take the shortest route and head straight for the minotaur.'

SNAKE'S EYES WIDEN. He starts to speak, shuts his mouth, then rubs his hands through his hair. 'Are you mad? Do you honestly believe you can fight a minotaur and win?'

I laugh. 'Of course not.'

'Good, because for a moment there, I thought you had lost your freaking mind and were suggesting we head straight into the heart of the maze and fight the minotaur.'

'I did, and I am backing us to make it past him and into the centre to claim our prize,' I finish.

Snake stares at me as if he's only just met me. He begins pacing around the room, which is quite a feat, since it's so cramped. He's agitated, and he's trying really hard not to fly off the handle. After a couple of circuits, he stops in front of me.

'Please tell me you're joking. I mean, we want to finish this as quickly as possible to ensure our parents aren't harmed while we're gone, but this is madness. We can't beat a giant half-man, half beast warrior.'

'Mandor just said we had to fight him, not that we must win,' I point out.

Again, Snake opens his mouth to speak and closes it. He tilts his head to the side and considers me for a moment before asking, 'Do you have a plan?'

I smile. 'I think I do. What if the minotaur guards the entrance, and all we must do is pass him to get inside. We're smart and we're resourceful. I'm sure, with the three of us working together, we can do that.'

For the first time since we entered the maze, I feel confident. This is not about magic or learning about who I am—this is a battle against a larger foe. I am trained to fight, and mostly that involves outsmarting your opponent before they pummel you. Combined with Percival's knowledge of the World Below and Snake's ability to find options when there aren't any, I'm sure that with a little bit of planning, we can do this.

Snake runs a hand through his hair; this usually means he is working something through. 'You're sure this is better than the one-day option and facing more traps?'

I nod. 'I am. We won't be able to predict what we will face there, so it will be next to impossible to prepare. If we choose the minotaur option, at least we know he'll be on the other side of the door, and we can make a plan.'

His hand goes to his hair again, and he pushes it out of his eyes. It's getting quite long and needs a cut. 'You make a fair point,' he admits.

'Besides,' I start. I'm not sure how to say this without sounding paranoid, so I just come out with it. 'While I'm sure Bernais and his cronies are plotting their next moves while we are out of their hair, Mandor's comment makes me wonder if Bernais has the power to ensure we don't come out of the maze—ever?'

Snake's eyes widen. 'I can't believe…. Percival, is that even possible?'

Our sprite friend has been strangely quiet since Mandor left, and I am not sure he has even been listening to us. However, he shrugs at Snake's question. 'Of course, there is always a chance someone could influence or bribe some being in the maze, but it would be a very brave creature who tampers with an official quest. They would have to answer to the minotaur, after all.'

'But he could, couldn't he?' Snake presses. 'I mean, Eleanora asked Mandor to come here, so she has sort of interfered.'

'Eleanora would never tamper with the quest. She only asked Mandor to come because she knows he will always do what is right, no matter what the cost to himself.'

Percival's words are bitter, hinting at their shared past. Although my curiosity is piqued, we don't have time to go into that now, so I say, 'I believe we can outsmart the minotaur—the three of us working together.'

Snake's eyes widen, telegraphing his surprise. 'But Percival is not a part of the quest. I'm sure the little boost of magic he gave to get us here would not be beyond the rules of helping….'

Snake looks at Percival for confirmation, but the sprite is silent. Instead, he rubs his chin thoughtfully and stares at the three doors.

'Yes, perhaps the three of us together could do this—defeat the minotaur,' he finally says.

Snake looks helplessly from Percival to me. 'Our only weapons are knives,' he points out. 'I mean, there is the bow and arrows, but I never got a chance to practice with them.'

'We are going to outsmart him, not face him head-on, just like we did with the troll,' I explain. 'What we have should be enough to distract him so we can get past him to the centre of the maze.'

Snake is quiet for a moment. I'm not sure he is convinced, but then he slips his pack from his shoulders. 'We'd best make sure our weapons are handy before we go through, then.'

I smile. I took the lead and made a decision. My team are supporting me. It feels good to be back to my old self.

Snake hands me some of his arrows. 'You might be able to do something with these—you know, change them with your magic.'

I nod and gaze at them. What could they be? I hold them together with my knife, and an image takes shape. I concentrate, and soon the wood and iron are re-formed into a sword. All right, it's not an amazing sword like magicians make in the movies, but it is sharp and serviceable and will suit my needs.

Snake hands me some travel bread, and I chew the berry-flavoured grains to recharge my energy while we plan out the battle.

'When we go through, I will take the front position. Percival, you go to my right and Snake to my left. Our best chance is to split up, forcing him to battle on more than one front. If you see a chance to make it to the maze's centre, take it. At least one of us will win through to the end.'

Before the others get a chance to comment, Mandor reappears and stands by the doors. 'Have you decided?'

'Yes,' we all say together.

Mandor's right eyebrow rises as he regards Percival. 'So you decided to fight for your future?'

'That is my business.' Percival's tone is tart. 'Your only job now is to let us through the third door—allow us to face this minotaur.'

'So be it,' the wizard says, and my stomach clenches as he presses his hand to the wood.

As the door swings open, my mouth goes dry and the travel bread sits heavy in my stomach. I hope I haven't made a foolish mistake—I mean, this is a minotaur, not a karate instructor ready to teach us a lesson. He will be focused on stopping us from getting to the centre of the maze at any cost. I square my shoulders. Too late to back out now.

As I step through the entrance, Mandor says, 'Percival, when you see Ellie, please tell her my heart is still hers and hers alone, and I miss her every day.'

'I am not sure how that helps her or you, but yes, I will tell her.'

Percival's voice follows me as I walk into a cloying black void. Silence swamps me, and I can barely breathe. I am here alone with no idea whether or not the others have followed. This is not at all what I expected.

CONFRONTING THE MINOTAUR

MY FEET SLIP from under me as the darkness around me changes. From within the void, I hear the wizard Mandor's voice echo. 'Use your head and your heart.' The words reverberate around me in the viscous air.

I try to walk forward, and I feel like I have walked face-first into a wet sheet. I gasp for air as I stumble. I am choking and falling and… then there is ground beneath my feet and I can breathe again.

As I struggle to stand, the pack on my back throws me a little off balance. Grasping my sword, I swing around, holding it in front of me. I raise my head, and my vision adjusts and shows me I am standing in the centre of a room about the size of my school gymnasium.

My gaze is drawn to burning red eyes inside a shadowlike bull's head. My eyes slide from the vision, as if they cannot quite believe what they are seeing. Behind him is a door—the door to the centre of the maze. I frantically search the room for my team, and my stomach clenches in fear. Has the minotaur decided to take me on in single combat?

The beast takes a step to the side, blocking my view, and I am forced to confront the beast that he is. Even though I try to stand straight and meet him front-on, my knees buckle, and I have to fight to stay on my feet. He must be seven, maybe even eight feet tall from his cloven feet to the tips of his horns. And that body is all bulky muscle and sinew lightly covered in brown fur. It would take both of my thighs to take up one of his biceps alone.

I fixate on his head, on the red glowing eyes and the snout that is twisted into a smile as if he has been waiting for this confrontation and is going to enjoy it. He dips his head in a parody of a welcome, allowing the light to catch the sharp points of his horns.

I shiver, then tear my gaze away and assess his other weapons. A sword hangs loosely in one of his large hands, and a mace swings hypnotically in the other. The spiked ball at the end of a chain is something I've never seen before. How do you combat that?

I am distracted by the sound of shuffling feet behind me. The minotaur's smile widens as Snake and Percival enter my peripheral vision. My heart rate calms a little at seeing them, at knowing I will not have to face our final test alone. They move into the positions I outlined before we entered the void. I'm relieved they're following the plan even though none of us could have imagined this entrance.

The minotaur roars, and my insides turn to liquid. Why did I choose to do this? Is there any way I can save us from our imminent defeat? Wait, can we refuse the challenge and choose another option? No, that is fear talking, and fear has no place in a fight.

This *is* the best option. Besides, Snake and I made it to the World Below, we have come this far through the maze, we have overcome every obstacle the minotaur placed in front of us, and the three of us will get to the centre. There must be a way around the behemoth guarding the door.

The room is slightly oval, with us at the apex and the door we need to reach at the furthest point. If the minotaur stretches out his arms with his weapons in place, there might almost be enough room for a piece of paper to slip past. The floor is flagstone, and the wall is stone. There really isn't much to work with.

As if he senses my brain working out a plan, the minotaur grasps his weapons and speaks. 'Ah, songsmith. Have you come to serenade me?' he asks Snake. His voice is mellow and cultured, which sounds odd coming from his beastlike face.

'Would it send you to sleep?' Snake quips in a rather jaunty tone. His voice is a little on the thin side, but I'm proud of him for not being cowed by our opponent.

The minotaur roars with laughter. 'No, young gentleman. You must know by now, nothing in my maze is that easy. I am here to test your mettle.'

Now that is just plain rude, I think. *Who does he think he is that he can boast of his right to test us?*

I straighten my spine and, ignoring my trembling legs, say, 'We wish entry to the centre of the maze.'

The minotaur laughs, a great rolling laugh that comes from deep in his belly. 'You two? Surely you jest. You come armed with a knife and a toothpick to fight me, the mightiest of the Queen's subjects?'

'How rude!' I say out loud this time. 'We came here on a quest. We earned the right to face you, so you could at least show us some respect.'

From the corner of my eye, I see Snake shuffle uneasily. 'Don't rile him up, Pris,' he tells me. 'He will be difficult enough to fight without you making him angry.'

To my surprise, the minotaur nods. 'You're right, of course—that *was* rude. I apologise. I don't get many visitors, and I do sometimes forget my manners. I guess the proper forms should be followed before I break you to smithereens.'

His apology does not reassure me. In fact he is so certain about the outcome of our contest, my resolve wavers a bit. I narrow my eyes at him. Perhaps this is just a tactic to put us off our guard, make us more fearful, as if his height and bulk are not intimidating enough. Or is this display of overconfidence something we can use to our advantage?

Ah, he still thinks Percival is only an observer in this dance. Is there something we can do with that? Even if he knew, he probably wouldn't see the sprite as a serious challenge.

If I have read the minotaur correctly, then Percival is our best chance of one of us getting to the centre. But how can I tell him of the change of plan without giving the game away?

'Percival,' I whisper without taking my eyes of the minotaur. 'Do you remember what I said about what we should all do if we get the chance?'

'I do.' His voice is soft, almost a whisper.

'How about you concentrate on doing just that.'

'Enough whispering,' the minotaur bellows as he leans his weapons on the ground and then relaxes. 'Who comes to challenge me for entry to the centre of the maze?'

This is it. This is the formal challenge before the fight begins.

'I, Princess Priscilla Crown,' I say.

'I, Sneak Thief,' Snake follows.

'And I, Percival of the Wyld Woods Tree Clan.'

The minotaur blinks twice, looks down at Percival, and asks almost conversationally, 'Are you sure about this, Percival? I mean, you have not crossed the line yet. You can still claim the role of advisor and sit this one out.'

I start. Did he just offer Percival a way out? Will he take it?

Percival takes a step forward so he is in line with me before squaring his shoulders. 'I, Percival of the Wyld Woods Tree Clan, seek entry to the centre of the maze.'

THE MINOTAUR'S MAZE

The glow in the minotaur's eyes softens a little as he regards the sprite. 'That is a shame. You know I cannot treat you any differently to the others.'

Percival nods. 'I am aware of that, and I would be insulted if you did.'

The minotaur raises his weapons and crosses his arms. The friendly chat with his mate is obviously over, and we are back in quest mode.

'All right. Prepare to be obliterated.'

THE MINOTAUR'S CHALLENGE fills the room, freezing me in place. Okay, so this is real now. I need to fight. Legs, move. Legs?

My legs are not listening. Taking a deep breath, I hold it together—just. Then the minotaur swings his mighty weapons. Finally, my legs get the message, but they move ever so slowly. I'm only saved from being crushed because the minotaur is so tall, I am able to step to one side and duck. Still, the wake of his swinging arm nearly causes me to lose my footing.

'Split up,' Pris yells, and I edge away from her sideways.

Actual sparks fly up from the stone as the sword strikes it at the end of its arc. The minotaur lifts his weapon for another attack. I don't move fast enough, and a burning slice of pain near my ankle causes me to stumble.

I glance down to find the blade cut right through my boot. I expect to see blood gushing from the gash, but there is barely a trickle. If a nick hurts like that, I hate to think what a full-blown strike will do.

I rejoin the fight to find the minotaur bearing down on Pris. He is totally ignoring Percival, which is allowing the sprite to slip in behind the beast and run for the door. Now I understand what Pris was whispering about before the fight.

When he reaches it, I expect him to slip through to safety. Instead, he turns to watch the battle. He can't be planning to help out in some way, can he?

A change in the air alerts me another swing is coming my way, and I dodge. For the second time, I am not quite quick enough. One of the mace spikes catches my arm and slices through both shirt and skin. At this rate my fight will be less of a battle and more a death by a thousand cuts.

I block out the pain and bite back my dismay as the minotaur raises the mace and prepares to take a swing at Pris. She is backed against a wall with nowhere to go. My eyes widen as the mace shimmers before my eyes.

'Duck,' Pris yells, and I do as she commands, shielding myself from splinters of wood and metal as the mace is blown apart.

I shake off shards of debris as I steal a quick glance at Pris. Apart from a couple of wounds on her face, she is okay. She wipes hair out of her eyes and looks up defiantly at the minotaur. Is she grinning? Yep. Then again, so would I be if I had come up with a move like that.

My relief turns to fear as the minotaur grips his sword, preparing to retaliate. There is no thinking, just action. I reach over my shoulder and grasp one of the arrows sticking out of the top of my backpack. I rush at the creature, yelling at the top of my lungs. With all my might, I force the metal tip into a meaty part of the minotaur's calf and dodge away.

The minotaur turns as if in slow motion, sword raised above his head, and glares at me, I think less in anger, more in shock. He's already pegged Pris as the main threat, but now he can't ignore me. I may not be the warrior Pris is, but I will not let him hurt her if I can help it.

I'm dizzy from fear and the adrenaline rush as the minotaur reaches down and removes the arrow as if it were a minor irritation. He flings it behind him, narrowly missing Percival, and swings back around to face his prey—Pris.

I may not have injured him, but I did buy Pris enough time to slip further around past the minotaur and towards the door. When he sees this, he roars in anger, his red eyes blazing. He moves forward, swinging his gleaming blade at Pris. She ducks and dives, trying to turn the creature around, but even I can see she is slowing down. She will not be able to keep this up for much longer.

I only have my knife left, and I'm not sure what I can do with that. Whatever I decide to do, I must do it soon, or goodness knows what will happen to Pris.

I rake the room with my eyes, searching for something… anything that might help me. Pris is using her magic to pick up shards of the mace and is flinging them at the minotaur. He swats them away like flies, but they are distracting him. A sliver of metal finally hits home, and the minotaur ignores it. Pris's shoulders slump. Desperation and exhaustion shine in her eyes as they meet mine, but what can *I* do against the huge beast?

At the back of the room, Percival is jumping up and down, trying to get my attention. It is difficult to make out what he is saying over the minotaur's grunts and roars.

His voice finally breaches my ears. 'Snake, it is up to you now. Use your magic.'

Use my magic? What does he mean? What use is lock picking when the beast is bearing down on Pris?

In a last-ditch effort, I yell, 'Hey you, big and ugly—over here.'

The minotaur turns his head and grins. 'I'm saving you for dessert,' he says and turns back round to Pris.

Again, all I have done is gain her a moment to catch her breath and a slightly better position to make a run for the door. It is not enough.

Percival yells again. 'Remember who you are and what your magic is.'

What is he saying? Who I am? I'm a gnome? No, hold on, I'm only part gnome—I also have elf blood. Does that mean my bindings are not as strong as the other gnomes? Can I do some higher magic? Can I move or change something to save Pris?

I study my surroundings. It will have to be small, as I haven't done anything like this before. There's nothing in the room. It's bare except for… the pavers. I focus on the stone directly under the minotaur's foot as his big fist comes down towards Pris. I move a paver up, then quickly drop it again. The minotaur loses his footing, and the blow that would have certainly knocked her out only glances past her cheek.

While Pris shakes her head and tries to refocus on the fight, I move the paving stone under his other foot, and the minotaur stumbles to one knee. He turns his head to glare at me before launching back to his feet.

I might be your dessert, but I'm going to give you indigestion.

Pris runs a hand over her eyes and wobbles a little. That blow must have been harder than I thought. When she catches my eye, I direct her gaze to another paver and move it. Her wide eyes meet mine, showing me she's worked out my plan. She wobbles the stones in front of the beast as he turns and steps towards me. He trips and is forced to use his sword to stop from falling.

I glance towards Pris, and she slips closer towards Percival while shaking stones around the minotaur's feet. I do the same, concentrating on moving him away from the door when I can. One last effort and we raise the stones he stands on so the minotaur almost touches the roof, then drop them to the ground. As the beast falls, arms swinging, we rush to the doors.

Percival frantically reaches for the door handle, misses, then grabs it firmly and turns it. There is a thud behind us, and the sprite yells, 'Hurry, before he regains his feet.'

The minotaur's roar shakes the foundations almost as much as our magic did, and I slip, banging into Pris as footsteps thud from behind.

Percival wrenches open the door, and we pile over the threshold in a tangle of gnome, elf, and sprite limbs. The floor rocks and another roar sounds out, and I cover my ears as the sound almost bursts my ear drums. I grab for Pris, wanting to have her close by as death meets us. Then I realise the roar is not one of anger or a battle cry. Is that the sound of the minotaur laughing?

DID WE WIN?

I DISENTANGLE MY limbs and try to sit up. My body doesn't want to obey, so I sink back on the cold stone and try to get my bearings. Everything is fuzzy and the room is spinning. That blow to the head must have affected me more than I thought.

I need to take stock of the damage. Okay, a little at a time. I wiggle my fingers, then try to lift my arm. I push down panic as I realise I can't feel it. Snake groans, and suddenly my arm is free. I blow out a sigh of relief.

Concentrating, I move my toes inside my boots. Yep, they're working, but something pressing against my right ankle. I manage to raise my head enough to identify the problem. My foot is stuck between the door and the jamb. The minotaur swims into view as my vision clears, his sword slung casually over his shoulder. My ears are ringing, and everything sounds like someone has turned the volume down, but I'm pretty sure from the way he is baring his teeth that he is laughing.

Anger burns in my gut. He is laughing at us. We fought against a mythical creature from legend, and although we didn't defeat him, we made it to the centre of the maze.

'I have not had this much fun in years. You have done well, my little friends. You almost made it,' he says, leering, or is that a grin?

'Wait. What do you mean we "almost" made it?' Snake asks before my brain is able to form the words.

The minotaur points at our feet, which slipped back into the room as we tumbled to the ground. 'You have not yet crossed the threshold.' He reaches down to the floor as he speaks.

Snake and I draw our legs back, but Percival is still trying to sit up and is unable to move quickly enough. The minotaur's massive hand closes around him, hauling him into a bear hug.

The creature stares down at us, and I notice his eyes no longer glow red, but are dark and liquid like a cow's, or a bull's, I suppose I should say.

The minotaur offers us a choice. 'So my friends, what say you now? Will you finish your quest and leave your friend to his fate? Or will you try and save him?'

I rise shakily to my feet and turn to Snake. His eyes plead with me, but I don't know what he is asking. I want to get away from this monster, but I won't leave Percival behind. All I want Snake to do is say we are a team, that we stand together, but a small part of me fears he might put saving his mother first, and no one would blame him if he did.

'Go,' Percival begs. 'I was not truly a part of this quest. I was only a helper. You can still retrieve the object and ask the Queen to save your parents.'

'No, we wouldn't be here if you hadn't helped us,' Snake says. My heart glows as he confirms he and I stand as one on this.

'We won't leave you behind,' I agree as Snake rises to his feet and tries to shake off his injuries.

He stands shoulder to shoulder with me, and together we face our common foe.

'Put Percival down, and we will finish our fight,' I say.

'No.' Percival wriggles in distress. 'You must not fail because of me.'

'But what about the boon you wish to ask from the Queen should we succeed?' I ask.

He shakes his head, and the sorrow his eyes pierces my soul. 'I am not sure that matters any more. I believe what you are doing here is part of something much bigger, something that affects us all.' The words are said so softly, I'm not sure I hear him correctly. Then he announces loudly and firmly, 'I waited this long. I can wait a little longer.'

Snake's fingers entwine through mine. I lean into him and whisper, 'Something happened to Percival last night. He seems both… well… broken and resolute. We can't leave him behind to be the minotaur's plaything. It wouldn't be right.'

'You can barely stand, my shoulder is killing me, and our weapons are gone. What can we do?' He sounds exhausted, defeated. Then he stands straighter and squares his shoulders. 'Can we try a distraction and hope he lets go of Percival?'

I consider the idea, but my head is still swimming, and I can't think of anything that might work. Finally, I admit defeat and tell him, 'I don't think so.'

'Then we must bargain for the minotaur to take me. If you free your parents, they are highborn enough they may be able to pull strings to help my mother. And you are more likely to succeed with Percival than with me because of his friendship with Eleanora.' I lean on his shoulder, and he squeezes my hand. 'You know this is the best option for everyone.'

I hear what he is saying, but I can't agree to this. I can't lose him just when we're… I am not sure what we are, but I am sure I am not going to let him go that easily again. 'What if the minotaur kills you?'

'I'm hoping he won't.' Snake releases my hand and steps over the threshold. I reach out to stop him, but I'm too late.

'I offer myself up instead of Percival,' he announces.

The minotaur bares his teeth, 'I knew there was nobility as well as music in you, boy. You have the heart of a true hero. And you will be a worthy opponent.'

He drops Percival to the ground and waits until the sprite scrambles back over the threshold before taking a battle stance, sword at the ready.

I can't do it. I can't let Snake face the minotaur alone. I glance down at Percival. He meets my gaze square-on, and in answer to the question he reads in my eyes, he moves to stand beside me. We step back into the room and join Snake, ready to fight as a team.

'Stop,' a voice rings out from behind the creature of legend. 'Surely this has gone far enough.'

FROM THE RECESSES of the room, someone asks the minotaur to stop. It takes a while to register, perhaps because my knees are knocking and my heart is pounding so loud, I can hear very little else. I have no idea where my attempt at bravery came from, but it disappeared pretty quickly.

I'm too scared to take my eyes off the minotaur, yet someone is moving behind the beast. Part of me wants to check this isn't another threat, but quite honestly, I am too bone weary to care.

'Come on, Aeron. I like a good contest as much as the next person, but they won fair and square. You are only drawing this out because they are entertaining you.'

The voice sounds familiar, but I can't quite place it.

'Ah, but the boy stepped back over the line….'

'Only after you taunted them with the sprite. You had your fun. The rules of the maze have been met. You all acquitted yourselves with honour, but you were outsmarted by the children in the end.'

I wanted to argue that we are not children, but I bite back the words. Aggravating our rescuer with petty details will not help our cause. Pris is not so circumspect.

'We're not children,' she says, placing her hands on her hips.

The minotaur laughs, his belly shaking. 'I am hundreds of years old, little elfling, and my friend here is at least three hundred…. You have scarcely begun to breathe by comparison. Hush now, and let your elders talk.'

Pris's jaw is tightening, a sure sign she is annoyed, but even she must admit we *are* children when you consider how old the minotaur is.

'I must say, I am impressed by how the elf and the gnome stood up for the sprite…. They have spunk, I will give them that.' The minotaur strokes his chin with his free hand. 'And they fought with vigour.'

While Aeron is diverted, Percival grabs at mine and Pris's hands, taking the opportunity presented to urge us back into the hallway.

'Aeron, the rules state all the questers need to do is get past you to the door. They did that.'

Our champion is a little closer now, still hidden behind the minotaur. The voice is *so* familiar. No, I still have no idea who it is.

'But how can I hold my head high and admit I was beaten in combat by two children and a wood sprite?' Aeron wails, carrying on as if his whole world is crumbling. 'The Queen might decide I can no longer be her champion.'

'Oh, really, that's what this is about? You don't want to admit to being beaten by us?' Pris steps forward, hands on hips. She glances at the ground, careful to check she did not inadvertently cross the threshold again. 'You can't admit we won, so you are making things up?'

'Pris!' I force through gritted teeth. 'Must you poke the bear? He may decide to decapitate us just for fun—quest be damned.'

'I take offence at that, young man. I will face anyone in combat, but I do not kill indiscriminately in a fit of pique.'

Honestly, what is going on here? Have I fallen down a rabbit hole into a bizarre new world where common-sense is absent? 'So she can call you a baby, but I can't say you might kill us?'

'I am an honourable creature—'

'It's all right, Aeron. Snake did not mean anything by what he said, did you, Snake?'

A figure moves out of the shadows to the minotaur's right. I stiffen with fright, then relax as I see Fairburn nodding, encouraging me to agree with him.

I guess needs must. 'Um, yes, I am sorry. I did not mean to call you dishonourable,' I tell Aeron, when what I really want to say is, 'What in the hell are you doing here, Fairburn?'

'Good.' The centaur smiles. 'Now, are we all agreed that the children made it to the door and so are allowed to proceed?'

'No, I will not admit defeat.' Aeron crosses his arms over his chest and refuses to budge.

Fairburn and Pris both sigh, but it is Percival who breaks the deadlock. The sprite steps around me so he can be both seen and heard. 'You were not defeated, Aeron. Not in battle, at least. I slipped behind you, and Pris and Snake used magic to outsmart you to get to the door.'

Aeron ponders his words for a moment, and I almost blurt, "You can't seriously be considering this?", but I wisely bite my tongue.

After a long while, the minotaur agrees. 'Yes, I can live with that. I am happy to tell people I was outwitted.'

I shake my head, unable to believe I am part of this madness. I'm too tired to argue that this is merely semantics and means nothing. Besides, it means we won, and we get to enter the centre of the maze—all three of us together.

I TURN ON my heel, thinking it might be a good idea to move before Aeron changes his mind. I mean, he might throw another hissy fit and decide Snake and I should fight him again.

Striding down the darkened corridor, I head towards the light in the distance. I pull up short as the light is blocked out and a dark shadow moves towards us. I slump against the wall. I can't do it. I just can't deal with any more surprises today. The shadow can bleeding well have me.

The shape saunters closer, resolving itself into a dragon. It is a sign of how exhausted I am that it takes a moment for my mind to process that I am staring at an honest-to-god dragon.

My new nightmare towers at least two feet taller than I am and glows a deep purple in the half-light. I want to reach out and touch the pearly scales, but I'm pretty sure that's not the done thing. Especially not when it is smiling down at me like I'm its next meal.

My first thought is, did Percival know about this? I mean, he did mention dragons. When he pulls up beside me and exclaims, 'What now? A dragon? What more are they going to throw at us?' I am thinking perhaps not.

Some part of me is aware Snake is not with us, but by now my whole world is those dragon eyes. They are drawing me in. A part of me knows this is not a good thing, but I am powerless to do anything about it.

Little elf, what do you want here?

The voice in my head is deep and vibrates through my body. The dragon is talking to me in my mind. Cool! Deep in the recesses of my consciousness, someone is screaming, 'Wake up! You're caught in a dragon thrall.' I think it might be me, but I'm too blissed out to listen.

'Away with you, my young friend. I granted these three entry, and they are under my protection.' Aeron's voice comes from far away. It really is a very dreamy voice.

The dragon snorts, and the bliss disappears, but it doesn't release me. *What is it you want?* The dragon almost whispers the words, and I sense it is seeking an answer to the question rather than trying to frighten me away.

A way to free my parents, I tell it, trying not to appear cowed even though my knees have turned to jelly under his lizard-like gaze.

I am a female, and I think you want more than you are admitting to even yourself. The dragon snorts again. *You seek your place in the world—in both worlds. I hope you find what you are looking for.*

She blinks, and it is like there was an elastic band holding me in place, and as she releases it, I stumble backwards into Snake, and he wraps his arms around me.

'Are you okay.'

'I'm not sure,' I tell him, and he pulls me closer.

'What are we waiting for?' Aeron grumbles.

He must have pushed Snake in the back, because he throws himself forward and I move with him, landing face-first in the belly of the dragon.

I freeze. The sensation is not unpleasant. Her skin is soft and cool, and I imagine this is what faceplanting into a very large snake would feel like. I turn my head to breathe, and one of the sharper scales surrounding her belly cuts into my forehead, and my blood trickles down her skin. Instinctively, I try to reach up, but I find I can't move.

The dragon steps back, and I'm frozen in place by a blanket of warm air. The air gently pushes me upright until I am on my feet, then it simply dissolves.

'Th-thank you,' I stutter.

The dragon bares her teeth, and I wonder if she's decided to eat me after all. She snorts. 'You would not even make an entree. We princesses must look out for each other, so it is written.'

She turns away, sweeping her long tail in close so she doesn't bowl us over, before dropping onto all fours and leading the way into the room at the end of the corridor.

Amazement tinges Snake's next words. 'So, that was a smile?'

I don't respond. I sense something portentous in the dragon's words, and her tone suggests I should understand what she means. Her words distract me as I head towards our goal—the centre of the maze.

'Does Snow White spring to mind?' Snake asks as Percival drops to a knee, mumbling something about Queen Ariana.

'What?' I drag my gaze back from the undulating form of the dragon as Snake's words sink through the haze in my brain.

Snake is right. Directly in front of us, in the centre of the room, is a woman asleep in a glass coffin. Her red-gold hair frames a delicate, fine-boned face. The lines are too sharp for her to be considered beautiful, but she could be described as regal. She has been dressed as if for a funeral in an emerald-green gown piped with gold, and her hands had been laid across her stomach. Apart from her pallor and the fact that her chest does not rise or fall, she could be just sleeping.

Curled up in front of the coffin's plinth is a huge emerald dragon. It opens a yellow eye and glares balefully at us before turning its attention to Aeron and Fairborn. The flicker of its snake-like pupil tells me it is probably communicating with the elder creatures.

I allow myself to relax a little and be dazzled by the fairy-tale display of magic. In my dreams, this was what the World Below was like until I stepped through the gateway a few days before and saw the reality. Then it hits me like a sledgehammer—the dragon and the woman are the only things in the centre of the maze except for us. Are they what we were sent to retrieve?

Snake must have arrived at this conclusion at exactly the same time. His eyes widen before his face settles into a mask of dismay.

Leaning in towards Snake, I whisper, 'Who is she?'

Snake half turns, but can't take his eyes off the woman. 'I have no idea.'

I shift my focus to Percival, but his face is blank and he is lost to us again. Before I can ask Fairburn, Snake's voice fills the chamber.

'Are we here for the woman or the dragon? And just how do you expect us to take either of them out of here?'

MY VOICE ECHOES around the room, and I try not to start at the sound. I really hope someone will step forward and tell me I'm wrong. I want them to tell me it is the ring the woman wears, or perhaps a dragon scale, that we are to take back to prove we made it to the centre of the maze.

The room is silent, and the longer it stays that way, the more I'm sure that

my first guess was right.

The smaller dragon curls up by the larger one—her mother, I assume, because dragons are generally solitary creatures—as Fairburn and Aeron take up positions behind the glass case.

Percival has dropped to his knees and is muttering something about the poor Queen and us of all being doomed. Is that Queen Ariana in there? No wonder people haven't seen her for a while.

I raise my gaze and stare directly at Fairburn. 'What's going on here?' I ask. 'Did the council send us on a false quest?'

The centaur does not answer. His head drops and his face softens as he looks at the Queen.

I do not get annoyed often, but I am angry now. I risked everything to try and save my mother, and they played me for a fool. The Queen is dead. How will I ever save Mum now?

'It is time for the truth, Fairburn,' a voice rumbles through the cavernous space.

I sweep the chamber with my gaze, but no one else has entered. I can't make out who spoke. The larger dragon raises her head and stares straight at the three of us. A sigh from Fairburn draws my attention back to him.

'No, Snake, it was not in vain, but nor were we completely honest with you either,' the centaur admits.

Pris moves beside me and takes my hand before saying, 'I think it is well past time for the truth, don't you?'

I don't know if it is because she is such a force to be reckoned with, or whether it's because she is a princess, but people listen when she speaks. And I'm beyond grateful they're listening now.

'I think it is the least you owe Snake, Percival, and me after what we went through the last few days,' Pris finishes.

The younger dragon snorts, in approval I think, and Fairburn colours. He glances at Percival, who is still on a knee.

'Percival, I am so sorry to find out about your father. His end is quite close now, but I know he asked you to come back and finish what you started with Princess Priscilla and Snake. I want to thank you for your sacrifice,' Fairburn says.

What? Something happened to Percival's father? That must have been where he was last night.

I place a hand on his shoulder. 'Percival, you should have said. I'm so sorry.'

Pris helps him to his feet and bends down to hug him. Percival bristles at her touch but does not move away from her. He doesn't speak, but then again, he is a very private creature.

We place Percival between us and turn back to Fairburn. 'Percival's sacrifice makes it even more important that you come clean with us,' Pris says, her arm still draped over the sprite's shoulder. As she faces Fairburn, she looks fiercer than I have ever seen her, like a momma bear protecting her offspring.

Aeron smiles. 'Yeah, Fairburn. Time for the truth.'

I think he is enjoying the fact that Fairburn is now the one being brought to task.

Fairburn sighs. 'I am a guard, a soldier. Words are not my tools, and I did not want to be the one to tell you this… but… as Queen Ariana's protector, I am the only one allowed to come here.'

'Is she still alive?' Pris demands.

'In a way,' Fairburn responds. 'Magic is holding her on the precipice between life and death.'

So, it *is* the Queen in the glass box. She is alive, but she is definitely not in a position to help us.

'Where do I start?' Fairburn speaks as if to himself. 'Do I explain the magic or the politics or….'

'For goodness sakes, centaur.' The larger dragon's voice rumbles in my head. 'Let me. Children, I am Am'rena, Queen of the Dragons and soul sister of Queen Ariana. Together we have tended the magical core of our world for over three hundred years.'

'You were there…,' Percival whispers, awe in his voice. 'I remember… not quite… but….'

The dragon continues over him. 'The magical flow has been slowing for some time, and the work we are doing to keep it moving made the Queen sick. Fairburn brought her here a month or so ago, placed her in stasis, and we have been trying to cure her since then.'

Everyone knows the Queen, or King, in rare instances, of the World Below is the only creature able to access the magical flow, but this is the first I have heard of a dragon partnership. I am still processing this while Pris kneels to better converse with the dragon. I guess not having learnt about magical history means she is more able to just accept this and feels able to talk to a dragon without being invited.

Pris's head drops to one side as if she is trying to make some sort of connection with Am'rena. 'Do you know what the problem is with the flow of magic?' Pris asks out loud.

'In the past, the Queen of the Seelie Court and the King of the Unseelie Court would work with their dragon sister and brother, and everything flowed smoothly. When the World Below sealed itself off, something happened to the river, and it was never quite right again, not even after the barrier was partially opened.'

'I'm not surprised,' I blurt, immediately identifying the problem. I falter when all eyes in the room turn to me.

'Why not enlighten us, then.' Fairburn's words drip with sarcasm. 'I mean, it took our scholars almost a hundred years to come up with a solution.'

Am'rena snorted. 'Don't be so quick to dismiss him, centaur. Your scholars are hampered by politics and a limited view of the world. This elf-gnome has the benefit of a different education, and I see he knows the answer.'

I raise an eyebrow. *Are you reading my mind?* I ask in my head.

Snorting again, which I now believe might be a dragon laugh 'Yes.' There is no apology. 'Tell them.'

If the Queen of Dragons has faith in me, I won't doubt myself. 'Once you block a river, dam it, so to speak, the water changes course. If you unblock it again, it might flow as swiftly, but will probably take a different path. If you only unblock some of it, it will never run the same again. I imagine the magical flow to be the same.'

Fairburn nods curtly, confirming my assessment. 'Although it is much worse. Magic flows like an infinity sign. We blocked the flow at the crossover point, which left magic stagnating in the World Above and the World Below. This caused a blight in our world, and the Dark Ages in the World Above. When we opened some of the gates and allowed some of our people to go back and forth, the blight was eradicated, but magic was never the same.'

'While I work with The King of Dragons in the World Above to do our bit, your King and Queen have not worked together to do theirs,' Am'rena added.

'You're telling me a dragon lives in my world?' Pris laughs out loud.

This is what she finds astonishing? Sometimes I have no idea how her mind works, but I guess that's part of her charm.

'No,' Am'rena rumbles. 'He does not live there. We all live in the Dragon Realm, in the World Between. He does visit through the portal at Loch Ness though.'

'The Loch Ness Monster,' Pris and I say together, then lock eyes, laughing.

This story is too bizarre, and amusing though it is, it does not explain why we are here. I decide to take a leaf from Pris's book and go the direct route.

'I appreciate your need to sort out magic and wake the Queen, but why involve us?'

'Yes,' Pris says, rising to her feet so she can better face Fairburn. 'I think it's about time you tell us why you brought us here.'

I AM FILTHY, tired, wounded, and a little unsteady on my feet. I want a soak in a bath and sleep a comfy bed, but even more, I want to know why we are here in the centre of the maze when we cannot remove anything to finish our quest.

Fairburn clears his throat, and his hooves shuffle. 'Right, the Queen has been sick for a while, something her closest advisors and I kept from the rest of the realm. Unfortunately, Bernais's network of spies found out about it.'

'He has always been a snake in the grass, putting his own interests before the realm. I banned him from the maze. I will not allow him near me,' Aeron states, banging his sword on the floor for emphasis.

I don't need convincing. I already knew Bernais had something to do with what is going on. Even so, I'm not sure he would harm the Queen, as that would not serve his purpose. He would, however, try to save her so he could claim the glory.

'You're not telling us anything they aren't talking about in every village market,' Snake says, earning a dour look from Fairburn.

I flash Snake a "let him finish" look before encouraging the centaur. 'Go on,' I urge.

'Hoping for the Queen's imminent demise, Bernais began jockeying for position, hoping to counter anyone she nominated as heir. You, Snake, are here because the Queen indicated your clan's punishment was at an end and that you all should be raised to elven status. Bernais could not permit this because the balance of power would change so much, and it might shift out of his—'

'He accused my mother, hoping he could delay proceedings,' Snake interrupts, bitterness in his voice. 'My family already worked that out.'

Fairburn nods. 'I am afraid this is just his first move—'

'Because he will raise the fact that my father married a person of mixed race,' Snake finishes again. Then he stands straighter, as if he has just thought of something. 'Bernais wanted me to do this to get me out of the way and to further sully the name of my family. Wouldn't it be useful for him to leak that the reason I failed was because I was not of pure blood?'

Percival stirs beside me. 'That would be just like him, to use that against you. He despises anyone who is not an elf, but, if it is at all possible, he despises those of impure blood even more.'

Snake takes a step forward. I can see he is excited about something. 'You, or perhaps the council and you, wanted me to come on this quest, didn't you?'

Fairburn nods encouragingly. 'Can you see why?'

'You want me to help the Queen because by helping her return to full health, she will not only counter Bernais, but it will give her even more reason to raise my family to their proper status.' Snake finishes, then stops, a frown creasing his brow. 'What made you think I would be of any help?'

Fairburn smiles and my heart literally flutters. 'Because you are the son of your father and grandfather.'

Snake seems to accept that answer, and I can see he is about to ask what Fairburn wants him to do, but the centaur is still speaking. I am sure I know what he is going to say, but I want to hear it.

'And you, Priscilla—you are here because your mother is the Queen's closest relative but chose a life in the World Above. When she did, she relinquished her claim to the throne—'

'But she didn't relinquish mine,' I finish. 'Bernais wanted to bring me to the World Below to get rid of me so no one could stand against him.'

All the pieces click together. I know who I am and why I am both listened to and hated so much, and why I was attacked in the World Above, and why my parents kept me away from their home. They were protecting me from this.

'And now you want me to help the Queen so Bernais does not rule in the World Below,' I finish.

Although I am pleased I finally have some answers, I'm not sure how I feel about this. Okay, Bernais can never be King, that is clear, but I don't want to be Queen of the World Below—ever.

Am'rena snorts. 'You get ahead of yourself, girl. Your Queen can still live for a few hundred more years if we save her in time, and there are others who might be pardoned with a stronger claim to the throne than you.'

'Oh.' I hadn't thought about where my mother might sit in the order of succession. And perhaps I have other cousins and such.

'The most important thing is to save the Queen and bring stability back to our realm,' Fairburn tells us.

Snake cuts straight to the point. 'So, what do you want us to do?'

'We want you to finish your quest. You were tasked with bringing what is in the middle of the maze out, and that is Queen Ariana. Only she can't be moved until she is cured and the magical flow is restored,' Fairburn says.

I close my eyes. My brain is sluggish, but it is putting together the puzzle in front of me, and I am sure I know what Fairburn will ask.

'You must all go to the Unseelie Court and convince the King to return here to at least help heal the Queen, and preferably to work with her to heal the magical flow.'

I knew it. Something else occurs to me. Although I do not want to leave Snake behind, perhaps he can go back to the Capitol and keep an eye on our families. And Percival will want to return to his family so he can say a proper goodbye to his father.

'I know that I must go to the Unseelie Court to petition on behalf of my—is she my great-aunt?—but why must Snake and Percival go with me?' I ask.

Percival takes my hands, and I force myself not to start in surprise, but my eyes are instantly drawn to him.

'My father told me something bigger than us was happening and that I had a role to play. He would not tell me what it was, but I see what it is now. I am to be the one to introduce you at the Unseelie Court,' he tells me.

'You are?' I ask.

'Of course. I knew many people there before they were sent to the World Above. I must go and help you.'

I want Percival to come with me, but it would be selfish to pull him away from his family at a time like this. 'But, Percival, what about your father?'

He shrugs. 'We have said our goodbyes. I will celebrate his life at the thirty days gathering. I am at your disposal until then.' He gives my hand a small squeeze and warmth fills me. While I could do this alone, I don't really want to. Percival being there will definitely make things easier for me.

'None of you have to go,' Fairburn interrupts, 'but I believe you are more likely to succeed if you all go together. We will give you some privacy so you can discuss what you want to do.'

SAVING THE WORLD

I AM ANGRY at Eleanora for not telling me everything about the quest and what the council had been up to, yet I'm also grateful. I have cut myself off from my true self while I have been her familiar in the World Above, allowing her to direct my actions rather than making choices about my life.

I now realise that she wanted me to be a part of this quest because she understands me. She knew if Pris and Snake were going to fail, I would help them and become a part of the quest, and therefore be able to petition the Queen to see her way clear to returning me to a full sprite. This is what Princess Petunia had always intended once her sister took the throne, but she was never able to do it because she was banished.

Now I see Eleanora wants more for me. She wants me to believe I am more than her eyes and ears. She wants to show me my own value so that when I face a Queen and ask for my reward, I know exactly what I am asking for and that I deserve it.

I will go to the Unseelie Court. I do not need to listen in on Pris and Snake arguing about who should go. I leave them to withdraw into the hallway for some privacy and join Fairburn and Aeron, who seems much more friendly now that he is not trying to cut me down with his sword.

What I need to do before we leave the centre of the maze is have Fairburn tell Pris the one piece of information he is holding back. It is only fair she knows exactly what she is getting herself into. As I approach, I try not to look at the Queen. It disturbs me to see her so lifeless. I clear my throat.

'You need to tell Pris *everything* before we leave,' I say, and Fairburn turns in surprise. He crosses his arms over an impossibly muscled chest. 'Why, Percival?

What good will it do?'

I stare at him in wonder. I know a centaur's heart beats differently to the hearts of other creatures. They run in herds and do not mate for life. But Fairburn cannot be this insensitive to how finding this out from someone else will affect the princess.

'Coming to the World Below and trying to save her parents is unsettling for Pris. She is trying to get a sense of who she is, and that changes almost every day. Surely it would be better if we told her everything,' I argue. 'Having her whole history would give her confidence in the court.'

'It is her family's job to tell her about this. I have been given no leave to pass on that information, and I expect you to keep it to yourself as well,' Fairburn instructs me.

He is very scary when he uses that commanding tone. I also sense he will not be swayed from his position.

'As you wish. But do not complain to me when things fall apart later,' I sniff and turn on my heel.

Pausing before going through the door, I turn back. 'Out of interest, who ordered you not to tell the princess?'

There are only a few creatures who Fairburn would consider able to command him, and I am curious about who is pulling his strings.

Fairburn strokes his chin. For a moment I think he isn't going to answer. Then he says, 'Her father asked me not to say anything.'

From Fairburn's smirk, I have not succeeded in keeping my surprise from showing on my face.

'There is nothing sinister in this,' the centaur adds. 'You know more than anyone does that Princess Pricilla's family situation is rather… um… complex. Malachi simply requested that she be told about her heritage by her family. I believe that request should be respected.'

His dark eyes pin me, and I glare back at him. I can see Pris's father's point, but he would have no way of knowing how much Pris craves that knowledge, or how this could impact her emotionally to have it withheld.

I turn and watch her as she argues with Snake, and I hope that Snake refuses to be left behind because I sense she is going to need him when we get to the Unseelie Court.

THE DETERMINED SET of Pris's jaw tells me her mind is made up. I would bet my entire instrument collection that she believes I will go along with whatever she says too. Clearly, the knock to the head scrambled her brains.

'You aren't Queen yet, so don't even try and command me.' I'm aiming for levity, hoping to charm her.

'But someone needs to be looking after our parents,' she presses.

She knows my weak points, but I can come up with something better. 'I think Fairburn can handle their security more effectively than I can.'

As I mention the centaur, her eyes take on this funny, googly, glazed look. Hold on, does she fancy that musclebound oaf? After all his double-dealing? Jealousy gnaws at my stomach. 'Pris, is this because you don't want me around?'

Her eyes clear and she frowns at me. 'What? No!'

The green-eyed monster then gets hold of my mouth and says, 'Would you prefer Fairburn escorts you?'

'Oh my god, you're jealous. Just because I admire his muscles—'

'I'm not—really, I'm not. That was just....'

I'm not sure what it is. I am tired, and I thought this would all be over when we made it to the centre of the maze. Now here I am, arguing with Pris when all I want to do is pull her into my arms and tell her I am going with her, and no argument she can come up with will change my mind.

What a great idea!

I wrap my arms around her and pull her to me. I draw her in closer. She leans into me, and just for a moment, I simply enjoy the feel of holding her.

'I am going with you,' I say gently but firmly. 'Not because I don't want to let you out of my sight, although that is part of it. I am going because I need to, if only to prove to Bernais that I am every bit as good as he and his elf friends are.'

She sighs and her body finally relaxes in my arms. 'I know you are better than him.' Her voice is muffled as she speaks into my neck.

'Thank you, but I think I want to prove it to myself. I want to stand up and be counted. Besides, I believe Fairburn is holding something back, not only about you, but about me as well. Something is going on at the Unseelie Court, something I can help with, and I want to find out what it is.'

Pris snuggles closer into my neck. 'I like this new you, and I love how you haven't told me that you shouldn't be with a potential heir to the crown.'

I laugh. 'You know, I hadn't even thought about that. Anyway, Am'rena told you not to get too ahead of yourself.'

Pris's laughter tickles my neck, and I smile. I step back, bend my neck, and touch my lips to hers. She tilts her head and slightly parts her lips, and I accept her invitation. Closing my eyes as the kiss deepens, I lose myself in the feel of her body against mine.

'Have you decided?' Fairburn's voice booms from the other room.

I groan. For a moment I had forgotten where we were and that we weren't alone. 'I hope we get a good night's sleep in a real bed before we head out,' I whisper.

Pris's lips twitch into a smile. 'Sleep?' she jokes, and I groan again.

WE WALK HAND in hand back into the centre of the maze. The cool air brushes against my hot cheeks, and I am sure my lips are swollen from the kiss. Fairburn takes one look at us and smirks knowingly. My face is burning, and this is one of the times my darker complexion comes in handy, hopefully hiding my embarrassment.

Beside me, Snake glares defiantly at the centaur, daring him to say something. My lips curl into a smile—my hero. I slide an arm around his waist so we present a united front, and Snake responds by slipping his arm around me. Percival moves to take the place on my other side, and I drop a hand onto his shoulder. My team is here.

'We will all go to petition the King of The Unseelie Court,' I say.

'Excellent,' Fairburn says as if he expected nothing less. 'Am'ratha will fly you, and her brother Ed'rathe is waiting outside to transport Percival and Snake.'

What did he just say? 'You want us to fly there? On dragons?'

He must be joking. I mean, this is like something out of a fantasy book, not something I ever expected to happen in my actual life.

'How else did you think you would travel from here to there?' Am'rena rumbles. 'My children will transport you in the blink of an eye. There is no time for dilly-dallying.'

Besides, it will give us a little time to bond, Am'ratha says.

I do a double take. *Bond?*

I look at Snake to get his take on this, but he is still engaged in a staring contest with Fairburn. Males!

Am'rena raises her head, and her golden eyes capture mine. *This is just between us,* she tells me, confirming my suspicion that no one else can hear our conversations. *Am'ratha is one of my potential heirs. She has been paired with you, and your travelling together will give her an opportunity to assess whether or not she can work with you in the future.*

My first instinct is to object. Tell them I am not an heir and never will be.

Unaware of what is going on with the dragons, Snake asks, 'You want us to go now? What about our packs and things?'

'And you can't expect them to turn up at the Unseelie Court looking like this.' Percival indicates our outfits. He, of course, looks like he has showered and changed, which he might well have done while we were… um… talking. 'And they smell,' he adds, his nose wrinkling in distaste.

Fairburn shrugs and his muscles ripple. I try to contain myself, as I don't want Snake getting the wrong idea again. A sigh escapes me. Snake and the promise of that kiss pop into my mind, and I realise that if we are to travel now, it will have to remain a promise. I lean against Snake, and I can't help thinking this is more like a punishment than a reward for making it to the maze's centre.

Snake leans his head against mine and whispers in my ear, his tone teasing, 'While you were fixated on his muscles, he said we can leave our packs behind.'

I smile and squeeze his hand. No need to tell him it was the memory of our kiss that distracted me.

'I am sure those at the Unseelie Court will take care of your needs when you arrive, including providing bathing facilities and… beds….' His eyes sparkle. 'For sleeping.'

I'm not sure I like his innuendo. It is too close to where my own thoughts were for comfort.

'So, if you are ready.' Fairburn gestures to a door that miraculously appears to his right. It swings open, giving us a glimpse of the sun setting over the top of the Wyld Woods. Have we only been in here for a few hours? It feels like days.

I step outside to find myself face to face with the most magnificent golden dragon. *Wow.*

Why, thank you, he says into my mind, and my cheeks heat.

'Em'rethe, it's not polite to read the thoughts of other creatures without their knowledge,' his sister admonishes as she exits behind me.

'I know, but she does think I'm beautiful.' Em'rethe preens.

'She thinks you're showy and conceited.' Am'ratha sticks her nose in the air, exuding superiority as she joins her brother. They both lower themselves to the ground before looking expectantly at us.

'Time to mount up,' Fairburn orders.

I want to argue, but everything in this moment is so surreal. There are two dragons behaving like human siblings, and I still can't believe I am supposed to ride a dragon like something out of some fantasy tale. With all the things I have been through in this maze, it is this one thing that has me frozen to the spot, unable to even twitch a muscle.

It's easy. Place your foot on my leg, grip a scale, and pull yourself up. Your legs go around my neck. Hold on to any scale, and I will keep you in place with my magic. We are not flying far, just a hop through the portal, then on to the castle. You'll be fine, Princess. I will keep you safe.

That's easy for you to say.

Am'ratha snorts and Fairburn pushes me gently in the back. 'It is said to be one of life's most exhilarating experiences,' he encourages.

Snake and Percival are already around the other side of their mount. *If Snake can do this, I can*, I tell myself, although I would really rather it was me riding with him than Percival.

No, you do not. I am by far the better flyer, Am'ratha chuckles.

It's Am'ratha's snipe at her brother that finally moves me. Their interplay is so… normal. It allows me to relax a little.

I follow the dragon's instructions and am soon in place. The ground is so far away even though she is still sitting. I sense her muscles bunching, and I am thrown forward. I grip one of the hard scales protecting her neck. It is cool and silky beneath my fingers.

Sorry, you are my first ever rider.

I smile. *Then we are well suited because you're the first dragon I've ever ridden.*

I sense her relax beneath me before she pushes herself onto her hind legs. The evening sun reflects on her skin, colouring it in swirling purple hues. My grip on her scales tightens as my body rocks forward with her movement, and my stomach lurches as she leaps upwards.

'Safe journey and good luck,' Fairburn yells as Am'ratha's powerful wings unfurl and we take to the sky.

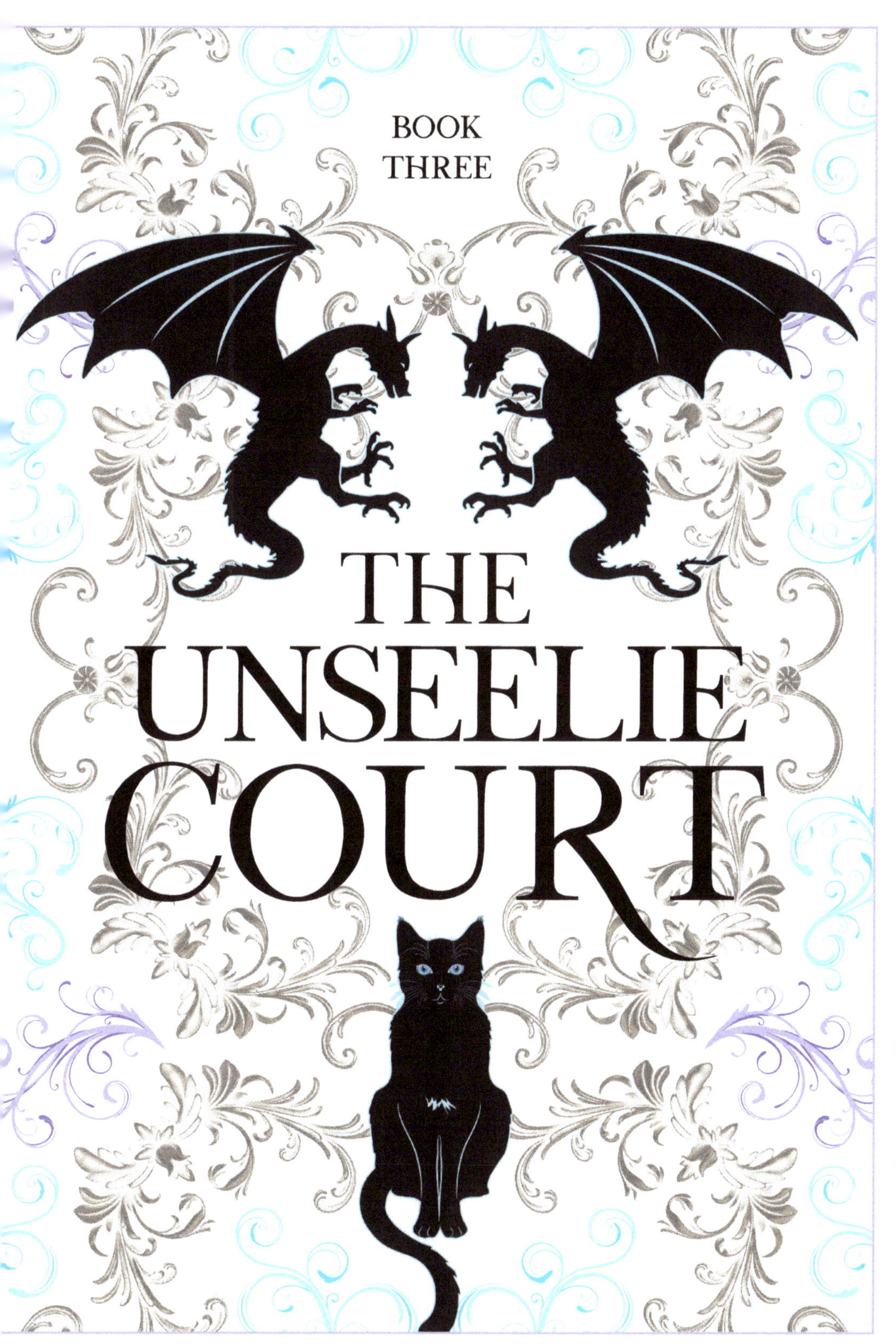

BOOK THREE
THE UNSEELIE COURT

THERE BE DRAGON

ED'RATHE PUSHES OFF with his powerful hind legs, and we are airborne. The ground drops away and the wind whips at my face. We rise higher, and my stomach plummets as I watch the world fall away.

I bury my face in Snake's back and wrap my arms more tightly around him, holding on for grim death. It would be ironic if I fell and died minutes after embracing life again.

'Percival, are you okay?' Snake's voice drifts past me, and I struggle to catch his words as they're carried away on the wind.

'Yes,' I mumble into his back.

'Then can you ease off a little. I'd like to be able to breathe.'

I loosen my grip before immediately tightening it again as we climb higher still. As Ed'rathe banks I catch sight of the mountains of the World Between, the home of the dragons, just beyond the minotaur's maze.

I shudder. That maze tested Pris, Snake, and me to the very edge of our endurance. We were lucky to escape with our sanity and friendships intact.

We level out over the mountains, and I am able to make out the edge of the Wyld Woods. My eyes are drawn to the home I have avoided for so many years. I am aware of the irony that now I do not want to leave it—not least of all because somewhere in the dense forest, our mother tree is sheltering my family while they mourn my father's passing.

Father and I were never close and were even less so after a curse turned me into something less than a sprite. However, I believe that in the end, he was proud of me.

I do not know why knowing that gives me solace. I thought I was past worrying what he, or anyone else, thought of me. Or maybe it is simply his prediction that I am integral to events happening in our world now has given me a purpose again—given me the motivation to act after so many years shying away from living—of allowing the shame of my actions and punishment to control my life.

Ed'rathe alters our course, and I shut my eyes, hoping this will help keep the food safely in my stomach. Riding on the back of a dragon is not how the legends tell it. It is not heroic. It is cold, uncomfortable, and quite terrifying. Still, if we are to reach the Unseelie Court tonight, I must endure this horror.

Of course, I have visited the court before with my friend Eleanora, and I know what to expect. No one has told Pris and Snake anything, so I fear this visit will try my companions even more than their adventure in the maze did.

This is where I can help. Some of the more senior members of his court are old friends of mine. They once played creature politics at the highest level. Their skills will be essential in the coming days if we are to save Queen Ariana and fix what is wrong with magic.

As the miles fall away and we draw closer to the portal between worlds, doubt begins to worm its way into my mind. Perhaps I have hidden myself from the worlds for too long. Will I be able to work with other creatures again? Or has my distance and isolation from the creature world changed me too much? What if they don't remember me? What if I am no longer able to influence them? Without that ability will I be of any help to Snake and Pris?

I straighten my spine and lecture myself. *Do not doubt yourself, Percival. Your friends will be happy to see you. They always are. Remember, you are one of the first lesser creatures to graduate university. You were part of the team that fought the blight and saved the worlds from disaster. You once stood up to the strongest governor in the land. You can be that person again.*

Perhaps my new sense of well-being is a result of the magic rolling off the dragon beneath me, or perhaps I have found my inner resolve. Whatever the cause, I am determined to hold on to this new-found confidence. I *can* help Pris and Snake convince the King of the Unseelie Court to visit the World Below. With his help I am certain we can restore Queen Ariana's health.

It was a shock seeing the Queen in the glass coffin held in stasis in the centre of the maze. She sleeps so the disease she caught does not have the chance to kill her. Even the dragons, the most powerful of magical beings, have not been able to save her.

The dragons believe the King of the Unseelie Court could awaken her, and together the two monarchs can restore the magical flow that has been waning for years. It must be something to do with the balance the dragons are so keen to maintain.

I hope they know what they are doing, because if they do not, then the World Below will be left without a monarch—and Bernais Baaronson and his cronies would just lap that up!

That want-to-be King would give anything to step in and take over from Queen Ariana so he could carry on his crusade to return the World Below to what they see as the glory days. If it were up to him, he would have lesser creatures like myself in virtual servitude in no time flat.

I shudder, and not just from the cold. We must convince the King to save the Queen and help restore magic. The alternative is too horrific to even contemplate.

The horizon draws closer, and I can sense a thrum of energy from the portal to the World Above. My head spins from the height and speed we are travelling. I take a peek around Snake, then immediately hide my face again. *Are we heading straight for a mountain?* My heart thumps in my chest, and I take another look and squint at the huge rock that looms in front of us, getting bigger and closer by the second. A tiny crack in the surface grabs my attention. There is a cave entrance, but we are going too fast to make that tiny pinprick of a hole—even with dragon magic.

As the portal draws closer and closer, I close my eyes, squeezing them tightly shut. If I block out the scene, I might be able to control the terror threatening to overwhelm me. I send a prayer up to the goddess for good measure and tell myself, *We will fly through the cave housing the portal and into the World Above. It will be no different than when I walk between the worlds at the Underground Ball Room.*

'No!' I wail, my eyes flying open as the consequences of moving between worlds hits me like a brick wall. *How could I have forgotten…. Above ground I will be a….*

The world around us drops away, sounds turning to echoes and white noise as we emerge from the darkness of the cave into dusk in the World Above. I have enough time to take in the grey depths of the water below us before my grip on Snake's back slips. I try to find purchase on the dragon's back, but the force of the wind is too much. I am falling, and the water is coming up fast. I hate water.

ADRENALINE PUMPS THROUGH me as the World Below falls beneath us. My body wants to slump with exhaustion, but fear of falling keeps me upright and my knees locked. Ed'rathe's muscles move rhythmically beneath me in time with the beat of his wings.

I force myself to relax and admire the scenery, trying to keep my mind off the fact that those golden wings are the only thing keeping us in the air. The woods below may appear as a moss-green carpet from this height, but I'm sure it wouldn't feel like it when I hit those trees.

With that thought, my mind finally processes the fact that I'm flying on an honest-to-gods dragon. Me—Snake Fieth—on a dragon, just like the elves of old. I'm sure I have a stupid grin plastered all over my face.

Ed'rathe's voice rumbles through me. *You are a natural flyer, Noble One. Perhaps when you and the princess join, you can request me as your dragon.*

'What?' The dragon's words jolt me from my reverie, and I play his words through again, trying to identify what had rung warning bells.

'We are not…. We have not….' I shake my head. What's the point of trying to explain what I don't understand myself?

Humph!

Did he just snort? Does he know something I don't? Can he see the future?

No, Noble One, but I can sense things.

'Oh.'

From the first moment I met Pris in the World Above, I was attracted to her. Since then, we have slowly built… something. Unfortunately, Pris and I have been so busy finding the key to the World Below and traipsing through the minotaur's maze, we haven't had a chance to find out what we are to each other.

I allow myself to remember the feel of her body against mine in the minotaur's maze. Was that only a few minutes ago?

An uncomfortable heat sends my body tingling. I glance over at her flying beside us on Am'ratha, the dragon she is bonding with as a Princess of the Royal Blood—a princess in line to the throne of the Seelie Court.

Slumped across her dragon's neck, she looks as exhausted as I am and a little less comfortable on the back of her dragon.

That isn't surprising, really. We have been on the move for the last couple of weeks, which has been tiring enough. In addition to the physical stress, she has had to process a lot: that magic and magical creatures are real, that there is another world running parallel to the one she grew up in, and the fact that her family is elven—and royalty to boot.

After all of that, we thought we had reached the end of this nonsense when we made it to the end of the minotaur's maze, only to find the creatures who were supposedly helping us had their own agenda. They'd conspired to send us to convince the Unseelie King to rescue the Queen.

At the Midnight Ball it was obvious we were being manipulated by the unscrupulous elf, Bernais, and his faction of the council. Now the supposed good guys had joined in. We had to play along if we wanted to keep everyone safe.

Pris and I kept telling ourselves we would find the time to spend with each other—time to figure out what we are to each other—once we got to the centre of the minotaur's maze. Now we'll have to wait again.

I turn my head and glance back at the maze, now not much bigger than a pinprick in the distance. It was a dirty trick, luring us there only to let us into the secret being kept from the rest of the magical world.

How can they believe the three of us will have enough influence to change the King's mind? Yet the Queen's dragon was adamant that we are the only creatures who can, and that was the excuse they used for deceiving us.

'Are you all right, Snake?' Percival's muffled voice comes from behind me. 'You seem a little tense.'

I bark out a laugh. 'A little tense? No, I'm a lot angry. Every time we think we have done enough to free our parents, someone puts up another barrier. I'm a tired of being a pawn in someone else's game.'

I force out a breath and try to release the building tension. Pris, Percival, and I had agreed we would go to the Unseelie Court and do our best to convince the King to perform his duty. Allowing my emotions to get the better of me will not make the experience any more pleasant.

I hope there are decent showers at the court. Clean clothes and a soft bed would also be great. At the thought of bed, my eyes drift to Pris, and the memory of our kiss in the maze brings a smile to my lips. Maybe tonight we will find time to explore what we mean to each other?

Beneath me, Ed'rathe shifts, altering our course, and I watch as Am'ratha does the same. Pris ducks lower on her dragon's back. The mountain's surface splits, making way for the cave, as we enter the portal between worlds. Her white hair streams behind her, making her look every inch the elven princess she is.

We are plunged into darkness, and the magical barrier clings to me as Ed'rathe forces his way through. We emerge into evening in the World Above, and Pris is once again the girl I first met, bronze skinned with black curly hair—very human, but no less regal.

I smile at the vision she makes riding her dragon over Loch Ness. For the first time since we've taken to the air, Percival's grasp finally loosens, allowing me to breathe. Suddenly, I don't feel him at all.

I turn in my seat only to find a black cat staring at me with wide, frightened eyes. I grab for it, but I am too late. The cat slips and plummets towards the depths of Loch Ness.

AS PERCIVAL AND Snake swoop ahead of us, I try to focus on anything but my fear of falling. I use Am'ratha's wingbeats to measure my breathing. Eventually it works, and I have almost convinced myself that travelling by dragon is normal.

My eyes droop, exhaustion weighing heavy on my mind and body as I lie against Am'ratha's neck. I shake my head, trying to clear the fog. Is it possible I'm dozing while flying on the back of a dragon? I should be excited at the very least, but all I can think is, I hope I don't fall asleep and end up plummeting to the ground.

Don't worry, Royal One, I will protect you. My magic will keep you on my back. Am'ratha has directed her voice into my head, and I know this conversation is for me alone. Still, "Royal One" is new.

What's with the formalities?

Am'ratha snorts. *The Dragon Queen has warned me to follow the rules. That means I can only talk with creatures who are titled royal, noble, or dragon friend.*

So, since I'm royal, you can talk to me. Can you talk to Snake and Percival?

Snake is your consort, so he is noble.

It's my turn to snort. *Consort? You're getting a little ahead of things.*

Am'ratha chooses to ignore me. *Also, he is the son of one of the Seelie Queen's advisors, which also confers this status.*

Was she teasing me? I'm not quite sure, but I think she was.

Percival has long been a friend of the dragons.

What? Now that's interesting. How come?

That is a long story, Royal One, and is perhaps best saved for another day.

If flying on the back of a mythical beast isn't mind-bending enough, I'm having telepathic conversations with a freaking dragon, and she's winding me up about Snake. *If only my friends could see me now!*

It's hard to believe it was only a couple of weeks ago that a boy burst into my home, announced he was a gnome, and informed me my parents had been taken to some magical world.

I've come a long way from being the girl who lived a sheltered life in London, far from the magical world my parents grew up in. Now I ride dragons, travel with a sprite and a gnome, and have almost accepted that I'm an elven princess who could one day be Queen of that magical world.

No, that'll never happen. I may have taken on their stupid quest and agreed to be their emissary to the Unseelie Court, but I will never be Queen. I have not chosen this, and I have to draw the line somewhere, or I fear this magical world will take over my life.

Before all of this, I was going to be a human rights lawyer, but that was before I found my parents had hidden this whole world from me. Now my future path is not so clear. Could I forget all of this and go back to my real life, to being a university student, and perhaps dating Snake in the real world?

Will he be able to go back and take up his position studying physics at university? Or has finding out he is part elf changed what he wants for the future? Certainly, if I were him, I'd be annoyed at how the other creatures treated me and my family, and I would want to do something about it. That's me. I haven't had a chance to ask Snake how he feels about it all. Maybe when we arrive at the Unseelie Court, we'll be able to make some time to talk.

As we speed towards an opening in the mountain, I keep low over my dragon's back. I tighten my grip as the world around us goes absent of sight or sound, temporarily shocking my senses as we fly through the film of the magical portal. I hold my breath until Am'ratha stretches her wings over a lake. I catch sight of a derelict castle on the shore and wonder if this is Loch Ness.

Now that we have successfully made it back to my world, it occurs to me Snake and I may not even be able to choose our own futures. If the Queen is not placed back on her throne, will Bernais ever let us leave the World Below? Or will he send us to the World Above and prevent us from ever returning?

I resist the urge to close my eyes and hide from the overwhelming uncertainty that question invokes. There are too many variables and so little we can control.

I shiver as the cold air sends icy fingers through my clothes. Actually, the thing I want most at the moment is a hot bath, or even a shower will do, and to fall into a blissfully warm bed.

'Percival!'

The shout jolts me from my dreams of soft sheets, heat, and cleanliness in time to watch a cat falling toward the loch below.

Poor friend Percival. Of course he would return to cat form when we left the World Below, Am'ratha purrs inside my head.

'He returned to what?'

I am sorry for the intrusion, my Queen, but we forgot about Percival's curse.

'Who are you talking to?'

Shh, Royal One. There is no time for explanations.

A new voice enters the conversation.

You may use magic to stay the curse for seven days. If the deed cannot be done by then, the curse will be returned.

Thank you, my Queen.

The cat is still falling towards the water as if in slow motion. As it is about to plummet into the icy water, it turns into Percival. He pinwheels his arms and legs chaotically, desperate to slow his descent, and my heart practically burst out of my chest in panic and fear for my friend.

His terror-filled scream rips through the air, just as a dark silver dragon leaps from the water, catching the semi-wet sprite on his back. Crisis averted, I let out a breath, relaxing against Am'ratha's back as the three dragons head to the ruins of an old castle at the edge of the lake.

Just when I am getting used to things in my new life, another twist throws me off-balance.

When we are all safely on the ground, I ask, 'Am'ratha, why is Percival a cat in the World Above?'

Shh. My uncle speaks.

If the dark dragon who emerged from the loch had eyebrows, they would be raised. Instead his thoughts in my head are laced with skepticism. *These are the ones our Queen believes will persuade King Maddox to do his duty?*

They are, Uncle.

My jaw clenches as I let go of Am'ratha's scales and rise to my full height. *Who is he to judge us?* At the same time, the full force of the magnificent dragon's presence hits me, and I have to stop myself from bowing before this creature.

They are our last hope, Am'ratha says before I can tell the dragon exactly what I think. *The Queen believes the King will listen to these three.*

As the dragons talk, Percival dries himself with magic before climbing back onto Ed'rathe. He appears unhurt, but he won't meet my eye. Something is not quite right with him.

How fares the world here, Uncle? Am'ratha asks.

Already the lack of magic is being felt, youngling. Weather patterns are changing and crops are failing. If we do not fix this soon, both worlds will suffer beyond repair.

No pressure, I think, and the new dragon raises his head to look at me. Of course he is reading my mind.

Royal One, this is no time for larking about.

I tamp down the anger beginning to surge within me. I'm tired of being both underestimated and used by creatures in the magical world, but an angry outburst will get me nowhere.

Ignoring the older dragon, I direct my thoughts to Am'ratha. *Why is Percival a cat in the World Above?*

He has not told you? The curse is part of his punishment for unknowingly spreading the blight centuries ago. In the World Below, he takes human form, and in The

World Above, he takes the form of a cat. In neither world can he be his true self.

It takes a moment for her words to sink in, then it hits me like a freight train as I begin to understand the burden Percival has been under. *You're joking, aren't you? He has endured centuries of punishment for something he did unknowingly—how barbaric.*

It is worse than that. As I understand it, he can no longer commune with the trees or be with his soulmate. Their story has touched the heart of many a bard, and he features in many of our favourite tunes. Many dragons hope he will save your Queen and have his punishment lifted.

I'm stunned into silence, and believe me, this does not happen often. My heart breaks as contemplate Percival's agony at being separated from his soulmate, and, worse than that, he can never truly be himself. Suddenly all my worries pale into insignificance. Percival chooses that moment to look towards me. He takes in my expression and frowns.

'What are we waiting for?' he asks.

Good luck, the Loch Ness dragon says as Am'ratha leaps for the sky. *I fear you will need it.*

LOCH NESS

SHIVERING WITH BONE-CHILLING cold, I grip Snake tightly as Ed'rathe prepares to follow his sister into the sky. The dragon takes pity on me and sends waves of heat through my body until my shaking subsides.

Although I am now warm, my arms still tremble with fear. Returning to cat form was bad enough. Doing it while on the back of a dragon above a lake shocked me out of my complacency. I had become so comfortable being in human form, it did not occur to me I would transform as soon as we left the World Below.

And that look Pris gave me. She is clearly aware of my past, and she pities me. Her dragon must have told her everything. No doubt Ed'rathe will tell Snake as well. How will I be able to face them as an equal, let alone a guide, now?

Are you ready to leave now, Dragon Friend? Ed'rathe asks me, doing me a great honour by speaking directly to my mind.

'I am.'

The dragon from the loch turns his intense gaze in my direction, and his golden eyes narrow to slits. *Our Queen has given you seven days in this form before the curse will return, Dragon Friend. The graveness of the situation is the only reason she allowed us to do this.*

Could you not have done something sooner? Sprites hate water. I lash out as my shame burns.

The air by the loch stills, and it is like the whole world holds its breath at my audacity. The water dragon throws back its massive scaled head and laughs.

You are either very stupid or very brave, Percival. Let us hope it is the latter because you will need it if you are to help sort things out at the Unseelie Court.

'What do you mean by that?' Snake asks, and I feel another wave of shame at finding out he has been included in the conversation all along.

It is not my place to tell, Noble One. Besides, you will find out soon enough.

I am tired of the games and the half-truths. I want to be on our way. The sun is setting, and the air is cold. All I desire is to curl up beside a blazing fire. Snake does not seem to feel the same way.

He points at the ruins of Urquhart Castle. 'Is that where we're going?'

No, young creature. The court once resided in Urquhart Castle because kings of old preferred to be close to the portal. The new King prefers human amenities, so he moved his court to a city and set up a guard post here.

'I guess it is a bit of a ruin, but I thought… you know, that the court might be hidden.'

The crumbling stone is indeed an illusion. The gatekeepers and their family reside in the castle.

'Ah, I thought the ruins were veiled in a shimmer of magic.' Snake shifts in his seat so he can face the dragon. 'Which city did the court move to?'

'It is in Inverness, Snake,' I say, unable to keep the impatience from my voice. 'And I would like to go there if you have finished your history lesson.'

My companion's body tenses, and I expect him to snap back, but he does not. 'Yes, we're all tired, and we've dealt with a lot these last few days.' His voice is calm and controlled as he smooths things over.

And you should not linger too much longer because our glamour will fade, the Loch Ness dragon says. *Once it does, people will talk of the monster in the loch. There are always some who can pierce the glamour we place to hide our presence, but those individuals are often treated as if they are crazy. If a whole busload of people was to see us, there would be nothing less than total chaos.*

Taking a deep breath, I force my voice directly into the large water dragon's mind. *I am sorry I was so rude to you. I appreciate you saving me from drowning.*

The dragon holds my gaze as if he is assessing the weight of my words. *It has been a difficult road in life for you, Percival. You have paid so much for your youthful mistake. Do not fail in this chance to end your suffering.*

As far as pep talks go, it's a little lacking. I have to remind myself that for a dragon to show even a little empathy for a creature is way out of character. Acknowledging the favour he has bestowed on me, I bow my head.

Not wanting to dwell on my embarrassment, I turn my thoughts elsewhere. Until I fell from the dragon, I was looking forward to returning to the Unseelie Court. I thought I could contribute something towards Pris and Snake's efforts to persuade the King to return to the World Below. Dropping from Ed'rathe's back put an end to that.

All my doubts and fears are back, and they are fighting for space in my mind. I cannot continue like this. If I cannot control my doubts, I may as well stay here and wait for my young friends to return.

Ed'rathe bunches his muscles, preparing to take off. 'Ed'ruven, can you tell us anything else that might help us at court?'

The dragon who had emerged from the water shakes his head. *The court is not how you remember it, Percival, and the change has not been for the better. Tread carefully and rely on your old friends to guide you.*

I duck back behind Snake to avoid the cold night air as we take to the sky. The dragon's cryptic comment replays in my head as we travel towards Inverness. Is there more to the King's reluctance to help solve this problem than Fairburn, the head of the Queen's Guard, had let on when he sent us on this mission?

I push aside all my self-doubts, and I begin to worry about what sort of mess we are walking into.

ED'RATHE PUSHES OFF, taking us upwards before levelling out and following his sister. The pressure of Percival against my back raises my anxiety levels. I'm still not over the shock of seeing a cat falling towards the loch, and I'm still getting my head around the idea that the cat was Percival. I'm now wishing I put him in front of me for this leg of the journey. The loch dragon assured us he won't turn back into a cat, but still… better to be safe.

The fact that Percival is a cat in the World Above is still a surprise—and a black cat at that. A black cat? I saw a number of black cats when Pris and I were in the World Above, including the one at Eleanora's place….

'Percival?'

'Yes?' His voice is muffled, as if he is pressing his face into my body.

'It wasn't a coincidence that Pris and I kept seeing black cats on our journey to the World Below, was it?'

I wait for a response and am thinking he probably won't answer me when his voice drifts forward, tentative and reedy.

'It was me. Eleanora sent me to protect the two of you.'

'It must be so cool to shape-shift.' The words slip out before I engage my brain.

'It might be if I were able to actually decide when I wanted to shift.' Percival's voice is tight and controlled.

I sense a story there but one Percival is perhaps not quite ready to tell.

His body tenses and relaxes, as if he is sighing. 'I was transformed as a punishment for spreading blight when I was around your age.'

Surely I didn't hear right. 'Transformed? Into a cat?'

Percival doesn't answer for a few wingbeats. 'Yes. It was partially reversed, so I am human in the World Below and a cat in the World Above'

'Don't you mean you're a sprite in the creature realm?'

'I am no longer fully sprite.'

Percival's words are a whisper on the wind but filled with such pain. I take in the enormity of his revelation, and I'm shocked to the core. Transformation of a creature is forbidden and is punished more severely than murder.

'By who? I mean, who would impose such a horrific sentence?'

'Magnus Baaronson.' Percival spits the name out like it's a vile taste in his mouth, and those two words rock my world.

'Baaronson? Bernais is a Baaronson.'

'Yes, he is. Magnus is his father, and he also happens to be governor of the region where Eleanora and I grew up.'

'But that's monstrous. Transformation has been outlawed for hundreds of years.'

Percival's body tenses against my back, telling me this conversation is difficult for him. 'I am aware of that. I was the last to be punished that way. Your great-uncle, Drow, and I worked together to ensure a law was passed that prevents other creatures from going through the physical and emotional trauma I endured.'

So many questions swirl around in my head as anger and sorrow war for a place in my heart. Percival was the sprite who made history by taking a governor to court and making sure no lesser creatures would be punished by an imposed transformation. It was one of the early steps that led to equality for lesser creatures. My great-uncle was a part of it? Percival knew my great-uncle?

'Hold on, how old are you…? You must be old if you've been this way for over a couple of hundred years. One small mistake changed the course of your whole life?'

Wow, Snake, way to go. You could have handled that better.

'I deserved some form of retribution for spreading the blight. You need to understand how big a deal the blight was at the time.'

This is Percival as I have never heard him—meek and uncertain. It's like he's reverted back to the boy he once was. This is so out of character.

'Percival, I can't see you doing something like that to the forest.'

'I would never…. Not on purpose. It was an accident, but I deserved to be punished because I was a thoughtless young sprite.'

'Okay, I get that. But really, overkill much?'

We are silent as Ed'rathe transports us towards the lights of a city. Then another thought hits me.

'You had a decision to make when we were in the minotaur's maze. In the end, you chose to stop being an advisor and join our quest. Did you do that because the Queen might be persuaded to commute your sentence if you help redress the balance between worlds?'

'Perhaps,' Percival agrees. 'Yes. But mostly I am doing this because, before he died, my father convinced me something big is going on here. Something even bigger than the blight.'

I'm struggling to remember my history of those years, and how Percival, now that I know he's *that* sprite, might have fitted in.

'Didn't you work with Princess Petunia and some others to stop the blight's spread? Wasn't that enough to earn you a commuted sentence?'

'Apparently not. I don't want to talk about it anymore.'

In the short time I've known Percival, I've found that when he decides something, he can't be moved. I try another tactic.

'Percival, my family doesn't talk much about Drow. Wasn't he banished?'

'Yes—well, no. He left along with most of Princess Petunia's court when she was exiled, but I don't believe he was ever formally banished.'

We fall silent, both lost in our own thoughts until Ed'rathe interrupts us.

We are almost there, Noble One, Dragon's Friend. When we land, you must depart quickly, as there is not enough magic to hold our glamour for long.

Soon we are swooping over a city, and Inverness Castle comes into sight. The dragons circle the castle by the river, giving us a bird's-eye view of the historic city of Inverness as darkness falls. I want to be excited about the view and landing in the courtyard in front of the castle while riding a dragon. In reality, though, I'm so tired, I can barely keep my eyes open.

As Ed'rathe's wings fold inwards, Percival holds himself away from me, stiff and formal. I think it's because he is a private creature. He's done sharing his past and he wants things to go back to the way they were.

'Percival, what we just talked about….'

He is silent, almost as if he is holding his breath.

'It can stay between us, but… if you ever want to talk about it, I'm here.'

The silence continues, and I wonder if he has heard me.

'Thank you,' he eventually says, and perhaps that's all he is capable of saying given the circumstances.

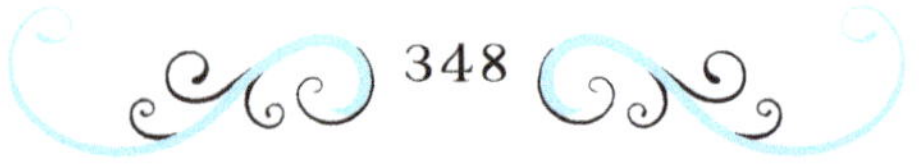

THE UNSEELIE COURT

Ed'rathe lies down to allow us to dismount. When my feet hit solid ground, I reach up, stretching out my back. Then I take a couple of steps, making sure everything still moves. I catch a whiff of something foul and scan the courtyard for the source—perhaps an open sewer or drain. Sniffing again, I realise it's me. My nose wrinkles in distaste. Boy, I need a shower, and the sooner, the better.

BY THE TIME we arrive at Inverness, the sky is dark and the town is a twinkle of lights below. We fly over the city, and I marvel at how the modern town blends with the old. The castle stands as a beacon on a rise beside the river, which Am'ratha informs me is the Ness.

Welcome to the Unseelie Court, Royal One.

Inverness Castle is the court? It's a traditional Norman structure—not at all what I expected. I can't believe they have it out in the open like this. The World Below is so secretive, and all about not showing magic to humans.

Am'ratha snorts, something I'm beginning to notice she does when she thinks I'm saying, or thinking, something stupid. *This is simply the doorway to the court. Like the Underground Ballroom through which you entered the World Below, the Unseelie Court is held slightly out of the World Above. Creatures can come and go through the special entrance, but few in the World Above know it is here.*

Magic is so cool, and kinda scary because it's existed right beside me for my whole life, and I never realised.

With the court so close, butterflies begin to flutter in my stomach. In the maze, I had been so certain that I, a Princess of the Royal Blood, would be able to talk the King into doing what others were unable to persuade him to do. Now that I'm actually here, I begin to wonder, what help can I be? I've never spoken to royalty, so why would a king listen to me?

Then, it's like my anxiety is on a roll. My concerns pop into my head one after another before I have time to fully process them. I've never been to court. How should I behave? If I'm royalty, will they expect me to conduct myself as if I am? I mean, I only found out I was an elf a few days ago. Oh, and will they use magic? I'm still quite bad at controlling mine.

Suddenly the war cry I owned when I formed my first magical flame—I'm a freaking elf princess—sounds so hollow. I couldn't convince a trumped-up court to release my parents. How will I ever be able to convince the King of a magical court to do something he so obviously doesn't want to? I tighten my grip on Am'ratha's scales. Perhaps she can fly me back to London—to normalcy.

Being expected to be a princess isn't the only thing that worries me. Always there's that nagging doubt that I haven't been told everything about who I am. My parents kept everything from me, and each new revelation hits like a punch to the gut.

I'm not sure they will ever reveal the full truth. I only uncovered my magical heritage because Mum and Dad were taken to face Bernais's charges of using magic for their personal gain in the World Above.

My mother is a princess, a niece of the Queen of the Seelie Court. No one will tell me why she and my father live in the World Above, denying their heritage and lying to me. Everyone else knows what happened, but they say I must wait for my parents to tell me.

Straightening my spine, I imagine my father telling me, 'Focus on the things you can control and influence, Pris, everything else is a wasted effort.' Now more than ever his words ring true.

As Am'ratha drops down so I can dismount, I think I might throw up.

You are a Princess of the Royal Blood and way stronger than you are letting yourself believe at the moment. Enter the court and do us both proud.

I wish you'd stop reading my mind.

Perhaps I will when you stop broadcasting your thoughts so loudly.

Although I don't like that she invades my head, her words bolster me. I slide from my dragon friend's back and stare up at the sandstone walls of the castle and the steps that lead to the enormous wooden door. No lights shine through the thick glass windows. It looks deserted, as though it's been locked up for the night. What if no one's home?

Go knock on the main door. I have sent a message of your imminent arrival. Someone will come for you.

Suddenly I don't want Am'ratha to leave. I am stronger by her side. *Can you stay until they do?*

You have Snake and Percival. Besides, there is not enough magic around for me to stay shrouded for much longer. Ed'rathe and I will find a place to hide near Loch Ness. If you need me, just call.

How will you be able to hear me? I ask, as much to delay her departure as wanting to find out the answer.

You are talking to me now.

So distance doesn't matter?

She drops her head to look me in the eye. *Sometimes it is easy to forget how little you know of our world. No, my princess, distance does not matter. We are linked, you and I, and we can talk to each other anywhere.*

Oh. Oh! That might be something to keep in mind next time I kiss Snake.

Don't worry. That is private, and I would never intrude. We dragons place strict boundaries on our links, and I would appreciate it if you followed them too.

My face heats up, and I try to change the subject.

Won't you be bored waiting around for us?

No, Ed'rathe and I enjoy playing around and scaring the humans who come to Loch Ness searching for monsters. We will be fine for a few days.

She steps away from me and prepares to leap. I'm almost toppled over by the force of the wind her wings create as she and her brother take off, leaving us to face the Unseelie Court alone.

WELCOME TO INVERNESS CASTLE

SNAKE AND PERCIVAL join me at the foot of the stairs, watching the dragons as they fly off into the night. Moments later they disappear, their glamour hiding them from sight. We're left standing in the empty courtyard in front of the foreboding locked wooden doors of the deserted castle.

The chilly evening air seeps through my clothing and into my bones, and I shiver. After the balmy weather in the maze, it's a shock to the system. Trying to ignore my growing unease, I take a step forward. Snake moves with me, dropping an arm over my shoulders. I lean into him, enjoying the shared warmth of our bodies.

'What now?' he asks.

Percival has not moved. 'Is he all right?' I ask, nodding towards our friend.

'I think so. The cat thing was a shock, and for his story to come out that way…. Well, it can't have been comfortable.'

'He knows it makes no difference to us, doesn't he?'

'He can hear you,' Percival says sharply. Then adds a little more softly, 'But thank you. I appreciate that.'

Snake chuckles. 'Yeah, he's okay. So, any ideas on how we get in?'

'Am'ratha said she told them we are coming. So, I guess we knock.'

Percival takes a step forward and says over his shoulder, 'Well, we certainly cannot stand around here all night, chit-chatting. We will catch our deaths in this cold.'

We follow him up the stairs and wait while he pounds on the door. The sound echoes in the night air. We wait. No one answers. Exhausted, I snuggle closer to Snake and as I do I remember our kiss in the maze. I nuzzle into his neck, and he pulls me closer.

Percival kicks the door, and this time the wood shimmers as a smaller entrance appears within the larger door seconds before it opens, throwing a shaft of light across us.

A female voice sounds from within. 'Show some patience. It takes time to deactivate the wards.'

I blink a couple of times and tense. Is that our au pair, Susan? Leaving Snake's protective embrace, I step through the opening and find myself staring into her familiar grey-green eyes. When she disappeared at the same time as my parents, I'd worried I might never see her again.

She steps towards me as if to wrap me in a hug before stopping short. My face must have shown my confusion at her being here. Not to mention the hurt and anger her abandonment had caused. Now I add betrayal to the list. For her to be here in the Unseelie Court means that she must have known what my parents hid from me for all those years.

'Susan, I didn't expect to see you here.' I try to keep my voice even, but my tone is chilly.

She flinches a little, but her eyes shine with sympathy and understanding. 'You are upset with me. I would expect no less from you.'

'So, what are you doing here?' I ask. My words are as clipped and unemotional as I can make them, hopefully masking my shock at her presence.

'I am a member of the Unseelie Court. When I found out your parents had been taken, I came to report to the King and also to beg him to help as was my duty.'

'Was it also your duty to lie to me about who I was?' Another thought occurs to me. 'Were you also spying on us for the King?'

'Never spying, only guarding.' She opens her mouth as if she is about to say more, then closes it. She settles the mask of polite host on her face and says, 'It is cold and late. Come inside. Rooms have been prepared for you all,' before lowering her voice and saying only to me, 'We can talk about all this later.'

'Indeed we will,' I mutter under my breath.

Snake slips his hand into mine, giving it a gentle squeeze. 'Is that your nanny? The one who left us that amazing lasagna.'

I don't want to be reminded that Susan thought to make sure I had food before she disappeared, leaving me to face the last couple of weeks on my own. Focusing on her lies and betrayal allows me to retain my animosity.

'Yes, it is. And it appears she's always been an agent from the Unseelie Court.'

'That's interesting,' Snake says as Susan leads us along the corridor, Percival in her wake. 'I wonder if she's friend or foe?'

My eyes narrow as they latch on to Susan's back. 'I'm not sure, but I aim to find out.'

Our footsteps echo in the empty building as we follow Susan through a cold, dark castle. I expected sumptuous furnishings and great works of art covering the walls, but everything is stripped bare. Soon our journey takes us past scaffolding and plastic sheets, indicating that this part of the castle is undergoing restoration, which explains the sparse decorations.

We stop in front of a white plastered recess that looks as though it was once a door to somewhere. Susan walks through the wall and disappears. Percival follows. Snake and I look at each other.

'Shall we?' he asks.

I take a deep breath, then nod. Together we step through the wall, and I shiver as the familiar chill of a magical portal washes over me. On the other side, we find ourselves in a luscious castle hallway that is everything I'd imagined a castle would be. I turn slowly, taking everything in.

If I had to describe it, I would say it was over the top turn of the 19th century—all wood and stone and wall tapestries—but it was a whole other level. It was luxury gone mad.

'Impressive,' Snake understates as he studies the surroundings.

'When Huntley remodelled Inverness Castle in the World Above in the 1850s, the old King of the Unseelie Court took the opportunity to build a parallel building,' Susan tells us as we regroup. 'The new King finished the work, expanding the court to house hundreds of creatures. Lately we have been having problems with magic in the World Above, so some of the courtiers returned to their homes, and the King placed part of the court in storage.'

'In storage? What does that even mean,' I mutter.

Susan taps her index finger on her lips. 'How do I explain this? The central court is attached to physical elements of Inverness Castle—the portals, the windows we look out of, and the like. The King uses magic to set this up, but once it is there, it takes very little effort from the King to maintain, and maintenance creatures are used to keep the barrier between us and Inverness Castle strong.'

She cocks her head to the side as if waiting for something. Ah, she's waiting for me.

'I'm with you so far.'

'Good. Now, the King is then able to extend the court from that core by using magic to make rooms larger, add on floors, and even extend beyond the boundaries of Inverness Castle.'

I think back to my magic lessons in the minotaur's maze. Particle magic allows things to be changed by adding stray particles in the air to what you already have, making it bigger or changing shape. I have used it to change small items, but…. My eyes widen, and Susan grins.

'I see you understand now. It takes a great deal of magical strength, a high concentration of magic, and a large number of extra particles to keep the larger court operational. As magic has decreased, the King has been forced to reduce the size of the court.'

Snake asks, 'So you're saying it's more like a country house than a castle now?'

Susan chuckles. 'Hardly. At full capacity the court is more like a small village. At the moment we still have enough creatures attending for the castle to be full. In fact, with you arriving, we are a little pressed for space.'

I send Snake a questioning glance, wondering if he caught her comment about the problem with magic. He shrugs, and I lean in to whisper, 'If they're already aware of the magic problem and it's impacting them, why isn't the King leaping at the chance to help fix it?'

'It is odd,' he says, stifling a yawn.

I yawn myself in response, and suddenly remember how bone tired I am. I tug on Snake's hand, and we catch Susan up.

'Is it far to our rooms?' I ask her. 'We've had a long day, and all we want to do is wash up and get some sleep.'

Susan pauses a moment and studies us in the light, a slight frown drawing her brows together. We must make a sad picture.

'Of course. Your dragon did warn us that you were in no state to be presented at court immediately, although I had hoped to tidy you up and at least introduce you to the King tonight.'

She pauses again, and I wonder if she is waiting for us to say we would like to meet the King. None of us moves. I suspect Snake and Percival are as exhausted as I am after our experience in the minotaur's maze, and none of us are in a state to make a good first impression on the King.

Susan's shoulders rise in a shrug. 'I will arrange time with the King tomorrow, so you can rest tonight. I have done the best I can with your accommodation given the short notice and—'

'The problem with space,' I offer.

Turning on her heel, Susan leads our motley crew down the rest of the corridor and around the corner. If we had thought the corridor opulent, we were mistaken. We find ourselves in the entrance hall of the Unseelie castle, and it is spectacular.

Chandeliers send light up the three floors of the building, bathing the sweeping polished wooden staircase in a dappled spotlight. The parquet floor below reflects the sparkling lights above, and the walls are almost completely covered in portraits and scenes of the World Below.

Susan sweeps up the stairs, not giving us much of a chance to take in the scenery. After hustling her along, I can't ask her to wait while I gawp at the room like a tourist in a National Trust museum.

As we reach the middle floor, Susan turns left, and we head away from the river. At any moment I expect to run into another creature or for the sounds of dining and dancing or something to fill the air. All I hear is our muffled footsteps. Are magical courts supposed to be this deserted?

I'M NOT SURE I was expecting a warm welcome to the Unseelie Court, but I certainly wasn't expecting empty corridors and an almost eerie silence, especially as the court is supposed to be full. Pris keeps her hand in mine while Percival walks almost stoically in front of us. Our procession reminds me of a death march.

I glance sideways at Pris. Her eyes bore into Susan's back. She is not as angry as she was when she found her former au pair answering the door, but she isn't quite happy with the situation either.

I understand where she's coming from. I only recently found out that my mother had not exactly been truthful with my heritage and that my grandmother was an elf. Inter-creature relationships are frowned upon in the World Below, and mixed-race children are often shunned. So, while I get why she didn't tell me, it still hurts.

Pris's parents' betrayal is so much more comprehensive. They kept her entire family and her magical heritage from her. Then to find out that the one other person you trusted your whole life was part of that deception—it's gotta hurt.

The silence is oppressive, and I feel the need to break it. 'Where is everyone?' My voice sounds loud in the too-quiet hallway.

Susan doesn't break stride as she answers. 'They're at dinner in the dining hall on the ground floor. I had thought you might be able to change and join them, but as you're all so tired and, well, you smell like you haven't bathed for a week, I will have food sent up for you.'

Percival glares at our host, and she obviously feels the burn, as she turns and says, 'That last comment doesn't apply to you, Percival. You are as immaculate as always.'

Percival preens, and I can't help but smile.

'Thank you,' he says. 'And thank you also for understanding that we are far too tired to make polite conversation with strangers tonight. We have had rather a trying time these past few days.'

As I consider the option of dinner, my stomach rumbles, and my cheeks heat up.

Susan half turns, eyeing my stomach as it continues to grumble. 'Perhaps I had better make food a priority.'

I nod, too embarrassed to speak. At the end of the passage, we turn right and find ourselves in a guarded corridor. Pris's eyes widen as she clocks the guards, and Percival stops moving.

'I have never seen guards in the residential suites before,' he mutters.

'Why are the soldiers here, Susan?' Pris asks, her voice wary.

Susan closes her eyes momentarily before answering, and I fear we're trying her patience. 'Strange things have been happening in the court lately. So, the King believes we can't be too careful with security when strangers arrive unexpectedly in the night.'

'Are they here to protect us or protect others from us?' Pris attempts to clarify.

'Here we are. This is the suite of rooms you will be sharing.' Susan looks at Percival and me as she reaches for the handle, avoiding answering Pris altogether.

The doors swing open, revealing a sitting room with two chairs and a sofa arranged around a fire. By the window sits a table with four chairs. Four doors break up the walls on either side of the room—two on the right and two on the left.

'The guest bedrooms are through the doors on the left,' Susan informs us. 'There is a shared bathroom between. Thank goodness the new King arranged to have the plumbing modernised so you can have a bath without someone having to haul water up for you.'

'I was kinda hoping for a shower,' I say, too tired to hide my disappointment.

Susan laughs. 'We are getting there, but we're not that modern yet. I see you arrived without a change of clothes. I'm sure the Royal Wardrobe will have something for you. I will arrange for clothes to be brought up while you bathe.'

'Two guest rooms?' Pris raises an eyebrow. 'Where will Percival be? We would like him to be accommodated with us.'

'I'm sorry, Princess, I haven't been quite clear. Snake Fieth and Percival of the Wyld Woods have been invited to stay here by the suite's occupants. You are to stay in the royal quarters.'

Pris drops my hand and glares at Susan. This isn't going to be pretty.

'I want to stay here with the others.'

Susan is clearly used to dealing with Pris in her demanding mode. 'I'm afraid that is not only not possible, but it's inappropriate.'

'So what do I have to do to make it possible and "appropriate"?' Pris air quotes appropriate, underlining the sarcasm dripping from her words.

'When the King heard who was in your party, he arranged where you were to stay himself. I am unable to go against his wishes, Pris, no matter how much it annoys you.'

Annoyed is a bit of an understatement. Anger is rolling off Pris in waves.

'So, let's go talk with him and arrange something more suitable.'

Susan sends Pris a hard stare. 'This is the Unseelie Court, Priscilla, and you do not go barging in and demanding the King cater your every whim— especially not when you are dressed like a navvy.'

The door swings open as if to punctuate Susan's words, and a guard's head appears. 'Do we have a problem here, Lady Susan?'

Susan doesn't respond, as she and Pris are locked in a battle of wills.

I take Pris's hand. 'Pris, it's only for tonight. We shouldn't make waves before we've even met the King.' I lean in closer and whisper, 'Besides, we have waited this long to spend time alone together. We can wait a little longer.'

A smile curls the corner of her lips. 'Or I could just sneak back here later,' she whispers, her breath tickling my ear.

I lean my forehead against hers for a moment, simply enjoying her being close, then pull away.

'Percival, look after Snake and see he doesn't cause any mischief,' Pris says, brushing past the guard as she leaves the room.

Susan barks out a laugh. 'I don't think Snake's the one we should be worrying about.'

The door closes, and I almost collapse on the floor. Percival eyes me critically, and his nose wrinkles in distaste.

'You take the first bath. I wouldn't want to upset our hosts with your odour if they arrive before we are clean.'

'I'll try not to be offended by that,' I tell him, but without malice. If I'm honest, I'm so relieved to be bathing, it's all I can think about.

I head for the closest guest bedroom and make my way to the adjoining bathroom before Percival changes his mind. Compared to the public areas of the castle, it's relatively modern with blindingly white subway tiles and an enormous claw-footed bath. I turn the taps, and the water runs hot, steam gently filling the room. I groan as my muscles tremble in anticipation.

Quickly stripping out of my dirty clothes, I leave them in a pile behind the door. Finally, I slip into the water, emerging myself fully before leaning back and half lying down, allowing the glorious heat to soothe my body and soul. I've a lot to think about, and maybe even a lot to plan for, but I clear my mind and sink beneath the surface again, blocking everything out.

THE LAST TIME I visited the Unseelie Court with Eleanora, the hallways were packed with courtiers and their hangers-on. To arrive and find everything so quiet is strange and quite unsettling. Given my experiences on the way here, I do not need anything else to throw me off balance.

When we walk through the portal, not a single sound emanates from the staterooms, where no doubt everyone is eating. No music, no laughter, and no sounds of fun being had? I will admit, I was a cat last time I was here, and so my hearing was a little more acute, but this is still way too quiet.

I wander over to the fire, and I add another log before taking a seat in the chair closest to the blaze. What was I thinking? I should have asked to speak with Eleanora's sister, Euphemia. She is the witch responsible for creature care in the north of the World Above.

She always has her finger on the pulse. Effie would be able to fill me in with what is going on, because, make no mistake, there is something other than the failure of magic turning the court into a shadow of its former self.

Agitated by my thoughts, I wander over to the window. Leaning my forehead against the lower pane, I watch the activity in the streets of Inverness below. It is early evening, and the humans are heading for their homes, or perhaps they are leaving for an evening out. The scene is so normal, it only serves to accentuate the uncanny atmosphere in here.

The Unseelie Court uses the windows of Inverness Castle to view the outside world, but the glass shimmers if you look closely. That slight distortion tells me the court's wards are operational, keeping us all just out of time and space. The wards are still working, which is a relief, so it must be something else. A light tap sounds at the door, and I pull myself away from the view.

'Come in.'

Moments later a female servant—a brownie, judging from her slight form—enters dressed in a floor-length black dress and white apron. She bobs a curtsey before carrying a covered tray over to the table. I barely have time to say thank you before she backs out of the room.

The scent of spices sets my mouth watering. I lean over the trays and lift a cover. Haggis and mashed potatoes—excellent. On another plate, the bread is still warm enough for the butter to be melting through. Lovely.

Another knock on the door has me dropping the cover back on the dish. 'Come in,' I say again.

A new servant enters with clothes draped over her arm.

'Where do you want these, sir?' she asks.

'The smaller set in the farthest guest room and the larger in the other.'

She silently distributes the clothes and leaves without making another sound, and I am once again alone. I debate whether to start eating without Snake. After all, I do not want the food to get cold. Good manners win out over abject hunger, but I will not wait forever.

I knock on the door to Snake's room and say loudly, 'Food has arrived. I give you five minutes to dress before I start eating.'

My stomach rumbles, and I must admit, I am sorely tempted to start without my friend. I also want a distraction to keep my mind off the feelings of inadequacy and shame transforming into a cat stirred up. The whole experience shook my resolve to help Snake and Pris, reminding me of how out of practice I am at taking action.

To fill the time, I open the door to our suite and step into the corridor. A guard is beside me before I can leave the shadow of the doorway.

'Can I help you with something, sir?' he asks. His tone is polite, but I am under no illusion—he will not let me take another step further.

'Yes. If you could, would you please send a message to Lady Euphemia? Let her know that Percival would like to speak with her as soon as she is free.'

'I am sure I can arrange that. Now, if you would please step back inside.' He pushes the door open behind me.

For some reason, even though he is being polite, his gesture irritates me more than his words. 'And would it also be possible to have some tea and cakes sent up?'

He presses his lips together at my request, the only sign my treating him as a servant has annoyed him. 'Of course, sir,' he replies, his tone somewhat less polite than before.

'Thank you.' I smile smugly and return to the room. The guard shuts the door firmly behind me.

Snake is standing by the fire, wrapped only in a towel. 'Have you eaten all the food, or did you leave some for me?' he asks.

'I have not even started, and I am sure I can wait until you get dressed.'

'Dressed?' he asks. 'In what?'

I draw in a breath and call on what little reserves of patience I have. In some ways my travelling companions are so capable, but every now and again, I find myself behaving like their parent.

'A maid brought clothes up. They should be in your room.'

He stares at me as if I am mad.

'I walked through there and didn't see anything.' He glances over at the food as if he is expecting me to say that we should eat and he can dress later.

Instead I open the door to his bedroom and point at the clothes laid out on the bed. 'Those clothes? Yes, I can see how you would miss them.'

Snake mutters something under his breath as he holds up the shirt. He slumps on the bed. 'You may want to start dinner. It might take me a while to get into these.'

'I know they look too small, but this is a magical court, after all.'

He stares blankly back at me, clearly not his usual self.

'Take your time,' I tell him. 'I will have my bath and will heat up the food for us when I am done.'

He nods, and I slip into the bathroom. While the bath fills, I reach through the portal in the pocket of my trousers to find my own suit of clothes from my room at Eleanora's.

I bathe quickly and then find myself having to wait for Snake. To fill the time, I wander around the living room, trying to work out whose rooms we are occupying. I do not find much in the way of ornamentation except for a couple of books on creature history beside one of the chairs, so I am guessing the inhabitants are most likely male, or perhaps they, like us, are only here temporarily.

From my previous visits to court, I know we are in the royal followers wing of the castle. Eleanora and I generally stay with Euphemia, so I have spent little time here. The witch is a great friend of Princess Petunia, the sister of Queen Ariana, and her rooms are in the royal wing, close to the princess's.

The best I can do is hope that we have been placed with friends rather than foes and that they will be prepared to help us convince the King to join us in the World Below.

If we can do that before I turn back into a cat, all the better.

FAMILY REUNIONS

SNAKE PICKS AT the food on his plate, eats a forkful of mashed potato, then raises his eyes, his fork hovering over the haggis. 'What's this?'

'It's oats, and spices, and meat.' What I don't tell him is that the meat is mostly offal. I mean, the boy needs to eat, and I see no reason to put him off his food.

He takes a mouthful, chews thoughtfully, then smiles. He follows it with another. I stop watching after those initial mouthfuls because the way he is shovelling food into his mouth will surely quell even the most ravenous appetite. Taking a sip of water, I am surprised to find it's spring water. It refreshes me and is almost as good as a glass of wine—almost.

Before he has even cleared his plate, Snake's head is drooping.

'You should get some rest.'

He jolts awake. 'I thought Pris might come back,' he tells me as his face flushes red. 'For some planning,' he adds.

'Of course,' I agree, but I am not fooled. 'I will be awake a while longer. I can wake you when she arrives.'

'If you think—'

'Go. You are no good to anyone like this.'

He stands and reaches up in a stretch before tidying his plate and mug onto the serving platter. As he does so, there is another knock at the door, and Snake is suddenly alert.

'Come in.' I watch the door expectantly.

Snake smiles hopefully as the door slowly pushes open, and a servant enters

with a plate of small cakes and a carafe of wine. No tea though, but I am sure the wine will do very nicely. A crestfallen Snake grabs a couple of cakes from the plate before disappearing into his bedroom.

'The Lady Euphemia sends her regards and says she will join you soon. She also suggested wine would be better for your conversation this night instead of tea.'

'She might well be right,' I say dryly, but the servant has already left the room.

I finish eating my meal and tidy the dishes before scanning the bookshelves on either side of the fire for a readable volume of something. I'm pleasantly surprised to find some modern fiction has made its way onto the shelves. As I choose my book, I wonder if these belong to the room's inhabitants.

With a copy of *Great Expectations* balancing the plate of cakes and a goblet of wine in my other hand, I make my way to a chair by the fire. With the food and wine settled on a table within easy reach, I curl up with my book. The red wine is delicious and goes well with the cinnamon cake. I am well into Pip's tale when the door creaks open.

'Did you not hear me knock?' a female voice asks. Euphemia, or Effie to her friends, is a slightly older, curvier, miniature version of Eleanora. She has the same startling green eyes and black-brown hair, but whereas Ellie is statuesque, Effie is petite. She also exudes the warmth of a witch with their power based firmly in the earth.

She is wearing an off-the-shoulder, full-length evening dress complete with crinoline undergarments that would not have been out of place in the late 19th century. This is not surprising, as the Unseelie Court never moved with the times—Victoriana has been the fashion here for as long as I can remember.

I struggle to uncurl my legs, my muscles complaining at being asked to move.

'Percival, please, do not get up. It is so good to see you, my old friend—I mean to see *you*, and not you the cat.'

Effie's smile is warm and welcoming, but there is a shade of sadness there as she mentions my usual form. She perches herself on the edge of the chair opposite, arranges her skirts, and pours herself a goblet of wine.

'You could have changed into something more comfortable,' I tell her. 'I would have waited.'

She smiles as she takes a sip. 'I am used to this,' she says, sweeping her hand above her dress. 'Besides, I am only here for a minute or two. I am sure you are tired. We can have a proper catch up tomorrow.'

'I am afraid we may not have time for that. Our mission is time critical, and we do not have long to achieve it—only seven days, in fact. So, if you have time now, I would like to find out what is going on with the court.' I place my book on the table. Untangling my legs from under me, I sit properly on the chair.

'Seven days?' She raises an eyebrow in the same way Eleanora does, and I want to smile, but the bitterness of my next sentence stops me short.

'I am here with two others at the request of Queen Ariana and the dragons. The Dragon Queen has granted me a stay of punishment for seven days to allow me to complete my task.'

'Oh, Percival,' Effie says, covering her mouth with the hand not holding the goblet. 'How we all have failed you over the years.'

I shake my head, not wanting to dwell on this particular aspect of our mission. 'We haven't time for this now.'

She drops her head a fraction, accepting my words. 'Are you able to tell me why you are here? Rumour has it you have two very interesting companions.'

'I am sure I can tell you a little. My role is more that of an assistant to my companions, Snake of the Fieth Clan and… well… Princess Priscilla.'

Effie's eyes widen as she recognises the name, and she leans forward in excitement. 'Well, this is a turn up for the books. You really must tell how this came about.'

Sitting by a warm fire, a drink in hand, I want to unburden myself, to tell my old friend everything, just like I would have in the old days. However, I am conscious that not all of this is my story to tell.

'While I want to tell you everything, Effie, Princess Priscilla is the emissary on this mission, and we have not yet spoken with the King.…'

Effie studies me for a moment before asking rather shrewdly, 'So I take it Cecily and Malachi still insist on keeping Priscilla in the dark about our world?'

I nod.

'All right. I will wait and find out what is going on with everyone else tomorrow. So, how can I help you now?'

'Thank you for understanding,' I say, then take a gulp of wine. I require fortification before approaching what has been worrying me since I entered the building. 'Effie, what is going on here? I mean, the Unseelie Court is subdued. We are aware there is an issue with magic, but that cannot be the only reason why a court once so flamboyant and full to bursting with creatures is now virtually a ghost town.'

'Ah, so you noticed?' she chuckles. 'Then again, how could you not?'

'So this is not only about reducing the size of the court because of the lack of magic?' I prompt.

She twirls the goblet between her fingers. Why is she so reluctant to answer me?

'Effie?'

'There have been attacks on members of the Unseelie Court,' she says, tears welling in her eyes.

I wait for her to continue, but she says nothing. 'Members of the Unseelie Court have always been prone to attacks,' I say, hoping she will elaborate.

She shakes her head. 'These attacks are different. This is not just a small group of crazies having a go at those who are different. These are co-ordinated, targeted attacks aimed to kill or, at the very least, maim creatures.

A gasp escapes my lips. 'Who would do that?'

She tilts her head to the left, and the expression of her eyes turns from sorrowful to flinty steel. 'Really, Percival, you have to ask?'

'No, Effie, you must be wrong. Magnus, Bernais, and their cronies may be purists, but so long as the Unseelie stay above ground, they leave them alone.'

Effie nods. 'They did… until they decided to make a bid for power. They were not able to gather enough followers by using the usual tactics, so they turned to the tried-and-true method of finding a target for everyone to hate. After all, hate bands people together to fight a common enemy, and the Baaronsons chose to use our court as their target. The attacks have been so violent, court members have been reluctant to return from their homes for some months now.'

I stare at Effie, not quite able to believe what she is saying, but at the same time, her words resonate with what I know to be true.

My friend still will not meet my eyes, so I am guessing there is more to come.

'Then, a little over a month ago, the King's consort was returning from a visit with his family when he was brutally attacked. He managed to make it back here, but when he arrived, he was barely breathing. The poor creature did not last the night.'

'But… but he was so young…. Only a little over 200 years old.'

'As I said, the attack was brutal. He was not meant to survive.'

'How did we not hear of this?' I ask, still stunned and unable to comprehend what this means to our mission.

'I guess you could say the King and the court went into immediate mourning. We battened down the hatches and withdrew into ourselves. None of us have any idea how to respond to creatures who have such malicious intent against us, and, until we do, we will remain in hiding.'

I study Effie as she stares into her wine. It is only now I notice the tightness around her lips and the fine lines around her eyes that were not there when I last saw her six months ago.

She takes a deep breath before continuing. 'A couple of weeks or so ago, Lady Susan arrived with the news that Prince Malachi and Princess Cecily were taken to face charges in the World Below. Priscilla disappeared soon after. The King panicked and sent his men to bring Princess Petunia to court, worried she might be a target too. Few people have come or gone since then, and under the circumstances, it is difficult to be joyful when we live under such a dark cloud.'

'Oh, Effie, if only we had—'

'You would not have been able to do anything. Nor would Ellie or Eugenia. Still, you are here now, and I cannot help but think that your mission is somehow tied to all of this.'

We drink our wine in silence as I attempt to fit all this new information into my picture of the worlds.

'Effie, I am not sure how all this goes together, but I am sure we have the right people here to figure it out. We have overcome these creatures before, and we will do so again.'

Even as I try to boost her morale, my words sound hollow to my own ears. Last time we faced the traditionalist in our world, we had the Queen standing by our side. Now we are alone.

A door opens, and a fully dressed Snake pops his head into the room before his body follows.

'I heard voices. I thought perhaps Pris....' His smile slips as he catches sight of Effie.

'Snake Fieth, may I introduce you to my friend, Lady Euphemia.'

Snake blinks a couple of times, his eyes adjusting to the light.

'Pleased to meet you,' he says politely, but he is clearly distracted. 'I think I'm going to find Pris. I hate that she is alone, and she said she'd be here.'

I rise to my feet. 'Snake, you cannot. The guards will not let you.'

As I take a step towards him to put a restraining hand on his arm, the door crashes open, and a booming voice announces, 'I see our guests have arrived. Perhaps we can stir up a party in here, since no one in the dining hall wanted to join in.'

STANDING IN THE middle of the room, shaking my head slowly from side to side, I feel like I've lost it. I must look that way too. Overtired and restless, I thought I heard a female voice next door. To be fair, I did hear a woman speaking, but it wasn't who I expected it to be. Instead of finding Pris, I find a mini-Eleanora.

Part of me wants to make polite conversation because that is what is expected in these situations. The bigger part of me wants to find Pris and make sure she's okay. As I tried to sleep, my anxiety levels rose as I managed to convince myself something was wrong. If she was all right, she would've found a way to come to me.

At that moment the door flings open, and someone whose face I have only seen in a picture is standing in the doorway. A little worse for wear and sporting what appears to be an alcohol-fuelled grin, but he's recognisable as my grandfather nonetheless.

My grandfather's eyes slide over me, dismissing me as unimportant.

'Percival, me old mate, great to see you in the flesh, so to speak.'

He attempts to stagger forward, and the creature holding him up struggles to prevent him from falling. 'Heart tried to single-handedly motivate the court into a singalong,' the other creature tells the room.

The gnome leads my grandfather to the sofa and helps him to sit, then moves the carafe of wine away before grandfather can take a drink. When the gnome guard sits down, he seems to be protecting the wine.

I am frozen in place, but I force myself to turn and face the creatures seated by the fire. Percival is eyeing me warily, as is the creature who arrived with my grandfather. He too looks strangely familiar, but all my attention is for the creature trying to keep himself upright while grinning stupidly at Percival.

'You're not a cat.'

Percival presses his lips together as if he is trying to stop himself from saying something. Unable to keep quiet, he says, 'No, I am not.'

My grandfather doesn't even have the wits to ask why. He stumbles on. 'So you are staying here with us? Excellent. And you can use a guest room rather than curling up by the fire.'

'You? You are here?' The words slip out as a whisper. 'You were in the World Above the whole time.'

The eyes my grandfather turns to me are cold and rather more focused than those of someone who is completely blotto. He leans forwards and peers at me before dismissing me again.

With his attention back on the others, he says, 'Euphemia, I might have known you'd be here, gossiping, no doubt. I could have used your help jollying everyone along.'

'Heart, you do know that you are a bard and not the court jester, do you not?' she asks dourly.

For a moment the creature's face clouds over. 'I know better than anyone that you cannot wallow in self-pity when you have lost the love of your life. So what are the two of you doing here? Catching up on the family news?'

Percival takes a deep breath. 'Actually, Heart, you could say we have been catching up on some of your family… ah… news.'

'What? Percival, why are you staring at me like that? And Drow, you look like you have just discovered a miracle, or at least something very interesting in one of your books. Why have you all gone quiet? And you have not introduced me to your young friend. I am sure he would love to meet the famous bard of the Unseelie Court.'

'Mmm,' Percival starts, his voice dry. 'He might have, had you not made such an ass of yourself.'

I remain where I am, not believing this is happening to me right here, right now.

Percival stands up, takes a step forward, and says, 'Snake Fieth, may I present your grandfather, Breaker of Hearts, called Heart by his friends. And this is your great-uncle, Drow Fieth.'

If I was shocked by my grandfather's appearance, he was more shocked when Percival introduced me. He mumbles something, stands up, sways, grins at me, steps forward as if to catch me in an embrace, stumbles, then collapses back into the chair.

I follow his actions, unable to move as a war rages inside me. Once the initial shock at finding Heart here at the court settles, little waves of anger travel through me, taking its place. He lived so close and could have helped my mother and me, and he didn't. This thought is followed by gut-wrenching hurt because none of this appears to be a big deal to him.

My grandfather was living in Scotland while my mother and I struggled in the World Above, not even knowing he was here. In the end, anger wins out, and I take a step backwards. Heart makes to stand again, but Drow, perhaps reading the room, stands up and lays a restraining hand on his shoulder.

'If you were in this world, why didn't you help Mum and me? How could you leave us to fend for ourselves like that?' The words tumble out, and my voice cracks with pent up emotion.

Heart stares at me, and I watch his face as he sobers. Was his drunken babbling all an act? I fear it might have been, because there's no sign of it in his voice as he says to me, 'Your mother worked so hard to distance herself from me and from the Unseelie Court.'

He stares down at his hands for a moment, as if gathering his thoughts. 'She ignored my letters and did not answer my calls. After a while I stopped trying to contact her and let her drift away.'

He pauses and runs a hand through his hair. 'Once her mother died, she wanted to be seen as a gnome. She did not enjoy being in the spotlight, and she did not want to join our fight for creature equality. She would not be a part of this court, and, after all we had been through together, I could not desert my friends. We were at an impasse, so I decided to let her live her life her way. I promised not to contact you or her directly but always thought she would relent.'

He glances up at me, and I glare back.

He blinks back tears and attempts a smile. 'Over the years Eleanora kept me updated on what your mother was up to. It was through her I learnt that you were born. When your father left, I sent money to ease your path a little, and Eleanora saw that you got it.' He stares me straight in the eyes as he tells me, 'I always hoped you would find me when you were old enough, and now you have.'

Astonishment and anger are now joined by confusion, and they are vying for dominance in my head.

'How would I find you?' I choke out. 'I didn't even know you existed until a couple of days ago.'

I expect him to say that was my mum's decision, but Drow interrupts. 'Many see our court members as outcasts, and it is easier to ignore our presence than face our existence. I am afraid your mother was one of those. And to be fair to her, I think she always wanted Heart to choose her rather than us. It cannot have been easy for her to stay behind.'

'I couldn't stay,' Heart's voice breaks, and this time he lets the tears run freely down his face. 'To stay with her required me to deny her mother, and I could no sooner do that than pluck out my own heart.'

Families are complicated. I don't know where the thought comes from, but it pops into my head anyway. Perhaps I was better off not knowing who mine are?

'Whatever your reason for being here, I am happy you are here now,' Heart says, giving me a look of such hope, I find the ice around my heart begin to melt.

Still, I'm not ready to forgive him, and I remain rooted to the spot.

'Well,' Percival says into the awkward silence. 'Fun though this is, we are not exactly here for a social call.'

At this Drow's attention moves back to the sprite, but Heart still holds my gaze.

'We are here to present a royal petition to the King,' Percival finishes.

Drow's eyes crinkle with a smile. 'So, once again you and I must work together to petition royalty, old friend. Let us hope we are just as successful this time.'

It is then I remember that it had been Drow who worked with Percival to have transformation banned as a form of punishment. Pulling my gaze from Heart, I study the creature who is my father's uncle.

'Will you help us?' I ask him.

Euphemia learns forward in her chair. 'It is perhaps more pertinent to ask, will the King allow him to help?'

To be honest, I had almost forgotten she was in the room.

Drow raises his eyebrows. 'I do not see how he can deny me time with my family and friends. If we happen to spend that time working in the library....'

The room falls silent again. I want to say so much more, but where do I start?

Euphemia stands up and stretches. 'Come now, it is late. We are all tired, and we should perhaps start afresh in the morning.'

I turn to the door. 'But I was—'

'Going back to bed,' Percival finishes for me. 'I don't think now is the time to take on the court guards and rock the boat.'

'What had you planned?' Drow asks me, his eyes narrowing.

'The other member of our party is a female,' Percival says, and Drow nods understandingly.

'Look, Snake, sneaking round corridors for illicit liaisons is not the way to make an impression on the King, and I am sure your friend's chaperone is telling her the same. Best you get a good night's sleep. Tomorrow is not that far away, and you will see her again then,' my uncle counsels.

I'm not sure which of my newfound family members I prefer. Heart, who wears his heart on his sleeve, or Drow, who is coolly practical. If I am honest, at this moment, I wish, instead of meeting either of them, I were well on my way to finding Pris.

'All right,' I say. 'I bow to your superior knowledge—this time. Good night, everyone.'

Heart stands up to do... I don't know what. Fortunately, Percival intervenes. 'Let me have a word with him, Heart. This has come as a bit of a shock to him. Besides, there will be plenty of time to build bridges tomorrow.'

I sense rather than see Percival follow me into my room. He shuts the door behind him, blocking out the tangle of trouble in the room next door.

'I know this is difficult. If I had known we were staying with your family, I could have warned you.'

I flop down onto the bed. 'It's not that.'

'I know, you want to make sure Pris is all right. I understand, but please believe me when I say that what I learnt about the Unseelie Court tonight…. Well, let me just say, it is best if we do not break any of the rules.'

I sit up and study Percival. He is so serious and clearly worried about something, and he has not led us astray yet. 'This is why you are here with us, isn't it. Not only do you know these people, but you're here to make sure we don't do anything stupid.'

Percival laughs, and the sound eases some of my tension. 'I guess I might be, at that.'

'All right. But if Pris is angry with me, I expect you to back me up and tell her how you virtually locked me in my room.'

'Deal,' Percival says. 'Now, get some sleep. We have a lot of work to do tomorrow.'

He closes the door, and I crawl beneath the blankets, still in my clothes, planning to wait until everyone is in bed before I go find Pris. I'm asleep before my head even touches the pillow.

I WANT TO scream, 'Just leave me alone for a minute'. There are so many creatures dressed in maid uniforms from some bad gothic movie crowding me, all vying for attention, asking if I need this or that. I don't want anything except some peace and quiet.

I frantically scour the room and finally find Susan. I send a silent plea to her, and she nods once before ushering the others not only out of the bathroom, but out of the entire suite.

'I'm out here if you need me.' Susan closes the door behind her, leaving me in blissful silence.

I strip off my filthy clothing, and I leave them in a puddle on the floor before stepping into the steaming hot bath. I shiver as I slip under the mass of lavender-scented bubbles, then I relax and allow the water to work its magic, easing away my stress while cleaning the dirt from my skin.

The bath is the most enormous claw-footed affair I've ever seen. It is so large, I can lie back with my legs stretched out and still not touch the end. All right, I am not as tall as I am in the World Below, but I'm not short in my human form either.

I curl a strand of black hair around my finger and am surprised I kind of miss the white it turns when I'm in my true form in the World Below. One thing I don't miss is my pointy ears. It's disconcerting enough to grow a couple of inches and have white hair without my ears changing shape as well. That transformation is so much more… personal.

Enough self-indulgence. I need to plan a way to get to Snake. I sink a little lower under the bubbles, leaving only my face exposed, and begin to plot. This corridor may not have guards placed at either end, but there is the gaggle of maids who I'm sure have not gone far. I'll have to dodge them if I'm to meet up with him.

The door handle rattles, and I shift so I can growl at the maid who has dared to interrupt me. I catch a glimpse of pink floral silk—this isn't a servant. Closing my mouth, I warily eye the door.

The woman who enters is dressed in a silver-and-pink off-the-shoulder gown with an impossibly slim-fitting bodice flaring out to a skirt caught up at the back, making her bum look enormous. Her auburn hair is swept into an elaborate bun held by a sparkling comb. My eyes widen. Are those real diamonds in the comb? And in the drop earrings and the choker around her neck? She could buy a small country with that set.

This woman is so put together and has such presence, I'm suddenly all too aware I'm lying naked in a bath. Thank goodness for the modesty-saving bubbles.

Without saying a word, my visitor glides over and perches on the rim of the bath before studying me, her face not giving anything away.

'So you are Cecily's daughter,' she says, her voice a rich purr.

I nod.

'And the rumour amongst the maids is that you have come to petition the King on behalf of Queen Ariana?'

I nod again, not quite sure where my voice has gone. Somehow this woman's imposing presence has robbed me of the power of speech.

'My sister has sent numerous creatures begging for his help, and he has sent them all away. But perhaps you might stand a chance where others have failed.'

I stare warily at the creature beside me as my brain puts together the breadcrumbs she has dropped. She is the Queen's sister, Princess Petunia. Princess Petunia is Mum's mother… and my grandmother. This woman is my grandmother. These thoughts flood my brain as a more practical part considers her comment. What does she mean, 'I might stand a chance where others have failed'?

'Do you speak, child? Because it will be difficult to petition the King if you cannot.'

Her tone is tart, and she gives no indication that she knows who I am or that I'm part of her family. Or does she speak like this to everyone? Holding her gaze with what I hope is defiance, I order myself not to apologise because the sudden appearance of a family member I only found out existed today is throwing me off my game.

Slowly my brain kicks back into gear. Is this what Fairchild was hiding from me in the maze? That my grandmother is here? Was that what I overheard Percival asking him to tell me?

Princess Petunia watches my face, still waiting for me to speak as I process what is going on. In my most sarcastic tone, I say, 'You'll have to excuse me. I'm not used to complete strangers barging in on me when I'm in the bath.'

The princess's blue eyes flash. 'I am hardly a stranger. I am your grandmother.'

Anger bubbles inside me so quick and so white hot, it's a wonder the water isn't boiling. 'I don't know how it works in your world—I couldn't, of course, because it was kept a secret from me—but someone you have never met is a stranger where I come from, even when they are a blood relative.'

A flash of something crosses the princess's face. Is it pain? It is gone in an instant, replaced by the mask Petunia arrived with. The silence after my outburst is heavy, and I wait for a haughty putdown. Then her face softens as she laughs. It's a full, throaty chuckle of pure mirth, giving me the merest glimpse of the person beneath the princess mask.

'Yes, Priscilla, you and I are going to get along just fine. For a minute I thought you would crumble under the weight of your responsibility, but I should have realised Cecily's daughter would have a backbone of steel and a whip-sharp tongue to go with it.'

I don't quite know what to say to that or how to take this creature. I'm saved from having to respond by the entrance of a maid carrying a bundle of clothing draped over her arm.

'No way,' I mutter as I catch sight of what I assume are a bustle and a corset. 'I am not wearing those.'

Rescue comes from a surprising quarter. 'Goodness, girl, do you have no common sense? The princess is not going anywhere tonight. Bring her a nightgown and robe.'

Minutes later when the maid returns with the requested items, my grandmother rises, takes them from the trembling girl, and places them on the chair in the corner.

'We shall speak more when you are dressed,' my grandmother says as she leaves the room.

Not wanting to keep the princess waiting, I drag myself from the now cooling water, regretting that I had so little time to enjoy my long-awaited bath. I dress quickly and plait my hair loosely, hoping it won't frizz too much.

The clothing is silky and smooth, and it completely covers me, but I'm reluctant to leave the bathroom, feeling somewhat exposed without undergarments. A part of me appreciates that this is normal for the period in history the court appears to be stuck in, but still, it feels odd. I'm about to slide my feet into slippers when there is a knock on the door.

'Yes?'

Susan enters, her modern clothing now changed for a dress appropriate to the period the court prefers. She hands me a plastic packet. 'Many of us here prefer some of the comforts of the outside world.'

I look down and find a multi-pack of underwear.

'When the shops open tomorrow, I'll send someone to buy a selection in your size.'

I smile at Susan, her thoughtful kindness breaking through the wall of ice around my heart. 'Thank you.'

'No worries.' She smiles as she leaves me alone.

I slip on a pair of knickers before slumping into the chair behind the door. It's the underwear that does me in. A wave of homesickness washes through me, and I wish I was home in my own bed. I'm tired of this adventure. I want some normalcy, and I want Snake.

To be honest, what I want most is to walk out of here and find Snake lying on my bed. To then lie beside him and have him wrap his arms around me and tell me we will make it through this. And I would believe him because the two of us can do anything together.

Tears well in my eyes, and I let them run down my cheeks. The door opens, and my grandmother, now in bedclothes herself, enters. I hastily brush the tears away.

'Come, child, I have ordered some soup and bread. You will feel better after you eat.'

She leads me to the sitting room, which is between what I now believe is her bedroom and mine. The fire is blazing and the chair comfortable. She places a bowl of soup in my hands, and at the smell of chicken, my hunger returns, and I almost inhale the liquid.

Once I am finished and the soup has been replaced with a mug of tea, the princess asks, 'So, granddaughter, how did you come to be sent on this mission? Last I heard, your parents were taken and you had disappeared.'

I tell her about the trumped-up charge of using magic for personal gain in the World Above, which saw Mum and Dad taken to the World Below. Recounting how I met Snake brings a smile to my lips, and I'm sure the eagle-eyed creature in front of me has noted that down.

In an attempt to distract her, I reveal that Snake's mother had been taken for the same reason, and we had decided to work together to save them. Then I recount our journey to the Midnight Ball to speak up for our parents and how Bernais had tricked us into the quest in the minotaur's maze to retrieve what was in the middle.

Princess Petunia is quiet as I speak, although minute changes in her facial expressions give me an idea of what she is thinking. She refills my empty cup and asks me to go on.

'When we finally made our way through the maze, we found Queen Ariana held in stasis at the centre. She was what we needed to retrieve, only to remove her, we have to convince the King to return with us because only he can heal her. Then they can fix magic, and the Queen can return home.'

I stop suddenly. Have I said too much? Should I have saved this for the King? While I'm berating myself for oversharing, Princess Petunia is sitting quite still.

'My sister is so ill, the dragons have placed her in stasis?'

Her lip trembles, and I think she might cry, but her face again returns to what I'm beginning to realise is the public mask she hides behind.

'Things have become more precarious than we thought. And with the Queen out of the Capitol, that explains the boldness of the attacks we have been experiencing. We must take care how we introduce you to King Maddox tomorrow. It is important he understands the severity of the situation, and that is why they have sent you in particular as an envoy.'

'Me and my friends,' I correct her. 'Snake and Percival have a role to play here. The dragons were insistent.'

The princess frowns before saying, 'Well, I am not sure they will have the same impact as you, but yes, your friends as well. Now, I can see you are exhausted. Time for bed. You need to be at your best tomorrow.'

I want to say I am fine, but the combination of food and tea and unburdening myself has worn me out. The princess leads me to a room with an honest-to-god four-poster bed in the centre. As I slip between crisp sheets smelling of roses, my feet touch something warm—someone has put a hot-water bottle down there. I'm so tired, I'm dozing before I can fully appreciate the gesture.

FAMILY COMMITMENTS

STRETCHING MY LIMBS between the sheets, I marvel at how strange it feels to sleep in a bed. It has been well over a hundred years since I have spent the night in one. I slept well, but cramps in my arms and legs tell me I slept curled up in a ball as I have every night for centuries now.

Rubbing the sleep from my eyes, I sit up and resist the urge to arch my back and stretch. A sharp knock on the door has me shooting back under the covers.

'Yes,' I say tentatively.

At my bidding, a maid enters. 'Sir, Princess Petunia requests your company for a light breakfast in her rooms.'

Now, this is interesting.

'All right. I'll join her as soon as I am able,' I tell her.

Her cheeks turn red. 'Begging your pardon, but I am to wait and escort you.'

A summons, not a request. Even more interesting.

What can Petunia want to talk to me about this early in the morning? I doubt very much that it is a social call. After dressing in my usual black, I check my appearance in the full-length mirror. Satisfied with my presentation, I allow the maid to lead me along the corridor and up a set of stairs to the royal suites.

Not only am I surprised the corridor is no more richly furnished than ours, but that Princess Petunia's suite is smaller than ours. Although keeping with the style of the court, everything is plush and comfortable. I wonder if the furnishings are modern reproductions. The windows face out over the Ness, framing a cloud-laden sky.

Petunia and Effie are already seated at a table overflowing with breakfast options. At the smell of freshly baked muffins, my stomach rumbles.

'Come, Percival, join us,' Petunia says, never one for formalities.

As I take a seat, she pours me a cup of tea just the way I like it and pushes it towards me. I fill my plate with blueberry muffins and toast and jam. She waits to speak until I am done choosing.

'I spoke with my granddaughter last night. She has had quite an adventure.'

Do I hear a gentle rebuke in that comment? No, Petunia is not usually that subtle.

'She has, and she has shown herself to be a capable young woman,' I say neutrally, wondering where this is leading.

'Creature,' Petunia corrects me.

I pause before responding, wanting to frame this comment as inoffensively as possible. 'I am not sure she yet sees herself as one of us, Petunia. She was brought up human and only recently learned of her true heritage.'

The princess looks down her nose at me, and I feel a lecture coming. 'I am aware of her history, but she is a creature, no matter how she identifies herself, and a high ranking one at that.'

I take a bite of muffin and chew. It is not worth arguing with Petunia over this. Still, until she sees Pris for who she is, our mission is going to be made more difficult.

'Petunia, you did not bring Percival here to discuss your granddaughter,' Effie prompts.

'Indeed I did not. We need to plan, and to do that, you and your new friends need to be made aware of everything going on here.'

I pause, a muffin halfway to my mouth. I glance at it reluctantly before placing it back on the plate. 'Pris and Snake should be here for this,' I tell my old friends.

'I do not know my granddaughter or this Snake. You I do know and trust, and I can speak openly with you,' Petunia says.

I could tell her she can trust Snake and Pris, but experience has taught me that when Petunia makes up her mind about something, it takes time to change it—time we do not have.

'All right, but when we are done here, I will tell them everything we discuss.'

Petunia slowly inclines her head in an almost nod, indicating this is an acceptable compromise.

She places her cup on the table and folds her hands in her lap. 'Over the last few months, we have experienced an increase of attacks against the Unseelie Court. The increase is both in number and severity.'

'Substantially more than normal?' I ask. There have always been people in our world who see the court as unnatural for accepting things Seelie high society would not.

She nods. 'I believe this is a campaign of activity targeted at destabilising the court.'

Effie leans forward, resting her arms on the table. 'Many of us believe it is a result of higher creatures working to regain their positions of power in the World Below.'

'I fear Effie is right, Percival. Things are changing in the World Below, and it is seeping into what was our haven here. Priscilla told—'

I wince. 'She prefers Pris,' I tell the princess.

She arches an eyebrow. 'Really?'

'Yes,' I confirm, undaunted by her display of hauteur.

Petunia's eyes flash, but she chooses not to question me, which is out of character. My senses go on high alert. Something is wrong—very wrong.

'When Priscilla told me about the Queen's absence from court, I knew it had to be Magnus and that son of his, Bernais, at the centre of these attacks. They are trying once again to twist society to their vision of what it should be.'

'To make matters worse, magic is waning both in the Unseelie Court and in the rest of the World Above. There has been little I can do to help the King keep it strong,' Effie adds.

Just as we get to the nitty-gritty, the door behind Petunia opens, and Pris emerges, her face set in morning grumpy mode. I brace for a bumpy ride.

'Ah, Priscilla, good of you to join us,' Petunia greets her.

Pris pulls out a chair, and Effie beams at her. 'It is such a pleasure to meet you, Princess. How like both your mother and father you are.'

'How nice it is to be continuously spoken to as though people know me well.' Pris reaches for a muffin, pulls an edge off, and pops it into her mouth.

'Priscilla, that is unforgivably rude. Apologise at once.' Petunia's tone is steely, and I am surprised when Pris does not react to it one bit.

Effie regards Pris for a moment, her gentle eyes showing warmth and concern. She places a hand on Petunia's arm. 'Blunt though she may be, Pris is right. Her parents chose to keep her away from our world while they themselves continued to visit us. We've watched Pris grow from afar, and it is as if we have known her her whole life.' She turns to Pris. 'How irritating and hurtful it must be to have been left out, then suddenly treated as if you have been a part of this world all along.'

I expect Pris to say something about being spoken about as if she is not here. Instead, she stares at Effie, an unreadable expression on her face. Her eyes fill with tears. She opens her mouth as if to speak, then pushes back her chair before rushing to her bedroom. For a moment no one moves.

'Well, I thought she would have more backbone than that,' Petunia says breaking the silence.

'Petunia, have some heart. She is young and a long way from home in so many ways. And think of all she has been through in the last couple of weeks,' Effie scolds.

As I stand up to go check on Pris, her door swings opens and she re-emerges. Although her eyes are red, she has clearly got herself back under control. She returns to the table and calmly carries on eating as if nothing has happened.

'I am sorry, Priscilla, I should have introduced you. This one of my dearest friends—the Witch of Westhill, Euphemia of the Wyld Woods.'

'And, as you already know, I am delighted to finally get to know you, my dear,' Effie says.

Pris raises her eyes and forces a smile. Her eyes widen and she says, 'You look just like—'

'An older, frumpier version of Ellie?' Effie supplies.

'Ellie?' Pris splutters, and Effie laughs.

'Oh, she's still doing the Eleanora thing, is she? She can be imposing when she pulls that one. I find it difficult to see her that way. I remember her as a scrawny, grass-stained youngster playing with Percival in the woods all day.'

Effie always knows the right tone to put creatures at ease. She would say it is because of her strong connection to the earth, but I think it is because she grew up having to navigate her way through the stormy waters Eleanora and Euphemia left in their wake. As the middle sister, she was often the glue that held them together.

Pris's shoulders relax, and she smiles at me. 'Were you and Eleanora childhood friends?' she asks.

'Hard to believe, but yes, we were,' I say as I return to my seat.

Pris helps herself to coffee and fruit, and, ignoring her grandmother, she half turns to Effie. 'Did I hear you say this court accepts… well, outcasts?'

'Yes. For instance, although your grandmother is wed to an elf, many of their friends have mixed marriages. When given the choice of denouncing them or being exiled…. Well, as you can see, she is here now.'

Pris's eyes widen. 'My grandfather is here? In the castle?'

Petunia returns her cup to the saucer before answering. 'Sadly not. He is at our property near Loch Ness—Urquhart Castle. We are the first port of call for people changing courts, so someone must remain to ensure a smooth transition.'

'Oh.' Pris manages to inject so much disappointment into that single word.

Petunia plows on though, refusing as ever to give in to the negative. 'There are other creatures here I would like you to meet. Your travelling companion—Snake, is it?—is breakfasting with his grandfather and his great-uncle. They are old friends of mine too. Drow in particular will be able to help with preparing you to meet with the King.'

'Snake's grandmother was an elf, I believe,' Pris says, turning to her grandmother.

Petunia seems to hesitate, her eyes glistening with tears. 'Yes, she was a good friend of mine. I still miss her every day.'

Pris gaze softens a little at Petunia's display of emotion. Then she has to go and ruin the moment by saying, 'If I am to meet the King today, can you tell me more about him? Like, has the crown been in his family for long? Is he happy, grumpy, evenhanded?'

I sit forward in my chair. 'Pris, there is something you should know about the King—'

'He lost his husband a couple of months ago,' Petunia interrupts, 'and he has not been the same since. He became closed off, and this once vivacious court has been in prolonged mourning ever since.'

The room is silent for a moment. I had no idea about the depth of the King's despair, and I try to imagine Maddox as a creature withdrawn from society, but it is difficult. All I see is his smiling face and his personality bringing to life any room he enters.

'Another thing you should know,' Effie adds. 'The line of Unseelie Kings does not go from father to son, but often from uncle to nephew, and sometimes passes to non-family members.'

Pris does not respond for a moment. 'Why, are the kings unable to have children?'

Effie nods. 'In a manner of speaking.'

I shake my head. 'Effie, stop beating around the bush. Pris is from the modern world, and her generation discusses differences in people more openly.' I turn to my travelling companion. 'The Unseelie Court was founded when the doors to the world were closed in medieval times. The brother of the Queen of the Seelie Court decided not to return below because he would not have been able to live with his male partner there. Because the King had no heirs, he established the tradition of passing the crown on to a male member of the court.'

'Except in 1482 when King Eron's niece became Queen,' Petunia interjects.

Pris's brow furrows. 'So the court accepts creatures who are outcasts from the Seelie Court but doesn't have queens?'

'Yes, except for that one blip in history, due to the fact that no faction would support any of the male candidates,' Effie explains.

I interrupt. 'We have gotten a little off track. Pris does not need the details of various successions in order to represent the Queen. A simple outline will suffice—although I must confess, I am interested how you found all this out.'

'Drow and I have been looking into court succession,' Effie says.

Drow has been spending time on succession? I cannot help but frown as I consider this new piece of information. He is one of the great legal minds of our time. What is going on here?

I keep my mouth shut and carry on eating breakfast while Petunia and Effie discuss what Pris should wear for her court presentation.

SO, SOMETHING IS going on at court. Big surprise. Why would I have thought it would be otherwise. Nothing has been easy since I found my parents had disappeared, so why should it start now?

I wish Snake were here so we could share our disdain at all this courtly stuff. Last night I was strongly discouraged from finding him. This morning he is with his family as I am with mine. It's as if now that we have found each other, fate is doing its best to keep us apart.

We will be together at court, at least. That is if he can recognise me after I've been primped into someone acceptable of being presented. As Grandmother and her friend chat, I turn imploring eyes to Percival.

'Percival, they want me to wear some monstrosity of a dress…. A pink dress. Can't you get me out of this?'

Percival deftly sidesteps the issue. 'I am sorry, Pris, but female creature fashion is not my area of expertise.'

'The dress is blush,' my grandmother interrupts, 'and it is quite the fashion at the moment.'

I'm not sure what to make of my grandmother. Sometimes she is quite friendly, and at others she is tart enough to sour cream.

When I don't respond, Euphemia says, 'The fashions have not changed since the court was set up. However, within reason, we can accommodate something a little more to your tastes, can we not, Petunia?'

Why isn't she my grandmother? She is much less… prickly.

'All right.' Petunia pushes herself to her feet. 'Come this way, Priscilla. We shall check my wardrobe.'

'If you are dressing, I will say my good-byes.' Percival stands up, and his gaze follows us as Euphemia and I trail after my grandmother.

I throw a 'save me' glance over my shoulder at Percival. He smiles and waves his fingers before slipping out the door. How I wish I were going with him.

Grandmother's room is decorated in pinks, but no frills, and is actually quite comfortable. When she opens her wardrobe, it is a different matter. There are frills and sparkles and all manner of bling and bows. Now, don't get me wrong, I don't mind a little bling when the occasion calls for it, but this is over the top. My thoughts must be written on my face.

'We have not kept up with the times, have we? Not much has changed here since I was a girl of your age,' Grandmother says.

I force myself to smile. 'I mean, it's all beautiful, and I am sure you turn heads all the time. They're just not… me.'

'So, let us find a compromise. Court rules dictate legs must be covered at all times. During daylight hours, so must arms and shoulders. That is non-negotiable.'

'Do I have to wear a dress for this appearance?'

She raises an eyebrow.

'All right, it has to be a dress, but no corset.' I'm adamant on that. 'And I don't want one of those.' I point at what I think is a bustle that makes her bum look enormous.

'That is a shame, because they do highlight womanly attributes, and you certainly have those.'

'So fat shaming is a thing here as well,' I say in a dry monotone, well aware that my figure will never meet the waiflike standard of fashion models, nor would I want it to.

'My dear, you are not fat. In fact there is not an ounce on you. I am merely commenting that you have a shapely figure, and it would be a shame to hide it.'

I place my hands on my hips. 'It would be an even bigger shame to believe I must meet some physical standard to be taken seriously.'

My grandmother glares back at me.

Effie steps between us. 'It would also be a shame to flout conventions simply to make a point when you want to get the King on your side. There must be a middle ground.'

Grandmother closes her eyes, and I can almost hear her mentally saying, 'Goddess give me strength.' She pushes some clothes aside.

'Thank goodness this is a formal court, not your debutante ball. Mmm…. Something with no corset or bustle, how about a day dress?'

I stare at my grandmother's and my reflections in the mirror. With her petite stature and slim figure, she is tiny beside my more athletic build. How are her dresses ever going to fit me?

She chooses a muslin number with capped sleeves. When she holds it up for me, I notice it's lightly gathered under the bust and has a skirt intended to fall to the floor.

More my style, but instead of saying that, I blurt out, 'It's pink.'

Grandmother purses her lips. 'What colour would suit you, Princess?'

'Purple,' I say, scanning the wardrobe for any hint of my favourite colour.

Before my eyes, the flowers on the creme dress change to lavenders and purples and greens. It is very pretty, perhaps a little too pretty, but better than before. It also appears to have grown to a size that will most likely fit me.

'Thank you,' I manage to force out, grateful she has tried to meet me halfway.

'We are not done yet. We will have to "pimp it up," as you young people say, for the court. Effie, I believe Lady Susan left some underclothes out for Priscilla. Would you mind getting them while I look for some accessories?'

A few minutes later, I'm pulling on the dress, which might have come right out of a Jane Austen movie.

'Now, to make it suitable for court,' my grandmother says.

Feeling a little like a rabbit in the headlights, I attempt to reason with her. 'It's beautiful as it is. I'm happy to go like this.'

The two older creatures turn to each other, then to me, shock written on their faces.

'My dear, I cannot let my granddaughter turn up to court so unadorned. It would be an insult to the King as well as reflect poorly on me and the Seelie Court. You must make the appropriate first impression.'

Okay, this is not a battle I'm going to win. If I'm honest, although I don't like it, my job will be easier if my clothes meet local expectations.

Grandmother produces a rose-coloured underskirt that she proceeds to turn lilac. I slip it underneath the dress, and she kneels in front of me. With practiced ease, she uses two small flower broaches to gather two front sections of the skirt so the underskirt can be seen.

Euphemia stands back and studies the dress, chin in hand, a frown forming between her brows. Honestly, they're taking this dressing thing way too seriously.

'I think the dress needs to be darker, Petunia. What do you think?'

Grandmother joins her, mutters something, and the dress shifts as if a breeze has caught it. Now when I look in the mirror, the fabric is cream raw silk with embroidered flowers. This is too much. Or apparently not. Effie and my grandmother are beaming.

Grandmother nods once. 'There, much better. Now for some jewellery.'

She strides to a dressing table and opens a box and rummages around before returning with a pouch.

'Put these on once Lady Susan has done you hair and makeup.'

On autopilot, I take the heavy velvet bag from her.

'Do not just stand there gawping. I still have to dress, and Lady Susan is waiting for you. No, wait a minute. Tell Susan to put your hair up, and I will bring in a tiara.'

I'm jolted out of my stupor. I've reached the end of my patience.

'No tiara,' I say.

Grandmother stifles a sigh, as if realising she has gone as far as I will allow her to. 'All right, there are enough pearls in there for her to do something appropriate with your hair. Now go finish getting ready.'

This time I'm bundled out the door, followed closely by Euphemia, who tells me, 'I must get ready too. I wouldn't miss court today for anything.' She sends me a wink before leaving, and I'm left wondering why she finds this whole thing amusing.

Susan meets me in my room and sits me in front of the oval mirror.

'Just something simple,' I tell her, and she snorts.

'I have instructions from Princess Petunia and, to be honest, she is way scarier than you.'

I meet her gaze in the mirror and smile. 'You're right. But can you somehow manage to keep me looking like myself rather than some painted doll?'

Susan smiles back at me. 'That I think I can do.'

After arranging my hair on top of my head, Susan threads some pearls through the front so it mimics a tiara but is way less flashy before pulling some curls down around my face. She completes the outfit with a pearl choker and some pearl drop earrings.

I turn so she can do my makeup. Normally I would just whip on some mascara and lip gloss, so I'm grateful for her expertise. When she turns me back around, I survey her handiwork. My eyes are outlined in smoky purple and framed in black. Something she has done has given me cheekbones, and my lips are a subtle dark pink gloss. It's me, but not me. It's kind of like when I change in the World Below.

'Thank you,' I say to Susan as the door opens. A maid enters carrying a pair of low-heeled purple pumps. The shoes don't appear to be big enough for my feet, but like everything in this strange world, they manage to fit perfectly.

'I feel… strange,' I say, slipping the shoes on and then standing up. 'And over-dressed.'

'Yes, I bet you do.' Susan laughs. 'You aren't used to all this finery. Unfortunately, here, as in your world, it is important to make the right first impression.'

I shrug. 'And what does all this say?' I ask. 'That I am a girl to be dressed up and preened?'

Susan shakes her head. 'No one there will be dressed like you today. They will all be shiny silks and glittering jewels trying to stand out from the crowd and be noticed. What all of this says is, 'I see your rules and I have made them my own. I acknowledge your conventions, but I am me.'

'Oh' is all I can think to say as tears of gratitude prick at my eyes.

'And most of all, it says, "I am an ambassador of the Seelie Court, and I am someone to be listened to."'

I stare at myself in the mirror, trying to see what Susan does. Dressing like this is like putting on armour for battle. I nod—ambassador me will do. She can pull off a regal show at the Unseelie Court, and she won't have butterflies swooping in her stomach, making her feel ill.

'Now, there are a few things we need to go over—can you curtsey?' Susan asks.

I frown. 'What? Curtsey?'

'When the King enters, you curtsey, and you do not rise until he is seated.'

I curtsey as I had been shown in etiquette class. Somehow it feels easier in this dress.

'All right, not bad. Now, you do not approach the King or speak to him unless he gives you leave. You never, ever initiate a conversation.'

I turn and face Susan. 'What if he chooses never to speak to me? How will I be able to plead our case?'

Susan raises an eyebrow as she always does when she thinks I am overthinking something. 'I am sure he will want to speak with you. If for some reason he does not, or if he does not appear for the court session this morning, then you will need to petition his secretary for a private audience.'

'What about my grandmother? Can she arrange an audience for us?'

Susan gives me a strange look. 'She is the disinherited sister of the Queen of the Seelie Court. In this court, you have more standing than she does.'

I process this for a moment, then realise it is likely because I am still in line for the throne. 'Oh, this is going to take some getting used to.'

Before I have time to ask anything else, my grandmother appears in all her pink frills and finery.

'We should go, or we will not be able to make our entrance before the King arrives.'

Her tone is commanding. For a moment I consider disobeying her, then change my mind—being with her is better than making my entrance to the court alone.

I TUG AT the ruffle collar around my neck. It is choking me. Grandfather frowns.

'It's hot in here, and this coat is making me sweat.' I resist the urge to tug at the green brocade tailed jacket. At least my tight-fitting trousers and boots are comfortable.

'Just be grateful you are not a woman,' he whispers and nods towards a group standing by the window.

In fancy dresses lifted from goodness knows what period drama, they're like a gaggle of peacocks. I have to admit, I wouldn't like to be wearing all of that. Still, this collar has to go.

I undo the fastening and slip it from around my neck before realising the only pockets I have are in the trousers. These trousers are tight enough for the collar to make an unsightly bulge. I sidle a little closer to the potted tree and drop the offending item under the foliage.

'Hey, that's Drow's second-best collar,' Heart says, rocking his own even more frilled collar like a second skin.

'I'll come back and get it later,' I tell him.

'But you look so… plain.'

'But I'm not choking.' I smile. 'For that alone I am happy to have just a simple Mandarin collar.'

'Well, it is too late to do anything about it now,' Heart says as he schools his face into a neutral mask.

After spending breakfast with my grandfather, I still don't know how to take the gnome. During the meal he was polite and asked questions about mine and Mum's life but revealed very little about his own.

Every now and then, I would tell him something, and he would relax and smile and really engage. Then he would stop, and the mask would be back. It was as though he didn't want me to meet the real him. The atmosphere remained awkward until Drow joined us.

Drow is different to anyone I've ever met. He loves the law and works tirelessly to change things to be more egalitarian. I would have thought we would have gotten on better given that we have so many ideals in common, but he is awkward and difficult to like.

I make sure no one is close enough to overhear us, then lean close to my grandfather and ask, 'Heart, why Drow is so hard to talk to?'

'Ah, I believe it's because he is married to his cause and has forgotten how to be with people.'

'That's sad.'

My grandfather nods. 'Indeed it is.'

'Still, he had some great tips on how to deal with the King.'

Drow had helped me outline a draft petition. When I was happy with what we'd done, he advised me the court today was not the time to present the details. We would need to request a private meeting to do that.

'What is today for, then?' I asked.

'For the King to meet you and for you to be accepted into the court,' Drow explained.

Court protocol is so complex, I'm relieved we have people to help us navigate it.

I scan the fifty or so courtiers in the room while I wait for Pris to arrive. The one time I tried to leave our rooms this morning to find her, a guard persuaded me it was in my best interests to remain in the suite.

Percival has assured me she is fine with her grandmother. Still, we are meant to be doing this together, and I would be less nervous with her by my side.

The room is cavernous, with windows down one side and chandeliers hanging from the ceiling in line with each one. Standing alone in front of the dais, I feel isolated and alone. All right, Heart is here, but it's not the same.

Where are Percival and Pris? Finally my scanning pays off. The crowds part, and I glimpse Euphemia, dressed in emerald green. It must be a family favourite, I think, remembering Eleanora's slinky green number at the Midnight Ball. Like her sister that night, Euphemia is escorted by Percival, who is dressed all in black and not a frill or any adornment to be seen. How does he get away with that?

Walking behind them is a petite woman decked out in pink, and looming over her is Pris. My heart literally leaps at the sight of her, and not because she looks amazing. I mean, she is stunning, but it's because it is her, and she is here.

Her dress is simple compared to others in the room but all the more stunning for it. And I for one appreciate the amount of her… um… chest peeking above the neckline. I thought she looked amazing when we dressed for the Midnight Ball, but this is a whole other level.

I take a step to join her, but Heart grabs my arm. I glare at him, and he nods towards the dais. Drow and a tall, gaunt elf have appeared. When they are standing on either side of the small wooden throne, a young elf dressed in royal colours announces that the King is ready to hold court.

Everyone bows or curtsies, and I rush to copy them. They're all so stately, I feel like a country bumpkin who has no idea what he's doing—largely because I don't.

We have been down so long, my back starts to cramp. Heart nudges me, and I straighten up to find that the whole room is not only silent, but is caught up in a drama playing out before them.

The elf who entered is standing in front of the throne. I do a double-take—he is a mirror image of Pris's father. Then it hits me, and I look from Pris to him and back again.

She is staring at the King of the Unseelie Court. Her eyes flicker. She must be putting together the same puzzle I have. I know the exact moment she realises why everyone believes she might be able to tip the scales in the Seelie Court's favour.

Pulling my eyes away from Pris, I turn back to face the King, who is now seated on the throne.

'I see the Seelie Court has seen fit to surprise me with their newest envoy,' the King chuckles. The rest of the room joins him, easing the tension somewhat.

Pris is standing still, and I thread my way through the courtiers until I am by her side. Who knows what rules of etiquette I'm breaking, but I don't care. The only thing I care about is being here to support Pris. Her hand is trembling as I place it in the crook of my arm.

'Come on,' I whisper into her ear. 'We've got this.'

She leans her head against mine for a moment, then stands tall as the King nods, and the petite pink-clad woman leads our party forward.

'Princess Petunia,' the deep voice booms in the hall. 'Can you please introduce the emissaries from your sister's court?'

'Your Majesty, may I present: Percival of The Wyld Woods, Snake of Clan Fieth, and Princess Priscilla Crown as envoys from my sister, Queen Ariana.'

The King ignores Percival and me, his focus turning directly from Princess Petunia to Pris.

'Hello, niece. Welcome to my court.'

THE SURPRISES KEEP COMING

THAT'S IT? WELCOME to my court.

I'm trembling with resentment as the reality of why it is important for me personally to be here hits me. It is not just because I am the Queen's niece, but because I am also the King's.

King Maddox is still talking. I can see his lips moving, but I can't hear what he is saying for the pressure building in my head.

Why didn't they tell me? And why haven't I met this man before. Scotland isn't so very far away from London. After all, he paid for my education and my extra karate lessons….

I stand there shaking while the fragments of my life click into place. Members of the Unseelie Court have been attacked over the years—I have too. They weren't random like my father told me. Snake suspected as much, and I wasn't quite sure I'd believed him. Now I'm certain they were because I'm related to the King of the unpopular Unseelie Court.

Did Snake know? I turn accusing eyes on him, but either he is a good actor, or he is as stunned by all of this as I am.

As if sensing my gaze, he squeezes my hand and whispers, 'Pris, are you okay? The King is waiting for an answer.'

'I… I….'

I have dealt with so much. My parents going missing. Finding out about the magical realm. Being hoodwinked into a quest. Finding out I'm a potential heir to the throne of the Seelie Court. Now this—my uncle is the King of the Unseelie Court.

Each piece of solid ground I fight to gain shifts beneath my feet, sending me hurtling towards another truth from my past. Only this time I fear I can't find a way forward.

It's all too much. I shake myself free of Snake and spin around, the other court attendees appearing as a kaleidoscope of colours through my tears. When I entered, there had been so much expectation on those faces—so much hope that I'm here to save them. I'm not up to this.

'Pris?' The concern in Snake's voice and the murmurs of the crowd follow me as I run from the room.

I've no idea where I'm going, except that I want to be away from here. Paintings rush past as I run along corridor after corridor until I reach a dead end. Turning back the way I had come, I stop to catch my breath, unsure of where I am.

Further along the hallway, a maid is carrying a laundry basket. As she disappears around the corner, I push myself off the wall and rush after her. Taking the same left turn she did, I feel the slimy coolness of a portal and find myself outside in the World Above.

A few feet away, a couple of tour groups are assembling in front of the castle. They turn to stare at me as I emerge from the portal, surprise showing on their faces. I can't tell if it's because of the way I'm dressed or because I appeared from nowhere—and I don't really care. Ignoring them all and blocking out their startled comments, I hurtle down the grass bank leading to the river. My heart pounds in my chest. Once I reach the pathway running alongside the Ness, I halt, unsure what to do next.

All I can do is replay the scene in the audience chamber over and over. Why didn't anyone tell me the King is my uncle? Why did they allow me to make a fool of myself like that? Is there more they're not telling me? All the while tears stream down my face, and the Ness swirls and roils as if nothing in the world has changed.

I shake my head to clear my thoughts. This is not me. I don't stand by while things happen. I'm a planner. I am calm. I process facts and come up with a strategy. Only how can I do that if the facts keep changing? There is only one creature who I can trust. One creature who can take me away from this mess.

Am'ratha, please come and take me home.

I choke back a sob as I wait for her to answer. Can she even hear me? She said I could talk to her from anywhere.

Am'ratha?

I pick up my skirts and start walking along the river, away from town, looking for a space where Am'ratha might land.

I hear you, Royal One.

Relief floods through me.

Thank goodness! Can you come and take me away? I can't be here anymore.

Silence again.

I am sorry, Princess, but it is daylight, and too many people wander the grounds of the castle. I cannot risk them seeing me.

Biting back another sob, I tell myself I won't break down here, dressed like some flaming historic heroine, in front of all these people.

Tonight? I send.

Perhaps. I will have to consult with my Queen.

I stare out across the churning waters, frustrated and alone. Okay, so I can't rely on anyone to take me away from here. I stare down at my clothes. Damn, I can't very well head back to London dressed like this. I don't have any money, or a credit card, or any identification. Who can I call? I can't even do that because my phone is still in the World Below.

'Are you all right dearie?,' an elderly woman asks, and I stare at her with unseeing eyes, my brain unable to process her words.

'It's okay, she had a bit of an upset. We're doing a photo shoot up at the castle and, well… photographers can be a bit… abrupt,' a familiar voice answers for me, and if I weren't so sad, I'd be grateful for his quick thinking.

The woman pats my arm. 'Dinnae let the buggers get ya down, lassie.'

I force my lips into a smile, and she walks off, muttering something about the pressure people put on young girls nowadays.

Resisting the urge to follow her, I turn to Snake, ready to face the music. Instead of leading me back to the court, he wraps his arms around me and pulls me into the circle of his embrace. For a moment I try to stay strong, to make like I don't need his comfort. When he leans his cheek against mine, the dam breaks.

The tears flow, and they flow, and they flow again, along with huge sobs that wrack my body. I can't remember a time when I've cried so long and so hard. And as I bawl, Snake holds me in his arms and says nothing.

I've no idea how long we stand there, or how long I cry for, but after a while, the tears stop flowing, and I simply lean into Snake, allowing myself a chance to recover. Finally, I take a deep breath and step back. Snake's arms release me, and he steadies me as I turn to lean on the barrier.

'You're not going to jump?' he asks, only half-joking.

I give him a watery smile. 'Not yet, but one more revelation like that, and who knows what I might do.'

A group of girls walk past, gape at me, and huddle together before bursting out laughing.

'I must look like a drowned rat,' I say, and Snake smiles.

'You're always beautiful to me. And maybe raccoon eyes will catch on.'

This time the smile I give him is genuine as he uses his thumbs to gently clear away the worst of my makeup.

'Wanna go back?' he asks when he is done.

'Can we just stay here for a bit so I can pull myself together?'

'We can stay as long as you need.'

I lean against his shoulder and watch the river flow by, satisfied I do have someone who will help save me after all.

STANDING WITH PRIS, leaning our arms on the wall overlooking the river, I try to imagine what she's going through. It was difficult enough finding out she was in the line of succession to the throne of the Seelie Court. Then to find out that the King of the Unseelie court is her uncle….

That is not what's bothering her though. It's the fact that everyone who knew just let her walk into the room without saying a word. How can you do that to someone? And how can Pris trust them after that?

I slip my arm over her shoulder, and she leans against me.

'I had no idea he was your uncle.'

She doesn't respond, and I worry she may believe someone had told me. Or, worse still, that I've always known.

'Believe me, if I'd found that out, I would have fought my way through heaven and hell to you to tell you.'

'That's a bit dramatic,' she says.

'And this from the creature who just ran out on the entire Unseelie Court?'

She chuckles, but the sound is still hollow.

'I understand, you know. Your family and mine seem to be expanding by the minute.'

Pris faces me and places a hand on my chest. 'Oh, Snake, I've been so wrapped up in my own problems, I haven't spared a thought for you. How are you getting on with your new family?'

I shake my head. 'My grandfather is an enigma, and my great-uncle is…. I'm not sure how to describe him other than extremely serious. How about you? What do you think of your new grandma?'

She chuckles softly, and a smile tugs at her lips. 'After having no one but Mum and Dad, I now have a clutch of royal relations—a pink princess, and a Scottish king right out of Othello.'

'You think that's bad. I've gained a rebel bard and a revolutionary.'

Now she is laughing for real, and I join her.

Finally, I say, 'What do you want us to do now, Pris? You say the word, and we're out of here.'

She shakes her head. 'I already thought of that. My credit card and both our IDs are back in your family home in the World Below. And we're not going far in these clothes.'

I'm a little surprised she has actually considered running away already.

'What about the dragons? Can they take us back to the World Below?'

She shakes her head again. 'Not in the daylight.'

Okay, even more surprised she'd attempted to call her dragon.

'So, we can wait until tonight and have the dragons spirit us away, or we can go back to the Unseelie Court and finish what we started—that is, if I haven't screwed everything up by being such a drama queen.'

I hug her closer. 'If it were me alone, I would choose option two. I originally started out trying to save our parents, so I would focus on that. However, now that we've found out why you're really here, I can't ask that of you.'

She leans into me, hiding her face so I can't tell what she's thinking.

Her voice is muffled when she asks, 'Do you think my being his niece will make the King change his mind about helping Queen Ariana?'

Part of me wants to tell her, yes, of course it will, and we'll be one step closer to getting our parents out of Bernais's clutches. I can't do it though. Too many people have put their needs before Pris's, and they've hurt her too much.

'Honestly, Pris, I have no idea. He may listen to you, but he may not. I spoke with Drow this morning, and he was helping me draft out a request based on creature law and history. Perhaps if we can combine that with your family connections….'

'How long would it take to pull a full petition together?'

'I'm not sure. Drow spends most of his time with the King and his other advisors, but he did say that Percival would be able to guide us. Did you know Drow and Percival are famous for bringing a compelling case to the Seelie Court that changed the law forever?'

Pris pulls away from me, her face stony. 'I can't work with Percival. He knew the King is my uncle. I thought I could trust him.'

'I think you still can. When you left the court, Percival literally went ballistic at your grandmother. Apparently he would have told you today, but the princess changed the subject.'

Pris closes her eyes before nodding. 'I think he might have tried.'

'Whether he did or not, he was telling her she should have listened to him and that they all should have told you the truth because you finding out this way was unfair.'

Pris is so still, and her jaw is tense. Time to lighten things up again.

'Then he paced about, saying, did they listen to him—no, they didn't. He finished by going into a rant, saying that for all their friendship, they still treated him as a lesser creature, and from now on his allegiance was to you and you alone, and the others could go to hell for all he cared. It was all very intense, and he was kinda bad-ass.'

'Percival ranted?' she asks, and this time she manages a full-on smile.

'And that's what you chose to take from all of that.' I'm relieved I've got her back.

The smile has now reached her eyes. 'So you, Percival, and I really are a team?'

'I believe so.'

'Save the world to save our parents?'

'Yep.'

'No,' she says so quietly, I almost don't catch it.

'No?' I ask, wondering what she's planning now.

'Save the world, save Percival, and our parents.'

I grin. This is something I can get on board with. Pris's eyes turn fierce—she has more to say.

'Then, once they're free, I'm going to kill my parents for not telling me about all of this.'

I know how she feels. I'm only now realising how much my mother kept from me. All families have secrets, but this is getting beyond a joke. Somehow holding Pris in my arms makes it less hurtful. A couple passes by, rubbernecking, but they avert their gaze when I glare back at them.

'Pris, we're getting a few stares out here. Do you think we could head back inside?'

She smiles. 'Lucky we're in human form. How would they take the white hair and pointed ears?'

'Perhaps, but then again, there are so many fantasy programmes being filmed now, we might actually be more accepted.'

Pris sighs. 'Can't we stay out here? Maybe find a cafe and talk? Just the two of us, without this… mess?'

How tempting that sounds, and for a moment, I consider taking her somewhere for a coffee so we can pretend to be two normal people on a date for a while. Then I remember our clothes. 'Another time, when we're more appropriately dressed.'

I hold her for a moment longer before leading us back inside. We head for the portal Susan took us through last night, but there are too many people around for us to enter.

We go back outside and eventually find the entrance Pris had come through. As we wait for a tour party to pass so we can enter, Pris leans her head on my shoulder, and says, 'I missed you last night.'

'I missed you too.'

We step through to the other side, and Pris touches my arm as I move towards the main entrance. 'Wait.'

The hesitancy in her voice makes me pause.

'I can't go back to the court just yet,' she says. 'Not until I've processed this and regrouped.'

Her eyes are filled with pain, and all I want to do is take her away from here. Unfortunately, the stakes are too high for us to simply run away. So, I slip her hand through the crook of my arm.

'Let's go to my rooms. The notes Drow and I were working on for the petition are there, and we can go over them if you like.'

Her hand slides down my arm until we are palm to palm, and she entwines her fingers with mine. 'That sounds perfect.'

ANGER IS NOT an emotion I give into often. In fact, over the years since my curse, I have buried most of my feelings so deep, it would take years to uncover them. Perhaps it is because I have decided to fight to return to my old life, or perhaps it is because I have watched that poor Pris being battered emotionally—because others wish to have their secrets—that I am consumed with rage.

As I berate them all for not telling Pris about her heritage, I am aware someone has cleared most of the courtiers from the room. I punctuate each point I make by banging my hand into my fist, but that is not enough to work off my agitation.

I pace in front of them as I list the way my so-called friends have let Pris down and then patted themselves on the back for doing what her father wanted. What about Pris? Why should she pay for her parents' decisions?

Normally I would worry that I was putting on a show, preferring to keep my opinions to myself. I would melt into the background. At the moment all I can think of is how hurt Pris must be and of how we... *I* have let her down.

My rant goes on for a while, but no one can sustain that high a level of emotion forever, and I soon find myself slowing down and taking a breath. When I finally run out of steam, I finish with a final blow. 'I warned them not to do this, that this would go better if you told her who she is. And look how it has turned out.'

I glare at the group left around me: Petunia, Effie, and Heart. The King and his first advisor are still on the dais, with Drow at their side. King Maddox's eyes bore into me as if he is testing the truthfulness of my words, and I quickly turn away from his gaze, hoping I have not angered him.

'It was her father's wish that she not be told about any of her heritage unless he and Cecily were doing the telling. It was in her best interests not to say anything,' says Petunia.

I find I still have some anger left, and I snap, 'You do not even know her. How could you make that call? She was bound to find out—everyone can see Maddox and Malachi look alike.'

Petunia presses her lips together and glares at me. 'I was simply adhering to his request, as I have done since she was born.'

'And that was fine when she had no idea any of this existed. How do you think she has felt, finding out she is fey and part of a magical world before being told she is in the line of succession for the throne in the World Below, and all of that in the space of a couple of weeks? And she had to find this out from other creatures, not her parents. How was not telling her the King of the Unseelie Court is her uncle the best course of action?'

'If she did not come to take her rightful place in our world, why is she here?'

King Maddox's voice comes from behind me, and I jump before turning to face him, surprised he's joined our group.

I step back so I can see his face when I answer, 'She has come because she believes this is the only way her parents will be released.'

'So, she has come to ask for me to intervene with the Seelie Court, and in return someone will release Malachi and Cecily?'

I shake my head. 'No, she has come to petition you to help Queen Ariana so the Queen can release her parents.'

The King glances away but not quickly enough to hide the disappointment in his eyes.

Petunia rubs King Maddox's arm. 'Oh, Maddox, can you not see? Until she saw you, she had no idea she was related to you. She came to meet with the King, not her uncle. Now that she is aware of who you are, that might change.'

King Maddox's face when he looks at Petunia is schooled back into the royal mask. When he speaks, his voice is a monotone. 'Oh, I understand. Malachi has not relented and told her about me.'

Giving his arm a gentle squeeze, Petunia says, 'You know the plan was to bring her to Scotland on a family holiday in a month and then to bring her to court to meet us. Unfortunately, Malachi and Cecily were taken to the World Below before that happened.'

King Maddox's eyes slide to the window. 'So she came as an envoy?'

'I am sorry, sire, that is correct,' I tell him.

The King sucks in some air and lets it out before returning to his throne. 'That is disappointing, but it changes very little. You—' He points at me. '—go find my niece and bring her to me.'

I bow to the King, and back out of the reception hall. When the doors close behind me, I relax, but only for a moment. The King wants me to bring Pris. He will not wait long, and I have no idea where she is.

Snake went after her, this much I know. Where would he take her? Not back to Petunia's suite of rooms, that is for sure. Perhaps the music room? No, I am sure I have not mentioned there is one, let alone where it is. Ah, there is only one place he would take her—our rooms.

I walk up the flight of stairs and follow the corridors until I reach the one our rooms are on. The guards have been removed, so I guess that is something. As I reach for the handle to open the door, I hear voices inside. I blow out a breath, relieved they were so easily tracked down.

Inside, I find the two of them at the table, their heads bent over some papers.

I announce my presence. 'Ah-hem.'

Two heads rise, and I am pinned with two pairs of eyes. Pris smiles. 'Great timing, Percival. Have you seen this?' She gestures at the papers.

I am relieved Pris appears to be all right, but the knot of my own guilt sits heavy on my stomach. 'Ah, no, but—'

'You should come and take a look. Drow and Snake have been drafting our petition.'

'I am sorry, Pris. I should have said something. I tried, but—'

She grins at me. 'Snake said you gave our families a roasting, and in front of the king too.'

I look at my feet, suddenly embarrassed about my outburst. 'Um, yes, I was perhaps a little too vocal.'

'As I see it, you were probably about vocal enough, and I appreciate it. Now, come look at this.' She points at the paper.

'Ah, thank you, I think. The King has requested you return to the court, so perhaps we should….'

Pris's face turns hard as stone. 'Tough. I am not ready to go back yet.'

Snake drapes an arm over her shoulders and whispers something in her ear. If it is possible, her face hardens even more than before.

'I'm tired of being sent here and there by everyone else. I will go to him, but in *my* time.'

Snake stares at me. He is asking something of me, but I am not sure what it is. I shrug, unsure what to say. Pris needs to take some control of things, but what can I do against a king?

'Is it possible that you might take a little time finding Pris?' Snake suggests.

Ah, I understand. 'Of course, it is unlikely I would find her in the first place I search, so I have time to peruse the petition before we head back to court.'

Pris relaxes, her face softening once again. She and Snake make room for me at the table so I can join them and the document. I can see Drow's fingerprints all over it. He has started by outlining the history of co-operation between the two courts and their commitment to keeping the flow of magic between the worlds. Then he moves on to the issues caused by the Queen overtaxing herself and finishes with outlining the potential impact on both worlds of not resolving this issue as soon as possible.

Under each section is a list of supporting documents and references that should be found in the library to fill out the argument and support our case. Reading this reminds me of the last time Drow and I petitioned a court.

It should bring back happy memories of our friendship, but instead it has my stomach churning. This time, as with the last, my future relies on the success of a petition. Last time I only got part of what I asked for. This time I need everything to go well so I can finally be free of the curse that keeps me from being a sprite.

'It is thorough. Then again, I would expect nothing less from Drow.'

'How long do you think it would take to pull this together if we all work on it?' Pris asks.

I rub my chin and try to remember how long it took Drow and me last time. 'Will Drow be helping?'

Snake shakes his head. 'He's offered to review what we do, but he's pretty tied up with the King.'

'Then two, perhaps three days,' I say.

Pris smiles. 'That's what we thought. So, let's get started.'

I hate to say it, but I must remind Pris we still have to face the King. 'Perhaps we can drop Snake at the library on our way back to court, and he can make a start.'

Pris sets her jaw, and I sense a fight brewing. Then Snake says, 'The sooner you get this over and done with, the sooner you can concentrate on why we are here.'

For a moment I think Pris is going to refuse. Then she closes her eyes, and when she opens them, our Pris is back.

'Come on, Percival, let's go and meet with my uncle.'

PLEASED TO MAKE YOUR ACQUAINTANCE

PERCIVAL TAKES MY hand as we walk down the stairs. He gives it one last squeeze before we turn left and find ourselves outside the court reception room. I'm touched by his concern but also worried because he thinks I need the extra support.

'King Maddox is in his study, Princess.' The guard on duty nods to a smaller door to the left of the huge double doors of the public room.

Percival and I step forward, but the guard places himself in front of us. 'Just Princess Priscilla,' he says, moving his body to cut Percival out.

I lean around the guard, trying to catch Percival's eye. Instead I watch my friend puff out his chest and say, 'I am the princess's advisor. Where she goes, I go.'

I grin at his cheek—I'm loving this new, improved Percival.

However, the guard is not so impressed. He folds his arms across his chest. 'I am informed this is a family meeting, not a state affair, so advisors are not required.'

'It's all right, Percival,' I say, preventing any further arguments. 'Go back to the library, and I'll meet you and Snake there once I'm done.'

Percival opens his mouth as if to object, glares at the guard, then looks at me. 'I will wait here for you.' His pronouncement made, he walks over to one of the chairs dotting the walls, sits down, and crosses his arms, not taking his eyes off the guard.

Stepping between them, I smile at Percival. 'I'll call for you if I need to. Hopefully this won't take too long.'

He waves his hand in a shooing motion, and I take the hint. The guard escorts me to the door and knocks. At some sort of signal only he can hear, he opens it and announces, 'Princess Priscilla for you, sire.'

'Send her in,' a voice barks from within.

The guard steps aside, and I pause for a moment to settle the butterflies dancing in my stomach, then enter. My eyes are immediately drawn to the figure seated behind a desk which dominates the room. His head is bent as he writes. He no longer wears his crown, but he is still dressed in his formal court clothes. I stand just inside the door, waiting for him to notice I'm here.

The guard takes pity on me and says under his breath, 'Go stand in front of the desk and curtsy. He will command you to rise when he is ready.'

I slide a glance at him, checking whether or not he is joking. No, he's not. Thinking it best to follow his advice, I stand in front of the desk and drop into a curtsey. Unfortunately for me, adhering to protocol does not gain the King's attention.

'You may leave us,' he says without raising his head.

Soon after the latch clicks, so I assume he is talking to the guard and not me. I continue to stand, knees bent and head lowered, waiting to be acknowledged. When the King still doesn't stop working, I decide I've had enough of this, and stand up.

The King is still engrossed in whatever it is he's doing, so I take the opportunity to study my surroundings. The room is narrow, with the King's desk opposite the door I entered. To his left is another doorway that I assume opens into the court's reception room. Running along the top of that wall are some narrow windows letting in some natural light from next door.

The opposite wall is lined with shelves that are overflowing with books and papers and folders all shoved in haphazardly. I suspect this is the space where the running of the Unseelie Court occurs.

I drag my eyes back to the figure behind the desk to find a pair of almost-black eyes studying me.

'So, you do not curtsey before your King?' he asks, his face deadpan.

I can't tell if he's being sarcastic or not. Either way, I dismiss his comment, thrown off balance by how much this man resembles my father. Not only could they pass as twins, but his voice is the same rich baritone. Hearing it sends a jolt of pain through my heart as I think about the position my father is in.

I'm speechless, but only for a minute. Then the rage from earlier rears back to life. I'm angry at my grandmother, angry at him, and angry at my parents for keeping secrets from me all these years. This rage is much more empowering than the fear that overwhelmed me by the Ness. My fury allows me to express myself, and I channel it all into my voice when I respond.

'I did, but you chose not to acknowledge me, and it was getting a little uncomfortable.'

Something flashes in his eyes. It could be amusement, but it disappears so quickly, I'm not 100 hundred percent sure.

'I will let it go this time, but in future you should remain in position until I see fit to release you.' He leans his elbows on the desk and steeples his fingers.

I hold his gaze and say nothing. I will not agree to this, but I'm smart enough not to say so. We stay like this for what seems like minutes but at a guess is probably only a few seconds. Eventually he relents and sweeps a hand towards one of the two seats in front of the desk.

'You may sit.'

I take up his offer but choose the other seat. It's petty, but I'm tired of being ordered around.

'So, we finally meet, Priscilla. Your parents have told me so much about you that I feel like I know you already.'

Everyone here knows me, or so they think. Rage bubbles almost to a boiling point in my veins, but I keep it under control. 'Funny, because I know nothing at all about you. And I prefer Pris.'

He shoots me a dark look, then sighs. I can almost hear him saying, 'So, this is how it is going to be.'

'All right, niece, I get your point. I do not know you, I know about you. And you know very little about your family. These are facts we cannot change, and we must move past them.'

Well played, Your Majesty. 'I suppose we must if I am to do what was asked of me. I am here as an envoy from the World Below, and I request a time to formally petition you on their behalf.'

He rests his chin in the palm of one hand and studies me… really studies me, and for a moment he seems almost human.

'So, you will not accept your role in *my* family, but you will represent your family from the World Below in my court.'

Why is he so annoyed? He's not the one who's been kept in the dark and shunted around to meet other's needs. I'm seething, but I don't want to show weakness in front of him, so I keep my next words clipped and precise.

'To be fair, when I agreed to this, I'd only just found out I was important enough in the Seelie Court to be considered suitable for a role. Secondly, Snake Fieth and Percival of the Wyld Woods are also part of this delegation.

Thirdly, I had no idea my mysterious uncle would even be here, let alone rule the Unseelie Court.' I force myself to relax and try to keep the tremor from my voice. 'And finally, I believed I had no option but to come here if I ever want to see my mum and dad safe again.'

He doesn't respond immediately, giving the impression that he is choosing his next words carefully. 'Fair enough. I want my brother and his wife safe as well.'

If you do, you have a strange way of showing it.

'If that's true, why have you refused requests to help Queen Ariana?' The words tumble out before I have a chance to parse them.

The flash of anger on the King's face has me immediately regretting my lack of control. I wish Snake or Percival were here to help me keep a check on my temper.

'I am King. I have to put the needs of my people first.' It is King Maddox, not my uncle speaking now.

I wait for more, but he says nothing. Closing my eyes, I breathe deeply until I have my emotions under control and I can speak as dispassionately as he did. 'This is important. If you won't help because it's the right thing to do, or for your brother and his wife, then you should do it because if you don't, magic will fail.'

The King's eyes are now like black ice, and his fists pound the arm of his chair. Surprisingly, his voice is all controlled fury when he responds. 'The Seelie Court despises us, and your father rejected a position here. I have enough magic to protect the Unseelie Court, so why should I put myself out to help those who would rather we did not exist?'

I lean forward, making eye contact and trying to reach the heart of this foreboding man. 'You won't lift a hand to save your own brother? What happened that you would cast him adrift like that?'

He runs a hand through his hair before leaning back in his chair. 'Our history is complex. When your father and I arrived at the Seelie Court of Britain as goodwill ambassadors from the Court of Africa, royal elves in our own right, they rejected us because of our skin colour. While I was fighting for a place in their world, Malachi was falling in love with their princess— foolish boy that he was.'

He pauses, and I wonder if he's going to say anything else. He shifts in his chair and clasps his hands on the desk in front of him. 'When I left to come to the Unseelie Court where I knew we would be accepted, he stayed with your mother. They were so in love, they made that stupid pact to renounce everything and live in the World Above—all so they could stay together.'

Although the King's voice is monotone, his eyes are heavy with sadness. A twinge of sympathy wriggles into my heart but not enough to take his side over my parents.

'What was so wrong about them choosing to stay together?'

'It is not that. They did not have to be alone. They could have come with me, and their marriage would have been accepted here.'

His words pierce my heart. Could they have? My life would have been very different if they had made that choice, I would have known my family and who I was. No, they must have had a good reason to do what they did. I would reserve judgment until I had a chance to talk with them.

'I believe they did the best they could to protect themselves at the time,' I say stubbornly.

'What good did it do them? In the end they came to me anyway. When you, the fruit of their union, began to experience attacks from creatures who didn't like your dark skin—or perhaps they didn't like me—either way, Malachi turned to me. I paid for your fancy school with high security and your fighting lessons, but they still only visited once a year. And they kept you away from the court—away from me.'

I shuffle forward on the seat as my uncle speaks, the hurt and loneliness in his voice drawing me in. Had he wanted a relationship with me? To be a part of my life when I was growing up?

King Maddox rubs a hand across his forehead and draws in a deep breath. 'None of that matters now. You were to come and meet me in a month or so anyway, but it is better you are here now. It is a this time of great disruption, and I need someone by my side to help keep the court running. With Tomas gone, that will fall to you.'

'What?' I am so cut up by the loss underpinning my uncle's words, I'm sure I misheard what he said.

'My deal with your father was that when you were finished with school, you would abdicate from the Seelie Court line of succession and join my court. You are here now, and I expect you to remain by my side.'

My jaw drops, and I stare at him. He can't be serious. Does he expect me to go along with some deal he and Dad made when I was a kid? No way is that happening!

'I'm thankful for you helping Mum and Dad out when I needed protection, I really am. But all this magical world stuff is new to me, and I'm not sure where I fit and what, if anything, I want to do about my family affiliations in either court.'

The royal mask falls back over King Maddox's face, hiding the man underneath. 'It makes no difference what you want. Your parents and I already agreed.'

'I don't care what you all agreed. I'm an adult now, and I'll make my own choices.'

Our eyes lock, and this time neither of us is prepared to give way. Tension is sucking the air from the room. I'm shaking, and I don't know whether it's from disappointment or anger. Either way, I won't back down. I'm tired of being pushed this way and that to meet others' needs. There is no way this unknown uncle will dictate my future.

King Maddox's lips draw into a grin, and it sends shivers down my spine.

'You will choose to stand beside me at court, or I will refuse to accept your petition.'

Is he seriously blackmailing me? Using the fact that my parents are in danger to force me into something I don't want to accept? I search his face, looking for any sign that this might be some sick sort of joke. He stares back, not giving away anything.

King Maddox has backed me into a corner, and he thinks he has won because there is no way I can say no when my parents' lives are at stake.

I rise to my feet and turn my back on the King, vaguely aware there is some protocol about leaving the monarch's presence but not actually caring if I've insulted him.

'I have not given you leave to depart.' King Maddox's voice is a low rumble as it follows me to the exit.

'Go to hell,' I growl as I slam the door behind me.

AS I DROP the books I've gathered onto the table, a grin lifts my mouth as they send a resounding thump through the room. It was easy enough to find most of the volumes Drow suggested for background details and legal precedents. Now all I have to do is search for the correct information, copy it out, and reference it.

'Just like a school assignment,' I say out loud as I take a seat.

I'm about to open the first book when the library door is flung open so hard, it thuds against the wall, then bounces back. Pris pushes it aside as she storms in, followed by an almost running Percival, and slumps into the chair opposite me. I wait for her to speak, but when she says nothing, I turn to the sprite.

'So I take it the meeting didn't go so well?'

He shakes his head as he tries to catch his breath. 'I do not know,' he manages to say. 'She won't tell me anything.'

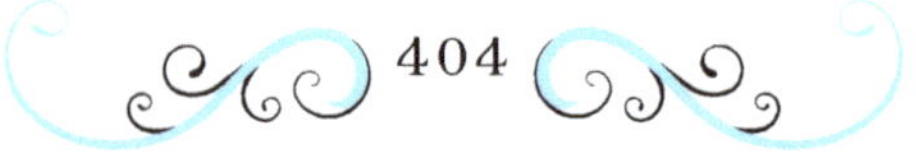

Percival pulls out the chair beside Pris and sits. We both eye her hesitantly.

She stands up and begins pacing. 'If he thinks I'm going to fall into line because of some deal he made with my parents, then he's got another think coming.'

I turn to Percival, but he shakes his head again. He has no idea what she is talking about either.

'But if I don't, he won't hear our petition. And I can't have that.'

'Pris?'

She carries on pacing as if she hasn't heard me, so I stand up and grab hold of her arm. She stops and glares at me. As her eyes focus, her glare softens, and tears well in her eyes. I gather her into a hug.

'Come on, Pris, talk to us. We're a team, remember?'

She nods against my shoulder, and I lead her back to a seat. Sitting beside her, I take her hand in mine.

Pris draws in a couple of deep breaths. 'My uncle, the King, wants me to lead the Unseelie Court with him because of some deal he made with my parents. He says if I don't, he won't allow us to present our petition.'

A punch to the gut couldn't have taken the wind from my sails this quickly. Luckily, Percival is on the ball.

'What did he say when he asked you to lead the court with him? Are you to be his heir? Or just his consort, a ceremonial Tomas replacement?'

Pris's voice is so quiet, I almost miss what she says. 'The second, I think.'

'That's a shame because if he said heir, we could argue that there has never been a Queen of the Unseelie Court.'

I look from Percival to Pris and back to Percival. 'So, are you saying we can't do anything about the other one?'

Percival's brows draw together in a frown. 'What exactly did the King say to you, Pris?

Pris draws her bottom lip between her teeth. 'He said I should give up my claim to the Seelie Court throne, join his court, and be by his side.'

'Interesting. And if you don't do this, we won't be able to petition the King?'

Pris nods.

'This is whacked!' I explode, and the others turn to me with identical quizzical looks. 'Your own uncle is blackmailing you.'

'I'm aware of that,' Pris says. 'We're discussing this because I want some ideas on what to do about it.'

She looks hopefully at me, and I have nothing—no ideas on how to avoid this. Nor has she. A thought tickles the back of my brain, and I wait for it to form. When it emerges, it's something else. All I have to do now is persuade Pris.

'Well, obviously you have to do it.' *Okay, perhaps not the best start.*

Pris blanches, and I see the hurt in her eyes. 'You want me to do as he says? Give in to blackmail?'

I squeeze her hand. 'Sometimes you have to give a little to get what you want. Then once you have it…'

I nod at her, willing her to catch on. She just stares back, her eyes still full of hurt.

'I think what Snake is trying to say is, you agree with what the King wants until we have presented the petition,' Percival pipes up. 'Or, worst-case scenario, until he leaves for the World Below.'

Her expression changes from hurt to hopeful. 'When can you have a somewhat reasonable petition ready?' she asks.

'If we work through the night, I think by lunchtime tomorrow,' I tell her.

'Percival, do you think you could ask Drow to give it a quick check tomorrow morning?'

The sprite nods.

'Okay,' Pris says, her eyes narrowing. 'Percival, how do I renounce my claim to the Seelie Court throne?'

'You have to attend the court and announce it to all those assembled. After it is noted in the official records, it is done.'

Pris grins. 'I can't do that at the moment, but I can hint that I will in the future. I'll tell my uncle later today and endure an evening and morning of being a court follower until we present our petition. Then I'm home free.'

The air feels lighter, and Pris laughs.

'At some stage, though, you will have to make this right with your uncle,' Percival says. 'He is not a bad man, just one who is feeling alone.'

The light fades from Pris's eyes. 'I know, and I will. But before I tell him, we have to sort out the Queen, fix the decline of magic, and get our parents freed.'

'Agreed,' I say, but I'm not as happy as Pris about all of this. With all the family complications we've run into, I'm finding it's no longer easy to see what Pris's and my futures will be when this is over. She has royal responsibilities, and I'm being slowly drawn into my own family issues.

Some of my turmoil must have shown on my face, because Pris places her hand over mine and says, 'Hey, it's only playacting and only for a couple of days. How hard can it be?'

I force myself to smile. 'Now you've gone and jinxed it.'

'You may believe this will be easy,' Percival says, 'but do not underestimate the King or his advisors. Drow may be able to keep his opinions on the depth of your commitment to himself, but I doubt Chancellor Rimould will. He is the King's man through and through. If he senses any deception, he will go straight to the King.'

'He's right, Pris. If you do this, you must do it properly. No sneaking away, no snide comments—'

I stop talking when I see a smile tugging at Pris's lips.

'You don't think I can do it, do you?' She moves so she can include Percival. 'Either of you?'

I'm shaking my head when the castle shudders. Pris's eyes go wide, and the building rocks again. I brace myself, gripping the table as books tumble from their shelves and bits of plaster fall from the ceiling.

'What the—?'

'I think…. I think someone is attacking the castle… with magic.' Percival sounds like he can hardly believe what he's saying. 'Perhaps we should take cover under the table.' His eyes dart around the room, a little panicked.

'Or in a doorway,' Pris suggests, 'like in an earthquake?'

A loud *crack* sounds, and we all dive under the solid oak table as the castle shakes again.

We huddle together, and I reach for Pris's hand, gripping it tight. Shouts and the sounds of footsteps running ring out from the hallway, but there is no more shaking. We wait a good few minutes to make sure whatever it was has stopped before emerging from the table's protection. Pris heads straight for the window.

'I would not stay there,' Percival tells her. 'The windows are the weakest part of the castle's protections.'

Pris appears not to have heard. I move to her side. 'Come on, Pris, we need to find out what is going on.'

'Look,' she says, pointing at a figure running down the street. 'Isn't that—'

'Grossman Green,' I say before she does. 'What is that slimy rat doing here?'

My lips curl back into a snarl. I have not forgiven him for selling us out in Wiseman's Woods or for taking part in the plot against our parents. Now he's here during a magical attack on the court. It can't be a coincidence.

I drop an arm over Pris's shoulder and lead her away. 'Come on, there's nothing we can do about him, but we may be able to help with repairs or something.'

I lead Pris to the door, with Percival following behind. Before I can open it, a guard enters.

'Is everyone all right in here?'

We all nod, but his attention is on Pris.

'Good. We have experienced a direct magical attack. The King has ordered all the entrances and exits closed until we find the culprits.'

Pris's hands clench at her sides, and she leans into me and whispers, 'Great. The enemy is in town, we can't leave, and I have to play princess—'

I hold up my hand. 'Please don't say it. You've already jinxed us enough for one day.'

Pris chuckles softly, and the guard frowns at us. 'This is no laughing matter. If you could please return to your accommodations, we need to do a head count to make sure there were no casualties.'

At the mention of casualties, Pris's smile quickly fades.

Chastened, we slip past the guard and make our way to Drow and Heart's suite, sidestepping a surprising amount of debris on the way.

AS I FOLLOW Pris and Snake along the rubble-strewn corridor, I shove my shaking hands into my pockets. I have never been so scared in my life—not even when I realised Magnus Baaronson had turned me into a cat. My life had not been threatened then.

Thank goodness for the wine in Heart and Drow's suite. I fill three glasses, then gulp mine down in a single swallow. As I pour myself another, I see Snake's hand tremble. I do not have it in me to reassure him that everything will be all right. Fortunately, Heart arrives in time to take the pressure off me somewhat.

'Ah, Princess, you are here. Your grandmother, Princess Petunia, is worried about you, given that you have not shown up in her rooms.'

'I've been with Snake and Percival,' Pris says, not picking up on Heart's actual concerns.

'You left the King in… less than… optimal circumstances,' he says as I hand him a glass of wine. 'Perhaps you would like to return to her suite and let her know you are all right?'

'I am fine here, thank you,' Pris tells him. She does not add that she has had enough of her family for one day—although I sense she wants to.

Heart shrugs. 'It is your call, but I think we should get a message to her. You were the last person unaccounted for, and she was certain something had happened to you.'

'If you think we should,' Pris says, taking a sip of her wine.

Heart presses the buzzer to summon a servant. I am surprised when one appears only a few minutes later. I had assumed they would all be busy cleaning up and that seeing to our needs would be a long way down on their list of priorities.

'Piers, please inform Lady Susan that we have found Princess Pricilla and she is well,' Heart instructs the brownie.

Before Piers leaves, Pris adds, 'And if you can ask her to organise a change of clothes for me—normal clothes, not these archaic dresses—I'd appreciate it.'

Heart raises an eyebrow.

Pris stares him down. 'Susan said we don't have to dress like ghosts from the past when we're not at court. So I assume she'll be able to find me more comfortable clothes.'

Heart's eyes crinkle around the edges when he smiles at Pris. 'You are as feisty as everyone says,' he comments before turning back to the servant. 'You heard the princess.'

'Add me to the list for normal clothes too,' Snake says.

I have no idea why he wants to change. He is very smart in his courtier garb. Why swap that out for jeans and a T-shirt?

The servant darts from the room before we can find anything more for him to do. Thanks to the wine, the slight tremor in my hands finally subsides, and we head for the seats around the fire. We are not long seated when another servant knocks before bringing in a tray of sandwiches and coffee. I had almost forgotten it was lunchtime, but my stomach remembers as soon as I smell the food.

'Cook says the dining room cannot open until evening meal time, so this is to tide you over,' she says before backing out of the room.

We all move to the table, and for a short time, we push our worries aside and eat lunch, happy to be alive.

Snake is the first to break the silence. 'When they say we can't leave our rooms, do they mean we can't go anywhere at all? I'd like to go back to the library and finish our petition.'

Heart answers before I can. 'Most of the guards are holding the outer barrier in place while the magically gifted find and repair any smaller holes. It would not be safe to move too far until they are done.'

At that moment yet another maid taps on the door and enters, carrying Snake's and Pris's questing clothes and footwear. 'Lady Susan sends her apologies. She has not had time to purchase any other clothes for you, and she hopes these will do. They have been cleaned and mended.'

'They are perfect. Can you thank her for me?' Pris says, taking her clothes from the creature. 'Where can I change?' she asks.

'Come, I'll show you the guest bathroom,' Snake tells her, grabbing her hand.

Heart chuckles as they disappear. 'I think there may be a little more than getting changed going on there, eh, Percival?'

'I am certain Snake will be a gentle—'

I do not get to finish as Drow barges through the door, all anger and fury. 'This has got to stop. They have dared to attack the court directly. They would only do so if they believed there would be no retribution.'

Heart, perhaps used to Drow's dramatic interruptions, does not look up from his coffee. 'Will there be? I mean, we have not done anything about the other attacks—not even Tomas's death.'

'A few of the guards have been sent out to hunt down the creatures who did this, and they are on orders to bring them back here. But no, there will be no counterattack and no retribution in the World Below. How can there be when the ones causing the problems act on their own initiative?' Drow drops into a chair by the fire, catches sight of the food, then gets back up to join us at the table.

I wait until he has a cup of coffee in his hand before I say, 'Drow, you do know our only hope is to persuade King Maddox to assist the Queen? Once she is back on the throne, she will be able to deal with these attacks on the court, and magic in both realms will be stronger.'

'You are right, Percival, and I have already thought of a way to extend the petition to include retribution for the Unseelie Court as being one of the positive outcomes.'

'Do you truly believe we can convince him?' I ask.

Drow grimaces. 'I fear it is not him we need to persuade but Chancellor Rimould. King Maddox has been off his game since Tomas died and relies more heavily on his advisor, who counsels against taking action in this matter.'

I tap my fingers on the table as I force my brain to work the way it used to when I played politics along with the best of them. 'And is he maybe a conservative? I seem to remember Eleanora saying something to that effect.'

'He is, but he can be persuaded to act given the right motivation and if it's in the Unseelie Court's interest.'

As Drow and I talk, it is like we are back in our university days, nutting out a problem together. I stop as a memory dislodges from the recesses of my brain.

'Drow, Effie said a lack of magic has been causing problems, but has someone been recording the incidents like we used to record the effects of the blight?'

'Not officially, but I think there is someone who might be able to help—Tomas's

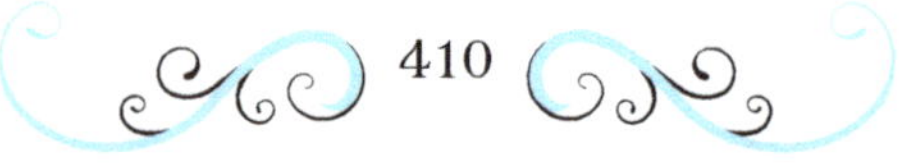

nephew, Dinian, has taken it upon himself to collate what reports we receive. You all head to the library, and I will search him out.'

'Are we allowed to leave?' Heart asks.

Drow pauses on his way to the door. 'Oh, yes, did I not say already?' Then he is gone.

Heart rolls his eyes and turns to me. 'Who is going to tell the lovebirds?'

I sigh as I stand up. 'I guess that will be me.'

PULLING IT ALL TOGETHER

SNAKE HAS INDEED been a gentleman if what I witnessed when I entered his room was anything to go by.

'Oh, you're alone,' I say, pointing out the obvious.

Snake laughs. 'It's difficult to be too romantic when you're worried someone will barge in at any moment.'

'Ah, then how did Pris get out of her dress?'

Snake winks. 'I did say not too romantic.'

The door to the bathroom opens, and Pris enters. She's rather further along in the dressing process than Snake, and as her eyes drift to his bare chest, her cheeks pink up. He slips past her into the bathroom, leaving the door open.

I am getting a definite third-wheel vibe and rush to say, 'I have come to collect the two of you. We are all heading to the library so we can work on the petition.'

'But I haven't had a chance to tell King Maddox that I accept his offer.' Pris says. 'I should go now.'

I raise my eyebrows.

She glances down at her travel attire, then back at me. 'I guess I can't go dressed like this?'

'No, you cannot.' I bite back a smile. 'Perhaps we could send a servant to request a few minutes of the King's time before the formal dinner tonight. That way you will have time to plan with us and also to dress appropriately.'

'Sounds okay. What do you think, Pris?' Snake says, doing up the last couple of buttons of his shirt.

Pris draws in a breath and lets it out slowly. 'I guess it'll have to do.'

'Fine. I will ask Heart for some paper and a pen, and you can write a request for the King.'

Pris wrinkles her nose. 'I guess I should write one to Susan too, asking her to make sure I'm dressed suitably for a royal consort.'

'How very forward thinking of you,' I tell her with a small smile. She is already starting to get used to how the court works. 'Now I shall wait for you outside. Please do not be long. We have much to do this afternoon.'

Heart is still trying to find a pen when Pris and Snake appear from the bedroom.

'Ah, found it,' Heart says, brandishing an ink pen. He unscrews the bottom and checks the ink before handing it over to Pris.

'This is a bit posh for a quick note,' she says, and Heart laughs.

'This is the Unseelie Court version of a biro. King Maddox likes us all to write with quill pens, but most of us have an ink one hidden away.'

Pris sits at the table and stares at the two blank sheets of parchment in front of her, bottom lip drawn between her teeth. 'So does that mean I have to write differently as well?' she asks Heart.

'The one to Lady Susan should be fine to write normally, but when writing to the King, it is best to use formal language. If you can, make your writing look a little fancy. He will appreciate the effort.'

Snake snorts. 'It's all a bit much isn't it? All this old-world playacting.'

Heart's shoulders tense, and I fear Snake is in for a bit of a dressing down. I am proven wrong when Heart speaks.

'It may be hard for someone with as few years as you have under your belt to understand that sometimes hiding in the past or playing a role can be comforting. And especially so when life has not been kind to you.'

My heart is heavy as my friend speaks. He lost his wife more than forty years ago, and he still misses her. His grief also brings shame to me. Heart cannot be with his wife, but I could be with my bond-mate Nisha, and I have chosen not to be. Still, I am finally on the road to setting things right. It is such a shame that I have waited hundreds of years to do it.

Heart's words must have touched something in Snake too, and he makes his way to his grandfather's side before placing a hand on his shoulder. 'I am sorry. I didn't mean to criticise.'

'It is all right, son. We all mock that which we don't understand. If you think of the Unseelie Court as a bunch of misfits trying to make a place where there is a space for everyone, then you may find its foibles easier to understand.'

'But not the lack of modern amenities,' Snake says, wrinkling his nose.

'King Maddox did start but was forced to slow down because there wasn't enough magic around,' Heart says.

Snake catches my eye, and I sense he's wondering if King Maddox is feeling the impact of a lack of magic, why is he not fixing it? I do not have an answer, so I say nothing.

'I'm finished,' Pris says, waving the two folded documents in the air.

I pull myself away from the touching family scene to join her at the table. 'Would you like me to check the one for the King?' I ask her.

Pris's eyes twinkle with mischief. 'Why, Percival, that is so sweet... or is it that you don't trust me?'

'Rumour has it your last words to him were something about going to hell, so can you blame me?'

She grins as she stands up and tucks the letters into her back pocket. 'While I appreciate your offer, I think I had best deal with King Maddox on my own terms, otherwise he'll never respect me. Now, we'd better get moving, or Drow will have everything sorted, and we'll have to waste time convincing him of any changes we want to make.'

'This should be good,' Heart says to me as we follow the princess to the door. 'If she thinks being there will prevent Drow from putting exactly what he wants in the petition, then she is in for a bit of a surprise.'

I chuckle. 'Or maybe Drow is. Pris is very adept at turning things to her advantage.'

Heart raises his eyebrows. 'Care to place a wager on that?'

I think about it for a moment. Drow and Pris are pretty evenly matched. Still, I think the princess may have a slight advantage. 'You are on. And whoever loses has to endure dinner this evening without the benefit of wine.'

Heart looks pained at my offer of a forfeit.

'Either you back Drow or you do not,' I tease him.

He laughs. 'It is a wager.'

'What's the bet?' Snake asks, dropping back to walk with us while Pris hands her notes to a passing servant.

Heart taps the side of his nose with his index finger. 'Never you mind, young Snake, never you mind.'

I cannot help but smile. I'm enjoying being back with my friends again. My smile fades as I enter the library and see who Drow is sitting with. I remember the elf from my last visit here as a cat. When he thought no one was looking, he played a rather nasty trick on a brownie maid and said nothing when she was dismissed for incompetence.

Drow stands up as we enter and frowns at his companion until he too rises to his feet. 'Lord Dinian, may I present Princess Priscilla, Snake Fieth, and Percival of the Wyld Woods. Everyone, this is Tomas's nephew, Dinian. He has been collating reports of fluctuations in magic for the King.'

The elf pushes a fringe of black hair out of his eyes as his gaze brushes past Snake and homes in on Pris. He glides around Drow, then takes Pris's hand and kisses it. 'I am so very pleased to meet you, Princess. As we are to be working together, may I call you Priscilla?'

Pris's lips tighten a little, and I wait for her to tell the upstart elf her name is Pris.

'You may,' she tells him, withdrawing her hand and tucking it through Snake's arm.

I cough to hide my laugh. The princess has the measure of Tomas's nephew.

As Snake leads Pris to the table, Dinian's eyes follow her trouser-clad figure, and he smiles appreciatively. I want to say something, but fortunately Heart steps in and gently slaps the back of the creature's head. 'Show some respect. She is related to the rulers of both creature courts.'

I expect the young elf to blush or show some sign of embarrassment, but he does not. 'I am beginning to see a reason to move the court towards more modern forms of dress,' he says. 'Perhaps it won't be that long until we can.'

Not only does his leering at Pris confirm my initial impression of the creature, but it also sounds warning bells, although I cannot quite put my finger on why.

'Perhaps we could start,' Pris is saying, and I draw my attention back to the petition. 'I am expecting to be called to meet with the King in a couple of hours, so we need to make the most of our time here.'

'Ah yes,' Drow starts. 'Perhaps if Percival could take the lead on completing the initial outline we had. He knows how these things work, and with Snake and Heart helping, we should have a decent draft ready in no time.'

My heart warms at his trust, and I smile my thanks. Snake is already sliding the books he found earlier down to the other end of the table. I pick up the papers, and Heart and I join him. As we set up, Snake sends dagger glances towards Dinian, who is standing far too close to Pris for anyone's liking.

'I don't like that elf,' Snake whispers as Pris moves away from him and takes a seat, making sure Drow is between her and her would-be suitor.

As we work silently through the texts, Dinian asks, 'How are you enjoying your time in the Unseelie Court?'

'I'm not here for a family visit,' Pris responds in her iciest tone. 'I am here on business.'

Dinian carries on as if she has not spoken. 'It cannot be all business. You must make time for me to show you some of the delights of the court.'

'I know what I'd like to show you,' Snake mutters. 'The business end of my fist.'

'Be calm, Snake. I am sure Pris can more than handle that creature,' I say.

As if to underline my words, Pris says, 'I am here for business and nothing else, and the only interest I have in spending time with you is if you can contribute something to our petition. Now, do you have any information that might help, or not?'

'Of course, Priscilla. Your wish is my command.'

Snake sniggers as Dinian uses Pris's full name, the one she hates with a passion.

The elf pulls a sheet of paper from the pile of documents in the middle of the table. 'This is a summary of the reports below in order of number of reported incidents. I've found the reduction in magic in the World Above has meant healers have not been able to heal some illnesses. Some have even lost their ability to help other creatures and have reverted to using natural medicines.'

'I had no idea things were that bad,' Drow mutters.

'There is more. Additionally, some of the magical races are not having as many offspring—brownies and sprites have been experiencing a steep decline in numbers. Perhaps the worst sign of magic waning is that many creatures report it more difficult to fight human pollution and to counter the damage it does to the world.'

Drow leans forward and picks up the stack of papers. 'This is good work, Dinian. We should slot this in after the legal arguments and our reference to the obligations the crown agreed to—for both monarchs to support each other in keeping magic clean to benefit both worlds.'

'What exactly is the legal argument based on?' Pris asks, and Drow tuts.

He never used to be this curmudgeonly. In fact, he used to enjoy teaching creatures about their history.

He looks down his nose at Pris as he answers her, and I wonder if there is more going on here. Life was so much clearer when I did not have to worry about such things.

'Well, Princess, once upon a time, magic used to flow freely between the World Above and the World Below. When people with magic began being noticed in the World Above, the Queen closed the gates—'

'Between the worlds.... I know that. I also know that magic was tainted in some way by this. I assume the agreement you all keep talking about between the courts came about when some of the gates were reopened?'

Drow locks his fingers together and studies the princess for a moment, as if he is taking her measure. A twitch at the corner of his lips suggests that, contrary to outward appearances, he might actually be enjoying this conversation.

'You are correct. When the council refused to open the gates to prevent the spread of blight, the dragons intervened. Many were already beginning to feel the loss of magic, the dragons included, and they stepped in. The Queen of the Seelie Court was already bonded to a dragon who boosted her magic in times of need. The Dragon Queen threatened to sever that link if the doors were not opened.'

'I get that,' Pris says, 'and I also know that Queen Ariana was cleaning the flow of magic when she became sick. What I don't know is where the Unseelie Court fits into this.'

Heart leans closer to me. 'Ah, the impatience of youth, eh, Percival?'

'It is indeed wearying,' I respond.

Drow's demeanour has softened, and I can tell he is warming to his subject. 'At the same time, the Queen of Dragons offered to raise the Unseelie Court to the same level as the Seelie one if they promised to work with the monarch of the World Below to cleanse the magical flow.'

'So the King was bonded to a dragon?' Pris asks.

'Yes, he was, as was King Maddox when he was named heir. I believe you met Ed'ruven when you came through the portal.'

Pris smiles. 'We did.' She places her arms on the table and sits forward. 'If I understand you correctly, the agreement with the dragons is what you're calling legal precedence?'

'Correct.'

'So, if everyone was keeping up their side of the bargain, how did magic get in such a bad way? Was someone not doing what they needed to?'

'It is amazing how someone new can size up a situation and cut right to the meat of the thing,' Heart chuckles.

I put a finger to my lips. 'Hush a minute. I want to hear how Drow deals with this.'

'There are many reasons magic has been failing, but I believe the two main ones are that Queen Petunia faced so much political opposition, it took almost all her time and energy to hold on to the throne, so she and her dragon were not as active as they once were.'

'And my uncle?' Pris prompts.

'He decided to move and extend the court and so was perhaps not as diligent as he should have been either.'

'And there was always the problem that when the two worlds were sealed off, some gates disappeared,' Snake adds. 'So magic did not flow as easily as it once did and needs constant attention.'

'Very good,' Drow praises his nephew.

The room falls silent, and Drow leans back in his chair.

Pris stares at the table, tracing the pattern of the wood with a finger. She stops and looks at Drow. 'I disagree.'

'With what?' Drow asks dourly.

'About where to put the impact of the loss of magic,' Pris answers. 'When I spoke to the King, he said he would only consider our petition favourably if it were in the Unseelie Court's interest to do so. I think we show him the impact the loss of magic has, follow that up with the reasons why, and wrap the whole thing up with family and legal obligations.'

The room is so quiet, I expect to see tumbleweeds roll by.

Finally Drow speaks. 'I have years of experience in arguing cases in court, and—'

Pris edges forward on her seat. 'And if this were a court case, it would be based on law, but it isn't. King Maddox is already aware of his commitments, and he has not only refused to meet them, but he's put the court squarely before them. We need to try something different, something that might shake him up a little.'

All eyes are turned to Drow, but he is staring straight at Pris, his head cocked to the side. 'What about his family ties and the fact that his brother is being held in the World Below?'

Pris's brows draw into a frown. 'I will take your guidance on that. From the little I've found out so far, Uncle Maddox still holds a grudge because my father chose my mother over him. So pressing family ties may backfire.'

Drow blinks, then nods a couple of times. 'All right, we will lead with the impact on the Unseelie Court, using not only the lack of magic but also the attacks because the Seelie Court is weak without the Queen to guide it. We should leave family ties out.'

Beside me Heart gasps, and I chuckle. My wine with dinner is no longer in jeopardy.

'Drow must be losing his touch,' Heart mutters.

'Is there anything we are able to offer from the Seelie Court, perhaps an olive branch that Queen Ariana will uphold?' Pris asks Drow.

'Well played,' Heart murmurs. 'First she beats him with logic, now she draws him back in by asking for his expertise. Drow had no hope.'

Drow smiles, apparently agreeing with Heart's whispered assessment of the situation. 'I like the way you think. One thing you could offer that I believe King Maddox will agree to and that Queen Ariana will jump at accepting. And I also believe her council will not be able to disagree with the collapse of magic at stake. Reinstate Princess Petunia as heir to the Seelie throne.'

'Oh, I like that,' Pris says. 'It closes Bernais down because it gives an alternative to him should the Queen not be able to take up her duties for any reason. And will appeal to King Maddox because it strikes at his enemies in the World Below.'

'And it puts you one step further from the throne,' I mutter.

Dinian leans forward. 'Is that wise? I mean, won't such a strong alignment between the courts mean the attacks will get worse, not better? Won't they try harder to take the Unseelie Court down?'

'I believe it is more likely it will weaken the Baaronson faction and the attacks will stop,' Pris responds.

The set of Dinian's jaw shows he disagrees. He opens his mouth to speak, but Pris closes him down.

'While we appreciate your input, I would like to find out what Snake and Percival think. After all, we three must stand behind this document.'

'You know me, Pris. I'm behind anything that will weaken Bernais and help my mother.' Snake grins.

I take a while to respond. Much as I hate to admit it, Dinian might have a point. Will throwing a spanner in Bernais's works make him even more violent? Given his nature, it is certainly a possibility. Still, if more magic is available in the World Above, then they will be better able to defend themselves. And the threat of persecution could put off some of his more lukewarm followers.

'I do have misgivings,' I start, gathering my thoughts as I speak, 'but I think it is better to offer it rather than leave it out.'

'Excellent,' Drow says. 'We have a plan. Dinian, thank you for your help, but we have it from here.'

It appears as though the elf will object, but he picks up his papers and moves to a smaller table on the other side of the library. Although he seems to be carrying on with this work, every time I glance his way, he is more interested in us than the papers in front of him.

EVERY NOW AND then, Dinian mutters under his breath, as though he wants to draw everyone's attention to the fact that he's still here. His antics make it difficult to concentrate on what Drow and Pris are saying. I want to be able to block him out, and usually I'm easily able to do that, but something about the guy gets right under my skin.

I'm about to say something to him when a knock on the door has everyone falling quiet. A servant enters with a note on a silver tray. He takes it straight to Pris, who reads it and then tells the creature she will be there.

As the servant leaves, she catches my eye. 'I have fifteen minutes with the King in an hour.'

I smile. 'Great. Let's keep working.'

'Actually, we're almost done,' Drow says, putting down the papers Percival handed him before the interruption. 'I think Percival and I can pull this together into a final copy while you go and dress, Pris.'

'I don't need an hour to get dressed,' Pris exclaims.

Drow chuckles. 'Tonight's dinner is a formal meal and is timed to begin directly after your meeting with your uncle. I think an hour will be almost enough time for you to dress.'

The shock on Pris's face makes me laugh too.

'You might well laugh, young Snake, but I requested a suit of formal wear be laid out on your bed.'

Pris smirks.

Okay, now this isn't as much fun. 'Please tell me the outfit doesn't have a fancy collar.'

Drow tries to keep a straight face but gives up. 'No, I got the message when one of the servants found a collar in the pot plant. I have tried to keep it plain and in our family colours.'

'Thanks, unc,' I say, rising to my feet.

Drow grimaces. 'I will never get used to this modern language.'

'We'll see you at dinner,' I tell Percival as I move to join Pris.

At the door, we are met by Dinian. 'Perhaps I can accompany you back to the royal accommodation, Priscilla. I believe you are with Princess Petunia, and my suite is next to hers.'

I roll my eyes. In spite of everyone else calling her Pris, Dinian uses her full name as if it's a privilege she has granted only to him.

'Thanks for the offer, but I'm going to wait while Snake changes, then we'll head to my grandmother's room together.'

Dinian turns to me and takes me in as if it's the first time we have met. His lips curl in almost disgust, but he is too well-mannered to show his true feelings. I raise an eyebrow, daring him to say something, but he schools his face into a polite mask before turning back to Pris.

'As you wish, Pricilla. Please, if I can be of any further assistance to you, you only have to ask.'

I want to tell him Pris will never need his help, but I'm wise enough not to speak for her, aware it will only get me into trouble. Still, I smirk when Pris tells him, 'I can't imagine I will need your help, but I'll keep your offer in mind.'

She slips her hand into mine, holding me back so Dinian can leave first. I wonder if Pris is worried about him following us. There is something off about that guy.

We walk in silence back to my suite, and Pris waits in the living room while I go and change. True to his word, Drow has picked out an almost-black dark-green tailcoat and a slightly lighter-green waistcoat. I have a pristine white shirt to go under them. The top part of the outfit is finished off with a bow tie, which I shove into my pocket to put on before the meal. I send a mental thank you to Drow, as these clothes are positively modern compared to my last outfit.

For the bottom half, I have black knee-length boots to go over stretchy, fitted black pants. I study the pants, which are almost like thick leggings. I can't wear them. They're going to be too revealing.

There's a knock on the door. 'What's taking so long?' Pris calls through.

'Um… hold on, just coming.'

I drag on the pants. I can hold my hands over the front to protect my modesty until we're seated. I pull on the boots, then check myself in the mirror, expecting everything to be on show. The pants are very discreet—so discreet, in fact, that I pull out the waistband to check everything is still as it should be.

I chuckle in relief.

'What's going on in there?'

'Nothing.' I tuck myself back in and run a comb through my hair. It has grown in the past few weeks and could really do with a cut. Perhaps I can—

'Snake!'

No time. Grabbing my jacket, I open the door.

'Mmm,' Pris says, grinning. 'Don't you look smart. Hold on, shouldn't there be a… um… bulge about there?' She points, a cheeky grin on her face.

'I could tell you about that, but then I would have to shoot you,' I quip back.

Pris nods solemnly. 'So, magic it is, then.'

I laugh. 'Come on, let's go and see what Victorian wonder they have for you.'

That soon wipes the grin from her face.

Time is ticking on, so we walk briskly to Princess Petunia's suite. Pris barges in without knocking, only to stop in the doorway. I pile in behind her, almost pushing her over.

'Oh, Grandmother. I didn't think you'd be here.'

'I am surprised you took the time to think of me at all, given that I have had no word from you since you rushed from the court this morning,' a tart voice responds.

Pris colours, and I know she is embarrassed rather than angered because her eye doesn't have that telltale glint.

'I'm sorry, Grandmother. I've been busy working on our petition, and now I've got to dress for my audience with the King.'

The princess's gaze turns to me. 'Are you presenting your petition now?'

'No, Snake is here to accompany me.' When her grandmother does not respond, she adds, 'Because of the attacks on the castle.' When the silence continues, Pris goes for a more formal approach. 'Princess Petunia, may I introduce Snake of the Fieth Clan. Snake, this is my grandmother, Princess Petunia.'

I bow. 'It is an honour to meet you.' When I rise, I detect the tug of a smile at the corner of the princess's mouth, but it is gone before I can be certain.

'I am pleased to meet you. Your grandfather and great-uncle are good friends of mine.' She turns her attention back to Pris. 'Lady Susan is waiting in your room. You had best hurry and get ready while I entertain your friend.'

Pris throws a worried glance over her shoulder as she heads to what must be her room. I smile back at her, showing more confidence than I'm feeling.

'Take a seat, young man. I will not bite.'

I do as she bids, although I'm not sure a bite is the worst to be endured from this woman. The keen-eyed gaze she sends my way sets my stomach churning, and I'm ready to tell her anything she wants just for a moment's relief.

'So, Percival tells me you are quite the musician. Do you intend to become a bard like your grandfather?'

Oh my god, is this a take on 'What are your prospects?' and 'What are your intentions towards my granddaughter?' I hope my face shows nothing of my internal shock. 'Although I love music, I intend to study physics at university. I have an interest in how magic operates in the World Above. I'd like to do everything I can to ensure the flow remains strong and perhaps even remove our reliance on the dragons for help.'

As I say the words, I wonder if any of my plans are still feasible. Magic is waning, and recent events have me questioning whether or not I will ever be able to return home.

Princess Petunia's eyes narrow, and I squirm a little in my seat.

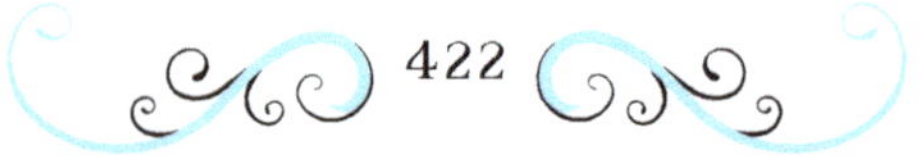

'Is that a job? Can you make money from it?'

My brows draw together in a frown. Mum and I had never had much money, so thinking about my future in terms of how much I can make is a bit of an anomaly. I won't lie about this though, not even to make Pris's family happy. 'I've no idea, you know. Mum discussed it with my uncle, and the gnomes were going to support my research, so I should be fine.'

I wait for her to say something along the lines of 'How will you support a family?'

She surprises me when she says, 'Your family are renowned for looking after the magical community. It is pleasing to see you take after them. Have you thought about asking for sponsorship from the Unseelie Court for your work? I am sure King Maddox would be interested.'

I study the princess, trying to assess whether she has an ulterior motive for bringing this up. Does she want me to become part of the court? Or does she think Pris will be likely to visit more often if we are aligned with the King?

Before I have considered her motives, Princess Petunia laughs. It is more like a bark, but it contains real mirth. 'You have much of Drow in you, Snake. I meant nothing more than to say you could have a position in the court and that it might benefit your studies and your purse to follow this up. It won't hurt that Drow is one of the King's chief advisors and that you are... friends with Priscilla.'

'Pris,' I correct automatically, and the princess laughs again. She should laugh more often. She is so much less severe when she does.

'Yes, I should remember that.'

We fall silent for a while, and as I fidget a little in my chair, I consider some possible conversation topics to make things less awkward. I come up empty, but it doesn't matter, as Susan soon slips through the bedroom door holding a brush and a hair tie.

'Pris is almost ready,' she informs us. 'She asked me to come out and do something with your hair.'

I blanch. 'You're going to tie it back?'

'Yes, I can do that. Unless of course you would rather restyle it yourself.'

'Restyle it,' I repeat. 'You mean cut it?'

Now Susan and Princess Petunia are laughing, but it's the princess who answers. 'My boy, we are in a magical bubble separated from the human world. The use of magic is not forbidden here. If your hair is not what you want it to be, just envision what you want, send some magic, and it will sort itself out.'

Are they joking? They don't seem to be. I try to imagine my hair as it is after a trim, and I send out a little magic. My hair tingles, and I run my hand through it. It feels shorter, but as there's no mirror, so I have no way of knowing if it's an improvement.

'Much better,' Princess Petunia tells me. 'You are quite the dashing young creature now.'

I'm mortified to feel heat rising from under my collar, and I hope I'm not blushing.

'Indeed,' Susan adds. 'I'll just go and finish sorting Pr—'

The door behind her opens, and Pris, a vision in dusky pink, enters the room. The floaty dress she wears is off the shoulder with a fitted bodice and a bustle thing at the back—at least, I think that's what it's called, from memory. Pris's hair is up, and the only jewellery she wears is a tiara.

'Wow.' The word escapes my lips before I can put a thought to it.

Pris blushes. 'You like it?'

'It's….'

'What Snake means to say is, it is perfect,' Princess Petunia finishes for me. 'Now, you two had best run along. King Maddox hates it when creatures are late.'

'Thank you, Susan.' Pris gives her old nanny a quick hug while I rise. 'Will I see you at dinner, Grandmother?'

The princess nods.

'Good, I have a lot to fill you in on,' Pris says as she takes my hand and leads me to the door.

'It was nice to meet you,' I say to the princess.

She grins at me. 'Good of you to say so,' she laughs as Pris closes the door behind us.

'What was that about?' she asks as we head down the corridor towards the stairs.

'Nothing,' I say, not knowing if Pris has the bandwidth to deal with my conversation with her grandmother with everything else on her mind.

'You'll tell me later though, right?'

I sigh. 'Of course. Do you want me to come in with you when you see the King?'

'No, I'll be fine,' she assures me. 'If you could wait outside though, I might need some moral support when I come out.'

'Heart mentioned there's a music room across the way from the reception hall. I can wait there for you.'

We come to a stop outside the door to the King's personal study. Pris takes a deep breath, then knocks.

A command comes from inside. 'Enter.'

'Wish me luck,' Pris says before taking a deep breath.

'Luck,' I say as she reaches for the door handle.

I watch her disappear before crossing the foyer to the music room. Wow, they have a grand piano. My eyes slide over the array of guitars and lutes—and even a saxophone—placed around the walls, all shining in the late evening light.

Today it's the piano that calls to me. I sit down and let my fingers glide over the ivory keys as I play a couple of scales to loosen my fingers. The sound is deep and resonates around the room, cocooning me in a bubble of music.

'Ah, you are a court musician like your grandfather. A noble calling, but is it what is right for Priscilla?'

The voice comes from behind me, but I recognise it instantly.

'Dinian, how lovely to see you,' I say as I launch into 'Creep' by Radiohead. It's a message to him to leave me alone, but he either doesn't know the song or is pretty thick skinned, as he doesn't move. It seems I will have an audience while I wait for Pris.

HOW BAD CAN this be? I ask myself as I open the door to King Maddox's study. Play at being princess for a day, get the King to agree to help Queen Ariana, then I can be done with it.

The study is darkened in the evening light. There is only one lamp lit, and it sits to the left of him on the desk. The King sits a little straighter as I enter, the lamp throwing shadows across his drawn face. Behind him stands the Chancellor, hands loosely clasped in front of his dark robes. He reminds me a little of a pointy-eared Professor Snape from *Harry Potter*.

'Ah, Priscilla, I see from your dress you have come to see things my way,' King Maddox says as I drop into a curtsey in front of his desk. 'No need for these formalities between us. Please, take a seat.'

There is every need for these… formalities, as he calls them. I want to keep this man at arm's-length while I neither know nor trust him. Standing in front of the desk, I unconsciously mirror the Chancellor's stance. 'If this is to be a private chat, perhaps the Chancellor could be excused.' I really don't want anyone to witness what I say to the King. Not least because it will be easier to deny what I have agreed to later.

'He and I have no secrets… but… if you insist.'

'I do.'

The Chancellor sends me a hard stare as if he's trying to assess my motives, then bows his head to the King and leaves via the side door. Once we are alone, I take a seat in front of the desk. The King leans back and waits for me to speak. I need to choose my words carefully. I don't want to lie to him because I might get caught out later. On the other hand, I don't want to sign myself up for something for the rest of my life either.

'I agree to be your consort for the time being, but only until I can speak with my parents.'

A smile tugs at King Maddox's lips. 'You don't trust me?'

This time I have no problem with being completely honest. 'I don't know you, so I have no idea if I can trust you.'

His eyebrows rise, and that almost smile is still there. It's almost as if he is enjoying my discomfort.

'Before I commit fully to anything, I need to understand Mum and Dad's intentions for me. They have always been involved in planning my future, and this never came up.'

This time he nods a slow, thoughtful nod. 'I can agree to that.'

'And in return you will listen to our petition?' I don't want him to forget his promise.

'I only agree to listen—'

'And you will take into account the best interests of the court.'

This time his frown is sterner. 'If you will let me finish.'

'I'm sorry, it's just this is very important to me.'

'I appreciate that, but you must understand that you will be asking me to leave my court in a time of great peril—'

'To try and lessen that danger.'

King Maddox glares at me.

'I'm sorry,' I mumble. 'It won't happen again.'

'I would look at things a little more favourably if my succession were assured, but alas, it is not.'

He can't be thinking of me as his successor, can he? Wait, I'm sure someone mentioned the court is always ruled by a King.

'Have you named your successor?'

'I have. It is to be Lord Dinian.'

Of course, the one person I have met here who makes my skin crawl. 'It's good that your succession is assured. You'll have someone to look after the court while you are away.'

King Maddox continues to stare at me.

'It is good, isn't it?' I ask, a little less certain.

'The creatures of my court will acknowledge him as my successor when I formalise it, but many think I could do better for them by choosing someone who is a little less… self—' He clears his throat. 'Someone who has their best interests at heart.'

He could definitely do better. 'Do they have someone in mind?'

'They do. Petunia's boy, Yves.'

Petunia has a son? I have another uncle? How many more family members are going to be sprung on me?

I hope my thoughts don't show on my face, but the twitch of King Maddox's lips tells me my expression has betrayed me.

'Then why not have him? Is he unsuitable in some way?'

'No, except for the problem of Petunia's role in the succession of the Seelie Court. Were she ever to be forgiven, he would be in the line of succession for the World Below. And then… there's Tomas's wish. He wanted a future for Dinian. I have been thinking about it, and Dinian's position would be stronger if I could announce you and he were betrothed.'

'Absolutely not! No way is that ever going to happen.' The words are out of my mouth before my brain can react to the King's manipulation.

King Maddox leans back in his chair and watches me through hooded eyes. 'Think about it. Not only would it strengthen his position, but I'm sure you could round off some of his rough edges.'

This is the total opposite of what I came in here to achieve. My idea of a short alliance has somehow slipped into a lifelong commitment—and it could be a long life.

'I notice all the benefits are for Dinian and the Unseelie Court. What about me? What would I gain from this?'

'An elevated position in my court. Surely that is enough.'

Flabbergasted. The word pops in my mind and sticks there. I never really knew what it meant before, but now….

'An elevated position? I don't want to be a part of your court—or any court, for that matter.' I spit the words out. 'All I want is to get my parents' names cleared and return to my old life.'

'I see I have taken you by surprise—'

'That's an understatement,' I mutter.

'Perhaps it is best if you take some time, mull things over, and let me know your decision… say, in the next couple of days.'

'I will not change my mind.' I rise to my feet, struggling to contain my emotions. I need to get out of this room and away from the King. 'Will you hear our petition after dinner?'

'I will, as we agreed. But bear in mind, I will not be in a position to consider leaving until things at court are settled.'

My fists clench, and for a moment I imagine myself punching that smug, self-satisfied smirk from his face.

Instead, I don't say anything further as I calmly walk to the door. I can't believe my own flesh and blood is blackmailing me into becoming betrothed to save his court. And to a creature like Dinian!

The door thuds behind me. At least this time I haven't stormed from his presence. I close my eyes and try to calm myself a little as the sounds of a waltz being played on piano come from across the hall. Ah, Snake. My jaw unclenches. He will know what to do. He always has a more balanced perspective than I do.

Before I reach the door, Dinian appears from nowhere, blocking my path. 'How did it go?'

His smile and the triumph sparkling in his eyes hit me. He knew all along. He's been a part of this.

Shooting him a withering look, I say, 'Stay away from me, you… you…. Argh!' I push him aside, which gives me a small amount of satisfaction, and open the door.

Snake is still playing as I enter the music room. I slide onto the seat beside him and lay my head on his shoulder.

His fingers continue to dance smoothly across the keys. 'So, it didn't go well.'

I shake my head, and his fingers pause. 'No, keep playing,' I whisper. 'Dinian is outside, and I don't want him to hear what we're saying.'

The music starts again. 'What is it?'

'King Maddox says that unless I become betrothed to his heir, he cannot leave the court.'

Snake's body tenses, although you wouldn't know it from the music. 'Who is his heir?'

'It's… um—'

'Let me guess… it's Dinian, isn't it?'

I don't respond.

'Of course it is. And that's why he's hanging around. He was waiting for you to come out. I can't believe the one person I would hate to see you with is the one person you must play up to.'

'What?' I ask, sitting upright.

He laughs bitterly, and his tone is resigned. 'You have to play along, Pris. It's all part of the same game we were playing before. You have to find some way to make the King think you are on his side until we have Queen Ariana back on her feet.'

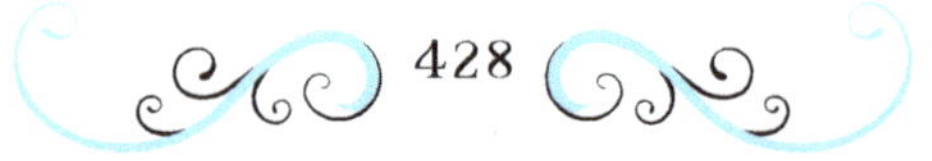

'I don't. We can find another way,' I insist.

'Perhaps if we had time, we could, but time isn't on our side—and I suspect they are better at this game than we are. We have to play along with this in the same way you played along with King Maddox's first demand.'

Frustration is curling like a serpent in my belly. 'Where does it stop, Snake? Where do I draw the line and say I am not prepared to do this anymore?'

He stops playing, then half turns and draws me into his arms. Speaking close to my ear, he says, 'When it gets too much for you, that's when. There is no way you are *ever* marrying that prat.'

I lean into him. He smells of lavender and… Snake. With his arms around me, I am home, and I can't believe everything is conspiring to keep us apart when all I want to do is be with him.

'Do you think you can do it?' he asks. 'Because if you can't, we will find another way.'

I stay where I am, wishing the world away. Then the gong sounds for dinner, and I know I can't stay here forever.

'I can try,' I say. 'But I'm not promising I won't kill him before this is over.'

Snake's chuckle rumbles in his chest. 'Back at ya.'

THE FORMAL APPEAL

WHEN I STEP out of my room, I am surprised to find a servant waiting by the door. When I ask him why he's here, I'm even more surprised by his response.

'The King requests your presence. He has decided to receive your petition before dinner.'

My gosh. We are not ready. My hands shake. My eyes slide to the table where our petition is laid, all ready to be given to the King.

I breathe in through my nose and out through my mouth until the shaking stops. Picking up the documents, I straighten my shoulders. 'All right, lead on.'

When we arrive at the public reception rooms, the servant tells me Drow is already with the King, then he leaves me outside the King's study. I tug at my jacket, checking I am presentable enough. Dinian saunters my way, followed by Pris and Snake a few steps behind.

'Have you any idea what this is about?' Pris asks.

'I believe we are to meet with the King before dinner,' I say.

A frown draws Pris's brows together. 'I wonder why he's moving things up. After our meeting earlier, I can't believe it means anything good.'

I move closer to Pris and Snake as they entwine fingers. My move was meant as a sign of support, but I realise it isolates Dinian, making him an outsider. I cannot say I feel guilty about that. There is something about the boy I do not like.

'I'm surprised King Maddox is still going through the motions of considering your request. The attack today showed how vulnerable we are. The Chancellor is concerned that too many more such attacks will pull the court out of its time and space,' Dinian says.

I study him a little more closely. There is a tone in his voice I cannot quite place. Is it disdain? And is it for the King, or for us?

'Perhaps that wouldn't be such a bad thing,' Pris mutters. 'Not only is this court stuck in the past, but it's also out of touch with the world it sits within.'

Dinian turns a cold gaze her way. 'Do you mean the magical world, or the human world?'

Pris glares back. 'Both.'

Looking from one to the other, it is clear there is something going on here I am not aware of. With everything else happening, I do not have time to sort out their spat. Instead I turn to Pris, hoping to add a little to her understanding of the creatures who live here. 'You need to understand that many of the Unseelie Court's creatures have been persecuted, and to them this is a safe haven. Many find the lack of change here a comfort when so many other things in their lives are uncertain.'

'True,' Dinian says, 'but Priscilla is right about one thing—we could do with modernising our court. Perhaps allow a larger council than the King has at the moment.'

I bristle at the lad's comments. I am aware he merely voices the impatience of youth, but I take offence at his criticism of King Maddox. 'When you are King, you can make all the changes you want. At the moment you are still yet to be formally named heir, so—'

'So I should keep my mouth shut and offer my support.' Dinian's lips are pursed, like he has sucked on a lemon, and his voice drips disdain.

He turns back to Pris, and his demeanour changes. He smiles and winks. 'I'm sure you agree with me though, don't you, Princess. Things will change when it's our turn.'

Snake's jaw tenses. Pris's grip on his fingers tightens as if in warning, and she mutters something under her breath.

Dinian chuckles. What is going on between the three of them? I raise an eyebrow in question. Snake shakes his head and mouths, 'Later.'

I turn my back on Dinian, dismissing him. It is time for us to focus on the task ahead. My voice is firm when I say, 'We must concentrate on the meeting. It is all part of the same problem anyway—freeing the Queen, which will help bring magic back to full strength, then she can put a stop to these attacks on the Unseelie Court.'

'We're with you on that,' Pris says.

Snake is strangely quiet.

'Snake, what is it?' Pris asks.

'I'm wondering about something. If the dragons are so powerful, why haven't they forced King Maddox to help?'

How do I explain the complex relationship between dragons and creatures to someone in the few minutes we have here?

'Dragons are…. Let us say they hold themselves apart from all other beings. They have immense power and could probably rule creatures and humans if they so desired, but they do not.

Dinian perks up at the mention of dragons. 'I bet there is a way to harness their power,' he says almost as if to himself, sending a cold shiver down my spine. I pity the dragon who has to bond with him. I angle my body to cut Dinian from the conversation and continue.

'Although dragons can compel those they call lesser beings to do their bidding, their one guiding principle appears to be to never use their magic to force another being to go against their nature.'

'Not even if magic were to disappear?' Snake asks.

'It appears not,' I confirm.

'We could do with a little less freedom and a bit more governance,' Dinian interjects.

'You want the dragons to lead us?' Pris asks.

'What? No! I meant our court could do with a strong leader—one who is not afraid of imposing his will.'

'A minute ago you were saying the King needs more councilors. Now you're saying he should be more of a dictator,' Pris says, and I am surprised by the scorn in her voice.

'They are not mutually exclusive, my dear Priscilla. Having more advisors does not prevent the King from making a decision, then enforcing it. At the moment this limbo helps no one.'

I am a little disconcerted at finding myself partially agreeing with Dinian. I may not like the lad, but his point about leaving the court in limbo is a valid one.

'Well, let's hope he decides in our favour this evening,' Pris says.

Dinian's brows draw downwards. 'I'm not sure that it is in the best interests of the court to have the King absent when we are under attack.'

'Then it's a good thing you're not invited to this meeting,' Snake snaps.

A smirk tugs at Dinian's lips. 'Oh, but I am.'

Snake and Pris lock eyes, and something passes between them. A sense of unease ripples through me. I wish they had time to tell me what is going on. Before I can ask, the door to the King's study opens, and Drow appears.

'King Maddox will see you all now,' he tells us before standing aside to allow us to enter.

AS WE CROSS the corridor, I overhear Dinian muttering, 'Of course the gnome is here. He's virtually running the court. I don't know how Maddox can let a non-elf have so much power.'

I ball my fists as I lead everyone in. Catching Drow's eye, I have no idea whether he has heard or not, but from the cold stare he gives Dinian, I'm pretty sure there is no love lost between them.

There are not enough chairs for everyone to sit, so I stand behind one. Pris and Percival join me, but Dinian slides into the other chair on this side of the desk. The rather dour creature standing behind the King frowns down at him and says, 'Lord Dinian, I had no idea you were one of the petitioners.'

I bite my lip to hide my smirk as the smarmy elf realises his mistake. He rises and follows Drow around the desk. As my uncle takes his position on the other side of the King, Dinian is forced to stand beside him, even further from the action. The scowl on his face tells everyone what he thinks about being relegated to second string.

He stares daggers at me, and I get the impression he believes us to be in some sort of tug-of-war over Pris. Perhaps in some ways we are, but as soon as we get out of this joint, any claim he may believe he has over her will disappear.

Once everyone is in position, Chancellor Rimould clears his throat and begins proceedings. 'Your Majesty, may I present Princess Priscilla, Snake of the Fieth Clan, and Percival of the Wyld Woods as ambassadors sent from the court of Queen Ariana. They request to present a petition on her behalf.'

'Welcome to my court,' King Maddox says as if we haven't already been in his presence today.

Percival takes a step forward, bows, then holds out our document. Everyone in the room seems to hold a collective breath while the King leans back in his chair and stares at Pris. Beside me, Pris tenses, and I suspect she is gearing up to give her uncle a piece of her mind.

I reach out and place a hand on her arm, hoping to remind her we need to show a little restraint here. King Maddox's eyes drop to my hand, then he raises his eyes to meet mine. In the past I would have removed my hand when challenged in this way, but Pris and I have come too far for me to be cowed by the King. I stand tall under his scrutiny, and my hand remains where it is.

Unfortunately, Pris witnesses our silent communication, and it must be the final straw for her. She shrugs off my hand and joins Percival. Taking the scroll from him, she glares at her uncle.

'We had a deal,' she forces out through gritted teeth. 'I am ready to stand by your side before the court tonight. Now it is your turn. Take the petition.' She slams the document down on the desk.

Honestly, Pris is one part magnificent and two parts downright scary when she's like this. The battle of wills shifts between uncle and niece, and I don't like King Maddox's chances of coming out on top.

Chancellor Rimould reaches over and takes the scroll, saving face for both Pris and the King. He unrolls the parchment and scans the document before sending a sidelong glance towards Drow. Rolling it back up, he says, 'Thank you for presenting your argument so succinctly, and so comprehensively. I am sure the King will want a little time to consider his response.'

King Maddox, still locked into a staring match with Pris, grunts something that the Chancellor takes to be assent.

Percival reaches out and touches Pris on the hand. 'It is time to leave.'

'No, Priscilla stays,' King Maddox barks. 'She promised to attend court by my side, and attend she shall.'

Percival does not move. For a moment I think Pris is going to refuse, then she turns to the sprite. 'It's all right, Percival. You take Snake through to the dining room, and I'll speak with you both after we've eaten.'

Pursing his lips, Percival answers, 'If you are sure?'

She nods before turning a pleading glance to me. I smile, understanding it will be easier for her if we do as the King asks. 'Come on, Percival. You might not be starving, but I am.'

I lead the way out, remembering to walk backwards, Percival at my side. Once we reach the door, we bow, and the King nods his dismissal. I'm not completely happy about leaving Pris alone in there, but I have to trust that she knows what she is doing.

When the guard closes the door behind us, I blow out a long, slow breath. 'That was intense.'

Percival nods as he studies the door. 'Something else was going on in there.' He leads me across the corridor. 'Do you know what it is?'

I want to tell Percival about the King's demands, but Pris told me in confidence. Still, I don't like keeping Percival in the dark—we're a team. 'Pris and her uncle are having a disagreement about her role at court.'

Percival strokes his chin. 'Interesting. Given that Pris cannot be in line to the Unseelie throne, I wonder what….' He stops stroking and raises surprised eyes. 'He cannot.'

'I think he can,' I say.

Shaking his head, Percival reiterates, 'He cannot. She is in line to the Seelie throne. There are protocols.'

'Are you sure?'

Percival simply stares at me until I catch on. Of course there are protocols. I grin. 'We should tell Pris. She will be so relieved.'

'We will later. It may not do her any good, though, if King Maddox is using her as a bargaining chip.'

I shrug. 'She's already considering playing along for the moment, but I'm sure she'd feel much better if she knew she had an out.'

'Come, we had best head in to dinner,' Percival says as some of the court begin to drift into the dining room beside the music room.

I place a hand on his shoulder. 'Percival, why would King Maddox choose Dinian as his heir? He doesn't seem to be an outcast or have the creatures' best interests at heart, and he also doesn't appear to be close to the king.'

'He is the nephew of King Maddox's husband.'

I nod. 'But I thought the position of King was not hereditary here.'

'It is not, but it does tend to be passed on to close family. Dinian has been here a couple of the times when Eleanora and I visited. He was always charming and the apple of his uncle's eye. I believe Tomas convinced King Maddox that he would be able to breach the gap between the Seelie and Unseelie courts, as he lived in both worlds.'

'I didn't know the court here wished to reconcile.'

'According to Drow, they do not. What they do want is for the two courts to be on an equal footing. And to do that, they want to change the view that the Unseelie Court is comprised of outcasts. King Maddox has taken Tomas's advice to heart and believes the best way for the two courts to live in harmony is to place someone who is not an outcast on the throne.'

'Ah, so their way of stopping the attacks on the court is to go, "See, we're not so different"?'

'Something like that.'

'I don't see it changing the minds of creatures like Bernais. And I don't see Dinian being a fit ruler—he prances around like a peacock. And I'm not sure he has time for anyone who's not an elf. And, most of all, I don't like the way he looks at Pris like she's something to be devoured.'

Percival grunts, and I take that for agreement. 'He is showing a lot of interest in her.'

My hands clench into fists at my sides at the thought of Dinian and Pris spending any time together.

Percival chuckles. 'Are you worried he might sweep her off her feet?'

I laugh, but it sounds hollow.

Am I worried Pris might be attracted to Dinian? To be honest, I'm pretty sure she doesn't like him. What I'm worried about is us not being able to spend much time together while this charade continues. What I'm sure of is that Pris and I have an intense attraction, but with everything going on, we haven't had time to explore what that means.

I run a hand through my hair. If only I were certain of where we stand and could count on us having a future once this is over. Or maybe if Dinian weren't continuously niggling me….

'I was joking, Snake.'

Percival's voice jolts me out of my reverie.

'I know, Percival. It's just…. Never mind. Let's go find the others before I talk myself into believing he might just be able to do that.'

KEEPING MY FACE impassive and my back to the door, I wait for Snake and Percival to leave. The snick of the latch tells me they're gone. My palms are slick with sweat, but I rein in my nerves and attempt to appear calm.

'What now?'

I expect King Maddox to answer, but it is his Chancellor who does the honours.

'We will review your petition—although I suspect Drow is fully aware of what it contains—and then decide on how to respond.'

I close my eyes for a moment, wondering if there is a way to have the King step up and do the right thing. I open them again to find King Maddox smiling at me, and his smile offers no comfort.

'Of course, you have it within your power to influence the outcome of that process,' King Maddox says.

I resist looking at Dinian. I've a sneaking suspicion he is in on the King's plan and is happy to get on board with it.

There is a flicker of exasperation in Drow's eyes, and he sneaks a sidelong glance at Rimould, who is too tense and tight-lipped to notice.

'Perhaps we can leave that discussion until later,' Drow says, and I find myself absurdly grateful for his interference. Turning to the King, he asks, 'Would you like me to summarise their petition for you, Your Majesty?'

A brief look of displeasure crosses King Maddox's face, but when he turns to Drow, he presents his usual mask. 'I think that can also wait until later. I believe we will soon be expected at dinner.'

Drow checks his watch. 'We have a few minutes, sire.'

'Very well. Dinian, perhaps you can entertain Princess Priscilla awhile.' The King gestures to two chairs and a table tucked in behind the door.

'But—'

'It is in your best interests to get to know each other.'

I'm not quite sure who the King directed this at, Dinian or me, but I'm sure I have no desire to know the elf any better than I already do.

'I'm fine,' I said. 'I'll read a book.'

Dinian watches the King for a few minutes before returning his attention to me. He clearly wants to be a part of their discussion, but he also doesn't want to miss an opportunity to spend time alone with me.

'Go,' the King says, and Dinian's decision is made for him.

While the three older creatures gather around the scroll, Dinian joins me at the other end of the room. Instead of sitting, I feign interest in the books on the shelf.

'Can I perhaps suggest something suitable for you to read?' Dinian offers.

Never in my life have I needed anyone to tell me what to read. A quick glance at the King tells me he is watching us, so I bite back my snarky retort and say with saccharine sweetness, 'And just what is it you would suggest I read?'

The sarcasm was lost on Dinian. Reaching past me, he chooses a book and places it in my hands.

'I think you will enjoy this. It should give you some guidance on how you should behave while here in the Unseelie Court.'

I look down and find myself holding a copy of Jane Austen's *Sense and Sensibility*. Dinian is attempting to make a statement with his book choice, but I'm at a loss as to what it is.

'I'm not quite sure what you want me to take away from this, Dinian.'

He smiles at me, and I'm sure he thinks it is a charming smile, but it's a bit too practiced for my tastes. 'We expect a certain standard of behaviour at court, and I am sure you can take some cues from this.'

A laugh escapes before I can hold it back, and Dinian's charming expression turns sour.

'Have you read this?' I ask.

'Well, no, but it is set in a genteel time when women knew their place,' he blusters.

I place the book back on the shelf and turn away from him. Let him wonder about Jane Austen's true message—that women should not constrain their behaviour according to societal expectations. I take a seat.

He sits opposite and leans in rather too close. 'You shouldn't reject your uncle's proposal out of hand. Together you and I could be a force to be reckoned with in both the Unseelie and Seelie Courts. And if you showed yourself to be a willing partner, I might be persuaded to ignore your little flings with the lower creatures.'

I can't move. In my mind, I'm raising my hand and slapping Dinian across the face, but I don't move a muscle. He can't possibly be serious, can he? Does he actually think I'm in this for the power? And that Snake is a passing fancy? Is he so totally wrapped up in his own world, he thinks I'll go along with this?

I'm about to tell him what I think of his suggestion when a voice behind me interrupts. 'You two seem to be having… fun, but I am afraid the staff are waiting dinner for us.'

Rimould's voice is stiff and formal, and do I detect a note of displeasure? I risk a quick peek and find him watching Dinian, lips curled in disdain. I quickly look away. Have we got a friend there? Or at least an ally when it comes to Dinian?

Carefully schooling my face into a mask of bland courtesy, I ignore the elf who intends to spend the rest of his life with me and slip around the Chancellor.

As I wait for the King to join us, Drow places himself in front of the desk. I suspect it's because he doesn't want me to see what they were working on. How can he be so on our side one minute and on the King's the next? It must be difficult. If I didn't know that he believed it was best for King Maddox to help the Queen, I'd be suspicious of his motives.

I'm relieved when the King offers his arm to escort me into dinner. Dinian follows close behind, ahead of Rimould and Drow. I guess it's important to him to show his superior position in court.

When we reach the top table, I am sandwiched between the King and Dinian. My appetite has disappeared. Dinian makes a show of pulling out my chair, and as I sit, he pulls his own chair closer to mine. This should be a fun night.

Once our party is seated, servants start bringing in the food. While one of them places a platter in front of me, I risk a glance at Snake's table. He is sitting beside his grandfather and opposite Percival, with his back to me. Percival catches me staring and smiles. I take that to mean 'you can do this,' and I straighten my spine as I smile back.

I can do this. I mean, it's only for tonight and perhaps tomorrow. How hard can it be?

A BRICK WALL

ALTHOUGH I'M SURROUNDED by friends, family, and well-wishers, without Pris by my side, I feel as if I'm eating alone. I took a seat with my back to the royal table because I didn't want to face her sitting with him. Now I'm wishing I hadn't been so petty, because I want to see her, and I worry she may need my support before the evening is done.

'Bunch over,' a voice says close to my ear.

Heart digs me in the ribs. 'You heard the lady. Move over so she can sit.'

We all shuffle along by one seat, and Lady Susan sits beside me.

'What's up?' I ask her, and she raises an eyebrow in response.

'Well, I'm pretty sure it's not great etiquette to ask us to bunch over,' I say with a smile.

Susan laughs. 'Would you believe me if I said things are less formal in the court at the moment?'

It's my turn to raise a quizzical brow.

'All right. I wanted to warn you guys.'

'Why not speak to Pris?'

Sorrow briefly crosses Susan's face before she tucks it away behind her court mask. 'I don't think she's forgiven me for the things I didn't tell her.'

I place a comforting hand on Susan's arm. 'She will. Just give her time.'

'I hope so. I think it might help when she finds out I've managed to buy some normal clothes for you and her.'

Now I'm surprised. 'How did you manage that? I thought we were in lockdown.'

'We are, but I still have my mobile. My sister and her family are in Inverness, so I got her to shop for me. Your clothes arrived with the food delivery today.' She eyes me critically. 'I had to guess your size. I hope everything fits.'

I want to hug her. I've never been much interested in clothes, but when you have to primp up every day for court, jeans and a T-shirt begin looking mighty good.

'Thank you.'

'You're welcome.'

The conversation fades as a server removes our plates and another one lays the next course in front of us. I expected it to be a main after the Waldorf salad appetiser, but I'm surprised to find a sliver of salmon on a bed of green beans. Yet another server drizzles some lemony-scented sauce over top. When they leave we're free to speak again.

'You didn't make all this effort to tell me about clothes,' I say before my mouth closes round a forkful of salmon. 'Yum, this is excellent.'

'It should be. Our chef ran a Michelin-starred restaurant before returning to the court.'

Susan's face softens as she talks about the chef, and I wonder if there is something more there. I want to ask, but I don't want her to become distracted. She finishes her fish before speaking again.

'There are rumours amongst the servants and ladies-in-waiting that the King is going to betroth Pris to Dinian.'

My jaw hardens at the mention of the King's manipulation.

'Ah, I can tell from your reaction that he has spoken to her already.'

Before answering Susan, I sneak a quick glance to make sure Pris is okay. She is nibbling at her food and looks quite miserable. Dinian leans towards her and says something in her ear. Smiling wanly, she says something back and continues eating. I will her to look at me so I can send her some courage, but she doesn't.

'He has,' I admit.

'And I assume being Pris, she rejected the King outright.'

I chuckle. She knows Pris so well. 'Yes, but he would not take no for an answer. She is "taking some time" to consider her options.'

Susan nods. 'The King wants stability in the court, and for some reason, Dinian has convinced him his marrying Pris will bring that.'

I let her words sink in before blurting out, 'What? This was Dinian's idea? How do you know?'

'Those of us in service to the court know almost everything that goes on within these wards. Also, I've made a point of keeping up on the gossip, and

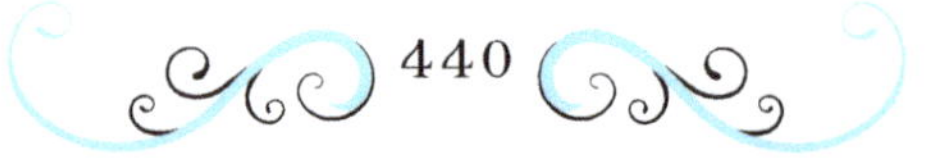

I've been updating Princess Petunia on court goings-on.'

Out of the corner of my eye, I survey the high table. Princess Petunia is chatting with my uncle. They keep glancing up as if to check no one is paying any attention to them. I wonder what they're talking about that they want to keep secret.

'And she needs to be kept up on what is going on because?'

'It's a good thing you're not at court often, Snake, because you'd be eaten alive.'

'Thanks,' I say dryly.

'No, that's a good thing—keeping out of the politics.'

'I'll take your word for it. So why does the princess want to know what's happening?'

'Princess Petunia has been the Unseelie Court's unofficial ambassador to the World Below for years.' Susan's voice has dropped so low, I have to lean in to hear what she's saying. 'Mostly she works through the witches, Eleanora, Euphemia, and Eugenia. They've been carrying messages back and forth for her for years.'

'How have they gotten away with that?' I ask.

'They are responsible for ensuring the wellbeing of the land and the creatures in their areas, and they have quite a bit of leeway in how they do that.'

'I guess that makes sense. But it doesn't explain why you're gathering information for the princess.'

'I was getting to that. Petunia was once one of King Maddox's advisors, but she pressed too hard for him to help her sister, and he cut her out. Now she has had to resort to finding out what's going on by other methods and using her influence with Drow and Rimould to steer the court.'

I chuckle. 'This sounds like something out of a spy novel.'

Susan smiles. 'It sort of feels that way too.'

We wait for another change of food before Susan gets to her real reason for joining me.

'I need you to convince Pris to play along with the betrothal—'

'But—'

'She has to, Snake. Not only will it keep the King happy, but she needs to keep onside with Dinian.'

'We've already planned to do that, Susan. Especially because King Maddox has said he won't do anything about our petition unless she does.'

Susan blinks a couple of times, then stares at me. 'I didn't know that. It makes it all the more important the King thinks she is going along with things.'

'If I can, I'll weigh in, but you can't expect me to push too hard. I don't want her to end up being forced into marrying that smarmy elf.'

Sympathy clouds Susan's eyes. 'It must be hard for you, but it's not forever.'

I sigh and concentrate on my plate, suddenly weary of court intrigue. I don't want to tell Pris to play nice with Dinian. I want her uncle to do what's right and help Queen Ariana without playing all these games.

I blow out a long breath. Even if that happens, what will it mean for Pris and me? There is something much bigger going on here than the Queen being sick. All we can do is let events play out. Once it is done, I doubt very much if we'll be able to return to our old lives. My appetite has disappeared, and I need some time alone.

'If you will excuse me,' I say to my dinner companions before rising and leaving the room.

A footman closes the dining room door behind me, and I start to head up to my room, then change my mind. I'm almost at the music room when a hand drops onto my shoulder.

'Are you all right?' Drow asks, his voice laced with concern.

'Sort of,' I say without turning. I don't want my uncle to find out how upset I am over what is happening with Pris. We haven't spoken about it, but I'm pretty sure he's not happy about our being together.

'Come, let's sit,' Drow says, using the hand on my shoulder to direct me to the closest chairs.

I shrug the hand off. 'I just need some time alone.'

Drow moves in front of me. 'This must be very difficult for you.'

I raise my gaze to meet his. 'What must be difficult?'

'Coming to court, realising your friend Priscilla has a role to play here—'

'And here I was thinking you meant meeting my family and finding out about their checkered past. And Pris is not just a friend.'

Pain flashes in Drow's eyes, which soon turns to sympathy, and I can't bear it. So I duck around him and carry on to the music room.

Drow's voice follows me as I walk. 'Snake, it is not wise to become too attached to Princess Priscilla. She is not meant for you.'

That's it, the final straw. My whole body tenses as I turn to face Drow and let loose. 'You can't be serious, warning me off Pris. Not you who campaigned for freedom for lesser creatures and creatures' rights. How can you lecture me on who I can and cannot date?'

There is now real pain on Drow's face, and for a moment, I regret my outburst—but only for a moment. As I open the door to the music room, he says, 'I only say this to save you from pain. I can't control the King, and he has his heart set—'

I slam the door, cutting off his last words.

Too angry to play, I pace circuits of the room, waiting for my heart rate to return to normal. I'm almost there when the door swing inwards and Heart's large form fills the opening. Not wanting another lecture, I stare out the small window at the back of the room.

'Those long meals get too much for me too sometimes,' he says.

I stay silent as I watch the people of Inverness wander past the castle. Then the sound of an acoustic guitar being gently strummed fills the room. I lean my forehead against the cool pane and allow the music to soothe me.

'It's been a tough couple of days for you, son, and it's not going to get better any time soon.'

Heart's voice is almost lyrical as he speaks, and I am lulled as he continues.

'I've lived a few years longer than you. And, like you, court is not where I am at home. If you will take a little advice from an old man, I will tell you, all any of us can do is be true to ourselves. Many will tell you what is best for you, but only you know what is in your heart and what you are able to live with.'

I am about to turn and join my grandfather when my heart almost stops. Below, mingling with the locals, are Grossman Green and Giles Regis, the elven representative in the World Above. What is he doing out of London and hanging out with Grossman? The last time I had seen them together was when they were giving evidence against Pris's and my parents. A ripple of fear runs up my spine. This is bad.

DINNER IS EXCRUCIATING. Unlike Snake, I can't leave before the King does, and I find myself angry at him for deserting me. I pick at my food. The King has ignored me the entire meal. He isn't talking to anyone. He just moves his food around his plate or sips his wine, seemingly lost in thought.

I'm left with only Dinian to talk to—and what a joy that is. His conversation consists of sniping about every noble in the place. According to him, he's the only creature at court I can trust. How little he knows me. He has no idea he is making me even more sure I don't want to count him as a friend.

The servers bring out coffee and, to my relief, King Maddox leans in and says, 'Would you join me?'

It's not quite a request, but it doesn't sound like a demand either. I rise, relieved at finally being away from Dinian and the critical eyes of the members of the court, and follow the King across the hallway to the audience chamber. Our footsteps echo in the empty space as King Maddox leads me to one of the window bays.

I wait for him to speak, but he simply stares out at the Ness. Then there's a tickle in the air, a light stroke of magic against my skin. The same tickle I feel when I'm talking with Am'ratha, and I realise King Maddox is talking to his dragon. The conversation is obviously private, so I lean against the window ledge and try to contact Am'ratha.

Royal One, I am happy you have called me. Are you well after the attack? I am sorry we could not come to your aid, but flying in broad daylight risks revealing ourselves and the Unseelie's home to the humans. I sensed you were not physically harmed or in distress, so Ed'rathe and I have remained hidden.

The voice in my head brings a smile to my lips. Communing with Am'ratha is like a phone conversation with an old friend.

Am'ratha, it did not even occur to me that you could help or should help, but I appreciate your concern. We're all fine. I'm pleased to find out you are still at the loch.

'I believe King Maddox is talking to his dragon. I have not been given mine yet. Apparently I won't get one until I am formally named heir. Hopefully that will happen after the King announces our betrothal.'

Dinian's voice comes from so close to my ear, it makes me jump.

Excuse me, Am'ratha, someone is trying to get my attention.

How rude. No one should interrupt our conversations. Tell him to go away, Royal One.

'Priscilla, I was talking to you.' Dinian's tone is all impatient command, and it stirs a fire inside I was barely able to keep in check during dinner.

'Firstly, Dinian, I do not appreciate being spoken to in that tone.'

His eyes widen with what I can only assume is shock at the way I'm speaking to him.

'Secondly, I was talking with a dragon, and you've rudely interrupted us.'

'You have a dragon?'

'That's what you take from that?' I seethe.

Dinian's eyes are sparkling and bright with excitement. 'I understand you're annoyed at me, but do you have a dragon?'

Honestly, can anyone be more self-absorbed?

'You don't *have* a dragon. You are paired with one to see if you bond. And yes, I am in the process of bonding with a dragon.'

Let me talk with him, Royal One. I am sure I can convince him to go away.

The threat in Am'ratha's scares me, and I am tempted to let her deal with Dinian.

I can handle him, but I'll keep you in mind should I need to scare the pants off of him.

Am'ratha chuckles. *I am here if you need me.*

'How come you have one?' Dinian's tone is sulky and petulant. He reminds me of an infant who's been told he can't have a toy.

I shake my head. How has no one strangled this creature before now? How am I going to get through the next couple of days without doing it myself?

'As I am in line for the Seelie throne, I have been asked to bond with a dragon.'

Before Dinian can respond, and I can tell from the frown drawing his brows together that it will be something cutting about why he hasn't got a dragon as he is the heir to the Unseelie throne, the King interrupts us.

'My dragon advisor, Ed'ruven, is in favour of your petition, and Drow is leaning that way, but Chancellor Rimould is worried about leaving the court without the protection of both my dragon's and my magic.'

'Surely you cannot seriously be considering abandoning us—not when we need you here at court, sire,' Dinian says.

The dirty, rotten turncoat. Only this afternoon he was helping us with our petition, and now here he is, trying to convince the King to stay. Where does he really stand on this matter? Or is his only position one that benefits Dinian the most? And if that's true, what does Dinian stand to gain by the King staying at court?

'And I worry that the waning of magic needs to be dealt with—but I am still undecided,' the King says, ignoring Dinian.

This lack of action is doing my head in, and—I can't believe I am thinking this—but Dinian might be right: the court is in need of some leadership.

'If you're undecided, why did you ask me to come here?'

King Maddox's eyes drift back to the view out of the window. 'I had thought Ed'ruven would persuade me one way or the other, perhaps even offer a way I could protect the court and help the Queen that I haven't thought of.'

I force myself to take a couple of calming breaths before I respond. 'Didn't your dragon warn you of the dangers of not acting?'

'Aye, he did. And that is the only reason I have not rejected your petition out of hand.'

I'm at my wit's end. 'Then what will convince you to act?'

'I will act when I know my court is safe.' His eyes slide to Dinian, and the implication is clear—the court will be safe when he has his successor in place, and I know what I have to do to guarantee that.

Dinian's smug smile strokes the flames of my anger, and I find myself unable to respond in case I speak my mind and ruin everything.

'Once you take your position at court, I will have my family with me, and

I will have a stable succession plan,' King Maddox says, almost wistfully.

'You can have all of that if you help resolve the magic situation,' I tell him.

The King closes his eyes and says nothing. I hope he is considering my words, but when his eyes open, he sets his jaw and says, 'My word is final. This is how it has to be.'

We shall see about that! I silently promise him.

The King turns his gaze back to the river, and I consider myself dismissed. I push myself off the wall and head for the door. Dinian catches me up.

'Let me escort you,' he says, offering his arm.

'I don't need an escort,' I snap back.

Dinian grabs my arm, halting my progress. I spin around, eyes blazing, ready to give him a piece of my mind. The words freeze in my mouth when I find a puzzled look on his face.

'I don't understand why you are so against this. It's not like this has to be a real marriage. After all, the Unseelie Court does not expect its king to provide heirs. And I've already said you can keep your pet gnome—'

I wrench my arm from his grasp, and, seething with suppressed fury, I stride towards the music room, anxious to put some distance between me and the elf who is determined to marry me.

FLAMES LAP AT the coals as I attempt to prod the library fire into life. Effie leans in closer, drawn by the warmth.

'If he won't listen to Petunia, is there anyone else who might sway him? Heart, perhaps, or what about Tomas's brother?'

Effie leans back in the chair. 'Heart is an entertainer and a drinking buddy, not someone King Maddox would discuss affairs of state with. And Raymond rarely comes to court now. He did not come often when Tomas was alive. Now I suspect we may not have the pleasure of his company at all.'

I cannot just leave it there, and not just because my future relies quite heavily on King Maddox doing what is expected of him, but because there is something very wrong with magic, and it's affecting the courts and creatures. 'Then it is up to you and me to make him understand. He must listen to you when you have the best interests of creatures as your motivation.'

Effie slowly shakes her head. 'I have tried. Besides, King Maddox is like a caged animal when he thinks he is being backed into a corner.'

I pace the rug in front of the fire. 'I will not give up. There must be something we can do.'

Before Effie can answer, if indeed she was going to, the door opens, and Drow enters. 'Ah, I see we are holding a war council,' he says as he takes a seat beside Effie on the sofa.

I study the two longtime friends who are so relaxed in each other's company and wonder, not for the first time, why they are not together. I worry that they both spend so much time looking after others that they do not take the time to take care of themselves.

Drow sits forward, rests his elbows on his knees, and clasps his hands.

'The attack today was a reminder that the court is vulnerable. He is worried and possibly a little scared. He does not want to be the last King of the Unseelie Court.'

'Of course not, but can he not see now is not the time to hunker down and wait things out?' I ask.

Drow stares into the fire for a moment, as if collecting his thoughts, before answering. 'The best I could do was have him agree to consult with Ed'ruven. Perhaps his dragon can persuade him.'

'Let us hope so,' I say.

'Anyway, fun as it is sitting around the fire with you both, I'm on a mission to find something to help shore up the court's defences. I am sure King Maddox would feel easier leaving to assist Queen Ariana if the court was more heavily protected.'

'A good idea, Drow. Perhaps Percival and I can help you.'

'Thank you both.'

'Also,' I start, but am not sure I should be bringing this up. My friends eye me expectantly. 'I wonder if we should also search for books on battle magic.' They both open their mouths to protest, but I hold up a hand to stop them. 'I know it has been banned, but I would not trust Bernais and his cronies to ignore the edict, and we should be prepared to defend ourselves against anything they may throw at us.'

Effie frowns. 'While it would be good to find something to counter magical attacks, Percival, you know how damaging such magic can be to the environment. Also, I worry that our knowing this magic may increase the probability of it being used.'

'Let us consider that as a last resort, then,' Drow says.

'And perhaps agree we would only use the defensive elements in response to a magical attack?' I say, not wanting to completely alienate Effie.

Effie reluctantly consents to at least see what is available. With nothing left to say, we disperse down different aisles of books.

Scanning the titles, I quiver with excitement when I come across a tome entitled *A Study into the Establishment of The Unseelie Court*. I reach up and pull it from the shelf, then decide that rather than gathering more books, I will start on this one now.

Effie and Drow have already piled some books on the table, so I move to the end and set myself up, ready to scan the text for information. I have only just sat down when Pris flings open the door. She is followed into the room by an amused Dinian and Snake, who has a face like thunder.

'Hi, Percival. What's happening in here?' Pris asks.

Snake takes a seat beside me, and as he does, he leans in close to whisper in my ear, 'Don't say anything. I don't trust that elf.'

As Dinian approaches I slip the book I was studying onto my lap. Drow appears from behind a book stack and blocks his and Pris's view of the table. 'We were just chatting about old times and got into a bit of an argument about something, and now we are each trying to prove the others wrong. Childish, really.'

Pris glances my way, and I force my shoulders to relax. Heeding Snake's warning, I do not want to give too much away in front of Dinian.

Effie then appears from another stack. 'We have been caught out, boys. Anyway, it's about time we put an end to this nonsense and head for bed.'

There is hurt in Pris's eyes, as she knows us well enough to realise she is being excluded because of Dinian's presence. She tries to catch Snake's attention, but he appears to be busy doing up the buttons on his jacket. I elbow him in the side, and he sends me a look like daggers. I nod towards Pris, and he finally takes the hint.

'C'mon, Pris, time for bed. Unless you want to stay and mediate their argument.'

'Yes, Princess, come. I will escort you to your rooms.'

Dinian holds out a hand for Pris to take. She ignores him and starts towards the door, with Dinian trailing behind.

'Go,' I tell Snake. 'I will catch you up later.'

As he stands up to go after the others, I hear Drow hiss, 'When I told you she is not for you, I was trying to save you from all of this.'

Snake does not even indicate he has heard, and I hope he does not listen to his uncle's advice. Drow may think he is protecting Snake, but he does not understand the deep connection the events of the past few weeks have forged between Pris and his nephew. I know better than most what it is like to be kept from the one you love. I do not wish that sort of heartache for my young friend.

ULTIMATUMS

THE WALK BACK to my room is tense. Dinian insists he is more than capable of escorting me without Snake tagging along. Snake's face is thunderous, and I fear he is holding in a storm. Even so, he says nothing. I suspect he's waiting for me to send Dinian away. This seems such a petty thing for me to do, as his rooms are close by mine.

By the time we reach the door to my grandmother's suite, I'm fuming. Snake should have left me alone with Dinian. He knows I can't stand the elf, but surely he knows me well enough by now to trust me not to lose my temper and reveal our plan. If he's going to chaperone us everywhere, then no one will believe we are resigned to our fate.

As for Dinian, for all his assertions that if we were together, he would 'allow' my relationship with Snake, he's certainly getting a lot of pleasure needling him at every opportunity.

If this is what the next couple of days are going to be like, then someone's head is going to roll—and it won't be mine. As I turn the door handle, my frustration is climbing, and have to force myself to slip inside without saying anything to either of my tormentors in case I make a bad situation worse.

The suite is only dimly lit. Grandmother must have already retired for the night. In one way I'm relived I don't have to make polite conversation, but in another, I wish she were up so I could ask her advice on how to best navigate the turbulent waters I've found myself in. Then again, my bed is cosy and calling me. The sooner I'm between the sheets, the better.

As I undress, I go over the events of the day, wondering how I managed to get myself into this situation and if there was anything I could have done to prevent it. I worry we won't be able to convince the King to do the right thing and that my parents will spend the rest of their lives in captivity. My mind is buzzing so much, I'm sure I won't sleep a wink. As my head touches the pillow, my body makes a liar of me.

In spite of my angst last night, I sleep like a log until I hear someone shuffling about in my room. Forcing an eye open, I can't see a thing. So I push my body upright and find Susan placing some plastic bags on the floor.

She sends me a cheery smile. 'Oh, you're awake.'

'I wasn't,' I grumble back.

'But now that you are, I can tell you I've some clothes and shoes in the bags for you and Snake.'

Suddenly wide awake and excited, I throw off the covers and leap out of bed. Susan hands me two of the bags. I open the first to find a couple of pairs of blue jeans, a couple of T-shirts, a purple hoodie, and some socks. In the second bag, there's a pair of purple trainers. I pull them out and squeal.

I throw my arms around Susan. 'You're the best.' Then I remember I'm supposed to be mad at her for lying to me, and I step back.

The grin on Susan's face falters, and guilt sends my stomach churning. Perhaps it is time to put all this behind us.

'Susan, why did you do it? Why did you lie to me all those years?' I ask, as I start pulling the clothes out of the bags.

Susan places a hand on my arm, stopping me. 'Your uncle has requested your presence at breakfast this morning, so you'll have to leave changing into these until later.'

I allow my displeasure to show on my face, and Susan chuckles.

'Trust me. I've found the perfect outfit for you.'

She lays a white blouse on the bed along with a slightly flouncy petticoat and a long purple skirt. The outfit is much plainer than anything my grandmother would have given me. She follows it up with a pair of lace-up Victorian-style boots. She runs her hand over them, and they are purple, a perfect match for the skirt.

As I dress, Susan tidies my room like she used to at home.

'You know I can clean up after myself,' I tell her as I have many times before.

'Yes, but I am still feeling bad about how you found out about being a creature. I never wanted to lie to you about who you are.'

I pause, hoping she will say more, but she doesn't. 'Why did you?'

I hear a sigh, but I remain silent, giving Susan time to answer.

'My parents had been part of the Unseelie Court for years when I arrived—an unexpected late-in-life gift. Dad was the butler, and Mum ran the serving staff. I grew up here, as did many of us who wait on the royals. When I was almost eighteen, my father had a heart attack. When he died, my mother took it badly, and I believe his not being here broke her heart. She followed him soon after.'

I turn to find Susan staring out the window, tears gathering in her eyes.

'I'm sorry, Susan. I had no idea.'

'I don't like talking about it. I still miss them.'

'What happened to you after they passed?'

'My sister offered for me to go live with her, but she had her own children to worry about. Your grandmother suggested I stay at court, and she would train me to be her companion.'

Susan's face softens as she talks about my grandmother. The two must be very close.

'Not long after, the attacks on you started, and both Princess Petunia and King Maddox begged me to go and look after you. They were worried that with your parents being so busy, they would need help. I agreed. Your father accepted my presence in your house so long as I pledged to never, under any circumstances, tell you about your extended family or talk to you about magic.'

'And you agreed.' This was more of a statement than a question because she never mentioned a word about magic—ever.

'I did. At first you were too young to understand and never questioned your parents. As you grew older, I tried to convince them that you had a right to know. Eventually they gave in and agreed to bring you here, but before they could… well, they were taken.'

Although I'm beginning to understand why Susan did what she did, I can't let go of the betrayal I feel.

'Couldn't you have told me anyway? I would have kept it secret.'

Finally Susan looks at me, and I find pain in her eyes. She shakes her head. 'If I had done that, I would have had to go. Magical promises are binding, and I would have had to leave you. By that time we were so close, I thought of you like a younger sister, and I couldn't desert you.'

It takes me less than a second to rush to Susan and pull her into a hug. At first she resists, then she hugs me back.

'I would rather have had you there than the truth,' I reassure her. 'And while I'm not happy about the lies, I will be forever grateful to my Unseelie family for sending you to me.'

Susan squeezes me before stepping away and wiping her eyes. 'Come, we had best go to breakfast. The King wasn't in a good mood this morning, and we don't want to make it worse by being late.'

With the sun streaming through the windows and the tables moved to a more informal setting, the dining room is less glamorous than the night before. It is also not so full of creatures.

King Maddox has foregone the high table to sit with Petunia and Drow. He has left a place for me opposite my grandmother but beside Dinian.

Susan steers me towards it, whispering in my ear, 'I know you want to sit with your friends, but you want to keep your uncle sweet, don't you?'

My uncle doesn't notice my presence as he carries on talking to Drow, but Dinian is solicitous in a rather possessive way, pulling back my chair to enable me to move my skirts around it and then calling over a servant to take my breakfast order. I am about to snap at him that I am perfectly able to look after myself when I catch Susan shaking her head. I bite back the retort, and Susan, happy I received her message, sits down beside Euphemia.

As I eat I try to catch Snake's eye. He is down the other end of the table, eating with Percival and Heart, his back partially turned to me. I eat a couple of bites of toast, waiting for Snake to look my way. He appears to be avoiding me—or me and Dinian together.

I stare at my food, trying to will myself to eat, but my stomach is roiling, and the thought of food is making me ill. Is this what it's going to be like for the next few days? My friends keeping things from me because Dinian is close by and Snake not able to look at me when he is near? Tears well, and I blink them away. I excuse myself by saying I need to go to the bathroom.

I'm leaning against the wall, trying not to allow the tears to fall, when a comforting hand drops onto my shoulder.

My grandmother's voice comes from beside me. 'No one said being a princess was easy.' She turns me around, then forces me into a hug. 'Tell me what is the matter. Maybe I can help.'

'It's just… well, everything, but mostly it's Dinian. King—'

Grandmother steps back and studies me. 'I am aware of what King Maddox wants you to do, and even should you agree, it is not a done deal. You are in line for the crown of the Seelie Court, and that position takes precedence over your being related to King Maddox. The Queen would have to agree to the betrothal before it is formalised.'

I stare down into Petunia's bluer-than-blue eyes, assessing whether she is joking or not.

'I shouldn't have to rely on that to stop this madness. It's the twenty-first century, and people are not chattel.'

A smile tugs at her lips. 'You need to be smarter than that, though, when playing politics. You do not want to anger the King at the moment. So this may be a case of holding your tongue and using what tools you have to negotiate. However, you will always hold the trump card, and that gives you room to manoeuvre.'

She stares at me as if waiting for me to catch on. Then I get it. 'Queen Ariana can't agree to anything in her current state.'

'That's my girl.' She pats my arm.

I bask in her pride for a moment before remembering Snake won't even look at me.

'Snake isn't taking this well.'

'He is playing along with your ruse. Don't expect him to be all sweetness and light when he has to allow Dinian to escort you everywhere. Especially not when that elf likes making a show out of everything.'

Although I'm aware that I was annoyed at Snake last night for not allowing me to just get on with things with Dinian, and now I'm annoyed at him for doing just that, I refuse to let him off the hook that easily. 'Would it hurt him to smile at me occasionally though?'

My grandmother gives me a hard stare, and I bow my head. 'I know, it's probably hard for him.'

She pats my hand. 'You are not alone in this, Pris. I am here for you, and so is Effie. When it all gets too much, come and see us.'

My eyes fill with tears again, but this time it's because of the offer of support and the realisation that sometimes having family is a good thing.

'Are you ready to go back in?'

I nod.

My grandmother links her arm through mine and leads us back into the fray.

WHAT A FRUSTRATING meal breakfast is turning into. The King is setting the tone. He is barely talking, and when he does speak, his words are clipped. An air of sadness has settled around him, and he appears not to want to do anything about it. I know he has lost his soulmate, but life has to go on.

I pause a moment, my fork halfway to my mouth. Did I really just think that? I, the sprite who has been mourning the loss of his soulmate for hundreds of years? And Nisha is still alive!

Taking a mouthful of sausage, I chew thoughtfully, wondering whether Snake is glowering at Drow or Dinian? Or perhaps both? I study him, following his line of sight. No, it is definitely Drow he is shooting daggers at. He is studiously ignoring Dinian and the empty seat beside him.

On the way to breakfast, I tried to explain to Snake that his uncle has seen how love can mess up people's lives. His best friends were banished from the Seelie Court because of the creatures they loved. While I think Snake understands that Drow is trying to save him from heartbreak, he would prefer his uncle to butt out.

'Percival, old man, would you be so kind as to pass me the butter?' Heart asks, pulling me from my thoughts.

I hand him the dish and take an opportunity to study Snake once more. He needs a distraction. Before I can think of a suitable topic, my young friend asks, 'Heart, why has Drow never married?'

Heart laughs. 'I have asked that question many a time, but I have not come up with an answer.'

Effie leans forward. 'It is because your uncle will not let anyone close enough to him to fall in love.'

She should know, I think as Snake speaks to the witch over my head.

'Is it because someone has hurt him? Or is he simply against love?'

The tinkle of Effie's laugh brings a smile to my lips. 'No, Snake, to the best of my knowledge, no one has broken his heart. I think it's more that he is a rational man, and love is sometimes irrational, so it is to be… feared? No, that isn't quite right. I think he avoids it because he cannot explain it.'

'Ah.' Snake nods and returns to his food, then glances up again. 'And yet he chose to leave the World Below with his friends. Is that not a sort of love?'

Heart places his cutlery on his plate and stares at Snake for a long moment before answering. 'It was so long ago, and we were much more passionate about things then. I suspect Drow left as much to make a political point as he did to support all of us.' Heart smiles sadly, as if his thoughts are still in the past, then picks up his tea.

'Given he is so caught up in creature politics, why is he still here when he could be back in the World Below, helping Elias?' Snake asks.

I startle as Drow's voice comes from behind me. 'Because Elias has my family to support him.'

'And because your father didn't want you rocking the boat,' Heart adds around a mouthful of breakfast.

'True. My brother is Fieth now, and he would welcome me home, but I am used to my life as it is. Besides, my friends are here. What sort of a life would I have back home without you all?'

As I listen to my old friend, I realise he no longer speaks with the same fire he did when we were younger. We are all a little older and perhaps not so inclined to be radical, but Drow used to fight vehemently for creatures' rights. It was his passion and, I thought, his calling. He and I had both fought to change our world.

I shift in my seat so I can see Drow, who is leaning on the back of Effie's chair.

'What happened to us, old friend?' I ask him. 'We once pledged to fight injustices and make life better for all creatures in the World Below.'

Drow turns sad eyes to me. 'We did, I remember, but it seems so long ago. I was powerless to stop my friends from being banished, just like I could not save you. I guess I began to question whether or not I was capable of changing anything.'

Effie leans a cheek on Drow's hand. 'You could never get it into your head that you only lost a couple of battles. The war is still there to be won.'

The room blurs as my thoughts turn inwards. Drow and I have both been sleeping, and while we slept, we allowed a war to carry on around us. By withdrawing from the fight, he and I are just as responsible for what is going on with the Unseelie Court as Bernais and his cronies are.

'The war is not lost yet,' I say slowly. 'Nor is the battle for the Unseelie Court. We are back, Drow—and Bernais had better beware because this time I will not leave the field until one of us has lost.'

A slow smile forms on Drow's lips, and a spark flashes in his eyes. 'Percival, your words shame me. How can I not take up the challenge you have thrown down? Once we have finished our work for the Unseelie Court, I think it is time you and I returned to the World Below and offered our talents to Elias.'

Drow holds out a hand, and I shake it.

'I would come with you, but I am afraid my banishment is still very real,' Heart says.

'I'll join your crusade,' Effie adds. 'I believe the welfare of the creatures here in the World Above will best be served by sorting out the problems in the World Below.'

Heart chuckles. 'Is that not what Eleanor came to tell you a few months ago?'

Effie frowns at the bard. 'You know how to take the shine off a declaration of action.'

'Or perhaps it is just that I will miss all of you when you ride off on your crusade,' Heart admits.

'And we will miss you too,' Effie says. 'But we will come back home after, and we will begin lobbying for you and Petunia to be reinstated at court, and this time we will succeed.'

'I hope so,' Heart says quietly. 'I really do.'

MOVING FOOD AROUND my plate, I can't raise an appetite, and the conversation at the table doesn't help. I tried to dig up some interest but gave up when my tablemates began to plan their return to the World Below.

I sneak a glance at Pris and Dinian. I know we agreed she should play along with the King's plan, but at the time, I had no idea how jealous I would be. Each time she speaks to him is like a knife being stabbed through my heart.

Okay, I get the irony. At first I let other things get in the way of us, so I have no right to condemn her for playing along with the King's wishes now—especially not when I believe it's the right thing to do. It's just, sometimes you can't help the way you feel.

Dinian catches me watching and smirks. It doesn't help that he loves rubbing my nose in the fact that he's with Pris. Even knowing that the joke will be on him when Pris and I leave before they can be formally betrothed does nothing to improve my mood.

I will get through this. Mum, I hope you appreciate what I'm doing to free you.

'So, Snake, what are your plans for today?'

Maybe Heart is at a loose end at the moment too.

'I don't know,' I answer, drawing my eyes back down our end of the table.

'Perhaps you and I could finish off what we started last—'

Crash! My head jerks up in time to catch the main doors violently swinging open. Standing in the entranceway are Grossman Green and Giles Regis, smiling bold as brass.

A collective gasp fills the air. How did they pass through the wards closing off the court? With magic waning, they shouldn't have had the power to do that… unless they are pooling magic… or they have help… or they're drawing it illegally from lesser creatures. The thought of them using creatures for a magical boost sickens me. Someone must have let them in. I scan the room, trying to identify the culprit. No one is smirking. Every creature here appears as shocked as I am at the intrusion. Perhaps I'm wrong, and they made their own way inside.

Pris's hands are balled into fists on the table, and I hope she doesn't do anything hasty. As far as everyone in the World Below is concerned, she and

I are still on our quest, so it is best if we keep out of sight. Fortunately she remains in her seat, shielded from view by Dinian. The elf stood up when the king did, ready to face down Giles and Grossman.

'What, no welcome for your brother creatures, King Maddox?' Giles sneers along with the last two words, turning the King's title into a farce.

Two guards belatedly appear behind them, swords drawn, but when they attempt to get close to the interlopers, they are thrown back—there is obviously a shield around the two creatures. The guards can do nothing except stand there helplessly. Another pair of guards slide into place, flanking the King, ready to give their lives for him.

'No need for all this aggression,' Giles drawls, a supercilious smile on his face. 'We have only come to serve a warning from the Council of the World Below. Stay out of matters that do not concern you, or we will pull down your court. What you saw the day before yesterday was a small demonstration of what we can do.'

King Maddox draws himself up, and for the first time since we arrived, I see him for the leader he is. There is an aura of power around him that is undeniable. Euphemia appears from nowhere and begins an incantation. How did she do that without being noticed?

'On whose authority do you send this threat?' King Maddox asks, his voice calm and commanding. I can't tell whether he is playing for time to give Euphemia a chance to use her magic or if he is gathering information.

'Bernais, the newly elected head of the Council of the World Below,' Grossman Green announces, initiating another communal gasp.

King Maddox glares at the intruders, his jaw clenched. When he speaks, his words drip with ice. 'I do not believe you or Bernais Baaronson speaks on behalf of all creatures in the World Below. So you take yourself back to your puppet master, and tell him he can take his demand and shove it—'

'Guards, remove these creatures from the court,' Euphemia commands, and the guards snap to attention. They grab the two creatures. With their shield countered, Green and Regis have no option but to move.

'You have until sundown tomorrow to change your mind, or watch your court crumble,' Giles yells as he is hauled out.

The room is silent.

King Maddox turns his gaze to Euphemia, and I wonder what the punishment is for interrupting a monarch. His voice is low when he speaks. 'Thank you, Euphemia, for dealing with those two and for—' He pauses for a moment. '—preventing me from losing my dignity.'

'My pleasure.'

King Maddox straightens his spine, and I don't quite know what he does, but it is as though I can see the crown on his head when he next speaks. 'Guards, ensure everyone returns to their rooms. The court is in lockdown until tomorrow morning.'

The king makes a dignified exit, followed closely by Euphemia, Drow, and Rimould.

For a moment everyone is frozen in place. Then it is as though someone says, 'Go,' as they all move at once.

'I guess our music session is cancelled,' Heart says as he rises to his feet.

I glance at Percival, not wanting to waste a whole day locked in our suite—away from Pris. 'Do we really have to spend all day in our rooms?'

'I guess we had better do as the King commands, for the moment,' the sprite says. Then he smiles. 'You go on ahead with Heart, I have to stop by the library on to pick up some things.'

Heart smiles. 'Come, young man. If Percival can take a detour, so can we. Let us go and help ourselves to a lute and a guitar or two as we make our way back to our rooms.'

My spirits lift at the thought of a day of music, but they plummet again as Dinian escorts Pris and her grandmother out.

She glances back over her shoulder as they walk towards the door, and her look clearly says, 'Save me.' It is wrong of me, but I'm a little happier knowing she's not enjoying spending time with Dinian.

As we leave the dining room. I ask Percival, 'Why did they set the deadline as sundown tomorrow? I mean, why not lunchtime, or the usual twenty-four-hour threat?'

'Because if they manage to pull the castle out of time, the resulting wash of magic and the influx of strangely dressed people into Inverness is easier to hide at night.'

'Oh,' I say. 'Can they do that—pull the court back into time and space?'

Percival shakes his head. 'I have no idea, but let us hope not.'

AND IT CHANGED
IN A HEARTBEAT

I ROLL OVER and press my face into the pillow. Susan is moving about, making enough noise to wake me, but I want to stay here—hiding. I'm not sure I can stand another day of playing nice with Dinian while the King stays holed up in his study.

The only good thing about yesterday was that the guards would not give in to Dinian's request to spend the day with Grandmother and me. He stormed off in a huff, saying he would have it out with the King.

When Euphemia dropped by later in the afternoon, she told us King Maddox would not admit Dinian to his office and had sent a guard to see that he remained in his rooms as ordered. That was the brightest spot in the day.

Susan brought us food and gossip but nothing more tangible. Even Euphemia, having spent the morning in his company, could not anticipate what the King was going to do.

Grandmother and I spent some time discussing how Bernais had managed to get control of the World Below's council, and came to no conclusion. That he poses a real threat to the stability of the creature world is obvious. The conversation raised concerns about her family, and she asked her dragon, Am'ralla, to join the others at Loch Ness to protect her husband.

Am'ralla agreed to keep an eye on her family but unfortunately didn't have any news about what was happening in the World Below except to say that it appeared to be chaos.

With no information, my main worry was what Bernais being in charge will mean for my parents and Snake's mother, but after fretting the morning away, I came to the conclusion that I can't do anything about their fate. Nor am I able to influence anyone to help them. All I can do is carry on trying to convince the King to go to Queen Ariana.

Besides, Grandmother reminded me that it would take time for Bernais to consolidate his power in the World Below. Until he did, our parents would be relatively safe.

'How come?' I'd asked.

'Because they are from prominent families. Bernais will have to ensure everything is done by the book with them, or he risks losing what support he has. Besides, if he touches a hair on my daughter's head, he will have me to contend with.'

My fears somewhat calmed, I'd thought I would go and share what Grandmother had said with Snake. Only, I hadn't been able to persuade the guards to let me leave our suite, let alone the corridor. Maybe with the curfew being lifted, I can do so today.

'You can't hide in there forever,' Susan says.

'Who says I can't.' I speak into my pillow. 'Besides, I'm not hiding, I'm thinking.'

'Of course you are. Would it help if I told you the King has called a gathering of the full council, and you're invited?'

I sit bolt upright.

'Ah, so that got you moving.' She chuckles.

'I'm so stupid.'

'What?'

I *am* stupid. There was one creature who might be able to provide some information about unrest in the World Below. *Am'ratha, are you there?*

Yes, Princess.

Are you able to tell me what has been happening in the World Below?

'Pris, come on, you're going to be late.'

Hold on a mo, Am'ratha.

'Shh,' I tell Susan, 'I'm busy.'

She raises an eyebrow, a look I well know means don't cross me.

'I'm trying to get an update from the dragons,' I tell her.

'Okay, you have a couple of minutes.'

There is chaos in the World Below. The palace is under siege, and a shadow council backed by local garrisons has taken control of the Capitol.

Oh no, it's worse than we thought. It sounds like the beginnings of a civil war.

Do you have any news of my parents? Or of Snake's family?

As far as we can tell, your parents and Snake's mother are still in the castle, along with Elias. They are protected by the Queen's Guard. Many creatures still support him, but calls for the Queen to appear and put a stop to all this nonsense are growing louder.

Dammit, I thought we still had a few days to change the King's mind, but we've run out of time.

Am'rathaa, does anyone there have a plan?

Elias has admitted that the Queen is sick from cleansing the flow of magic, Royal One. Yesterday he told the people she will appear in ten days' time, which is when the doctors have said she will be well enough to walk.

So, he bought us some time.

Yes, a little.

No pressure, then.

Yes, Royal One, there is much pressure on you to make the King change his mind.

Note to self: dragons don't get sarcasm.

I am not sure if the King will hear what I have to say. He is wrapped up in grief and focused on protecting his people.

If he stays away and the Queen does not appear, Bernais will take over, and any chance of healing the breach and fixing magic will be gone.

Am'ratha, he says if I marry the heir to the Unseelie Court, he will help heal magic.

In times of need, we all have to make sacrifices.

I expected a little sympathy because of our growing bond, but her response is delivered in a matter-a-fact tone, which irritates me.

Why can't he make the sacrifice?

Am'ratha does not answer.

Maybe the threat of his court being ruined will be enough to motivate him.

Perhaps, perhaps not.

My head is spinning, trying to figure a way through this new mess. *Hey, if the problem with magic will get worse if Bernais is crowned, does that mean he doesn't have a dragon?*

He does not. He was just a baby when his family was removed from the royal line. The bonding process will take time, then he would need to be trained to work with his dragon to cleanse magic. Why?

What happens if he declares himself ruler without the support of the dragons?

The sacred bond is broken, and the dragons will have to try and keep magic going by ourselves. We will be fine, but it will not be the same in the human and creature world.

Would we lose our bond? I'm surprised to find that the thought of losing Am'ratha makes me feel sad.

No, Royal One. Those of us with existing bonds will keep them. And the ruler of the Seelie Court will still bond with a dragon so we can keep lines of communication open.

What about the Unseelie Court?

No, once the sacred bond is broken, the Unseelie Court will lose its special status, and those who come after King Maddox will not have access to our magic to protect them.

Does Bernais know this?

I believe he does, Royal One.

Oh my god, does Bernais hate the creatures of the Unseelie Court so much, he's willing to risk magic in both worlds to ensure its downfall? This is madness.

Another thing you should know, Royal One. Bernais's mother is in our world, the World Between, begging for an audience with our Queen. We believe she wants to reinstate their line as heir to the throne and is asking for dragon support.

That news strikes at my heart more than everything else I've heard. Not only do the Baaransons want to be rid of the Unseelie Court, they also want to overthrow the monarchy in the World Below. I freeze as icicles of fear tingle all over my body. These are the creatures who thought transforming Percival into a cat was a reasonable punishment—and they did that when they weren't even in charge.

Our last hope is getting the King to come and help us, isn't it? I ask my dragon, my thoughts conveying my growing dread.

Yes.

Thank you for your help, Am'ratha.

Tread carefully, Royal One. A lot rests on your shoulders.

Great, the fate of two worlds is in my hands. My course is clear. Dinian is smarmy and possessive, and I'm not sure I can hold my temper around him, but I must keep up the ruse even though I can see how hard it is on Snake.

I take a deep breath and slowly let it out. Snake looked so lonely yesterday, and I've not been able to update him about anything I've learnt. The burden is too heavy for me. If I could just see him and share the load….

'Come on,' Susan urges me, swatting the bed to get my attention.

I launch myself into motion. I'll be damned if I will fall completely into line. I dress in jeans and a white T-shirt before lacing my trainers and throwing on the purple zip-up sweatshirt. Susan doesn't even comment on my outfit choice. She just leaves me to finish off and plait my hair.

There is no one in the sitting room when I finally emerge. Tiptoeing, I open the door to the corridor, determined to see Snake before breakfast.

I am stopped by a guard before I reach the end of the hall.

'I'm sorry, Princess, I have orders from the King. Your breakfast is on its way up, and after you eat, I am to escort you directly to his study.'

'Where's my grandmother?'

The guard frowns at me. 'I am not sure I'm supposed to—'

I glare at him, and he shifts uncomfortably from foot to foot. I guess being royal has some perks.

'I believe she is breakfasting with Lady Euphemia. I am to pick them up on the way downstairs.'

I'm about to tell him what the King can do with his plan when Dinian's head pops out of a doorway further down the corridor. He turns his head, sees me, then grins.

'I'll tell you what,' I quickly improvise, 'I'll go back to my room and not cause any problems if you promise to keep him away from me.'

The guard's face splits into a smile, and he says, 'It will be my pleasure, Princess.'

I let the princess thing go in the spirit of conspiracy and return to my grandmother's suite. While I wait for my meal to arrive, I spend my time wondering why the guard was pleased at being able to thwart Dinian's plans and thinking how I might arrange a meeting with Snake before the council.

I SIT DOWN at the table in Effie's sitting room, again finding myself between the witch and her friend, Princess Petunia. It is not the most comfortable position to be in, especially not when the two are in planning mode.

And make no mistake about it, they are clearly up to something. The fact that they are meeting away from Pris signals that more than anything. They too have been invited to the council this morning, and they are strategising how best to make the King understand that this battle will be fought and won in the World Below.

'I do not know why you are even bothering with the meeting today, Petunia,' I interrupt. 'Surely you would be best deployed using your dragon to return to the World Below to fight Bernais for the throne.'

Petunia stops mid gesture and turns to me. 'You think I have not already considered that option, Percival? All it will do is give Bernais someone concrete to direct his ire at, and I will not be able to help with the battle up here.'

I lean my elbows on the table and steeple my fingers. 'That is likely true—'

'You agree she should stay?' Effie asks.

I shake my head. 'No, she should definitely go. If you are there, it is likely the dragons can be persuaded to grant you Queen-in-Waiting status regardless of what the creature council wants. Even if you could not take the throne, you would have access to the magical flow, and you could carry on cleansing it. That would help reinforce magic in both worlds, and the creatures here would be better able to fight off their attackers.'

My theory is met with stupefied faces and silence.

Petunia sighs. 'That is a possibility, but there are still problems with your plan. The Queen's Guard is sworn to her until she dies, so while she lives, they cannot protect me. In fact, given that I am not the named heir, they would have to treat me as they would Bernais—as a usurper.'

I am still not convinced. 'That would only be if you took the fight to the Capitol. There is still support for you in the countryside, and the people there would protect you.'

'True, but it won't be enough. Only Queen Ariana can rally the people who are undecided, so we need her to be there to challenge what Bernais is doing.'

'That would be the best-case scenario,' I concede.

'And, even if the dragons accept Petunia as heir, she will still not be connected fully to the magical flow. That means there is a possibility she will only have a small impact on the waning magic. You of all people should appreciate how that will limit her abilities given your current state.'

I remember back to the night Magnus cursed me, and how Petunia, with the help of her mother's dragon, tried to heal me. It had only been a partial success, but I always thought that was because the Dragon Queen required some punishment to stand for my misdeeds.

'I am not sure that is true,' I say. 'My punishment is the result of my actions, not of Petunia's inability to access the full magical flow.'

Petunia reaches out her hand and takes one of mine. 'So we were told at the court hearing, but I have always wondered if I had been bonded to my own dragon and given full queenly access, would the outcome have been the same?'

Petunia's eyes well with tears. I had not realised that even after all these years, she still blamed herself for not being able to fully reverse the spell.

'I am sure it was through no fault of yours,' I reassure her.

She shakes her head. 'I am not so certain. We were told you had to face some punishment for thoughtlessly spreading the blight—but three hundred years, Percival. That is too long. I fear I should not have interfered that night.'

I squeeze her hand. 'Petunia, I am forever grateful for all that you did for me then and after. Anything beyond that is on my head.'

'You are sweet to say—'

'Goodness, you two, leave the past in the past. We have enough to worry about without bringing up history.'

Effie's words have the desired effect. I withdraw my hand and smile. My witch friend is right. We have to decide the best course of action for now.

'Need I remind the two of you, Am'ralla informed me this morning that Elias has promised that the Queen will be back at court in ten—'

'Nine now,' I correct.

Effie's brow draws down in a frown, and I find myself squirming a little in my seat.

'That means there is only one way we are going to sort this mess out,' she says.

'I agree,' Petunia chimes in. 'We must persuade the King to intervene.'

They both turn expectant gazes towards me. 'What? Do you think I can persuade him? If no one else has been able to, what can I do differently?'

'You can have words with that granddaughter of mine and persuade her to do whatever it takes to get King Maddox to help Queen Ariana, short of betrothing herself to that nincompoop, Dinian.'

'I believe she is doing that already, but we should not place all our eggs in one basket.' I say. 'We need a plan B.'

'Percival, it will not do for me to go Below and declare myself heir. I have been away too many years, and it will take time to get enough people to support me to make a difference.'

Effie sits forward on her seat. 'Pris might be able to do it though.'

Is this the type of conversation that got Pris and Snake caught up in this in the first place? Pushing responsibility onto the two of them because we are too tired or too scared to fight?

'Yes, that would work, Effie. Percival, you should—'

'No, I will not speak to her about it. These problems we face are not of her making, and we should not sit here comfortably by the fire and throw her to the wolves.'

After my outburst, Effie and Petunia appear confused. 'You don't think Pris will be able to mobilise support?' Effie asks.

I bow my head for a moment. 'What happened to us? We were so full of fight when we were younger. We were prepared to take on the world.'

Effie places a hand over mine. 'We were younger then. We had much less to lose. Fighting is for the young.'

I remove my hand from under hers and stand up, staring them both in the eye. They are quite content sitting here, moving pieces on the chessboard. I find myself appalled by their lack of action.

'We know how difficult it is to fight for change. Goddess knows we made little impact when we were younger. Perhaps if we had some of the elders onside back then, helping us, even, we would not be in the position we are in now.'

The fire crackles behind me as Effie and Petunia consider my words, but I am not done yet.

'Our worlds have been on shaky ground for a while, and all we have done is chip at the edges, perhaps even destabilising it further. You must decide here and now if you are happy with how things are turning out, or do you want to make changes for the better? None of us have the luxury of sitting on the sidelines anymore—the time to choose a side in this battle is here.'

'I think you are over—'

'No, Effie, Percival is right. When we cleansed the blight against the orders of the council, we began something—we were just too young to see it.' Petunia rises to her feet and begins pacing. 'We challenged the old guard, and when they slapped us down, we accepted our fate, giving power back to them. And they have used that power to shore up their position, and now they are wanting to drag creature-kind back centuries.'

'That may be so,' Effie says, 'but I do not see what we can do about it—not when magic is tainted.'

'As Percival says, we need to plan.'

I smile. This is the Petunia I remember. She has a fire in her belly and is ready to lead us all to battle. Effie and I watch her as she paces, knowing that while she walks, that brilliant political mind of hers is working.

She stops abruptly and turns to us. 'Let's get the important things out of the way first. Percival, will your family be safe?'

This was the same question I asked myself last night, and raising it again also raises my anxiety. Sprites are pacifists by nature, and they tend to stick to their groves. However, that will not prevent them from being drawn into the coming battle. At the moment I have to trust that Ellie would find some way to get a message to me if they were in any danger and that we have enough friends who will protect my clan.

'I do not know. They are still in the grove, mourning the death of my father. Ellie is close by in the village with your mother, Effie, so I believe my family will be protected for the moment, especially while all unrest is focused on the Capitol.'

As I answer something tugs at the back of my mind—something important to this discussion. The wizards!

'And Ellie is in touch with the wizards, or at least with Mandor. She persuaded him to participate in our maze trial.'

Petunia taps her index finger against her lips. 'Interesting.' She begins pacing again.

'Right, we have Pris and Drow working on King Maddox. It is now more essential than ever that he agrees to help Queen Ariana. Not only will his intervention hopefully enable her to return to her duties, but it will reinforce relations between the courts. Both outcomes should give those attacking the Unseelie Court something to consider.'

Effie and I exchange glances. There must be more to come.

'Percival, you and Effie should continue trying to find a way to protect the Unseelie Court from attack. If we can take that worry from King Maddox, he will be more inclined to leave. Also, once the court is protected, the rest of us can return home and see what we can do to help.'

'Not much of a plan,' I say, earning a scathing look from the princess.

'Until we know exactly what is happening, we cannot be precise. If Drow, Heart, Effie, and I go to the Wyld Woods, we can offer support to Eleanora. I am sure she, Elias, and Fairburn already have some plan of action, and we would be better served to strengthen their efforts than do something that might run counter to them.'

I open my mouth to speak, then close it again. While I would love to have a more solid plan of attack, Petunia has agreed to leave the court and return home to fight. That is a massive concession.

'All right,' I say before asking, 'Petunia, what about your husband, daughter, and son? Will they come with us?'

Petunia closes her eyes, but I catch a glimpse of pain in them before she does. She turns away from us before answering. 'When we stayed at the castle, we took on a sacred duty to maintain the portal between worlds. They cannot leave, but they will be safe. Because the portal is also an entrance to the World Between and also bypasses the usual gatekeeper from the World Below, the minotaur, the dragons will not allow anything to befall its defenders.'

It will be difficult for Petunia to fight this war away from those she loves most, but war ofttimes splits families and friends. We will be there to support her, and her family will be safe. That is what matters.

A gong rings, summoning us to King Maddox's study.

'Well, this is it. Make or break time,' Petunia says as she leads us out.

TAKING A SIP of coffee, I watch as Heart places the remains of his breakfast on a serving tray and makes ready to leave.

'Are you coming to this morning's council?' I ask.

Heart smiles and shakes his head. 'Court bards do not get invited to councils, no matter how good a friend they are to the King.'

'But wouldn't you want friends amongst your advisors? At least you can trust them.'

Chuckling to himself, Heart does up the buttons on his jacket before answering. 'Snake, if I were on the council, I would have to care about all the minutiae of court life as well as all the big issues, and that would leave me no time for making the music that soothes everyone after they have dealt with those things. Besides,' he says as he opens the door to leave, 'Maddox already knows what I think on the matter.'

Heart closes the door behind him, and I finished my coffee, wondering to myself if Heart hadn't perhaps got it right. Look where getting involved in politics had gotten me: eating my breakfast alone while the person I most want to be with is spending time with someone else.

My fork is halfway to my mouth when there is a knock at the door. I consider the bacon and egg and wonder if I have time to eat it before answering it when the decision is taken from me. Pris sweeps in, her face like thunder. Following close on her heels is Dinian. So close, in fact, she almost shuts the door in his face.

'I thought I was escorting you to the council,' he tells Pris brightly, ignoring her slight.

'Wait for me outside, then,' Pris snaps back at him.

Dinian's only response is to grin more widely.

Pris glares at him, but he doesn't move, so she turns her back to him.

I place my fork back on my plate before taking a rueful look at the remains of my breakfast. I guess I'm not going to get to finish it. As if intent on aggravating Pris even more, Dinian moves to her side.

'Why are we here?' he asks.

Pris rolls her eyes as she answers, 'I'm here to discuss tactics with Snake before we meet with the King. Lord only knows why *you* are here.'

'We are a team,' Dinian says. 'Where you go, I go.'

This finally gets a rise from Pris. She turns on Dinian, hands on hips, and lets him have it. 'Snake and I are a team. Percival, Snake, and I are a team. My dragon and I are a team. You and I are....'

Okay, time to put a stop to this before Pris says something she'll regret later.

She doesn't have to be friends with Dinian, but our plans require us to keep him onside. I push my chair away from the table, stand up, then walk the couple of steps to Pris's side. Placing a hand on her arm, I lead her away from Dinian before she uses some of her advanced karate on him. Fortunately, Dinian has taken her words to heart and is staring out the window as if ignoring us.

When we are far enough away that Dinian cannot hear us, I whisper, 'What's up?'

Pris turns angry eyes on me, and slowly they soften. She takes a deep breath as if to calm herself before she answers, 'Nothing.' She rubs her hands over her face. 'Everything.'

I wrap my arms around her, and she leans into me.

'I'm tired of having a shadow. I'm tired of being relegated to the role of "princess," and I want to be with my friends—with you.'

I know what she means. Having her in my arms feels so right, and all the tensions of the last few days begin to melt away. I want to tell her how much I have missed her and how hard it has been seeing her with Dinian, but I don't. I don't want Pris dealing with my crap while she's so close to the edge, dealing with her own. Unfortunately, my body has other ideas, and I am no longer able to hide the effect her being this close is having on me. She raises her head and smiles.

Boy, do I wish we were alone so I could—*no, stop that.*

I lean in until my lips are close by her ear. 'It's only for a couple more days,' I whisper.

She tenses in my arms, and I realise I've said the wrong thing. Then again, I don't know what the right thing to say would be under the circumstances.

'It's all right for you,' she hisses. 'You get to spend time with your family and Percival while I'm primped and pampered and pimped out to the most irritating person I've ever met.' Her eyes flick to Dinian, and she shudders, emphasising her distaste.

'Elves can be rather supercilious creatures.' The words are out before my brain connects with my mouth. Then I follow up with strike number three. 'And you aren't too primped today.'

Like me, she is dressed in the clothes Susan's sister smuggled in, and she appears much like the Pris I met in London less than a month ago.

As she steps away from me, I know I'm going to pay for not connecting my brain before I spoke. I brace myself for an earful, but what I see in her eyes is pain, not anger. That changes my entire perspective. Hard though this not being together has been for me, I have had friends and family for support. She is doing this alone.

I touch my forehead to hers. 'I'm sorry. I'm an oaf. It's just… I don't know—'

'I miss you,' she whispers, hugging me closer.

My heart thuds in my chest, and I pull her closer and lean my cheek against hers, savouring the few moments we have together. 'I miss—'

'Although I am enjoying this little love fest, that sound a few minutes ago was the bell calling us to council,' Dinian says. From the tone of his voice, he appears pleased that Pris and my time together has been short—and chaperoned.

I press my lips to Pris's forehead, holding her to me a moment longer before reluctantly releasing her. With one last look at my barely touched breakfast, I take Pris's hand, and we follow Dinian to the court rooms.

Outside the doors to the room where the King holds court—I guess it's something like the throne room—we find Petunia, Euphemia, and Percival already waiting. From the music room, I hear Heart picking out something on the piano. How I wish I could miss this meeting and spend the rest of the morning playing with him.

Instead, we join the others, and Pris lets go of my hand. Dinian manoeuvres himself so he is between Pris and me. I lean around him to catch Pris's eye, but she is staring intently at the door, already getting into character for the meeting ahead.

The doors are thrown open, and a guard steps through to usher us in. Dinian holds out his arm, and Pris places her hand on it, then the two lead us inside. I smirk at what an odd couple they make right now—Dinian in his Regency finery and Pris in her jeans and jumper.

We enter as a group and bow to the King. He is sitting at a round table. How very King Arthurish! In Arthur's court the table was intended to signify that all voices were equal, but with the King flanked by Drow and Rimould on one side and Dinian and Pris taking the seats on the other, it is easy to see where the power lies here.

I slip in beside Drow, which places me almost opposite Pris. Percival sits beside me. Petunia sits beside Pris and takes her hand, offering her a smile of support before looking up and acknowledging me with a slight nod. I smile back, grateful Pris has the support of her grandmother. Euphemia is the last to take her seat, at the end of the table opposite the King.

Chancellor Rimould clears his throat. 'Now that we are all here, we can begin. We are here to decide whether or not King Maddox should grant the petitioners from the World Below their request to have him aid Queen Ariana.'

While his Chancellor speaks, King Maddox's eyes remain fixed on a point at the opposite side of the room. His face is grey, and his eyes are tired and

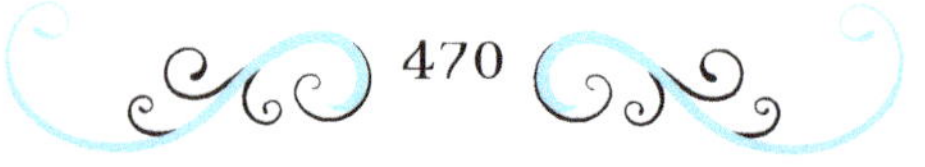

drawn, as if he's been up all night. If the time when Drow returned to our rooms is anything to go by, he was working for at least a good part of it.

When the Chancellor finishes speaking, King Maddox raises his head and scans the creatures seated around the table. 'After the discussions last night, I believe my duty to the sanctuary that is the Unseelie Court must remain paramount. Like the captain of a ship, I must defend what was entrusted to me, so I deny your petition.'

My head is ringing, and my hands form two tight balls.

Someone gasps, 'No.'

And all I can think is, he can't do this. Not only is he endangering his own people, but he is allowing magic to disappear from both worlds, and he is sentencing my mother to banishment.

Before I can voice my objections, Princess Petunia stands up. 'You stubborn old goat. You have allowed the bigots to scare you into inaction. And in all this time, you have not realised that the Unseelie Court is not a place, it's an ideal. It's where those of us who don't fit traditional society can band together. Your job as our leader is to fight for us and what we stand for, not to hide away and wait for things to blow over.' She speaks with passion and fury, and I couldn't have said it better myself.

King Maddox and Princess Petunia are locked in some staring contest, and my eyes move from one to another. The princess appears determined, and the King…. I'm not certain what he is. Princess Petunia's words appear to have rattled him, but I'm not sure he has it in him to rise to her battle cry.

It is the King who looks away first. 'I will not abandon my people.'

'Then at least let me send out a call for those who want to come and defend the court to join us,' Petunia counters.

King Maddox sighs. 'They will not arrive in time. Those who wish to may stay and help defend the court. Anyone who wishes to leave should do so as soon as possible.'

Pris leans around Dinian to plead with her uncle. 'Come with us and—' Pris starts.

King Maddox holds up his hand to stop her. 'No, Priscilla. I must see to my court first. When this current threat has been dealt with, then perhaps we can help with the problems in the World Below. Now, I have to prepare for the coming battle.' He turns to Rimould. 'You will see the announcement is spread?'

Rimould's face is as inscrutable as always. 'Of course, sire.'

I scan the faces around the table. This wasn't a council, as there was hardly any debate. It can't be over.

The King rises and exits the room. Every single eye follows him. When he is gone, Pris pushes her chair back and bangs her fist on the table as she glares at Drow and Remould. 'How can you two allow him to do this? He is sentencing this court to death and all but ensuring magic will die out in both our worlds.'

Dinian places a restraining hand on Pris's arm, and she turns her anger on him. 'Don't touch me!'

The elf appears unperturbed by her outburst. 'There is nothing you can say here that will change anything. You must petition the King again.'

If looks could kill, Dinian would be flayed alive.

'If you will excuse me,' Rimould stands, 'I must see if the King needs anything.'

'He needs something, all right,' Pris spits. 'A backbone.'

'Priscilla, enough.' Princess Petunia's tone is steely, but I detect a flicker of approval in her eyes.

Pris drops into her seat.

'Your anger will change nothing. We must now put all our effort into a plan B, as Percival would put it.' The princess turns her gaze to Dinian. 'Do you not have somewhere else to be?'

Ignoring the dismissal, Dinian says, 'No, I don't,' and leans back in his chair as if to emphasise his point.

Before anyone can eject him, the door opens, and Heart joins us. 'I have just been updated by Rimould. I've come to say my good-byes.'

'Good-byes?' I repeat as Heart joins us at the table.

'Yes, lad. I have hidden away here for too long. I will try to go home to my family in the World Below. I want to make sure they make it through the coming conflict, and I need to see what I can do for my daughter.'

It takes a moment for the enormity of Heart's words to sink in, then I find I'm too choked up to speak. Tears make their way down my cheeks, and I finally manage to say, 'You're going to try and help Mum?'

Heart drops his hand onto my shoulder. 'Yes, lad. It is about time I did something for her. Will you come with me?'

I glance over at Pris, trying to work out what is going on in her mind, but she is staring out the window, her thoughts elsewhere.

'I understand, lad. I have some packing to do. You still have an hour or so to make your decision before I leave.' He turns to go, but I tug at his sleeve. In a moment I am standing up and drawing him into a hug.

'Thank you,' I mumble into my grandfather's shoulder.

He pats my back. 'No, son, I should be thanking you for reminding me

I have a family and friends. And for helping me realise I have been in mourning for too long, and it is high time I returned to the land of the living.' He pats my back once more. 'We will do what we can if you feel you are needed here,' he says, then he is walking away.

'Wait up, Heart,' Drow says. 'I will come with you. There is little left for me to do now, and I fear that my family will need me if we are to free your daughter and Pris's parents while preventing Bernais from taking the throne.'

It's like we have all been held in suspension, waiting for the King's decision, and now that he's made up his mind, we can all act.

What will I do now that the King has stated he won't be going to the World Below with us? My eyes trail after my uncle and grandfather, torn between leaping up and going with them and wanting to stay with Pris.

Beside me, Percival rises to his feet. 'Well, Petunia, what is our plan B?'

'It seems I will have to return to the World Below and petition for my place as heir to be reinstated, after all. What about you, Effie?'

'I am tempted to come with you, but while we are under attack, my place is here, protecting the court and the creatures in Scotland. I will go back to the library and continue our search for something, anything, that might help shore up the court's defences. When it is time to fight, I will stand alongside King Maddox.'

'I will join you in the library, Effie—at least for a while, as I have very little in the way of possessions to pack,' Percival says. 'I have decided to journey to the Wyld Woods to help protect my family and to join those working to prevent Bernais from taking the throne.'

The sprite turns to Pris. 'Will you come with us, Pris?'

Pris drags her gaze back to the room and wipes a tear from her eye. 'No, Percival, I can't go. Much as I want to be there for my parents, I don't believe there will be a Word Below or an Unseelie Court unless the King works with the Queen to fix what is happening with magic. I'm afraid I have to stay.'

As I process Pris's words, my heart pounds in my ears, and I'm not sure whether it's because I feel her pain or because I'm disappointed—no, I'm angry—I'm completely gutted she made this decision without even talking it through with me first.

She stands up and rounds the table until she is beside me, then she speaks to me like there is no one else in the room. 'I'm sorry, Snake. I don't see any other option for me. I'd be no use in the World Below, and I still think there's a chance the King might be persuaded to change his mind.'

Her eyes show the depth of her pain and uncertainty but also her determination to do what she believes is right. She reaches out and touches my arm, begging me to understand, melting my heart as she does.

My insides feel like they're being pulled apart. My path is not as clear-cut as hers—this is not a political decision for me but a personal one. I want to do everything in my power to save my mother, but the thought of leaving Pris to face what is coming alone tears me up.

Percival joins us and takes hold of my hand. 'Stay with her, Snake. You know we will be doing what we can for your mother. She has family and friends working on her behalf. And Pris, well—she needs allies here. She needs you.'

I stare into Pris's eyes. They ask what she will not put into words. They plead with me not to leave her here alone.

'Okay, I'm staying for as long as Pris needs me.'

Somewhere in the background Dinian snarls, I'm sure he thought he was rid of me. I dismiss him from my mind. All I'm interested in is being here for Pris.

PREPARING FOR BATTLE

TEARS FLOW UNCHECKED down my cheeks as I hold Snake's gaze. It is like we are suspended in time, and I want to stay there with him forever, but the noise in the room soon comes back into focus, and reality takes over.

'Thank you,' I mouth, not trusting my voice.

He smiles, then reaches up to brush away my tears.

I want to say more. To tell him I understand what he's giving up to stay here with me. To explain to him that everyone else has a purpose now, and this is the only place I can be useful. All too soon, though, he is hustled away to the library with Percival and Euphemia, and the moment has passed.

Dinian mutters something under his breath. I'm too emotionally drained to take him on, so I ignore him and ask my grandmother, 'What do we do now?'

She doesn't answer. Instead she stands up and strides over to the door leading to the King's study. She knocks firmly, and the echo fills the room. The door opens a crack, and she speaks to someone—I assume it's Rimould, as I can't imagine King Maddox is in any state to do anything for himself.

Grandmother's footsteps clip-clop over the floor as she returns. 'Rimould has informed the King that we are waiting to speak with him, but he does not think the King will see anyone before the deadline.'

My head drops and my shoulders slump. Of course the King won't see us. I doubt even promising to marry Dinian here and now will change his mind. Is there anything that would alter that? Perhaps there is.

'Grandmother, how many people in the court would likely favour the King saving magic over the court?'

Her eyes widen with surprise. 'You're thinking of calling for a vote?'

I nod. 'I'm not—'

Dinian's chair scrapes back, then crashes to the floor. 'You cannot call for a vote. The King's word is absolute, and I will not let you do anything that might change that.'

I study the elf for a moment, wondering about his motivation. Of course he sees himself as leading the court one day, and he therefore wants to ensure his own power will be absolute… but there's clearly more to it.

'Perhaps you can worry about the future of the Unseelie Monarchy once we have ensured the court will live on after today,' I tell him, not bothering to hide my distaste. With King Maddox having made up his mind, I see no value in keeping up the charade.

The annoying elf is not cowed. A sly smile tugs his lips into a sneer before he quickly hides himself back behind the courtier's face he normally wears. 'I do not think I need to worry about that either way.'

What does he mean by that? I'm about to ask him when the doors crash open, and Snake rushes in. 'Pris, Princess Petunia, you need to come quick. Percival and Euphemia think they've found a way to save the court.'

The three of us start to follow Snake out of the room when I step in front of Dinian. My unease about his last comment is still fresh, and I decide he should sit this out. 'Sorry, Dinian, we need someone to stay here to find out if the King will see us and to come and collect us if he will.'

He stares at me, and I wonder if he senses that I don't trust him. 'What if I can help?'

'Then someone will come and get you,' Snake tells him.

'Please, Dinian.' I hope a little pleading will flatter his ego. 'We will only be gone a little while, and I'll fill you in when we get back.'

He huffs out a breath and says, 'All right, but if you are not back in an hour, I will come and get you. I'm not sitting here by myself all day.'

I beam a smile at him, hiding my dislike perfectly. 'Thank you.' I rush to catch up with the others before he changes his mind.

'I don't know how you can be so nice to him,' Snake says as we race up the stairs.

'Me neither.' We slow our pace as we approach the library, and I ask, 'Do you guys think Dinian would work against the King and the court?'

Grandmother stops in the middle of reaching for the door handle. 'Why do you ask that?'

'I don't know, it's just a feeling.'

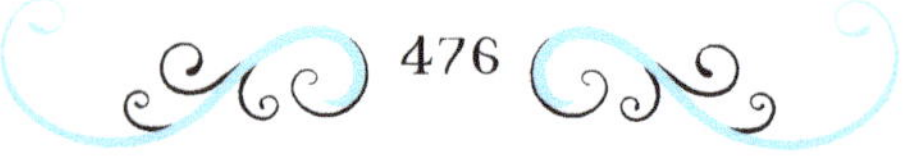

'Well, I don't trust the guy.' Snake manages to instill a whole heap of feelings in those few words.

'That may be jealousy talking, young man, but I know what you mean. While I don't think he would actively work against the court, he's certainly known for looking after number one at all costs,' my grandmother declares as she opens the door.

Once we are all seated around the large table in the library, Euphemia briefs us. 'We believe we have found a way to counter the magical attacks on the court, but we will have to act fast.'

'Effie,' Grandmother interrupts, 'slow down. Start at the beginning.'

Percival leans forward and butts in. 'I picked up a book yesterday which told how the Unseelie Court was built and managed. On our way to the library I was telling the others about it.'

'And he said the Kings of old used to place the court in stasis—in a sort of a protective bubble—when they departed on a royal tour.' Snake carried on. 'Everyone would leave the court except for the castle caretaking staff, and the building would be placed in stasis so it would not drain magic unnecessarily.'

'Cool,' I say.

Percival smiles. 'We talked about it and thought maybe putting the Unseelie Court in stasis might be an answer to our problem. The court would be safe, and King Maddox could concentrate on saving magic.'

Petunia leans in. 'I am sensing a "but".'

'There always is,' Euphemia laughs. 'The spell requires a lot of magic. Magic has been waning since the times of the blight, and this spell was last done centuries ago, when magic was in abundance. Also, it has only ever been done to Urquhart Castle.'

Percival points at the page of the book in front of him. 'It takes an elf, a gnome, and a witch to join magic and cast the spell of protection.'

I stare at the sprite, sensing there is a problem but not seeing what it is. 'We have enough of those types of creatures to do that. In fact there's enough of them here that we could have two or three of each combining their magic—if that's a thing.'

'It is a thing, but that is not our problem. We need to find somewhere that has enough magic for the spell,' Percival says.

Okay, now this is more like it—some action we can take to get things sorted. 'I take it there isn't enough in Inverness?'

He shakes his head. 'There are very few places in the World Above or Below that would have the amount of magic we are talking about.'

'Okay, you need Snake and me to find the magic? We'll do it, won't we, Snake?'

It's Euphemia's turn to shake her head, and Percival leans over and takes my hand. 'No, Pris, we need Snake and Petunia to go. Your job is still to stay here and convince King Maddox that we can protect his court and get him to leave with you before the castle is placed in stasis.'

I stare at him, not sure I've heard him correctly. I look at Snake. 'You don't want me to come?'

He sounds torn when he says, 'Of course I want you to come, but you're also needed here.'

Percival squeezes my hand. 'Apart from ensuring the King leaves before the court is sent into stasis, we still need some creatures with strong magic to stay and shore up the wards.'

'What happens to the court when it goes into stasis? Will the people left behind be able to carry on as normal?' I ask.

'From what we can tell, it will be like in the story of *Sleeping Beauty* when the court sleeps—'

'Or like cryogenics,' Snake expands on Euphemia's explanation.

'So we really don't want to be here when that happens,' I say.

Percival nods. 'The risk of staying is twofold. If the barriers fall before we can put the court to sleep, then anyone who remains will be at risk. Because of that, we have suggested all vulnerable creatures leave before the deadline tonight.'

'The other risk is to those who are caught in the stasis spell. They will not be released from suspended animation until the spell is reversed,' Euphemia finishes.

'And what will happen if magic disappears completely?'

I think I already know the answer, but I have to ask anyway.

'They are as good as dead,' Percival tells us.

I don't want to dwell on that thought for too long. 'Will the creatures who need to leave be able to get away in time?'

Euphemia's face breaks into a grin. 'Many of them have already left the Unseelie Court and are blending in with the people of Inverness. I believe they have a few surprises up their sleeves for our attackers.'

We sit there in silence, and I know they are all waiting for me to support this plan.

My fingers twist into knots, an external visual of what is happening to my stomach. 'I can't do this,' I tell them. 'I can't be the one who is responsible for getting King Maddox out.'

It's Petunia's turn to take my hand. 'You can, you know. You are the last hope for the Unseelie Court to be saved and keep the balance in our two worlds.'

All the fears that plagued me when using my magic in the minotaur's maze return in a rush. 'We're doomed if I'm the one you're all relying on.'

'You won't be alone. You will have Am'ratha and Ed'ruven to feed what magic they can. And they will be there to help you escape,' my grandmother tells me.

'Ed'ruven?' Snake asks.

'King Maddox's dragon,' she tells him.

'What about Ed'rathe?'

Euphemia answers. 'Am'ralla, Petunia's bonded one, and Ed'rathe will be needed to transport us to the source of magic we are to use to cast the spell.'

I don't know why, but I blurt out, 'Dinian is going to be so pissed that Snake's riding a dragon.'

There's a moment of silence before everyone laughs, and the tension in the air dissipates. I check around the room and see that we appear to have consensus on a way forward. 'I guess this is our plan B, then?'

Those around the table nod their agreement.

Percival catches my eye. 'Pris, a lot of responsibility rests on your shoulders. Once the court starts going into stasis, you will have only moments to get out. If King Maddox does not come with you, he will play no further part in this conflict.'

I try to make light of it. 'So, no pressure then.'

'Yes,' he says, straight-faced, 'there is pressure.'

I smile at him. 'I know, Percival.'

'Ah, sarcasm.'

I nod, and he smiles.

'The only thing I worry about is, how will King Maddox and I know when to leave?'

Petunia answers, her lips curving in a wistful smile. 'We can communicate via the dragons, just like the leaders of old did.'

The room falls silent for a moment, then I realise there is something we've forgotten. 'Who's going to inform King Maddox of our plan?'

ESCAPE INTO MUSIC has always been my refuge, and I find it calms me today as all around me is in chaos. When I walk to the music room, I feel a little guilty—I should be preparing to leave like everyone else. Well, almost everyone. This time Pris will be staying, or more accurately, I will be leaving her behind.

The guitar is my go-to instrument, but today the piano is calling. I warm up with a couple of scales before starting Ludovico Einaudi's 'Walk.' I'm a little rusty, but soon I'm lost in the flow of the music.

I sense Pris enter. She hovers in the doorway, listening until I finish playing. As the last notes linger in the air, she joins me on the piano bench.

'That was beautiful.'

'I'm not a pianist, but some pieces of music are just made for the piano.'

She leans her head on my shoulder. 'I've missed your music—and you.'

I lean my head against hers. 'Stay a while, then.'

She draws in a breath, and I know this will only be a stolen moment.

'Let me guess, you have to rush back to the King and Dinian.' I try to say the words in an even tone, but my hurt leaks out.

Pris places a hand on my thigh. 'Please don't be angry with me, I can't bear it. It is difficult enough not being able to spend time with you, but being forced into Dinian's company makes it all the harder.'

I place a hand over hers. 'I'm sorry. I've missed you too, and it's driven me a little crazy.'

I attempt a smile when I find that her face reflected in the dark wood of the piano is serious—almost haunted.

'King Maddox is still waiting for an answer about Dinian. For a while during the council, I thought I'd been let off the hook, but now we still need the King onside, and….' She sighs. 'And while I put off talking to him about it, Dinian is behaving like we're already betrothed. I feel like the two of them are herding me like a couple of sheep dogs.'

I knew the charade had been hard on her, I hadn't realised how hard. My heart aches for her, and I feel… sad. I don't know what to say to make things better. 'Have I lost you?' It's all I can come up with.

'To Dinian?' Pris scoffs. 'Hardly.'

I'm not ready to laugh yet. Her relationship with Dinian is not my main concern. 'I'm more worried that I may have lost you to the duties you'll be compelled to fulfil as part of the royal line,' I admit quietly, hating the fact that Drow has managed to get under my skin.

She slides her arm around me. 'You will never lose me to that. I just have to find a way to get out of this without alienating King Maddox. We can worry about what the Seelie Court expects from me later.'

In an uncharacteristically fluid movement, I stand up with her in my arms as the piano stool scrapes across the floor. I'm not gentle when my lips find hers as all the pent-up emotions of the last couple of days break through the wall I built around them. I slip one of my hands down her back and rest it on the curve of her hip, pulling her close to me.

A moan escapes her lips as her fingers entwine in my hair, and she pulls me closer. My world shrinks to the feel of her body against mine and the heat and need that is threatening to overwhelm me. There are too many clothes between us. I slip my hand beneath her T-shirt and the feel of her smooth skin sends another wave of desire through me.

I raise my head to suggest we find somewhere more comfortable, but it's as if that move in itself breaks the spell. As her fingers trail down my face, her eyes catch mine, and mixed with the smoke of her desire is regret.

'You didn't come here for this.' My voice is husky, and I struggle to control it—and myself.

Her lips curl into a wicked smile. 'Well, no, not exactly, but I can't say I'm disappointed.' She pulls my head down, and this time her kiss is sweet and teasing.

'Pris,' I groan, 'if you don't stop….'

She smiles wistfully. 'I don't want to stop… but we have to. We both have things to do.'

I take a half step back. With her body moulded to mine, the blood my brain needs to function is in the wrong place. It takes a minute for my body to settle and my head to kick into action.

'Don't we always?' I ask.

'Yes, only this time there is a battle looming, and goodness knows what we will find when we return to the World Below'.

I entwine my fingers with hers. 'I wish we were able to face this together.'

Pris gives my hand a squeeze. 'Me too, but at least with you gone, Dinian will stop trying to one-up you.'

'And you being with Dinian will keep King Maddox happy.'

Her laugh is deep and throaty. 'No, me agreeing to marry him would make King Maddox happy, but at least he will be distracted by what is coming.'

I pull her to me, but she resists. 'Snake, we can't.'

'Because someone might see?'

She shakes her head. 'No—well, yes, but that isn't what I was thinking of. Petunia and Euphemia are explaining our plan to King Maddox. When they are done, you and Percival will be leaving with them.'

'I could stay, you know. Drow or Heart could be the gnome.'

'Euphemia says Heart's magic hasn't been the same since he lost his wife. Besides, Drow and Heart have already left.'

'So soon?' I ask, surprised at how disappointed I am that I didn't get a chance to say good-bye.

Pris leans in and hugs me. 'They left a letter with Percival for you, but they couldn't wait. The guards are closing off the doors any minute now.'

A door bangs in the corridor, followed by the sound of two familiar voices.

'That's it,' I say. 'Time to leave.'

Pris hugs me tight. 'Percival said to tell you your questing clothes are clean and in your room.'

I don't want to let Pris go, and I hold her for a moment longer before pulling away.

'I don't want to leave you.' I lean forward and brush my lips against hers. 'But this is only good-bye for now. We will hurry back and meet you in the World Below.' I kiss her once more, and it's a kiss full of the promise of things to come.

I walk away without looking back, because I know if I do, I will not have the strength to leave.

LADY SUSAN LEADS us out of the castle through an underground passage. It is dank, and wet, and it smells like a disused sewer system. Footsteps echo off the walls, interspersed with sloshing water and an almost constant scratching.

Something runs over my foot. I sweep my torch downwards and up again quickly. Our pathway is scattered with rats. Not the harmless rats found at home in the Wyld Woods, but mean and hungry rats that look as though they would eat you alive given half a chance.

Finally we reach a ladder that Lady Susan says opens into an alleyway not far from the castle. She climbs up first, and once she's checked there is no one around, she motions for us to join her. As Effie spells the stench and sewerage off our clothes, Lady Susan starts back down the ladder.

'You're leaving us here?' I ask.

She nods. 'I let Pris down once before. This time I will stay with her. Besides, this is my home. No one is going to chase me from it.'

'But you risk getting held in stasis,' I say.

She shrugs. 'Perhaps, or perhaps we might get enough of a warning to get out. Now go, the lot of you, before someone realises you're here.'

The manhole cover clangs as she drops it back into place, startling us enough that we move towards the alley opening. We are just about to step into the street when Snake motions us back into the shadows.

'There are an awful lot of lesser creatures around—more of them than normal.' It is the voice of Grossman Green. 'Do you think some of them may be getting out from the castle?'

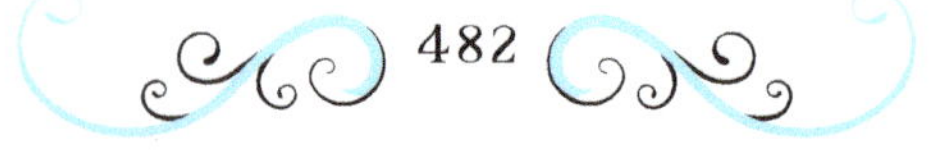

Whoever he is talking to answers, 'They can't be. We have all the exits covered. No one is getting out.'

'I am not so sure…,' Green starts to say, then trails off as if he has become distracted.

'Perhaps they are lesser creatures come to help defend the castle from the outside. They will make little difference in the long-run.'

'Say, where has Bernais disappeared to? Wasn't he supposed to join us? We will need his magic if we are to drive the Unseelie from their court once and for all.'

'Never you mind. Just keep an eye on your part of the plan.'

Once the creatures have passed by us, Snake leads our small group back onto the road and round some back streets. The plan is to walk to where Petunia has asked the dragons to wait.

'Hey, look!' The call comes from behind us.

'Go!' Snake hisses.

I glance over my shoulder.

Grossman Green is less than a block away, pointing at our retreating backs. 'I told you they were getting out somehow. After them,' the goblin says over the sound of running feet.

We speed up and make it to a busy main road before our pursuers almost catch us up. Petunia waves down a taxi, and we all pile in. As Petunia reels off the address, the taxi door locks just as Grossman Green grabs for the door handle. The goblin bangs the window with his fist as the taxi takes off.

'Would you believe the nerve of some people?' the driver says. 'Think they own the world, they do.'

The taxi pulls into traffic, and the driver checks his rearview mirror. 'They'll have a bit of a wait for another ride this time of day. You all going to some fancy-dress thing?' he asks as he moves through the traffic.

I frown. Snake, Petunia, and Euphemia are in trousers, shirts, and jackets, and I am in my normal black trousers and jumper. I think we look pretty normal, but apparently not.

'Sort of,' Snake tells him. 'We are going to a Dungeons and Dragons party.'

The taxi driver nods as if this is normal. Moments later he turns into an industrial estate and pulls over.

'Are you sure it's here?' he asks doubtfully, scanning the deserted street.

'Yes, this is perfect, thank you.' Petunia pulls out some cash and pays the driver.

I am surprised as I catch a glimpse of the bundle of human money she has stuffed into her inner coat pocket. She catches my eye. 'Just in case,' she whispers. 'You never know when you might need a little ready cash.'

'Have you not heard of banks and plastic cards?' I ask as we get out of the car.

'Of course.' Her tone is haughty. 'However, if I want a little something while I'm at court, I need cash.'

We make our way between the industrial units to a field behind them. Once the taxi is gone, there is a rush of wind, and the dragons land.

Hurry, Ed'rathe says. *We cannot hold the invisibility spell for long, there is not enough magic here.*

Snake climbs up onto his back, then gives me a hand up to sit in front of him.

'I will feel better with you where I can see you,' he chuckles, no doubt referring to my fall last time we travelled by dragon.

I want to answer back with a snarky comment, but I am not looking forward to riding a dragon again, and I do feel much safer with Snake in behind me.

As we take off after Petunia's dragon, Am'ralla, my stomach lurches, and I grab hold of one of Ed'rathe's scales.

Flying high above Inverness, Petunia asks the dragons to do a loop of the city. From our vantage point above, we spot a number of creatures gathered in groups at what they believe to be all the castle entrances. A shimmer of magic pulses over and around each group. There are a lot of them, but not as many as I had imagined. Perhaps the rebellion is not as widespread as we first thought.

I am also able to make out lesser creatures setting up wards and traps around the castle. Inverness Castle itself shimmers as the creatures still inside weave their own wards of protection.

'I hope they can hold out for long enough,' I say.

The word is out, and any creature nearby who is true to the court is coming to help.

I hope they get there in time, Ed'rathe rumbles.

'Where are we heading?' Snake asks as the dragons climb and swing away from Inverness.

'The Isle of Skye,' Percival says.

'That's where we're going to find a store of magic?'

'Of course. The Old Man of Storr should have all the magic we need to work the spell.'

I lean back into Snake and try not to let my terror at the speed we are travelling and the height we are flying turn me into a total wreck.

SAVING THE UNSEELIE COURT

I MUST HAVE dozed off, as I awake to Snake prodding me gently in the ribs.

'We're here,' he says, his voice close by my ear.

From the position of the sun, I think it is midafternoon-ish, and we are flying over the Skye bridge. The dragons land near the rocky pinnacle that towers high over the west of the island. There are a smattering of tourists on the path, so they use the magic that shrouds them to make it appear like we are walking out from a patch of mist.

As we walk, Effie says, 'Legend has it that the Old Man of Storr was a giant who lived on Trotternish Ridge. When he was buried, they could not cover his thumb. This small part of the giant still juts out of the ground, creating the famous jagged landscape.'

Snake smirks. 'But you're going to tell us that the legend is actually true.'

'Young man, I don't like your tone of voice,' Petunia tells him, and when Snake blanches, she winks. 'But you are right, of course. It is more than a legend dreamt up to bring tourism to the area. One of the ancient giants is sleeping here and has done so for many years, ever since magic in the World Above dropped below the levels needed to sustain such an enormous magical creature.'

'What they got wrong, though,' Effie butts in, 'is that the giant is a woman, not a man. And as she sleeps, she gathers magic into a power stone in case of great need.'

'Cool,' Snake says, then his brows draw into a frown. 'If she's been building the magic for perhaps hundreds of years, do you think she's going to give her magic to us without a fight?'

'Well,' Effie says, 'I am sure if we ask in the right way, she will. We simply find a way to explain that this is a time of dire need.'

Now Snake's eyebrows go in the opposite direction, and his voice drops with sarcasm. 'Of course she will, because everything since I got caught up in this crazy mess has gone to plan.'

I turn to tell Snake to stop being so negative, but I swallow my words when I see a tightness around his eyes and mouth. He puts on a good front, but these last few weeks have taken a toll on him. I am sure he is worried about Pris, about what will happen to her if this does not work, as well as his own role in casting this spell.

'She will be all right,' I try to reassure him. 'King Maddox's magic is strong, and she has Am'ratha with her.'

He forces a smile, perhaps acknowledging my effort at support. 'I know, but—'

'But you will not be there to make sure?'

He nods. 'And she doesn't have full control of her magic yet. So I'm not sure how much she will be able to do.'

'Then we need to be successful here,' Petunia says brusquely.

Sometimes when Petunia cuts straight to the point, she can be abrasive, but today I welcome her certainty.

Effie leads us away from the main body of tourists, and we three make a barrier so no one can see what she is doing.

Snake leans down and whispers, 'Percival, how are we supposed to get to the magic?'

Surely he heard our plan, then again perhaps not. We did a lot of fine tuning while he went to get Pris. 'A simple exposure spell should reveal the power source.'

'It can't be that simple, can it?' he asks.

I straighten my spine, pulling on the role of advisor, and I have so often had to with him. 'No, it is not. The real trick is convincing the giant to let us access the magic she has tended for hundreds of years.'

'Do we have a spell for that?'

I snort. *Where does he get these ideas from?* 'I believe we should leave that bit to Effie, as she is more experienced in talking to a wide range of magical creatures.'

Snake stares at me, as if he does not believe what I am saying. 'So you're telling me this whole plan relies on Euphemia convincing the giant to give us her magic?'

I nod.

Beside me Snake mutters, 'If I had known how flimsy our plan was, I would never have left Pris alone to face the upcoming battle.'

Too late now, I think as Effie begins to chant the reveal spell to open the earth and expose the stone containing the giant's magic. As the music increases in intensity, the tingle of magic fills the air, and the ground beneath our feet shivers.

'It is done,' she says, and we turn as one. It will take all of us to lift the stone into the open.

Finding a grip on the stone is difficult. It's not just that the stone is relatively smooth, but it is also dirt-encrusted and slimy. Once we all have a hold of part of the stone, we heave. Nothing.

'How about if we all push from one side,' Snake says, 'you know, laws of physics and all that.'

We all move to one side and crowd together, and push. It doesn't budge an inch. We try again, giving it all we have, but it will not move. Euphemia tries another release spell, but the giant will not let go of her treasure.

Petunia's eyes glaze over as she asks her dragon for help. 'Am'ralla says there are too many people around for them to come. Hold on, the Queen of Dragons wants me.'

Closing her eyes, Petunia speaks with the Queen. Minutes later she sighs and opens them. 'It seems the dragons and the giants have a pact. Neither the dragons nor the giants will interfere in one another's business. If we want to use the stone, we must retrieve it ourselves.'

'Of course,' Snake mutters, 'and for our next trick, we'll find the needle in a haystack.'

His shoulders are hunched, and he stares despairingly out to sea. My poor young friend is losing heart. That is a worry because this is only the beginning of what we must face if we are going to ensure creatures remain free and equal in the World Below.

I for one am not prepared to give up. Too much rests on us saving the courts, not the least of which is my future. For the first time in hundreds of years, I now believe I have one, and I will not let it go that easily.

I make my way to his side and pat his arm. 'Come, Snake, we must continue fighting.'

'Why?' he asks, his voice bleak.

I wish I could tell him it is because if we carry on challenging the Baaronsons and their people, life will get better. He is my friend, and I cannot lie to him. 'Because the alternative is too horrendous to contemplate.'

Snake laughs, and some of the tension leaves his shoulders. 'Not much of a pep talk, Percival.'

It may not be, but it has worked. Snake turns back to the stone, and I ask, 'What now, Effie?'

The witch turns and walks towards the outstretched fingers of the giant's hand, then places her palm on the rock before pressing her forehead against the stone. We all go silent.

'Come, sister, do not guard your secret so well. There is unrest here in the world of humans, and magic is waning. It is time to use what you have stored to benefit the two realms you used to protect.'

It is mine and it keeps me warm while I slumber. It is so cold here, sister, and I am so lonely. Come lie with me.

The last sentence has some compulsion behind it, and I find myself considering how I might lie down with the giant. Fortunately Effie appears not to be affected.

'I cannot, sister. And you need rest for only a little while longer. Soon your work will be done and you will find peace with your kinfolk.'

'What does she mean?' Snake asks.

'If what Effie believes is correct, once we take the magic she has stored, she will no longer have a purpose and will join her kin in their own realm.'

Nothing happens for a moment, then the ground appears to roll like waves in the sea, and the stone is free. At the same time, a group of tourists rounds the headland.

'Hey, what are you doing? Anna, something's not right here—where's your phone?'

A woman stops and stares open-mouthed while she fumbles in her backpack. I cannot help with the spell, but I can help with this. I walk towards the group as my companions move into position around the stone.

'There is nothing to see here,' I tell them. 'We are just carrying out some routine maintenance.' I put some glamour behind the words, reinforcing the idea that there is nothing unusual going on.

'Bobby,' the girl named Anna says, 'you had me worried. It's just maintenance workers.'

A frown furrows Bobby's brow. He has seen more, so the magic is taking a little longer to work on him.

'You were having a little bit of a joke,' I suggest to him. 'Now you want to return and find somewhere to warm up.

His face clears. 'Don't get huffy, Anna, I was just mucking around. Come on, we've seen the stones. Let's go and have a pint somewhere warm.'

The group heads back the way they came, and I stay on the path, ready to deter anyone wanting a closer look at the Giant of Storr. I half turn so I can watch both the path and my companions. The three greater creatures are

holding hands in a circle around the stone. Another tingle of magic reaches me, pricking my skin, telling me they are ready to begin casting.

MY MOTHER OFTEN talked of spells worked with the power of three. I've never seen a spell cast this way because in the World Above, we try to keep magic hidden from mortals. Humans are able to explain away small magical feats as tricks—they do it every day.

However, magic on a large scale would be difficult to ignore. Not just because three chanting creatures would make a spectacle but because magic on this scale would have an impact on the physical world. The world would be drained of magic and would soon show signs of decay.

As I take the hands of a royal princess and the Witch Protector of the north, the enormity of what I'm about to do hits me. I can't believe I'm about to cast a major spell with two of the most notorious creatures of our time. Me, the gnome who tried to stay hidden most of his life, to blend in, to not cause ripples.

I breathe in through my nose and out through my mouth, attempting to calm the panic rising from my gut. If this is to work, I need to focus on saving Pris and the Unseelie Court. I push away my awe of working with these two women and just concentrate on the magic pulsing from the stone, tasting the feel of it and steeling myself not to recoil from its intensity.

Euphemia squeezes my hand, and I turn my attention to her. 'All right, listen carefully to the words of the spell. You need to memorise them.'

'What we need is to get a move on, or there will be no court left for us to save,' Princess Petunia says dourly. She reminds me so much of Pris, my heart aches.

'Hush, this will take as long as it takes. Now listen:
Out of time, it doth reside,
In dire peril, heart and mind.
To save it all, the court must hide,
One point in time must we bind.'

I repeat the words in my mind, my experience learning song lyrics no doubt helping me memorise them quickly. I nod when I'm ready. Princess Petunia is still mumbling, but a minute or two later, she tells us, 'I am good.'

'We must repeat this out loud while holding the court in our minds.'

'Sounds easy enough,' I say.

Euphemia shakes her head. 'Not so easy. We must sing it to this tune to use the stone's power as well as the magic around us.' She hums something that sounds a little like 'Greensleeves.'

I can't help the grin that splits my face. Finally something is going my way. This will be much easier than parroting the words.

Princess Petunia tugs at my hand. 'It is nothing to smirk about, Snake. This is a serious business.'

'But it's "Greensleeves,"' I say, stupidly pleased.

Her frown softens, and she smiles slowly. 'I believe it is. Well, that will make things easier.'

'Are you two ready?' Euphemia asks.

Princess Petunia says, 'Yes,' but I ask, 'How long will we need to sing—I mean, how will we know if the spell has worked?'

Princess Petunia smiles again. 'The dragons are communicating. Am'ratha is circling Inverness. If the spell works, the magical light of the Unseelie Court will begin to dim to a blue glow. This is the sign for her and Ed'ruven to fly Pris and King Maddox out of the castle. Once they are free, or when the court is fully in stasis, she will tell us we can stop.'

The princess's words have a sobering effect. Pris could well be stuck in the court should things not go to plan. I suck in a deep breath in an attempt to calm my nerves, then slowly let it out.

'Are you ready?' Euphemia asks again.

'As ready as I'll ever be.' I draw in a breath, filling my lungs in readiness for a long singing session.

'Right, prepare yourselves. Draw on a little magic, and let us begin.'

We link hands and draw on magic. My hands tingle, and I almost fall to my knees when the magic the others are drawing rushes through me. Combining the power of three intensifies the levels, and I am vibrating to my very core. It is all I can do to hold myself together and maintain the circle.

'Snake, concentrate. Do not lose yourself to the flow, or this will never work.'

Petunia's tart tones act as a beacon grounding me. I focus on her, and it helps me find my sense of self in amongst the magic.

Euphemia starts singing the spell, and we join in. I hold Pris and the Unseelie Court in my mind while also trying to keep myself whole as the magic intensifies to a whole new level.

As the magic increases, I can sense every individual molecule in my body, and it feels like they are unbinding. I struggle to maintain my chanting while channeling the magic and keeping myself whole. I miss a word, then I hear Ed'rathe in my head.

You are almost there, Snake. Don't let go!

I hear his words and wonder who Snake is. Am I Snake? Yes, I am Snake.

It is as simple and as difficult as keeping that name in my head while I work the spell.

Well done, my friend. I would hate to lose you as my creature just when I am getting used to you.

Ed'rathe's my dragon. The thought sneaks into my mind as I repeat the spell. I'm not going to be able to keep this up for much longer. All my worry is for nothing because at that moment, Euphemia's hand slips from mine, and the circle is broken. I stumble to my knees and lean forward onto my hands, panting, trying to draw breath.

Did we do it? I ask Ed'rathe as the stone swims before my eyes. Then the world goes black.

I STUDY THE sprites and hearth elves outside the window of the court audience chamber as they shore up the wards around the castle. Apparently they're laying a few nasty little traps. King Maddox paces behind me, muttering under his breath. Dinian is slouched over a chair, reading a book, completely disengaged.

'Shouldn't we be doing something?' I ask, running my sweaty hands down my trousers. I changed into my questing clothes to be ready for action, and here I am, twiddling my thumbs, waiting while others work.

King Maddox stops. 'We are to stay here and stay safe, for the court is as much about us as it is about the place.'

'What a waste of our skills,' I say.

My uncle studies me, a quizzical expression on his face. He's trying to work out if I'm being serious. This is confirmed when he speaks, his voice taking on a lecturing tone.

'No, we are preserving our magic. We are the last line of defence. When everyone else has fallen, it is up to us to protect them and escort them to safety.'

'Oh.' Not a great comeback. Then again, I'd thought King Maddox was hiding out here, making like nothing was wrong, so I'm thrown a little off balance by his explanation.

'Only problem is, I don't know how to use my magic well enough to do that.' Deep down I'm embarrassed to admit this, but I hold my head high— after all, it isn't my fault I never learned.

King Maddox stares at me, almost as if he is seeing me for the first time. He sighs as if all of this is too much for him. Or perhaps it's me who is adding to his burden. 'Of course not knowing about us would mean you did not grow up with magic. You will be of little use to us now.'

I close my eyes and absorb this blow. I am sick of creatures dismissing me because I know nothing about their world or because I can't use my magic. I want to scream, 'It's not my fault! You were all part of the conspiracy that kept me from my heritage.' The only thing that stops me is that we have bigger things to worry about.

My uncle resumes his pacing just as the door to the chamber opens, admitting Susan. I still can't call her Lady. Then again, I can't get my head around my being a princess either.

She bobs a curtsey. 'They made it out, Your Majesty.'

'Excellent,' King Maddox says and continues pacing. 'Now we must wait.'

Susan starts walking backwards out of the room.

'Wait,' I say. 'What are you and the others doing now?'

'We are strengthening the internal wards. It should help with staving off the attack, but we also need strong wards to protect the court in case it's in stasis for months rather than days.'

'Oh. I'm not sure my magical abilities are quite at that level yet.'

'It is not difficult. I can teach you. You're a quick learner, and you come from two lines of powerful elves. And if you can't master the technique, I can use your magic to bolster mine.'

'She is needed here,' King Maddox says.

Why is he being so difficult? It makes me all the more determined to go with Susan.

'You won't need me until the attack begins. I will return as soon as it starts.'

He flicks his hand in a shooing motion. 'Go. Perhaps you will be of some use in defending the castle after all.'

The anger I have been keeping under control while we waited threatens to bubble up and overflow. I half turn, ready to give him a piece of my mind, to remind him it is not my fault I was kept from my true heritage. The only thing that stops me is Susan. She places a hand on my arm and shakes her head. I follow her out of the room, and as the guard shuts the door, she says, 'He is worried for his court and his people.'

'I know, but that doesn't excuse how mean he's being,' I tell her.

Susan's smile is sad. 'It is not you he is mad at, it's your father. Family is everything to King Maddox, and it broke his heart when your father stayed in the World Below with your mother. He visited, of course, but it was not enough. King Maddox made the court his family, and now he's worried he will fail us.'

'If he had helped Queen Ariana sooner—'

I stop mid-sentence. If my uncle had helped sooner, would the attack on his court never have happened? I was no longer quite so certain about that. Bernais and his cronies were too well-organised, and they had quite a following. They and their creature purist cronies must have been planning the overthrow of the two courts for some time. Queen Ariana's absence is merely a convenient opportunity for them to launch their attack.

'So, how do we do this?' I ask, changing the subject.

She leads me through the hallways and shows me how to look for weaknesses in the spell weaves—it's kinda like blurring your eyes, and anything that's clear holds a weakness. It's a slow process, and I find my mind drifting. Then I see it. I see the molecules moving and how Susan pulls the rents together and adding more molecules to strengthen it, sort of like darning.

She draws so little on my magic as she works that I'm sure she asked me along just to give me something to do, and my heart thaws a little more towards her.

'King Maddox sent me to care for you when you were little. He went a little mad when the love of his life died. Then your father went missing, and he called me back with a message spell. It was only when I arrived back here that I realised he had meant me to bring you too. By that time, you had disappeared.'

'But the lasagna? You knew you were going?'

'No, I was meant to be out that night at a birthday party with a friend.'

Steeped in the memories of that night, it suddenly strikes me. 'You're friends with Giles Regis's daughter?'

'Yes, Verona and I've been friends since we were children.'

'But you're—'

'Older? Only by a few years, which is no time at all in our lifespan.'

'I meant—'

'That I'm a gnome? That has never mattered to Verona, and in the World Above, her father has had to accept my presence, although there has always been an underlying hostility.'

'And now—'

'Giles Regis and I find ourselves on different sides. Verona's and my friendship will not stop me from giving that creature exactly what he deserves should he and I come face to face.'

Susan stops what she is doing and studies me. 'Are you ready to try now?'

'I… How did you know?'

'I have watched you learn things over the years. You get a certain look when something clicks with you.'

I find the next patch and give it a go. I stare at the ward, going almost a little cross-eyed, until I can see the particles that make up the shield and the extra particles floating around in the air. I will the stray particles to fill in the gaps. They wrangle with me a little, but eventually I will them into place.

The end result is not as tidy as Susan's, and I expect her to smooth it over for me, but she smiles and says, 'That'll do.'

My heart is lighter, and we work through the corridors, mending as we go, and I am soon working as quickly and neatly as Susan. Not long after, the light above us blinks out, and the ward I'm working on trembles.

Susan covers my hand with hers. 'The battle has begun. You must return to the King now.'

I don't move, reluctant to leave the fighting to others. 'So I can hide away during the battle?'

'No. I told you, he wants to protect us. Also, I shouldn't tell you this, but he holds the thread that keeps the court out of time. He will need your strength to keep it there.'

'He has Dinian. Let me stay and fight with you.'

'That elf is no better than he should be and will be very little use.' Susan places her hands on my shoulders and pushes me back towards the audience chamber. 'Go, help your uncle. Whatever you may feel about him, he is very important to all of us—he literally holds the wellbeing of my world in his hands.'

I do as my old nanny requests, her words ringing in my ears. My uncle could not be all bad if someone like Susan respects him.

THE BATTLE IS WON

BY THE TIME I reach the audience chamber, I feel like I'm wading through a balloon being collapsed from the outside. The air is thick, and it's difficult to breathe or move. Having focused so intently on the wards to strengthen them, I can almost see them bend under the external pressure, then move inwards.

When I enter the room, I find Dinian still slouching in the chair, reading. I storm over to him and grab the book from his hand.

'We're under attack in case you haven't noticed,' I snap. 'Why aren't you doing something to help?'

He raises an eyebrow. 'I am holding myself in reserve. If the King fails, it is my job as heir to take over.'

I follow his gaze as he checks on King Maddox. Framed by the window, his forehead leaning against the glass, he appears to be watching the activity below. On a closer inspection, the lines of strain around his eyes stand out— eyes so very like my father's.

I stride over to him and place a hand on his arm. 'Use my power.'

He turns his head towards me, his eyes two pools of sadness. 'No, girl, this is my duty.'

'And you are to be my wife, so you should wait and share your power with me when the King is depleted,' Dinian says from behind me.

Does he sound almost gleeful at the prospect of the King collapsing? What am I missing here? Is he hoping the King will die in his attempt to keep his court and people safe? Does he want to be King that much?

I throw Dinian a disdainful look, drawing my lips back in a sneer. 'I'm not your wife yet, and if I have any say in the matter, I never will be.'

I move closer to my uncle. 'King Maddox, Uncle, take my power. Your people need this place to stay where it is, and you need to keep it here for them.'

The plea on behalf of his people works. King Maddox reaches out and clasps my hand. His palm tingles as it touches mine, followed by a gentle tug. I almost swoon as my blood sings in response to his call. I'm locked in place by the spell, but it is working. The tension around the King's mouth lessens, and I sense the palace stabilising as the wards repulse the worst of the attack.

'I do not think I can hold this for much longer,' King Maddox whispers. 'Your power is helping, but they are strong.'

'So are you and your people,' I tell him. 'And don't forget, we don't have to hold this forever—just long enough for the others to cast their spell.'

While my words bolster the King, my own fears grow as the edges of the magic holding the court out of time begin to fray. At the same time, something else tugs at my senses. It is like a slow, warm wind heading towards me.

Crash. I jump as the window beside us caves in. Is this it? The end of the court?

A dragon nose appears. *Come, help the King onto my back*, Ed'ruven says. I lead my uncle to the opening, and, after making sure no sharp edges will cut him, he hauls himself out and slides onto his dragon's back.

In a moment Am'ratha takes his place. *Your turn.*

I move to slide across her neck, but I'm tugged back into the room.

Dinian holds my wrist in a vicelike grip, and his lips curl into a snarl as he says, 'You are mine. Do not ever forget it. You will stay with me, or take me with you.'

I twist my arm out of his grasp and snap, 'I am nobody's, and I thought the plan was for you to stay here so the people would have a leader when they're brought out of stasis.'

His lips curl again, baring teeth. 'I am not spending my time sleeping. Who knows when we will be awakened. I come with you, or you don't go.'

Am'ratha's voice rumbles in my head. *Come, Princess. We have little time.*

I glance towards the other side of the room. A light film is advancing towards us at the pace of a man walking.

Bring him, Royal One. Your people will need you in the coming battle, and I can carry two.

Against my better judgement, I allow Dinian to grab hold of my arm, and we jump onto Am'ratha's neck together. As my dragon shoots into the sky, the filmy wave touches the window, and I breathe a sigh of relief. I settle in for the ride to Loch Ness and survey the town as we fly over. No one would know a battle is waging—or is it?

Something itches at the back of my neck, and it isn't Dinian. Grossman Green and Giles Regis easily breached the wards yesterday, and yet they did not make it in today. Also, even though the castle is being held in stasis, smaller battles would still be occurring outside. Why aren't we seeing more fighting? I want to talk to the King about my concerns, but his dragon is too far away.

'This is so amazing, my first dragon ride,' Dinian almost purrs in my ear. 'I cannot wait until I get my very own dragon.'

I shudder as he leans his head against mine. I can't pull away without unseating us, but I send an elbow backwards, digging him in the ribs.

'Ouch, what was that for?'

'You're too close,' I tell him.

I can ditch him in the river if you want, Am'ratha sends for my ears only.

Best not, I tell her, although I'm sorely tempted.

In the moments before we left the court, Dinian had shown himself to be a selfish, self-serving git. Not only am I more determined that I will never marry him, but I'm also not prepared to keep up this sham of friendship, not even if it keeps my uncle onside. I wriggle forward, trying to put as much distance between us as I can.

'You should be nicer to me,' Dinian says, his voice taking on a threatening tone. 'You never know when it might be useful to have me as a friend.'

I suppress another shudder. I would rather kill myself than ask Dinian for help.

Hold tight, Am'ratha says, *We are almost at the loch.*

AS THE SUN begins its descent over the Isle of Skye, the air around me thickens with magic. It is like being enveloped in a wet blanket. Then, all of a sudden, it is gone.

I walk the few paces back to where the others had stood around the power stone. The ground has closed back over, and all sign of the stone is gone. Around the place where it had appeared, Effie, Snake, and Petunia lie, limbs akimbo.

The ground is cold, and I rush over to check that they are still alive. My heart thuds in my chest as I try to find Effie's pulse. It is there. That gives me hope for the others. I take my time checking Snake and Petunia. They are alive. Shaking each of them in turn, I try to wake them. They remain asleep. I will have to move them somewhere warmer so they can recover.

Ed'rathe, I call, *I need your help.*

We cannot come, Dragon Friend. You have taken all the magic, and there is not enough left to make a glamour. We are forbidden from revealing ourselves to mortals. I will find a place close by where we can draw on magic, then let you know where you can find us.

I am on my own. Should I go for help, or wait until they wake up? The chill in the air bites at my face, and I fear if I leave them for too long, they may still die. I reach for Effie's and Petunias' hands and send what little warmth I can into their bodies. I keep a little magic in reserve for Snake.

They are going to die of exposure, I tell Ed'rathe. *Are you able to help in another way?*

Give me a moment, Dragon Friend.

'Ugh. What happened?' Snake is slowly pushing himself up off the ground.

Thank you, I tell the dragon.

Snake stands up, surveying the scene in a bit of a daze.

'Snake, we need to move the others to somewhere warmer where they can recover.'

'What?' He shakes his head as if trying to clear it.

'Can you help Effie and Petunia to that bench by the path while I search for some food?'

'Ahh.' He turns his eyes to me, though I am not sure he actually sees me. 'I guess.'

I leave them and head for the lights of the township. The smell of fish and chips wafts towards me, and I increase my pace. Without slowing, I reach into my pocket and search around the supplies I left at Eleanora's place in the World Above. I touch something papery. No, that is my stash of books. And that hat is the bell Eleanora's daughter put out for me to request tea. I pause. Tea would be nice. No, I need to concentrate on hot, warming food.

Ah, there it is. I grasp a wallet filled with money Eleanora insisted I have. At the time I had laughed because money is only useful in the World Above, and I was going on a quest in the World Below. Besides, in the World Above, I am a cat. What use would a cat have for money? She simply smiled at me and said, 'You can never predict what will be useful and what will not. Best to be prepared for every eventuality.'

Now, as my hand comes back through the portal and I draw the wallet out of my pocket, I am ever so grateful she ignored me and left it anyway.

Half an hour later, I am walking back to the spot where I left the others, my mouth watering at the aroma of freshly cooked fish and chips wafting from the parcel under my arm. The three of them are huddled together on the bench, sharing their body heat and looking like they have not eaten in a week. I open the parcel, and the hit of salt and vinegar is heaven and sets my taste buds tingling. They fall on the food like ravenous beasts.

Finally they slow down, and I step forward to take my share.

'We should be going,' Snake says. 'We should call the dragons.'

'There is no magic left in the area to hide them,' Petunia says.

Alarm flashes on Snake's face. 'But how are we going to get to Loch Ness?'

Petunia shrugs. 'There is no rush. Our task was to put the court in stasis, and we have done that.'

'I need to go to Pris and make sure she is okay.'

'Ah, the impatience of youth.' Petunia smiles.

'The boy is in love, Petunia, cut him a break,' Effie says. 'Besides, don't you want to go to Loch Ness and check up on your family?'

I wipe my fingers on a napkin. 'Snake, I think the next bit is up to you and me. I don't like doing this, but needs must.'

He looks at me suspiciously, not getting my meaning at all. When we arrive back at the town, I lead our team away from the main street into a residential area. It is not quite dark enough for this, but I think I still have enough magic left for an invisibility spell.

We find a quiet street, and I have Effie and Petunia wait at the corner. The first house has a car, but we walk until I find a dwelling with two vehicles parked in the driveway. 'We need to break into the house and steal the keys,' I tell Snake. 'This is where your skills come in.'

'I can do one better.'

He tests the doors, and to my surprise, the driver's door of the second car opens. 'Always worth a try just in case.' He smiles crookedly.

'We still need to get it going,' I whisper.

'Hop in,' Snake says. He slides into the driver's seat, reaches under the dashboard, fiddles with some wires, and the vehicle sparks into life.

'How?' I ask

'Dad taught me when I was little. In the magical object retrieval business, it was always important to have getaway options. I never needed to use it, but he and Mum both made me practice.'

We back out of the driveway and onto the road before stopping at the corner. Effie and Petunia shuffle across the back seat. Once Snake has convinced them to buckle up their seatbelts, he directs the car towards the bridge to the mainland.

'I hope the dragons aren't far,' Snake says, pointing at the petrol gauge. 'I don't want to have to explain a hot-wired vehicle to a service station attendant.'

He smiles, and I can't stop myself from chuckling at the thought as we make our way across the bridge to the mainland.

THE CAR HURTLES across the causeway. I'm not used to driving on the open road, and my knuckles whiten as I grip the wheel. My stomach is churning. Initially I think it's because I want to get us to the dragons as quickly as possible, but as we leave Skye, the certainty that something is not quite right begins to grow.

'Are you sure the court is in stasis?' I ask.

'Am'ratha reported it was and that the King and Pris were on their way to Loch Ness,' Princess Petunia tells me.

Ed'rathe, are you there?

Yes. Am'ralla and I are settled in a field outside a place called Boardford.

I check the next signpost. *We are a little over ten minutes away.*

Your time means nothing to me, Noble One.

We will be there soon.

I focus on the road and try increasing our speed. I almost roll the car as I take a corner too fast, and I ease my foot off the accelerator a little. Arriving a couple of minutes earlier is not worth risking our lives.

The car is silent as the others rest. Although I try to calm myself, my anxiety grows. I can't shake the feeling that something isn't quite right.

Ed'rathe, can you ask Am'ratha how much damage was done to the castle at the Seelie Court?

Certainly.

It seems like a lifetime but is probably only minutes later when the dragon gets back to me.

Am'ratha said the castle took very few blasts and remains intact. Only a few of the attackers managed to force their way inside. Also, she carries Dinian as well as the princess.

Thank you, Ed'rathe.

So the slimeball wouldn't stay and protect the court—typical, but I am sure that is not what has me even more worried than before.

'Are you all right, Snake?' Percival asks.

'I'm not sure,' I answer honestly. 'Something doesn't feel right.'

'What do you mean? Everything is going to plan.'

Percival has hit the nail on the head. 'Yep, and that's the problem.'

The sprite shifts in his seat, and a sideways glance shows his concern for me. 'You are not happy our plan is working?'

'It's all been too easy, Percival. I worry that we're missing something, because when have things ever gone right for us?'

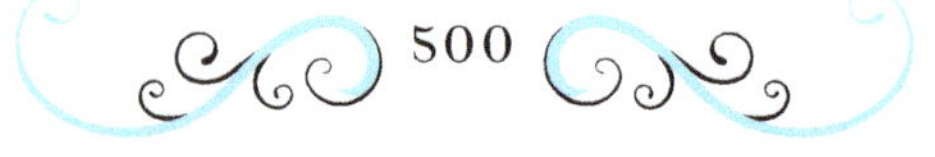

As the words leave my mouth, it hits me like a punch to the gut, and my dinner threatens to make a reappearance.

'Percival, when we placed the court in stasis, we locked a large portion of the Unseelie guard in the castle.'

'Of course. They remained to defend the court and any creatures who decided to stay.'

'Ed'rathe told me that when the court was frozen, only a few of the attackers were caught inside. And if none of the court managed to escape before the spell took….'

Out of the corner of my eye, I see Percival blanche. 'That means Bernais's cronies are free to carry on the fight while many of our team cannot help until we find enough magic to restore the court.'

I nod. 'Even worse, though, I fear it means they knew our plan. Only a dozen or so people were aware of what we were doing. So, that means there is a mole in our midst.'

The car falls silent as everyone comes to terms with our betrayal. I press my foot to the floor, and the car lurches forward. Now that Pris might well be in danger, every second counts.

'What is going on?' Effie asks as she grips the seat in front of her.

'We have to get to Loch Ness and warn the others. We had a spy in the court,' I tell her, 'and I think he escaped with Pris.'

My heart is pounding so loudly in my ears, I almost miss Princess Petunia saying, 'Why not just tell Ed'rathe to contact his sister and have her warn Priscilla and King Maddox to be careful?'

Of course, what was I thinking? Obviously I wasn't thinking at all. If we're to help the others, I need to keep my cool.

Ed'rathe, can you please pass a message to your sister? They might be heading into danger and—

She says they are just coming up to Loch Ness, and…. Hold on, Noble One…. I have lost contact with her.

Euphemia leans forward. 'Do you really think it might be Dinian? Or are you letting your dislike cloud your judgement?'

'I don't know,' I tell her as I take the next corner at breakneck speed, and someone in the back gasps as they are flung across the seat. 'But I do know someone leaked our plan.'

'We will be no use to the others if we die,' Princess Petunia says sharply as she pulls herself back into a sitting position.

It is all I can do to keep the car on the road, so I don't comment. We turn another corner, and I can make out the dragons resting in a field. Well, perhaps not resting, as they appear to be eyeing up the Highland cattle in the next paddock.

There is no time for eating, Ed'rathe.

I am sure I hear him humph as the car screeches to a halt by a wooden gate set into a hedgerow. Everyone tumbles out, and I remind them to lock their doors so no one else steals the car. Princess Petunia reaches into her pocket and then throws a handful of notes onto the back seat. When she catches me watching, she smiles and says, 'That should compensate them for their trouble.'

Damn straight, it should. I counted at least half a dozen £50 notes.

Any update? I ask as I run across the paddock towards the dragons.

No, Noble One. We cannot contact either of the two dragons meant to be at Loch Ness.

Is that normal?

No, Noble One, it is not.

Percival and I climb onto Ed'rathe's back and wait while Princess Petunia and Effie settle onto Am'ralla. The wind rushes past as Ed'rathe pushes into the air. Unfortunately, he doesn't have an accelerator, and all I can do is will him to go faster and pray we will be in time to rescue Pris from whatever is happening at Loch Ness.

OR IS IT?

WITH DINIAN'S ARMS wrapped around my waist, I try to put as much distance between our bodies as I can without falling off Am'ratha. I tolerated him while we were in court, but now that he has shown his true colours, I no longer want to be anywhere near him.

Every time he touches me, I suppress a shiver, and he does it so often, I can't relax and appreciate the spectacular countryside we fly over. I begin to suspect he is enjoying my discomfort.

I work at blocking him out because at the back of my mind, a kernel of a thought is growing into a big problem. Something feels wrong about the attack on the castle. There was no great storming of the battlements as Giles and Grossman had promised, and there were very few creatures fighting in the streets. In fact, most of the creatures I saw outside the wards were standing round, chatting. As we flew over Inverness, I found very little magical activity anywhere, and not even any human type fights.

My unease increases as we leave the city behind. Finally I have to admit that what went on in Inverness felt less like a siege and more like a feint. If that was the case, what did Bernais have to gain?

'This is amazing.' Dinian's voice comes from close by my ear. 'When I get my dragon, I will fly everywhere.'

As you can imagine, my brothers are queuing up for the honour, Am'ratha says.

A chuckle escapes even though I try to bite it back. *I thought dragons couldn't do sarcasm.*

You have a lot to learn.

'What are you laughing at?' Dinian asks, his voice suddenly cold and hard.

I don't answer. It's none of his business.

'You do not take me seriously. When we are married, that will change.'

That's it, the final straw. It's time I put the elf in his place. My only regret is that I can't deliver the words face to face so he can see how determined I am.

'Dinian, you need to get it through your thick head that there is nothing on heaven or earth that would make me marry you.'

'I have been promised your hand, and I will have it,' my would-be husband says from behind me. 'If not with your permission, then by force if need be.'

Gone is the charming courtier, and I find myself sharing my ride with a petty tyrant in his place. In my head I'm ready to tell him I don't believe for a moment that my uncle would force me down the aisle kicking and screaming. Besides, as an heir to the Seelie Court's crown, I require the monarch's permission to marry.

Fortunately I don't open my mouth, because I suddenly realise that this high in the sky, I do not trust Dinian not to lash out when he is faced with my particular reality.

I would drop him and rush to save you, Am'ratha reassures me.

Tempting, but no. I need to handle this myself when my feet are firmly on the ground. And I might just deliver it with an un-princess-like punch, I promise myself.

Am'ratha snickers, *I can hear you.*

I know.

It seems an age before I can make out the crumbling ruins of Urquhart Castle in the distance as dusk begins to dull the sky. Almost safe. As we approach the castle, Am'ratha sweeps in a circle to find the best place to land.

Perhaps you should let the dragons in Skye know we have arrived.

When we are on the ground, Royal One. There is some unrest down there I do not like the look of.

I can't make out anything, but then again, my eyesight isn't as good as the dragons'. We drop and begin our approach towards a flat piece of ground near the castle. I catch a glimpse of a small cohort holding off a larger group of creatures by a cattle grid on the road into the lake. That must be what Am'ratha saw.

Are some of Bernais's followers trying to get back through the portal? I ask. *And is Petunia's husband holding them off?*

Perhaps. Am'ratha sounds less certain, and I wonder what she can see that I can't.

Why didn't they simply go through the fields and wait until night? I wonder. *They could have snuck through to the portal under the cover of darkness, and no one would ever have known.*

Royal One, we must change our plans. We cannot wait here for the others, but it is too dangerous to fly directly to the portal, as our undersides are defenceless. Ed'ruven commands that we land until the path is clear.

Am'ratha's tone tells me there is no room for argument here.

'What's going on?' Dinian asks as the dragons land behind the defenders.

I dismount as quickly, wanting to get as far away from Dinian as possible.

'Should we help out, or stay with the dragons?' I ask the King.

He doesn't have time to answer as bodies emerge from nowhere, and we are embroiled in a two-pronged attack with the dragons at our backs.

I take my defensive position, ready to fight, but neither King Maddox nor Dinian has moved.

'Shields,' King Maddox barks as something whizzes past me.

'What the hell was that?' I shout.

'Magic,' my uncle answers. 'Raise your shield.'

'I don't know how to,' I admit.

King Maddox mutters something under his breath, then the air around me thickens. 'Move away from the dragons. We do not want them hurt by a stray pulse.'

'Perhaps we can join up with the portal guards,' I suggest.

'Good thinking,' the King says, and I'm pleased I'm finally good for something.

Moving slowly as a group, we inch closer to the guards, but our attackers figure out what we're doing, and they stop us a few feet from our target.

'If we all stand back-to-back, we can concentrate on maintaining a forward shield only and save our energy,' King Maddox commands.

We move into position, and I feel a little more secure. Something pings off the shield level with my face. 'Aren't we going to fight back?'

'Using magic to harm others is outlawed. While I believe that will not matter to these creatures, there is still a chance they may stop short of hurting us,' King Maddox warns.

Another shot pings by.

'Are you sure we shouldn't attack?' I ask.

'Yes, niece. Let's save our strength. Besides, I think I see reinforcements arriving. They may think twice about attacking Petunia and Euphemia.'

I hope so because I fear I am not going to be much help in a magical battle. I glance over my shoulder, relieved to see there are indeed two dragons heading our way. We may just get back to the World Below in one piece after all.

WIND WHIPS THROUGH my hair, but Ed'rathe is flying so fast, I daren't let go to hold it back. When this is over, I really need to get a haircut—if it is ever over. I'm beginning to feel I will be trapped in this nightmare forever.

I don't have time to wallow in my self-pity because, in what seems no time at all, the dragons are circling above Loch Ness, allowing us to observe the scene below. Pris, Dinian, and King Maddox are surrounded by a handful of creatures, and they're standing back-to-back, ready to fight. I peer down. There is a small knot of creatures, perhaps dwarves, hiding behind a hillock, waiting to attack.

Behind the royal party, a small contingent of creatures is holding back a larger group from entering the fight, keeping them on the other side of a cattle trap. They can't help the royal party, but at least they are preventing them from being over-run. Am'ratha and Ed'ruven wait beside the ruins of the castle, seemingly watching the action.

I gesture to the two of them, *What are they doing? Why aren't they helping?*

Unless the flow of magic is threatened, we stay out of directly involving ourselves in the affairs of men and creatures, Ed'rathe informs me.

'*But you took us to Skye and then back here,*' I argue.

Yes, because you were trying to save the Unseelie Court so King Maddox could concentrate on his duty to clean the flow, Nobel One.'

My hands ball into fists, and I resist the urge to pummel the dragon's hide—we are still too high for me to survive the fall should he decide to eject us. How can they stand by and do nothing? Is there another way they can contribute?

Is there anything you dragons can do?

The air thrums, and I recognise this as the dragons talking to each other.

We can protect King Maddox if his life is threatened. He is the one tasked with protecting the magical flow, so he has special consideration.

And if he dies? I press.

He does not have a confirmed heir, so we would have to go to our Queen for direction.

This is so maddening. What is the point of having dragon allies if they can't do anything to help? Ah…. If they can help King Maddox, perhaps they can also help Pris.

Ed'rathe, Pris appears to be Queen Ariana's only heir. With the Queen held between life and death, Pris is, in effect, the leader of the Seelie Court.

Interesting. I shall find out what I can, Noble One.

I sense the dragons talking again.

Ed'ruven believes we are obliged to protect the princess as well as the King.

That's at least something, I guess. Surveying the scene below, I consider our best options for joining the fight—not that I really have any training.

Petunia's dragon swoops down and lands. When the princess and Euphemia are on the ground, she takes to the air and circles the skies. I watch as the dwarves hesitate for a moment, allowing Euphemia time to join the royal party and Petunia to go and assist her husband.

'Why aren't the dwarves attacking?' I ask Percival.

'I think the brains of the outfit are in the group trying to get over the cattle stop. Either that, or they are tasked with making sure none of the Unseelie Court get through the portal.'

'Or perhaps both,' I say after watching them a while longer. 'What do you want to do? I'm going to help Pris, but Ed'rathe could still take you to the World Below.'

'We fight. There is no point going back home if we leave King Maddox behind.'

Ed'rathe drops to the ground, and we slide from his back. He bows his head and says, *Fight well, my friends. I would be sad to lose you when I have just broken you in.* Then he smiles, and I wonder which is more terrifying, him or the battle we are running headfirst into.

Thanks for the confidence boost, I tell him as he rises to join Am'ralla.

There is no reaction from the dwarves as we join the others. Now that I'm on the ground, I quickly realise there is a battle going on, it's just that the fighting isn't physical. The air around us is thick and shimmers slightly with magic.

'What are they doing?' I ask Percival.

'From what I can make out, everyone has erected personal shields, and they are testing each other out to find a weak spot.'

'Pris doesn't know how to do that.' Come to think of it, nor do I.

'I think King Maddox has her covered.'

'How do we probe a shield?'

'You send finger bolts of power at the creature, targeting different areas around them.'

My eyebrows almost fly off my head. 'But we're taught that directing magic at another creature is a grave sin. From what I've heard, it's somewhat like getting an electric shock. Misdirect it, and it can be fatal.'

Percival turns a fierce face to me. 'This is a war we are fighting, Snake. There will be casualties.'

My mind can't process what Percival's saying. Creatures are at war? We are actually going to be attacking each other—with magic. I shake my head. Of course we are, and we must use magic too, otherwise the war will be lost before we start.

It started when Grossman and Giles used magic to enter the castle. If I hadn't known it then, the lesson is driven home when a shot of energy clips my ear a moment later.

'Raise a shield,' Percival commands as I reach up to touch the wound, and my hand comes back down bloodied. In seconds I'm following Percival's instructions and surrounding myself with an energy shield.

'We will not let any of you back into our lands. You are not welcome,' one of the dwarves says, and it is as if what he says lets loose the others.

Where the fighting had been controlled before, now the dwarves are attacking with everything they have.

'The royal party have combined their shields,' Percival says. 'We should too.'

In moments Percival and I are sharing bubble.

'You're stronger in magic than I am, so I will maintain our protection, and you concentrate on attack,' he says as a small contingent breaks away from the main group and heads towards us.

I am sending out shards of magic, fearful one might strike, but also afraid none will, when everything stops.

'I have Priscilla. Stop now, or I will kill her.'

I KNOW THAT voice. My worst fears are confirmed when the dwarves part, and I see Dinian is holding Pris from behind with a knife at her throat. Of course, it makes sense now. Nothing would be able to penetrate a bubble maintained by King Maddox and Effie. The threat would have to come from within.

Beside me, Snake tenses, and I move quickly to grab his arm. 'You can do nothing from here. You must play the long game.'

'I knew that slimy elf couldn't be trusted,' Snake snarls. 'I will break every bone in his body when I get my hands on him.'

I understand his anger, I feel it too, but I need to calm him if Pris is to get out of this alive. 'You might have to wait in line,' I tell Snake. 'If looks could kill, King Maddox would have taken Dinian's life already.'

His body relaxes a little, but the tension around his lips tells me his mind is still working through possible scenarios to rescue Pris. The fighting around us has stopped for the moment while everyone waits to see how this plays out. Perhaps we can use this to our advantage.

'She can take care of herself,' I remind him. 'What we must do is be ready to react when she makes her move.'

'Can't the dragons help in some way?' Snake asks.

'Not while Pris has a knife to her throat.'

'Of course not, so what do you suggest?'

Now I have his attention.

'There are too many of them for us to win in a straight-out fight, so at some stage, we have to make a break for the portal to the World Below. While they are watching Dinian and Pris, we have the best chance we're going to get to take them by surprise.'

'Okay….'

'Can you speak with Ed'rathe and have him ask the others to be ready to make a run for the portal on my command?'

Snake studies me, a thoughtful expression on his face. 'Percival, who knew you were such a great tactician? We really could have used your help in the minotaur's maze.'

'You're wasting time,' I tell him impatiently, not used to accepting praise, but feeling pleasure anyway.

'Done,' he tells me, and I know the others understand when King Maddox sends a subtle nod our way.

Then it happens almost as if in slow motion. Pris moves a fraction, and she jolts her head backwards into Dinian's face, then, almost too fast to see, her knee comes up and she stamps down hard on Dinian's foot. As his hold on her loosens, she elbows him in the stomach and turns so that as he bends slightly in reaction, she kicks him in the shin.

It isn't as pretty as the kata I have seen her practice, but it is effective. Dinian releases his hold, and she turns and swings an almighty punch, landing it right on his chin. Dinian, not having expected her to be able to defend herself, staggers back as Pris pulls back for another punch, but King Maddox grabs her arm and drags her away. Then, as one, Pris, King Maddox, and Effie run through the gap towards us.

'Now,' I yell as loud as I can. 'Meet us by the loch.'

The air thrums as King Maddox puts up a new shield around our group, and I turn to head for the water. Snake does not move. His eyes are fixed on Dinian, who has recovered and is running after Pris, calling for the dwarves to support him.

It is as if Dinian's voice alters reality, and everything moves back into real time. Still tracking Dinian, Snake sends out some bolts of magic, aiming for the ground, and the dwarves hesitate, allowing Pris, Maddox, and Effie to run past us. Dinian is close behind, and as he reaches out for Pris, Snake steps out of the protection of the circle, draws back his arm, and punches the elf, his fist landing full force on the backstabbing elf's jaw. As Dinian collapses to the ground, Snake turns to us, a self-satisfied smile on his face.

'Snake, watch out!' Pris rushes towards him and knocks him out of the way of a magic bolt.

Snake stumbles to the side, and Pris falls at his feet. Am'ratha's roar fills the air, signalling that Pris hasn't fallen over Dinian as I first thought but that she's injured. Snake is staring at the scorch mark on her back.

I freeze, all thoughts gone from my mind. King Maddox rushes back and picks up Pris.

'Run,' he yells as he sprints towards his dragon.

Next thing, Snake has my hand, and he is pulling me and Effie towards the water. Without dragons, the only way to get to the portal is to spell the water under our feet. Effie takes the lead and transforms the water. I am in the middle, keeping up the shield. Snake takes the rear, sending out magical bolts to keep the dwarves at bay.

The dwarves are in disarray. They do not appear to be able to walk on water and keep up a shield at the same time. Working as a team, we are pulling away from them. In front of me, I see King Maddox's dragon enter the portal. Sanctuary is but a few feet away now. Am'ratha and Ed'rathe follow the older dragon.

Effie stumbles in front of me, and I almost trip over her.

'Not far now, old friend,' I tell her. 'You can do this.'

My heart is racing, filling my ears with its thudding. We are so close.

King Maddox is standing at the entrance of the portal. 'Hurry, the dragons are getting ready to close the door. They will not allow fighting so close to their home.'

What does he mean? The dragons never close their portal.

Then the whole pathway in front of us firms up as if there is a barrier between us and the water. King Maddox holds out his hand, lending support to Effie. We speed up. Effie is running full force, and I turn to grab Snake's arm.

'We must run,' I tell him.

He sends one last bolt of magic at the dwarves, swings round, and dashes towards us.

In front of us, the edges of the portal are shrinking inwards like someone is tightening a knot. Snake makes a dive for the shrinking hole, dragging me behind him. I look over my shoulder just in time to see the portal disappear completely.

I suck in great gulps of air. We have made it. No, hold on—where is Petunia? I look this way and that, dread clouding my senses. We have left her behind. Who will lead the rebellion now?

Effie places a hand on my arm. 'It was her choice. She wanted to stay with her husband and protect her home.'

'But what about our plan, Effie?'

Snake stands and dusts himself off and stretches his limbs. 'In all the movies, they say the first casualty of any battle is the plan.'

Effie pats my arm. 'We will regroup and do the best we can with what we have.'

Snake stills for a moment. 'Am'ralla's told Ed'rathe that Princess Petunia and her people made it safely to the castle while the attackers were distracted. They are as safe as any creature can be in these times.'

I slip to the floor, exhausted, but still aware this is not an ending but the beginning of something much larger.

THE WAR TRULY BEGINS

SNAKE SLIPS DOWN the wall beside me, and I lean into him. I do not like personal contact but, after the turmoil of the last few hours, his presence is comforting. He is not restful though. His head turns this way and that as he scans the cave.

'Where is Pris?' he asks, his voice shaky with panic.

'Don't worry, lad, Am'ratha has taken Pris to safety so someone can tend to her wound.' King Maddox sounds weary, almost like he has had the stuffing knocked out of him.

'That is good,' I say. I mean it, but I do not feel it. I am numb. What started as a personal quest to stop Bernais from playing havoc with my world has now turned into creature fighting creature.

If I am honest, there has been something bubbling in the creature world for the last few hundred years, ever since Petunia and her followers were expelled.

We lost many potential leaders as others chose to support her by leaving too. Still, I always thought we would find a solution without coming to blows. Most creatures do not like change, King Maddox's court is a testament to that, but we have to bend or we will break, or so I believed until now. Never in a century would I have thought we would choose to break.

'Percival, are you okay?' Snake's voice washes me with concern.

I suck in some air and breathe out slowly. Now, there is a question. Am I all right?

'It is a lot to take in, Snake.'

'It is,' he confirms. 'I'm feeling a little overwhelmed too. I keep telling myself what my mum always says—when you are asked to eat an elephant, the only way to do it is one piece at a time… or something like that.'

I cannot help but chuckle. 'I understand what you are saying. This is huge, but all we can do is take one step at a time.'

'Yes, and that first step must be to go save Queen Ariana.' Effie's voice comes from across the cavern and bounces loudly off the stone walls. 'Moving forward will be easier with her on our side. Not least because she and King Maddox can begin restoring magic, which will appease some of Bernais's current supporters.'

'I guess now that I am here, I may as well go and see what I can do to help.' King Maddox's voice booms in the confines of the cavern.

'About time,' Snake mutters under his breath, and I snort, trying to hold in my laugh.

King Maddox sends a look that under any other circumstances would have me shaking in my boots. Now I am too tired to react.

'No time like the present,' Effie says, pushing herself to her feet.

I follow suit, but Snake says, 'I'm not going—'

Effie does not wait for him to finish speaking. 'We haven't time to argue. Come, King Maddox,' she commands. 'This madness has gone on long enough. Time to put an end to it before anyone else gets hurt.'

I smile at the King's back as he simply obeys. Ed'ruven allows them onto his back and waddles towards the opening. There is a gust of wind, and they are gone, leaving us behind.

'Ed'rathe, will you take me to Pris?… What do you mean, if you're able?'

The air buzzes with their conversation. While they work out what they are going to do, I think about where I want to go now. I had thought we would all stay together once we left the World Above, but obviously we're not going to. Now I must decide where to best focus my efforts.

Even though I am concerned for her, going to check on Pris does not seem like the best use of my time. Then again, neither does going to the end of the maze to help the Queen. In either place I will just be a spare part, and I am no longer satisfied with the role of bystander.

'Ed'rathe says Pris was taken to their home, the World Between, and he must ask their Queen's permission to bring us there,' Snake says.

The air tingles with magic, and Ed'rathe drops to the ground for us to mount. *I have permission for both of you to enter our lands.*

I do not even need to think about it. 'Thank you for your invitation, but I am afraid at this moment, I have other commitments.'

The Queen thought you might refuse, Dragon Friend. She gave me leave to take you to where you need to be. And you are welcome to join us any time you feel the need.

'Thank you, Ed'rathe, and you too, Snake. If you do not mind a diversion before heading to your home, I would like to go to mine.'

'Are you sure, Percival?'

'Very. I need to check up on my family and say a final farewell to my father. Then I must consider where I will best be placed to help with the coming battle.'

Snake smiles. 'I will miss you.'

'And I you. Pris not so much.'

A chuckle erupts from Snake. 'Percival, you wily old fox, you've been hiding a sense of humour all this time.'

Ed'rathe inclines his head, and Snake and I climb on his back, Snake still laughing to himself. The dragon stands up and moves to the entrance, and a cool wind brushes my face as he takes flight.

He flies out from the cavern for a few wingbeats before banking left. In the distance I can just make out Ed'ruven as he swoops down over the minotaur's maze. Ed'rathe glides over the maze before peeling off and dropping down on the outskirts of the Wyld Woods, just in sight of the village.

I scramble down and bow to the dragon. 'Thank you.'

Snake leans over Ed'rathe's neck. 'I can't believe this is good-bye, but I understand—family is important.

He is right, family *is* important, and I have neglected mine for long enough. Still, that is not my only reason for coming here.

'I have a suspicion that Eleanora will need my help over the coming days, so no doubt we will meet again soon.'

What I do not add is that for the first time in a long time, I am ready to do more than follow orders; I am ready to fight. It will be strange without Pris and Snake, but we each have different paths to follow now.

'It will be weird without you—without your guidance,' Snake says. 'If you get a chance, do you think you could…. No, you will have enough to worry about.'

'Of course I will see what I can find out about your mother and Pris's parents' too.'

'Thank you. Not just for that, but for everything.'

His words make my chest squeeze. I dip my head and offer him a smile.

'Now go, look after Pris. She will need your support to get through these next few days. Many will have expectations of her, and it will be difficult for her to decide which path to take. Farewell, my friend.'

'Good-bye, Percival. Stay safe.'

I watch Ed'rathe take off, and continue to follow his flight until he and Snake are almost out of sight, the empty feeling in my stomach increasing with each wingbeat. Taking in a deep breath, I tell myself it is time to look forward, not back, and start towards the woods, only to find two figures walking towards me.

As they get closer, they materialise into Eleanora and her sister Eugenia. Their faces are pinched and grim. I hasten my steps towards them, knowing I am not going to like what they have to say but also knowing I am no longer the sprite who hides from the truth.

I FORCE OPEN an eye and close it immediately. We are high above a mountain range, and I hurt so much, I can't even cling to Am'ratha's back. She must be keeping me on with her magic. I don't like this lack of control, but I'm too sore and groggy to do anything about it. Everything blurs, and I let go, knowing Am'ratha will keep me safe.

The air is warmer. We must be close to or on the ground. *Landing,* I guess as I am jolted, waves of pain sent through my shoulder and arm. The world swims again as hands help me off her back.

Be well, my friend, Am'ratha's voice hums in my mind as I descend into full darkness.

At first I thought I had passed out for a long time, but I open my eyes to find myself being carried on a stretcher down a long, dark corridor. Who is transporting me, and to where? My heart is pounding, and I try to sit up, but I'm forced back down by a wave of dizziness.

I breathe in and out, slow and steady, until my heart calms, and I'm able to think. Am'ratha would not take me anywhere I would be in danger, I trust her to keep me safe, so all I need to do is wait and see what happens. This is so against my nature. However, I force myself to relax.

Finally we arrive at a huge cave. The ceiling is so high, I can barely make it out. Globes hover high above me, generating enough light to see by—barely. I try to twist, but just that slight movement sends burning pain through my body. As my stretcher bearers make their way forward, the room is silent except for the occasional shuffle as someone changes position.

It seems like hours later, but is probably only minutes, when my stretcher is placed on the ground. Again I try to sit up, but my head swims. I slowly and gently turn my head towards the direction I was travelling and gasp in a breath.

If I could move my arms I would rub my eyes, but I have to settle for blinking a few times to make sure I'm truly seeing what my brain is telling me I am.

A deep velvety voice engulfs me. *Ah, Priscilla Crown, we meet again.*

I can barely comprehend the enormous ruby glow of the dragon's scales or the deep unending black of her eyes. She fills the cavern with her presence, and even without looking directly into her eyes, she has me in her thrall.

Still, I have the presence of mind to say, 'Again?'

The room shakes with a rumble, and I realise she is laughing. I am injured, lying on the ground with no dignity, and now I am being laughed at.

Little one, all those of royal blood are presented to me when they are first born so I can confirm they are worthy to be included in the line of succession.

Little one? Seriously, I am over this, but I can't find the will to do anything about it.

Careful, little one. I will forgive some things, but outright disobedience in my court will not be tolerated.

Of course she can read my mind!

And you need to learn to control your thoughts. Now, lie back and relax. The magic has damaged the muscles in your shoulder and has given you a mild heart attack. If you will allow me, I can repair the damage.

Magic. Someone hit me with magic!

You can rant, or I can heal you.

I close my eyes and try not to think anything uncomplimentary the Dragon Queen might hear. 'Healing, please.'

This may hurt a little.

That was an understatement. Fire burns through my muscles, and I bite back a scream as pain wracks my body. I hold it in. I won't show weakness in front of my unknown audience. Who knows what they might do if they believe I am not strong.

The white-hot pain disappears and is replaced with a cool soothing flow. Then there is nothing but numbness. I lie back, exhausted.

When I wake, I've been moved to the side of the room. I have a much better view of the Queen of Dragons, and it is just as shocking as the first time I saw her. She is at least the height of a three-storey building, and her head is as large as a lorry. She reclines sideways on a chaise lounge carved out of the rock and is by far the most magnificent thing I have ever seen in my life.

That is the glamour talking, Royal One.

I turn my head to find Am'ratha beside me.

THE UNSEELIE COURT

She is glorious, but she does like to use the glamour to invoke awe.

'Thank you for coming back for me.' I am voicing my relief. 'And for bringing me here.

I was summoned, otherwise you would not have been allowed here, she says pragmatically.

Alarm bells ring in my head. 'Why?' I whisper.

Princess Adina and her dragon, Am'nera have been waiting to petition the Queen. Our Queen would not grant her an audience without both sides of the conflict being represented. Now you are here, the princess has been summoned.

'Wait. What? I've just been injured and healed. Now I'm expected to what? Represent Queen Ariana in the Dragon Court?'

Yes.

I flop back on the stretcher. Just when I thought things could not get any more ridiculous. I've been betrayed, shot at with magic, and now appointed as a royal ambassador for a second time! Seriously?

Can you stand?

'Sorry?'

Can you stand? Princess Adina is not the type of creature you want to give the upper hand to. You will want to meet her on your feet.

I struggle to stand up and look down at my clothes with dismay. I look like I've been dragged through a hedge backwards before being shot at with magic.

I cannot do anything about that in the time we have, but I can make it so creatures will not notice what you are wearing.

I smile at Am'ratha. 'Thank you.'

You are welcome. Come, we must approach the Queen.

'Wait,' I say as my friend steps forward. 'Who exactly is Princess Adina?'

Am'ratha's large saucer-like eyes regard me, and I imagine I see pity in there.

She is your great-aunt, Prince Bernais's mother. She has petitioned our Queen to appoint her Queen of the World Below given that Queen Ariana is missing and has no named heir.

The world shifts, and I sway on my feet. I knew there was a battle to be had, but I didn't think it would be here so soon, or that I would be alone when it happened.

You are not alone, Royal One. I am with you and will remain by your side.

We reach the podium in front of the Queen just as a blue dragon peels off from a group at the side. I expect a snarl and am surprised by her polite nod.

Am'ratha chuckles. *We are not like you creatures. Manners and respect are everything in this court—something you would do well to remember.*

Point taken, I tell her.

The woman who joins us moments later obviously did not get the message. She glowers at me as she moves beside her dragon. I would have reacted except I'm so taken aback by how much she looks like a tall, angular, pinched version of my mother, I'm momentarily shocked into silence.

Welcome back to my court, Adina.

'Your Majesty, thank you for seeing me. If I could—'

This is your niece, Priscilla. Priscilla, this is your great-aunt, Adina.

Remembering Am'ratha's warning, I school my voice and say, 'Pleased to meet you, Aunt, and you too, Am'nera.'

The dragon inclines her head, acknowledging my greeting. My great-aunt studiously ignores me.

You may proceed, Adina.

'As my emissary outlined, the people of the World Below grow restless. Queen Ariana has not been seen for months, and our world is in disarray. She has not named a new heir, so I request you name me Queen in her absence. Once that is done, I will name my son my heir, and I would request that he is paired with a dragon as a sign of his new status.'

She has been rehearsing that, I send to Am'ratha, who bites back a snort.

The Dragon Queen's eyes swivel to me. *Have you something to share, Priscilla?*

She is so reminiscent of one of my schoolteachers, I instantly feel chastened. Then I realise she is actually inviting me to speak. This is my moment, and I've not prepared anything. Taking a deep breath, I marshal my thoughts. This will not be perfect, but I put all those years of debating into practice and start.

'I saw Queen Ariana myself, just a few days ago. I can assure you, she has not disappeared. She is merely ill from cleansing the magical flow.' I cross my fingers superstitiously behind my back. 'I have just returned from the Unseelie Court with King Maddox. He has come to help restore magic to all of our worlds. Once the core of magic in both worlds is repaired, I am sure Queen Ariana will return to the Capitol and ease everyone's worries.'

The Queen of Dragons lowers her head, accepting my words.

'How do we know she speaks the truth?' Adina almost spits the words out.

The Dragon Queen tenses, and I get the impression Adina has moved beyond impolite to rude. The Queen's cold tone when she next speaks confirms my suspicions.

You question whether or not I can read truth in the words of a creature?

Adina hastily recovers. 'No, of course not. It is just we cannot go on like this forever.'

True. I will give Queen Ariana and King Maddox ten days to sort out the problem with magic. By then, if the Queen has not returned to the Capitol, we can consider other solutions.

'On that matter, she has no named successor, Your Majesty.'

I do not take a hand in creature affairs, as you well know, but as I am aware, there is a line of succession already. Princess Petunia is the named heir and was never formally removed from the line of succession when she chose to exile herself. If the Queen does not return to the Capitol, and Petunia returns to the World Below in the next ten days, she will be Queen-in-Waiting.

'But she has been exiled and cannot return here,' Adina says.

Then as, I understand it, with Princess Cecily having renounced her claim to the throne, Princess Priscilla is next in line, and she appears to be in good enough health to appoint or produce her own heir.

The air around us thrums with tension. Adina turns to me, and there is so much hatred in her eyes that Am'ratha shuffles between us.

I'm torn. There is no way I want to be Queen of the World Below, but I can't let Adina know that because she'll use it to her advantage. However, I need to know my options before I make a decision.

'Can I please check something with you, Your Majesty?'

You may speak.

'If Princess Petunia is physically back in the World Below, then she is still next in line to the throne.'

That is correct.

Adina sniggers. 'Good luck with that. My son is in control of the council and will never overturn her banishment.'

I ignore my great-aunt's vitriol and carry on.

'Do you know if my mother can resume her place in the hierarchy?'

Perhaps. As far as we are concerned, she is still a Princess of the Royal Blood. She and her dragon still maintain contact.

Wow, another thing I never knew about my family. They just keep stacking up here.

As far as I understand it, there is an agreement between your mother and Queen Ariana. Cecily would raise you in the World Above, but she could return at any time and take up her duties, thereby resuming her place in the succession.

'Over my dead body,' Adina hisses.

I would love to arrange that, I think. I'm circumspect enough not to say it, but I'm pretty sure Am'ratha and the Dragon Queen can hear me, as Am'ratha snorts in agreement.

I tire of this creature mess. I will not see either of you again for nine days. If Queen Ariana has not appeared by then, you may both approach me.

We are definitely dismissed. Even though I am mentally spiralling, I keep my back straight and my head high as Am'ratha leads me out of the cave and into the fresh air. I expect Adina to follow and brace myself for a confrontation, but by the time we reach the entrance, she has not emerged.

Your great-aunt waits in the chamber, hoping our Queen will speak with her alone.

Of course, I should have expected something underhanded from Bernais's mother. 'Should I go back?'

No, our Queen has spoken, and she will remain bound by her word. Come now, I will take you to the creature guest quarters where you can clean up and rest.

Both those things sound really good right about now.

ED'RATHE SKIMS LONG snow-topped mountains before spiralling down into a valley surrounded by tall peaks. He stops on a ledge outside a cave opening and lets me down.

You have been allowed into the World Between, but you must not leave the creature compound without a dragon escort, Noble One, he explains.

'Is this where Pris is?' I ask.

I am not sure. I think not though. I must return to my home now. The others here will tell you all you need to know and make sure you are settled.

He spreads his wings and glides out into the valley. I watch him for a while. He is truly magnificent and more so as the sunset bounces off his scales. A blast of cold wind buffets me and reminds me I'm not dressed for altitude. I turn to seek the shelter of the cave.

As I enter, warm, soft light bounces off the smooth walls, highlighting that it is so much more than a simple cave. About ten feet in, I push back a heavy curtain to find myself inside a huge, cosy cavern. A fire roars in a central pit surrounded by scatters of cushions and thickly woven rugs.

Three corridors lead off from the main room. From the one directly to my right, I hear voices, and the smell of food wafts towards me. Following my nose along the dimly lit tunnel, I find it opens up into a dining room filled with around twenty or so creatures from a variety of races. I'm surprised to find a face I know in the crowd. She breaks away and joins me by the door.

'Priscilla Crown's guard. I'm surprised to see you here,' Verona says as she greets me, her face beaming.

'Not as surprised as I am to see the daughter of Giles Regis,' I respond wearily.

Verona grimaces, then shrugs. 'If my father had not wanted me to make friends amongst the creatures in the World Below, he shouldn't have banished me here as a punishment.'

'Yeah, then again, how was he to know you would meet so many handsome and interesting creatures?' a blond sprite says as he joins us. 'I'm Fergus,' he says, holding out his hand.

'Snake,' I respond, grasping it.

For a moment the room falls silent, and it's as if everyone is frozen in place. Next thing, I'm surrounded by creatures, and everyone is asking about our quest and wondering where Princess Priscilla is.

Verona catches my eye, then takes me by the arm and hauls me back towards the central room, announcing loudly, 'This guy looks and smells like he needs to wash up and get into some clean clothes. While I show him the amenities, perhaps someone could rustle him up some clean clothes and a bowl of stew.'

Clearly used to her bossing them about, the others melt away and she pulls me down the opposite corridor.

'Thank you, that was getting a bit intense.'

Verona smiles and leads me deeper into the cave.

'Okay, baths are that way. It's a hot mineral pool really, but it's amazing. I'll get someone to drop some clothes inside the door. The third room on the right is free. We are two to three to a room, so you'll have to share with someone at some stage, so don't spread out too far, as some more of us are arriving in the next couple of days.'

I laugh. 'What you see is what I have with me, so there's not going to be a problem there.'

She smiles. 'Many of our numbers are refugees from the fighting. We are well provisioned, so we can set you up with everything you need.'

I'm weary, and the baths are calling me, but I'm not too tired to ask, 'And who are the "we" you refer to?'

She laughs. 'Don't worry, you're amongst friends here. We are a loose affiliation of groups who have been fighting for equal rights for all creatures. With the change in the makeup of the council, there have been crackdowns on our activities, and the dragons offered us sanctuary of a sort.'

I nod, storing the information away to process later.

'So, just to clarify, you and your dad….'

'Are on opposite sides. Look, go clean up, eat, and grab some rest. And don't leave your room until you're up to being questioned.' She smiles and winks at me. 'Although… before I go, I have to ask, is it true you and Priscilla went on a quest to the minotaur's maze?'

I nod wearily, and she literally claps her hands together in glee. 'Man, I can't wait to hear about that! He was so imposing when he tested us as we came through from the World Below that he's become a little bit of an idol. Now go.' She pushes me through a door.

The room she sends me into has a floor of polished rock, and in the middle is a sort of roundish pool of water bathed in a cloak of steam. I stumble in the rush to remove my clothes and sink into the bath. It is bliss, and I can't stop myself from groaning as I submerge myself in the pool's soothing depths.

I'm in spa heaven. My aches and pains slip away, and I even feel the tension in my shoulders ease. Finally hunger forces me from the water, and I dress in the simple linen trousers and shirt someone has left for me. I pad barefoot to the room Verona said I could use.

It is a simple affair, containing two beds covered in homespun blankets, each with a chest at their foot and a small bedside table. On one of the tables is a steaming bowl of stew. I wolf it down, barely tasting it, before lying back on the bed, my hands clasped behind my head.

Sleep is calling, and every muscle in my body feels like it weighs a ton, but I can't relax until I know where Pris is. I'm not sure what the protocols are here about contacting him, but if I don't try, I'll just worry.

Ed'rathe, do you know where Pris is?

To my surprise he responds. *She should be with you, Noble One.*

The words spur me to action, I push myself up and swing my legs around just as the door is gently pushed open. I've never been so happy to see someone in my life. Pris stands in the doorway, dressed identically to me and carrying her own bowl of stew. Her eyes catch mine, and she smiles, tucking a stray strand of white hair behind a pointed ear.

No sooner does she put her food down than I sweep her into my arms. She melts into my embrace, and everything else leaves my brain. I hold her tightly as if I never want to let her go. Then I remember her injury, and I gently remove my arms and step away.

'Your wound?'

She smiles before snuggling back into my embrace. 'I've been fixed—by the Queen of Dragons, no less.'

There is a story there, and part of me wants to hear it, but mostly I want to hold her. She tilts her face, and I respond to her invitation, crushing her lips with mine. As one, we move back until I can feel the edge of the bed. I draw her down with me, and for a while there is nothing in my head but the two of us. We have waited so long for this moment, to be together alone, and I'm not going to let anything come between us.

SOMETIME LATER, SHE is wrapped in a blanket, leaning against me, and picking at her lukewarm meal. Drawing on some magic, I heat it for her, and she smiles appreciatively. While she eats, she tells me about her meeting with the Dragon Queen. I listen, but am too exhausted to even comprehend the meaning.

'What do you want to do about it?' I ask.

She puts her bowl on the table and snuggles back into me.

'I'm not sure. There is so much we still don't know.'

I lean my cheek on her hair, and the smell of her sends a pulse through my body. I pull her closer.

'There is one thing I know,' I say.

'Yes?' Her voice is low and seductive.

'Whatever is happening, it can wait for one night.'

I turn her towards me, and she leans to plant a sweet kiss on my mouth. 'It most certainly can.'

BOOK
FOUR
THE
WORLD
BETWEEN

IN THE SHADOW OF DRAGONS

LIGHTS FLICKER IN the distance, illuminating the shadowy trees lining the path as I follow Eleanora and Eugenia to Wyld Woods village. Their sharp whispers and the beat of dragon wings are the only sounds breaking the stillness of the night.

I resist the urge to watch Snake leave. Although my witch companions are two of my oldest friends—and we are talking centuries here, not decades—I feel alone without Snake.

Perhaps because the past few weeks, he and the elven princess have been my constant companions. *Ah, Pris.* I replay the vision of her falling in battle and another of her being swept away by her dragon, Am'ratha. I hope she is all right. She has to be. I will not countenance any other outcome.

Ours is a friendship forged in adversity. Perhaps that is why I feel so hollow. Or perhaps it is because being with them helped me remembered who I was—no, who I am.

Ellie and Genie are pulling ahead, their longer legs covering the distance to their house more quickly than mine. It hurts that they have not noticed I am not with them.

Their disregard sparks a flash of anger. For years they pushed for me to do more, to be a part of their plots and plans for the World Below. Well, I am here now.

My fists ball up in frustration. I take in a couple of deep breaths before forcing my fingers to relax. Returning to myself is new, and my friends were not there to witness it. It is not up to them to make space for me to join them; it falls on me to remind them that I am a force to be reckoned with, and that

I will help them defeat Bernais and his elven cohort.

I am *the Percival*. The Percival who helped rid the world of the blight. The Percival who worked with the gnome Drow to prevent the use of transformation to punish lesser creatures ever again. This is who I am, and I should live this.

'Ellie, Genie, wait up,' I call into the night.

The two witches half turn and wait for me.

'I'm sorry, Percival,' Ellie says. 'Genie and I have to hurry back. A leader of a group we hope will join us in the fight against Bernais and the faux council he has set up is stopping by.'

'*We* need to be back for that,' I correct her, my voice firm.

Her eyebrows rise, and she sends a sideways glance towards Genie, a smirk playing on her lips.

'About time, Percival,' Eugenia says matter-of-factly. 'Then *we all* must make haste.'

Is it as simple as that? Have they been waiting all this time for me to stop being a cat and remember that I am a sprite with a voice?

As we reach the outskirts of the village, we take the left-hand fork in the road and head towards a rambling house built in the shade of an enormous oak tree. Even though we don't venture into the village itself, we can see that the streets are eerily deserted for this early in the evening.

Genie follows the direction of my gaze and places a hand on my shoulder.

'We have much to catch up on, my friend. Given the current state of political unrest, creatures are reluctant to leave home after sundown.'

Before we reach the house, the door opens, spilling light out in a welcoming arc and illuminating the figure of the woman who is my second mother.

'Hello, Percival. You have made it safely. Welcome home.' Seraphina's voice is warm as she greets me. 'Daughters, Gregor is already here. He hasn't much time before he travels to the World Between.'

Seraphina stands aside, allowing us to enter before her. While Ellie and Genie remove their cloaks, she studies me. 'You look like you have been in the wars, young creature.'

'That is an understatement. I literally had to fight my way past dwarves to the portal at Loch Ness to get here.'

'Would you like me to organise a bath for you?'

In the past, I would have killed to bathe and change into a clean set of clothes from the store I leave here. Gregor is the most powerful witch of his generation, and he is also the leader of a group of young people challenging the existing order in the World Below. The new Percival is going to attend this meeting.

THE WORLD BETWEEN

'No, thank you, Seraphina. Perhaps later on. I will join the others for now.'

She inspects me silently, her eyes black pools of concern. 'Something is different about you tonight, Percival. We must speak after Gregor has gone. In the meantime, would you like some tea and something to eat?'

My stomach gurgles and Seraphina laughs. 'I will take that as a yes.'

'Yes, please,' I say as I follow Ellie and Genie into the living room. Seraphina retreats to the kitchen, leaving both doors open, something she does when she wants to hear what is going on.

'Eugenia, Eleanor. I was worried I would have to leave before I had spoken to you,' a young man says as he rises from a chair by the fire.

Genie waves a hand at him, gesturing for him to remain seated. 'If we stand on ceremony, we'll be here all night, Gregor.'

The young man relaxes back into his seat and runs a hand through unruly auburn hair. 'Is it safe…?' He glances my way as his voice trails off.

'You've met Percival before,' Ellie says, sitting on the sofa opposite their guest, and Genie joins her.

'Yes, of course. But normally….' Again he does not finish his sentence.

'Yes, yes,' I say impatiently. 'Normally, I am the cat on the sidelines. Tonight I am the sprite taking part. Do you have a problem with that?'

Gregor's eyebrows are not the only ones in the room to rise at the brusqueness of my words.

'No, of course not.'

'Good.'

I take a place on the sofa opposite the fire, close to Genie. Soon after, Seraphina comes in carrying a tray with a teapot, mugs, and some slices of fruit cake.

When we are all seated, drinks and food distributed, Gregor begins.

'I came here tonight via the Capitol. When Bernais took control of the city, many students ended up stuck, unable to go home. Some of us made it to the World Above before they placed a barrier on the portal. We've been returning in small numbers via the mountain gate in Essendore.'

He pauses to sip some tea. 'I would not have stopped here, except I had to wait for permission to join my friends in the World Between.'

Everyone else nods their understanding except me. This is not right—creatures do not just ask for permission to enter the dragon realm.

'What do you mean you are going to the World Between?' I ask.

Everyone turns my way as if I have said something strange. Then Ellie's eyes flicker with understanding. 'Of course, you were in the Unseelie Court when the Capitol fell.'

'I was.' I lower my eyes as a twinge of betrayal tugs at my heart. Ellie was one of the creatures who had plotted to send Pris, Snake, and me to the Unseelie Court. Hurt though I am that she had not let me in on the plan, that is a discussion for another time.

'Let me bring you up to speed,' Ellie says. 'The university has always encouraged liberal thinking and challenging the status quo.'

'It is the way of the young,' I agree, wearily hoping she will get to the point soon.

'Well, Bernais and his new council took exception to their protests and declared them, and some of the more radical protestors in the Capitol, outlaws.'

'That *is* surprising, but it does not explain how the dragons are involved?'

Gregor leans forward and places his now empty mug on a side table. 'The dragons have offered us sanctuary while the monarchy is under dispute.'

I massage my forehead. This is a lot to take in. Dragons do not take sides in our internal politics. They were clear that they could only assist Pris, Snake, and me when we were actively working to help Queen Ariana so she could restore the proper flow of magic between the worlds. Had things now become so bad that they have no option but to intervene? And what does that mean for our future?

'I see what you are thinking, Percival,' Seraphina says, 'but you are wrong. The dragons have not taken sides. They are only offering sanctuary for those outlawed by a government the dragons do not consider legitimate. If Bernais's faction is successful in overthrowing the queen, then the dragons will withdraw their offer of a home when they accept Bernais as king.'

My weary lids droop closed. I have only been gone a few weeks. When had this all become so complex? Or was it always, and I just had not noticed?

'Percival?' Seraphina places a hand on my arm. 'You are clearly tired. Your room is prepared. Perhaps it is time to sleep.'

I force my lids apart. 'It has been a long day for me, and there is much I need to tell you all, but that can wait. However, I would like to know what Gregor came to tell us before I rest. He did not choose to wait here by accident.'

Gregor nods. 'I came to warn you that we are going to attack the Capitol. We have to do something before the elitists become intrenched and definitely before they take over the palace. While the Queen's Guard holds out there, there is still some hope we can oust them.'

No one speaks. Effie and Ellie share a look that suggests a lack of surprise.

'You are not the only ones thinking this way,' Genie says. 'Ellie contacted the Wizard Council, and, while they will not support any action we take, there are some who will abdicate from the order and help our cause.'

'If you send word when you are ready to move, we will join you and bring all the strong magic users we can muster,' Ellie adds.

'And what about the other creatures?' Gregor asks.

I stare from my witch friends to Gregor and back again. Are they discussing what I think they are—civil war?

'Some local communities are already calling a muster. The Wyld Woods village and sprite representatives are meeting tomorrow. We believe they will also agree to join the muster at the base of the Essendore Mountains,' Seraphina tells the young witch.

'Those of us who have fled the Capitol, or have come back from the World Above, are ready whenever you are,' Ellie says. 'The only creatures we have not heard from are the elves and gnomes from the villages within the Wyld Woods. They never accepted the rule of the Crown family, and as Magnus Baaronson has left them to their own devices, they probably do not feel they have a stake in this fight.'

Gregor shifts in his chair. 'Can we win without their support? What if all the greater creatures decide to opt out?'

'Then that will make your position all the stronger when we win,' Seraphina says dourly.

'His position?' I ask.

'Gregor and his rebels want to use Bernais's takeover to upend society. They want to support inter-creature marriages and restore lesser creatures to equal status in society,' the witch protector of the Wyld Woods says, her tone sour enough to turn milk.

'But Seraphina, I thought those were your aims as well,' I say.

'They are, but I believe those rights need to be won through the court, not on the battlefield.'

'What would you have us do, Mother? Sit back and wait for Ariana to retake her rightful place and hope that is enough to stop Bernais?' Ellie asks.

'Or would you rather we stop him before he gets started?' Genie presses.

I have clearly opened a can of worms that I should have left closed.

Beside me Seraphina huffs. 'Bernais and Magnus would destroy our realm. They have no interest in seeing magic restored, although they might change their minds when there is no more magic for them to use. However, I would rather not see war in our land.'

'That is not within our control, Mother, but in Bernais's. He has had a taste of power, and he will not let go unless we force him to,' Genie says somewhat sadly.

Ellie stops refilling her teacup. 'It is like this is the last stand of the conservatives. If they don't grab power now, they will lose everything because the forces for change are getting stronger and challenging their privilege.'

Seraphina folds her arms and leans back in her seat. 'You are right—this is necessary, but I still do not want to see creature fight creature.'

I stare into the fire and wonder what is becoming of my home. Can I really do anything to save it from destruction?

SOMEONE'S IN MY room. I'm immediately fully awake, holding still, listening. Beside me, Pris's body is nestled into mine, her chest gently rising and falling. There isn't much space in the single bed, but it's worth the discomfort to have her this close to me. I bury my face in her hair, the scent of her washing away the loneliness I'd felt at our distance when we were in the Unseelie Court.

'Ugh,' she groans as she tries to turn over. This is the noise that woke me. There isn't an intruder after all.

Before our reunion last night, the Dragon Queen had used her magic to heal Pris. I pull Pris closer as I remember that reunion, then mentally shake myself—*focus, Snake Fieth*. Although she is outwardly fine, her body will need a lot of rest to recover, and we certainly had not spent the early part of the night doing anything remotely restful.

There is another bed in our room, but I don't fancy the idea of crawling from the warmth of our shared nest and moving over there. I have a better idea. Not far away from our room is a bathroom containing a tub filled with naturally warm springwater.

I slip from under the covers, making sure not to let any of the cool air disturb Pris, then pull on some loose trousers and grab my shirt. Pris rolls into the warm patch I've left, snuggling deeper under the covers. For a moment I consider climbing back in beside her, then remember she needs to sleep.

The bathroom is free, and as I sink below the gloriously warm water, I stretch and allow my body to relax. Percival is with Eleanor, Pris is safe, and the injury she sustained as we battled to reach the World Below is healed—I am done for the moment. I am so tired of being ready to react to the next thing the World Below has to throw at us. It is so liberating to be safe.

The tension of the past few weeks seeps from my shoulders as my body floats free. From the time I found out the Bad Fairies had taken my mother to the World Below to face trumped-up charges of illegally profiting from magic, I have been on one quest after another to get her back.

THE WORLD BETWEEN

It started with convincing Pris to come with me to save her own parents from the same fate. First, we found our way to the Midnight Ball in the World Below, and then Bernais hoodwinked us into accepting a noble quest to bring back what was in the middle of The Minotaur's Maze. We reached the centre to find Queen Ariana locked in stasis, and we were duped into going to the Unseelie Court to petition their king for help. After all of that, we still don't have our parents back, and rescuing them will now have to wait until we save the world.

I duck under the water again, trying to block everything out and just be in this moment, but I can't. Once I might have been able to forget about my commitments, but not now. The journey Pris and I took to get here has taken its toll, and I am no longer the gnome I was—hell, I'm not really a gnome at all. What a revelation that was, finding out my grandmother was an elf, and that my mum being half elf was why Bernais had really arrested her.

Unable to hold my breath any longer, I break the surface of the water and shake my head, trying to clear my thoughts. There is no value in rehashing the past few weeks. What matters now is how we move forward.

Unlike Pris, who is being nudged in a direction she doesn't want to go, no one is manipulating my actions. I can't rescue my mother, and though I will always help Pris, I need more than in my life than supporting her. Just what that will look like… goddess only knows.

I push myself from the bath and towel myself dry before dressing in the clothes provided by the outlaws. They are a little crumpled from being discarded on the floor while Pris and I greeted each other, but they will do for now.

Cleaning the bathroom to make it ready for the next creature takes a couple of minutes, but it wakes me up. I pop my head into our room, but Pris is still asleep. There are voices down the other end of the hallway, coming from the communal room sitting at the hub of the cave complex. Joining them is an option.

I pass several doors before hiding in the shadows of the common room opening. The creatures there are deep in conversation, and I don't want to interrupt anything personal. A mixture of creature races circle the fireplace in the middle of the room, most of them relaxing on large cushions. It's difficult to believe these creatures are being hunted simply for wanting to change things. Just as I can't believe that in the week Pris and I were at the Unseelie Court, so much changed in the World Below, and all because Bernais Baaronson is now the self-proclaimed Chancellor-Soon-To-Be-King. He and the councillors he hasn't dismissed are intent on returning the world back to a time when elves were supreme and every creature knew their place.

'I don't want to live in the Unseelie Court just because I love Gregor,' Verona Coronas is saying as I force my attention back to the group around the fire. She is the only creature I recognise, and I'm surprised she's with the outlaws, as her father is one of Bernais's staunchest supporters. 'But I will if I have to,' she finishes.

Stepping out of the shadows, I decide it's time to give them an update about the events in the World Above and the Unseelie Court.

'I'm afraid the Unseelie Court is no longer an option,' I say, and everyone's attention turns my way. I suck in a breath to calm my nerves. *This is no different to singing to a room full of strangers.* 'In order to protect the Unseelie Court from an attack, we had to place it in magical stasis. The World Above will need to produce an awful lot of magic before anyone can cast the spell to bring it back.'

The room falls deathly quiet, and the atmosphere is so tense, you could cut it with a knife. The fire hisses and crackle as I wait for someone—anyone— to respond.

Someone across on the other side of the fire laughs, 'Good one, mate. You had us going there.'

I don't know what to say to that. It is a fact, but I can't prove it, and I'm too mentally exhausted to debate the issue.

'Snake, come and join us,' Verona says, smiling her encouragement as she waves me over.

I'm grateful for her save, but I'm uncertain if I want to be here now. Verona moves over to make room for me on her oversized cushion. I accept her invitation and sink down beside her.

'Do you feel up to telling us what happened in the Unseelie Court?' she asks.

I don't think I'll ever be able to bring myself to share the story of how I helped wake a giant, stole its magic, and put an entire court to sleep in order to prevent it being destroyed forever. Or describe the soul-destroying revelation of betrayal just as we were fighting our way back to the World Below.

I find myself fixated on the fire, regretting not having returned to bed. Then again, if I don't help these creatures understand that there is no Unseelie Court to offer them refuge, who will?

I begin at the beginning, with the queen needing King Maddox to help her cleanse magic. I tell them about the king grieving because attacks on the Unseelie Court killed the love of his life. Then I tell them about the battle that has already begun in the World Above. I don't tell them I worry there will soon be a battle in the World Below; admitting that out loud will make it too real.

'If we can't go to the Unseelie Court, then we must stand and fight here,' Verona says, and many around the fire agree with her.

'If the king and queen restore magic, we can cast the spell to bring the court back. I'd rather go there and forget about this backwards realm,' the girl beside me argues.

'Yeah, even if the queen is back in charge, nothing will ever change while the elven lords rule their fiefdoms as governors,' the boy across the fire adds.

How long have the creatures in the World Below felt like this? To me, the creature realm has always been a place with unfettered magic where creatures don't have to hide their abilities. On closer inspection, there are as many problems here as in the World Above.

'We will never have a better opportunity to change perceptions than this. If we help Queen Ariana put Bernais and his followers back in their place, then she will have to listen to us,' Verona argues.

I close my eyes as the debate rages around me. Suddenly I'm overcome by a bone-deep weariness as the past few weeks catch up with me, and I'm too tired to take part in the discussion. As my mind drifts off, a thought worms its way into my subconscious, pulling me back from the edge of sleep. Should these creatures achieve their goals, they can marry whomever they wish. In the world they want to make, there will be room for an elf and mixed blood gnome—Pris and I would have a chance, and that is worth fighting for.

PRINCESS?

The insistent voice interrupts my dream. Ignoring it, I focus on Snake, his arms around me, him leaning in….

Princess!

Why are we always interrupted just when things are getting interesting? No, wait. We—

Princess, I do not need to know that!

My eyes fly open. Was I just about to relive Snake's and my reunion for Am'ratha?

Yes, you were. And thank the Mother I reached you before you did!

I sit up, rubbing the sleep from my eyes as I note the absence of another body in my bed. The place Snake occupied is cold, so he's been up for a while.

Princess, please focus. You must get ready to fly to the Minotaur's Maze.

I'm still searching the room for signs of where Snake disappeared to, so it takes a moment for my bonded dragon's words to sink in.

What? Why?

I was not given a reason. As soon as it is light, I am to take you to the Maze. That is all I have.

The Minotaur's Maze? Really? My memories of that place are not particularly fond, and I have no desire to head back there. What would happen if I refused to go?

That would not be a good idea. The Dragon Queen wants you there, and it is best you never find out what would happen if you did not go.

Sometimes it is disconcerting to have someone able to speak directly into your mind, let alone read it. And it's even more off-putting when they deliver information with a thread of dread that leaves you reeling.

I will be ready.

After last night's physical activities, I need a bath. I hope I have time. It's hard to tell because there are no windows inside the dragon's guest caves.

Throwing off the sheet and colourful woven blanket, I swing my legs over the side of the bed, wincing as I force myself upright. The Dragon Queen may have healed most of the damage done to my body from the magical blast I received, but my side is still tender.

Moving slowly, I retrieve my clothes and shuffle towards the bathroom. The corridor is empty, but voices drift down from the common room, so I either slept for a short time, or I was out for the count and it's morning already. I quicken my pace, not wanting to keep Am'ratha waiting too long.

The warm water is bliss. I slide back, allowing my hair to stream out behind me. It's still disconcerting to see it white instead of its natural black. I guess my eyes changed from brown to blue when I arrived here too. I trace my fingers round the slightly pointed form of my left ear. Although I can feel the touch, the shape does not register as belonging to me. I'm still not used to changing into elf form every time I leave the World Above.

My change in appearance makes it difficult to deny who I am now. I'm no longer the girl about to embark on a family holiday before starting university. I am an elven princess who is part of a strange, magical world. That's not strictly true. I am not a part of this world. I am part of the royal family who governs the World Below.

No longer relaxed, I sit on the ledge running round the edge of the pool. All my recent problems come back to the fact my mother is the niece of the queen. That means I'm actually in line to become ruler of the Seelie Court in the World Below. Worse still, the Dragon Queen will bump me to the front of the line if Queen Ariana doesn't get better soon.

No, I don't want to go there. If I accept my fate, I'll have to give up ever having a normal life—and I'll probably have to give up Snake. My body tingles at the memory of last night. We had waited so long, and it was so worth the wait.

If only we could spend some more time together… but I've been called away again. Will I always have to put duty first? Is this my life now?

I lean my head back against the lip of the tub and stare up at the ceiling. If only I were back at home in my bathroom with its white tiles and fluffy purple towels. Everything in the dragon's guest quarters is grey and spartan. Still, it's amazing to have a real bathroom in a cave. How did the dragons do it?

Magic, of course. Everything here is magic.

If someone had told me a few months ago that magic was real, I would've thought they were nuts. And that's exactly what I thought when Snake told me. Even when I used magic to make my first flame, I still couldn't quite believe it existed. Then Snake and I stepped through a doorway to the World Below to attend the Midnight Ball, and there it was—a magical world straight out of a fantasy story. If I hadn't physically changed when I stepped through that door, I would probably still be denying I belong here.

I shake the water off my hair and force myself out of the bath, no longer able to relax. If the World Below had been a revelation, the Unseelie Court had been a bombshell. My parents had hidden the World Below from me, but they had also kept the fact that my father's brother was Maddox, King of the Unseelie Court.

I roughly dry myself, almost like I think I can rub away my parents' betrayal with the towel. I can't. Nor can I wash away the fact they brought me up believing it is my duty to contribute to society and to make the world a better place.

Argh, it's so frustrating. The sense of obligation they instilled in me means I couldn't ignore it when I was asked to help Queen Ariana and the Seelie Court. It's also why I'm getting dressed so I can do the Dragon Queen's bidding now.

Oh my god, have Mum and Dad been preparing me for my royal duties all along?

The thought burns like acid in my stomach. Have they really been that deceitful? I'd like to believe they haven't and that they have good reasons for what they've done. Perhaps I should reserve judgement until they have a chance to explain themselves.

I pull on the linen trousers and shirt given to me when I arrived, plait my hair, then quickly tidy the bathroom. Our room is still empty, so I wander down the corridor towards the voices.

Feeling unsure if the bunch of strangers will welcome me, I search for Snake. I find him curled up asleep beside a petite platinum blonde creature who looks vaguely familiar. Was she at the Midnight Ball?

'My father's as big a hypocrite as any of them. I mean, look at the size of me. There is no way an elf would be this short if there wasn't some creature-mixing somewhere in our past,' the girl says. 'So why's he so against my being with a witch?'

At the mention of her father, I study the elf closely. Those sharp eyes and the sardonic quirk of her lips transport me back to the house in London where Giles Coronas, the elf who later spoke against my mother at the Midnight Ball, attempted to talk me out of finding my parents. Snake is sharing a cushion with Gile Coronas's daughter, Verona.

My chest tightens. The two of them seem so comfortable together. Jealousy is not something I'm used to feeling, but here it is, rearing its ugly head. Before I can do anything stupid like act on it, Snake's eyes blink open, and he groggily searches the room. He spies me and jumps to his feet, startling his pillow mate.

'Pris.' He's by my side in seconds, worry twisting his face. 'I left you to sleep. I figured you'd need it for healing, and after, you know….' As his voice trails off, his face flushes. He takes his hand in mine. 'Come join us.'

I resist his pull. 'No, I can't. I've been called to the Minotaur's Maze.'

He stops in his tracks. 'Why?'

'I don't know. Am'ratha just said her queen would be upset if I refused.'

Snake's lips quirk into an almost smile. 'You still thought about not going, didn't you?'

'For a moment. I'm tired of feeling like a piece on a chessboard. I'd like to stay in one place for a while.'

Snake slips his arms around me, and I snuggle into his shoulder. 'I'd like us to be together, too, and I keep saying we will be soon, but—'

'Unfortunately, in these times of unrest, romance must wait.' The voice comes from behind Snake, and I untangle myself from his embrace to find Verona Coronas smiling up at me.

'Sorry to interrupt, but we've had a dragon messenger arrive. They asked us to kit you out for flying. I'm Verona, by the way, and you're Priscilla?'

'Pris,' I say automatically, that little worm of jealousy writhing in my stomach.

The elf smiles with a warmth I'm not able to return. 'Yeah, Snake said you prefer that. If you come with me, there's a surprisingly good clothes stash in a cupboard in the dining room.'

I reluctantly let go of Snake and follow the girl. Snake trails behind as we go through a curtained archway into a room containing three long wooden trestle tables with benches down either side. The smell of sausages frying distracts me for a moment, and Snake nudges me forward. On the other side of the tables is a large cupboard stuffed with gear.

'Where did all this come from?' I ask.

Verona rummages through a shelf and hands me some moleskin trousers and the softest white woollen jumper.

'Most of us arrived with only the clothes on our backs. So, the dragons made a run down to the villages in the Wyld Woods, asking for spare clothes. Do you have boots?'

'Yes, they're back in the room.' I hold the clothes up, wondering whether they'll fit.

'They're magical, so they'll do fine,' Verona tells me matter-of-factly. 'Snake, are you going with her?'

'Umm, I don't know if I've—'

'He wasn't expressly invited,' I tell Verona, before placing a hand on Snake's arm, 'but if you want to come….'

'Do you want me to come?' he asks, and it's the perfect response.

'Of course I do,' I reassure him. 'But it is the maze, and if you haven't been invited, then, we don't want to upset the Minotaur.'

'So it's probably better if I stay here?' His eyebrows rise in a question, his tone all too eager.

The sigh escapes before I can suppress it. I understand his reluctance, I'm not looking forward to meeting Aeron again either. This is yet another thing I must face alone when I would rather have Snake with me. 'I guess so.'

Drawing me near, he gently kisses my hair. 'I'll be here when you get back.'

'What will you do while I'm gone?'

'Sleep,' Snake says as another male voice chimes in, 'Help us prepare to march on the Capitol.'

Our attention shifts to the doorway, and we discover a tall creature with dark auburn hair standing there. In the blink of an eye, Verona was by his side and then in his embrace.

'Gregor, I wasn't sure—'

She stops mid-sentence as the creature bends down and kisses her as if there's no one else in the room. My little worm of jealousy does a deep dive of shame as Snake leans in and whispers, 'Gregor was stuck in the Capitol, and Verona was worried something horrific had happened to him.'

'Why?' I ask.

'Because he's a leader of the creature rebellion.'

I make myself busy folding my clothes, wondering how I'm going to get past the reuniting couple to get changed, when Verona turns in Gregor's arms.

'Hon, this is Priscilla Crown and Snake—'

'Fieth,' Gregor finishes. 'Percival told me you'd be here, although he said you were injured, Princess.'

'Pris, please,' I tell him.

Verona turns to me. 'How about we organise you some breakfast while you go get changed? She has been called away by the dragons.' This last is directed towards Gregor.

Snake picks up my clothes and prepares to follow me.

'She won't have time for you and food, Snake,' Verona says.

Snake glances at me, and I'm caught between wanting to spend as much time with him as I can and wanting to eat.

'I'll be quick,' I tell him as I take the clothes and slip between Gregor and the door.

POSTURING

CROSSING THROUGH THE now empty common room, I pull back first one, then another treated leather curtain blocking the cave entrance, making a gap big enough to glimpse the rising sun turning the sky pink. I rush to get changed, waiting a beat for the clothes to adjust to my size, before returning to the dining room. As I enter, the smell of a cooked breakfast sets my stomach rumbling. Sending a quick prayer to whoever is listening not to send Am'ratha until I've eaten, I scan the room for Snake.

Creatures crowd around two of the tables, eating, talking, and laughing. Snake, Verona, and Gregor are at the far end of the third table, separate from the other creatures, who are casting curious stares at them. I slide into the empty seat beside Snake and serve myself from the platter of food on the table.

I take a mouthful of the steaming cup of coffee someone thoughtfully left for me, and groan in pleasure before wolfing down some sausages, eggs, and mushrooms. Letting the food settle, I notice quite a few of the creatures are watching me.

'They know who we are,' Snake whispers. 'We've become kinda famous.'

I cover my mouth before I snort out coffee. 'In a good way, I hope'

A wry smile appears on Verona's face. 'In an iconic "we'd follow you to the ends of the earth" kinda way.'

I almost choke again, and she laughs. 'Aren't you pleased about that?'

I turn halfway to check out what's happening behind me, and some of the other creatures shift position, pretending they weren't staring at us.

Leaning towards Verona, I ask 'Why?'

Her chuckle is low and throaty. 'Because you stood up to Bernais Baaronson, and you went on a quest and met the Minotaur, and you're in love with each other. It's the stuff of songs and epic novels.'

'It's what?' Snake splutters, and I say, 'We're just friends.'

Verona and Gregor share a look that screams, 'Can you believe these guys?'

Under the table, Snake squeezes my hand. If ours is a love story, and we haven't had time to figure that out, then I'm certain neither of us wants it to be such a public one.

'Stop teasing them, Verona. From what I've heard, they've been through a lot, and it's not over yet,' Gregor says.

Verona's face turns serious. 'We've all suffered, Gregor, and we're all risking so much. That's why it's so important to remember why we're doing this—so you and I and Snake and Pris can decide whether we want to be together, not have some outdated and restrictive set of laws tell us who we can love.'

Verona is so intense. She clearly feels deeply about this and it makes me wonder how many other creatures feel the same. However many, it's comforting to find someone else who is passionate about change in the World Below.

Clapping breaks out from the tables behind us, and Verona colours, perhaps unaware of how her voice has risen. Gregor hugs her. 'If our little movement has a heart, it's you, Verona.'

'We have the heart and the brains. What we need now is a leader we can rally around, someone to inspire us,' Verona says, looking expectantly our way.

'What?' Snake forces out while I'm still searching for words.

'No, you can't mean us,' I finally say.

'No one here knows us,' Snake adds.

Verona smiles and leans closer to us over the table. 'No, but they know *of* you, and they know what you've risked, and that is even better.'

'Man, I'm pleased you're on our side,' I blurt out, in awe of Verona's cool, calculated approach.

Gregor grins with obvious admiration, 'I know, right?' He turns to us. 'In all seriousness, we do lack inspiration, and we're going to need it because I want us to join up with the other groups opposing the new council and help them take back the Capitol.'

It's like someone has thrown a bucket of ice water over me. After fighting the dwarves to get here, the last thing I want to do is walk into another violent confrontation, let alone a full-on war.

Under the table, I grip Snake's hand, wanting to feel the comfort of his touch.

Snake whispers, 'Pris, are you okay?'

I'm far from okay, but I can't find the words to express how I feel right now. Squeezing Snake's hand as if I'm clutching onto a life raft, my eyes find Gregor's and I beseech, 'There must be another way.'

'If you have any ideas, I'm all ears. The last thing I want to do is lead my friends into battle against trained soldiers.' There is a heaviness to his words that convinces me this is not a decision he's taken lightly.

'Can't you wait for the queen to make good on her promise to rise from her sickbed and reunite the country?' I ask in desperation.

Gregor studies me with such intensity, I have to resist the urge to squirm. 'Do you know something I don't? I mean, my contacts at the palace say no one has seen her for some time. They fear she is dead.'

'She isn't dead,' I blurt out as Snake says. 'It's more complicated than that.'

Snake lets go of my hand and leans forward, lowering his voice, 'Please, this is just between us. The queen exhausted herself trying to keep magic flowing. We convinced King Maddox to help her even though his court has been under attack, but it will take time for the two of them to sort things out. Surely we can wait until then.'

I school my face not to react to Snake's words which, although aren't strictly lies, skirt the edge of truth. Maddox and the dragons must wake the queen before they can restore her health, but that makes little difference to what we're asking Gregor to do.

'The Elven governors have sent most of their forces to the Capitol. They have control of the council and have imposed martial law. The only reason they haven't overrun the palace is that the Queen's Guard stands strong there. However, once the palace falls, so will most of the resistance to the new council,' he says.

'I don't understand how the conservative faction got enough votes to remove Elias as Chancellor,' Snake says.

Gregor barks out a laugh. 'Oh, that was easy, and a politically genius move. Bernais brought forward a resolution to have the wizards removed from the council, stating that, although they hold themselves apart from the rest of witch-kind, they are still witches and so should not have separate seats. Of course, the dwarves and goblins jumped at that because they've long complained that witch-kind had six seats to everyone else's three.'

'But how could that pass?' I ask. 'If there were six witch votes, three gnomes, and Elias, that should have passed 10 to 9.'

Verona grimaces. 'Unfortunately, wizards couldn't vote on a motion about them.'

'Oh,' Snake and I say in unison.

'Yes. And it gets worse,' Verona continues. 'Once the wizards were removed, a dwarf brought forward a resolution stating that, as gnomes are lesser elf-kind, then the same rules should apply to them. That passed, and the elves then controlled the council. They appointed Bernais Chancellor, and the queen was not there to object.'

My stomach churns, and I worry my breakfast might make a reappearance. Two simple resolutions were all it took to change everything in the World Below.

Beside me, Snake balls his fists. 'Our race is hundreds of years old. Sure, we were once elves, but we have evolved and flourished as a separate race.' His voice rises in protest. 'We have lost our voice and our identity in one fell swoop.'

Gregor nods sympathetically. 'I understand your anger, but that is just the tip of the iceberg. By limiting the council to elves, witches, goblins and dwarves—'

'Elves and their cronies are running the World Below,' Snake finishes.

'And any chance of lesser creatures joining the council has been pushed back hundreds of years,' Verona adds.

How can this happen? Surely their constitution has checks and balances to prevent these sorts of decisions. 'I don't understand how they can get away with it.'

Verona grimaces. 'Unfortunately, you're thinking like I used to, that things here work similarly to the World Above, but they don't. It is up to the Crown, or its representatives, to ensure there is fairness and justice for all.'

'It took generations for the queen to give the council decision-making powers,' Gregor says. 'Initially, the council were simply advisors to the Crown, and the monarch would choose three from each of the greater races. Queen Ariana's mother turned the advisors into councillors who could suggest changes to the laws of the land. She then allowed the greater races to choose who represented them and expanded the council to include wizards.'

Gregor cups his hands around his mug and stares morosely into his drink. Rubbing Gregor's arm in a comforting gesture, Verona picks up the narrative.

'Things changed again under Queen Ariana. The witches proposed that the gnomes should join the council, and a single vote passed it. At that point, there was an even number of councillors. Queen Ariana decided the Chancellor was to have a deciding vote when the council was tied.'

'My family speaks of this as one of the greatest days in gnome history, and perhaps even in the history of the World Below. Elves treat gnomes as lesser creatures, and many thought this change would pave the way for other lesser creatures to join the council,' Snake finishes up.

'And in the last couple of days, Bernais and his cronies have rolled back centuries of change,' I say, as disappointed by their actions as the others.

Gregor bangs the table with his fist. 'Oh, we will fight this. But first we must prise the Capitol back from the conservative's grasp. Did you know, when I left, they were rounding up insurgents and throwing them in prison?'

My gaze flies to Snake. What about his family? And the witches? Eleanora and Eugenia had been working with the witch representatives on the council. Snake's eyes widen in fear as they meet mine.

'Don't worry, Snake, your father got your family to the palace. The witches refused to take a role in the new council, and they warned senior gnomes and witches in time for them to either flee the city or take refuge in the palace.'

Snake's worry lines ease as he replaces fear with resolution. His eyebrow rises in query, and I nod. He doesn't have to ask for my support, but I'm pleased he still considers us a team.

'I'll join your fight, but only as a foot soldier.'

Verona turns to me. 'And you, Pris? Will you join us?'

I take in the creatures around the room and Verona's hopeful face. I so want to say yes, but I promised the Dragon Queen I would take over Queen Ariana's duties if she didn't recover. If I hadn't, she might have agreed to acknowledge Aunt Adina's line, which would see Bernais seize not just the chancellorship, but the Crown.

Snake drapes an arm over my shoulder, and I lean into him. 'She can't. She is the only one who can prevent the dragons from acknowledging Bernais's claim to the throne. Her first duty is to make sure that doesn't happen.'

It sounds like a copout. I want to fight, and I'm more capable at fighting than Snake. Honestly, he'd be better with the dragons than me. He's way more diplomatic. If only we could reverse roles.

Am'ratha interrupts. *Princess, I am waiting.*

On my way.

'I reckon your battle is the tougher one.' Verona chuckles. 'I've met your aunt in the court of the Dragon Queen. She is very keen to see her son on the throne. Watch your back, and your front, with that one.'

'I've got to go,' I say reluctantly, taking one last gulp of coffee as I stand up.

'We'll talk more when you get back,' Gregor says.

Snake follows me out of the dining room and pulls me to a stop when I get to the treated leather curtains leading outside.

'Be safe,' he says, brushing his lips against mine.

I want him to hold me, but I fear if he does, I'll be tempted to stay.

'You too. And don't start any wars before I get back.'

His lips quirk into a lop-sided smile. 'I'm not promising anything.'

Snake leans in and touches his forehead to mine. I close my eyes and relish this moment of togetherness. Drawing in a breath, I squeeze his hand before I force myself to break the connection—I'm not great at goodbyes.

Am'ratha perches on the ledge outside, her purple scales glinting in the morning sun and her yellow eyes sparkling with humour. *Oh, this is going to be a fun trip.* I climb up her leg and nestle in a comfortable spot on her neck.

You have made the most of your short time here, my dragon friend says.

I don't know what you're talking about.

Our bond is different. You have mated.

OMG, is nothing sacred? And what does she mean by mated?

Ed'rathe will be pleased. He can request to bond with your mate.

Woah, hold on…. Back up there a mo. Snake and I are… close, but we're not mates.

Wow, how backward this place is if sleeping together means you're mated.

It is not about physical relations, Princess, it's about the bond between creatures. Surely you can feel the change.

I'm not talking about this—at least not with you. It's between Snake and me.

I should have guessed that my bonded dragon would feel obliged to weigh in on what happened last night. However, one night together does not a relationship make. We haven't talked about things between us yet, so I'm hardly going to discuss anything with Am'ratha.

Can we just get going? The sooner we get there, the sooner we can return.

Am'ratha humphs her displeasure as she pushes off with her powerful back legs, and I'm thrown backwards. I grip on to her scales as Am'ratha flies towards the snowcapped mountains of the World Between, then banks and comes back full circle.

What are you doing?

Before we go to the maze, the queen has decreed we must complete the bonding rites.

Sorry? What? I thought we were bonded.

Am'ratha snorts. Clearly we aren't actually bonded, but how was I supposed to know? I'm learning this as I go.

So, tell me, what do we have to do?

I am sorry, Princess. I sometimes forget no one has schooled you in the ways of an heir. We were granted permission to bond and given time to get to know each other. Today, the Dragon Queen asked me if we were ready to declare our bond before the ancestors, and I said yes. I hope that was all right?

There is a smidgeon of doubt in Am'ratha's question, which surprises me. This is clearly a big deal for her. As I believed we had already bonded, I can hardly object.

Yes, Am'ratha, it was the right thing to say.

I'm certain I sense a relaxing of Am'ratha's muscles beneath me, then she drops down below the cloud line and lands almost immediately on the ledge of a cave. As she folds her wings, a wave of hot air wafts over me.

Where are we?

The cave of the ancestors. You must stay on my back, as no creature can ever set foot on the ground here.

Okay, I say as Am'ratha drops her head and waddles into the cave.

If I thought flying on a dragon was difficult, maintaining my seat on her neck is near impossible as she makes her way through the cave entrance. I'm concentrating so hard on staying put that I almost lose my balance when Am'ratha stops moving. When I've regained my seat, I take the time to get my bearings and to appreciate the importance of this place.

Delicate crystalline stalactites hang from the roof that are so long, they must have been millennia in the making. They sparkle in the glow of the sconces around the walls, giving an ethereal air to the cavern.

The cave itself is awe-inspiring, but it is nothing to what rests in the centre of the floor. Surrounded by a colourful array of sleeping dragons are hundreds of silver, white, and gold eggs sitting in the glowing embers of a fire.

The eternal fire of life, Am'ratha explains.

Where are the ancestors?

They are here. When a dragon passes, a new egg appears. When an egg is ready, it hatches, and we are born.

I've been struck speechless very few times in my life, but now is definitely one of them. Am'ratha has brought me to the heart of the dragon world, and the honour not only steals my voice, but it takes my breath away.

What now? I ask.

We wait.

Wait for what?

As I finish speaking, I know what it is I have to do; what I have to say—it is as though the ancestors are placing the words in my head.

Great ancestors, we come before you to declare our sisterhood and that henceforth we will support each other as family. We will care for our brothers and sisters and the magical world to the best of our abilities until our dying breath.

We say the words together, and it takes less than a minute, but I know the weight of that declaration will remain with me for the rest of my life.

No doubt if I'd had more time to think this through, if I'd had some idea of what I was committing to, I would have stressed over whether or not to complete the bond. However, this way is perhaps easier.

As we leave the cavern, I lean down and hug Am'ratha. *Sister?*

Yes, we are sisters. But do not think that means you can take advantage of me.

The laugh escapes my lips as we reach the outside ledge.

Never, I tell her. *I feel….*

I trail off because I really don't know how I feel or what this means for my future. On the one hand, I have made a commitment to the World Below in a way I never have before, yet my mother made the same commitment and left this realm behind. Oh, and Adina must also have sworn the bonding oath, and look at how she behaves.

Do not overthink it, Princess. Now that you have made the bond, the bond will tell you if you are acting contrary to your oath.

So, I simply carry on as normal?

Of course. Just do what you believe to be right.

It can't be that easy.

The bond works on intent. If the ancestors believed your intentions are bad, then they would not have given us the words of the oath.

Oh. I don't know whether I find it disturbing that the ancestors assessed me without my knowing, or whether I think it's cool that magic works in this way.

Come, it is time to journey to the maze.

As Am'ratha pushes off and her wings beat, I can't help but think there should be a more dramatic ending to such a spiritual event. Then again, perhaps that is more of a creature or human perspective. The dragons seem to take all these amazing magical things in their stride.

Once we're above the jagged points of the mountain range encircling the dragon stronghold, the chilly air fingers its way under my clothes. Am'ratha banks, then flattens out.

Soon after we have left the mountains behind, the landscape turns orange and gold, and the breeze brushing my face turns balmy. I pick out the Wyld Woods to my left and the walls of the Minotaur's Maze to my right.

Beyond the maze, I can almost make out the forest that kept Snake from me so he could meet his great-grandparents. That seems so long ago, but it has only been a few weeks.

Leaning forward, I wrap my arms around Am'ratha's neck, suddenly needing something solid to hold on to. So much has changed over the past months, and it doesn't look like it'll slow down anytime soon.

I close my eyes and block out the world, turning my thoughts to Mum and Dad. If what Gregor said is true, they aren't in any immediate danger, so long as they have the Queen's Guard to protect them. In fact, they're safer than everyone else in the World Below because creature kind will soon face off in a civil war.

If I had a choice, I'd be back there with the others, plotting revolution rather than joining the establishment and supporting a regime I don't believe in. This is not who I am, but it's who I have to be until I can get someone else to take over.

Blowing out my frustration, I hug Am'ratha again. At least I am not alone in this. I have her, and I have Snake. They have my back. And, hopefully, I still have Percival.

We are almost there, Princess.

I want to bury my face in my dragon friend's neck and hide. Below lies more strangeness, more responsibility, and there's no one there with my best interests at heart.

I am here. I will look after you.

But only if you can without displeasing your Queen.

Am'ratha snorts a chuckle. *I will not let anyone hurt you.*

I guess that's something.

Am'ratha circles towards the ground, and I straighten in my seat, blanking my expression to one of cold confidence, unwilling to let anyone else see how tired and disheartened I really am.

THE SUN SLIPS through the gap in the curtains, falling across my face and forcing my eyes open. I can no longer feign sleep. The presence I sense in the room shifts in the chair as I roll over. Nathanial, an elder from my home grove in the Wyld Woods, stares unblinkingly at me.

'Percival, good, you are awake. Seraphina sent me to ready you before everyone arrives.'

Forcing myself into an upright position, I rub a hand over my face. 'Everyone?' I ask, frantically trying to remember why creatures would come here today.

'Yes—the local leaders attending the meeting to discuss what we are going to do about the unrest in the Capitol.'

A thought forces itself through the fog clouding my brain. The lesser creatures want to fight, to start a war against the armies of the ruling fae. Fear keeps me still as I contemplate how many might die should we fight. Our side has the numbers, but they have the trained standing militias. They also have the will to go to any extreme to win.

'Are you all right, Percival?' Nathanial asks, resting his elbows on his knees. 'You have gone quite pale.'

The sprite elder's concern touches me. I have missed him.

'I am… fine, Nathanial.'

He cocks a bushy grey eyebrow, and it slips under a fringe of almost white hair. *My uncle is old*. The thought hits deep. When had that happened? He is so old that he should be back in the grove, enjoying his last years, not here preventing a war.

Preventing a war? Is that what the sprites will do? Work to stop bloodshed and, when they cannot, retreat to the grove and wait out the violence?

'Yes, fine,' I say, although we both hear the lie. 'I will ready myself and meet you downstairs.'

Nathanial does not move. 'Your brother is here.'

I grin, my mood lightening. *Wait, he should be at the grove, overseeing the mourning of my father—preparing everything for the last farewell.* If he is here as our spiritual advisor, then things must be worse than I thought. Emrys's being here is a clear sign the sprites see recent events as impacting their well-being and security.

'And Nisha is with him.'

His words hit me like a punch. 'What? Nisha's here?'

To see me? No one else knows I am in the World Below.

'She is here to represent us at the meeting.'

I'm surprised—both by the fact that Nisha agreed to come and that we are old enough to represent our kind.

'Thank you for letting me know, Nathanial.'

Nathanial stands up to leave, then pauses. 'The witches want you to be a part of this meeting, and I can understand why—you have been involved in their machinations for years. However, I must make it quite clear that you do not speak for the sprites.'

His words are another blow. Nathanial has never treated me any differently since my punishment made it impossible for me to return to sprite form. That he should say these words to me now. Betrayal is not a strong enough word to describe my feelings.

'Oh, I see.' I fail at disguising my hurt.

Nathanial's face softens, and he takes a step closer, 'I have not spoken clearly. Sprite-kind chose us to represent them. We did not foresee your being here, so you can have no official role.'

'I understand,' I say, although the familiar old feelings of rejection and shame wash through me. It is so much easier to believe I am unwanted and unworthy—to assume the worst. Nathanial clears his throat, pulling my attention back to him.

'Also, it occurs to me your direct involvement in recent events means you can paint a bigger picture, one that includes all creature-kind. That is why your input will be valuable today.'

I *am* wanted, maybe even needed. The spectre of my own inadequacies releases its hold on my heart, allowing me to breathe again.

I swing my legs around. 'I guess I had better get ready, or I will not be attending, let alone representing anyone.'

Nathanial nods. 'Of course. We will wait for you downstairs so we might walk to the meeting hall together,' he says before letting himself out.

Before getting up, I ensure the door is closed. Someone has laid fresh clothes at the end of the bed and brought a bowl of water and a towel, which are on the dresser. I place my hands on the metal bowl and speak a warming spell, then give myself a quick wash, allowing the water to cleanse away the last of my hurt feelings.

The clothes are black, the only colour I have worn since my transformation into something not quite sprite, but they are from the World Below. The trousers are moleskin, the shirt linen, and the fine jumper I pull on over top is woollen. Someone has cleaned my black boots, and I pull them on gratefully. All clothing in the World Below is spelled to fit the wearer, even shoes, but a new pair of boots is never as comfortable as ones that have been with you for some time.

Checking myself in the mirror, I grimace. My hair has grown and is a little messy. I take a moment to imagine my hair shorter and draw in some magic. My scalp tingles as the strands shorten and my hair tidies itself. *Perfect.*

I could lie to myself and say that I always take pride in my appearance—and I do—but I also cannot bear to have Nisha see me disheveled. Since we bonded, I have put my mate through a lot, including spending years away from her. Now that I understand her belief we can have a life together regardless of my not being a full sprite to be true, I want to make a good impression on her.

Voices drift up from the living room, and I attempt to calm the butterflies flitting in my stomach as I descend the stairs. I am always excited to see Nisha, but this time I am also wondering why my healer wife, who rarely leaves the grove, has done so now.

My hand hovers over the door latch, and I attempt to catch a little of the conversation before entering. The stout wooden door filters everything into indistinguishable murmurs. I take in a breath as I press down on the latch and push the door open.

Genie greets me as I scan the room for Nisha. 'You're finally here, Percival. We can leave.'

She swoops past me, followed by Ellie, who squeezes my arm in a gesture that I perceive as support before exiting. Nathanial follows last, leaving two creatures standing in the middle of the room.

Emrys, my brother, and the new spiritual leader of the grove since our father's death, steps forward and pulls me into an embrace. 'It is good to see you so well.'

I return his hug, but all the while, my eyes are on Nisha. It is almost surreal to see her in the human form she dislikes taking. How graceful and fragile she appears, standing with her hands clasped in front of her. Her liquid black eyes hold mine while I finish greeting Emrys.

My brother releases me and follows my gaze. 'We shall talk later. Nisha, we have very little time before the meeting starts.'

Emrys's message is obvious—do not take too long. He leaves Nisha and me alone, firmly shutting the door on his way out.

She holds her hands out to me, and I step towards her.

'I did not expect you to be here,' she says as she clasps my hands.

Resting my forehead on hers, I breathe in her essence. 'Is it a pleasant surprise?'

She pauses before answering. My mate has never found it easy to lie, nor is she practiced in the arts of demurring.

'It is neither good nor bad, Percival. Or perhaps I would be more accurate to say it is a little bit of both. I am always happy when you are with me. However, having you here may divert my focus from effectively representing our grove.'

I press my lips to her hairline and whisper, 'What is it you are here to do?'

She pulls away from me and straightens her back, her countenance stern. She is such a warm person that it is easy to forget the rod of steel that runs through her.

'Percival, please do not ask me what the grove wants. I am not your spy or your agent. What I have to say today may run contrary to your beliefs, but it will be in our community's best interest.'

I run my hand down her arm in what I hope is a reassuring manner—it is hard to tell, as we have never spent long enough in each other's company to build the level of unspoken communication other couples have.

'Nisha, I am proud that you are here for our kind, proud that you have stepped forward. I will do nothing to compromise your work. This day we will both need to be true to ourselves and our beliefs, but I hope that does not lessen our bond.'

Nisha blinks slowly, considering my words. 'We have disagreed on many things in the past and that has not happened.'

I send her a smile that is tinged with sadness and regret. The distance between us is the result of my decisions. I want to rectify that, but does she? After years apart, I know who I am and that I want to be with her, but I cannot expect her to simply fall in line. I must work to win her back.

Holding out my arm for her to take, I say, 'Perhaps we can find some time to spend together later—we have much to catch up on. However, for now we should join the others, or they may leave us behind.'

Nisha slips her arm through mine and remains beside me all the way to the meeting hall. I walk a little taller with her by my side. When we arrive, she leaves me to join Emrys and Nathanial.

The tables, which are usually reserved for banquets and weddings, have been repurposed for this meeting. Someone has pulled them together to run the length of the rectangular room. Wooden chairs stand down either side with name tags in front of each one.

Genie walks along the sunshine-dappled floor in front of windows looking out over the town square. She takes a place at the top of the table beside a giant of a creature, his face obscured by a bushy brown beard. Thomas Mulligan, Wyld Wood Village's Head Creature, and head, too, of the dwarves here, bangs a gavel, and the creatures in the room take their seats.

On the right-hand side, facing the windows, are the lesser creatures—the sprites, brownies, pixies, and dryads. Opposite them are the representatives of the greater creatures—the dwarves and goblins, witches and gnomes. The seat beside Ellie and her mother, Seraphina, is vacant. They must be waiting for a third witch.

Although the creatures are greeting one another, the air in the room is tense, as if each group is poised to do battle. Politics in the World Below have not encouraged creature unity, but I hope they can over-come this antipathy today.

There is a row of seats on either side of the double entry doors, and I choose one on the lesser creature side of the table. I have just made myself comfortable when Thomas Mulligan calls the meeting to order and begins.

'We can wait no longer. We must start if we are to finish before any of the fey in residence at The Manor realise what is going on and send the guards out.'

The room falls silent, and the dwarf gestures for Genie to start.

'Good morning, all. We have an update on the Queen today, thanks to our friend, Percival.' She pauses as everyone turns my way. I lift my head and sit a little taller as I meet every gaze before they return their attention to the head of the table. 'King Maddox arrived in the World Below yesterday. We hope he and the queen will join forces and begin repairing magic once they have dealt with the threat to our govern—'

'I apologise for being late, but I ran into a couple of old friends, and I insisted they join us,' a voice booms from behind me, carrying to every nook and cranny by force of magic.

I do not need to turn around to know that Mandor the Wizard has entered the room—he must be the third representative of witch-kind. However, I am interested in finding out who he has brought with him. Shifting slightly in my seat so I can watch the party enter the main hall, I let out a gasp of surprise as Drow and Heart follow Mandor in.

ONCE PRIS IS gone, I no longer have the stomach for breakfast, but I've no idea what to do with myself. The refugees are limited to the guest cave for the time being, as dragons don't like creatures wandering through their realm, so I'm stuck inside. The cave itself only has two accommodation corridors, a common room, and the kitchen/dining area, so I can't really go exploring here either.

A few creatures have drifted back to the common room and are sitting round the fire pit chatting, so I drop onto a free cushion and listen while I wait for Verona to finish eating. Perhaps she can help me find something useful to do to pass the time.

'I appreciate this is an opportunity for us to force change, but I'm not sure a physical revolution is the answer,' the small elf girl to my right says.

'If you were as committed to forcing change as the rest of us, then you would fight,' a burly dwarf boy says with a sneer.

The girl rises to her feet and stares down at everyone. Her intense blue eyes are so like Verona's, I wonder if they're related. She places her hands on her hips and sneers right back.

'You write me off because I'm an elf, and because of that, you assume I can't be as committed to change as all of you. You're like children playing at revolution. The reason I believe we're not ready to fight is because we have no plan for after. If we completely overthrow the current government, we'd best be ready to rule—and we aren't.'

She turns on her heel and strides away.

'Johan, that was cruel,' another girl says. 'Orissa's parents threw her out when she defended Verona and Gregor. She could have stayed quiet and lived a comfortable life, but she is every bit as committed to change as the rest of us.'

'And she's not wrong,' someone else continues. 'We don't have a plan for after, and we don't want to pull everything down with no idea of what we will replace it with. That would be worse for creature-kind than what we have now.'

The cushion shifts as someone leans down and whispers close by my ear, 'So, what's the answer?'

'What?' I ask, turning to find Gregor crouched beside my cushion. 'I'm not a part of this. I have no experience living in the World Below.'

'True, but everyone has a view on the future of creature-kind, no matter where they live. And I'm not asking you to fix it single-handedly. I'm simply asking for your opinion.'

I stare at the flickering flames of the fire, fully aware of what Gregor is doing. If he draws me into the debate, I'm more likely to become their figurehead and rally everyone behind the plans for war. I answer him anyway.

'Life doesn't have to be all or nothing, Gregor, and it doesn't take a revolution to change things. If I were in your shoes, I would see Bernais and his followers as the principal threat because they represent a step backwards. You can't fight on two fronts, so I would consider working with the Queen, perhaps leveraging her need for your support to have her agree to a programme of change.'

Where did that come from? I'm not normally a political person. Perhaps spending time with Pris has rubbed off on me.

Gregor stands up and stretches. 'I didn't know gnomes were mind-readers.'

'We're not. Hold on, is that what you're planning to do?'

Gregor gnaws at his lower lip for a moment, and I get the impression he's trying to decide something. He studies me intently, like he's weighing up how much to trust me.

'Come with me,' he says, turning to leave the room.

I follow him down the corridor opposite the entrance. It also has bedrooms coming off it, but there isn't a bathroom at the end like there is down our corridor. To the left is a dark passage that smells slightly sulphuric, and to the right is a curtained doorway. Gregor pulls back the curtain and ushers me inside. I step into an almost empty room about double the size of the bedroom I shared with Pris. There's no furniture, just a few large cushions arranged around a small fireplace set into the opposite wall.

The curtain swishes closed behind me, and Gregor gestures for me to sit. Nestled between two of the cushions is a tray with a teapot and cups. Gregor clearly intended us to talk, no matter what I had said.

When I have a mug of tea in my hands, Gregor begins. 'What do you know of creature history?'

My brows draw together. This is not what I was expecting. 'That's a broad question. Although we all learn about the same events, I think our creature race colours our understanding of it.

'Of course.' Gregor sweeps a hand as if brushing away my comment. 'Let me clarify. How much do you know about creature history and the origins of magic?'

'Oh.' I place my cup on the floor and run a hand through my hair, attempting to dredge up lessons from long ago. 'Well, let's see. Dragons produce most of our magic. Some of it seeps through to the World Above and the World Below. Taking care of the environment and growing things supplements magic in these realms.'

'Well done.'

I'm surprisingly pleased by his praise.

'What about the waning of magic?'

This is easier to answer, not only because the history is more recent, but because I've always been interested in magic in the human world. 'In the World Above magic began declining as Christianity took hold and witches were persecuted. The Industrial Revolution, which saw more and more people leave the countryside for cities to work in factories, followed this. With fewer people working the land, and even fewer remembering the old ways to care for it, there is little magic left there.'

Gregor nods for me to continue.

'I knew little about the World Below until recently. As I understand it, magic bounced back after the blight, but lately the flow of magic between the worlds has become sluggish, and I guess we're using more than we're creating.'

Gregor nods. 'You have the gist of it. I have a book in my room on the history of magic and magic usage in the three worlds which I think you would find interesting.'

Is he kidding? I'd love it. Before all this adventuring, my plan had been to study physics and how it affects magic at a university in the World Above. Apart from music, this is what I am most passionate about.

'Let's go back a little further,' Gregor continues. 'Long ago, the three realms were separate. We each produced our own magic and kept to ourselves. When the ways between worlds opened, the dragons were worried some of their kind would force dominion over weaker creatures, so they cast a binding spell, keeping dragons in their own world, and have always limited who can come and go in the World Between. However, to ensure no one tried to sneak in to take magic, they allowed some of their store to flow through to the World Above and the World Below.'

'And that led to the Bargain of Dragons,' I say.

'Yes. The Dragon Queen summoned the most powerful magic wielder of each generation to step forward and form a bond with a dragon. Then the two would help channel magic into the flow between the worlds.'

'I thought it was the king or queen who was called to serve.'

'Back then, the World Below had no monarch. It was several separate territories, each with their own leaders and laws. A contest was held every fifty years to choose the next creature to bond. The elves consistently won every competition, which granted them a degree of power over other creatures, and they eventually held the leadership of most of the territories. Then, one family line showed most able, and our monarchy was born.'

I lean forward, fascinated by this new view of history. It explains a lot.

'What about mages and witches in the World Above?'

Gregor blows out a breath. 'Okay, the quick version of the history of the human world closest to ours, which maps onto Great Britain and Ireland, is that for generations, mages chose which of them would bond with a dragon. When the persecution of witches became a thing, mages and witches went underground. It became harder and harder to find magic wielders of sufficient ability to keep magic flowing.'

'If I have this right, originally a creature in the World Below and a witch in the World Above bonded with dragons to keep the flow of magic going,' I clarify. 'Did that change when the elves took the Crown?'

Gregor grins. 'It did indeed. Many creatures objected to the new monarchy, and especially to them imposing one rule of law on all creatures.'

'The first of those were the elves who didn't want the Crown family taking control,' I say.

'I should have known you'd be all over the gnome history. Unfortunately, the Crown family were too powerful, and when they won the battle, they restricted the amount of magic their enemies could access, creating gnomes.'

It hurts to have the birth of our race talked about so casually. The humiliation of serving the elven race since that day to earn back what is rightfully ours sours the stomach of every gnome.

It's also odd to be reminded that had the Queen not fallen ill at the Midnight Ball, my family would no longer have limits placed on our use of magic. Then Bernais would have less to complain about because my half-elf, half-gnome mother would have been more acceptable. A little ball of anger stirs in my gut. We are not lesser than elves because of our ancestors' actions. Nor should anyone treat my mother and me differently because we are mixed race.

I don't want to dwell on these thoughts, so I change the subject.

'There were other creatures who decided not to confront the elves directly, and they left the World Below to set up the Unseelie Court in the World Above.'

Gregor nods. 'Go on.'

'From that day on, the dragons allowed the monarch and their heir in both courts to bond with dragons to maintain the flow of magic between the worlds. Is that why we have people like Princess Petunia and Princess Adina bonding with dragons? Is it because they were heir to the throne at one stage?'

'Yes, that is exactly why,' Gregor confirms. 'And here ends our lesson on creature magic.'

Although I already knew most of these events, the new way of viewing them has my head spinning a little.

'Hold on, creatures keep magic flowing in the World Below, and the King of the Unseelie Court has taken on the job for the World Above, so what happened to human magic users?'

'There are very few people able to use magic in the World Above today, and much of their lore was lost when magic users went into hiding during the witch trials.'

'Wow, it must have been horrid to have an entire culture wiped out,' I say.

Gregor's lips twist into an almost secretive smile. 'That's the common history in the World Above. The story told in the World Below is different.'

Eager to learn something new, I urge him on. 'So, what really happened to human magic users?'

'Well, some of them had found a way into the World Below. The witches who arrived here were essentially refugees and had no place in this realm. Fortunately, the sprites and dryads offered them a home. They were used to dealing with all kinds of magical creatures in the World Above, so of course they became advocates for creator creatures in the World Below.'

'Creator creatures?'

'That's what creatures who tend to the environment used to be called. We call them lesser creatures now because they can't wield a lot of magic.'

'That is so cool. So, if witches came from the World Above, are they creatures or humans?'

'We have been here a long time, and we have assimilated into the culture, but yes, we are essentially human.'

Wow, and I thought I had problems.

'Is that why the conservative elves hate witches so much? Because you're not creatures?'

'It depends who you ask. Some of them dislike us because they hate humans, and some of them dislike us because we are as powerful as them—some of us more so.'

My head is spinning. 'Can I just clarify? Now that we have elves seizing power in the World Below and rewriting the rules to suit them, creatures who disagree set up the Unseelie Court.'

'Exactly. Then we have the ways closed between the worlds to consolidate elven power, which causes the blight here and the Dark Ages in the World Above. And magic has never been the same. And that's a potted history of magic in the Worlds Above and Below'

'Hold on, how do the creature villages in the Wyld Woods fit in? They're mixed communities and they follow their own rules.'

'Since they keep to themselves, no one bothers too much about them. There is just one more piece for me to fill in,' he says, 'and this is not a part of history that is often shared beyond my kind. When witches came here from the World Above, we could wield magic at a similar level to elves. In return for sanctuary, we agreed we would put no one forward to bond with a dragon.'

I can't believe what I am hearing. 'You're saying you agreed never to challenge elven superiority?'

'Correct. But it gets worse. Witches have a tradition of studying and developing the use of magic, and that didn't change when we came here. Add this to the fact that magic in the World Below is richer and runs deeper than in the World Above, our people soon began to develop spells and use magic in a way elves never could.'

My eyes are almost popping out of my head. 'You mean witches are stronger than elves? Why don't you all just take over?'

'Our original agreement. Any witch wishing to study advanced magic must leave the World Below and make a magically binding promise to never challenge the leadership of the Seelie Court.'

'And that's why witches formed the Wizard Council?' I ask. Mandor, the wizard who'd helped us enter the Minotaur's Maze, had given up his life with Eleanora to join the Wizard Council.

'Yes.' Gregor stares into the distance. 'We have such a wealth of power, and we can never use it because once a wizard breaks that basic rule and challenges the Crown, everything they have learnt since taking the vow is ripped from their memory.'

'That's harsh.' I can't imagine what it would feel like to have years of learning gone. 'Can't they just bind their magical ability like the elves did to the gnomes?'

Gregor's laugh is harsh. 'As you already know, it is possible to reverse that spell. Once wiped, a wizard's memory is irretrievable. Also, no one has ever triggered the spell, so we don't know how much of a wizard's memory is wiped. It may just be their knowledge of magic, but it also might be their life experience until that point.'

After Gregor finishes, a heavy silence lingers in the room. Finally, I state what is now all too obvious. 'So, basically, what it boils down to is elves acting to keep elves in power.'

'Of course.'

'I can't believe Queen Ariana or Princess Petunia would be a party to that,' I protest. 'Well, not Princess Petunia. She did defect to the Unseelie Court after all.'

'Perhaps she isn't part of it, but her sister definitely is. To her credit, she's made some minor changes, but she's not had much support from those who hold the balance to her power—the council and the regional governors.'

'I can't believe I'm defending her, but she's spent a lot of time trying to sort the flow of magic.'

'True, but the rise of elves and the failure of magic are linked. She should put as much effort into ensuring we produce more magic and use less.'

This is blowing my mind. It all goes so much deeper than we ever thought. There's too much to take in, too many problems, and no straightforward solution. I close my eyes and attempt to pull my thoughts into some sort of order.

'What I don't get is what could Queen Ariana do to make sure we produce more magic?'

Gregor's eyebrows rise. 'That's a fair question. Let's see. Take a dryad—a tree spirit. They take in magic from the world and feed it to the trees they tend, and in return the trees spread even more magic into the world.'

'Yep.'

'When we cut down trees, there are fewer trees to create magic. If we planted more trees that would help, provided we planted them in the right places. Because dryads and sprites don't do so well in villages and towns, trees planted there are not tended properly and produce no magic.'

'But if we set up groves for sprites and closes for dryads, they could live in villages,' I suggest.

'Exactly, but we're not even having those discussions. Meanwhile, greater creatures continue to use magic with abandon, while creator creatures are finding it harder and harder to work.'

I bark out a laugh. 'So we're caught in a vicious circle.'

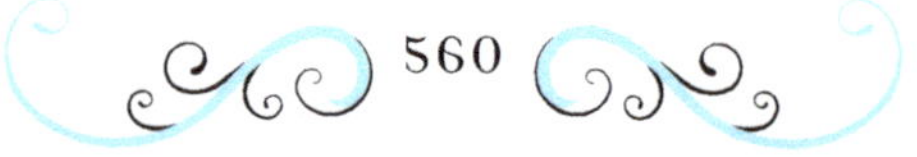

'Yes, one that will only get smaller and smaller if Bernais and his friends strengthen their control over the world.'

I run my hand through my hair, trying to sift through everything I've just learned. While I understand why magic is failing, and also why Pris and I, being from the World Above, might see things differently with all the climate change debates, what I don't understand is what Gregor expects me to do now.

'Gregor, what do you want from me?'

He starts as if the question is unexpected, and then he grins. 'What I'd hoped was that you'd be so overwhelmed with compassion, you'd say, "Gregor, I'll do whatever you ask to fix this".'

I chuckle. 'If you think I can do anything to fix something this thoroughly broken, then you're madder than a box of frogs.'

'True, and I might well be.' He sinks back into his cushion, his gaze drifting to the fireplace. 'Part of me *was* hoping I'd inspire you to help. Our world is being stifled to death. We have one lot of leaders who want to smother it more quickly, and the other lot is moving so slowly, it'll suffocate before anything changes.'

'You have inspired me, but I don't know what I can do to help.'

'To be honest, I don't know what any of us can do. We're all so young, and we have no clout, and there aren't many of us. Yet, if we sit back and do nothing, we won't have a world to live in by the time it's our turn to run it.'

Gregor's despair is a heavy weight. Pris and I were aware something much bigger was happening in the World Below as we ran around trying to save our parents, but until now we hadn't had time to stop and find out what was really going on.

Now that I know, I almost wish I didn't because how can I sit by and do nothing? Equally, I can't see what one person can do to change any of this. I slump back on my cushion, the weight of the world now squarely on my shoulders. And that was what this was about. I turn and stare at Gregor, and he nods, the ghost of a smile on his lips—he knows he has me now.

'It was Verona's idea. She said anyone who went to so much trouble to rescue their mother wouldn't be able to walk away once they knew what's at stake.'

Dammit. I can't leave, but I'm tired of being manipulated. If I'm to take part in this fight, it has to be on my terms.

'I won't help overthrow the government, nor will I manipulate Pris or her position to help us. What I *will* do is help you forge an alliance with Queen Ariana's court, if that is the path you choose to take.'

Straightening in his cushion, Gregor pins me with an intense gaze. 'And will you help our leaders formulate our demands?'

'I… I'm not a politician or….'

'Think about it, please.'

Before I can refuse, the curtain rustles, and Verona pokes her head through the gap. 'I thought you two might like some fresh tea and sandwiches for lunch.'

A SLOW MARCH TO WAR

MANDOR'S FOOTSTEPS ECHO as he strides the length of the room. All eyes follow his progress except for mine. I watch my friend as the husband who foreswore her for a life of study takes the spare seat between her and Seraphina. Ellie's face is blank. Only her eyes betray the tumult of emotions she is feeling.

Their living apart for the last few centuries was no more their choice than it was mine to live as neither sprite nor man. We had all suffered the consequences of disobeying the council. Although Ellie had married again—more than once and had children—she'd only taken mortal lovers. I believe that was because no one could dislodge Mandor from her heart.

Mandor places a hand on Ellie's shoulder, and she raises her eyes to him. I cannot see what passes between them, but the wizard takes his seat moments later.

'Pleased you could join us,' Genie says somewhat tersely.

Mandor bows his head towards Thomas and Genie. 'My apologies for the tardy arrival, but now that I no longer have access to the wizard's source of power, I can only take one creature with me when I portal. As I thought you would want to hear from both my guests, it took us a little longer to get here.'

Heart and Drow remain in the doorway while Mandor speaks. The wizard motions them in, and as he does, he notices me sitting in the back. A smile brightens his face, taking the harshness from his next words. 'Perhaps I shouldn't have bothered, since Percival likely has more current news than we do.'

I force myself to acknowledge Mandor's greeting. When everyone's attention returns to the front, Drow and Heart move into the seats beside me.

'Did I hear correctly? Has Mandor renounced his wizard status?'

Drow leans past Heart to better see me. 'Hello to you, too, Percival. And yes, Mandor, as well as about half of the wizards, have renounced their affiliation and have joined the other creatures readying themselves to march on the Capitol.'

'So there really is going to be a rebellion? Who are they intending to fight? The council or the Crown?' A knot of fear forms in the pit of my stomach as I wait for their answer. 'And how come Mandor still has his memory?'

'The Wizard Council refused to take part in this battle even though they have a lot at stake, so some of their number renounced their positions. Because of that, they are cut off from the wizard's pool of magic,' Drow says.

'But who are they fighting for?' I ask.

'The Crown of course. They can't renounce their vow, which means they have to fight for the leader of the Seelie Court or lose their memories. Now, if you two would stop nattering, I want to hear this,' Heart hisses just as Nisha stands up to speak.

I miss my mate's first few words as my head spins with worry. It is a good sign that the wizards are joining the fight, but they will have to walk a fine line if they are to retain their abilities—and their minds. With their help we increase the likelihood of removing Bernais, but if we topple the government and court at the same time, the backlash could devastate the ex-wizards.

'…and I speak for the sprites from the Wyld Wood Grove. We creatures prefer peace to war, but we are prepared to fight for change in the World Below… provided that change benefits *all* creatures.'

The table erupts as almost every other delegate's voice rises either in support or disapproval of Nisha's words. She does not let the dissent cower her, and her poise makes me proud.

Thomas Mulligan holds up a hand. 'Come now,' his voice booms, 'if we carry on like rabble, we will be here for an age.'

When the table has quietened down, Thomas turns his attention to my mate. 'Nisha, you must be aware that we as a committee do not favour overthrowing the Crown.'

Nisha's head drops, and I worry she might sit down. She does not. Instead, she raises her head and studies every greater creature on the other side of the table. 'Ever since the council formed, we have allowed you greater creatures to play politics while we so-called lesser creatures have tended to the lands, and the air, and the water. Look where that has brought us…Magic is disappearing from our realm, and we are on the brink of war. We sprites have had enough of standing by while others destroy our world. We want a say in our future.'

Pride wells inside me as Nisha speaks for our people and expresses what is inside my heart. The dryad to Nisha's right rises. Their voice is low and melodic when they speak.

'We dryads of the Oaken Stand say we have had enough of the distinction between the creators and users of magic. Our world needs all our skills and talents, and we all should be a part of the government.'

The delegates alongside Nisha murmur agreement, while stony silence reigns opposite. A brownie delegate stands up, followed by a pixie. The brownie, a young male, speaks first.

'We came expecting that we would have an equal vote here and that we will have an equal vote once we have ousted the current council.'

Heart leans back in his seat as Drow sits forward, and we wait for the next creature to speak. There are a number of private discussions, but no one speaks up. I contemplate whether I should.

This issue is the very one Drow, our friends, and I fought for when we were younger. Lesser creatures had understood that the blight had to be stopped at any cost, while the council were more worried about the political fallout of reversing their decision to close the ways to the World Above.

It is Thomas Mulligan who speaks next. 'I…. We may agree in principle, but I am not sure exactly what we are agreeing to.'

Mutterings on the greater creature side of the table increase, but before they raise an objection, Mandor says, 'I believe what we are agreeing to is that we do not want Bernais and the current council to continue to hold power. The problem is, we can't agree on what changes we want after that. If my summary is correct, then let's move on and leave the details for later, as we have much to decide.'

'Yes,' Thomas Mulligan agrees. 'A good idea. After this meeting is over, those of you who are interested in hammering out the details of this accord might form a group led by… umm.'

'How fortunate that I brought one of the eminent lawyers of our generation with me,' Mandor says, rescuing the dwarf. 'I am sure he would love to spend time drafting an agreement. Although this will be the first formal agreement in this war, I do not believe it will be the last.'

'A show of hands?' Thomas Mulligan asks.

A few hands are slow to rise, but the vote is unanimous. Drow sits back, a smile splitting his face. As Genie calls the meeting back to order, I catch Nisha's gaze on me. I nod my encouragement, hoping she senses my admiration. Her cheeks colour, but she raises her head a fraction and straightens her spine before turning her attention back to the meeting.

Over the next half an hour, I listen to the debate, which is way less emotionally fraught now that they have sidelined the most contentious issue. I am so weary that I find it difficult to maintain focus, and my mind wanders, only to be brought back as the group hits another bump on the road. The dwarf contingent are on their feet, ready to walk away. It would be a disaster to lose such ferocious fighters.

'We are here because we believe the elven stranglehold on our land should not continue,' their leader says.

'Your representatives were happy to take their side on the council,' the brownie leader heckles.

The dwarf reddens, but he stands strong. 'Our brethren in the city have forgotten their roots. They are nothing but hired stooges for the elves. We in the country prefer our independence, and many will be happy to see the council fall.'

Others around the table nod their agreement. If they are in concert, why the disagreement? What have I missed?

Drow rises to his feet. 'If I may?'

No one hears him.

'Silence!' Seraphina does not appear to move, but her voice fills every nook and cranny in the room. The response is immediate.

'Drow, do you have something to add to the… discussion?' she asks.

'Thank you, Seraphina, I do. As I understand it, this is a problem essentially of who we are fighting—our immediate foe or the entire system. In our hearts, I think we would like to choose the latter, but we then strike a problem. And our problem is one of capacity.'

'Capacity? We're talking about fundamental issues with how our world is run,' the leader of the dwarves says, puzzlement crossing his face.

Drow grins. He is enjoying this debate. 'Should we choose to enter as a third party, we will fight not just the regional militias, but also the kingdom's most skilled military unit, the Queen's Guard.'

'We can take them all on,' one dwarf brags.

'Huh.' The laugh slips out, and I immediately wish it had not, as everyone turns to stare at me. Not so long ago, I would have wilted under such scrutiny, but not now. I glare at the dwarf.

'We will have numbers, it is true, but we are not soldiers, and we don't have military discipline. To fight a battle on one front will be tough enough, but on two fronts….'

'Not to mention,' Genie adds, 'there is a balance in the world to respect. Who knows what will happen to magic if we descend into all-out war for months on end.'

'Does that mean we should not fight?' Nathanial asks.

'I didn't say that. Fighting will damage our world by using magic as well as by taking creatures away from creating it. The shorter the war, the less damage there is. What we don't want is a prolonged war that might leave our world in a worse state,' Genie explains.

The leader of the dwarves leans his fists on the table, and I fear our words have fallen on deaf ears. 'If we just oust the council, nothing changes. What is the point?' His shoulders slump, and he sinks back into his chair.

'Not to mention, we wizards cannot fight with you if you are working against the Queen and the Seelie Court,' Mandor adds.

'Well…,' Drow starts, his eyes still twinkling, 'there may be a way. If we take on the council on the Queen's behalf, we have leverage. I believe if we produce a list of demands in return for our support, we have a unique opportunity to force change.'

'A nice idea,' one of the goblin says with a sneer, 'but all of this started because no one could get access to the Queen.'

'We might have a way.' Drow's eyes lock on me.

'Do we?' I ask, somewhat bewildered.

Genie raises her eyebrows. 'I don't believe *we* do, Percival. I believe you might, though.'

My heart skips a beat. I *did* help the Queen out by bringing King Maddox here. She might grant me an audience when she wakes up. Can I do it?

Everyone is watching me. I find Nisha in the crowd. Her presence exudes empathy, and I'm embarrassed by my uncertainty.

'We each have our role to play, Percival,' she says, her tone encouraging.

Thomas Mulligan slaps a hand on the table. 'I propose we expand the remit of the group working with Drow to extend our alliance agreement to include a proposal for the Queen. We will offer to fight in support of her if she will agree to our requests for changes to be made.'

When no one disagrees, Thomas Mulligan continues. 'Moving on. Can the designated military leaders stay here and work out logistics? We must consider how to move creatures into position and keep them concealed until we are ready to attack. Mandor, can you join them and work out how many of your witches we will need for this?'

'I can,' the witch says.

Crash! The doors beside us swing open and bang against the wall. A young dwarf enters, shouting, 'The guards are coming.'

'Break into your groups,' Thomas Mulligan shouts.

'Planners to the tavern,' another voice adds.

'Medical and support to mine.' Seraphina's voice carries above the noise of shuffling papers and chairs scraping as the creatures ready to leave.

Nisha joins the witches as they depart through a side door.

Mandor hurries over. 'Drow, those of us wanting to work on the agreement for Queen Ariana are also heading to the tavern.'

Drow rises to his feet and follows Mandor as he exits through the doors beside us. Heart and I wait amidst the chaos. Through the window, I see that the sun is high in the sky. We are soon alone in the empty hall.

Heart pushes himself to his feet. 'Well, old friend, it seems we are surplus to requirements. Shall we head to the tavern? I could do with a pint of ale.'

'Shouldn't we be doing… I do not know… something?' I ask.

His face turns serious. 'Once things wind up here, we will be busy. I will go into the Wyld Woods to canvas the villages for support, and you will go to meet with the Queen.'

I rise, then Heart's words sink in, and I sit back down. 'Wait, you're going home?'

Heart's mouth breaks into a crooked grin. 'Yes, imagine that—I'm going home.'

'Well, this is turning out to be the oddest of days.'

'To the tavern for some Dutch courage?' Heart asks hopefully.

I shake my head. 'Sorry, Heart. Much as I enjoy your company, I want to make sure Nisha can find me when she's done.'

He claps a hand on my shoulder. 'And you'll want a sober head for that conversation, too, no doubt.'

'Indeed. Let's go back to Seraphina's. She will have food and ale, and maybe we can be of some help.'

'Okay,' Heart says, and I lead the way out.

As I open the door to the street, two young guards bowl through. They don't even stop us to ask what we are doing here. If they're who Magnus Baaronson has left to police the village, we have nothing to worry about.

AFTER WEEKS OF being on the move and having Pris and Percival with me, I thought it would be relaxing having time for myself and absolutely nothing to do. Perhaps it would have been if everyone else wasn't busy doing something. In the end, boredom gets the better of me, and I make my way to the kitchen and offer to help with dinner. I'm not much of a chef, but I can peel a potato with the best of them.

After answering an initial flurry of questions about Pris's and my adventures, the cook and his helpers forget about me. As it turns out, working in the kitchen is a great way to hear what's going on in the worlds. This must be why spies work as hired help.

I hand the full pot of potatoes to the head chef. He passes me an empty one. 'If you could fill this also. I hear we are to expect some refugees from the Unseelie Court for this evening's meal.'

I almost dropped the pot. 'From the Unseelie Court? I thought they were all locked in stasis.'

The brownie scratches his head. 'Some escaped. From what I hear, a few are camping out with our main forces—of course, I can't tell you where they are—loose lips and all that. Some leaders are coming here for the big meeting tonight.'

I place the pot on the bench and begin peeling. The dwarf working beside me is busy making some sort of pies, so I'm careful not to take up too much space as I get back to potato peeling. She nudges my arm. 'I heard it was mostly servants who escaped. They made it to the Birmingham gate.'

'They had to go there because the dragon's closed the Loch Ness one, no doubt,' I say.

She nods as she crimps a crust. 'The renegade wizards secured the Birmingham gate for us because it comes out close to their sanctuary. It's a good thing they did because the gate to the Underground Ballroom exits in the Capitol—'

'Which means it's under elven control,' I finish for her.

'Yep.'

'Renegade Wizards? You're having me on, right?'

She laughs. 'No, I'm not. Some of the Wizard Council decided they could not sit this out and renounced their vows.'

The potato I'm peeling slips from my hand and tumbles across the bench. 'You're kidding. I didn't know they could even do that!'

'Nope. Not kidding, and apparently they can.'

'Wow' is all I can manage after that as my brain tries to process the enormity of this news. It simply can't. Massive changes are happening in the World Below, and it's so chaotic that I can't see where it's all heading.

'Have you heard anything about the creatures who attacked the Unseelie Court?'

'Nope. Only good thing is, they'll have to head south in the World Above to get here, so our forces have a one, maybe two, day advantage.'

'But that will fly by. Our enemies are mustered in the Capitol already, and we are still trying to recruit. If only the ex-wizards could portal more than a person at a time,' the chef says.

'I sincerely hope you're not discussing tactics in here,' a familiar female voice says from the doorway.

'Susan!' The chef drops his ladle and rushes to throw his arms around the elf.

'Steady there, George. I still need to breathe.'

The brownie apologises and lets go of Susan. 'We thought you were lost,' he says.

'I made it out of the castle before the stasis spell took hold, along with many of the servants.' She catches my eye and shoots me a smile. 'See, Snake, it all turned out okay in the end.'

'Did any guards get out? It sounds like we could use a few trained soldiers in the coming days.'

'Why Susan, I'm so happy to see you,' Susan says sarcastically, and I bark out a laugh.

'Of course I'm pleased to see you. I can't imagine what it would be like to be held in stasis. It's just….' I drop the potato and peeler onto the bench and suck in a breath. 'After all that effort, all that energy and planning, we were duped. Giles Coronas and Grossman Green didn't commit any of their forces to the castle, and Dinian had been feeding them information all along.'

Susan steps around George and crosses the distance between us before placing a hand on my shoulder and giving it a quick squeeze. 'We did the best we could, Snake. I heard from Petunia how dwarves ambushed you at the Loch Ness gate and how we were double-crossed by that slimeball Dinian. We couldn't have predicted that. At least the castle is safe, and King Maddox is doing what he has to do. All *we* can do is regroup and move forward.'

Her words, meant to soothe me, don't quite work. So many thoughts and worries curl their way through my brain, but I can't grasp hold of them. I'm so weary, I'm beyond thinking. As I slump against the bench, she drops her hands and gives me a little nudge with her elbow to make some space for herself before picking up the peeler and dealing with the potato.

'How's Pris? I heard she was injured?'

'She's fine. The Dragon Queen healed her.'

'Really?' Susan grins. 'That must have been awesome to watch.'

'It probably was, but I didn't get to see it.' My voice comes out all sulky, but I'm finding it hard to feel anything but exhausted.

Susan plops the potato into the water. 'And where is she now?'

'She was summoned to the Minotaur's Maze after breakfast, and I haven't heard from her since.'

Glancing at me, Susan radiates sympathy, and I can't bear it. 'She has her duties, no matter what she and I might want.'

'She does,' Susan starts, her voice tentative, 'but they don't need to control her life.'

I drop my head, not sure how to answer that. The closeness between Pris and me is so new, and after last night, I still have a lot to process.

'Anyway,' Susan says, 'you haven't told me where the others are. I assume King Maddox went directly to the maze.'

'Yes,' I answer, relieved at the change of subject. 'Euphemia went with him. Susan, what's happening with the others in the World Above?'

She stops peeling and studies me. 'Petunia was warding her home and preparing to come to the World Below with some of the unit that guards the Loch Ness gate—she may even have arrived for all I know. Most other creatures, my sister and her family included, have hunkered down, waiting for this to all blow over. A few realise the significance of this battle and have returned home to right the balance of the worlds, but most don't even know anything is going on.'

'The balance of the worlds?' This is the first time I've heard that phrase.

Susan runs a hand through her hair. 'Interrupting the flow of magic is not the only thing that might throw the worlds out of balance. Extreme social change and war can do that too.'

'If that's true, then why aren't all the creatures from up there down here?'

Susan releases a long breath. 'Most creatures have become so distanced from our home, they have forgotten the teachings. If you weren't here now, would you even have any idea there was something amiss?'

I think back to my life in London. I'd be busting my butt and saving like mad to start uni next year, and I probably wouldn't have even thought about the World Below unless my uncle Earth mentioned it. And I wouldn't have paid much attention to what he said anyway.

'No, perhaps not. Are you here to fight?' I ask.

'I'm here on behalf of the refugees from the Unseelie Court. We want our court to be returned to normal, but we can't ignore what's happening in the World Below either. If the Baaronson faction remains in control, the Unseelie Court will always be under attack. Besides, maybe it's time for genuine change, and that is something worth fighting for.'

George clangs some pots onto a work surface. 'Too right it is. It is time to remove these divisions. Time we were all treated equally.'

The dwarf on the other side of me snorts. 'As if that will ever happen.'

'It won't happen if we do nothing,' George responds.

Picking up another peeler, I help Susan finish up the pile of potatoes, leaving the other two to their bickering. Less than two months ago, my life was pretty normal. I had work, and university, and a future. Now I'm caught in the middle of a civil war I hadn't even known was brewing in a realm I left as a baby.

As is always the case, it is more complicated than that. My family are major political supporters of the Crown and Pris is herself a Crown, which places them on one side of this conflict. My mother and I are mixed race, which puts us on another. The only side in this triangle I don't have a stake in is the conservative elven faction. This is one of those times I wish I'd never tried to save Mum.

Then again, if I hadn't, I'd never have met Pris, and I would never have fallen in love with her. I stop mid-peel. *Hold on, that's a leap.* I shake my head. When had that happened? When had attraction and friendship developed into something more?

'Snake? Snake?'

'Sorry, Susan. I missed that.'

'You were miles away. I asked if you were coming to the meeting tonight? Verona mentioned you joining their group.'

'I might come, but I haven't decided. Pris and I have been on the go for so long, and I need some rest.'

Susan's shoulders visibly relax at my answer.

I give her a suspicious glare. 'Why do you ask?'

Susan leans in close to me and whispers, 'With your being so close to Pris, you want to be careful about making any political alliances. You might inadvertently end up putting her in a bind.'

I'm stunned. 'I don't make my decisions based on our friendship,' I say through gritted teeth.

'If it were simply a friendship….' Susan extends her hands, palms upwards.

'What Pris and I are to each other is nobody's business but ours,' I hiss. 'Just as what I do, or don't do, is my decision, and—'

I was about to say it wouldn't involve Pris, but that would be a lie. I really need some alone time with Pris so we can figure out how we navigate this minefield together. What I wouldn't give for a mobile phone about now. *Hold on, there might be a way to speak with her.*

'Susan, I've got to go.'

Susan's eyes widen in surprise, but I don't give her a chance to object. Moments later, I'm alone in my room, sitting on the bed Pris and I shared last night.

Ed'rathe, are you there?

I tap on my leg as I wait for a response.

I am, Noble One.

Phew.

Are you able to relay a message to Pris for me and then wait for an answer?

I really shouldn't…. Is it urgent?

It's urgent for me, but would the dragons think it was important enough to bend the rules?

Not if she's going to be back here tonight.

She will not be.

It would have been nice if someone could have told us that this morning.

Then, if you could pass a message on for me. There is a meeting here tonight. They want me to do some things, and I need Pris's input.

There is a hum in my head, something I'd not heard before. Then Ed'rathe comes back. *My cave mates say a brief message should be all right.*

Okay. Tell her the resistance wants me to fight with them. I believe in what they are doing, but I can see problems for her if I do this.

No.

No? You mean no, you won't send the message, Ed'rathe?

I mean, no, you cannot join in the fight with the rebel group. You are the Heir Consort, and that is not appropriate.

I'm the what? I splutter.

You and the princess have bonded, and so you are now her consort.

Bonded? Is this because we…. I trail off, not wanting to discuss what happened last night with my dragon friend.

Oh, no. Physical relations have nothing to do with it. Something happened between you last night and you started to form a mate bond.

What the hell? A mate bond? Like Percival and Nisha? Is that even possible? It wasn't unheard of, but it rarely occurred between greater creatures. Political alliances commonly formed the basis of their marriages.

If we *had* partially bonded, that would explain my deeper feeling for Pris, but hell, we hadn't had a chance to even discuss things between us, and now this?

Can you please just send the message?

Done.

My head thrums, and Ed'rathe is back.

The princess says things are moving fast. If you can put off deciding what to do until you two can speak, she would be pleased.

Thanks, Ed'rathe.

You are welcome, Noble One. Now, make yourself presentable, and I will be at the door in a few wingbeats—the Dragon Queen wishes to speak with you.

You're joking.

I most certainly am not. Indignation laces Ed'rathe's words.

The Queen? What does she want with me?

I'll be there, I mutter as I pull out my clean questing clothes and change as fast as I can.

Bloody hell! I'm about to meet the Queen of Dragons.

AM'RATHA DROPS INTO a courtyard behind a mansion in the centre of the maze. Last time I was here, I was so drained, I was in no position to appreciate the grandeur and magnitude of the Minotaur's residence. Now, as I slide from my dragon's back, I take it all in. The cream stone dwelling is impressive. The morning sun picks out shadows in windows half hidden by balconies in the upper two stories and throws the arched walkways circumnavigating the ground floor into shade.

A figure emerges from a side door. As she approaches, Am'ratha lowers her head and says, *Al'kyla has summoned me.*

Al'kyla?

Queen Ariana's bonded one. She needs my magic.

I'll come with you.

No, Royal One. With someone as exalted as Al'kyla, she must invite you into her presence.

I blow out a breath of frustration.

All right, but if I'm not supposed to help, why am I here?

I am sure they will reveal the reason in good time.

How do dragon's do it—remain so calm, and so obedient?

I was brought up to put community first.

Stop reading my thoughts!

Learn to shield them!

The good mood flying always brings evaporates, and I concentrate on suppressing my irritation. *Honestly, I'm going to come out of this whole thing looking ten years older than when I started.*

I take a couple of calming breaths. *Will you let me know if you hear any news from the Capitol or from the World Above?*

Of course.

Am'ratha waddles round the side of the building. When her tail is no longer visible, I redirect my attention to the creature who arrived to meet me. Standing just below my shoulder, she is wearing a simple knee-length black dress with white cuffs and collar and has a white apron tied around her waist. Is she a brownie?

'I am Xia, Your Highness, and I am to escort you to your rooms.'

'My rooms? I've only come for today. Perhaps you could take me directly to Queen Ariana, or even King Maddox will do.'

A slight flicker of shock passes over her face so quickly, I almost miss it. Was it because I asked to see the King and Queen, or because I questioned her orders?

She gives nothing away. She simply turns on her heel and walks back towards the building. Short of remaining outside, I have no option but to follow her.

Leading me, she takes me into a corridor through an open door. The whitewashed wall reflects the sunlight and my eyes struggle to adapt to the dark windowless space. My guide's feet click on the terracotta tiles, and I have to rush to keep up.

The corridor ends, and we enter an atrium that opens up to the sky. Skirting the fountain and gardens in the middle, our path takes us up a flight of stairs, then round the first-floor balcony. Xia stops in front of a set of double doors and waits for me to catch her up before opening them to reveal a large, opulent room in calming blues and creams.

A semicircular sofa dominates the space, giving anyone seated there a spectacular view of the desert through the open patio doors, and I can just make out the wall of the maze at its edge. To my right is a dining table laden with fresh fruit, nuts, and pastries. To the left is a set of three doors—this is definitely a guest suite rather than a reception room. How long do they expect me to stay here?

My guide gestures with her hand towards the sofa. 'If you will make yourself comfortable, I am sure someone will be with you soon.' She closes the doors behind her as she leaves.

I've not long had breakfast, but there is little else to do, so I head for the table. After loading a plate with fruit and pouring a coffee from a carafe, I take my snack out onto the balcony that runs the width of the room. Tucked behind the door is a wrought-iron table and chairs. Once seated, I close my eyes and allow the sunlight to warm my face.

The place is eerily quiet except for the occasional trill of birds and the rustle of leaves as the breeze stirs them into action. The lack of other creature sounds is unnatural, and I feel isolated and alone. Panic pricks at my skin.

Shaking my head, I try to relax and dispel my anxiety. I concentrate on enjoying my coffee while nibbling at the food. All too soon, the sun drenching the balcony makes it uncomfortable to remain here. I take my dishes indoors and place them on the table.

A quick circuit of the room reveals nothing to distract me. I open the doors to see that they hide generic double bedrooms with a bathroom between. They would not look out of place in a hotel. I flop down on the sofa and stare up at the ceiling. What on earth am I doing here?

With a grunt, I push myself to my feet, pad across to the entrance, and fling open a door. Before I can put a foot outside, a dwarfish guard in the Queen's livery steps into my path.

'May I help you?'

'You can let me out,' I snap.

She folds her arms across her chest. 'I'm sorry, I can't do that.'

My heart rate increases. How was I stupid enough to become trapped here? Forcing my fears down, I draw myself up to my full height, which is slightly taller than her, then arrange my face into haughty princess mode, 'Am I a prisoner?'

The guard isn't fazed. 'No, Princess.'

'I'm so sorry,' apologises a familiar voice. 'We have so many guests, and we are not prepared for this.'

The brownie who showed me to the suite appears as the guard steps away. 'I thought you might get bored while you waited, and I did not know….' Her voice drifts off as she hands me a basket.

Taking it, I peek inside. There are a couple of books, some wool and needles, what looks like it might be embroidery, and a large box that rattles in a way that suggests it might contain puzzle pieces.

I'm not here to knit!

'Someone summoned me here,' I say, hating the whine in my voice, but feeling too aggrieved to do anything about it. 'I could be with my friends doing something useful. Do you know who called for me and when they will actually appear?'

An apologetic facade appears on the brownie's face, intended to empathise and neutralise my irritation. 'I believe it was Al'kyla who requested your presence. There is….' She draws a breath. 'Things are happening, and I'm not sure I can talk about them. Someone should be here soon.'

She bobs a quick curtsey and disappears as the guard closes the door in my face. I glare at the solid wood, debating whether to let my temper loose on the bulky guard. Hoisting the basket up my arm, I step back from the offending door. One thing I have learnt from my time around creatures is that you have to pick your battles wisely, and this one isn't worth the effort. I curl up on the plush sofa and reach into the basket.

Pulling out the books, I study the cover of the top one—*Tess of the D'Urbervilles.* Yuck. I didn't like it at school, and I doubt I'll like it any better now.

Oliver Twist. Who chose these? I guess at a push I could read this.

Oh, what's this? Wilkie Collins's *A Woman in White.*

I pop the other two books back and place the basket on the floor. Curling up against the arm of the sofa, facing toward the window, I open the novel and start reading. I'm about a quarter of the way through the story when my eyelids droop. I've spent so much time rushing here and there these past few weeks, I can't remember the last time I could sit and do nothing. My body is certainly appreciating the chance to relax.

Sometime later, I force my eyes open. The sun has changed position, and I'm covered by a blanket. My head feels a little heavy, as if there's some sort of pressure building up behind my forehead. Blinking a couple of times, I allow my eyes to adjust and find them drawn to the figure sitting at the other end of the couch, *Tess of the D'Urbervilles* in his hand.

'Pris, you're awake,' the Minotaur's deep voice rumbles, and I resist the urge to leap to my feet and take a defensive position.

The last time I saw him, he'd tried to kill us. He then took part in the subterfuge that sent us to the Unseelie Court. Although this is his home, he was the last person I expected to see here.

Staying alert, I force myself to say politely, 'Aeron… ah… how, um, nice to see you again.'

LIFE LESSONS

THE BOOK ON my lap falls to the floor as I sit up. The Minotaur grins, his smile revealing his prominent lower tusks.

'Princess Priscilla, the pleasure is mine. I thought I would join you for lunch, given everyone else appears to be too busy to spare us any time.'

I swing my legs to the floor and glance behind the half man, half bull to find the table has been cleared and is now set for two people. Aeron stands up, his black trousers and a white shirt emphasising his massive muscular form. While they hide most of the hair covering his body, they cannot conceal his hooves or that he has the head of a bull.

He holds out his arm, and I rise, resting my hand in the crook. This is so bizarre! I have visions of *Beauty and the Beast* as the Minotaur of myth and legend escorts me to the dining table, where he takes his place at the head, while I sit to his right.

When we're settled, he reaches out and rings a small bell. Seconds later, Xia enters, pushing a trolley. She serves a soup course and leaves us alone.

I groan with pleasure as the spicy soup hits my taste buds, and my stomach rumbles as I crack the crusty bread to soak up the liquid my spoon can't reach. When the edge of my hunger is dulled, the absurdity of the situation hits me anew, and I question why I'm here with Aeron rather than with one of the two creatures who came to assist the Queen.

'Aeron, where are Euphemia and my uncle?'

Aeron places his spoon down and dabs daintily at his mouth with a napkin before answering. 'The Witch Protector of the North and King Maddox are still working with Al'kyla to heal the Queen.'

'If everyone is busy, why am I here?'

Aeron runs a hand through the course, stubbled hair on his head. 'I believe it is because the Dragon Queen wanted you trained to work with King Maddox at restoring the magical flow.'

'Oh.' That makes sense.

I eat a little more before my skin tingles, alerting me to the fact Aeron is watching me again. I pause and raise a questioning brow.

'You are happy to do that?'

I blink twice, then stop myself from saying, 'Of course I am.' Instead, I inquire, 'What am I missing, Aeron?'

'You are here because the Dragon Queen worries that Queen Ariana won't recover. With your mother in the middle of a potential war zone, the Dragon Queen wants you to take on royal responsibilities.'

Aeron continues his meal, but my appetite deserts me. I place my spoon down and stare out the window, longing to be back in the cave sanctuary with Snake—back where I can be just Pris.

The bell tinkles, and the brownie appears, again pushing her trolley. She clears our dishes, then places a covered plate in front of Aeron. As she moves to put one in front of me, I hold up my hand. 'I'm not hungry.'

After Aeron nods, she removes the plate. She tops up our glasses with a chilled fruit drink and sets a plate of flatbreads in the middle of the table before she goes.

'Some heir to the throne I am,' I mutter. 'I can't even get a brownie to follow my orders.'

Aeron snorts. 'Of course not. She has sworn her loyalty to me.'

I pick at the tablecloth. 'I thought brownies were servants. Shouldn't they do what anyone asks?'

'It is so easy to forget that you know very little of our world,' Aeron says as he lifts the cover from his food, revealing a platter of spiced meats, goat's cheese, and some dips. The smell wafting towards me sets my stomach grumbling. It seems my appetite has returned.

Aaron grins and pushes the plate between us. 'Please, share with me.'

'Only if you will tell me what I don't understand about brownies.'

He wraps some of the spiced meats in a flatbread and puts some cheese and hummus on top before rolling it all up and finishing the lot in one bite. It looks delicious.

'Please.' He gestures to the food. As I make a roll, he explains, 'Brownies are house creator creatures. They not only derive income by serving others, they also create magic and strengthen the status of their family as they work. Many unscrupulous masters take advantage of their need to serve, turning their brownies into virtual slaves.'

I nod. 'The strong take advantage of the weak. It's the same everywhere.'

'To protect them, the council issued a decree that brownies in service must sign a magical contract. They swear loyalty to their master, and in return, their master takes care of them, pays them, and agrees on a set of duties. The contract is then assessed by the council and, if it is deemed fair to both sides, they ratify it.'

'And that protects the brownies?'

'In most cases, yes, if the council is diligent. Brownies in my service have a contract saying they do not have to take orders from anyone else unless I ask them to.'

'I see. So the brownies in my uncle's court would have had their own contracts and their own set of duties.'

'I am not sure how things work in the Unseelie Court,' Aeron admits.

I take a bite of the wrap. The pleasure of eating the fluffy soft bread turns into agony as a sharp pain pierces my head, causing me to drop my food on the table.

'Are you all right?' Aeron asks, his voice gruff with worry.

Another wave of something indescribable rolls through the room, and my head pounds in response.

Concern tugs at Aeron's brow, but it is swiftly replaced with a look of understanding.

'Oh dear, they are using an awful lot of magic.'

I massage my forehead. 'This is because of magic?'

'We must fix this. You need to learn to shield against this, Princess. They could be at this for hours.'

'Hours?' I repeat, dismay seeping into every limb as my eyeballs feel like they might explode.

'Close your eyes,' Aeron commands, and I follow his instruction.

'Now, reach out with your other senses. You should be able to make out a sort of dissonance around you.'

'Yes, I can,' I whisper as magic buzzes around me, its sharp edges pricking my skin like hundreds of pins.

'Good, now concentrate on pushing it away from you.'

I try to do what he says, ignoring the increased pain and using what I already know of manipulating magical particles in the air. I imagine the particles bunching up and leaving a space around my body. They move sluggishly, and then they spring back, sending another wave of pain through me.

Gritting my teeth, I start again. This time I push a little more slowly, allowing the fragments to move and regroup, and then I nudge them once more. Slowly, I create a space around me, and the pain recedes.

'Have you done it?' Aeron asks.

'Yes.'

'Now, imagine a shield of air around your body creating a no-go zone for the dissonance.'

'Okay.' I attempt to do what he says, but as soon as I pull my focus from pushing the particles away to concentrate on my shield, they drift closer, and my head pounds again.

I instantly drop my shield and force the magic away until the pain recedes. This time, I use more power, moving magic further away to give myself a chance to erect a basic shield. I picture the air turning solid like a wall protecting the space around me. Only a little magic seeps back through the cracks in my shield this time, raising goose-bumps on my skin. I thrust it away again and strengthen my shield, filling the cracks and adding another layer so nothing can get through. I release my hold a little, testing its stability… and it holds. It is done.

Opening my eyes, I'm relieved the headache has gone, but I'm drained. Aeron is peering at me, his bovine features twisted with concern. I smile at him, and he relaxes a little.

'Well done. Your first shield is never easy. Come, lie down. You'll need to recharge after that,' he says, leading me back to the sofa, then placing the blanket over me. "You should check your shield frequently and repair it until it becomes second nature to maintain it.'

He returns to the table and rings the bell. When the Xia reappears, Aeron asks for tea and cakes. As the brownie tidies up our meal, he finds a seat on the sofa.

'You arrived in our world with so little teaching and knowledge, yet they want you to stand as heir and take responsibility for keeping magic flowing. It is wrong.'

'Wrong? How?' I ask. I understand my own reservations, but I'm curious to hear his perspective.

'Because you had a life, and they are taking it from you. No one is asking what you want. They all assume what they need from you is what you should be giving.'

Tears well in my eyes. So many people have been telling me I should do what is best for the World Below. It touches me that this creature who hardly knows me is more concerned about how it will affect me. Aeron may appear to be a beast, but the man inside is so much more.

Xia returns, and Aeron insists I drink some tea and eat some of the fruit, while he nibbles on the fruit and nuts from the platter placed on a small side table. The tea clears the aches and pains, but I'm still bonetired. I sink back into the sofa, and Aeron leans back, his hands clasped behind his head.

'What do you think of everything that's going on?' he finally asks.

'Which part exactly?'

'I am sorry, that was rather a broad question. I was there when Fairburn forced you to go to the Unseelie Court not knowing who you were or why it was so important that *you* specifically went. Now you are to become the Crown Princess and save the World Below—a world you didn't even know existed until a few weeks ago. Is this what you want for your life?'

'No,' I say, and it comes from my gut. I follow it with 'But I can't see any other way to stop things from falling into total chaos.'

'Youngling, there is such a weight on your shoulders, and it is evident your parents taught you to do your duty.'

There is a heaviness and sadness in his voice, and it cuts me to the quick. Aeron stares into the distance, his thoughts clearly elsewhere.

'Working out where you fit is the toughest part of growing up. Others see you one way, and they try hard to tell you that's who you are. The trick is to know yourself without being swayed by their preconceptions, or by what they want from you.'

I study Aeron as he speaks. The intelligence and sadness in his eyes are at odds with the face he presents to the world. I have faced a lifetime of scrutiny based on the colour of my skin, both in the World Above and the World Below. It's even worse here because I'm also judged based on my family. Despite how terrible it was, I doubt it compares to what Aeron's endured. As part man, part beast, finding a place to fit in would have been difficult.

'How would you suggest I deal with the Dragon Queen and her expectations?'

Aeron turns to me, his expression unreadable. Then he expels air in something between a grunt and a sigh. 'No one has ever asked for my opinion. How do I answer?'

'You could tell me what you would do if you were me.'

He slowly shakes his head. 'I would not feel right doing that. Perhaps I can tell you a little of my past instead.'

I'm about to tell him I know what the legends say, but I stop myself; maybe it isn't his truth. Instead, I make myself comfortable and wait for him to start.

'Poseidon deceived my mother, who is Helios's daughter, into mating with a bull as part of a power struggle between Minos and the sea god. I resulted from that union.' Aeron runs a hand over his face. 'My family despised me. Not just for what I symbolised, but also for my appearance. In an age where people admired learning and physical beauty, I was a beast—a monster, even.'

The last words are whispered, and my heart bleeds for the pain in Aeron's voice.

'They banished me to the centre of the dark maze, and every nine years, warriors came to fight me. In the months leading up to those battles, they starved me, and goaded me, and tortured me so that by the time the tributes arrived, I was the crazed beast they had been told to expect.'

'Oh, Aeron, that's horrid,' I say. Those details were omitted from the histories I read, and hearing them gives me a whole new perspective.

The Minotaur holds up his hand. 'That was not the worst of it. When my sister fell in love with a man, he vowed to kill me as a display of his devotion. He was a mighty warrior, and I decided to grant him his desire because I wanted nothing more than to end my loneliness and suffering. When he taunted me and boasted he would defeat me and return my head to my sister, I laid down my weapon and told him to run me through.'

Aeron stops speaking and stares into the distance, his face contorted in pain as if he is reliving the moment. I hold my breath, worried he might decide to end his story before it is finished, and I am desperate to hear the rest of it.

'One of his companions stepped forward and pointed out that I was not the beast they had expected, and to kill me would be wrong. I begged them to end my misery. The companion, a centaur, moved to my side as if to defend me. As he did, he talked of a place I would be valued. All we had to do was find a way to get me there. At first I dared not hope his words were true, but he was convincing. Then he and the warrior concocted a plan where the warrior would take back the heart of a beast and claim to have killed me while Fairglade spirited me to the World Below.'

'Fairglade? Any relation to Fairburn?'

Aeron chuckles. 'Yes, he is Fairburn's father. He is ancient now—as am I—but he still visits, and we wile away an occasional afternoon playing chess. The point is, I am here now because he convinced me I am more than my appearances.'

He captures my gaze with his own to drive home the point.

'I get it. I am more than a princess,' I tell him. 'But how did you end up here, doing what you do?'

Chuckling again, Aeron says, 'I had spent so much time alone, I did not feel comfortable around too many creatures. Queen Ariana's mother spoke with the dragons, and they made some space for me on the edge of both worlds. In return for my home, I test the nature of creatures and dragons when they want to travel between the worlds.'

'Are you asked often?'

'When we had more contact with the dragons, yes, I was. In recent years

I have not been called upon so much. Mostly I tend to my orchards, read books, and play host when creatures visit. It is a quiet life, but I am not lonely, and I am who I was meant to be.' Aeron rests his hands on his thighs.

I push myself into a sitting position and cross my legs. 'Have you found peace?' I ask.

The Minotaur nods. 'I have, Princess. It has taken time, but, yes, I have.'

I hug the blanket around me. Aeron did not choose to be born or to be treated as a pariah, yet he took a risk and found a place where he belonged and made a happy home here.

Deep down, I'm aware that I can't go back to my old life despite the part of me that desires it. In the past few weeks, I have been manipulated and pushed from pillar to post. I understand why this happened, but I'm done. It would be way easier if I had another option.

'So, my young friend, my challenge to you is for you to decide how you fit into our world. It will be tough, but you will not be at peace with yourself until you do.'

'You're right. It's just, I've been running round so much, I haven't had a chance to stop and think.'

The grin revealing Aeron's ginormous teeth would be terrifying if his eyes weren't twinkling. 'Then perhaps it is a good thing everyone here is preoccupied with bringing Queen Ariana back to health. This gives you time to consider your options.'

My nose crinkles. 'I'll go crazy in this room, just sitting round lost in my own thoughts. I have to move to activate my brain.'

Aeron slaps a hand on his thigh. 'Excellent! Perhaps you'd like to accompany me on a walk around my orchard.'

I leap to my feet, invigorated by the opportunity to do something other than try to fix the problems in the World Below.

ED'RATHE EYES ME stonily as I tidy myself after the short ride from the guest quarters to the Queen's Cave.

Is that the best you can do? he asks, huffing on his burgundy scales so they shine.

I didn't exactly arrive here with a suitcase of clothes, I say dryly.

His eyes widen in what might be the dragon version of raising your eyebrows. *You could glamour yourself.*

Glamour myself? I ask, because the idea hadn't even occurred to me.

Using magic for such frivolous reasons is frowned on in the World Above, while in the other worlds, it is commonplace. I turn away from Ed'rathe and reluctantly reach out for magic. I am almost blown off my feet by the weight off it, and I quickly let go. There is so little magic in the World Above that you have to grasp it and pull to use even a little. Here, that tug almost blew me apart.

This time I give a gentle pull and imagine myself in formal clothes. Releasing all but a trickle of the magic to maintain the image, I check myself out. I do look smarter, but I can't get rid of the guilt niggling inside at the frivolous use of magic and the ongoing cost. It lessens somewhat as my mother's voice in my head says, 'Now do us proud, son.' I roll my shoulders back and straighten up, ready now to meet the Queen.

Ed'rathe leads the way into the cave and down a torchlit corridor into an enormous cavern. We stop in the doorway and wait, which gives me an opportunity to survey my surroundings.

An enormous throne cut from the very fabric of the earth dominates the room, and on it sits a dragon, her scales glowing with such intensity, she eclipses every other creature. As if he can read my mind, Ed'rathe sends, *During court gatherings the Queen uses her own form of glamour—one that dulls her light. She is the most powerful being in the three worlds. If she did not hide part of herself, none in the room would be able to bear her presence.*

I wasn't nervous before, but now butterflies flutter in my stomach. I calm a little when we are joined by another dragon and an elf woman. The woman is vaguely familiar, but I can't place where we've met.

Ed'rathe, the new dragon sends, *do you know why the Queen summoned us?*

We should wait for her, Ed'rathe sends back. *Am'nera, this is Snake Fieth, of clan Fieth, and consort to Princess Priscilla.*

I'm about to remind my dragon friend I am no such thing when the elf hisses, 'Abomination! You should not be allowed in the presence of true creatures.'

Her face twists, and recognition dawns, she is Adina, Bernais Baaronson's mother. It takes all my will to not to tell her what I think of her and her narrow-minded family. I will not lower myself to her level.

Am'nera, I am pleased to make your acquaintance. Princess Adina. I acknowledge her with a bow of my head that meets the minimum requirements of respect when meeting royalty—something I know will annoy her, and I have to hold back my grin.

Pris's aunt opens her mouth, no doubt to spurt more vitriol, but a smaller dragon steps between us and advises us that the Queen will see us now. I step closer to the throne, but Ed'rathe holds back.

The Queen did not call for me, he sends.

Without Ed'rathe by my side, I'm even more apprehensive. When I'm in front of the Queen's throne, her power washes over me, which doesn't improve matters.

It takes all my strength to hold on to my sense of self as I bow before her.

Welcome to my court, Sneak Thief. I have been hearing great things about you.

My pleasure at her praise outshines my unease at her use of my private family name.

'Thank you,' I mutter.

Young creature, you need to erect some shields, or this meeting will not go as I planned, the Queen admonishes.

Shields? She's reading my mind. I move away a couple of steps and focus on erecting a barrier against magic before returning to my position.

The Dragon Queen bares her teeth. I hope it's because she finds my ineptitude amusing, not because she sees me as a delicious meal. Or maybe it's because she can no longer read my thoughts.

I requested your presence because I heard you are joining our refugees, and I want you to become their ambassador to my court instead.

My mind goes blank, and I struggle to find the words to respond. Adina steps forward.

'Your Majesty, I must protest. There is no precedent for your recognising these… *refugees* as a political entity.' She sneers as she says the word, like it's sour on her tongue and she can barely stand to even speak of us at all.

They are guests in my realm, and I allow who I will at this court. You are only here today as a courtesy—don't make me regret your presence.

'But…,' Adina splutters, 'you can't consider him a worthy ambassador. He… he's not pure.'

The whole cavern falls silent at her words. Am'nera shuffles away as if distancing herself from her bonded princess.

Adina, you are dismissed, the Queen sends, her voice icy as it chills the cavern.

'But—'

Am'nera steps between Adina and the Queen, cutting the princess off as two dragon guards appear from the shadows. The guards lead her out, and Adina mutters in protest every step of the way.

Sneak Thief, I apologise for the rudeness shown to you in my court. It will not happen again.

I'm still searching for words.

Ed'rathe mentally nudges me. *Snake, the Queen is waiting.*

'Um, I don't blame you for Adina's spite, Your Majesty.'

Good. As ambassador, I expect you at the morning court every day. As the Princess Heir's consort, I assign you Ed'rathe to begin the bonding process.

Ed'rathe's pleasure hits me in waves, but I'm still trying to process what's happened here, let alone what's happening between Pris and me. I can't do this. I don't want any of this. I'm not ambassador material, and my bonding with Ed'rathe …. It's too soon too, too much pressure. Finally I find the right words.

'While I appreciate your offer, Your Majesty, I am sure Gregor and the refugees would prefer to appoint their own representative to your court.'

The Dragon Queen's eyes narrow, and she studies me intently before snorting. *Verona Coronas has been doing an adequate job, but as the Princess Heir's consort, this is an appropriate role for you, and it keeps you from doing anything… politically unsound.*

Suddenly the reason for this meeting becomes clear—Ed'rathe and his friends have been doing some manoeuvring behind my back.

'About that, Your Majesty. I think I need to come clean. Princess Priscilla and I have no formal understanding. It would be… a little presumptuous of me to present myself as her consort before we've discussed matters.'

Again the Dragon Queen snorts, and I'm pretty sure that means she's laughing, or at least I hope she is.

Creature relations are so complex. It is a small matter. We can call you Consort- in-Training. Anything else?

Consort-in-Training? What the hell?

Ed'rathe sends a warning. *Snake.*

Is this how Pris feels when others make decisions for her?

Snake, Ed'rathe repeats, this time with a little more urgency.

I don't want to upset the Queen, or be thrown out like Adina, so I say, 'No, I'm good. Thank you, Your Majesty.'

Excellent. Your first job as ambassador is to remind your friends that they cannot launch any activities from their base here. We are happy to provide them with food and shelter while they are homeless, but we cannot support their political agenda any more than we can support Adina's son. We have no desire to become involved in creature politics.

'I will make that clear, but I'm not sure whether they will listen to me,' I tell her.

You have my backing, young creature. They will listen.

The usher brings forward two new dragons, and my audience with the Queen is over.

Without another word, I join Ed'rathe, and he leads the way from the court, a new swagger to his walk.

'Ed'rathe, did you organise all of this?' I ask dourly.

I did not. I merely reported to my Queen that you were thinking about becoming embroiled with the leaders of the rebellion.

I want to be angry with him, but he was only doing what he thought was right. How could he know it wasn't right for me? Hell, *I* don't even know what is right for me.

This consort business has me wondering if I've really thought about what being with Pris will mean for me. She has repeatedly told me how being in line to the throne impacts what she can and can't do, but have I really thought about how, if we're together, that will extend to me?

I care for her. Hell—I'm pretty sure I'm falling in love with Pris, but is it worth letting her being a princess control my future? We really need to talk.

Shall I return you to the guest caves, Noble One? Ed'rathe interrupts.

He lowers himself to the ground, and once I climb onto his back, I lean forward and say into his ear. 'Thanks for what you did. I appreciate it. In the future, perhaps we could discuss things before you take them to your Queen.'

He stretches out his wings, then tucks them back in before turning his head my way so I can see one of his eyes.

Once we fully bond, I will have a little more leeway. However, my allegiance to the Queen and my dragon community must always come first.

His gaze bores through me, and I appreciate he is making a point and that this is the first step in the dance of us becoming a team.

'Of course, I understand. Though if we are to work together, we need to ensure any actions one of us takes doesn't compromise the other.'

Ed'rathe doesn't move for quite some time, then drops his head slightly in acceptance. *Of course.*

He turns and launches himself off the ledge, making quick work of the leap to the guest caves. He drops me outside before flying towards the setting sun, heading off to goodness knows where. The heavy leather curtain is just falling back in place when Verona accosts me in the entranceway.

'We have company, and they want to see you.'

She drags me by the arm through the main room and down the corridor to where Gregor and I had spoken earlier. He is there, talking to a taller, dark-haired creature.

'Mandor.' The name escapes my lips in a whisper as the other inhabitant of the room steps out from behind the wizard.

'Hello, Snake,' the wiry academic-looking creature says, and I can't help the grin that spreads over my face as I step towards the gnome.

'Drow, you made it below.'

'I did indeed, and not a moment too soon for the state of our realm.' My great-uncle wraps an arm around my shoulder and gives me an awkward hug.

'What are you doing here?'

'I came with Mandor to speak at the gathering tonight. We have much to discuss and much to decide. Will you be joining us?'

'Snake is going to be one of our leaders, or so I hope,' Gregor says before I'm able to answer.

'About that,' I start, then search for the most tactful way to announce my new role. 'The Queen of Dragons wants me to be your ambassador to her court.'

Beside me, Verona barks out a laugh. 'You mean she told you it's your job.'

'I'm sorry, I know—'

'Snake,' Verona interrupts. 'Believe me, it's fine. I'm going to be so busy with logistics and planning, I was wondering how I would fit it in, especially as I can't portal backwards and forwards.'

'But what about you working with us?' Gregor asks. 'I was hoping you could convince some more creatures in the World Below to join the fight.'

Mandor clears his throat. 'We must discuss this, Gregor. Not everyone who opposes the elven elite wants to fight, and we should not force them.'

'And we will need some creatures to stay behind and help the refugees who find their way here.' Verona adds.

'Stay behind?' I ask.

'Yes,' Drow says. 'Those prepared to fight are going to be moving to the main camp over the next few days.'

I let out a breath, and Mandor smiles. 'Let me guess. You have strict instructions from the Dragon Queen that we are not to run a war from here.'

I grin. 'Yes.'

'Are you going to be the Dragon Queen's spy?' Gregor asks in a casual tone.

'I am supposed to report back to her about your activity, yes.'

Gregor's nose wrinkles, then his mouth splits into a smile. 'That means she thinks our rebellion is serious enough to keep tabs on.'

'It's weird that you find that a good thing,' I tell him, and he laughs, breaking the tension in the room—and in me, too, if I'm honest. I hadn't realised how worried I was that my new role would change the delicate balance of the friendships I'd been building.

'Now that everything's sorted, let's get something to eat before the meeting,' Verona says, attempting to hustle everyone out of the room.

As Drow and I make our way to the dining hall, I ask, 'Is Heart here?'

My uncle shakes his head. 'Your grandfather is going to the Minotaur's Maze in preparation to visit his parents. He said if I saw you, to tell you that he will leave tomorrow if you want to join him.'

My last few weeks have been all about duty. Surely I can take a day or so to visit my family. I'd love to get to know Heart's parents, Mender and Keeper, better.

Drow must have sensed my thoughts. 'While he's there, he will meet representatives of the local villages to discuss the rebellion. I am sure the Dragon Queen would see the benefit of your reporting back on that.'

'I'll think about it,' I tell him.

In fact, it was all I could think about during dinner and then again during the meeting. I paid enough attention to make mental notes about the fact that all but a few refugees would fight. Those not prepared to do so would go along and work on logistics. They hoped to use the sanctuary for anyone unable to carry on fighting—which meant those too injured to be of use. I would tell the Queen this when I next saw her.

The moment the meeting was over, I contacted Ed'rathe and asked his advice about joining my grandfather.

The Queen's advisor says that so long as you attend court early tomorrow, I am at your disposal to take you and your grandfather to the villages in the far Wyld Woods. You must, however, agree to report anything you learn to the Queen on your return.

I agree, I send, feeling happy for the first time today. Tomorrow I'm going with my grandfather to visit with his parents. Perhaps being an ambassador will not be so bad after all.

I will fetch you at dawn.

Or maybe it will be, I groan inwardly.

SERAPHINA CASTS A "keep-fresh" spell over the leftover food while Heart wipes down the bench and I put away the last of the dishes. He and I have been feeding creatures off and on throughout the day, but now most of the creature representatives from this morning's meeting have finally gone. Outside the kitchen window, the light is fading. Inside, the air is cooling as afternoon turns to evening. It is getting late. Hopefully Nisha will soon be finished.

The kettle boils, and I add water to the teapot before placing the stewing brew on the table. Heart pulls out a chair, and I join him, hoping to catch a few minutes' respite before we are called on to help with something else.

Footsteps drift in from the hall, and I pause, teapot in hand. The door behind me opens to admit Mandor and Drow. Heart half stands to give up his seat, but Mandor tells him to sit. 'We're not staying long. I have to get to an evening meeting in the World Between.'

'Seraphina, they want you in the lounge,' Drow says

She passes him a couple of cups before leaving. He places them on the table before taking an empty seat. Mandor leans against the bench as I pour.

Drow relaxes in his chair as he takes a sip from his cup. 'Seraphina makes the best teas. She swears she doesn't use magic in her mixes, but I don't know.'

'Huh, that's like saying you don't use magic when you brew a potion. If you don't hold the intent in your mind and activate the properties of the ingredients, the potion won't work,' I say.

Drow's eyes widen. 'You mean Seraphina mixes her teas like she does potions?'

Mandor claps a hand on Drow's shoulder and chuckles. 'For such an intelligent creature, sometimes you are quite naïve.'

Drow joins in the laughter, and somehow that as much as the soothing tea helps us relax. It has been so long since the four of us, once almost inseparable, have sat round a table and chatted about inconsequential things. We have not done this since Heart was banished and Mandor was forced to join the Wizard Council. As I sip my tea, I take a moment to enjoy the luxury of our finding this opportunity to reconnect amidst the turmoil.

We do not discuss weighty matters. Instead we catch up on the past couple of hundred years, keeping things light. When the dregs of the tea have gone cold, Mandor pushes himself to his feet. 'Drow, we must leave for the World Between if we are to make the evening meeting with the group there.'

'How come you're doing that?' Heart asks.

'Someone needs to talk to the refugees about what we decided today,' Mandor says. 'And Drow is the best person for that, as he has all the details about the petition to the Queen.'

'And Mandor's going because I need someone to open the portal there and then the one to the Minotaur's Maze after we're done,' Drow finishes.

My eyebrows shoot upwards. 'You're going into the maze?'

Drow nods. 'Yes, we have to if we want to petition the Queen—'

'Who is in stasis,' I remind him.

'If Maddox has done his job, she might well be awake. And it's best to get these things sorted out quickly,' Drow explains.

'Where are you two going from here?' Mandor asks.

I glance towards Heart, who adds, 'And I'm heading for the Wyld Woods and my home. It's past time I reunited with my family. Mandor has some witches spreading the word throughout the villages, and I will help them while I'm there. I may even lend weight to their call for the villagers to join the cause.'

'Oh,' I say, a little jealous of my friends' decisive actions. I should go with Drow to speak with the Queen, but until I have talked with Nisha, I won't be going anywhere. Our previous conversation today has made me realise that, although we may not be moving forward together, it is time we discuss our options and make some decisions together.

'Percival?'

Mandor's voice shakes me from my reverie. 'Sorry?'

'I asked if you wanted Alyce to take you to the maze to visit with the Queen before she takes Heart to the Wyld Woods?'

'When would I have to leave? I'd like to talk with Nisha before I go….'

'Soon.'

As I trace my finger along the woodgrain of the table, wondering what to do, Nisha and Emrys appear, deep in conversation, forestalling my decision.

'Percival, there you are. I was wondering if you wanted to journey back to the grove with me?' Emrys asks.

My eyes are glued to Nisha as my heart pounds in my ears, blocking out the murmur of voices around me. 'With you?' I ask my brother.

'Yes. Nathanial is staying here with Seraphina, and Nisha is going with the witches to Essendore to set up medical support.'

The pain in my heart is so intense, it almost stops beating. Nisha is going away, and she didn't discuss it with me? Even as I remind myself that I have left her on numerous occasions and she did warn me she had a role to play in the upcoming conflict, the hurt runs deep.

As I force myself to breathe, Nisha steps forward and takes my hand. 'If you will all excuse us, Percival and I need some time alone.'

Without waiting for a response, she leads me through the back door and along the path that runs by the edge of the Wyld Woods.

'I see I have hurt you in some way.'

I give her hand a brief squeeze. 'It is not you. It is me. I returned home at the realisation that I've been evading my life, ready to begin anew with you. In the meantime, you have committed to being a part of the opposition to the new council.'

Nisha stops walking and lets go of my hand, then turns to me, sadness written on her face. 'Oh, Percival. Your timing….'

I smile wanly. 'I know. As Snake would say, "it sucks."' I take her hand. 'I was proud of you today. You have so much to offer, not just to our grove, but to the creature world as a whole. I am here to support you in whatever you do. It's just… I do not know where I fit into your life.'

Nisha leans in and touches her forehead to mine. 'You belong with me, and, after this is over, we will be together.'

We stay there, our energies mingling, our spirits reconnecting, until the sound of the door opening behind us breaks the spell, and I reluctantly pull away.

'Emrys is going to the grove to ready the sprites for war. He would certainly appreciate your help,' Nisha says as we slowly wander back to the witches' house.

I shake my head. 'I must earn my place back in the grove, and now is not the time for that. It is more important that I talk with the Queen as the committee asked.'

Then another thought strikes me. I can do more than convince the Queen to sign this agreement. In this changing world, Queen Ariana will need new advisors, and at least one of them should be a lesser creature. Why shouldn't that be me?

'Percival?'

'I'm sorry, Nisha, I was thinking.'

'I asked if that was the best use of your skills, given your connections. If you are serious about accepting who you are, you need to recognise that you have a lot of influence in the higher realms of government.'

I turn my eyes back to her, surprised by her words and their closeness to my own conclusions. Can Nisha read my thoughts? I had heard of bonded couples being able to do that after many years together, but Nisha and I had not spent enough time in each other's company for our bond to strengthen that much.

'Do not look so shocked. You are connected to some of the most powerful non-elves in our realm. You should work with them.'

I chuckle. 'I was just thinking that I will present myself as an advisor to the Queen when she awakens.'

Nisha's lips spread into a smile. 'Perfect.'

Before we step into the light spilling from the kitchen door, I pull Nisha to a stop and turn her to me, then wrap my arms around her and hold her close, as if I am imprinting the feel of her onto my brain. 'I will miss you,' I whisper into her hair.

'Are you two ever going to come back inside?' Heart's voice booms into the twilight.

I suck in a breath, then reluctantly let Nisha go as Heart and Emrys join us, followed by a young witch.

'You took so long, Mandor and Drow left already,' Heart informs us. 'I've been talking with Drow, and he's going to see if Snake wants to come with me to the Wyld Woods. Alyce here is about to take me to the Minotaur's Maze to wait. She'll come back and get you.'

'Percival, you're not coming back with me?' Emrys asks, sounding dismayed. 'With father so recently deceased and Nathanial staying here to co-ordinate things, I could really use your help at home.'

His request is genuine, and I know he believes that I could actually help him. However, he forgets that there are still many sprites who have not forgiven me for the anger I brought down on them from Magnus Baaronson when I spread blight to his property, then challenged him in the Queen's Court. I have much to make up for before they will accept me back.

I draw my brother into a hug and hold him tight. 'Emrys, you know I would come with you if I thought I would be any help at all, but I think I can do more for sprite-kind working with the queen.'

I feel his gasp rather than hear it. 'You raise yourself too high.'

Taking a step back, I hold my brother's gaze. 'No, Emrys. These are creatures I have known all my life, and they have accepted me for who I am. It is time I encouraged them to extend that acceptance to all sprites. My only regret is I did not see that sooner.'

Nisha moves to my side. 'This is his role, Emrys. Let him do it.'

Emrys's head swivels from me to Nisha, then back again, his lips pursed. Then his face softens, and he looks me directly in the eye as he says, 'Perhaps, yes, this might still be as father saw.' He hefts a pack over his shoulder and includes everyone in his farewell. 'Until we meet again, may we all be successful in creating a better future for our fellow creatures.'

He drops a hand on my shoulder. 'You may not believe it, but the grove is still your home, Percival, and we all miss you deeply.'

Tears well in my eyes as I watch my brother make his way into the forest. With that parting sentence, he has hit at the heart of my worries. I send a prayer to the Mother Tree that I will earn my place back in the grove soon.

Heart breaks the moment. 'Right, Percival. Are you ready?'

'No, not quite. Just let me say my goodbyes and gather some things.' I make my way past him and into the house.

Eleanora is standing by the stove, waiting for the kettle to boil. She looks up, and I suspect that she's only making tea because she wants to catch me.

'You're not staying, are you?' she asks, tears glistening in her eyes.

My heart is heavy. For so many years, she has cared for me, championed me when I have not valued myself, and encouraged me to be more than the recluse I turned myself into. She must have known all the time that when I came out of my self-imposed exile, I would leave her.

'No. It is time.'

She takes my hand in hers. 'My friend, you and I both know it is well past time. Where will you go?'

'I am heading to the maze,' I tell her.

'Good. Ariana had better listen to you.' Her face is fierce.

'How did you—'

'Oh, Percival, Ariana herself has wanted you to talk to her about the life of sprite-kind ever since she met you.' Ellie wipes the tears from her eyes.

I want to hug her, but she will not thank me for making her cry harder.

'There is a pack ready and waiting in the hall, I bought some of your things from Wimbledon. My girls are on their way here to take part in the coming war—except for Mae, who is staying behind to look after the children and creatures who have not come to join us.'

'Is she to be the new Witch of Wimbledon?' I tease.

'Temporary Witch of Wimbledon.' She winks, then waves me off, 'Go grab your things. You don't want to keep everyone waiting.' She sniffs and smiles.

When I return with the pack, Ellie is making the tea, her back turned to me. I know she will not like a long goodbye, but I cannot simply leave.

'Ellie, there are no words I can say that will express how grateful I am for the years you allowed me to indulge myself. You are the best friend anyone creature could ask for.'

'It is what friends do,' she says in a tear-choked voice.

I place the pack on the floor and close the distance between us, standing patiently beside her.

Finally, she turns, bends, and hugs me. 'I didn't think it would be so hard when you left. We have done so much together…'

'And we will do so again,' I tell her as I squeeze her. 'Take care, and do not do anything reckless.'

I step from her embrace and walk away, aware there is nothing and also so much more to say.

Nisha waits by the door. In her face I find understanding and love, and it almost undoes me. My years of cat life were so much easier than this, and yet, they were also so much less.

Clearly aware of my fragile hold on my emotions, Nisha touches my arm and says, 'Stay safe, and stay strong.'

I nod. 'Until we are together again.'

With that, she disappears inside, leaving me with Heart and Alyce.

Taking a couple of deep breaths to steady myself, I force myself forward. 'Right, let us be on our way.'

TAKING A STAND

THE EX-WIZARD, ALYCE, transports me to an internal courtyard in the Minotaur's palace, narrowly missing dropping us in the water fountain as we land on the rim. I quickly jump down, and she disappears almost instantly to pick up Heart. Before she returns, a figure joins me.

'Percival, I did not think to find you back here,' Fairburn, the Captain of the Queen's Guard, says.

'You mean after you tricked us into going to the Unseelie Court while refusing to tell Pris about her family connection to the King?' I ask tartly, but I'm too heartsore to put any genuine anger into my words.

The centaur shifts uneasily, his hooves clattering on the tiles. How had I not heard him approach? He must have used magic to hide his hoofbeats.

'I promised her parents I would allow them to tell her about her family.'

Fairburn, although honourable, should have known that sending Pris to the Unseelie court without warning her of her grandmother's presence or that the King was her uncle would lead to problems.

'How is the Queen?' I ask, changing the subject.

'Maddox, Euphemia, and three dragons are with her. I am told it will take time to reawaken her. Then more time to cleanse her body of the poisons she has taken on for the good of our realms.'

There is a touch of sadness, and maybe a little fear, in Fairburn's voice. I study him from under lowered lashes. He seems more attached to the Queen than he once was—more attached than a Captain of the Queen's Guard should be. The Queen's husband died long enough ago for them to form a close friendship—or even something more. I refrain from comment; what goes on between them is their business.

'Are we talking hours? Days? Weeks? There is a war brewing—one the queen herself could stop by making an appearance and taking control of the situation.'

'Percival, do not be disingenuous—the Baaronson faction has gone beyond falling back into line once the Queen is better.'

His words ring true, but there is a large part of me that wishes it were otherwise, that there was a simple, non-violent solution to the impending war that is building. And still another part of me is aware that our realm needs a shake-up if lesser creatures are to gain our rights.

Once my friends and I were so passionate about change, we had put our futures on the line. Princess Ariana was there with us—back when we fought the blight. Our future Queen believed, as her sister did, that all creatures are created equal—although she was nowhere near as passionate about putting her ideas forward. As heir to the throne, she had to walk a tight political line.

Despite his attachment to the future Queen, our friend Allard had gone with Mandor, Ellie, and Genie to test out opening a gate to the World Above. The rest of us stayed behind to cover their absence. Upon their return, the council imprisoned them. Drow eventually freed three of the four—everyone except Mandor. Someone had to be held responsible, and their leader was their scapegoat.

However, we only realised the extent of our trouble when Magnus Baaronson attacked us, dispersing us and preventing us from causing any further trouble.

Using an old statute against inter-creature relationships, Baaronson had Heart banished to the World Above. After being convicted of treason, Mandor was saved from execution by Professor Xander from the University, who spoke on his behalf. They offered him the option of life imprisonment or joining the Wizard Council. Ellie had begged him not to choose prison, but he believed Drow would find a way to free him.

Unbeknown to Mandor, Drow was feeling the failure of not being able to save me or Heart, and he had left the World Below for the Unseelie Court. Euphemia had already taken up her position as Witch Protector of the North, and she offered to introduce him to the King.

In the meantime, the council appointed Ellie and Genie to positions in the World Above. Although it broke Seraphina's heart, she sent her daughters off with her blessing. She had worked with Magnus Baaronson for long enough to realise they were safer away from home.

Although Ariana's support of us weakened her position at court, she insisted on marrying Allard, which might have been what saved him from punishment.

As for me, I had returned to my home, the grove in the Wyld Woods, to lick my wounds. I tried to fit in, but I was still angry about my treatment.

Finally, Nisha had taken me aside and suggested that I might be more useful helping Ellie settle into her new position in the World Above. After a while I agreed, and I'd arrived on Ellie's doorstep with a letter from Mandor and curled up in Ellie's lap as she read it out loud.

My Darling Ellie,
You told me I should choose to live my life over rotting away in prison. I have followed your wishes, and I am with the wizards.
I have done what you asked. Now I ask you to do something for me. Live your life. Do everything we talked about doing—have a family and build a dynasty.
I will always love you, and one day, I hope we will meet again as friends.
Mandor

Drenched by Ellie's tears for the life she would never have, I had shared her grief. Together we helped each other with our losses, and we built a life in the World Above. Although we kept our connections with the World Below, our passion for change had slowly died.

When Ariana was crowned and took her place on the throne a hundred years ago, we'd hoped this might be our time again. She had started out with a great deal of promise. Then Allard died in a hunting accident, and something died inside our friend. Without her husband by her side, she became afraid to rock the boat lest it sink.

We understood her reaction, and we did what we could to help her. In the end, she lost faith in herself and left more and more of the day-to-day ruling to her Chancellor and cousin, Elias. This left a power vacuum that Bernais was more than happy to fill. If we had come back and helped Ariana earlier, would we have been able to avoid all of this?

'A song for your thoughts?' Heart's voice draws me from examining my guilt.

My head snaps up to meet his eyes. For a moment I'd almost forgotten where I was, so lost was I in my memories. I am in the Minotaur's home… and there's Fairburn talking with Alyce.

I offer my old friend a sad smile. 'I don't think they're worth a song, Heart. Besides, who would want to hear a lament for our lost ideals and the time we wasted getting ready to challenge everything that is wrong in our realm?'

Heart chuckles. 'Wow, Percival, if I had known you reconciling with Nisha would do this to you, I would never have pushed you into it.'

'Percival, Heart,' Aeron rumbles from behind us. 'Have you ever considered that the reason creatures enjoy such a long life is to give us time to come around to doing the right thing?'

Aeron joins us by the water fountain as Heart says, 'Perhaps, but it may also be so we have time to repair our mistakes.'

The Minotaur's laugh comes straight from his belly and soothes my heart.

'Percival, I was not told you were coming. I am having a room prepared for you, but in the meantime, I have a young princess who has been here since early this morning and would probably appreciate the opportunity to spend some time with her friend.'

'Pris is here?' I ask somewhat redundantly.

'She is. Up the top of the stairs and to your left—the room with the guard outside the door.'

I pause.

Heart raises a brow. 'Go ahead. I may have to wait some time for Snake before I leave.'

He does not need to tell me twice. I am up the stairs in the blink of an eye. The guard opens the door, revealing a pacing, pale Pris. She eagerly turns as I enter the room, then, perhaps seeing it is just me, her shoulders slump.

'I am sorry. Were you expecting someone else?' I ask, a little hurt by her reaction.

'Oh, Percival, I didn't mean to be rude.' She takes a step towards me, and for a moment, I think she is going to give me a hug. When she doesn't, I side-step her and make my way to the sofa in the middle of the room.

She joins me, and there is a smile tugging at the edge of her lips, as if she knows I rushed here and that I am pleased to see her alive and well.

'You look good, Percival.'

'Better than you do,' I say, concern for her gnawing at my gut. 'Are you not fully recovered from your injuries?'

'Yes—well, almost. It's just….' She runs a hand across her forehead as her brows draw downwards. 'It's just I felt a change in the air, and I'd hoped….'

She walks over to the window, and the light nighttime breeze ruffles her white hair. Now that she mentions it, something is different. I allow my natural barriers down and find the air is heavy with magic—healing magic. Has this been going on all day? A single glance at Pris, who is unaccustomed to defending herself against such enchanting accumulations, shows that it has. That she is not unconscious on the sofa suggests Aeron has taken steps to ensure her safety.

As I rebuild my walls, the magic drifts away, which suggests that the creatures with the Queen are no longer using it. *Is that good or bad?*

Pris stiffens before turning to me, her eyes bright with unshed tears. 'Am'ratha says the Queen is waking.' Pris staggers towards the room's central sofa and collapses onto it. 'She is alive. I don't have to be Queen.'

'You do not have to be Queen? Who said you needed to be?' The words escape before I can bite them back. 'What have they been doing to you in the day or so that we have been apart?'

SO, THIS IS WHAT having the stuffing knocked out of you feels like, I think while another part of my brain recognises that Percival is working himself into a fury on my behalf. I mentally shake myself and focus on answering Percival's question.

'The Queen of Dragons said I was the next in line to the throne, and, should Queen Ariana not recover, I would have to step up.'

Percival raises himself to his full height, which isn't much over four feet. 'How dare she! What about your mother?'

I lean my head back against the sofa and stare at the ceiling, unable to rouse the anger or the fear that kept me keyed up all day as I waited to find out my fate. A voice inside my head niggles, saying, *It might still be your fate,* reminding me that I'm still in the line of succession and the Queen waking has merely delayed the inevitable.

Percival crosses the distance between us and takes one of my hands in his. 'Pris, what is it? You have gone over all pale.'

I rouse myself for long enough to answer. 'I might not have to be Queen now, but I might have to be someday, if only to stop Bernais Baaronson from taking the throne.'

Letting go of my hand, Percival stands in front of me. 'Why don't you tell me what has been going on with you since you arrived in the World Between?'

His stare is so intense, and I sense there is more behind his question than idle curiosity. The door opens, and a brownie brings in a tray of tea and small sandwiches. He places it on the low table in front of the sofa, then withdraws.

'Tea?' I ask, raising a frown from Percival. I suspect he will demand a response, but he breathes out and moves aside so I can pour.

By the time I hand him a mug, he is sitting on the sofa, an expectant look on his face. I sit beside him, take a sip of soothing chamomile, then tell him about my interview with the Dragon Queen, finishing with her expectation that I will take over royal duties.

I didn't know what to expect from Percival, but I definitely didn't expect him to have no reaction at all. He stares into his tea, not moving.

'Percival? Are you okay?' I reach out to take his cup as his head jerks up.

'We creatures have made a mess of things, have we not?' He looks away, and it's quiet in the room again.

The weight of Percival's sorrow hangs heavy in the air. I reach out and touch his shoulder. When he doesn't move away, I rub his arm.

'The past is the past,' I tell him. 'What is important now is how we move forward.'

My words are platitudes, but I hope they help.

Percival slowly shakes his head. 'I have been dwelling on the past since I arrived, and it has made me… melancholy. And you are right—we need to act. It really is time we helped Ariana understand that we must change if our world is to survive.'

The sprite's words are full of a determination and a sense of certainty that is new to my friend. Something has galvanised him into action.

'Percival, what's going on out there?'

While I sip my drink and nibble on sandwiches, Percival tells me of the rebellion brewing in every corner of the World Below. It seems Bernais Baaronson's council coup lit the fuse of a powder keg that has been threatening to explode for years.

The group I'd encountered in the World Between is just the tip of the iceberg. Wizards have defected from their order, the lesser creatures—or should I say the *cultivator* creatures—are standing against creator creature domination, and many in the villages have decided to stand with them.

'A slow shift back to the old ways, or the good old days, as the Baaronson's would have it, had been tolerated. When they forced the pace of change in Queen Ariana's absence, years of resentment boiled over, and now there will be civil war.

'Creatures want things to change, Pris, and they are willing to fight for it.' His gaze is full of determination.

Things really are a mess. It's not just about kicking out Bernais Baaronson and putting Queen Ariana back on the throne. The people of the World Below want change.

'I guess I shouldn't worry about being Queen because it doesn't sound like there'll be a throne for me to ascend to,' I say, my voice dry.

Percival snorts a laugh. 'Yes, I think that is the least of our worries. Drow and Mandor will arrive here soon with a petition to present to the Queen. It says something like, "We will help restore you to the throne, but we want concessions."'

'You think she'll sign it?' I ask.

Percival shakes his head. 'I do not know. I would like to say yes because I know a young Ariana would have supported the sentiments. But a lot of water has passed under the bridge, and I am not sure where she sits—'

'Still on her throne, but somewhat restrained,' a familiar voice from the door interrupts. 'Excellent, you have tea.'

Euphemia sweeps by me, King Maddox trailing in her wake. She reaches down and places her hands around the teapot. I sense a whisper of magic, then she pours herself and Maddox a cup each. Euphemia sits beside Percival. I say nothing, waiting for them to speak as Maddox drifts over to the balcony doors, his gaze distant as he drinks.

'How is Ariana?' Percival asks.

Euphemia's chest rises and falls as she takes some deep breaths before responding. 'She will recover. She needs food and rest, but she should be back on her feet in a couple of days.'

Relief floods every fibre of my being, and I release a heavy breath. The Queen is alive. She will take back her throne and give her creatures the change they want.

'And then?' Percival asks.

'Then she and I must cleanse magic as we were supposed to do,' Maddox answers.

'What?' I demand, my blood running cold as the implications of this hit me. 'What about going to the Capitol and reclaiming her throne?'

Maddox's face tenses with stubborn resolve. 'You heard me, niece. The Queen of Dragons has demanded we uphold our side of the bargain and sort out the problem with magic once and for all. If we don't start work immediately, she will close off the World Between forever.'

'What about removing Bernais? What about my parents? What about the impending war?' Thoughts tumble from my mouth one after another.

Maddox runs a hand through his hair, accentuating the lines of weariness around his eyes. 'I believe you heard me. We must restore the flow of magic now or lose it forever.'

My jaw drops. Is magic more important than the loss of creature lives a war will bring? Perhaps my view is skewed by having grown up in a world without magic, but I think not.

Euphemia intervenes before I can argue my point. 'Pris, you must understand, dragons not only create magic, but they cannot survive without it. If we do not sort out the magical flow soon, they will close their borders to save themselves. The levels of magic in our worlds are so low that, when they do, magic will die here and in the World Above.'

The haunted look in my uncle's eyes reminds me that if magic dies out completely, the creatures locked in the Unseelie Court—the creatures he swore to protect—will be there for all eternity.

'Dammit!' I spit. Just when I see a way out of the mess, I get sucked even further into the mud. 'While you guys cleanse magic, we go to war. What happens if the Queen doesn't lead the creatures against Bernais? Will they accept her back as ruler once this is over?'

Maddox smiles, but it doesn't reach his eyes. 'The dragons suggest you should be her proxy while she cleanses the worlds. The Dragon Queen is impressed with you, niece.'

I'm not sure how to respond to that. It's exhausting always being the person everyone comes to. I just got out of school and haven't even had a chance to start my life, but now I'm expected to fix a problem that's been going on for centuries.

Percival places his hand on mine. 'Instead of looking at this as a death sentence, you could approach it as a once-in-a-lifetime opportunity to effect change.'

'Are you mad?' I hiss. 'No one is going to listen to me. They don't know who I am, and I'm not equipped for this.'

As I speak, a kernel of a thought forms in my mind. I know someone who has been fighting their whole life for the rights of others. Someone who the creatures of the World Below already know. I'm about to raise the idea when the doors burst open, admitting Snake and Drow.

'Snake, You're here.' I know I'm stating the obvious, but I'm so pleased to see him, I feel almost giddy with relief.

A nanosecond later, Drow demands, 'Have you initiated a coup?'

'What?' I look from one to the other, trying to make out what's going on.

A wry smile forms on Snake's lips. 'The Dragon Queen ordered us here because Queen Ariana has woken up. When we arrived, Ed'rathe told us to talk to you instead of the Queen.'

Percival slips off the sofa, holding his hands out in front of him as he tries to calm things down. 'I think you will find it is more to do with the Dragon Queen's orders than Pris's actions. In fact, we were about to discuss Pris's response, if you'd like to join us.'

Snake's eyes widen in surprise, but there is also concern in their depths, and all I want is to be alone with him to talk this through. Well, alone with him and Percival. Everyone else here has their own agendas, and none of them have my wellbeing at the centre.

'I'm sorry, but I need you all to leave—all of you except Snake and Percival.'

Drow voices his objection over Percival's head. 'But… but we have to—'

Euphemia rises from the couch and places her mug on the table. 'The princess has a lot to take in, and she has asked us to leave. The least we can do is give her space to think.'

Euphemia's glower stifles Drow's objections. I'd forgotten how empathetic Euphemia is. Her support warms my soul. Maddox follows the two of them out of the room. Once the door has closed behind them, Percival retakes his seat, and Snake, his eyes holding mine, crosses the room to stand in front of me.

He reaches out and cups my cheek, and I lean into his hand.

'Hey there, you,' he whispers quietly, and I feel some of the tension in my shoulders release.

I wrap my arms around his neck, needing the embrace. 'Hi back.'

His arms slip around my waist, and I feel him sigh against my hair.

After a moment, we step back from one another, and, hand in hand, we rejoin Percival on the sofa as Snake says, 'This mess is getting out of control.'

He sounds as weary as I feel.

THERE IS A fragility about Pris that wasn't there when she left the caves this morning. Part of it will no doubt have come from the heavy magical energy in the air. It's almost suffocating.

I squeeze Pris's hand. 'How are you coping with all the magic swirling around?'

A smile tugs at her lips. 'Aeron taught me to create a shield.'

I draw a little magic to reach out and test the barrier. It's solid, and I'm suddenly very grateful to the Minotaur, although not so grateful that I've forgotten that he was planning to kill me not that long ago.

'So, Pris, what's going on?'

She closes her eyes and sinks back into the sofa, and it's Percival who answers my question.

'The dragons are demanding Queen Ariana and King Maddox fix magic in the two realms before doing anything about the political crisis facing us all.'

'And,' I prompt.

'And they want Pris to act as regent.'

Pris removes her hand, stands up, and makes her way to the window, leaning her forehead against the glass. I move to join her, but Percival shakes his head. I'm so pleased to have the old team back together, I heed his advice, and we wait in silence for her to speak.

'This isn't my problem to solve,' she finally says. 'Until a few weeks ago, I was happy living my life away from these centuries-old feuds and disagreements.

If I had my way, Snake and I would walk out of here and leave you all to it.'

Feeling a sudden warmth inside at knowing she would choose me over the Crown, I respond in kind. 'Say the word, and we're outta here.'

'Huh, as if you could,' Percival says. 'Your parents did not bring either of you up to run away from a fight simply because it is not yours.'

Pris slowly releases a breath. 'No, they didn't, but they didn't encourage me to poke my nose into other's business either.'

'Still, here we are.' He crosses his legs, trying to appear casual. 'If you had carte blanche, what would you do to solve this little dilemma?' he asks.

Oh, he's good. I can see the cogs working in Pris's mind as she attempts to solve this puzzle.

'I don't know…. I've never lived here, so I'm not sure I'm qualified, but… perhaps using lessons from the World Above….. Mmm…. History teaches us that countries run by an oligarchy or a dictatorship often do not treat minorities well.'

I get where she's going with this. 'The most stable societies let all adults have some say in the government.'

Pris turns from the window, her gaze now more thoughtful. 'Mum often comments on how many refugees flee their homes because, rather than listen to them, their government has persecuted them, and they no longer feel a part of the community.'

Pris is coming back to life before my eyes, and she's sweeping me along with her.

'Much like Verona and the creatures in the World Between.'

Pris nods. 'Yes. They feel the council doesn't speak for them.'

'As do many of the creatures who cultivate and care for our land,' Percival adds.

'Any solution we fight for must allow all creatures to have a say in who represents them,' Pris announces.

'I believe that *is* what Drow's petition suggests,' Percival says.

Pris takes a step towards us, her eyes bright with excitement. 'I would go one step further. I would see the council ruling the World Below and the Queen being perhaps one vote on that council.'

'What if the role of Queen weren't just ceremonial, but more like the Vice-President of the United States? She would have the ability to cast a deciding vote when the council is deadlocked,' Snake suggests.

'And if we separate the legal court and the royal court…,' Pris muses.

'Whoa, slow down,' Percival interjects. 'This is more of a long-term vision. I'm not sure the World Below is ready for such radical change.'

A frown draws Pris's brows together. 'You did ask what future I might imagine.'

I resist the urge to support her with a 'Yeah,' because I understand what Percival is doing. He has inspired Pris to take a position. Now he's probably wanting her to find something achievable she can lead people to embrace. Something Queen Ariana will be compelled to endorse when she's back in charge.

Pris's shoulders drop, and she turns away. 'They're only ideas. Anyway, it doesn't matter because I am not the heir to the throne. My mother is. And I believe she should be the one to take this on.'

'What?' Percival and I say together.

Pris's chin juts out as she raises her head. 'Everyone is so keen to push me onto the throne, but they've forgotten my mother is actually next in line.'

'But…,' Percival splutters.

'I know. She's locked in the palace. But that doesn't mean we can't find out what she wants to do.'

I beam at Pris, proud of the solution she has found to our problem. Percival still looks confused. Pris takes a seat between us and turns to him.

'This is the perfect solution, Percival. Queen Ariana is part of the problem.' She holds up a hand. 'I get that she's your friend, but it's the truth. Even if she agrees to the petition, she has been so focussed on keeping magic alive that she has done very little to help creature-kind, which means many will question her true commitment to change.'

'I guess that might happen,' Percival reluctantly admits.

'Besides,' Pris continues, 'when this is over, her role will be to bring everyone together, including the elves. If my mother negotiates a deal and sets things in motion, then Queen Ariana can say she was forced into this position, and she will work with everyone to produce a compromise. She will be seen as the one healing the nation.'

Percival stares at his hands while he considers Pris's proposal. 'Can you explain to me why it has to be your mother and not you?'

Pris smiles wanly. 'Because she was born here. Because she left so she could be with my dad. Because this is what she's passionate about, and now I know why. And mostly because she will do it so much better than me.'

'How can she lead us all from captivity?' I ask.

Pris's brows draw into a frown. 'Well, obviously we use the dragons for communication—' she starts, then stops. 'Oh. Of course. This was what Gregor was talking about. The groups fighting Bernais are so diverse. We need someone to bring them together—a figurehead. A unifying force.'

'He was asking you?' Percival asks.

'He was asking *us*—Snake and me,' she tells him.

'It's because our quest has captured everyone's hearts,' I add. 'But—'

'You must do it, both of you,' Percival says with such conviction, it's difficult to argue with him. 'You're the future of our world.'

He is so earnest, I can't help but grin at him, ready to join him on the battlefield. Then I remember my promise to the Dragon Queen. 'I've sort of promised the dragons I will act as ambassador to them.'

Pris's and Percival's heads turn in unison 'What?'

'Gregor wanted me to act as poster boy for their cause, and he almost had me convinced. I wanted to talk to you first, Pris, 'cause I know you've been under pressure, but the dragons stepped in and offered me a solution. They want me to act as a go-between for the dissidents and the dragons.'

Pris frowns again. 'Percival, I thought the dragons didn't interfere in creature politics.'

Percival taps his finger on his leg and stares into the distance. 'It is unusual… but… I'm wondering if the state of magic has become so bad, they feel they have to intervene. I mean, if they are threatening to withdraw from the worlds… perhaps this is them showing they are giving us a chance.'

The room falls silent. The only noise is the tap-tap-tapping of Percival's finger against his leg. Finally, he says, 'I think the dragons deserve our consideration, and at the very least, they should be kept abreast of our activities.'

'I agree,' Pris says. 'Especially if we want them to aid our communication with my mother and one another.'

The two of them look at me as if waiting for my input. I agree with them, but I have reservations, mainly about my being the person placed in that role, but that is not my only concern.

'What is it, Snake?' Pris asks, quick to see my discomfort.

I suck in a breath, trying to relax before I voice my fears. 'I feel like events are controlling you and me again. You're going to be a spokesperson for your mother if she agrees to our plan, and I am going to be ambassador to the freaking dragons, for goodness sake. I want to say no, but I can't walk away either, even though every fibre of my being wants to return home.'

Pris reaches for my hand as Percival rises to his feet and begins pacing. Her fingers wrap around mine, and I draw some comfort from the gesture.

'Are you only staying because of us…. Because of me?' she whispers.

I shake my head. 'No—well yes, in part. But mostly I'm thinking about staying because I can't go back to my old life knowing what's happening here. If I do, then I am just as bad as the Baaronsons and their faction.'

Percival stops moving and turns to us. 'I feel sorry for the two of you, I really do, but I don't think this is exactly "happening" *to* you. I believe it's happening *because* of you. When Bernais took your parents, it was the beginning of his attack on the main power structure of our world. He believed it would crumble. Then the two of you came charging in to save your parents, putting a spanner in the works, so to speak.'

I turn the thought over in my mind as Pris says, 'Are you saying this coming war is our fault?'

Percival hides a cough that sounds suspiciously like a chuckle behind his hand. 'Well, I guess I am. If you and Snake had not come here, I believe Bernais would have succeeded in slowly relieving the Queen of her power. Instead, several very senior officials found themselves thrown together, trying to prevent Bernais from hurting you two. Keeping you safe and out of Bernais's clutches galvanised them into action, nudged them into working together to use the two of you to save the Queen. Your interference set all of this in motion.'

'And it was only the three of us who could have motivated those hiding out in the Unseelie Court to join the battle,' I add, understanding dawning.

Percival smiles. 'And your heroics inspired the discontented youth to stand up and fight, because if you could take on the establishment, so could they.'

I grimace as Pris's grip on my fingers tightens. Rather than soothing her concerns, Percival's theory has increased her anxiety level. I untangle her fingers and wrap an arm around her.

'Whether we're being buffeted by the winds of change or we're stirring them up, we're here now. If we work together, the three of us, we can at least channel the winds in a direction we're happy going in,' I say as I lean my head against hers.

'And when this is over? Where does that leave us all?' she asks.

'Hopefully together.'

She leans into me, and I want to stay holding her forever.

'So,' Percival starts, 'I'm going to go and make sure the proposal Drow has with him meets our needs and then figure out how we get it to Cecily.'

Pris pulls away from me. 'And I must talk with my mother and get her on board.'

'Do you want me to stay?' I ask.

'I want you to, but I think this is a conversation we'd best have on our own—well, on our own with our dragons.'

I rub her shoulder before reluctantly pushing myself to my feet. 'I'll leave you to it, then?'

She nods. 'Wish me luck.'

'You won't need it. This is a good plan.'

'But I don't feel good asking because—'

'You think you're using her to get out of doing this yourself?' I finish for her.

'Yes.' The word is a whisper.

'Do you honestly believe she's the best person to do this?' I ask. 'Because if you don't, there is still time for you to do it yourself. Percival and I will be here to support you if that's your decision.'

Her eyes slide to the side as she considers this. 'No, this is the right way to do it. I don't have what it takes to change the World Below—Mum does. It's like she's been training for this her whole life.' She looks at me, her eyes shining with wonder.

A smile tugs at the corner of my lips. 'Perhaps she has,' I tell her. 'But you'll never know unless you have that conversation.'

'Okay…. Something else to consider.' She grabs a hand as I turn to go. 'You're not leaving the maze, are you?' There is a note of panic in her voice.

'I'll be nearby,' I reassure her.

'Thank you,' she mouths as she shoos us both from the room.

WHO'S LEADING WHO?

PERCIVAL OPENS THE door, and Snake follows, then turns to me. 'Are you sure you want me to go? I can sit here in silent support.'

His mouth quirks upwards, and his half grin is so adorable, I almost change my mind. Before I allow myself the luxury of the distraction he would be, I shake my head. 'I appreciate the thought, but I think I need to do this alone.'

'Of course. Tell Am'ratha if you need me, and I'll come back.'

The door clicks shut behind him, and I allow myself a couple of minutes to clear my mind before reaching out to my dragon friend. Once our normal greetings have been dispensed with, I get straight to the point.

Am'ratha, if I wanted to talk to my mother, is there a way you and Am'rena can do that?

You mean other than our relaying your conversation? Am'ratha's tone is so dry, I imagine her raising a single eyebrow in disdain.

I think about it for a moment, then agree that that's exactly what I mean.

There is, but I will have to link my mind to yours, and Am'rena will have to link with your mother.

My mood lifts. Finally something is going in my favour. *Cool. Can we do that, then?*

Not so fast. If we do this, I will have full access to your mind—your thoughts, your memories, your dreams, your hopes, and your desires. No, don't answer immediately. Think about whether you are happy with anyone knowing that much about you.

But you can read my mind now.

True. But you can put up barriers, and I can choose whether to read your thoughts. I will have no choice if we do this.

Oh.

Yes, oh. And for this to work, your mother must agree to the same situation with her dragon. As they have only spent a short amount of time together since your mother left the World Below, they might feel uncomfortable being that close.

As with all magic, there is a downside. I've known Am'ratha long enough to know that my dragon friend will not rifle through my mind if we were to do this, but she would still be a part of me, a part of my consciousness.

Hold on a minute. If you pick up things from me and my private conversation during this process, do you have to report it back to your Queen?

That depends.

On what?

Well, everything is deemed private unless you are threatening the World Between—that I would have no option but to act on.

I would never do anything like that, I reassure Am'ratha.

Not knowingly, Royal One.

Okay, just so we're clear.

I should be all right on that front, but the reasons for possibly not doing this are building. *Dammit.* I can't risk this conversation being misunderstood because someone else is filtering our words. Why don't they have phones here? I hope I'm doing the right thing and that it doesn't backfire on us.

Am'ratha, would you ask Am'rena if my mother with speak mind-to-mind with me?

As you wish, Royal One.

My mind goes quiet as Am'ratha chats with Am'rena. I use the bell on the table to summon a servant. He agrees to bring more tea and is just returning with a tray laden with a teapot and a tiered plate of sandwiches, savouries, and cakes when Am'ratha returns to my mind.

Royal One, your mother asks if this level of communication is necessary? Am'rena has been keeping her updated with news from our Queen and from Queen Ariana. She sends that it would have to be something surpassingly important for her to consider mind-merging with Am'rena.

Dammit. Of course it's important. I'm not exactly looking forward to this myself.

Perhaps rather than blaspheming, you could give her an idea of the purpose of the conversation, Am'ratha suggests, but rather than criticism, I sense amusement in her tone.

Given how often Am'ratha picks up on my thoughts, merging our minds might not be too challenging. My dragon friend's chuckle reverberates in my skull before she says, *You have no idea how difficult this will be for you. Another presence in your head is uncomfortable and disconcerting to say the least.*

My gut ties itself in knots as I think about Am'ratha having full access to me, and I wonder if maybe we could do this via the dragons.

Tell my mother this has to do with the future of the land. If that isn't important enough to take this step, then I don't know what is.

A sense of pride in my strength filters through the bond as Am'ratha leaves my mind. While I wait for Am'ratha to return, I pour myself some tea and nibble on a cake, my stomach churning too much to eat anything more.

They agree.

I slowly release my breath. *Good, now how do we do this?*

It is best if you lie down and make yourself comfortable.

Odd, but I guess I can do that. Before I stretch out on the sofa, I position my tea and the rest of my cake on the table. As I study the cornice work on the ceiling, I try to relax.

I am ready.

Without any warning, I feel tendrils of… *alienness* worm through my head. My first instinct is to fight them, push them out. It takes all my concentration to let them in. Just as my head feels like it's about to break apart, the movement stops. I'm pleased I'm lying down because the excess weight would have had me keeling over.

Then pain assaults me, like my mind has been flayed open, followed by the shouting of strange voices. As I open my mouth to scream for it to stop, I am suddenly in a… void? The pressure is still in my head, and there is a roaring in my ears. It's like holding my breath underwater.

Breathe, Princess. That's it. Nice and slow.

I count in—one, two, three… and out. My heart rate slows, and the panic recedes.

Now, we will concentrate on the conversation. You must forget I am here. Doing both those things should keep the noise of my mind from intruding and overwhelming you.

Okay. The thought is a whisper.

Are you ready? Yes, I can tell you are. Please be quick, as the longer we are like this, the longer the side effects will last.

Side effects? Am'ratha, you didn't mention side effects.

Pris, is that you?

Mum? Mum's voice is so clear in my mind, I'm overwhelmed with longing to see her, to touch her. The pressure builds in my ears, and I remember

Am'ratha's words—concentrate on the conversation.

Yes, Pris, I'm here. What is it you needed to talk about?

Are you okay?

Yes, your father and I are fine for the moment. Tell Snake his mother, Ginth, is also all right. Bernais's men surround the castle, but our defences have not been breached. But you didn't go to all this trouble for an update, Pris.

Although I am happy my and Snake's families are unharmed, the almost unbearable pressure in my head, along with my mother's tone, force me to get on with the main event. *No, Mum, I didn't. I guess you know Queen Ariana is awake.*

Yes.

And do you also know what the dragons want me to do?

Yes.

I pause for a moment, hoping my mother will say something like, 'Don't worry, Pris, this isn't your fight. We have a plan.' There is nothing.

We have another idea.

We?

Snake, Percival, and I. We believe we can win the coming battle if we pull all the factions fighting Bernais together, but we need your help.

Mmm, and what about Ariana and the Dragon Queen? What do they think?

Our plan involves more of an 'ask for forgiveness than permission' approach.

Okaaay. And what is my involvement in this?

Well, you're at the centre of it.

When Mum doesn't respond, I outline how we want her to agree to enact the constitutional changes that we will proclaim in her name to galvanise the forces should we win this war.

And what about our ruler, the actual Queen?

Percival is going to work on her. He says she always broadly agreed with a move to a more democratic form of government, so we're just providing her with cover.

I wait for her reaction.

And you're hoping that by the time Ariana is back on the throne, she won't be able to reverse the changes.

I grin. Mum always picks up on nuances. *Yes.*

Another silence. Maybe the delay is because Mum is keeping Dad in the loop.

And you are aware that if I do this, I am accepting my place back in the royal line of succession, which means—

That I will also be in line for the throne? That we're making a commitment to giving up our lives and staying in the World Below?

When I discussed the solution with Percival and Snake, this hadn't seemed like a big thing. Talking to Mum about tearing our lives apart is next level.

Pris? Are you okay with that? Your father and I have always known this day might come, but we hadn't even had an opportunity to introduce you to your heritage before we were kidnapped.

She wants me to reassure her that keeping me from my family and my birthright was okay. I can't because the truth is, I'm still completely pissed that she and dad kept me in the dark and that I've had to feel my way blindfolded through this world.

We can talk about your parenting skills when this is over, Mum. In the meantime, we all have to do what is right for the creatures of this world and the World Above.

There is another pause, and this time I know for sure she is talking with Dad, possibly because my heightened senses are able to read her better—but more likely it's because Mum's tone of thought leads me to believe she's tiptoeing around me. Dad's always been better at handling me when I'm being 'emotional,' so they'll be strategising.

I've spoken with my mother, and she will never return to the World Below, so I am afraid if we want to keep the throne from Adina and Bernais, then you and I will have to step up.

The Dragon Queen as good as told me that.

Interesting. I must decide whether to take the reins and rule in a way you and I can agree on, or whether I should do what I know Ariana would prefer….

What Ariana would prefer? Would she prefer to keep things as they are and potentially lose her Crown? I suppress the idea before it can take hold.

Mum, is there really any question?

I mentally cross my fingers, hoping I've called it correctly.

No, I guess not. It's just… we might send the realm into further turmoil.

It's already spinning out of control and splitting into factions. If we don't pull everyone towards a common goal, then Ariana won't have a realm to rule when she returns.

I sense Mum's tension through our bond, and it adds to the pressure in my head.

Mum, we're going to work with as many groups as we can out here to build a new base of support for the Crown. In order to do that, we have to be sure we can promise them real change—definite changed. This is the only way we have enough power and numbers to stand up to Bernais.

And if you do it in my name, you have legitimacy, and we have continuity of power should anything happen to one of us when you speak for me.

Yes.

Okay then, Pris. Let's do this. Am'rena will come and pick up the agreement for me to sign.

Relief almost overwhelms me, and for a second, I'm again aware of Am'ratha in my mind, before I concentrate on Mum and my dragon fades into the background.

Great. And Mum.

Yes?

We are going to have to talk about what you kept from me once this is over.

I know, hon. In the meantime, keep yourself safe so we can have that conversation.

You too.

Love you, Pris.

Love you, too, Mum.

That is as close as my mum gets to being mushy. If I'd known she'd been brought up as a royal princess, I would have understood her need to be proper earlier.

Are you ready? Am'ratha asks.

For what?

Suddenly, the pressure in my head recedes, and the room spins. I barely make it to the bathroom before my stomach empties. After, I sink to the ground and lean my head against the cool marble at the base of the basin, wondering how long it will take to get over the worst hangover ever.

'FOR GOODNESS SAKE, Snake, would you sit down,' Heart snaps. 'She'll come find us when she's ready.'

I scowl at my grandfather. He glowers back.

'Come and help Percival and me sort this agreement out,' Uncle Drow suggests. 'We could use your help.'

I close my eyes, praying for the strength to deal with my family. In the end, I take a seat at the table. It's been a long day. I'm tired, and I don't have the energy to argue.

'There is nothing in there that says it must be Queen Ariana who agrees to the terms,' Percival says absently, flicking pages. 'In fact, isn't Princess Cecily a better signatory because Queen Ariana is going to be recuperating or working on restoring magic for the foreseeable future?'

Drow drags a hand through his hair, causing it to stand on end, which gives him even more of a mad professor air. 'All the creatures thought the Queen was signing it.'

They have been going round and round this argument for the past half an hour, neither one giving an inch. My head is spinning, and I let out a groan. The three creatures around the table stare at me.

'What?' I snark.

Heart pats my hand, and guilt turns my stomach contents to acid.

'I just don't get it. Whoever signs the paper, the creatures will get a more democratic form of government if this works out. What does it matter whether it's Queen Ariana or Pris's mother who provides it?' I demand. 'Or whether Pris leads the army or doesn't?'

'But the Queen…,' Drow starts.

'Let me handle Ariana,' Percival says. 'And no one, not even the dragons, can object to Cecily becoming regent, as she is next in the line of succession. And no one can object to Pris acting in her mother's name if Cecily agrees to it. And if there are objections from the World Between, I'm sure Snake can manage those.'

My heart beats faster as I realise he's alluding to Princess Adina. He wants me to handle that viper? It didn't cross my mind that she might be there when I next meet with the Dragon Queen.

'This conversation might be moot if Pris can't get her mother to say yes,' I offer hopefully.

'Pris did get her mother onside,' a voice says from behind me.

I'm on my feet in a heartbeat, and my arms are around Pris seconds later.

'You look terrible,' I say, only half joking. She's grey, and her body trembles in my arms.

As I lead her to the table, I detect a trace of flowers and mint. Has she showered? She sinks into a chair.

Percival pours her a glass of juice from the pitcher on the table and passes it to her. 'Here, drink this. It will help restore your equilibrium.'

Pris turns green as she picks up the glass. 'I can't.' She places it back on the table.

Percival nudges the drink closer. 'You can, and you should. I promise you will feel better with some sugar in your system.'

She takes a tentative sip, then a smile brightens her face, and she drinks the lot down before extending her glass for more. After she's drained her third glass, she appears done as she pushes the empty vessel away.

'Mum agreed to step up. She also agreed to the changes that will remodel the government of the World Below into a democratically elected council as soon as Bernais is ousted, followed by taking steps to move to a constitutional monarchy.'

'Then it is done,' Percival announces. 'We just need to get her to sign the document.'

Drow frowns. 'I really want to talk with the others about this… this change.'

Pris turns to me, eyebrows raised.

'Wait,' I mouth.

'Perhaps you could hold off on that until I have spoken to Queen Ariana. I have a meeting with her in the morning,' Percival suggests.

'A great idea,' Pris agrees. 'We could get together for lunch and make plans from there.'

Drow purses his lips as if preparing ready to disagree. Although he is getting what he wants for the various factions, he is such a stickler for detail, and not having the Queen endorse the treaty clearly does not sit well with him.

'Drow, Percival is going to get the Queen's approval for this plan, and that is as good as her signing the treaty,' I tell him.

He puffs out a sigh. 'I know, but so much could go wrong between winning the war and Ariana taking back control. There are other factions in the Capitol who can get to her and change her mind before she implements anything. We have walked this path before.'

Percival pats his hand. 'We won't let that happen, old friend.'

'Besides, don't we want to bring those factions on board once this is over?' Pris adds. 'Leaving them out will only provide them with an excuse not to support the changes.'

'And keeping Queen Ariana out of it means she hasn't allied with either side, and she becomes the perfect creature to negotiate the peace,' I finish up.

Drow looks at me, eyes wide with surprise.

'What? I have a brain and an education.'

Holding up his hands in surrender, Drow says, 'All right, all right. Your reasoning is sound. It's just that I haven't got anyone's agreement on the changes.'

'Everyone trusts you to do the best for them,' Percival says.

'If that's settled, then? I'm exhausted.' Pris stands up, and her chair scrapes against the tiled floor. 'Aeron has kindly invited me to stay the night, and I'm turning in.' She smiles at the others before capturing my eyes, and the message is clear—*Come with me.*

Heat rises in my cheeks. Everyone else probably gets the message, too, but I don't care. I take her hand and allow her to pull me to my feet.

'I'll escort you to your suite—you never know what might be lurking in the corridors,' I say as Heart mimes throwing up.

'I won't be long,' I tell my grandfather before following Pris from the room.

I've barely closed the door when Pris swings around, her eyes questioning. 'I won't be long?'

I tug her towards me, wrapping my arms around her. Was it only last night we were together? It seems like so long ago. Or perhaps that was a dream.

I rest my head against hers and say, 'I'm sorry, but I promised my grandfather that Ed'rathe and I would take him to visit his family.'

She stiffens in my arms. 'You're going? We're on the verge of war, and you're leaving me to face this alone?'

'This isn't just a family reunion. Heart's going to the deep Wyld Woods to convince the villages there to support the revolt against Bernais. Because of their distance from the Capitol, the villages have often ignored what is going on in the rest of the World Below, but Gregor thinks their numbers could change the tide in our favour.'

She relaxes. 'Sorry. I'm so emotionally strung out. I'd hoped we could be together tonight and… talk.'

I can't help the grin that lifts my mouth and my spirits. Mindful of the guard outside her room only two doors down, I whisper, 'Are you sure it's talking you want to do?'

Her laugh is breathless. She shifts in my arms and kisses my cheek. 'Although a repeat performance would be… nice… magic assaulted me for most of the day, then I've been pulled through a magical ringer tonight. I think anything strenuous would break me. Besides, it's moot. You've other commitments.'

Standing there with her in my arms, I wish I hadn't told Heart we'd transport him into the woods. It's bad enough that escalating tensions mean I must report back to the Dragon Queen, if not tomorrow morning, then at least tomorrow afternoon, and can only spend a couple of hours with my family when I drop Heart off. Now I'm missing out on spending the night with Pris as well. It's a double whammy.

'I could come straight back—is that okay?'

'I'll probably be asleep….'

'But I'll be there when you wake up. And maybe we can talk for a while before the worlds interrupt us.'

'I'd like that,' she says, and my heart skips a little knowing she still wants to be with me.

She steps out of my arms and gives me a playful push away. 'Go on, then. The sooner you go, the sooner you can come back.'

I take a step towards her, unable to stop the smirk crossing my face. 'Or I could stay a moment longer for this.'

Leaning forward, I reach out and entwine my fingers in her hair before capturing her lips with mine. The kiss begins as gentle, but it is soon anything but.

'Snake,' Pris groans as the guard coughs into her hand.

I lean my forehead against hers and say, 'All right, visiting the family it is, then.'

It takes all my effort not to turn back as I open the door to Drow and Percival's suite. Once inside, I lean against the closed door. How can she do that to me? I was so sure I was in control there.

'Right, young man. Time to leave?' Heart says, passing me my jacket.

'Give me a moment,' I say, and he laughs.

'If I give you any time at all, you'll be down that corridor quicker than a flash, and I won't get out of here tonight.'

I take the jacket. He's right of course. And I curse him every step of our walk downstairs and out into the courtyard where Ed'rathe waits for us.

About time, Ed'rathe says. *I've been standing here forever.*

I had things to do.

I know. He manages to transmit a smirk with his words, and I am reminded I need to strengthen my wards.

The flight over the treetops to my great-grandparent's village is short, and we travel in silence. Ed'rathe lands in a field about a mile away before saying, *I will stay here. It will be dawn in four hours, so please do not be too long. Creatures scare easily with dragons around.*

I intend to be well gone before dawn, but I don't tell him that. *I'll be back in an hour.*

I hope it is not an hour like at the maze, he sends as he settles down to wait.

We enter the village via a different path to the one I took when I was last here, and we're much closer to the house my father grew up in. Halfway down the street, Heart stops and places a hand on my arm.

I pull up beside him. 'Is something wrong?'

The look he gives me is full of anguish. 'I'm not sure I can do this. I haven't seen them in over a hundred years… and I took their granddaughter from them.'

He swallows, and the gulp is audible in the night air. I take his hand in mine, each of the calluses on his fingers telling the story of the music he's played.

'I told you, Heart, they don't hold a grudge. They are sad they missed out on some things, but they understand the reasons.'

Heart's hand trembles in mine. 'Would you mind if I did this alone? I am sure they'd love to see you and you them. But I think this would be easier if I didn't have an audience the first time.'

I swallow my disappointment. Breaker and Keeper helped me through my first trial in The Minotaur's Maze, and I would love to have seen them again.

However, this reunion with his parents is a huge step for Heart. I can give him the space he needs.

'Just initially, or should I save my reunion for when I come and pick you up?' I'm pretty sure he'll choose the latter, but I'm hoping to at least say a quick hello.

He sends me a sheepish look from under greying brows. 'Would you mind?' Heart squeezes my hand. 'I'm asking a lot.'

'Not at all,' I tell him—a little white lie. 'I'll wait a ways down the street. If they don't throw you out after five minutes, Ed'rathe and I will head back to the maze.'

'Thank you,' Heart says, then straightens his clothes and smooths back his hair before making his way to the house at the end of the row.

As he raises his hand to knock, I slip into the shadow of a doorway. He bangs twice before I see the flicker of a candle in an upstairs window. Moments later the door creaks open, and I can hear the gasped 'Heart, you're home,' from my hiding place.

Tears well in my eyes as I watch Mender take his son in his arms and haul him inside. Once the door is closed behind them, I don't wait around. Heart is home.

FLIPPING THROUGH A book on creature magic, I make my way through the deserted corridors of the Minotaur's house back to our suite. I could have asked a brownie to bring me the book, but I wanted some time alone.

Drow is still going over the proposed contract. Without a doubt, he's triple-checking that we have not let down any faction in the rag-tag alliance.

'I've ordered cocoa for both of us,' he tells me without raising his head. 'I hope it will help me sleep.'

'I have my own methods of sending myself to sleep.' I hold up my book.

Curling up on the sofa, I am soon engrossed. A brownie brings in the cocoa, and I drink mine while I consider the chapter I've just read on how magic came into the World Below. We all know the story, but considering recent events, it is interesting to study it again.

'Percival, why are you frowning so intently?' Drow asks as he sinks into the sofa beside me.

'Magic? Power? I do not understand how creatures and humans can put these things above the welfare of others and their worlds.'

Drow chortles. 'So nothing deep and meaningful, then.'

I rub a hand over my face. 'My instincts tell me Bernais's control over the council is a grasp for power by a dying regime—except they control most of the military

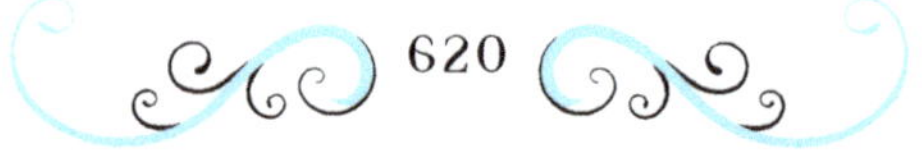

and the largest centre of population. They can also wield more magic than we can.'

'Do not forget, most creatures are too scared or cowered by years of mistreatment to stand up to them.'

I clasp my hands in my lap. 'Drow, I fear I am too old for this battle. I want to return to the grove and spend the last centuries of my life tending trees and spending time with Nisha.'

Drow quirks an eyebrow. 'What are your chances of being left to do that should we fail here?'

I'm saddened that his words ring so true. 'It is déjà vu. Or, if not a rerun, then we are about to fight the battle we were too scared to face all those years ago.'

Creases form around Drow's eyes as he smiles. 'Perhaps if we had had the courage back then… but we were young, and wounded, and we had so much still to learn.'

I rest my head against the back of the sofa. My purpose in studying history wasn't to evoke this sadness, but to find something to convince Queen Ariana that it's time for the elves to hand over power to the creatures of our world.

Will she consider it? Maybe if Elias, her cousin and chosen Chancellor, were here, she would listen to him. He had been the only one brave enough to stand by Ariana when we left, and he has earned her trust. Then again, at that time, he was recently betrothed, and perhaps he only stayed because he had more to lose than the rest of us?

I shoot a quick sideways glance at Drow. Once I had thought Drow would stay behind and help Elias. After all, his family were already advisors to the Crown. Then he had opted to follow Heart to the Unseelie Court.

'Drow?'

'Mmm.'

'Why did you decide to come back now?'

A brief look of worry crosses Drow's face, but it is gone so quickly, I am left wondering if I imagined it.

'Because everyone else was. Besides, what was the alternative? To get caught within a castle in stasis?'

I had forgotten about that. Still….

'There had to be a point when you were tempted to come home. What about when you heard about Ginth. Didn't you want to come back and advocate for her? Didn't Heart ask you to?'

Drow's fingers scratch against his growing stubble as he rakes a hand across his face. 'We talked about it. But Heart is still officially banished. And if I went alone, would I still hold any sway in a court I had deserted?'

'You would have had your family. They would have supported you.'

Drow sits forward, resting his arms on his knees. 'It is complicated, old friend. I am unsure if they would have welcomed me at court. He gulps as if the words are choking him. 'I am not sure *Elias* would have welcomed me.'

I study Drow carefully. His face and voice are guarded—then again, he has always been difficult to read when it comes to his feelings. He and Elias were once so close, the best of friends—then they grew apart. So many things had happened so close together when we dispersed, but had it actually been Elias's betrothal that had pulled apart the creatures who were once as close as brothers?

'Did something happen between you and Elias—something to do with you and Leesha?'

My friend's jaw tenses ever so imperceptibly, indicating I am getting close to the mark.

'Drow, did you and Leesha have a falling out? Or…?'

Oh my gosh, did Drow hold a torch for his best friend's betrothed and could no longer bear to be around the two of them? I thought everyone knew they had an arrangement. Once Leesha had produced two heirs, Elias would return to court, and she would have her own life in Essendore. The marriage had only ever been one of convenience.

Drow runs a hand through his already untidy hair, his brow furrowed the way it does when he's thinking. 'When I left the Capitol, I was so angry with Elias. Leesha had guessed our secret, and she gave Elias an ultimatum. Either he ended our friendship, or the engagement was off. She wanted no hint of impropriety.'

Hold on! Elias and Drow could no longer be together? Years of observing their friendship ran through my mind. How had I not seen this?

Drow is staring at me, his face showing concern. 'Percival? Are you all right? You didn't know, did you? I always thought you did. I hope….'

'Oh, Drow, it is nothing like that. I should have known, but I guess back then, I was so caught up in my own misery that I could not see anyone else's.'

'It is fine, Percival. We never made a big thing of it. I had always thought our lives would carry on as they had done forever. My family would never force me into a political union, but we hadn't counted on Elias's parents deciding he needed a family.'

Drow slumped and rested against the couch. 'In our youthful thoughtlessness, we thought Leesha would stay at the estate and we could continue to be together in the Capitol, sheltered from scrutiny by the guise of our friendship. We underestimated her, and I underestimated Elias's desire to be accepted.'

Drow is silent for so long, I think he's finished speaking. Then he says, almost as an afterthought, 'When Elias gave in to Leesha's demands, I thought my very soul would break. I could not be near him, so I exiled myself to the Unseelie Court. I guess part of me had hoped that amongst like-minded people, I could find someone who would mend my soul. But I could not stop thinking about Elias, and I finally had to admit that while he lives and breathes, he will still hold my heart.'

I reach out and drop a hand on Drow's thigh to show…. I do not know. Perhaps solidarity.

'Now Elias is in real trouble, and I cannot let him face this alone. I have to do whatever I can to get him out of this alive. I've a lot to make up for.'

It never surprises me how much the world can change in a matter of minutes. Who knew my eternal bachelor friend had been in love with the same creature for hundreds of years and none of us knew—well, at least I *think* none of us knew.

'Drow, I do not know what to say,' I tell him.

'I do not need you to say anything. In fact I would prefer it if you kept this to yourself. Ariana is the only other creature who knows, and I would like it to stay that way. Although I have come back because I cannot bear to let Bernais ruin everything Elias has worked for, I have not come back for him.'

'Of course, Drow. Whatever you need from me, you have it.'

I let out a chuckle. 'I always thought you and Effie might… you know. How wrong I was.'

Drow is so filled with sadness at my words that I wish I had kept my thoughts to myself.

'You have to tell her,' I say.

He nods. 'I guess I owe her that. I had always hoped she would find someone and realise we are like brother and sister.'

We sit side by side in silence for some time, Drow lost in his thoughts and me with my mind racing. Was it any wonder Drow was so intent on making sure this agreement was perfect? He was hoping it would save the one he loves. That made it even more imperative I convince Ariana to agree to our plan.

THE BURDENS OF BEING A HERO

THE PALACE IS quiet as I creep back inside. Perhaps alerted by the swish of my footsteps on the marble floor, or maybe Pris has told her to expect me, the guard has the door open when I arrive at Pris's suite. We share a curt nod as I enter, then she closes the door softly behind me.

Pris had left one door slightly ajar to make it easy for me to find her room. At least I think it's her room. I hope they haven't given her a companion in my absence as I slip out of my shoes, heavy jacket, and top, and crawl into bed beside a sleeping female.

The figure snuffles and roles onto her back, and I'm relieved to find it *is* Pris. Moonlight from the window falls across her face, and my breath catches in my chest. She is so beautiful, my heart almost stops. For a brief moment, I consider waking her, but I'm exhausted, and she was not great when I left last night.

I move further down the bed and snuggle into Pris, her warm body moulding itself to mine.

'You came back,' she mumbles, a satisfied smile forming on her lips.

I kiss her hair. 'Yes.' I wrap an arm around her, and with a feeling of everything being right, I close my eyes and let sleep claim me.

When I open them, I'm assaulted with bright sunlight. Rubbing the sleep away, I reorientate myself. The bed beside me is empty. I run my hand over the sheet, and there's no trace of warmth at all. She must have been gone for a while.

The sheet slips down my body as I push myself into a sitting position, and just as I do, Pris enters carrying a tray.

When her eyes land on my bare chest, she grins. 'Good, you're awake. I thought you were going to sleep the day away. I've got breakfast for us.'

She scans my body, and heat rises to my cheeks. I stop myself from pulling the sheet back up. I've never felt insecure about my physique before, but in the stark morning light, all my imperfections are on display. Running a self-conscious hand through my hair, I catch a whiff of something not quite savoury.

'Can I grab a quick shower first?'

She nods towards the other door in the room as she places the tray on the end of the bed. 'There are guest pjs in there too.'

She's obviously taken advantage of all Aeron's hospitality. Her hair is still wet, and she's wearing a cream silk camisole and pyjama bottoms that highlight her curves. I shake my head and leap out of bed before my thoughts become physically obvious.

When I had suggested a shower, I didn't expect there to actually be one; baths are as good as it usually gets in the World Below. However, Aaron's guest suite has both options.

I choose the shower, and, while it's not hot, the water I release by pulling a chain is pleasantly warm. When I emerge from the bathroom a few minutes later, I'm refreshed and wearing pyjama bottoms similar to Pris's.

She has snuggled back under the duvet and placed the tray beside her, within easy reach of us both. I sit on the edge of the bed and slide my legs back under the covers. Once I'm settled and the tray stops moving, she pours us both mugs of coffee and leans back against the headboard of the oversized bed.

'We could fit my whole family in here with us,' she says dryly.

'Pris!' The thought of her parents seeing us like this is actually shocking.

She chuckles. 'I wasn't suggesting….. It was the size…. I mean—yuck!'

I grin as I take a sip of coffee, enjoying this little piece of normalcy. This is the life. Food on tap, Pris by my side, and no reason to leave the room. I reach for a croissant, take a huge bite of the buttery pastry, and stare out the window.

The sun is more than up. Have I slept most of the morning away? Fortunately, when the Dragon Queen sent me here yesterday, she had informed me that I would not be required back to appear at court this morning. If nothing has happened while I've been recharging my batteries, I may get away with spending most of the morning here before returning to report last night's events. Although I wouldn't stake my life on being left in peace for that long.

'Pris, what's the time?'

'Chill—it's only about nine. The sun rises early here.'

With a few more mouthfuls of coffee, my mind is firing again. 'What time is Percival's meeting with the Queen?'

'He was heading her way when the brownie brought the breakfast tray.' With her mug suspended in mid-air, Pris pauses, and a frown appears. 'It's crazy to think that it's my first breakfast in bed with someone, and we're casually talking about meeting with royalty.'

'Ah, it's the first time you've had breakfast in bed with a boy.' I tease, hoping to keep the mood light for a while longer.

Spots of pink colour her cheeks. I reach for her hand and give it a squeeze. Perhaps this isn't the right thing to tease her about.

'Soooo.' I draw the word out. 'When you imagined having breakfast in bed with me, was I shirtless?

She almost splutters out a mouthful of coffee but presses her lips closed. 'That's pretty bold, thinking I imagined this with you at all,' she says once she's swallowed.

Now we're back on track. 'I thought we might talk about how much you love me and how you want to spend the rest of your life with me,' I tease.

Next to me, Pris tenses. Man, I keep hitting bum notes today.

I sit up and turn so I'm facing her. 'I'm just messing with you, Pris. I wanted this time to be separate from what's going on out there. A little slice of normal in the madness.' Pris squeezes my hand, and I carry on. 'I guess when you're about to go to war, thinking about the future is not as easy.'

'That's why it's so important to grab on to those moments when we can.' Pris draws her bottom lip between her teeth, then releases it. 'This *is* new for me, Snake. And I can't tell whether what we have is real, or if it's because we were thrown together.'

It's like a physical blow to my gut. For me, I'm certain my feelings for Pris are real. Then again, this is not my first rodeo. I try to put myself in her place, and realise she might not have anything to compare this to.

Trying not to make too big a deal of this, I say as evenly as I can, 'Are you telling me you want this to stop?'

A troubled look crosses Pris's face. 'Hell no. What gave you that idea?'

I try not to show how relieved I am as I withdraw my hand, then take her mug from her and place it with mine on the tray. After putting everything on the floor, I settle back against the headboard and draw Pris into my arms, then rest my head on top of her hair.

'If this weren't going on, and we met in the World Above and had a date and ended up in bed together, the next morning we'd have breakfast, and then we'd talk—okay, we might do other things, but then we'd talk.'

She relaxes and leans into me. 'And what would we talk about?'

'We'd get to know each other a little better. Not the deep things that you and I already know about, but the little things, like, why are you studying law?'

'I'm not. Well, not yet.'

She's so practical. 'Just go with it,' I urge her.

The silence grows, and I wait to see if she's going to play along.

'I guess because of my parents. They brought me up with a strong sense of helping others. They're both lawyers, although their jobs are different, and I guess I see that as a starting point.'

'That's interesting. And what do you want to do after graduation?'

'I want to work with my mother, helping refugees and immigrants and minority groups.'

We're in the flow now.

'So you've always wanted to work with your mum, not your dad?'

'Yes. I mean, Dad's organisation does good work providing housing and assistance for those less well-off, but I've always felt more drawn towards human rights.'

I nod, wondering if she sees the parallels I do.

'What about you? Why physics?'

Before I answer, I consider whether bringing magic into this fantasy world will ruin the vibe. It'll remind us we're not in the World Above, and once we're back here, the real world would intrude.

'The long answer?'

'Yep.'

'The world is changing. Global warming is increasing, and consumerism has become toxic. I want to find ways to repair the damage to the environment, and studying physics is one way I can do that.'

Pris forces herself up so she can look at me, her eyes twinkling with amusement. 'So part of what we're doing now is what you were going to uni to achieve.'

I pull her back to my chest. 'Pot, meet kettle.'

Her laugh rumbles through her body. 'Ironic, isn't it?'

'It is.'

And now, we have broken the spell. We're back in the World Below, attempting to save the creature realm.

'If we get through this—'

'*When* we get through this,' I amend.

'Okay, when we get through this, do you want to go on a date?'

The laugh explodes out of me. 'Oh, yes, I want to go on a date and do all those things we've missed out on.'

'Good, so do I.' Pris tightens her hug. 'Do you think it will be here, or in the World Above?' The question is barely a whisper, almost as if Pris is unsure whether or not she should give it air.

She has just confirmed her place in the succession to the throne. Does she really think she can go back home?

'I mean, my mother and father had time in the World Above…,' she adds.

That's true. For a moment I allow myself to believe I can go back to my friends and the life I had above. It stirs up a strong desire, but the idea of going back feels wrong. I would have to leave my family behind again just when I've found them.

Fear winds icy tendrils around my heart. 'Do you want to go back?'

'I don't know. A part of me wants to, but I honestly don't know.'

I hold her close, and it almost feels like clinging to her, rather than drawing comfort from her presence. Do we have a future? I'm not ready to give up on the idea yet, and I hope she's not either.

'Snake? Have I ruined everything?' There is genuine distress in her voice, and all I want to do is ease it for her.

I'm doomed. This woman has stolen my heart and my common sense with it. Or has she? How can any of us make plans for a future that may not be there? Still, I can't lie to her.

'I don't know, Pris. My world has turned around, and I don't see myself going back to my old life. Yet, I've no idea what the future holds for me… for us. The only thing I'm certain of is, I am falling for you. And that has been the only good thing about these past few weeks. Whatever my future holds, I know I want you in it.'

There, I have laid my soul bare. Pris hugs me so tight, I almost can't breathe.

'Is it wrong to long for normal, for home? When I was working towards getting Mum and Dad back and returning to our old lives, I had a goal and I could see a future. Now, I'm being swept along by events, and the only things that are constant, the only things stopping me from getting swept away, are you and Percival.'

I hate the despair in Pris's voice, and I want to make this better for her. Having grown up knowing I belonged to another world has given me a different perspective. Home has always been family for me, and now my family is down here.

Then again, if my mother decides she wants to return to the World Above, will that make me change my mind? I couldn't let her go alone. Dammit, it's not so simple, but we will not solve the future now.

'Don't tell me you think of Percival the same way you think of me?' I say in mock alarm, trying to lighten the tone again.

Pris slaps my leg. 'Snake! No! That's like fancying an uncle or some other family member.'

'Ah, so you still fancy me.'

Pris shimmies up my body, making it difficult for me to hold on to any playful thoughts. Then, when her mouth meets mine, all those thoughts are gone. As I run my hand along the length of her spine, a knock sounds at the door. We freeze.

'Who is it?' Pris asks.

'It's me, Maddox. We need to speak.'

'SERIOUSLY? NOW?' I groan. Giving Snake a quick kiss, I roll off him but pause for a moment, torn between duty and wanting to continue what we'd started. I get up and scrabble around for the clothes left in the room for me last night, pulling on each piece as I find it. Clothed in loose tan linen trousers and a white linen shirt, I'm tidying my hair when I become aware Snake hasn't moved.

'You're not joining us?' I ask, a little impatiently. While I'm not sure how my uncle will react to my being with Snake so recently after he tried to have me marry his heir, I'm willing to risk his censure rather than face him alone.

Snake tilts his head to the side as if he's considering joining me. 'I'm not sure my appearance would impress King Maddox.' A wry smile tweaks his lips. 'Besides, I need a little longer before I make any sort of public appearance.'

It takes me a moment, but then my eyes drift to where the bunched sheet covers his lower half. 'Oh, okay. I guess I can do this alone.'

In a nanosecond Snake is alert and about to leap out of bed. 'Do what?'

'Whoa, slow down. I simply mean face my uncle. I've no idea what he wants, but none of our previous conversations were exactly comfortable.'

A knot twists in my stomach as I finish plaiting my hair. So far my uncle has tried to blackmail me into joining his court. When that didn't work, he upped the anti by trying to marry me off to his heir, who turned out to be a traitorous leech.

He redeemed himself by ordering my dragon to save me from a magical attack and transport me to the dragon court, but that doesn't mean I entirely trust him now. I haven't talked with him one-on-one since, but his wanting to see me can't be a good thing.

'You'll do fine,' Snake says. 'You've managed to thwart every one of his plans so far. But if you wait a moment, I can come with you.' He leans over the edge of the bed and reaches for his clothes.

The knot lessens somewhat at his words and offer of support. 'No, I'm okay,' I tell him rather more confidently than I feel. I take a deep breath before opening the door and entering the sitting room with a breezy, 'Good morning.'

Aeron stands up and returns my greeting. I reward him with a smile.

My uncle simply turns from his position on the sofa and studies me, his face an implacable mask.

Ugh, I hate all this court formality. I lower my head to my uncle, acknowledging him as my social superior, before asking, 'How can I help you two gentlemen?'

A slight grimace crosses my uncle's face. Maybe he's looking forward to this as much as I am.

'Please, take a seat.' He gestures to the sofa.

I pull out a chair from the table and sit facing King Maddox. His eyebrows rise a little, but he carries on.

'Queen Ariana asked me to talk with you in light of instructions we have received from the Dragon Queen.'

'So you and she have been scheming,' I say, unable to stop myself from needling him.

'You could say that.'

'We've been doing a little planning too,' I announce before he can say any more.

The King's lips almost form a smile before he schools his face back into disinterest. 'So I hear. Percival is talking with the Queen now. Whatever you have planned, I hope you remember she and I will be busy for the foreseeable future.'

'We've taken that into account,' I tell him.

He nods approvingly. 'Good. What I want to talk to you about is your new role…. Your royal role.'

My eyes flick from King Maddox to Aeron and back again. Dammit, if Maddox still thinks I'm going to be a part of his court, it will really throw a spanner in the works. And I can't believe Aeron is part of this—not after our conversation yesterday.

'Hear the King out.' Aeron's voice is low, but it still rumbles.

Maybe he's not thrown me to the wolves after all.

'Queen Ariana and I have come to an agreement about your royal status.' Maddox clears his throat, and I sit forward in my chair. Did my great-aunt take him to task? 'It seems you are already in line to sit on the throne of the World Below, and according to the Dragon Queen, this claim supersedes any from my court.'

Yes! I resist the urge to fist pump the air.

'We have made a mutual decision that you will assume the role of Ambassador to the Unseelie Court once it is fully reinstated, with the intention of fostering new relationships.'

'Did you now?' The old anger at being manipulated flares inside me. How is it that two people who don't even know me feel they have the right to decide my future?

I turn to Aeron for help. There is a sadness in his eyes as he opens his hands palms upward. Is he telling me that this is my time to take a stand? Hell, this is scary. I wish Snake were here.

I keep my features calm, relaxed. I don't want to come off as being a brat or even as being unreasonable, but I'm not going to let them move me round like a pawn on a chessboard.

'The courts exchanging ambassadors is a great idea,' I tell Maddox, 'but we're a long way from making appointments.'

Aeron smirks as Maddox's lips tighten. I'm pretty sure he's suppressing a smile rather than showing displeasure. I decide to press my luck.

'I'm sure there's one thing we can sort now. I am not, and never will be, betrothed to Dinian.'

Maddox snorts out a rather un-kingly laugh. 'I think we can take that as a given, niece.'

There had been a small part of me that worried he might still expect me to marry his potential heir, even after Dinian had joined Bernais. To be fair, though, I would never have married the creepy elf. His sense of entitlement far outstrips any abilities he has as a ruler.

'Of course, Ariana and I will have to find you another suitable match.'

My fists clench, but then I catch the twinkle of amusement in Maddox's eyes. In our time in the Unseelie Court, Maddox had been every bit the epitome of the tyrannical king. Of course, he had just lost the love of his life, and his court was under threat. There is clearly another side to my uncle. Odd that it's appeared on the eve of a war that could decimate the World Below.

Aeron breaks the tension with a bark of laughter. 'You two are like two cocks in a ring, neither prepared to back down. Maddox, you know you will not marry Pris off any time soon. And Pris, you must know your great-aunt and uncle have more on their minds than your marital future.'

I turn my attention to the Minotaur. The more time I spend with Aeron, the more I appreciate what an accomplished political operator he is. In the past twenty-four hours, I've come to value his words almost as much as I would Snake's or Percival's.

I lean forward and pitch my voice low and neutral. 'Uncle Maddox, why are you really here?'

My uncle stares out the window, lost in his own thoughts. 'I am… not busy,' he finally says. 'I have spent so much time running my court, keeping everyone safe, and now I'm left… waiting for Ariana to recover enough to begin our work together.'

'You're bored?' I splutter. He's been teasing me all this time because he's bored? 'Have you spoken to the dragons about getting your court out of stasis?'

'Of course.' His tone is disdainful. 'The dragons believe it will take quite some time, maybe years, before magic builds up enough in the World Above to perform the spell to restore my home.'

He sounds defeated. He is a king without a court. And he's no doubt worried about his subjects caught inside. My old nanny, Susan, is probably there. I might not even be alive when she finally gets out.

'How many of your subjects are still inside?' I ask.

'In the end it was only the guards outside the room we were in. It seems Lady Susan had an evacuation plan and she got herself and the bulk of my followers away.'

Susan and the others made it out. That's a relief. I wonder where she is?

'Those left behind had volunteered to stay to make sure we were protected while we maintained the court barriers,' my uncle continues. 'When the dragons helped us escape, they were trapped.'

Those poor guards. I couldn't imagine being so devoted to a cause or a person that I would give up my life. Then again, isn't that exactly what I'm doing now—subjugating my wishes to the needs of the World Below? *No, don't think that. Be happy that most of the court got out before Snake, Euphemia, and Princess Petunia completed the stasis spell.*

Aeron clears his throat. 'Um, Maddox, you had some other reason for being here, did you not?'

Maddox frowns as he pulls his mind back to the present

'I did? Oh yes, of course. As I said before, Ariana and I have been talking. She and I are unhappy with you wandering around the worlds alone, especially given your close ties with both royal families. The danger you face is very real, and we both feel you need greater protection.'

'You're kidding me, right?' I inject every ounce of disbelief possible in those words. 'You're worried now? After I've faced down a multitude of foes and extracted myself from several dangerous, life-threatening situations? Snake, Percival, and I have been fine, thank you very much.'

Maddox does not give in. 'As I understand it, the World Below is about to go to war. Your mother is already in a compromised position in the Capitol. As second in line to the throne, it is even more important that you remain well-guarded.'

I rush to my feet. 'You are not going to lock me up as if I'm some simpering princess,' I protest.

'Pris,' Aeron says, and I am reminded of his words about deciding what sort of princess I want to be.

Taking a couple of calming breaths, I start again.

'I may be a princess, but I am also central to what is going on in the World Below. Mum and the leaders of the revolt agreed to work together last night. Percival is speaking to Queen Ariana about it now. I am very much a part of their plan, and if we want a world we are all happy to live in after this, I must do my job.'

A smile plays at the edges of Maddox's lips. 'I do not remember saying we were going to lock you up, but merely that we are concerned for your safety.'

My anger deflates like a popped balloon as I hold his stare. I lower myself back into my chair. 'What are you suggesting?' I ask, feeling more rational now.

'We have asked Aeron if he will become your Royal Guard until this is over, at which time Ariana will provide you with another.'

My eyes flick to Aeron, and he nods once, indicating he has agreed to this. My initial argument that I can defend myself stalls as I consider this option. It is true that the Minotaur is a mighty warrior, and his presence would make potential assailants think twice before attacking. However, there is another benefit to having Aeron by my side.

Well, there are a couple, really. He has proven to be an asset when it comes to politics. But even more, his presence in the meeting today has helped me react less and consider more. In short, he can help me become the princess I want to be.

'I agree—on one condition,' I say.

Uncle Maddox suppresses his surprise. 'And that would be?'

I turn to Aeron. 'If you are going to be around me all the time, then I would also like you as my advisor. We won't stand on ceremony, and you will give me your opinion whether I like it or not. Those are my terms.'

A Minotaur's grin is actually quite a fearsome thing to see, or it would have been if I hadn't seen the pride in his liquid brown eyes.

'I agree,' he says.

'And I guess I do, too, although I can see that is moot,' my uncle adds.

'Good, and the other thing?'

As I wait for an answer, King Maddox's cheeks actually redden. 'Well, umm, this relates to something I brought up before.' Maddox turns to Aeron for help.

'What Maddox is saying is that the dragons told Queen Ariana they are treating Snake as your consort. This is a breach of protocol for a proper heir, and she would like to meet with Snake to assess his suitability.'

My self-control flies out the window once more. 'Absolutely not! This is between Snake and me. Snake and the dragons too,' I amend. 'We are nowhere near the stage of anyone else needing to become involved.'

Maddox's eyes slide to the bedroom door, and it is my turn to redden. He has known Snake was in there all along.

'Oh, come on! We're not in Victorian times, no matter how much your court might like to pretend. Sleeping together is not a life commitment.'

'Actually,' Aeron says, 'In Victorian and Edwardian, times they were all at it all the—'

'Aeron,' Maddox rumbles.

The Minotaur grins at me, giving me courage.

'I appreciate I have royal responsibilities. So, I promise if Snake and I ever get to a stage where you and Queen Ariana need to become involved in "vetting" him, I will tell you. Then I'm sure he'd love to sit down and have a chat about his suitability as my consort,' I finish, mentally apologising to Snake for setting him up.

Before King Maddox can respond, the door opens, and Drow appears.

'Excellent, you're all here.' He scans the room. 'I was expecting—'

'Your nephew can join us momentarily,' Aeron says dryly.

Drow starts, then recovers himself. 'Queen Ariana has asked to meet with you and Snake, Pris.'

'If this is about Snake being here….'

Drow's eyes widen as a flush spreads across his cheeks. 'Ah… no. She wants to talk to you both about the agreement we made and your roles in the upcoming conflict.'

QUEEN ARIANA CLOSES her eyes and lies back against the pillows. Her grey-shot black hair is in a plait, and she wears a royal blue bedjacket, the sole evidence of her status. She is not as pale as she was when she was held in stasis in the centre of the maze, but she is not fully back to health yet either. Her skin is still a luminous white, and the fine lines around her eyes are a sign of the strain talking with me has put on her.

From her place in the garden, Al'kyla watches me through the patio doors with an eagle-eyed intensity. I promised her I would not weary the Queen, and I have tried not to. However, her realm is in turmoil, and discussing anything to do with its collapse would inevitably take a toll.

After outlining our proposal, I had thought we would discuss it. She had only stared thoughtfully at the wall, then called for a servant to fetch Snake and Pris.

I wring my hands as I pluck up the courage to ask her what she thinks.

A cool breeze ripples through the room, disturbing the cornflower blue curtains, and passes over my face. It must have disturbed the Queen, because she shifts restlessly in the yellow-damask-covered bed that almost swallows her and says, 'I am pleased to see you here on your own behalf, Percival, and not as Eleanora's messenger. How I have missed your incisive insights.' Queen Ariana clears her throat and reaches for a glass of water from the bedside table.

'Your Majesty is too kind,' I say, trying to mask my pleasure at her praise.

I've always been in awe of Petunia's sister. She is a little older, a little more aloof, and far more regal than her younger sibling. Truth be told, we all had a little bit of a crush on her, but she has only ever had eyes for Allard.

Fairburn, the head of the Queens Guard, appears in the doorway to the courtyard, startling me. His steps are so quiet, his sudden presence always seems to catch me off guard.

Queen Ariana finishes her water and leans back against the pillows. 'Is it done?'

He dips his head. 'It is. Are you sure this is for the best?'

'If we want to win, it has to be this way.'

The silence that follows fills the room with questions I cannot ask. What has Fairburn been organising? Why does the Queen want to see Pris and Snake? What does Queen Ariana think of the proposal? Will she accuse us of plotting treason? Is that what Fairburn has been organising? Our imprisonment?

'Percival, you look like you have eaten something disagreeable,' Fairburn says.

'Oh dear, Percival. You have had such a busy few weeks. I hope I have not overtaxed you.' Queen Ariana glances at Fairburn. 'Perhaps we should not have put things in motion without talking to everyone first.'

Something passes between the two creatures, and I get a sense that their relationship is more than that of guard and queen. Before I can explore this idea any further, the door beside me opens, admitting Snake and Pris.

They both look relaxed and well rested. They're dressed in the linen trousers and long-sleeved shirts most of Aeron's staff wear. Perhaps they both spent the night here. Holding hands, they step into the room and bow before the Queen. Behind them, a brownie appears with two more chairs and places them side by side near the foot of the bed.

'Snake Fieth, Priscilla Crown, I am so pleased to finally meet you,' Queen Ariana says. 'You may approach and be seated.'

Surprisingly, the two do as they are bid without any sarcastic quips or snarky remarks. Pris does slip a questioning glance my way as she takes the seat closest to me. I shrug, letting her know I have no idea what this is all about either.

'I believe you both know Fairburn,' the Queen continues.

I am not surprised when neither of the two acknowledge the centaur. It was he who broke the news that we had not completed our quest yet when we reached the middle of the maze. Fairburn assigning us the task of retrieving the King from the Unseelie Court to save Queen Ariana had not made him our friend.

Finally Snake breaks the silence. 'I guess you're happy now you have what you wanted.'

Fairburn shuffles a little but holds Snake's gaze. 'I will not apologise for doing what needed to be done to save my Queen.'

Snake shifts in his seat, dismissing the guard as he turns his attention to the Queen.

Queen Ariana studies the creatures in the room, and the air thrums with magic as she talks with her dragon.

'Peace, everyone. I am sure you have all done things you are not proud of while I have been gone. It was a trying time, and I take full responsibility for all actions carried out in my name. So, if you have a complaint, I am ready to hear it.'

It is Snake's turn to shuffle uncomfortably. While he may not have been happy about being moved from pillar to post, he would not raise such petty concerns with a creature so recently returned from the brink of death.

'Now that that is settled, and before we move on to more weighty matters, I want to thank the three of you for bringing Maddox here to help me. I know you were used by others, and it must have been frustrating. However, you could have backed out at any time, and you did not. For that, you have my gratitude.'

'You're welcome,' I say as Pris and Snake mumble similar sentiments.

'When things are settled in our realm, I will reward all of you, but I am not really in a position to do very much at the moment.' She smiles wryly. 'I acknowledge that I am thanking you one moment and then asking for more help the next.'

I stiffen with surprise. I am not sure I have another quest in me. Suddenly the mat in front of the fire of Eleanora's place in Wimbledon is very inviting. I push the thought away. I will not hide from my duty again.

Queen Ariana's laugh fills the silence. 'I am overwhelmed with your protestations of unqualified support.'

'With all due respect,' Pris starts as Queen Ariana laughs again.

'Usually that comment precedes something which shows a marked lack of respect,' the Queen says. 'In this room, here, today, I give you leave to speak freely. We do not know each other well enough to speak in courtly terms and still understand one another, and we do not have the time to rectify that.'

'Okay,' Pris says. 'We have not had such a great experience with members of your court, so we will wait and hear what you are asking before committing to anything.'

'Fair enough. Do you feel the same way, Snake? Percival?'

'Yes,' Snake says, but I hold back. Not that I do not agree with Pris, but I have a history of service to the Crown, and to Eleanora, that is difficult to set aside.

'Percival?' Queen Ariana asks.

If I do not stand up for myself and my beliefs now, when will I? 'I agree with Pris.'

There is a glimmer of a smile on Queen Ariana's lips. Does she approve?

'We know where we stand, then. So, let us get started. Percival, you and Drow, with the help of others, have worked on a near perfect response to the actions of the elven faction taking over the government.'

'Near perfect?' I ask, a little bewildered.

'Yes. I am not wild about being forced to move to a constitutional democracy, and with such a short timeline proposed. Nor am I happy about the implication that Cecily will take the Crown should I not fall into line.'

'It is not meant as a threat, Your Majesty. We offer it more as an option for you to step aside if you do not recover completely from your illness,' I say diplomatically. The worried look that crosses Queen Ariana's face has me regretting my words. 'I mean, uh, we weren't trying to depose you.'

The Queen composes herself. 'Relax, Percival. I will be fine, and I understand what you are saying. It is not that I disagree with what you are proposing. In fact, I have some sympathy with the ideals. When we were younger, Petunia and I often discussed how we hated our future being controlled by the actions of a long-ago ancestor who believed he should rule the world.'

I did not expect that. Neither Petunia nor Ariana had ever discussed this with us. Oh, they had talked about change and more equality, but not about how they felt about being part of the royal family.

'But that is neither here nor there. There are two problems I see with what you suggest. The first is that, although Petunia has stepped down from the line of succession, unless we have her on board, some factions could rally around her.'

I nod my understanding.

'But Grandmother isn't interested in taking the throne,' Pris interrupts.

'Unfortunately, what my sister does or doesn't want may not come into it,' the Queen says. Before Pris opens her mouth to object, Queen Ariana raises a hand. 'If I could finish?'

Pris nods for the Queen to continue.

'The second thing we must consider is the dragons. Al'kyla advises that I need to send representatives to the Dragon Queen to stop her from intervening in our affairs. Apparently, she has set some sort of deadline for me regaining control of my realm?'

'Yes,' Pris says. 'You have eight more days to do that, or the dragons will consider Adina's petition to have her family included in the line of succession.'

'That is what I understand you were told. What you may not know is that if Maddox and I cannot get magic flowing between the realms again, then the dragon realm will close itself off from the other worlds—meaning most of our magic will be lost forever.'

'We have heard,' Snake says.

'What you definitely do not know is that if we go to war to regain control of the World Below, magic will be affected. Instead of creating life, it will stop, and the worlds will begin to rot. While you fight, Maddox and I will work to ensure things do not get any worse than they are. If this battle is prolonged, he and I will not meet our commitment to the dragons, and that would devastate the world. Already the climate is deteriorating in the World Above, and creatures there are becoming sick. Very soon we will see that reflected here in the World Below.'

The stunned look on Pris's face likely mirrors my own.

'The Dragon Queen mentioned it would affect magic but not what that meant, exactly,' Snake says.

War stops magic from being created and taints what is there. The taint likely will seep through to joined worlds, making the blight seem as nothing, so my Queen is worried, the dragon, Al'kyla, says to us all.

'Thank you Al'kyla. I can take it from here,' Queen Ariana says.

'Man, this is huge,' Pris says under her breath, releasing the tension in the room. 'We're damned if we let Bernais take control and damned if we fight to remove him.'

'Indeed,' I respond, marvelling at how I am still learning about the world around me after all these centuries. 'I guess it is a choice between the guaranteed slow death of magic in our land and risking it all in the hopes we can recover.'

I glance from Pris to Snake, seeking their permission to ask the big question. They both nod.

'How can we help you sort this out, Your Majesty?'

The smile on Queen Ariana's face is filled with sadness. 'I am desolate at having to ask more of you. Pris, it is your birthright to serve your people, but you are new to this. And Snake, you come from a family of advisors, but I am asking you to step up and take a role you would normally take centuries to grow into.'

Snake takes Pris's hand, 'We understand these are difficult times and that you must make difficult decisions.'

'Thank you. First, I need the two of you to ask the Dragon Queen to remove her deadline. I suspect she will not because she will worry about an endless war and its impact on the worlds. When she refuses, I want you to have her confirm she will not give in to Adina's demands—no matter what—until after that deadline. You can tell her the request comes directly from me and would be seen as a personal favour. That should be enough to reassure her.'

Snake and Pris turn to each other, then back to the queen. 'We can do that,' Snake says.

'Then I need you both to meet with Petunia and have her agree to lead the army with Priscilla. As part of a united front, no one can rally dissent around her. She must also agree to relinquish her claim to the throne again when this is all done.'

'Sorry? You want me to lead the army?' Pris's eyes are wide with shock and apprehension.

Fairburn snorts. 'You'll be the figurehead. I will be the brains.'

'But who will protect the Queen?' The words are out of my mouth before my brain goes into action.

Queen Ariana leans over and pats my hand 'Thank you for your concern, Percival. I will have Maddox and our dragons. And this place is protected by Aeron's magic. If anyone gets through all of that, all will be lost anyway.'

My heart sinks at the thought of anyone attacking the Queen, but I will also be here to make sure she is all right. As if reading my mind, the Queen now turns to me.

'And you, my old friend—I have a special task for you. You must go with the others to the rebel camp and make sure my voice is heard, not just by Petunia, but by all the factions gathered there.'

'What? No, I am to stay here and advise you,' I protest, my head spinning as my plan is turned on its head. I am not to speak for 'lesser' creatures but to once again work for 'greater' creatures. 'Fairburn can speak for you.'

Queen Ariana shakes her head. 'No, Percival, he cannot. I have released him from his duties so he can lead the rebel forces. He has handed over his mantel to a Commander in the Capitol. You are a Dragon Friend, so Al'kyla can communicate with you if you both agree, and we can share information.'

'But Queen Ariana, my views are in opposition to yours. I want to fight for greater equality,' I protest again. I do not want to let the Queen down, but for once I want to stay true to myself.

'Perhaps we are not so far apart, Percival. Now that I know the time of the elves must come to an end, I think perhaps working with an advisor who sees things from a more egalitarian point of view is exactly what I need. I don't just want a yes-person. I want someone who can challenge me and others to make the best decisions for all creatures—and that creature is you.'

Queen Ariana squeezes my hand. 'Please help me with this, Percival. I know you want to convince me to work for equality for all creatures, but I am not against this. Your efforts will be better spent convincing others to take creator creatures seriously in the coming battle.'

With my free hand, I wipe a tear from my eye. How can I refuse her when she asks so prettily?

PREPARING FOR WAR

THE ENORMITY OF what we are facing follows Pris, Percival, and me from the room. Part of me would like nothing more than to walk away from this problem that seems too big for us to solve, but the main part of me knows I am too committed to do that.

'It's not too late to run away,' I say under my breath, hoping to convince myself of the truth of the statement.

'We had our chance to say no, to back out,' Pris says when we're a few feet away, 'and we didn't, so we're in this to the end.'

'Mmm,' Percival says, clearly lost in thought.

Pris slips her hand into mine. 'It's not all doom and gloom. At least she agreed to our proposal, which means we might have a slim chance at a brighter future.'

I want not to be so grumpy about where we are, nor so scared that we'll muck it up and make things worse. She's only asking us to talk to the dragons, and I've been doing that anyway. 'I'm not looking forward to telling Princess Petunia what to do,' I say, attempting to lighten things up.

'Percival or I can talk to her. She'll probably take things better coming from one of us,' Pris concedes.

'And I guess in return, you'll want me to beg a favour from the Dragon Queen?' I don't quite pull the quip off.

Pris tugs on my hand, drawing me to a stop. When I turn to her, her face is set. 'What's your problem, Snake? This doesn't have to be hard. These are the same things we were sort of doing before we saw her.'

She's right, but our visit to the Queen changed things somehow. I close my

eyes, unable to face Pris as I say, 'I don't know, Pris. I knew things were bad, that we're going to war, but having everything laid out like that? A few weeks ago, we were a couple of kids trying to find our parents. How can *we* fix this?'

Pris stares at me for a moment, then gently rubs my arm. 'I get where you're coming from. I'm scared too. I'm hanging on by a thread here, and the only things keeping me going are that I can't stand by and do nothing and also that we're not in this alone anymore.'

Her words strike a chord, reflecting perfectly what I feel. And it helps that she's scared too. She's so beautiful when she speaks from the heart like this, and I feel so connected to her. I only wish we could stay like this, in our own bubble. Unfortunately, she must have gathered where my thoughts were wandering, because she slaps my arm.

'Hey!' I protest.

Her blue eyes twinkle with mischief. She knows exactly what she's doing. 'Hey yourself. Mind on the job.'

I grin at her, and my mood lifts as I draw her arm through mine and follow Percival, who is now a few paces ahead.

'I'm sorry, I'm just having a moment. Let's put it down to my not looking forward to asking the Dragon Queen to forget her timeline. She's kinda scary.'

Pris shudders. 'No, she's full-on terrifying.'

Percival pauses. 'She would be easier to approach if we understood why she is paying close attention to the World Below now.' He taps a finger against his lips. 'We have had social upheaval before, and the problem with magic has been building for years….'

'Could it be because of the refugee creatures now being homed in her realm?' It seems like the most logical reason to me.

'Perhaps, but I feel there is more to it than that.'

The image of a sour-faced elf leaps to my mind. 'Perhaps Adina's petition to have her family recognised by the dragons has forced the issue?'

Before Percival can comment. a soldier rushes past us towards the vestibule.

Our eyes lock, then as one, we sprint after her, arriving just in time to hear her telling Aeron and Drow, 'Al'kyla says that the Royal Guard are holding strong for the moment, but the palace is essentially under siege.'

Drow is slowly shaking his head. 'The Royal Guard are intent on protecting Princess Irene as Royal Heir. If Bernais takes the palace, he can force Irene to stand down. That will cement his position as heir to the Crown, and the war will be over.'

'I do not believe that is his endgame,' Percival says. 'I think it is more likely he wants to remove Irene all together.'

Beside me, Pris gasps. She clearly had not understood the very real danger her mother is in. I wrap an arm around her and pull her close. 'We won't let that happen,' I whisper into her hair.

The Minotaur furrows his brow, and, deep in thought, he cups his chin with his thumb and forefinger. 'We get Fairburn back so he can take control, and then we can contact the rebels to urge them to take what forces they have and push forward.'

'But they are still waiting on some of the trained soldiers from the World Above to arrive. Without them, the army is basically a rag-tag bunch of civilians,' Drow says.

'I believe Fairborn has resigned his commission,' the guard says.

'What?' Drow splutters.

'It is true.' Percival says. 'He is going to lead the rebels.'

Drow runs a hand through his hair. 'I guess this just got real.'

Aeron claps a hand on my uncle's shoulder. 'It was real from the moment Bernais seized control.'

I understand how my uncle feels. Until now our actions were merely strategic moves on the chessboard, and the possibility of creatures dying in battle felt far away.

'Are you okay?' I ask Pris.

Leaning into me, she says. 'I guess so… or maybe not.' She shakes her head. 'Attacking the palace is now their endgame, and they want my mother dead. But my dad and your mum are there too.'

I am certain the worry and helplessness showing on her face are mirrored on mine. I hug her close as I turn to the others, almost too scared to ask, 'Aeron, how long can the palace hold out?'

The Minotaur's face twists into a grimace. 'That is like asking how long is a piece of string? Rest assured, the palace is constructed to withstand a siege.'

Pris takes a step forward. 'There's a but in there.'

Aeron nods. 'The palace will withstand a physical siege. However, it won't take Bernais long to figure that out.'

'And after what he did at the Unseelie Court, he will change tactics and use magic to attack it,' Pris finishes.

Remembering the magical attacks Grossman Green and Giles Coronas led in Inverness turns my stomach. The thought of my mother and the rest of my family being caught up in that is terrifying.

'Don't look so worried,' Drow says from beside me. When had he moved? 'Cecily is strong in magic, and she has her dragon to help protect the castle.'

I think about Ed'rathe having been assigned to me because the dragons believe I am Pris's consort. 'Does Pris's father have a dragon?'

'No, I do not think so. Malachai and Cecily left the World Below before anything was official between the two of them,' Drow answers.

Pris's eyes narrow. 'Snake, let's add that to the list of things to talk about with the Dragon Queen. With Mum's being Queen Ariana's heir, Dad should have a dragon chosen to bond with him, even if he can't complete the bond while he is being held captive.'

'We were meant to be on our way to the World Between' 'Now that things have changed, should we still go?'

'It's even more important we follow through on our plans,' Percival says. 'If Adina can prove Bernais is more likely to take control of the realm without an all-out war, that may play well with the dragons.'

'And she will be in the Dragon Queen's ear at every opportunity,' Pris adds, her mouth curling with distaste.

'Indeed,' Percival finishes.

'And on that note,' Aeron says as he points at two bags. 'Queen Ariana requested formal court clothing for the two of you. I also had them pack some more everyday clothes and footwear.'

Pris flashes him a smile. 'Thank you, Aeron.' She turns to me. 'I guess we should say our goodbyes and be on our way.'

'Not so fast,' Aeron says, stepping between us. 'I am coming too.'

Pris blanches. 'What? I mean, why? I'll be with Am'ratha.'

Aeron folds heavily muscled arms across his chest. 'King Maddox and Queen Ariana asked me to protect you, and protect you I will.'

I chuckle, remembering how obstinate Aeron can be from our encounter in his Maze. Pris is also stubborn, but I don't like her chances of out-stubborning Aeron.

She blows out a huff. 'You can come… if Am'ratha is happy carrying you.'

Smart move.

Aeron's unsettling grin suggests Pris has been outmanoeuvred. 'King Maddox has already sorted that. The Dragon Queen has approved my accompanying you everywhere.'

Pris turns on her heel and stalks out. I roll my eyes at Percival and Drow. Although I'm pleased Pris has the Minotaur covering her back, I am smart enough not to let on.

'She has been through a lot, and she has much more to adjust to,' Percival says. 'We understand.'

I stand there, caught between following Pris and saying goodbye to Drow and Percival. We may not see each other again for some time, if at all, and the loss is already seeping into my soul. I have to say something, but if I do say goodbye, what is appropriate in this sort of situation?

Drow slips an arm over my shoulders. 'Let us not dwell on this. We all know what is coming, and none of us can predict what will happen. I'll just say, I'm pleased to have met you, Snake, and I hope I get to know you better once this is over.' He gives me a brief squeeze, then turns away.

I stare at Percival. If I am to stay at the Dragon Court and he is to be with the army, he and I may well never see each other again. There is no way I can find the words to tell him what his friendship has meant to me these past months.

The sprite meets my gaze, a smile hovering at the edge of his lips. 'I know, Snake. There are no words.' He reaches out and clasps my hand in his. 'Until we meet again, my friend, in this world or the next.'

I withdraw my hand and drop to one knee before pulling Percival into a hug. For a moment, his body is stiff in my arms, and I think I've overstepped the mark. He relaxes and hugs me back. Then I rise, grab my bag from Aeron, and leave before the tears can fall from my eyes.

When I enter the courtyard, Pris is already on Am'ratha's back. Ed'rathe is waiting patiently, and his eyes twinkle with amusement as Aeron appears from behind me.

I do not know who is more displeased the Minotaur is joining us, my sister or the princess. Ed'rathe snorts in what I'm sure is a dragon version of a laugh.

I'm happy you find this so funny, I snap, then instantly regret it. This is not Ed'rathe's war. *I'm sorry, Ed'rathe, I didn't mean….*

It is all right. I was a little flippant, and I believe you have had bad news.

I nod, then climb onto the dragon's back, tucking the bag of clothes in front of me.

Back to my realm?

Yes. Pris is arranging to meet with your Queen, but we will need somewhere to change before we see her.

Ed'rathe launches into the sky, but not before I see the look of disapproval pass over Am'ratha's face as Aeron slips behind Pris. In contrast, the Minotaur's face glows with pure pleasure in anticipation of his first ever dragon ride.

It is arranged. You are to prepare for your audience with the Queen in one of the caverns near the court. I am to wait for you and then escort you inside. The dragon sounds proud.

Do you attend court often?

It is my first time. I hear the preen in his voice, and it makes me smile, eclipsing the dread pooling in my stomach.

The ride is short, and I'm soon inside a cool cavern at the entrance to the court, getting changed. Once again I am to wear the standard skintight black trousers tucked into knee-length boots, a ruffled white shirt, and a green tailed coat. Everything fits perfectly, and I luxuriate in the quality of the garments the Queen provided, happy not to magic something up of my own. I do use magic to tame my hair into something reasonable before joining Ed'rathe in the large cavernous space that joins our dressing rooms to the Queen's main court. He waits beside Am'ratha.

Where is Pris?

The tingle of magical communication pricks my skin seconds before a voice from just inside the opening says, 'Women's clothes take longer to put on, especially when there's no one else to help.'

Pris moves into view, holding up her hair. She turns her back to me. 'Can you finish doing these up?'

I fumble with the tiny pearl buttons closing the purple bodice of Pris's Edwardian-style dress. As my freezing fingers brush her neck, she shivers and, under the gaze of two dragons, I resist the urge to drop a kiss where her hair meets the nape.

'Thank you,' she says, dropping her hair back in place, then smooths down the silk skirt of the dress before turning to Aeron. 'And thank goodness you chose something simple.'

'Nice to know I'm useful for something,' the Minotaur says sourly.

Pris places her hands on her hips. 'There was no way you were coming inside while I dressed.'

'I would have turned my back to you and guarded the door.'

'You could guard it just as well from outside.'

I intervene, saying, 'And no one was hurt, so all is well,' before turning to Am'ratha. 'Are they ready for us?'

We must wait for Princess Adina, Noble One.

I let out a heartfelt sigh. 'Must we really?'

Aeron's eyes flicker, and he smoothly positions himself beside Pris, standing at attention.

'Goodness, Priscilla, this is overkill, is it not?' A testy voice comes from behind me, and I cringe, awaiting the inevitable insult.

'Am'nera, Princess Adina,' Pris says, dropping her head in formal acknowledgement.

I nod at Am'nera but ignore Adina, showing her the same disdain she sends my way.

Bernais's mother sweeps past us, followed more sedately by Am'nera, who sends us a look of apology.

Aeron scowls at the elf's back as I hold out an arm for Pris to take. We follow our two dragon friends into court with Aeron guarding our rear, muttering under his breath about manners and what he would like to do to Adina.

Am'ratha and Ed'rathe block our view as we enter the vast cave, but they can't block out the murmurs rippling through the court as we progress towards the throne.

At first I think the excitement is because we are here, or perhaps they enjoy Adina's public displays. Then I catch a word here and there and realise it's Aeron causing the excited buzz. It's so good to have everyone's attention on someone else for a change.

Upon reaching the throne, our dragon friends lower their heads and move to the side. Pris curtsies and I bow, awaiting the Dragon Queen's leave to rise.

Aeron, Mighty Minotaur of legend, welcome to my court.

Oh my goddess, is the Dragon Queen fangirling over Aeron?

'I am honoured you have allowed me entrance. And, if I may say so, Your Majesty, you are looking particularly radiant today.'

Now she's giggling.

I quickly glance at Pris to find out if she's seeing this. She mouths, 'He's flirting with her,' and I choke back a laugh.

You are too kind.

'I beg to disagree. I merely state it like I see it.'

Pris's grip on my arm tightens as she tries to suppress her laughter and keep her balance. She's in danger of falling and causing an incident and, suddenly, the flirting isn't as amusing. Fortunately, Am'ratha steps in and saves us from a potentially embarrassing situation.

Your Majesty, Princess Priscilla and her consort bring a petition on behalf of Queen Ariana.

Oh, yes. Please rise.

I swear I can hear Pris's knees creak as she stands up. While we await permission to speak, Princess Adina steps forward and breaks protocol.

'Your Majesty, I—'

This audience has been granted to Princess Priscilla and Ambassador Fieth. Your role is to watch and observe only, the Dragon Queen explains as if to a naughty child.

For a frightening moment, I think Adina is going to object, but she sees sense and steps back into the shadows.

What is it Queen Ariana wishes to petition me for?

Pris steps forward to respond.

'Your Majesty, Queen Ariana sends her greetings and wishes you to know she is healing well and should be able to return to cleansing magic in the next few days.

That is as it should be.

'Although her heart desires to see her realm settled, she is conscious of her duty and will comply with your request, but….' Pris pauses and takes a breath. 'She is aware it may take a little longer to sort out than the eight days she has left to return to her people and deal with the issues in the World Below.'

The room is still. Not a single whisper is heard. This is not good. I take the few steps forward to join Pris in front of the throne as she continues to speak.

'We appreciate you have been lenient with the creatures of the World Below and the World Above, especially as they failed to meet their commitments to you, but we are not simply asking for an extension. Princess Cecily will be governing the realm while Queen Ariana is busy.'

The Dragon Queen's eyes widen slightly, then almost pop out of her head as Adina rushes forward.

'No, you can't support this. Cecily has not lived in the World Below for years. She simply cannot succeed Ariana.' A sly smile forms on her lips. 'Besides, I hear Petunia is back. I bet she didn't agree to this.'

'Viper,' Pris hisses under her breath. I reach out and touch the back of her hand in warning. Schooling her face into a diplomatic mask, she says through gritted teeth, 'My grandmother has renounced her right to the Crown and is merely back to ensure my mother takes her rightful place.'

And what about you? the Dragon Queen asks.

Pris straightens her spine, turning regal before my eyes. 'I will be confirmed as second in line to the throne.'

Mmm, I see your family is working to rectify past wrongs and taking responsibility for securing the future wellbeing of the World Below, which is as it should be. However, my original ruling stands—if your family cannot sort out the rebellion in the World Below within the next eight days, then I will consider if granting Adina's petition will be better for our realms than the status quo. Or whether I should simply call my dragons home.

The cavern explodes with expressions of shock and disbelief.

'But you said you would give Bernais his dragon,' Adina yells.

SILENCE.

The command might have been imbued with a touch of magic, as there is an immediate hush throughout the room.

We have persevered with our centuries-old relationship despite recent betrayals as well as tainted magic entering our realm. It has come to a point where I must consider whether our relationship with your world provides any value.

I'm stunned into silence, but Pris doesn't cower or back down.

'I apologise for my ignorance, Your Majesty. Given that the other two realms have behaved with such bad faith, why do you still put up with us?'

If I'd thought Aeron's smile scary, it is nothing compared to the one the Dragon Queen displays.

That is a fair question. Perhaps it is simply an indulgence, or perhaps it is because my dragons believe you can do better—that you can rise above your petty disputes and return to tending to your worlds.

'We *can* do better,' Pris says.

The Dragon Queen drops her head, and her voice is weary, *I hope you can, but you need to be better soon because my time of indulgence is at an end.*

THE DRAGON QUEEN'S words reinforce for me how much I still have to learn about the World Below. The irony that earlier today, Maddox asked me to be an ambassador to his court is not lost on me as I'm given a lesson in inter-realm relations.

Why is the Dragon Queen staring at me? She expects me to respond. Heat rises to my cheeks, and I frantically search for something to say that won't sound stupid.

'Thank you for explaining things to me,' I start, playing for time. 'While I totally respect whatever decision you make, all I can do is thank you for your patience so far. And, I hope we can continue to work with you in the future, should that be what you desire.'

Then I remember Queen Ariana's other request.

'If I may, Your Majesty, Queen Ariana asked me to have you confirm that you will stick to your original timeline when it comes to considering Princess Adina's petition.'

As I wait for an answer, the air around me is chilly, and I worry I've gone too far.

It is only fair.

The Dragon Queen's tone is clipped, as if she's had enough of creature disputes. I bow and prepare to leave.

'Your father's dragon,' Snake whispers.

'Not the time,' I whisper back.

The Dragon Queen surprises us with a grin. *When will you two learn that if I can hear your unguarded thoughts, your whispers are like shouts to me?*

I cringe a little before forcing myself upright to talk with the Queen.

'With the succession confirmed and my mother becoming regent, we would like you to consider providing her consort with a dragon to bond with. Although I completely understand if that is out of the question, given what we discussed today.'

'You cannot do that,' Adina hisses.

The Dragon Queen turns her head away from Adina in dismissal.

While our agreement is in place, the consort can bond with a dragon. Ed'rathe, you were chosen to bond with the heir's consort. You have a choice. You can go to him now, or wait until Ambassador Fieth becomes an heir consort and finalise the bonding process with him.

Beside me, Snake pales, and the air around me buzzes with magic as he and Ed'rathe talk. Snake and I don't know what our future will be, so I'm almost certain he will encourage Ed'rathe to choose Dad. I understand how much Snake will miss Ed'rathe if he agrees. I couldn't imagine losing Am'ratha. I want to reach out to him, but I allow the two their private farewell.

'Please, Ed'rathe,' Snake begs out loud. 'It's not that I don't want you to stay, but I couldn't live with myself if you lost your position because of me.'

Ed'rathe stands tall and turns to face his queen. *I will stay. Rima is next in line. He will be honoured to become Ed'rima. You should send him to Prince Malachai.*

Snake brushes tears from his eyes, then catches his dragon friend watching him, concern written on his face. 'Thank you,' he mouths, and I feel the weight of another responsibility settle on Snake's shoulders.

'Thank you for your consideration,' I say to the Queen, aware of Adina snarling in the background. I ignore her. If it's good enough for the Dragon Queen to do this, then it's good enough for me.

It shall be as you request, Ed'rathe. This matter is closed.

The last was directed more at Aunt Adina, but we have all clearly been dismissed.

Aeron, perhaps we could have a private word.

It looks like not all of us are off the hook.

'Wait for me by the entrance, and stay close to Am'ratha,' Aeron demands, and we make our way to the exit of the audience chamber.

'Do you need any help changing?' Snake asks, and I am touched by his thoughtfulness.

Adina's furious gestures towards Am'nera catch my attention, causing Snake to move a little closer to me. She is clearly upset, and I am not in the least surprised when she storms off along the platform. Before she enters one of the caves, she turns and bellows, 'I will not allow my home to be ruled by half-breeds and interlopers.'

Before we can respond, she disappears. Nearby, Am'nera grunts, then bobs her head politely in our direction before launching herself into flight.

'Am'ratha, how come Adina is not staying at the creature compound?' I ask, watching the dragon bank and fly over our heads.

Argh! My dragon manages to load that sound with a wealth of disdain. *She would not want to stay with such lowly creatures—that one has always thought more of herself than she should. To keep the peace, Al'kyla allowed her to use a guest room in the Queen's compound to keep distance between her and the other creatures claiming refuge.* Am'ratha tilts her head to the side. *You know, you may use a suite there. It is much better appointed.*

A chuckle bubbles from my belly. 'Am'ratha, are you teasing me?'

The dragon's stare is so unwavering that I think she might have been serious and now I've offended her.

Then her great shoulders rise, as if in imitation of a shrug. *Perhaps.*

'Thank you for the offer, but I would rather not have to listen to Adina's complaints this evening,' I inform her.

'What's that?' Snake asks, turning his attention back from Am'nera's retreating figure.

'Oh, Am'ratha is informing me we can stay in the royal quarters on this side of the mountains. Upside is the rooms are nicer. Downside is—'

'Adina,' Snake finishes for me. Pulling me into a hug he says, 'I think I prefer where we are, thank you.'

I snuggle in closer, allowing his body to warm me. 'How long do you think the Dragon Queen will keep Aeron?'

'I am here,' the Minotaur says. 'Have you not changed yet? You can't fly in that ridiculous dress.'

I glare at him. 'You told me to wait here.'

'Oh, I did too. Come on, then. Let's get you dressed, and then we can head to the rebel camp.'

Turning my head to take in the setting sun, I say, 'I think we'll stay here tonight, with Snake and the other refugees, rather than fly in the dark'

Darkness does not bother me, Am'ratha says.

Let's keep that to ourselves today, please.

Aeron raises his eyebrows. 'I guess we're staying to be safe, not so you can spend the night with young Fieth.'

'I'm JUST here,' Snake mutters as I wink at Aeron.

'Purely for safety reasons.' I tug Snake with me into the small changing room. He helps with my buttons, then dresses quickly, giving me space to change. As I pull on a warm top, I'm annoyed to see Aeron blocking the doorway, his back to me.

'So, Aeron, what did the Dragon Queen want with you?' I tease.

'Nosey.'

'Yes,' I reply. 'I am.'

I take a seat on the bench, then retrieve the boots from the bag and proceed to put them on. I wait a moment for them to adjust to my feet before standing up—I do love magic apparel. Aeron still hasn't answered.

I start stuffing clothes into the bag. 'You don't have to tell me….'

Aeron crosses from one side of the entrance to the other, then adjusts his jacket. 'She asked why I had involved myself in this conflict, given I am not of these worlds.'

I pause. *Should I ask what he said?* But instead, I simply tell him, 'I'm done.'

Aeron half turns. 'Do you not want to know my answer?'

Of course I do, but I don't want Aeron to know that. 'If you want to tell me, I'll listen.'

His shoulders rise in a sort of nonchalant shrug. 'I have a pleasant life. I'm safe and secure, and I doubt very much that current events would threaten that.'

'That sounds more like a reason not to become involved.'

Aeron's lips curl into what I hope is a smile. 'It does, doesn't it. And, had my conversation with you yesterday not reminded me of my past, I would have forgotten how grateful I am for my life—and who I owe that life to.'

My eyebrows shoot up. 'Are you saying you are protecting me because you owe Fairglade a debt? I thought the King and Queen asked you to do it.'

With his grin widening, Aeron says, 'It is more that I am reminded why I chose to remain in the World Below. That in itself is reason enough to take some sort of action to save my home from certain disaster.'

'And protecting me?'

Aeron's grin fades, and his face softens, his huge brown eyes looking more cowlike than they had. 'When Fairburn and Maddox requested my services, they were asking me to commit to the future of our realm. Princess, you are our future. How could I refuse? And that is what I told the Dragon Queen.'

I'm speechless. The weight of Aeron's belief in me as the future of the realm is almost suffocating, ramping up the pressure of being the heir. My shoulders slump, and Aeron drops a meaty hand on my shoulder.

'Pris, my reason asks nothing more of you than you already agreed to give. Now, shake it off, and let's get ourselves to the guest quarters. After that meeting, I could do with a bowl of hot food and a cold tankard of ale.'

Aeron directs me past him and into the cold evening air, and my spirits lift a little seeing Snake is already atop Ed'rathe. At least I will spend tonight with him.

The trip across the canyon is short, and we do not waste time with long goodbyes. Am'ratha agrees to return a little after dawn before joining Ed'rathe in the sky. Pulling back the heavy inner hide curtain, we find the common room a study in chaos. There are creatures and bags and stuff everywhere. We attempt to sidle round the edge, but when the first creature spots Aeron, it's all on—calling to mind visions of rock stars being mobbed.

Snake tugs on my hand, and we try to slip away, but Aeron is having none of it. His strong fingers grasp my arm, and I'm going nowhere. He leans down and whispers frantically, 'Do not leave me to these…these… children.'

'Honestly, we have a war to fight, and you waste time clamouring over him?' The amused voice comes from behind the crowd. The "children" part to reveal the wizard Mandor.

Wait, he's not a wizard any more, is he?

Last time I saw the witch was when he set the final puzzle to get us into the maze, and he seems to have aged a decade since then. Maybe he aged when he gave up his powers. Or maybe that's what happens when you lead a rebellion. Given my role in things, I hope it's the former.

'Princess Priscilla, pleased to see you alive and well. Aeron, trust you to arrive and cause havoc with my well-organised relocation plans.'

'Old friend, it is my pleasure. But if you could point us in the direction of food, I'm sure we would be happy to leave you to it.'

The creatures rather reluctantly return to what they were doing, and Mandor leads us into the dining room. 'We have eaten, but I'm sure there will be leftovers. Just ask—'

'Susan,' I exclaim as my family's ex-au pair emerges from the kitchen. I rush to her, dropping my bag on the way. My body slams into hers and familiar arms come around me. I hug her tightly, never wanting to loosen my grip.

'I thought I'd lost you forever,' I whisper. 'Then, when Uncle Maddox told me you were all right, I didn't get a chance to ask where you were.'

Susan moves so she can see Snake. 'Didn't you let Pris know I was okay?'

What? Snake knew?

'Sorry, Pris. Honestly there's been so much going on, it never occurred to me you didn't know.'

'Well, I'm here now, and I'm fine,' she says, her voice close by my ear.

I bury my face into her shoulder, and for a moment, I'm the girl I'd been before a strange gnome burst into my home. Relishing the sense of security, I'm reluctant to leave her embrace. My rumbling stomach eventually forces me to pull away.

Practical as ever, Susan says, 'Take a seat, and I'll get you all some food and drinks. Are you staying?' she asks Mandor.

He shakes his head. 'No, I have to oversee the evacuation. I'll pop back before I go.'

'Are Verona and Gregor still here?' Snake asks Mandor.

'No, sorry. They have gone on ahead to the mustering site to organise the arrivals,' Mandor responds. 'Can I pass on a message?'

Snake looks so forlorn. 'No, it's okay. It's just….'

'I understand, son. You want to be with them. They appreciate that we each have our own roles to play, and yours is to keep the dragons informed and neutral. The last thing we need is them deciding the Crown line is no longer capable of ruling the World Below. Then all we have worked for will fall apart.'

Snake forces a smile. 'So, no pressure, then?'

Mandor slaps him on the back. 'I'm sure you're up to the job.' He scans our group before he says, 'if there's nothing else?'

When no one speaks, he leaves us to find seats while Susan heads into the kitchen to get our food.

'Is everyone going?' I ask Snake as we sit, wondering if he will be alone here when I leave to see my grandmother.

'I'm not,' Susan says as she places a platter of bread on the table. 'I'm staying to set up hospital facilities. The Dragon Queen has agreed injured rebels can return here to heal after their initial treatment.'

She returns to the kitchen, and Snake wraps an arm around me.

'I'd be fine, even if Susan weren't here,' he tells me, and I lean into his shoulder.

'I know, I just wish—'

Snake places a finger over my lips. 'It'll be difficult, but we'll get through this. Remember, we're going to enjoy what time we have.' He removes his finger and presses a gentle kiss to my lips.

'Get a room, you two,' Aeron snorts, but is then distracted as Susan places a frothing tankard of ale in front of him. He greedily licks his lips and gulps half of it down in a single mouthful.

With our companion's attention directed elsewhere, I snuggle into Snake, brushing a kiss at the base of his neck where it meets his shoulder. He shivers. I'm pleased I decided to stay the night.

When Susan places bowls of spicy stew on the table in front of us, all thoughts of what might happen later are gone from my head as other appetites take over.

ALYCE PORTALS ME to a spot under the trees behind a huge white canvas tent, right beside Drow. From here all we can see are trees and white fabric. The only sign there's an army mustering at the base of the Essendore mountains is the incredible mixture of voices shouting, metal clanging, and feet marching that permeate the air.

'Thank you.' She is gone before I even finish the first word.

'She looked exhausted,' Drow says. 'I guess portalling skills are in demand now the army is mustering.'

'Which is why they should be taking more care,' I say, more than a little dourly.

'The Dragon Queen's arbitrary timeline is placing pressure on us all,' Drow says.

I worry we will achieve nothing if we run our scarce resources into the ground. Then again, creature-kind has been very good at focusing on our immediate needs, willing to sacrifice the future for a little ease in the present. Perhaps if we learn one thing from this debacle, it will be to think long term.

Alyce deposits Fairburn beside us before wandering off to find somewhere to eat and sleep.

'This is the first thing we will change,' Fairburn says, 'To have the back of the command tent so exposed is folly!'

We round the corner, and I stop short. In front of us are row upon row of tents in an array of colours and styles. While some are still being pitched, others are already set up with inhabitants gathered around shared fires.

To the right, a raggle-taggle of creatures is being drilled by an imposing dwarf who is almost as wide as he is high—and he is tall for one of his kind. The drilling creatures are a mix of races, but they have clearly had some sort of military training in the past because, although they wear civilian clothes, their form as they march is precise, like their muscles remember long ago commands.

'Come,' Fairburn says, 'We have little time to gawp. We need to find out what is happening in there.' He nods towards the wall of the command tent.

As we approach, two strong dwarf guards halt us.

'A little late for this,' Fairburn snaps. 'If we had wanted to, we could have obliterated your command when we arrived five minutes ago. You—' He points at the guard on the left. 'Go get a couple of creatures from that platoon and clear a space for the command and royal tents in the middle of the army. Anyone wishing to get to the leaders of this rebellion should have to fight through every soldier we have mustered to gain their chance.'

Recognising authority, although not perhaps knowing who Fairburn is, the guard salutes and leaps to action. The remaining guard is not so gullible.

'And who might you be to give orders?' he challenges the centaur.

'I am Fairburn, previously of the Queen's Guard, and I have come to offer my expertise.'

'F-f… Fairburn? C-c-c… Captain Fairburn?' the guard stammers, straightening his back.

Fairburn flicks a hand as if dismissing his title. 'Former. Now can we go in?'

'Of course, sir, but I warn you, it will not be what you are used to.'

Fairburn snorts. 'But I suspect it will be exactly what I am expecting, which is why I am here. Lead the way, soldier.'

The guard pushes open the tent flap and gestures for us to enter. If outside is organised chaos, inside is its disorganised sibling. Standing around a table, approximately thirty creatures are studying a map of the World Below. Everyone is talking, each raising their voice higher and higher to be heard over the others.

The only creatures I recognise are Thomas, Nathanial, and Gregor. The rest are strangers drawn from all races of creature-kind.

I catch Drow's eye, and he frowns, deepening the worry lines on his face. We both look at Fairburn to see how he is reacting. He remains in the doorway, arms folded over his heavily muscled chest. He appears to be waiting for something, but I do not know what. After some time passes, he clearly gets bored with this and yells, 'SILENCE,' in a tone used to being obeyed.

And obeyed it is. Every mouth in the room closes, and every eye turns to us. Expectation hangs heavy in the air. The creature opposite us opens his mouth to speak, but Fairburn raises a hand to silence him.

'We have two, maybe three, days before we engage the enemy, and you are standing here, arguing like a bunch of market traders haggling for the best price.'

A few of the creatures have the grace to blush. The one across from us stands taller and is not happy about having what authority he does have questioned by a stranger. Again, Fairburn does not give them a chance to speak.

'Firstly, there are too many cooks here. If you are not the leader of the group you brought to muster, please leave.'

Some creatures come forward, and Fairburn moves to allow them to depart. A few look to their leaders for approval, and a couple throw rebellious glances our way. Fairburn is implacable. Eventually half the creatures in the room depart.

'Good. Now, have any of you had any military experience?'

No one moves.

A brief flicker of exasperation crosses the centaur's face. 'None of you have had any military training at all?'

One young creature, a goblin, perhaps, steps forward. 'I was part of the local guard until my brother passed and I was called home to run our vineyard.'

Fairburn's teeth flash the briefest smile. 'Excellent. And you are?'

'Brynn Bottas, sir.'

'Brynn you are now my Adjutant. If I am not around, then you will deal with everyone's concerns and questions.'

Finally the creature opposite can contain his ire no longer. 'And who are you to organise us so?' he splutters.

'I am the only one here with enough military experience to lead this force,' Fairburn says.

I lean into Drow and whisper, 'Why does he not introduce himself?'

Drow's grin is rather sardonic. 'He is so well known in the Capitol, he isn't aware that no one outside the city's confines has any idea who he is.'

Taking matters in hand, Drow steps forward. 'Elected leaders from the regions, may I introduce to you Fairburn, previous Captain of the Queen's Guard.'

Whispers circulate the room as eyes widen with shock. The creature who confronted Fairburn blanches. He quickly recovers and says, 'Well, sir, we welcome your leadership.'

Fairburn drops his head briefly, acknowledging the invitation and accepting it with the same gesture.

'You already know Drow, I suspect, as he has been working with Mandor to pull this alliance together. Once Mandor arrives, they will deal with any disputes you might have between yourselves. And this is Percival. He is here to represent the Queen's interests, but I want him to work alongside Brynn as my eyes and ears when I am otherwise engaged—that is if you accept me as your General.'

The last is less of a request and more of a statement. When no one objects, Fairburn seamlessly takes control.

'Right, our first order of business is to find out what we have to work with. I assume you have details of who has responded to the muster?'

One by one, the leaders step forward. Along with Thomas from the Wyld Woods and Brynn Bottas from the winemaking region of Avondale, there is: Angus Abernathy a dwarf from the mining region of Essendore, Toab Rowne, a gnome from the fishing region of Melliores, and Amelia Farrmer from the market garden region around the Capitol.

'We are still waiting for a response from the deep woods and there are still creatures arriving from the World Above. Also, Princess Petunia is here, and she brought a small contingent of soldiers,' Brynn advises. 'I believe they are drilling some of our recruits outside.'

'Thank you, Brynn,' Fairburn says, capturing Drow's eye. 'We must ask the World Above to send a representative to this war council.'

'I need to talk to Petunia on behalf of the Queen,' I whisper. 'Do you think I should go now?'

Drow shakes his head. 'I would wait until Fairburn finishes. Especially now that he has given you a role as his adjutant.'

'Now, next item on the agenda. How many of your recruits have military experience? And do any of them have weapons?'

Angus Abernathy from the mines steps forward. 'All my people can wield swords. We must all be able to test what we make. We each brought our own weapon and a second sword to arm someone else. There is also a wagonload of 200 pikes arriving on the morrow.'

Fairburn's eyebrows rise. 'You have done us a great service, Angus. Thank you. Brynn and Percival, can you pull together a list of what else we have available from those who have their details with them?'

A few of the creatures separate from the group and wait by a smaller table containing paper and inkwells in the corner.

'Drow, would you mind scribing for me as I tour the camp with the rest of the representatives?'

'Of course,' Drow says and grabs a notebook and pencil from the table. 'Happy to be useful.'

And useful we are. Before I even have time to take a seat, the representative from Avondale starts listing their contributions. The sun has set when Brynn and I finally finish with our lists. It was immediately made apparent that our main issue is not the number of creatures gathered, but finding weapons for them and feeding them over the next few days.

After we have summarised everything in a report for Fairburn, I rise to my feet, stretch, then roll my shoulders. Every part of me aches from sitting for too long.

'If we are done here, I have a message from the Queen for her sister,' I say to Brynn as I tidy my workspace.

Their eyes widen as they study me with a newfound look of respect. 'You're more than a secretary, aren't you?'

I nod.

'Who exactly are you and the gnome you arrived with?'

I stop mid-action and consider how to answer their question. There are a myriad of possible responses, but which one is relevant in this context?

'I am Percival of the Wyld Woods, and the gnome is Drow—'

'Drow Fieth?' Brynn finishes, their voice tinged with awe. 'Gosh, wait until my friends hear I worked with creatures we learnt about in school.'

'Thanks,' I say dryly, 'Now I feel ancient.'

They grin at me. 'Well, Percival of the Wyld Woods, it has been an honour to work alongside one of the creatures who changed our world for the better. It gives me hope to know that we have you, and others like you, on our side.'

My ears tingle as heat rises from my neck to their tip. Who knew my coming out of hiding would be met with such welcoming support?

'Well… umm… thank you, I guess.'

'If you need to speak with Princess Petunia, then you'd—'

Brynn doesn't get to finish. The tent flap is flung open as Fairburn returns with the representatives and Mandor by his side.

I return to my seat while everyone crowds into the command space. While they quieten down, Drow places his notebook in front of Brynn.

'This is the command structure Fairburn has agreed to. Lieutenant Howden from Princess Petunia's forces is to be his second-in-command, and, well, you can see the rest. He wanted a copy made for each of the leaders.'

We make space for Drow at the table, and we each begin copying what's on the page onto fresh sheets of paper. While we work, I listen to the discussion around the command table about splitting the volunteers into platoons, what weapons they will have, and how unarmed creatures will be assigned logistical support.

'Small well-armed groups will be more effective than large numbers for what I have in mind,' I hear Fairburn say. 'Now, I'm going to hand over to Mandor, as your signing of the accords that brought this group together is not a military issue.'

The centaur makes his way to our table in the back as the rest of the group gathers more tightly around the map. Drow joins them to answer any legal questions.

Fairburn taps my arm to get my attention. 'Percival, Brynn and I can finish here. Time for you to speak with Princess Petunia. Her agreement to this plan is critical.'

He does not need to tell me twice. I'm outside within moments, and I take my time walking the few paces to Petunia's tent, enjoying the fresh air and preparing myself for the interview ahead.

IT'S BECOMING REAL

FOR SOME REASON, I'm almost overcome with nerves outside the flap of Petunia's tent. I only saw her a couple of days ago. Could it be because then I saw her as a friend, but now I'm here for Ariana?

The guard stares down at me, an eyebrow raised. 'In or not?' he asks.

I square my shoulders. 'In.'

He slips between the opening. 'Your Highness, Percival of the Wyld Woods is here to see you.'

Petunia's voice drifts out. 'Oh, we don't stand on ceremony with Percival.' then I hear her say, 'Come in old friend,' a little louder.

Not a great start in my new official role. I step beneath the tent flap the guard holds up for me. 'Petunia, I am afraid this *is* a formal visit—Queen Ariana sent me.'

As my eyes adjust to the candlelit interior, I am aware of Petunia's eyes narrowing.

'Ariana sent an emissary? How so very her. I am surprised it is you, given our friendship. Then again, it must be something important to her if she is playing at this level of politics.'

Her words carry pain, making me feel uneasy. What have I walked into?

'I am an emissary to the military command. This is more of an… additional job… a one-off.'

Petunia gestures to the chair opposite her. 'All right. This is a little odd, but perhaps we can still talk as friends.'

I sit, my mind scrabbling for some safe footing. I had believed Petunia and Ariana were close, but I am getting the impression something has gone wrong.

'Tea?' Petunia asks.

I nod. 'Yes, please.'

Petunia rises and moves to the table, where she prepares the drink herself. This is a very different Petunia from the woman at the Unseelie Court. She is dressed in a brown woollen split skirt suitable for riding with a cotton shirt, and her feet are clad in boots. Gone is all the finery she wore in the Unseelie Court.

She returns with sturdy mugs of steaming tea. After passing one to me, she retakes her seat and waits patiently for me to start. I am even more reluctant to open my mouth now that I know there is something amiss between the sisters. What if I say the wrong thing?

'Percival?' Petunia prompts.

'Mother, did you know Howden is in the command tent?' a female voice asks as the tent flap rustles.

Moments later Princess Irene flops down in the seat between her mother and me.

'Did you really ask him to organise a force to breach the Capitol's defences?'

Petunia shakes her head as I ask her, 'How did you know about what Bernais is doing in the Capitol?'

'I sent Am'ralla to find out what she could. Did you know the city is under martial law, and there is a curfew in force?'

'No, but I'm sure those in the command tent are aware,' I respond, wondering why I had not heard anything about this.

Petunia leans forward in her seat. 'Lesser creatures are being herded into ghettos, and anyone who resists the council is being imprisoned. They are being held at the hospital. I believe they are being drugged so they can't use their magic.'

I shudder at her words. If this is true, then it is grotesque.

'See? This is why I could not just stand by and do nothing. Lieutenant Howden and I devised a plan to get a small force inside the Capitol to free the prisoners.'

I cannot help the tut that escapes. Petunia scowls back.

'If Ariana cannot, will not step up. Someone has to take control,' she says.

'Petunia, if only you had attended the council, you would know Ariana *is* stepping up.' I wring my hands in frustration. 'This is what she was worried about, which is why I am here.'

Petunia does not hear me. She is on her feet, talking as she circles the tent. 'If she's taken charge, where is she, then? Still hiding behind her commitment to the dragons so she doesn't have to face up to the chaos she let develop in her realm?'

I hold my hands palms outward, trying to calm things down, but Princess Irene continues the tirade.

'You only have to look at the disparate forces outside to know things are not right in the World Below. Most of the creatures gathered here are rebels wanting to overthrow the Crown.'

Petunia turns to me. 'Percival, how did we not know things were this unsettled in the World Below? We were remiss in staying away for so long, believing Ariana was handling everything. Now it is time for us to step up and sort this mess out.'

I place my tea on the side table between Irene and me, buying myself a little time to consider how to traverse the minefield in front of me.

As the silence grows, Petunia says, 'Just spit it out, Percival.'

'Petunia, have you considered asking how you might contribute to the coming war, rather than taking control?'

Petunia's face turns thunderous, telling me I have mis-stepped.

I run a hand through my hair, trying to clear the fog tiredness is creating in my brain. 'I am sorry, Petunia, that did not come out right. Let me start again.'

'Do you think I do not have the best interests of the creatures of the World Below and Above in mind when I take action?' Petunia asks tersely.

Perhaps I have gone too far to turn this around.

Princess Irene comes to my rescue. 'Perhaps we should hear him out, Mother.'

'Please, Petunia.' I'm not above begging at this stage. 'I have information you may not have, and I am sure you would like to be in possession of all the facts.'

Petunia's gaze is stony as she says, 'All right.'

I wring my hands together in my lap as I begin where I should have started a few minutes ago. 'While we were defending the Unseelie Court and Ariana was held in stasis, there were those in the World Below who were aware of what was coming and have been working behind the scenes. A young wizard called Gregor has been co-ordinating a group of young creatures who are tired of the slow pace of change.'

'I met Gregor earlier today,' Irene says. 'He has quite a force behind him, and they appear to be very anti-monarchy.'

I nod. 'It is true. They would like to see radical change. By the same token, there are those who have joined who prefer a more evolutionary approach to wrest control of the World Below from the elves.'

'How could Ariana let things get so bad?' Petunia whispers. 'Is there any way to come back from this?'

'Mandor and Drow believe so. In fact, at the moment, the leaders of various factions are signing an accord that will pull these disparate groups together.'

'How so?' Petunia asks.

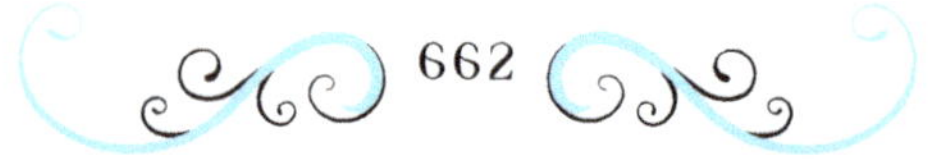

I spend the next half an hour outlining the agreement made with Princess Cecily and the factions and describing how Queen Ariana has sent her support. Petunia and Irene allow me to finish before responding.

'If I understand this, you want me to allow my forces to work under Fairburn, and you want me to stand aside and let my granddaughter lead this rebellion?' Petunia summarises.

She was always good at cutting to the chase. In fact, I had often thought it was a shame she was the younger sister because she would have made a magnificent queen.

'Yes, Petunia. We need you to take a step back.'

'I have never met Priscilla, and she's only young. Why should we trust her to lead?' Irene asks.

'I *have* met her, and she has potential,' Petunia tells her daughter. 'But Percival, you and I both know Priscilla was not brought up to this role, and she was ambivalent about taking on royal duties when we were in the Unseelie Court. If it were Cecily here….'

I nod my understanding. 'Pris is not wild about this, but she realises it is her duty to stand beside Fairburn. And this is the second reason why Ariana wanted me to speak to you.' I cross my fingers, hoping Queen Ariana will forgive the small twisting of her words. I am sure she would have asked me to set this up had she had time to think of it. 'Pris cannot do this alone. She will need your support if she is to do a halfway decent job.'

Petunia sits back down, and my shoulders relax for the first time since I entered the tent. 'Well, I guess this was Cecily's destiny when I left the court. And Pris has always been next in line. And, I do intend to return to Urquhart Castle after this is over, so….'

Irene jumps to her feet and paces in front of us—she is so like her mother, it is uncanny.

'Mother, I can't believe you're thinking of doing this. Cecily brought her daughter up outside our world. There's no way she can lead this army. She should step aside and allow me to step up—at least I have military experience.'

'I did not know you wanted a royal role,' Petunia says, somewhat bewildered.

Irene stops in her tracks. 'You've never asked what I wanted to do. Wilfred is trained to take over the garrison, and his wife will take over your position. What is next for me at Loch Ness?'

The blank expression on Petunia's face tells me she really had not considered Irene's future.

'Besides, I don't want a royal role. I just want *a* role,' Irene finishes. Her tone is a touch sad—perhaps because it has taken a war for this to be brought to her mother's attention.

I cross my fingers again, hoping Ariana will support me on this as it plays out, and maybe it will be better received now Irene is searching for her place in the worlds.

'Ariana wondered, Petunia, if you would help her strengthen relations with the Unseelie Court by becoming her ambassador there—once the court is restored, of course.'

Petunia draws her gaze from her daughter, stares blankly at me, then shakes her head. 'Well, it is about time she took a stance on that, but I am sorry. I am not the creature for the job.'

'Hold on, Mother. You've spent years saying the two courts should work more closely together. Now that it's happening, you opt out?'

Petunia is silent for a while, her gaze unfocused. When she speaks again, her words are considered and sad. 'It is not what I want to do, Irene. I was not happy to leave the Seelie Court, but it was impossible for me to stay. We have built a good life in the World Above since then, and I do not want to jeopardise it.'

'What if I want to go home to the World Below?'

'Then you should. Ariana would welcome you with open arms. In fact, *you* should help Pris. I am too old for this fighting nonsense. I'd be far happier working in the hospital tent with the witch sisters.'

'Mmm, I could do that.' A sparkle of excitement glints in her eyes, then her gaze turns to me. 'But I'll only help her if I think she is up to the job.'

Hold on, what is going on here? 'Queen Ariana wanted you to help Pris, Petunia. She knows you.'

'Oh, I'll help her with the nonmilitary things, but it would be good for Pris and Irene to get to know each other. Irene is an experienced soldier, and Pris can help Irene find a place in the World Below once this is over.'

'And the ambassadorship?'

'A discussion for another time, Percival.'

Do all emissaries lose control the way I did? Or *did* I? My primary mission was to get Petunia to support Pris rather than strike out on her own or gather followers, and I did that. I stifle a yawn.

'Percival, you are almost asleep there. Have they allocated you a bed for tonight?'

'I will sort something out later. I want to go to the hospital tent and find Nisha,' I say, pushing myself to my feet. 'So, I will bid you all a good night.'

'Good night, Percival. Sleep well,' Petunia tells me, and I leave, feeling quite pleased with what I achieved during my short visit.

The hospital tent is busy, although they are only treating minor cuts and bruises at the moment. Effie and Genie are running some sort of clinic, while Ellie is reviewing paperwork with Nisha.

I watch the two of them. Their relationship has never been easy. I always worried Nisha resented my closeness to Ellie, who in turn harbours a deep sense of guilt about the time I spent away from Nisha. Seeing the two of them now, I wonder if I had been less selfish, would they have been friends?

Across the room, a creature groans, causing Ellie to half turn towards the noise. Spotting me in the doorway, she motions for me to come in.

'Percival. There you are. Nathanial told us to expect you sometime this evening.' Taking the sheaf of papers from Nisha, she says, 'I can finish these up. Why don't you find Percival a bed before he collapses.'

'If you are sure….'

'I am.' Ellie flaps her hands.

As Nisha slips an arm through mine, I mouth, 'Thank you,' to Ellie.

Outside the tent the cool air hits us, and Nisha leans into me so we might share our warmth.

'When I heard you were here, I hoped you would come and find me,' Nisha says, her voice a little tentative.

I pull her closer. 'Of course I would come. We have been apart too long, and I intend to make up for that.'

She leads us to a smaller shelter to the side of the medical tent. Pulling back the flap, Nisha enters, and I almost groan with relief when I spy the nest of blankets set on top of tree branches. It is a while since I have slept in the sprite style. I sink into the cocoon bed, pulling Nisha down with me.

Although we still have much to discuss about our future, my eyes flutter close and exhaustion seeps through my limbs. I whisper, 'Peaceful night's journey.'

Her breath warms my cheek as she returns the nighttime wish, and I think that for all that is wrong in the world, this at least feels right.

A TRICKLE OF cool air seeps through a gap in the covers, and I snuggle into the warmth of Snake's body. He groans and wraps an arm around me, drawing me still closer. Sleeping two to a single bed does not make for the best night's sleep, but it'll do for the one night we are able to spend together before the crazy starts.

'Is it morning yet?' Snake mumbles.

'No, I don't think so. Go back to sleep.'

He nuzzles into my neck and is soon snoring gently. I attempt to relax, but sounds of creatures moving about in the hall make their way through the closed door. I'm awake.

I untangle myself from Snake's embrace, wrap the blanket from the end of the bed around me, and head for the bathroom. By the time I return clean and dressed in warm clothing, Snake is up and dressing too.

He glances at me through his fringe as I enter, and the grin he sends my way has butterflies fluttering in my stomach. I step towards him and finish buttoning his shirt, stopping to consider if unbuttoning it is a better option. No. Last night was a gift. This morning would be a selfish indulgence.

While I grapple with the last button, he gently places his hand over mine. I lift my head, and he kisses my forehead.

'There's so much I want to say, but….' He closes his eyes for a moment. 'But it all seems so… unimportant.' His lips brush my cheek, and his breath tickles my ear as he says, 'Except maybe I think I'm falling in love with you.'

The words rock me to my core, and I resist the urge to pull away. As my heart pounds in my ears, my first thought is *This is too much.* Then I wrap my arms around Snake and bury my face in his shoulder. Perhaps it is not too much. I don't want to be anywhere else but where I am now. As he holds me, I sense he's waiting for a response, but although my heart screams tell him, my head warns me to wait and see what the next few days bring.

Snake loosens his hold on me. 'We should go get breakfast.'

I may not be able to tell him how I feel, but I'm not ready to let him go either. 'Not yet. I want one more minute of it being just us like this. Burrowing my face back into his neck, I breathe in the smell of him, hoping to hide from my responsibilities a little longer. Snake's arms tighten, and, to my surprise, I find tears leaking from my eyes.

'Hey, I didn't mean to make you cry,' he says, gently rubbing my back.

'You didn't,' I snuffle, and I feel the vibration in his chest as he chuckles. 'I mean, it's not what you said, I just feel so…. It's all too much.'

I take a step away from him. What I want to tell him is now clear in my head. Gazing at him through a haze of tears, I say, 'I think I'm crying for what might have been between us. You know, getting to know each other, drawing closer, allowing our feelings to grow.'

He takes my hands in his, and I worry he's going to say something before I've got everything out. I relax when he gives my hands a squeeze, signalling for me to go on.

'Instead, we have snatched moments with no guaranteed future, and I'm feeling the loss.'

Snake's mouth twists into a wry smile, and his eyes glisten with understanding. 'We have what we have, Pris, and I'm insanely grateful we have that much.'

I lean in a plant a soft kiss on his lips before letting go of one of his hands and turning us towards the door. 'Don't get me wrong, I would rather have this than nothing, but still….' I leave the rest unsaid because we both know what I mean. 'Come on, let's get some breakfast before Am'ratha calls and I have to leave on an empty stomach.'

Snake hesitates, then obviously decides food will serve us better than more words. By the time we reach the dining room, we are both ready to face what the day will bring.

If the corridors were quieter than we expected, the dining room is even more so. Only Susan is there, sitting at the table, cradling a cup of coffee.

'Where is everyone?' Snake asks as we take seats opposite her.

'The last of the refugees left a few minutes ago,' Susan says as George appears from the kitchen and places two plates of sausages and eggs in front of us.

'What? No choice?' I joke.

'Not much point in a big cook-up for only a few people,' he snarks before returning to the kitchen.

'He wanted to go with the others,' Susan says. 'It took a lot of persuading to have him remain here. We expect a lot of casualties, and someone will have to feed them.'

'So, they're all gone?' Snake asks before tucking into his meal.

'Yep. There's only the four of us here now—three when Pris leaves.' Susan stares into her mug.

I reach out and touch her hand. 'You wanted to go too.' It's a statement rather than a question.

Her head moves in an almost imperceptible nod. 'Yes, but I guess someone has to remain and prepare for casualties.'

'Wait, four of us? Where's Aeron?' My eyes scan the room even though there is no way the giant creature could hide anywhere in here.

George bangs the coffeepot on the table before taking a seat beside Susan. 'He went to the camp. Said you were safe here and he would meet you there.'

'So much for his needing to be by my side at all times,' I mutter. 'Guess that's only when it suits him.'

Our quiet breakfast serves as a stark contrast to the lively one I had last time I was here, highlighting the seriousness of the upcoming fight. All too soon, Am'ratha calls me to the ledge.

Back in our bedroom, I pull on my jacket and finish packing my bag.

Snake watches me from the doorway, then escorts me outside.

It is as if the pall from the dining room follows us, or maybe it's because the words we have to say are too overwhelming. Too personal. Too close to the bone. I place a hand on his chest as we stand between the two curtains.

Before he can say anything, I stand on tiptoes and kiss him. 'Let's not make this a thing,' I say.

He squeezes my arm in understanding. 'I don't know what the Dragon Queen expects of me, but I'll try to find you when I can. In the meantime, fly safe and be well.'

I nod curtly and turn away before he can see the tears forming. This is still goodbye, even if we don't say the words.

Princess. Am'ratha bows her head as I emerge. *Are you all right?*

What a loaded question. How do I answer that?

Ah, I see.

Am'ratha doesn't say anything more, but waves of sympathy travel through our bond, bringing more tears to my eyes. She waits until I am settled before taking to the sky. I turn my face to lessen the sting on my skin from the sharp, crisp air as we circle to leave the World Between. Catching sight of Snake standing on the ledge, I finally allow my tears to fall freely, fervently hoping this is not the last I will see of him.

Sensing my mood, Am'ratha leaves me to my thoughts as we fly. This is my first actual view of the world my forebears have ruled for centuries. My first impression is of a land sparsely populated. Settlements are small and spaced far apart, for the most part, with the occasional larger village.

It is also a land stuck in the past. There is no sign of electricity lines or motor vehicles. In fact, with only one main road in sight, there would be nothing for them to drive on. On the other hand, the air is clear, and I can see for miles.

While I have an excellent view, my eyesight can't match Am'ratha's, and as a range of mountains appears on the horizon, she suddenly banks.

Princess, there are men approaching the position of the rebel camp.

Are you sure? I mean, I can't see anything at all, let alone an army.

An invisibility spell hides it to most. I am able to see through the working. I count about ten groups of guards heading directly for the camp.

Am'ratha's revelation has me worried.

Can we still land nearby without alerting them to our presence?

She is silent as she rises high into the sky and circles what I assume is the encampment, which seems to be nestled in a clearing at the base of some mountains.

No, we cannot.

She ranges wider, and I can make out a larger force of guards heading our way.

How long before they join the others?

I would guess they are just over a day's march away, even if they use magic to move more quickly.

Wait, they can do that?

Some creatures, yes.

As we bank again, a group of about twenty men detach and take off at a jog, but I can see they are moving more quickly than should be possible. Could they be slowly bringing up troops to surround us? If we hadn't seen them, their attack would have taken us by surprise. More worryingly, although they couldn't hope to win against the number of creatures we have amassed, they could cripple our forces.

We need to alert Fairburn. Can you put me down close by?

Princess, you cannot make your way to camp through those guards. It is too dangerous.

Do you have another suggestion? I don't even try to keep the annoyance from my voice.

As we complete another circuit around the camp, a group of guards look up, clearly aware we are in the sky above them. I tense, sure they will send a magical attack our way.

Do not fear. From that distance, they will only see me—they cannot tell I carry a rider. Besides, they will not attack a dragon.

You seem sure of that.

There is a smile in Am'ratha's voice when she answers, *I am. Not only are dragons neutral, but they will not want to anger us lest we take a side in this fight.*

I am smart enough not to point out that they sort of have taken a side when they elected to support the status quo. Instead I say, *But that will not make it safe for us to land near the camp, will it?*

I have contacted Am'ralla. She is going to have Princess Petunia send a wizard to meet us behind the posting inn to take you to the camp.

Couldn't we have discussed options, like perhaps telling Fairburn what's happening? I send.

Am'ratha snorts at my sulky tone and doesn't deign to respond.

I'm sorry, I tell her once we've landed, hidden from the road by the posting inn. I dismount, allowing my dragon friend to crouch and rest while we wait for my wizard escort. *I want to be seen as a leader, not someone who needs rescuing.*

I rest a hand on her shoulder.

She snorts again. *We all have different skills and abilities. A good leader encourages those around them to use what they have.*

She's right, of course, and I know it. Before I have time to overthink it, a wizard appears. Holding a portal open, he gestures for me to hurry through.

Am'ratha?

I will stay close by with Am'ralla. She waits in a cave in the mountains.

Can you let Snake know what's happening? I ask as I step through the opening.

The portal closes as Am'ratha sends, *It will be done.*

AM'RATHA FERRIES PRIS away. All too soon they have disappeared from view, and I try not to focus on the possibility that this might be my last glimpse of the person who's captured my heart.

I need a distraction. Back in the kitchen, Susan and George are stirring rather foul-smelling pots of liquid.

'I hope that's not lunch,' I say, attempting a levity I don't feel.

Susan's nose wrinkles as she adds something to her pot, causing it to bubble. 'Fortunately for you, it's not. We're making up sleeping and pain draughts. If you want to help, you can decant the pot we made up before breakfast into the green bottles. It should be cool enough to handle.'

Happy to have something constructive to do, I do as I'm asked. Once I've finished and corked the bottles, there are two more pots cooling nearby.

'Those are to go in the blue bottles,' Susan instructs.

She takes the pot I have emptied to the sink and begins cleaning it. Over by the stove, George is stripping willow bark, preparing to distill another batch of pain tonic. The three of us continue working throughout the morning until we have no more ingredients left to process. The work is tedious, but it keeps my mind off Pris and the coming war.

George brings the last pot over and returns to his workspace with a bowl of steaming soapy water and begins scrubbing down. Susan moves the bottles I've filled into a cupboard at the back of the dining room as I finish emptying the last pot.

When the kitchen is clean and all the bottles stowed away, George makes a plate of sandwiches, and I put on the coffee.

'What's next?' I ask as we gather round the table to eat.

'Slow down, lad. Enjoy the break,' George says.

'I think Snake is trying not to miss the love of his life.' Susan winks at George, and they laugh as if they're sharing a huge joke.

I want to join in, but the truth is, I want to keep busy—*need* to keep busy so I don't miss Pris.

'Don't look so worried.' Susan pats my arm. 'We had a delivery of camp

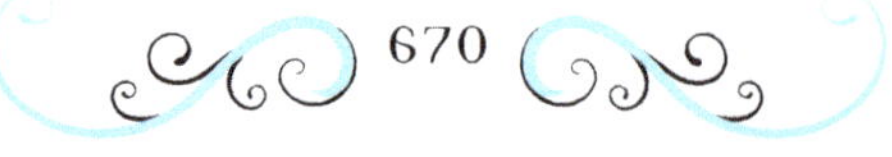

beds this morning, and they need to be set up in the dorm rooms.'

George groans, and Susan smiles at him. 'With three of us it should take no time at all.'

'I was planning to make some stocks for soups,' George protests.

Snake, are you there? Ed'rathe interrupts.

Yes, I'm here.

Can you be ready soon? The Queen has a job for us.

'Snake, are you all right?' Susan asks.

I focus back on the room. 'Just Ed'rathe. I'm afraid I won't have time to help with the beds.'

Susan flicks her hand as if to shoo me away. 'Go. I know you have work to do.'

Let me finish lunch, Ed'rathe, and I'll meet you out front.

Before I can take another bite of my sandwich, the air in the room goes cold, then shimmers. Next thing, an unknown creature appears on the other side of the table, my great-grandfather in tow.

I leap to my feet and am around the table in seconds. 'Mender,' I say, followed by, 'Why are you here? Is something wrong?'

The elderly gnome shifts the instrument case on his shoulder and draws me into a hug.

'Snake. It is so good to see you alive and well.' He turns to the stranger. 'Thanks for the ride, young creature. I can take it from here.'

The wizard draws a portal opening in the air and steps through without saying a word. Mender takes my arm and leads me back around the table, his face a picture of seriousness.

'What is it, Mender? Why are you here?'

My great-grandfather places his hand on my shoulder and urges me downwards. 'Sit, young Snake. Finish your food. There is nothing amiss. I have come to teach you.'

'W-what?' I stammer out as he leans his lute against the wall before pulling out the chair beside me.

'Yes, it was your grandfather's idea. He thought it might be useful for you to learn our family's magical secret.'

I am here, Snake.

'Wait. What secret?' My head is spinning. *Hold on, Ed'rathe.* I've gone from wondering what to do with myself to having everything thrown at me, and I'm finding it difficult to concentrate.

Mender chuckles, and Susan says, 'Snake, aren't you going to introduce us to your guest?'

I close my eyes, blocking out the world, and centre myself.

'Susan, George, this is my great-grandfather, Mender. Mender, I am afraid our reunion must wait. I have been called to work.'

Snake?

Coming.

Grandfather's eyes widen in surprise. 'I had heard you were ambassador to the Dragon Queen. Are you going to an audience?'

I shake my head. 'No. I'm not sure what I'll be doing, but my dragon friend is waiting for me.'

Mender's eyebrows shoot to his hairline. 'You have a dragon friend? Gosh, my family is rising through the ranks. I guess teaching you sleep magic can wait.'

I freeze halfway to my feet and drop back down into the chair. 'What? Hold on, you were going to teach me sleep magic? Is that even real? Or legal?'

Mender chuckles again. 'Semi-legal. We do not use it often, maybe to soothe a fretful child now and then, but I am assured this is something we might need in the coming days.'

Now I'm torn. I can't ignore the Dragon Queen's request, but wow…. sleep magic. That would be so cool.

Susan stands up and begins clearing the table. 'Snake, you need to go. I am sure Mender will be here when you get back.'

'Of course I will. Witch Lorin is not fetching me back until tomorrow morning. I'm told there is the possibility of a bed here?'

He turns to Susan, who in turn looks at me and grins. 'I assume there is a bed with unused bedding in your room?'

My face heats, as I'm well aware of what she's implying, and I mumble, 'Yes.'

'Good, now go. We'll keep Mender entertained while you do whatever it is you have to do.'

I push myself to my feet, grateful for Susan's pragmatic support and that Mender seems oblivious to her dig at me.

Mender places a hand on my arm and looks up at me, eyes twinkling. 'Wait. Would it be too much to ask to meet your dragon?'

It's sad that I have taken my friendship with Ed'rathe so much for granted that I've forgotten the awe and wonder dragon-kind inspires in others.

'Sure,' I say. 'Come with me to our room so I can grab a coat. You can leave your lute there.'

'And on the way, you can tell me why it's unusual for only one bed in your room to have been slept in,' Mender says, a cheeky grin crinkling his face.

I want to blot the next quarter of an hour from my mind, but I fear it's seared into my brain forever. Mender's questions about Pris and me create a new level of discomfort that is only superseded by my embarrassment as I translate a conversation between him and Ed'rathe—about me!

Your elder is a good creature, Ed'rathe informs me as we leave the World Between.

You're only saying that because he thought you were wonderful, and amazing, and awesome.

You say that as if you don't believe I am any of those things.

Ed'rathe manages to convey a little hurt in his words. I've gone too far with my teasing—after all, I *am* in awe of dragon-kind, and he has shown me nothing but friendship.

Dude, you are all of those things, and you know it. It's just me who sometimes forgets.

Ed'rathe grunts. Is he laughing at me? Before I can retaliate, my dragon friend chooses that moment to outline the Dragon Queen's orders.

We are to fly over the World Between, then report what is going on back to my Queen.

Can't she ask the other dragons who are out there with Pris? And don't Princess Petunia and Princess Cecily report to her?

Both sides protect those dragons, and they have special privileges. Reporting back activity relating to this war might affect their neutrality. However, if we fly over the World Below and happen to see things, we can tell the Queen.

Most of what I see as we fly is… well… nothing. There aren't even farmers in the fields, and the village streets are pretty empty. I guess creatures are lying low, or they have joined up to fight with one side or the other. This report will probably bore the Dragon Queen.

Look over there, Ed'rathe says as he banks right.

I can just make out uniformed creatures setting up shelters in the forest. When Ed'rathe straightens up, I study the surrounding area, searching for the object of their attention. I can't find anything.

What's going on? I ask.

The guards are encircling the rebel camp.

At first, I think he is kidding, but then I realise the camp is hidden from view. And, with that thought, fear for Pris takes over.

You must warn Am'ratha so she can get a message to Pris.

I cannot. We must not take a side in the coming battle.

I growl my frustration. *Then set me down, and I will warn them.*

Ignoring my request, Ed'rathe turns away from the forest and heads towards the Capitol.

Seriously, Ed'rathe. Put me down.

I am certain they know what is happening. They will have wards and scouts, and Pris and Am'ratha flew this way not so long ago. Besides, if their success in this endeavour relies on you and me, then they are doomed to fail.

How is he so calm? I fidget on his back, attempting to look back over my shoulder.

Please, be still. I do not want to have to pick your carcass up from the ground.

The reminder that I am flying stills me in my seat, and I resort to fuming.

I can sense your anger, but I assure you, all is well. The rebels have access to magic that allows them to see through the eyes of animals, and they will be using it to protect their position.

But we could help them by giving them a clearer picture of where the threat is coming from.

Not while you are with me and not using my mindspeak.

Is there a loophole there? I believe there is. Now my only thought is to get this mission over with so I can return to the World Between and alert the rebels.

In no time at all, Ed'rathe has us circling over the Capitol. The streets, much like the villages, are devoid of creatures. There are few guard patrols along the city's walls and fewer still on the ground. Has Bernais sent most of his force out to take on the rebels before they arrive at his doorstep? I really must warn Fairburn

Then all thoughts of the guards in the forest are driven from my mind as I see them—the hundreds, perhaps thousands, of uniformed humans camped out around the palace. This is why Bernais was able to send the governors' militias away—he has brought in mercenaries.

We know his plan. We can return home, Ed'rathe says.

Can we do another turn around—what the? My ears ring, and I grasp the side of one of Ed'rathe's scales as the mountains encircling the World Between appear beneath us.

When my balance is restored, I yell, 'What the hell was that?'

My Queen asked that we report back in a timely manner, Ed'rathe explains without answering my question at all.

I open my mouth to speak, but instead lean over to the side and lose my lunch.

Oh dear, time compression sometimes has this effect on mortals. Let me take you back to your quarters, and I shall report to the Dragon Queen for us both.

Time compression? You're kidding, right?

Ed'rathe settles on the ledge outside the creature guest quarters. As I attempt to get my breathing back under control, I slide off Ed'rathe, a little clumsier than normal. As a try to take an unsteady step, I find myself encased in a gentle pressure bubble preventing me from moving.

Wait. I will get someone to attend to you.

The call he bellows out almost splits my head in two. Susan appears moments later, followed closely by Mender. My legs buckle, one knee hitting the ground, and they help me to my feet and through the door as Ed'rathe says, *Rest for a while, and you will be fine.*

I'm not sure I'll ever be fine again. It feels like each part of my body is moving to a different rhythm—or perhaps operating in a different time?

'Apparently there is such a thing as time-shift magic?' I ask as my helpers lower me onto my bed.

'It's an urban myth,' Susan assures me, but my great-grandfather's brow wrinkles. 'There are old stories, myths even, that talk about dragon's compressing or warping time,' he informs me.

My stomach roils, and I close my eyes, certain it's no myth at all, but I don't have the capacity to argue with Susan and do what needs to be done to warn our forces.

'Susan, I need to speak to a rebel leader from the camp. Have you some way of contacting them?'

She pulls a blanket over my still-shaking form and says, 'You need to rest.'

'I will, but this is important. I have information they need.'

'All right, if you're certain?'

I nod, instantly regretting the movement.

'I will stay and care for him,' Mender says. Well, I think that's what he says, but his voice is drifting in and out.

My mind spins, and I try to catch hold of something that is just out of my reach… then I have it. Ed'rathe could have taken the flight over the World Below and reported back to the Dragon Queen himself. Although they had stuck to the letter of the law, they intended for me to have this knowledge and to pass it on.

Clarifying that thought leads me to another. The Dragon Queen would not have leaned this close to supporting us unless she was redressing a balance. Those humans should not be in the World Below. Does having them there breach some sort of agreement? No, that's not it. There are no laws against moving between the realms.

Then it hits me like a blow to the gut. There was only one way to get so many humans to agree to come to a magical realm, then follow the orders of mystical beings. Bernais and his cronies had done the unthinkable—they had bewitched mercenary soldiers from the World Above into our realm.

THE WAR DRUMS BEAT

STANDING ALONE OUTSIDE the command tent amidst the whirlwind of activity, I swallow my disappointment and rejection. Fighters are being trained. Weapons and armour are being cleaned. Food is being cooked and clothes are being mended. Everyone is contributing to the war except me.

They already knew, Am'ratha.

I am not surprised, Princess. They have their own ways of finding out information. Do they have a plan?

They're working on it.

You are with them?

I close my eyes, blocking everything out and attempting to sort through the emotions that have been surging through me since I stormed out. There is anger, and frustration, and… if I'm honest, humiliation.

When they said they wanted me to lead them into battle, they meant me to be more of a poster girl than an actual leader.

There, I've said it. I'm not worthy of being included in their planning. War and rebellion might be new to me, but I'm not totally useless in combat. Fairburn's rejection had stung. I may as well sit round in a pretty dress and smile all day.

Good. Now you have a job you can concentrate on.

That is the final straw. Being a pinup is not a job. How dare Fairburn tell me I can't fight either. I've been training in martial arts for most of my life.

Calm down. Your thoughts are being broadcast at full volume. He is right, though—you don't send the Queen or her representative into battle to be killed. If they get taken out, the army loses heart.

Dammit, there is a logic to that. Even though I'm not ready to let go of my anger, I try. I want to go back inside, but I'm worried if I don't get control of my emotions, I'll say or do something that will reinforce their opinion of me. That's why I had left in the first place.

I don't even know what a figurehead is supposed to do!

My tone is sulky. I sound like a spoilt child, and I'm annoyed at myself for falling back into this old pattern. I thought I had moved on from all this.

A figure slips through the tent opening and joins me. Percival. I almost sag with relief. He always knows how to bring the best out in me.

He gives me a knowing look. 'So, Princess, shall we go visit your grandmother? She has had more experience with this sort of thing, and there is no shame in asking for guidance.'

As he speaks, an elven woman dressed in guard leathers detaches herself from the nearby troop and heads our way. She looks familiar, but I can't place her—and that isn't good because she's someone I no doubt should be able to identify.

'Percival, they want your help moving the hospital,' she says, her voice displaying a slight Scottish burr.

Where do I know her from? Is it the Unseelie Court?

Percival's voice pulls me back into the conversation. 'I thought they were staying here.'

'Now that *they* know where we are, the wizards—sorry, witches—are moving the hospital to somewhere in Melliores tonight.

Percival's gaze drifts towards the tent emblazoned with a large red heart surrounded by black plants, then back to us, his brows drawing together. 'I was going to take Pris to visit Petunia.'

'I can do that.'

'If you are sure….'

'I am.'

I'm not. Something about this elf sets me on edge, and I don't want to be alone with her.

The elf places a hand between Percival's shoulder blades and gives him a gentle push. 'Besides, it's about time Princess Priscilla and I become acquainted.'

Percival throws a concerned glance over his shoulder, and I mouth, 'I'll be okay.'

I mean, who would attack me in the middle of the rebel encampment? Then again, this elf doesn't exactly seem friendly. Where is Aeron when you need him? I would feel a lot more confident dealing with this stranger if he were here.

Positioning herself directly in front of me and cutting off my view of

Percival's retreating figure, the elf says, 'I am Princess Irene, your—'

'Aunt! That's who you remind me of—Mum.' It clicks, and now it's so obvious.

My aunt's response to my revelation is tart enough to curdle milk. 'I wouldn't know if I resemble Cecily, as *your* mother stayed behind with Queen Ariana when *my* mother left the World Below, and I have had little to do with her since then.'

Hurt and anger at having to answer for things outside of my control well up inside me. 'You knew where Mum has been. You could visit her. Talk to her. Write to her, even. I didn't know I had any family other than my parents until a few weeks ago,' I snap.

My aunt's brows form a disapproving frown.

Shame closely follows anger, and I take a deep breath. 'Look, I'm sorry. It's been quite a journey, getting to know my family and the magical realms.

Rather than softening, the elf's gaze becomes even more stony, and her tone is scornful when she says, 'And everyone believes you capable of leading an army into battle.'

My jaw drops. I have met every challenge thrown at me these past weeks. Now, in the space of an hour, Fairburn's rejected me, and this… this *creature* is judging me and finding me wanting.

'You must feel so unprepared. Perhaps it is time to hand off to someone else.'

Although her words are consoling, I get the impression this is less about me and more about her.

Well, you know what? I've had enough.

Straightening my spine, I square my shoulders and meet her eyes. Does she want to lead the army? Is this some attempt to usurp Queen Ariana and my mother in retribution for an old grievance? My anger is bubbling below the surface, but I keep it locked down, careful to not let it show.

'I am sure my mother would be more than happy to step up and lead the army,' she finishes.

Okay, not her, but Grandmother. Is there something I'm missing?

'Queen Ariana doesn't want royal support becoming split between her and Grandmother.'

Irene's lips curl into a sneer. 'If she is so keen on family unity, why wouldn't she let Cecily live in the World Above with us? Maybe then we would have been better prepared to face this situation as a strong, united family.'

Well, this is something new to chew on. I assumed the Queen was putting the World Below first when she sent me here. Maybe I should have considered that she might have another, more personal, agenda.

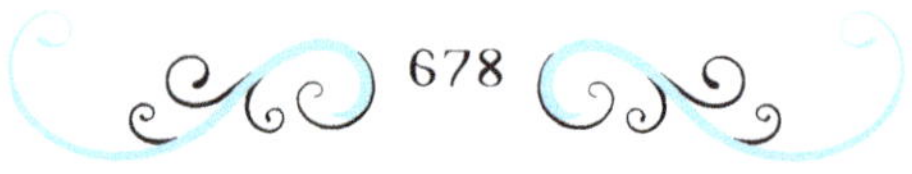

'It is a bit of a mess,' I concede, my anger receding a little. I'm sick of raking over old history. It won't achieve anything. 'And I'm sure many mistakes were made in the past. But I guess we are where we are.'

Irene studies me for a long time, as if she's deciding something. 'True.'

'And as we're moving the troops tonight instead of tomorrow, we should save this family reunion stuff for later.'

Irene turns away. 'I guess we should go find Mother.'

I follow her, feeling like I've been tried and found wanting.

If my aunt's welcome was less than effusive, my grandmother makes up for it.

'My darling Pris, I was so worried when I heard you were injured. Then, to have the Dragon Queen herself heal your wounds! You are blessed.'

I sit in an empty chair, surprised by the luxury of the tent she occupies in the middle of a battle camp. Although she is dressed in riding clothes, she still radiates royalty.

'I didn't feel blessed. All I felt was a whole lot of pain.'

She hands me a cup of tea, and I sip it gratefully while she and Irene settle.

'How is that young creature of yours doing? I hear he has his own dragon now. Does that mean you have something to tell me?'

My cup clatters on the table as I heavy-handedly place it down. 'No!'

Ignoring my outburst, Petunia turns to Irene. 'Snake Fieth is the gnome I told you about.'

For the first time since I met her, my aunt's eyes flash with approval. 'The one who helped place the Unseelie Court in stasis? Now *he* is someone I would like to meet.'

Unlike me, who merely convinced the King to leave his court and is clearly not up to much.

Something in my demeanour must have warned Petunia, and she turns back to me. 'So, if you are to be our leader, what do we have to work with? Can you ride a horse?'

Finally I have a chance to display my skills. 'Yes, I took lessons for a couple of years, but I haven't ridden since I started my A levels.'

Irene quirks a brow. 'Are we talking novice or competent?'

'Competent,' I respond, hoping her idea of competent and mine are the same.

Irene nods as Petunia asks, 'What about fighting?'

'What about it?' I ask, a little confused. 'Fairburn said I wasn't to fight.'

'You might not be in the thick of the battle, but we need to know whether you can defend yourself if you're isolated and attacked. It can devastate an army if their leader dies,' Irene explains as if speaking to a child.

'I know that,' I want to say, but I bite my tongue. 'I've studied martial arts since I started school.'

Irene frowns. 'What about weapons?'

'I have trained with a few, but I guess the most useful from horseback would be the Jian.' When Irene frowns, I explain, 'It's a double-edged straight sword.'

'Mmm… I think we could cover that.'

'How are your public speaking skills?' Grandmother asks, changing the subject.

I grin. Now we're talking.

For the next half an hour or so, Grandmother and I nut out some key phrases I can include in a rousing speech. When we're done, my grandmother excuses herself for a minute.

Irene takes this as an opportunity to study me thoughtfully. 'Better than I first thought, but I think I'll reserve judgement until I see you in action.'

'Just out of interest, what did you expect?' I ask, unsure how much my aunt knew about me.

'A spoilt, protected rich kid from London,' Irene says with a smirk, and I bark out a laugh.

Up until a few weeks ago, when I met Snake, that description would have been pretty accurate. In spite of her acerbic attitude, I find myself warming to my aunt. She's more like me and Mum than she'd like to think.

Grandmother returns with a sword in her hand. 'As I am to leave with the hospital crew, I think this will be more than suitable for you to use.'

She hands the sword and sheath to me as Irene gasps, 'No! Mother! It was Father's bride gift to you.'

Realising the weapon's importance, I shake my head. 'Irene should have it.'

It is Princess Petunia, not my grandmother, who responds. 'Symbols are important. This blade is known to be mine, and for you to wield it shows my support of you to everyone on both sides. I want it back, mind, because it will eventually go to Irene.'

Grandmother turns a questioning glance to Irene, who holds her mother's gaze then nods her consent.

Reluctantly I take the offered weapon. 'I will return it to you when I am done.'

'If you are able,' Irene adds, reminding me that this is no game we're playing. 'Come, we still have to find some suitable armour and a horse.'

I hug my grandmother goodbye, and she whispers in my ear, 'Be safe.' Then to Irene, she says, 'I am entrusting everything to you.'

Irene kisses her mother on the cheek. 'Goddess be with you.'

Thirty minutes later, I exit the armoury tent, tugging at my new leather armour. It is heavy and uncomfortable, and I can't get it to sit right. As it is similar to Irene's, I resist the urge to whine about it. I roll my shoulders again, and Irene pauses, studies me, then places her hand on the armour. The leather warms under her touch, but the armour now fits like a glove.

'Sorry, I forgot you aren't used to using magic. While all clothes are spelled to fit by their makers, you have to spell your own armour, as leatherworkers don't usually have the same skills.'

'Thank you,' I say, but Irene is already moving towards the makeshift field where the horses graze.

She calls over one of the creatures polishing tack and says, 'I believe there is a mount assigned to Princess Priscilla.'

The young female creature—a dwarf, I think, but can't be certain—nods. 'Yes, Princess. The dun-coloured one under the tree.' She points at a horse, who looks up as if she knows we're talking about her. To me, the creature says, 'She is strong and a little willful. If you let her know who is boss from the start, she will be fine.'

'Thank you,' I say.

Irene follows with 'She will be ready when we leave later on tonight?'

The creature nods. 'Of course.'

'Good.'

Irene turns and heads back towards the command tent.

'Thank you,' I say to the groom, and she smiles shyly at me.

'Her name is Gwen, and she's partial to an apple if you can find one.'

I smile back. 'I'll see what I can do.'

As I hurry to catch Irene up, Am'ratha sends, *She will not be as good to ride as me.*

You shouldn't be spying on me, I tease.

How else am I to protect you?

Fair point. And she might not be as comfortable to ride with as you, but she is a little bit less flashy.

I will take that as a compliment.

Gotta go. War council time.

I draw level with Irene as she reaches the command tent. It takes a moment for my eyes to adjust as we step inside, and before they do, a familiar voice beside me says, 'Well, it's about time you turned up.'

'Some guard you turned out to be,' I joke.

Aeron clutches his heart and moans, 'I have failed in my duty.'

Fairburn claps him on the shoulder. 'No, you haven't. Priscilla was never in any danger.'

Irene straightens by my side and says almost reverentially, 'I was with her, Mighty Warrior. Although I am not in your league, I am more than capable of defending my niece.'

To my surprise, Aeron bows. 'Ooh, am I in the presence of the legendary warrior elf, Irene? Your reputation in tournaments is celebrated across the lands.'

I study my aunt with a newfound respect, and I'm shocked to see the tiniest bit of colour bloom on Irene's cheeks under Aeron's scrutiny.

'I am honoured to share the protection of Princess Priscilla with you.' Aeron bows again, and Irene giggles. Actually giggles!

I roll my eyes. *OMG, really.*

Aeron raises an eyebrow. 'I would keep silent if I were you, given what I have witnessed between you and your consort.'

'He's not my consort,' I respond automatically before my brain kicks into action.

Aeron winks, and I curse myself for having fallen for his ruse.

'Let us get this council underway before we descend to kindergarten level,' Fairburn says, much to my relief.

I smirk as I catch Aeron and Irene sharing admiring glances as we gather around the map table.

'I WILL NOT say goodbye,' Nisha says. She carries on packing a chest with bandages, keeping her back to me.

'But—'

'No, Percival. We have unfinished business, not the least of which is saying a final farewell to your father once this is over. I will not entertain the possibility that we will not see these things through.'

She has become so defiant, my bond mate. Where did this change come from? Is it hubris to wonder if my past decisions changed Nisha?

I am startled from my thoughts by a hand gently squeezing my arm.

'There is no use worrying about the path not taken. We are here now.'

She cups my cheek, and her brown eyes capture mine. 'Go help Eleanora with the carts. We will meet again on the other side.'

I lean into her and touch our foreheads together, mingling our breath. How could I have spent so much time apart from her? How did I bear it? Reluctantly, I draw away.

'Are you all right, old friend?' Ellie asks when I join her beside a loaded wagon.

'I am getting there, as the young people say. At the very least, I know where I am going.'

We cover the wagon, and as Ellie pulls the last tie tight, she turns to me and smiles. 'It seems odd for you to be so certain of your future when everything around you is falling apart. You never used to be this contrary.'

I consider her words. It is true I used to bend with the winds when I hid from the world. Now I am back and ready to lean into them when the cause is right. Still, this is not a conversation to be had on the eve of a civil war. It is too heavy, and we need lightness.

Pulling on a mock serious face, I tease, 'So… Mandor is not a wizard anymore.'

For a moment, she stops, and I fear she might ignore me. Then she says, 'Meaning?'

'Just saying.' *I really have spent far too much time with Pris and Snake!*

'I am trying hard not to think beyond the next few days, Percival. And I certainly do not want to be pining for what might have been.' She pats the side of the wagon and turns to me. 'I am not as hopeful for the future as you are, my friend.'

Sadness brings tears to my eyes. Working things out with Nisha has given me hope for the first time in a long while, and I am desolate that my friend does not feel the same—especially as she has kept me from despair for so many years. 'There is not even a little hope?'

Ellie gnaws at her lower lip. 'It has been such a long time, Percival. Perhaps we are beyond those feelings.'

'You will never know if you do not try. Soon the battle will be upon us, and it might be too late.' I hated saying the last, but given that we may not come through this, we cannot waste a single opportunity.

'Hark at you giving me relationship advice,' Ellie says, a twinkle in her eye.

I see the irony. She married two mortals, aged with them, and saw them through their deaths. Still, this is Mandor, the love of her life.

Ellie rubs her forehead. 'I can't do anything even if I wanted to. He is off in the deep Wyld Woods, searching for Heart and the creatures he promised to bring with him.'

It is almost as if by speaking Heart's name, she summoned him. He and a group of creatures bearing arms appear from nowhere, with Mandor trailing close behind. Ellie gasps in shock at this sudden appearance and then busies herself as if demonstrating she doesn't care. I know better, though.

'No excuse now,' I say to Ellie before moving to greet Heart. 'Pleased you could join us.'

Heart claps a hand on my shoulder. 'Can't stop now, old friend. I believe I have the solution to your problem. Lead me to the command tent.'

'Our problem?' I ask, somewhat confused as I nonetheless lead him to the centre of the encampment.

'Your ring-of-guards-around-the-camp problem,' Heart clarifies.

Behind us, Mandor calls for someone to take the new recruits to the food tent before he and Ellie follow us.

When she sees us approach, the guard outside the command centre flicks the flap open, and the entire command contingent turns as we enter.

Before anyone can utter so much as a word, Heart announces, 'I have a sleep spell that can solve your problem of how to sneak out of here tonight without alerting our enemies that anything is amiss.'

It was like someone hit the Pause button on a TV—the world stops while everyone takes it in.

'Well, a sleep spell,' Fairburn eventually says. 'That would indeed be very useful.' He turns to Brynn. 'Now that we might actually sneak out, we need to be certain no one does anything to tip our hand. Alert the surveillance teams to notify us immediately if they think the enemy is getting suspicious.'

Brynn leaves, and Fairburn calls everyone around the map.

'With the human mercenaries in the Capitol, it is essential the creature enemy forces surrounding us are committed to attacking our camp for as long as possible. We do not have the numbers to engage them as well as the human mercenaries should they join up. Right, let us go over the schedule one last time.'

One delegate swings a blackboard round, and we all turn our attention to the details Fairburn summarises for us.

'At midnight we will begin moving the hospital to Melliores.' Fairburn's gaze turns my way.

'They are packed and ready to go,' I confirm.

'Excellent. Two hours later Percival and Drow will be portalled into the university at the heart of the Capitol to mobilise the students and security staff who have remained behind. We have been co-ordinating activities with them and training them to help us with some specific tasks.'

'Their most recent dispatch confirms they will be ready and waiting to receive their final orders,' Drow assures us.

'Good. The members of campus security will help us enter the Capitol through an assigned gate, and some students will be sent to rally creatures in the ghetto to create a demonstration to provide cover for our movements.

Another group has been preparing to free our people who are being held captive. Once they have been dispatched, Percival and Drow will then set up our command post.'

Drow steps forward and spreads out a map of the city. 'There is a curfew in the Capitol, but our student friends are no doubt well versed in moving around after hours without being caught.'

There were a few laughs in the tent.

Drow smiles, then continues. 'The security guards will make their way to the Avondale gate and capture the enemy guards there. This is of upmost importance, as our best chance is to sneak into the city and battle the soldiers outside the palace. If we have to fight our way there, we will waste time and resources, which will allow Bernais to mount a defence.'

'Won't the guards hear us arrive outside the walls?' Pris asks.

'Our transport site is five minutes from our entry point. The first troop will immediately move into position in front of the gates and will be held in a sound bubble,' Fairburn explains. 'Once the gates are open, they will secure the area, then fan out around the walls, immobilising the other guard posts as they go. The rest of our force will make its way through the streets to their positions, ready to engage the humans surrounding the palace.'

'And the demonstration is timed to make enough noise to cover the sounds of their movements?' Pris asks.

Fairburn nods. 'That is the plan.'

Drow takes over again. 'As Fairburn touched on, we know from Princess Petunia's report that lesser creatures were rounded up and are being held in the suburbs behind the university in a sort of ghetto.'

'Shame,' someone near me hisses, and I have to agree.

'Indeed,' says Drow. 'We will send some students there under cover of darkness to encourage them to protest against their conditions once the curfew finishes at dawn. They should create enough noise and a big enough disturbance to cover our troops entering the city.'

Now it is my turn. 'Another contingent of students will be sent to free those being held in increature conditions at the hospital.'

It turns my stomach to even talk about creatures being held in stasis. Controlling creatures using spells or bewitching them is worse than murder. Some never fully recover.

'The more magically adept will break into the hospital and counter the spellwork keeping the prisoners docile. They will then bring those released back to the university, where we will see about getting them further help.'

Fairburn stands beside the blackboard. 'We hope to have all creatures released and either receiving medical attention or protesting by just past sunup. Soon after, we will have our forces in place. Once the sun rises, the witches left at the encampment will join the healers ready to deal with any casualties, and…. Well, let us say, all bets are off after that.'

Irene chuckles. 'It's a great plan, Fairburn, but will it hold up when we engage the enemy?'

'Perhaps, but probably not. That is why we are trying to move into place without the enemy knowing what we are doing,' Fairburn counters. 'It will give us the greatest chance of success.'

'Do we have contingencies?' Irene presses.

Fairburn's front hooves shuffle. 'Had we more time to plan, I am sure we could have had contingencies. However, not only do we not have much time, but the enemy encircling our camp has cut what little time we had in half. I am afraid we have one shot at ending this quickly, otherwise we will withdraw and fall back on guerrilla warfare to prevent the elven faction from consolidating their power.'

'No,' Pris says. 'We have one shot full stop. If we don't sort this out before the Dragon Queen's deadline, she will allow Bernais to ascend to the throne.'

The room falls silent as everyone contemplates the disaster this would be for our land.

'Then we had best not fail,' Fairburn says. His gaze rakes the room. 'Is there anything we have forgotten?'

No one speaks, but Heart is studying the map, a worried frown creasing his brow.

'Good, then with Heart's offer to spell the enemy to sleep—'

'Umm, about that,' Heart interrupts. 'I had no idea the area would be so big. I am going to need some help.'

MMM, STEAK.

The thought permeates my consciousness and finally settles in my stomach, which rumbles loud enough to crash mountains, rousing me from sleep.

My room in the guest quarters in the World Between is empty and a little cool. How long have I been asleep? I was pretty groggy when the witch from the rebel camp questioned me about the human forces in the Capitol. Once she heard what I had to say, she had been keen to return to the camp as soon as possible, and I hadn't complained.

I push myself into a sitting position, and then I stretch and check myself out. I no longer feel like the world is spinning around me. Tentatively I swing my legs over the side of the bed and stand up. Yep, everything is good. My stomach grumbles, reminding me of why I am up and about at all.

As expected, Susan, Henry, and my great-grandfather are in the dining room. Henry has gone all out for dinner. A roast of beef sits between the creatures, slices of perfectly cooked meat steeping in aromatic juices. Roast vegetables are piled up on another plate sitting beside a large jug of gravy. There are even Yorkshire puds. I bite back a groan.

'Do not just stand there, boy,' Mender says, 'You of all of us could do with a hearty meal.'

I don't need a second invitation. Taking the seat beside Henry opposite my great-grandfather, I pile my plate high with food.

'This is amazing,' I tell the brownie as I stuff myself.

'It may be our last chance for a slap-up meal,' he tells me, and although my stomach sinks at the thought of what is to come, I'm thankful for tonight.

'There's lemon meringue pie for dessert,' Susan tells me. 'So leave some space.'

This time I do groan. I can't remember when I last had a traditional, home-cooked meal this good.

When we're done eating the main meal, Mender says, 'Dessert can wait until you've learnt the sleep spell.'

Before I can argue, he drags me into the common room while Susan and Henry clear away the first course.

We sit by the fire, and Mender picks up the lute he brought.

'In the coming days, you may need this sleep spell, and we haven't much time for me to teach you,' Mender says, tuning the instrument. When he's done, he quietly strums a tune.

I try to concentrate on what he is playing, and I expect to start falling asleep, or at least yawn, but I don't feel any different.

'Grandfather, I don't think it's working,' I whisper, a little disappointed that it doesn't. I mean, how cool would it be to be able to do a sleep spell?

Mender chuckles but carries on playing. 'The spell has two parts. The first is the music, or the tune, really. The second is the intent. Much like the dynamics that turn a tune into a performance from the heart, you must concentrate on willing the subject to sleep.'

I nod my understanding. He is speaking my language, after all. With the fear of falling asleep while learning eliminated, I'm able to quickly pick up the tune. The base theme is Brahms's 'Lullaby.' There are a few added arpeggios, but it's essentially the same.

When he's run through it twice, Mender stops and hands the lute to me. I've only tried playing the instrument a few times, and it feels kind of awkward, but not completely unfamiliar. It's like a guitar, and I get the best sound by picking instead of strumming.

It takes me a few tries, but once I have the basics, Mender makes me play it a couple more times just to make sure—he's an exacting music teacher.

Finally he is happy, and he takes the instrument from me. 'Now is the telling part. If you have inherited the ability to use the sleep spell, I should be able to play it with intent and you will not fall asleep.'

'Wait, you mean there is a chance I may not be able to do this?' I ask, feeling the loss of a spell I never had.

'Yes, I am afraid not everyone with our blood can cast it.'

'That's a weird way of checking.'

Mender chuckles, his eyes twinkling with merriment. 'Or a very sensible way.'

'Sensible?'

'Yes. You can hardly use a spell if you fall asleep while casting it.'

Of course—it's so obvious.

'The trick is,' Mender says as he plays, 'to believe with your whole being that you want the listener to go to sleep. Any doubt or distractions, and it won't work.'

The music he is playing changes. The sound is fuller and encourages me to close my eyes and drift away with it. I concentrate, trying to work out what he's doing differently. Whatever it is, it's so subtle, I can't identify it.

He stops playing and smiles. 'Well, you've passed the first step.' He hands me the lute. 'Now for the second test. Susan,' he calls, raising his voice to be heard in the dining room. 'Would you mind being our guinea pig?'

Susan appears in the doorway. 'What?'

'Would you mind allowing Snake to sing you to sleep?'

'I have a lot to do….'

'I will only let him start to send you to sleep, then,' Mender reassures her. 'That way you'll wake up as soon as he stops playing.'

'Okay then.' Susan wipes her hands on her apron and takes a seat across from me.

Taking a deep breath, I play the tune through once for practice, then the second time, I will Susan to sleep.

She stifles a yawn but is otherwise unaffected. A frown appears between Mender's brows.

'I could feel your intent, but it did not change the timbre of the music as much as it should.'

'So, you're saying, once more, with feeling,' I joke.

Mender nods solemnly. 'Yes, please.'

I try again. Then once more. Then again. My desperation lends the music a sharpness that counteracts my will, and the most I get from Susan is another yawn.

Mender rubs a hand across his brow. 'I do not understand it. I have never had this much trouble teaching one of my blood this spell.'

'Perhaps it's just that Snake is tired,' Susan offers. 'He's had a bit of a day.'

'Yes… that could be it.' Mender's tone is not convincing. 'We can try again—'

Mender stops mid-sentence as the air shimmers, and Mandor appears behind Susan.

'Good, you're both here. We need your help at the camp.'

'Snake and I?' Susan asks.

'No, Snake and Mender. We need them to play their sleep spell.'

'But I only agreed to teach Heart and Snake the spell. I am too old to involve myself in war,' Mender says.

'And I am presently serving the Dragon Queen,' I add. 'I can't go anywhere without her permission.'

Mandor frowns. 'This is really important. We are surrounded, and this is the only way we can see to move our troops into position without alerting the enemy that we are leaving.' He runs a hand through his dark hair, a forlorn look crossing his face. 'Is there any way you….'

Mender lets out a breath. 'I guess if this is all you will ask of me, then I could lend a hand.'

They turn to me. No one has mentioned that I can't actually complete the spell yet, so I don't either. No need to worry about that until I have permission to help.

'Okay, let me talk with Ed'rathe.' I look down at my crumpled clothes. 'And I'll get my gear as well.'

Back in my room, I grab a change of clothes as I contact Ed'rathe and explain the situation. He agrees to speak with the Dragon Queen on my behalf. He comes back before I've even pulled on my boots.

The Dragon Queen allows you leave until tomorrow morning. I am to wait with Am'ralla and Am'ratha and bring you back tomorrow.

You don't need to come until tomorrow.

That is too far away if something happens to you.

Oh. I hadn't thought this might be dangerous. *Can you thank the Dragon Queen for me?* I ask and grab my jacket. *For letting me go and sending you.*

There is one commitment the Dragon Queen asks for. She says if she calls for you, you must return immediately.

Of course. Nothing ever comes without strings in the World Between. *As she commands.*

I sense Ed'rathe leave, and I head back to the communal room. Mender has returned his lute to its bag and is waiting while Mandor talks with Susan. I hover in the doorway, a mess of uncertainty. I can't do this.

It's not nerves. Well, it sort of is, because this will be dangerous. I mean, I literally can't do this. I can't make the sleep spell work, and even if I could, I don't have an instrument to play on.

Mender must have sensed my concern. He steps towards me, takes my arm, and moves me back into the hallway.

'I know what you're thinking,' he says, 'and I don't want your inability to complete the spell to put you off. You were close, and I have an idea on how it might work for you.'

I hold up my hand. 'It doesn't matter, Mender. I don't have an instrument. The lute you gave me is in the Unseelie Court along with all my other possessions.'

Great-Grandfather claps a hand on my shoulder. 'Impatient imp, that was what I was going to tell you. You are competent with a lute, but it is not your natural instrument. However, you sang for my people when you were in the Minotaur's Maze, and your voice is as good an instrument as any.'

My nose wrinkles with distaste. My voice is not an instrument—it's an accompaniment. It complements the music I play.

'All right,' he allows, 'it is not an optimal solution, but you could try.'

He is so positive I can do this, I don't have the heart to let him down. Besides, if I go to the camp, at the very least I'll get to see Pris one more time before the battle.

'Are we ready?' Mandor calls.

I suck in a breath, 'As ready as I'll ever be.'

By the time we return to the fireside, Mandor has opened a portal.

'One at a time?' I ask.

Mandor shakes his head. 'We have modified the spell, and we can now hold the doorway open long enough for more than one person to travel at a time.'

'Good luck,' Susan calls as we step through to a clearing in front of a large tent.

To the left is a large fire, and I spot Drow and Heart sitting together on a log, both eating from wooden bowls.

'Go join them. You have some time before you're needed,' Mandor says before disappearing into the tent.

My heart races as I locate Pris sitting on the other side of the fire. She is sharing a log with Aeron and a female elf I feel I should know. I make my way directly to her, and as if sensing my presence, Pris glances up, and smiles a welcome as she reaches to pull me down beside her.

I lean in and whisper, 'I've missed you.'

She chuckles. 'You only saw me this morning.'

'And that was too long apart.'

I wrap an arm around her and pull her closer as I study the rest of the group. 'Where's Percival?' I whisper.

Aeron leans round Pris and responds, 'Saying his goodbyes to Nisha.' His smile suggests more than a simple goodbye, and I turn to Pris, my eyes wide.

Her eyes darken with emotion. 'They've been getting on really well. It's so lovely.'

I'm not sure whether I find that comforting or disturbing, like thinking about your parents being intimate is. The only way I can deal with it is to push the thought from my mind.

I nod towards Aeron, who is following the familiar elf as she speaks while looking up at him with doe eyes. I lean in close to Pris to speak into her ear again. 'What's their deal?'

She chuckles. 'It appears Aeron has a crush on my Aunt Irene.'

'That's Princess Irene? Wow, she's supposed to be this amazing warrior woman.'

Pris's voice is tinged with exasperation when she says, 'Great—everyone has a crush on my legendary aunt. Perhaps she should be the one leading the army.'

I pull Pris in and kiss her cheek. 'She's got nothing on you.'

She relaxes into me. 'Good recovery. And timely, too, as I was considering whether or not to show you what I found for you.'

I rest my head on hers. 'You have a present for me?'

'Sort of. Heart was telling us about the spell you guys are going to play and that you need instruments. We sent a witch to get a lute for him from Mender's shop.'

'And you got one for me too?'

'No, we did one better.' Pris looks up at me, her lips curling into a smile. 'Percival has been working with a creature called Brynn. They mentioned their brother brought a guitar back from the World Above and they said you could use it. We sent a witch to get it for you.'

As if by magic, a goblin appears beside me with a rather beautiful acoustic guitar in their hand. 'I hope you can play this, as my brother certainly could not,' they say, holding out the instrument.

I leap to my feet, gratitude filling me as my fingers curl around the neck of the guitar. 'Thank you for loaning this to me,' I say. 'Tell your brother I will take good care of it.'

Brynn stares at the ground. 'My brother has passed to the other side. I would be honoured if you would take this.' He chokes up at the end, and I reach out and squeeze his arm.

'What is your brother's name?'

'Gareth.' Brynn's voice is little more than a whisper.

'I will sing the sleep song in Gareth's name, and together we will fight for creature freedom.'

The gnome looks up, tears glistening in their eyes. 'Thank you.'

'Come, join us.' I gesture to the fire, and Brynn takes a place on the other side of Irene.

I lean against the log Pris sits on and tune the guitar. It has a beautiful, rich tone, and my fingers fly along the strings as if I've been playing this guitar all my life. I play the sleep spell through a couple of times, and I connect with the piece in a way I couldn't when playing it on the lute. Just to test things out, I send a little intent into the last few bars, and a few of the creatures around the fire yawn.

From across the blaze, Mender's eyes meet mine, and he sends a nod. For the first time, I believe I might actually be able to help our forces move.

Reluctant to put the guitar down, I strum a few chords, thinking about what I might play to capture the mood tonight. Mandor and Eleanor join us.

'The hospital group are safely in Melliores,' Eleanora announces.

Percival appears from the darkness and takes a seat beside Drow. My uncle places an arm around his friend's shoulders. Percival has been Pris's and my rock since we started on this quest. He was there for us even when we didn't know he was. This is the first time I have seen him so forlorn.

This more than anything brings home the enormity of what we face tomorrow. Yet here we all are, supporting each other through this, and in that moment, I so want to believe that everything we are giving up will be worth it.

Almost as though my fingers are moving of their own accord, they find the notes for Rachel Platten's 'Fight Song,' and the lyrics rouse everyone. By the last chorus, they're all singing along.

When the words are done, I carry on playing the tune. It then drifts into Bob Marley's 'Redemption Song.' When I sing the chorus, Pris and Irene join me.

Eleanora and Mandor stand and leave the fire, hand in hand.

'Do not do anything I wouldn't do,' Drow teases.

'Leave them alone,' Pris says, and Drow bows his head like a naughty child.

'Are they back together?' I ask.

Pris slips down the log and lays her head on my shoulder. 'Perhaps they are simply taking time to be together before tomorrow.'

I lean the guitar against the back of the log and wrap an arm around Pris. She nestles into my side, and I catch sight of Aeron and Irene sneaking into the dark.

'Creatures and humans alike crave connection at times like this. It may be for one night, and that is fine. For something longer term, you have to make a choice to be together and keep choosing to be together,' I muse.

The crackle of the fire fills the air as we're distracted by our thoughts. As I drift off I whisper in Pris's ear, 'I choose us.'

'I CHOOSE US.'

At least, I think that's what Snake whispers as he falls asleep. My heart flutters at the words, and I feel I can face anything tomorrow… no, *today*.

While I'm worrying that I should respond in some way, Snake's snores ruffle my hair, so he's clearly not waiting for me to do so. Still, I should say something, but what?

In his arms, I am at home, but is that enough? Can I make that leap and choose us—choose him too? I can't bring myself to say the words. Instead, I watch the flames and try to sleep until, sometime after two, Brynn stirs.

'I guess it's time,' they say.

I nudge Snake. 'Time to go.'

He looks so young, rubbing the sleep from his eyes, and I want nothing more than to take him in my arms and run away somewhere this war cannot reach us. Leaning in, he kisses the end of my nose, and I press my forehead to his.

'Stay safe,' I whisper. 'I couldn't bear it if….' I can't finish the sentence.

He pulls me close. There is nothing more to say. Aeron emerges from the darkness and helps me to my feet.

From beside him, Irene asks, 'Have you got your speech?'

I nod as they draw me away. I send one last glance over my shoulder to find Snake's eyes following me. 'Goddess, please don't let that be the last time I see him,' I whisper into the night.

In Grandmother's quarters, Irene helps me into my armour. I attempt to block out my worries and fears by going over my speech in my head. When

I'm ready, Aeron pulls back the curtain, and I almost throw up when I see the number of soldiers assembled outside.

Irene places a hand in the small of my back and gives me a gentle shove. 'If it were easy, anyone could do it.' She escorts me out and adds, 'Remember, Fairburn has arranged for a muffling spell, so speak loud and clear for those at the back.'

Aeron helps me onto my horse so I will be high enough for everyone to see me. Then he grabs the bridle to ensure my mount doesn't spook. I sit up straight in the saddle to survey the crowd, and I almost lose my nerve there and then. All these creatures are about to face death, and I don't want to let them down.

I suck in a deep breath, and find Snake who, along with Heart and Mender, is leaving. Snake looks back over his shoulder, and his gaze finds me. For a second, we connect, then Heart tugs his arm, and he's gone. I suck in a breath and tell myself, *They're prepared to give their lives for this, so this is the least I can do for these creatures.*

In the soldiers' faces, I see a mixture of hope, and fear, and determination. Suddenly, the speech I'd prepared seems inadequate. I shove the paper in my pocket and lean my hands on the pommel.

'I was going to give you a rousing speech about how we will win this war, defeat the council, and everything will get better,' I start. 'And while I do hope for all that, the words did not come from my heart.'

Unrest ripples through the ranks.

I'm losing them.

'What I want you to remember today as we fight our common foe is that we are all here for a reason. Your reason may be different to that of the creature standing beside you, or you might have come here together to fight for a particular cause. Whatever your reason for being here, we are all putting our lives on the line because we believe it is time for change in the World Below— time for all creatures to be heard.'

The crowd is silent now, and I frantically attempt to remember the ending of my planned speech. My mind goes blank. I look down and catch Aeron's eye, and I get a piece of divine inspiration.

'If a mere girl without magic from the World Above can defeat a Minotaur in his very own maze, then this creature army can topple mountains.' I hold my fist in the air. 'To victory!'

Crickets. You could hear a pin drop. Even hearing that would be better than the dead silence that fills the air. Then, as if a wave ripples through the soldiers, their fists pump the air. 'To victory!'

I get very little time to bask in my success. All too soon the troops are moving, and Aeron sends me a mock hurt look. 'Did you have to tell them about beating me. My reputation will be in tatters. What will Irene think?'

Over Aeron's head, my aunt winks, clearly amused.

'I think she'll be fine,' I tell the Minotaur as he moves my horse beside Irene's.

We wait for some signal from outside the dome that our watchers are asleep, then Mandor and two other witches open a portal wide enough for three horses to ride through. Behind them are three other witches to take over when they tire.

Ahead of us, the witches who will perform the sound suppression spells move forward, followed by Fairburn and the first wave. Our group moves behind, and seconds later, we're close to the Capitol walls. Fairburn is already urging his group forward—the advance party who will clear the way into the city.

Irene, Aeron, and I wait with the war council as the rest of our forces come through the opening. As the last of the troops emerge, a murmur ripples through the ranks.

I lean across to Irene. 'What is it?'

'It seems like there were fewer guards to send to sleep than we expected.'

'Is that a problem?' I ask.

My aunt waits until the portal closes before answering, 'I don't know. Then again, that's the problem with battle plans. They only hold up until first contact, and we're past that point now.'

11

AFTER FIRST CONTACT

WITH TREMBLING HANDS, I play the first notes of the sleep spell, loading it with intent and playing it through. It sounds eerie in the night air, and it's like the trees around me rustle in time.

Erina, the witch assigned to portal me back to camp should anything go wrong, gives me a thumbs-down.

What have I done wrong? It was working around the fire. Then again, I was relaxed, no one was relying on me, and no one would shoot me if they figured out what I was doing. How am I supposed to do this? How can I possibly block out everything else and concentrate on sending someone, anyone to sleep?

'Once more, with feeling,' I whisper as I close my eyes and bring up the vision of us sitting round the fire a couple of hours ago.

I start playing and humming the tune, wishing I could send my friends all to sleep where they would be safe. I send a little 'louder' spell along with the intent and carry on. Finally, I open my eyes and search for Erina. She sends a thumbs-up. Relief surges through me, encouraging me to play the song with more conviction. I even sing the words of the original lullaby under my breath.

'Lay thee down now to rest, may thy slumber be blessed….'

The bushes behind me rustle, and I stop. Erina returns and circumnavigates the plant, her sword at the ready. Chuckling under her breath, she returns to me. 'One of their scouts. He's completely out of it.'

I nod and carry on playing until Erina stands in front of me and chops her hand in a stop motion. When I'm no longer playing, she removes the plugs from her ears.

'Our watcher signalled that our section's all asleep.'

I lay the guitar in my lap. 'I expected that to be more difficult. Or at least take a little longer.'

'It *should* have been more difficult,' the guard says from behind Erina. 'Yesterday afternoon, there were three guard platoons in this section. Tonight, there are only perhaps fifty creatures in total.'

Erina chews her lip, considering our options. Should we check for more guards or return to camp? 'Is it possible some guards moved to another section, perhaps expecting us to head for the road?'

The guard shrugs. 'That's possible. However, it is not our problem. Our orders were to spell anyone in our section asleep, then return.'

I stare expectantly at Erina, who takes a moment to react, then opens a portal back to camp. Just as I'm about to step through, there is a noise above, and a dragon drops into the clearing in front of us.

'Oh my goddess,' the guard says, his jaw dropping at the sight of the enormous creature.

Noble One, you are called to the Dragon Queen's Court.

What? Now? We're just about to—

You promised, Snake. And she would not send me unless it was important.

I turn to Erina. 'Unfortunately, duty calls. I must return to the World Between.'

'You're going to the Dragon Realm?' the guard asks, assessing me with a newfound respect.

If the dragon being there wasn't enough, the guard is struck dumb as Ed'rathe crouches to allow me up.

I am afraid we must compress time, my dragon friend informs me as he leaps to the sky.

My dinner prepares to make its way from my stomach at the thought. *But if we do that, I'll be in no condition to talk to the Queen until perhaps tomorrow afternoon.*

Let me worry about that, he responds.

We land on the ledge outside the Dragon Queen's audience chamber seconds later. The only thing keeping me on Ed'rathe's back is his magic. The world swims around me, and I am about to lose the fight to save my dinner. Then a wash of healing magic sweeps over me, and the nausea is gone.

'So...' I turn to Ed'rathe once I reach the ground. 'You can cure sickness from time compression?'

I'm certain his face darkens, perhaps in a blush, but it's difficult to tell with dragons.

I was not given leave to heal you last time.

Right as I'm about to answer, Am'ratha comes flying down with Pris riding along. Am'nera, with the familiar figure of Adina on her back, follows closely behind. There's an old elf lord with them. It is clear from his resemblance to Bernais that this is Magnus Baaronson, the notorious elf responsible for transfiguring Percival. I feel the bile rise in my throat at his presence.

'So, time compression is a thing,' Pris says as she joins me, slipping her hand into mine so we can enter the hall as a united front.

I grimace. 'Yeah, it's not really my thing, though.'

She sends a side glance. 'You've done it before? When?'

'Later,' I say as the three dragons lead the way in, followed by the Baaronsons, who sweep past us as if we are beneath their notice.

'This is going to be a blast,' I say, wondering what the Dragon Queen could be thinking, calling this meeting now.

The audience chamber is deserted. Then again, it is the wee small hours before dawn. Our dragons lead us directly to the throne, and the Dragon Queen does not stand on ceremony.

There is to be war in your realm. Creature will fight creature, and there will be deaths. Some of you are prepared to go to extremes, perhaps even beyond the pale, to achieve victory. I wanted to take this opportunity to bring you here to broker a peace before it is too late. The Dragon Queen's tone is weary, and she pauses. Is she expecting someone to respond? No one does.

What is at stake here is more than the leadership of the World Below—it is the natural balance between all the worlds. On the one hand, I have two regents working day and night to restore that balance as fast as they can. On the other, I have thousands of creatures threatening to pull that all apart. Can we not spend a little time here and negotiate peace?

The Dragon Queen trains her fathomless eyes on each of us, ramming home her message. I'm guessing now is the time to speak. I tug at Pris's hand, pulling her back so we can talk privately as Magnus Baaronson steps forward.

'You cannot be serious about peace. Not when you bring me here with a dark elf and a half-breed gnome. They represent all that is wrong with our world, and they must be stamped out of existence. If we achieve nothing else with this war, we will ensure the purity of our races.'

'At the cost of draining magic from our world?' Pris splutters.

Magnus Baaronson does not turn our way. 'Then so be it.'

'This is madness,' Pris whispers. 'There is no negotiating with zealots.'

I give her hand a squeeze, urging her to try.

Pris turns slowly to the Dragon Queen and bows her head. 'Your Majesty,

I am sorry to say we cannot negotiate with anyone denying the rights of so many inhabitants of the World Below.'

Then, although it may tear families and communities apart and destroy magic in the World Below forever, it will be war.

'It was always going to be,' Magnus Baaronson says with a sneer, then turns on his heel and stalks from the room without waiting to be dismissed.

Adina tuts, then drags her eyes from her husband's back. 'If that is all, Your Majesty?'

Go.

Adina follows her husband, but Am'nera waits. The Dragon Queen and she are clearly talking, but their conversation is not for our ears. Soon after, she follows her bonded one out.

Priscilla, Am'ratha will take you back and make sure you are ready to fight. She will remain nearby until this is over. She cannot aid you in the battle, but she will ensure you remain as safe as possible.

'Thank you, Your Majesty.'

May your goddess go with you.

Pris and Am'ratha are dismissed, leaving Ed'rathe and me with the Dragon Queen.

Have you done what is required of you?

'Yes, Your Majesty.'

Good, then you and Ed'rathe can go. Your task is now to report on the progress of the war.

No. I can't watch my friends risk their lives while I do nothing. 'You don't need me to do that. Ed'rathe can keep you appraised. Let me fight.'

I swear the Dragon Queen tuts at me as if I'm being a willful child. Then I remember—Ed'rathe can report to the Dragon Queen, but he can't report to our Commanders. I will be in a position to provide information that could change the tide of the battle.

Something else that could change the tide of the battle would be having Queen Ariana and King Maddox join us. It's a shame the Dragon Queen will not consider…. Hold on, why did the Queen leave it to the eleventh hour to try and broker a peace? What changed?

'Your Majesty, if I may, can I ask you something?'

You may. I might not answer, but you will not be punished for your question.

'You seem worried about magic in the worlds. Are things not going well with Queen Ariana and King Maddox?'

Mmmm. You are very clever, Sneak Thief. Priscilla has chosen wisely.

It is not exactly an answer, but it tells me what I need to know.

'Can't Cecily be brought from the palace to help Ariana?'

Ariana wants to make amends for the mess she has created by saving magic for her people. She will not release her position as guardian. It may kill her, but she refuses to leave a mess for Cecily to clean up.

This is worse than I imagined.

There is little you can do about it, young gnome. You can only tread the path you are on.

'Thank you for sharing this with me, Your Majesty. And thank you for your consideration these past few days.'

You are welcome. I hope it has shown you that there are options for your future. Your family has served the worlds for generations, and there is no reason why you, too, cannot find a way to do so.

The Dragon Queen's eyes close, and I am clearly dismissed. For a being who doesn't want to become involved in the affairs of other realms, she certainly spends a lot of energy nudging creatures into positions she wants them in.

One of the Dragon Queen's eyes opens. Dammit, I forgot she can hear thoughts. I bow and leave before I can think anything else that might get me into trouble. Pris and Am'ratha are waiting for us outside.

'Are you able to tell me what she wanted you for?' Pris asks.

'She wants me to observe the battle,' I respond, not voicing my suspicions as to why she wants me there, as it's best not to acknowledge it in any way.

On the other hand, I don't think there's anything stopping me from letting her know about Queen Ariana, but this may not be the motivation she needs going into battle. Then again, the shock of finding out later could have an equally bad impact.

She leans in and kisses my cheek. 'Goddess be with you today.'

'And with you,' I say even though I really want to beg her to stay.

I draw in a breath. We can put it off no longer. Time to go to war. She quickly mounts, and a nanosecond later, she and Am'ratha vanish from view.

FROM OUR VANTAGE point to the side of the main gathering, Drow and I watch Pris give her speech. I was so worried about her, but she has come through. While not a conventional battle cry, it comes from her heart, and its impact is felt by everyone.

'I feel like a proud parent,' I say to Drow, and he laughs.

'Yes, it would appear your protégée has graduated. Now, can we go? We have a lot to organise in a short time.'

I nod, and the witch assigned to us opens a portal into the library at the university. The room is both different and familiar. I run my hand over the table where Drow and I had prepared my case for transformation reversal. I can still picture us sitting there, so full of hope and passion.

The library is empty. We had sent messages, anticipating the university activists to be waiting for our arrival. Through the stacks, I hear snoring. Perhaps we are not alone after all.

We wend our way through the corridors of books until we arrive at the front desk. Sprawled across it is a sleeping figure hidden under voluminous white hair. At our approach, the creature snuffles and turns, and I can almost make out the features of the university's head librarian.

'Jasper. Jasper!' Drow calls.

No response.

Drow strides over and shakes the elderly elf awake. Jasper rubs his eyes and glares at us. 'No need to be so rough.' He brushes his hair back from his face, then breaks into a grin. 'Oh, it is yourself, Drow. And you, too, Percival. Wait a moment.'

The librarian picks up an ornate bell and shakes it. There is no sound to be heard in the library, but somewhere in the halls, it will be ringing.

'We are so few now that we cannot waste resources waiting around for the likes of you to appear. Those you have requested to meet will arrive—'

Jasper's last words are drowned out by the scrape of wood on wood.

'I must get that door sorted,' Jasper says ruefully as about half a dozen young creatures barge into the room. Upon spotting Drow and me, they pull up and study us with wary eyes. My goodness, did Drow and I ever look that young? A male gnome follows behind them, entering at a more sedate pace.

'Are you sure this is them?' a tall, thin female with jet black hair asks Jasper.

'Oh, aye, this is them,' the librarian confirms.

The creature's eyes widen. 'I expected… I don't know… someone a little more… imposing.'

'Sorry to disappoint.' My tone of voice is as dour as I feel. 'Regardless of how uninspiring we are, we do have orders for you, and we have little time to waste.'

I catch Drow's eyes, and he's grinning. I'm pleased he finds this amusing.

'Right,' he starts. 'Let's get the lie of the land.'

He leads the way back to the large central table and draws out a map of the Capitol and surrounds from the tube he carried. We spelled it to show our troops, and he and I will update it as the battle progresses. A couple of the creatures provide books to stop the edges from curling.

'As you can see, our forces are already amassing outside the city. Do we have the head of campus security here?'

The gnome steps forward. 'I am he. My people are waiting by the entrance to the sewers for your orders.'

'Percival, if you would do the honours?'

I draw the gnome aside and hand him Fairburn's signed orders. 'The goal is to neutralise the guards at the Avondale Gate, keeping casualties to a minimum. Then you are to open the gates and let our forces in.'

The gnome nods once. 'Consider it done.'

He leaves more quickly than he entered. I return to the table and squeeze in beside Drow. Someone has helped him add the student teams to the map. In addition to our forces outside the gate, there is a team by the sewers and a couple of other groups congregating in the dining hall.

Once our creatures come in contact with enemy forces, they will send word via magical paper planes, and we will have a complete picture of the battle. Couriers will also drop in and out to provide updates and carry information back to Fairburn and the other leaders as the battle progresses. We hope no one will realise we are co-ordinating things from here, so Drow and I should remain safe.

Drow has finished setting up the map and has checked all the spells are in place. He is now briefing the students who will be sneaking into the ghetto.

'The idea is, you will mobilise the creatures and they in turn will take responsibility for spreading the word. Remember, they are to amass in groups large enough that the small number of guards will not want to stop them, and they are to be ready to move at sunup,' Drow explains.

'What if the guards call for reinforcements? Shouldn't they be ready to fight just in case?' a small gnome asks.

'That is why they are to wait until dawn before they move. By that time our forward platoons should have immobilised the main guard posts around the walls. Bernais will have been informed that we are attacking the Capitol and will be reluctant to release anyone from the palace precinct,' Drow explains.

'And please remind the lesser creatures to disperse when our army arrives. They are there to create a diversion, not to take part in the actual fighting,' I remind them.

They repeat their orders, and Drow says, 'Do not forget to send a note if you encounter enemy soldiers. The more information we have, the better this will go today.'

They pat their pockets to show they have the spelled paper, salute, then scamper off.

There are two leaders left, the tall female creature and her shorter male companion.

'You are leading the expedition to free the prisoners being held in the hospital?' Drow asks.

'Yes. We pulled together a group of the strongest magic workers in the senior class, along with a couple of witches who, like me, specialise in dismantling spells cast by others.'

'Excellent,' Drow says. 'I believe you have figured out a way to enter, but we have not been told about your strategy for extracting the prisoners. They will be weakened and disoriented due to insufficient sustenance, so you may need assistance.'

The girl grins, and I would not want to be on the receiving end of her malice.

'Oh, we're not getting them out. We plan to hold the building and get the creatures back on their feet there.'

'How are you going to manage that with so few in your team?' I ask, worried we might have to change their plan on the fly, and we do not have much time.

'We expect there will be some attempt to take back the building because some of the most vocal and connected creatures working against the council are being held in there, and at the very least, they would be useful hostages,' the girl explains.

'That is why we targeted the release of these creatures as being of the utmost importance,' Drow says. 'We think Bernais will attempt to regain control of the building. That is why we had asked for a plan to remove the prisoners and bring them here.'

There is that grin again. It really is most off-putting.

'That is a poor plan for several reasons.' The female holds up her hands and begins counting off. 'First, it would draw attention here, and the council may find out this is our command centre. Second, there are too many opportunities for ambushes if we move the prisoners. Third, some prisoners will need time before they're moved—time that we would have to defend the building and support an evacuation. And, finally, the hospital is easier to defend than the university.'

Drow is nodding, clearly impressed by this logic. 'It could work. How do you propose to hold the building and care for the prisoners with so few creatures?'

'The council has done most of the work for us. They have sealed the windows and closed off all but two of the doors. Once we have disabled the guards and sent them packing, our strongest magicians will seal the final two doors. After that, most of our efforts will be spent ensuring the wards remain strong, except for a few creatures who will head to the roof with some nasty little surprises we have been gathering. We aim to hunker down and wait the war out.'

'Nasty surprises?' I ask.

The grin is now almost gleeful. 'One student from the World Above got us a recipe for something called a Molotov cocktail.'

Drow and I share a look. 'I think she has defence covered,' I say.

'Defence is good, but what about caring for the prisoners?' Drow asks.

'Felix here is part of the Fieth clan, and they have a formidable network of creatures who are good at…. shall we say, working in the shadows. They have been gathering food and medical supplies and storing them in the sewers beneath the building. When we have control, they will begin bringing up supplies. I believe they also have some volunteer medical professionals who will assist once our spell breakers have worked their magic.'

Drow raises his eyebrows, and I nod my approval. I am impressed with the plan and how organised they are. I turn to Felix. 'And your family…. They are happy to be involved?'

Tears well in the young gnome's eyes. 'Some of my family are being held by the council, and still more are stuck inside the palace. We can't do anything about those in the palace, but at least they are not being tortured. We will do anything to get our creatures out of the council's grasp.'

Apart from the trembling of his bottom lip, Felix is stoic and shows a firm resolve. Snake's grandfather, the Fieth, would be proud of his young relation.

'We can find nothing to object to with this change of plan,' Drow says. 'You may proceed. Good luck.'

'We will not fail,' the girl says.

'If you do not mind me asking,' I say to her, 'What is your name?'

Again that grin. It reminds me of someone. 'I am Renata. You know my uncle, Mandor.'

I try to hide my shock, and she laughs. 'Everyone tells me I am a lot like him.'

'Indeed,' I say. 'He would be proud of you.'

For the first time, her sang-froid waivers, showing how young she still is. 'Thank you.'

When the two have gone, Drow and I watch the map and trace the departure of our young warriors.

'They should be in class, not undertaking missions that could end their lives,' Drow says, weariness tinging his voice.

'We all do what we must in times like this.' Jasper's voice drifts through the stacks, and he follows soon after it, a tray with steaming mugs of coffee and a pile of sandwiches preceding him. 'If you consider the consequences of not overthrowing this corrupt council, you will understand why they are taking such risks.'

The tray thumps down on the table beside the map. 'Make time to take sustenance now, because when the action starts you will need all your energy,' he instructs.

We do as he bids while watching the map. Jasper keeps the coffee flowing, and we adjust the map as spelled paper brings us written updates from the creature ghetto. As time marches on and we have not heard from the prison or from the contingent sent to open the gates, my anxiety rises, making my stomach knot. The only consolation is that we can still see them moving on the map.

Finally, a note arrives from the gates. There has been a setback, but they'll keep us informed.

'Oh well,' Drow says as he updates the map. 'It would not be a proper battle if everything went to plan.'

'Please, Goddess,' I pray, 'Help them get through the gates. If they do not, all will be lost.'

MAY THE GODDESS be with you this day, Am'ratha tells me before flying off to find a place where she can watch the battle that is close enough for her to rescue me should she need to.

I am still a little wobbly from the time compression even though Am'ratha swears she healed me, and my ears are still ringing from her lecture on the many reasons I should keep out of the fighting today.

The air is heavy with tension as I make my way through the army. From half-heard conversations, I gleaned it was partially battle nerves, but there is also growing concern that it was almost sunrise and we weren't moving.

Irene and Aeron are laughing like hyenas when I reach the front of the forces. I'm about to snap that this is not the time and place for jokes before it hits me—this actually *is* the time and place. Seeing their leaders so relaxed will only boost the confidence of the soldiers.

I reach up and scratch my mount's neck. 'Aeron, what's going on? Why are we still here?'

Irene leans in and whispers, 'Do not react, and laugh like we're sharing a joke. It's because the scouts have not called us forward.'

I grin inanely at her and hide my mouth as if I'm stifling a giggle.

'And why am I acting like a half-wit?'

'It's crucial that we appear unbothered by the fact that dawn is breaking and we are not inside the Capitol.' Aeron speaks close by my ear as he pretends to adjust my horse's tack.

'What do we do?' I ask.

At that moment the head of my grandmother's forces rides over.

'Is it time, Howden?' Irene asks.

'It is, Princess. If we don't go now, we will lose the cover of darkness. We must trust that by the time we reach the gates, Fairburn will have everything in hand.'

'Right you are,' my aunt says, hauling herself up onto her horse.

Aeron helps me up, then takes his position between Irene and me. Howden glances over his shoulder to ensure we're all ready, then leads us forward.

We don't have any magic workers to muffle the sounds like Fairburn's troops do, and I am surprised by the roar that moving so many soldiers makes. Darkness may still hide our exact numbers, but anyone awake on this side of the city will be in no doubt that we are coming.

Fairburn's troops wait in the shadows of the wall, and we approach them at a right angle. When we halt, the noise coming from inside the city makes it clear that Bernais's guards are fighting to keep the gates closed.

'We may need to blast our way in,' Howden says to Fairburn.

The centaur nods. This option is far from perfect because it will reveal our presence and allow Bernais to position his troops to mount a better defence. Fairburn is about to give the order when one side of the gate swings open.

As I release the breath I was holding, a voice inside the walls yells, 'Sound the warning.'

Into the night air, the single clang of a bell rings before a body falls from atop the guard tower. It is like the world holds a breath, wondering of that single clang has signalled the death knell to our plans.

Ignoring the interruption, Fairburn rallies his team to action. 'Take the other guard posts. We don't want anyone coming in behind our forces.'

As they scatter along pre-arranged routes, the Commander of our forces turns to Howden and says, 'Your path to the palace may not be as straight as we would have wished,' before following his troops.

'Right-o,' Howden says, 'We're going with plan B, the three-pronged approach. Irene.'

'Group one, to me,' she commands and swings to the right. Aeron and I follow, to make our way round the city walls towards the palace's delivery entrance. Group two is to go the long way round to the servants' entrance to the left, leaving the main force to take the most direct route to the palace.

'Why was this plan B?' I whisper. 'I mean, surely a single point of attack would be bad tactics.'

'Normally,' Irene says. 'However, the original plan moved our forces directly to the palace under a spell of silence, and we would have fanned out once we got there. This way will take longer. We don't have enough creatures able to use muffling spells on all three groups, and we're at greater risk of ambush because our forces are split.'

And this is why Irene is in charge.

Footsteps and the clink of metal on metal fill the air as we slink through the shadows. I strain my ears for any sign that the demonstration has started so we can pick up the pace. As the sun turns the sky pink, shouts ring out from closer to the palace, and Irene gives the order to speed up.

'I'm not sure that is the demonstration—it sounds more like a skirmish. Maybe they're barricading the roads,' Aeron says, hefting his mighty sword.

I draw my weapon as Irene commands, 'Eyes about.'

A handful of creatures peel off and scout ahead while everyone else prepares to fight.

A couple of turns later, we encounter several open doors. Aeron checks each dwelling before we pass, ensuring we are not ambushed from behind. When he returns to my side, he says, 'They are empty, and not just of creatures. They've been stripped bare.'

'Why would they do that? Are they leaving the city?' I ask.

Aeron barks a laugh, and when we turn the next corner, I understand the joke. Under the watchful gaze of a handful of soldiers, a stream of men, women and children are carrying furniture to a makeshift barricade.

The female gnome at the back of the line turns and screams when she sees us. She drops the wooden kitchen chair she's carrying, grabs two children, and disappears down a side alley. More civilians follow her as the guards scramble over the makeshift structure blocking the road.

Irene calls, 'Halt. Take positions.'

Aeron bustles me backwards as some of the troops melt into doorways along the street. Still others break away down the alley, and I can just make out shadowy figures climbing to rooftops.

'What are you doing?' I ask as Aeron leads my horse back around the corner.

'Keeping you out of range. We do not know what weapons they have, and I do not want to give them a clear shot if their human mercenaries have brought guns with them.'

'Oh, I hadn't thought of that.'

'Let Irene and her people clear the way. Then we can move forward.'

'I can't stay back here and let others fight for me,' I protest, a power struggle between fear and embarrassment going on in my head.

Aeron maintains a tight hold on the horse's reins. 'Most of these creatures fight for Irene as part of the Loch Ness battalion. They have this under control, and you will only get in their way.'

I nudge my mount forward so I can at least see what is happening while trying to find the right words to convince Aeron to let me join in. Before I form a coherent thought, arrows rain down on the defenders behind the barricades, and the air fills with their screams.

The soldiers in the doorways make their way towards the barricade under cover of the eaves. Instead of climbing over, as I would have done, they dismantle the structure piece by piece.

They are fast and efficient, and it is only a matter of minutes before Irene emerges from the alley and calls her troop back to her. We join the back of the procession through the gap in the barricade.

I've watched battles in movies and seen the aftermath of war on the news, but nothing could prepare me for how much blood runs over the cobbles. Nor for the tang of iron on the air or the smell of bodily fluids released from injured and dying creatures.

Although my gorge rises in my throat, I force myself to imprint the scene on my mind. I helped make the decision to fight today, and I am partially responsible for every wound, lost limb, and death that occurs as a result of that.

Irene dispatches a handful of soldiers to check for survivors to be taken prisoner or transported to the hospital. I don't like their chances of finding anyone alive, but it still has to be done.

'Does it get any easier?' I ask Aeron.

The Minotaur raises sad eyes to meet my horrified ones and shakes his shaggy head. 'Never. And it should not. If that happened, making the decision to go to war would be too simple.'

Would I have been so cavalier about going into battle if I had known what today would be like? Or would I have spent more time focusing on a diplomatic solution? It is difficult to say. But one thing I *can* say is, I don't want to see anything like this ever again.

As the sun shines brightly in the clear blue sky, shouts of creature protests ring through the air. I shake off my shock and heartbreak over the death that is all around me. We are in this now, for better or worse, and the only way is forward.

WAR IS MESSY

ED'RATHE GLIDES DOWNWARDS and gently settles on the clifftop. Am'ratha lifts her purple head, and the tingle in the air tells me the siblings are talking.

Am'ratha says Pris is back in place and that we have missed nothing.

'Thank you, Am'ratha.'

She blinks twice, then drops her head to rest it on her front paws, her gaze directed back towards the Capitol. The dragon on the other side of Am'ratha turns her head, appraises me, then turns away. I get the impression this unknown dragon has dismissed me as unimportant, and that irks me.

Do not mind Am'rena. Princess Cecily has forbidden any rescue attempts, and she has been sitting here brooding for days.

The pre-dawn light glints off the green dragon's scales as she opens an eye. *I do not need your pity, youngling. Save it for those who fight today.*

'I meant no disrespect. I was merely thinking how difficult it is to stand by while someone you care for risks themselves.'

Her eyes widen as if in surprise. *Yes, Snake, I see you do understand. But sometimes knowing you are nearby is worth something to those we love.*

Now it is my turn to be surprised. It hadn't occurred to me that knowing we are here might provide a comfort for those who are in the midst of battle.

Someone has to rescue them if things go wrong. Ed'rathe's tone is dry.

The sun peeks over the horizon, turning the sky pink. Birds in the nearby trees sing in the morning until unfamiliar sounds carried on the wind silence them. It has begun.

Ed'rathe lowers his head. *Come, Snake, it is time.*

With some trepidation, I climb onto Ed'rathe's back. When I'm settled, the dragon takes off out to sea, then turns back around and heads towards the Capitol. I know very little about the battle plans except that once the mercenaries have been engaged, the palace guard are to join in and create a second front.

In the palace courtyard, a mass of creatures is chanting and taunting the human mercenaries. The soldiers hold their positions but seem a little perplexed.

We circle wider and find three columns of soldiers wending their way towards the palace—one group fighting through a barricade to reach their destination.

Back at the palace, the mercenaries are being reinforced while the rest of their number pull apart their makeshift camp in the palace grounds. They are clearly aware this protest is the precursor to something bigger and are preparing for it.

While the grounds are a hive of activity, the palace is strangely quiet. On a balcony stands a lone centaur watching the action, but there is no sign the Queen's Guard are even up. Did the message not get through?

Ed'rathe, can you ask Am'rena if Cecily got the messages about the plans for today?

The air sings with magic, and the conversation between dragons goes on for much longer than I anticipated.

She says Cecily will not commit their force until they are certain we will win. Guard Captain Georgio advised that to strip the palace of its protections would be a disaster should we lose.

Really? Creatures are putting their lives on the line, and they are protecting themselves?

Even though these creatures are also keeping my mother and the Fieth family members taking refuge in the palace safe, their lack of action puts everyone else at greater risk, and that makes me angry.

They are only doing their job, Noble One. The palace guard's primary aim is to keep the royal line safe.

I huff because I can see the logic. Still, don't they understand that if they don't engage, all will be lost?

Ed'rathe banks again, and as he does, I make out a small group—mercenaries, judging from their dress—climbing the palace walls. There are not enough of them to take on the might of the Queen's Guard, but there are enough for an assassination attempt on Princess Cecily.

Let me down, Ed'rathe.

I can tell Am'rena about the men.

We don't know what they're up to, and I don't want to give the palace guards any excuse not to join the main battle.

I cannot help you if you leave me, and you cannot help the main forces from there.

True, I won't be able to follow the battle, but I must make sure Princess Cecily is okay. Also, it might help to remind her personally what is at stake today.

I have to do this, Ed'rathe.

My dragon's response is to take me out of sight of the climbing soldiers and lower me towards a balcony round the corner. I ignore the long drop to the ground three stories below, and I'm grateful Ed'rathe uses his magic to ensure I land safely on the balcony after sliding down his leg.

I will continue to circle. Come back here if you need me to pick you up.

After wandering through the empty suite in the dawn light, bumping into sofas and tables as I go, I fumble for the doorknob, then stick my head into the corridor.

To my right I make out two centaur-like figures guarding a stairwell. My immediate thought is to call them, but in the time it takes to explain who I am and why I'm here, the mercenaries will be long gone. I can always call for help if I need them. What am I saying? Of course I'll need them. I can't fight five men alone.

Ahead of me, the sounds of boots trying to creep across a stone floor attracts my attention. Crouching, I duck my head around the corner and quickly pull back. There aren't only five men, but more like twenty standing in the hallway, consulting a map by torchlight.

There is no way two guards and I can take on this amount of people. Or can we? Mender said singing the sleep spell should work. I guess I'm about to find out if that's true.

I crouch down and start singing the spell in a soft voice, filling it with intention and using a direction spell to send my voice along the corridor.

One of the soldiers glances over his shoulder. 'Hey, what's that?'

The others turn. Two of them rush towards me, and my voice cracks a little and I lose the melody.

There's no time for subtle now. I stand up, take a deep breath and bellow out the words, willing the soldiers to sleep as if my life depends on it. And it just might because the entire group is now bearing down on me, and they'll be here any second.

The lead soldier is about four steps away, drawing his sword, ready to attack, when the weapon slips from his grasp, and he drops to the ground. The man behind him falls over the prone body and is asleep before he hits the floor.

In a split second, the spell starts to take hold, and I can actually see the other soldiers' eyes droop. Slowly they crumple one by one, except for the three at the back. They act quickly and stuff their fingers in their ears. As their mates fall around them, they stride towards me.

From behind me the clatter of hooves on stone bolsters, my resolve and I force more intent into my song. It only slows the two men and one woman, but it's buying me some time for the cavalry to arrive. As two centaurs push past me, I drop to the floor, exhaustion pulling me under. The next thing I know, I'm being nudged by a hoof.

'Oi, you, up.'

I stare up into the brown eyes of a centaur guard whose face is way too close to mine for comfort.

'He doesn't smell like the others. He's creature, not human,' he says to the other guard.

'I think he was the one singing,' his female companion says.

'Were you?'

Again that intense stare.

'Yes, a sleep spell. Did you get them all? I think they were trying to get to Princess Cecily.'

'Well, obviously. But what are *you* doing here?'

'I need to talk with the princess?'

The centaur stands back and snuffles. 'Huh, you and thousands of others.'

Shaking my head to clear the magic hangover, I search for inspiration in the fog of my brain before crossing my fingers and saying, 'But I *really* need to speak with her. I have a message from the Dragon Queen.'

Okay, the Queen didn't specifically ask me to update Princess Cecily with what was happening with her aunt, but they don't know that.

Again the centaur snuffles, which I'm thinking is him laughing, but I can't be certain. His companion sniffs the air.

'Hermes, I think we might have to at least take this one to Georgio. He has the smell of the Fieth about him, and I think one of them was with the dragons. Can't you smell that other scent?'

Hermes shakes his head. 'Sorry, hay fever, my nose isn't working at its best.'

Okay, maybe not laughing.

'All right, Fiamma, but it's on your head. I can't take any more kitchen duty.'

'You all right managing this lot. I already called for backup to help take them to the dungeons.' She nods towards the shackled men.

Hermes tests the restraints and assures her he can deal with them. Fiamma leads me past the mostly sleeping soldiers.

'How did you get them tied up so fast?' I ask.

'We centaurs have little magic, but we can transport a few chains from the dungeon when we need to.' She looks towards the stairs where another couple of centaurs appear. 'And send a message for help.'

'Hey, can you wake them before you go?' Hermes asks.

I smile ruefully. 'Sorry, mate, I was only taught the sleeping spell.'

'Try a bucket of water,' Fiamma calls over her shoulder, laughing to herself at the thought.

OUT THE LIBRARY window, the Capitol stretches out towards the horizon. Ignoring the occasional shouts and clanging of metal and the empty courtyard, it feels like I'm studying here again. I rub a hand over my weary eyes and return to the table.

Jasper is asleep, his head resting on his arms. I gather the teacups and consider heading to the kitchen to make a fresh brew. Drow is gazing at the map, magical notes piled up beside him, and I'm distracted from my task.

'What is the matter?' I ask.

He points at a building close to the university. 'Renata and her group arrived a little while ago, but I have not received an update. I fear for them. And see here. We broke into three groups, so we are following plan B, but no one has informed me of the reason or let me know about enemy forces'

I place the cups on the table and move until I am beside my friend. 'We cannot worry about every deviation from the plan. We were aware it would not be a walk in the park and that changes would have to be made. That is why we maintain the map—so the Commanders can send for an overview and adjust their tactics.'

The paper plane updates have allowed Drow to spell in the opposition forces, and it is clear we have taken a number of captives.

'Where are we holding the enemy soldiers?'

Drow raises a weary head. 'We had planned to use the main guardhouse, but it is already full. I have sent word to bring the overflow to the university refectory.'

A knot of worry tugs in my stomach at these words. 'Was that wise? It may turn attention our way.'

Running a hand through already messy hair, Drow's gaze returns to the map. 'It was the only area within our control large enough to accommodate the numbers. They will be in chains and have guards with them. Besides, there is no way for prisoners to find out we are here.'

It all sounds reasonable, but worry claws at my gut. The map is a study in chaos and does nothing to soothe me.

'What does that mean?' I point at a swirling pattern outside the city walls.

Drow's brows draw together. 'I have no idea. It appeared there about ten minutes ago.'

'It is not something you spelled in from the dispatches?'

He shakes his head. 'No. But I did spell the map to pick up any seriously bad weather or large groups of creatures in the area.'

The knot pulls tighter. 'And the sky is clear… so, a group of creatures?'

'Mmm… perhaps. Or maybe livestock?'

I shake my head. Large herds of animals do not just wander around the World Below untended. And why would they be heading for the Capitol? There were no markets being held, with mercenaries camped out in the palace square.

'We will monitor it, and I'll send a message to Fairburn so he's aware.'

Drow picks up a clean sheet of paper and begins writing. We're so engrossed in the message that it takes a moment for us to realise a portal has opened into the room. It is only Jasper sitting bolt upright that alerts us.

Eleanora, Eugenia, and Euphemia step through the opening, followed by the half dozen witches who had remained with them at the campsite. Mandor is last through, and he closes the portal.

'I thought you were going on to the hospital with Mender and Heart,' I say to the witch sisters.

'We were,' Genie starts.

'Until we checked on the soldiers we'd sent to sleep before leaving,' Effie adds.

'Yes, we thought rather than let them join up with their friends, we'd take as many of them prisoner as we could with the handcuffs and shackles we had,' Mandor says as he joins us, 'but we found there were far fewer than our earlier reports had indicated.'

Drow stops writing, 'How many fewer?'

The witches look at one another.

'Perhaps less than half of what was counted earlier in the day,' Mandor says, and the others nod their agreement.

Drow and I lock eyes, then we both look at the map and the swirling mass moving closer to the Capitol gates. 'Is it possible surrounding our camp was a feint intending to force us to move before we were fully ready?' Drow asks, voicing my own concerns.

'We need to find out what that is,' I add.

'Alyce,' Mandor calls, and a witch steps forward. 'Go to the guard tower nearest to there and find out what is causing this disturbance.'

The room is silent while we wait for the young witch to return. Minutes later our worst fears are confirmed.

'It's the guards we saw heading to our camp yesterday. They must have turned around and headed back at a quick magic-assisted march when night fell,' she informs us.

'And I'll bet our missing guards from the perimeter are not far behind them,' Eleanora comments.

Jasper leans over for a better view. 'Looks like our creatures will be caught between them and the human soldiers.'

'Not if the Queen's Guard in the palace attack the mercenaries from behind,' I say, although a little doubt is worming its way into my confident tone. We should have had a note by now, telling us the guards have left the palace.

Effie has drifted over to the window. 'Worrying will not help, the die is cast, and we must now wait to see the outcome. Percival? Who is that coming into the courtyard—they look like prisoners.'

I join Effie, and Ellie and Genie cram in behind us.

'They are prisoners. Drow says we ran out of space in the guard quarters.'

'You can no longer stay here unprotected,' Ellie asserts, and her sisters mumble agreement. 'We'll send a message to the hospital that we're staying unless they desperately need us.'

'But you did not want to fight,' I protest.

'Defending you is not fighting,' Genie tells me.

We continue to watch the string of prisoners make their way into the building to the right, while in the background, Mandor gives instructions to the other witches. Once the prisoners vanish and the witches have left to deliver news of the new danger, we resume our positions at the table and witness the enemy's rear guard entering the city.

FOR THE MOMENT before we enter the square in front of the palace, it's like I'm watching something out of a movie. Hordes of creatures are shouting at the human mercenaries who are attempting to fend them off without breaking their lines. The soldiers are being forced backwards until they can move no more. It's like they've hit a brick wall, and perhaps they have.

'Have the Queen's Guard set up a shield around the palace? Is that how they've been keeping safe?' I ask Aeron.

His huge shoulders rise in a shrug. 'It could be them, but could be us.

Centaurs have little magic, so they cannot protect the entire palace. But I guess they could put up a targeted shield to slow down an attacking force.'

Irene signals that the other groups have arrived at the square, then sends one of her scouts to clear the area. Some creatures who have been protesting head for the streets, but others want to join the battle and are creating chaos.

In the confusion, a group of mercenaries surrounds some protestors and takes them hostage, then order the other creatures to leave or the hostages die. To prevent panic, Fairburn sends in a group of trained creatures on a rescue mission. Then it is all on.

We surge forward into the marketplace to support the initial troops as the scared protestors flee towards the emptying streets. The area is so crowded, Irene orders us to get off our horses and send them back out of the arena.

I've experienced fighting before, have even fought for my survival, but nothing can prepare you for confronting an adversary in battle. My ears ring from the noise, and my stomach roils from the smells—and not just blood either.

A few minutes in, my energy is draining fast, and my sword feels twice the size—and I'm only at the edge of the fighting, helping the protestors away from danger. There is no way to conserve energy when you are under constant attack, and I can't fight like this for long.

Beside me Aeron roars, and I half turn to see blood streaming down Irene's arm from a gash. Aeron makes his way to her, and I follow in his wake. By the time we arrive, she has bound her wound and is ready to fight again.

I glance towards the palace, hoping that by now they have sent out a force of guards to aid us. The building is eerily quiet.

'Get Irene to safety,' I order Aeron.

'No, I am fine. I've had worse in training. But you should get Pris out of here,' the princess tells the Minotaur.

I glare at her as she glares back. And the only reason we're not cut down is that Aeron is protecting both of us.

Irene pinches the bridge of her nose and closes her eyes. Finally she says, 'All right, we protect each other.'

I don't know what that means, but I get the idea when Aeron and Irene turn shoulder to shoulder, leaving a space for me to create a triangle. They have me angled towards the back of the fighting, protecting their backs, but Aeron hasn't carried me away, so I'm not complaining.

Am'ratha?

Princess, concentrate on the fight.

I grit my teeth and parry a blow from a mercenary who looks even younger than me. He's swept away by the crush of creatures still moving to the streets.

I need you to find out from Am'nera what's happening with the Royal Guard. We really need them.

All right.

There is a long silence. Then it stretches for even longer.

Am'ratha?

She is still talking with your mother.

Still talking? What's there to discuss? *Tell her to tell my mother to look out the window. If she doesn't want the creatures fighting for her to be wiped out in a single battle, then she should send out—*

'We're trapped!' a cry rings out.

Before my mind can process that, a blast comes out of nowhere and fells a creature beside me.

'They're using magic against us.' Aeron bellows.

'Who is?' I'm confused. That attack came from behind. Oh my goddess, we've been outflanked.

Am'ratha, get my mother! Now!

Then a shockwave sweeps over the marketplace, and in its wake, everyone holds still.

'Was that another magic attack?' I ask Aeron.

'I have no idea what that was, but it was nothing good.'

ALL OR NOTHING

'WHILE I APPRECIATE your help in foiling the enemy incursion this morning, the head of my guard and Ariana's chief advisor, Elias, have made it clear that if we were to lose the battle today having committed our forces to the fray, we might as well give up now. I promised to hold the throne for Aunt Ariana, so I must follow their advice.'

Although the woman in front of me is wearing jeans and a denim shirt, she is no less regal. She is definitely Petunia's daughter, and I can see where Pris gets her haughtiness from.

'That's the whole point,' I argue. 'Today is an all-or-nothing situation. And if you don't help, it will definitely be nothing.'

'I am aware of the knife edge we are on, and I am not standing idly by. Elias and Georgio are watching proceedings, and the guard is ready to go on their command.'

This isn't working. Telling her about Queen Ariana sacrificing herself for magic had only made Princess Cecily more determined to stay out of the battle today. What will make her change her mind?

'Pris is down there fighting.'

Cecily barely flinches, but something changes in her eyes. There was also a gasp from the creature standing by the door—Pris's father. The princess draws her bottom lip between her teeth, and it's so reminiscent of Pris when she's worried that it almost breaks my heart.

'And the Dragon Queen will not let this battle turn into a prolonged war without intervening.'

THE WORLD BETWEEN

Before Princess Cecily can respond, a wave of power travels through the room, then it's as if the whole world stands still. When it is over, no one moves.

We mourn the loss,
The Worlds all weep,
Her memory safe,
The dragons will keep.

The haunting words rumble through my very bones, and a sadness pulses in my chest like a heartbeat.

'What was that?' I whisper.

Princess Cecily places her hand on my arm. 'You heard that?'

I nod as I realise many in the room did not.

'It was a dragon sending.' Princess Cecily pauses as though listening to someone, then adds, 'Am'rena says Queen Ariana is dead.'

Gasps ripple around the room.

A taller, slimmer version of King Maddox moves to Princess… *Queen* Cecily's side.

'Malachai?' The word is a question.

In response, he wraps an arm around her. 'It was inevitable this day would arrive when you retained your position in the line of succession. It is no longer enough to keep the seat warm for Queen Ariana. Now *you* must decide what is right for the realm.'

She doesn't even wait a heartbeat before beckoning over a youngling dressed in palace livery. 'Tell Georgio it is time to release the guards.'

'Thank you,' I say, my entire body sagging with relief before it dawns on me that I am now in the presence of the Queen of the World Below. 'Your Majesty, I have much to do on behalf of the Dragon Queen—'

'You may go, Snake.' She gives my arm a squeeze. 'And stay safe.'

'I will, ma'am,' I respond before hurrying from the room.

Ed'rathe, I am ready.

I meet the dragon at the agreed place and find it's harder to climb up than it was to get down. Thank goodness for dragon magic, or it would be impossible. Ed'rathe takes to the skies, sweeping over the chaos in the courtyard. I can't see Pris anywhere, and worry churns my stomach.

Am'ratha would tell me if she is in danger, and you would see my sister dragon fly to her rescue.

That is a little comforting. Hold on, do they think of danger as mortal peril or wounded? I can't bear to think of either.

Let's go a little wider and see what's happening in the rest of the Capitol, I say.

Ed'rathe banks to the left and takes me out towards the university. As we sweep over the streets, my gaze is drawn to a group of about thirty creatures skulking in the shadows about five minutes out from the main university buildings.

No, that's not good. Drow and Percival are the only ones there, and we will lose our command centre if they are captured. I tap on Ed'rathe's scales.

Can you set me down in the university courtyard?

I feel rather than hear him sigh.

It is safer for you if we are together.

I can't let anything happen to my uncle and my friend. If there is a chance I can stop it….

I understand.

Ed'rathe sweeps around and gently drops to the ground. My feet have not quite found purchase when Ed'rathe snorts a warning, and I look up to find we're surrounded by armed creatures.

'Grossman, what luck. We come to ensure the students stay out of the battle, and we find ourselves a couple of traitors,' a familiar creature says.

Ed'rathe tenses beside me, and I can't believe Giles Coronas would be stupid enough to attack a dragon. As Grossman Green steps from behind Giles's left shoulder, his face twists into a mask of fear, and I worry that the elf may just be that stupid.

I hold up my hands in a placating gesture. 'Now, Giles, while I am a legitimate target, you don't want to start anything with the dragons.'

The elf sneers, and the malice in his eyes sends shivers down my spine. 'I've studied enough dragon lore to know that you and he are in some way bonded, and to get to you, I must go through him.'

I don't want Ed'rathe getting involved in this. 'I'll send him away.'

'He won't go. He will stay and defend you to the death if he must,' Giles spits. 'And the best thing is… if I ask even one of my creatures to not join the fight, he will not use his dragon fire in case he hurts them.'

Ed'rathe?

He is right, Noble One. I cannot return home head held high if I desert you.

And the dragon fire thing?

That is also correct. It would shame me to hurt an innocent bystander, and dragon fire is not a precise weapon. But I am still a formidable foe without it.

Resting a hand on his flank, I consider my options. I'm sure Ed'rathe can fight well, but the courtyard is not big enough for him to move with ease.

My gaze falls on Grossman Greene. The goblin has been strangely quiet. He shakes his head as if he's urging me not to fight. Why would he do that? The air pops beside me, and I jump with fright when Mandor, Eleanora, and Euphemia appear.

'I think this evens up the odds a little, don't you?' Eleanora grins with a ferocity I never thought I would see on the normally caring witch's face.

Giles sneers. 'You have no weapons!'

Pop.

Eugenia appears with an array of swords and parcels them out. There is even one for me, although I have no idea how to use it.

'Where?' I ask.

Eugenia winks. 'The university mess hall has an amazing display of ancient weapons. I don't know how sharp they are after all this time, so you might want to tend to the blade before we begin.'

There is a hum of magic as the others do as she suggests, but I think it's better if mine remains blunt so I don't inadvertently cut someone in my ineptitude.

If you position yourself near my flank, then I can use teeth and claws to protect your back.

I tell the others what Ed'rathe suggests, and we're just getting into position when the fighting begins. Grossman comes straight for me, sword in front, and it doesn't take me long to realise he's as incompetent at this as I am. After one ringing blow, my sword slips from my hand, and I think I'm done for. Then, as if he's evening up the odds, Grossman lets go of his own weapon and comes at me fists swinging.

I centre myself, ready for impact, then pull back my arm and land a satisfying punch to his jaw. As our struggle continues, I catch a glimpse of the scene around me, and it's not good. My team all have injuries, some more serious than others. Mandor is working hard to keep Giles at bay, but the elf is ferocious in his determination to beat us. This fighting for your life thing is terrifying, and the scene doesn't cut away when it gets too messy.

No one is going near Ed'rathe—I guess the wrath of a dragon is something to be feared after all. Still, even though Ed'rathe has our backs, we are outnumbered, and we're tiring. If something doesn't happen soon, then we're done for.

My distraction costs me as Grossman lands a blow that sets my ears ringing. I shake my head to clear it, but there appear to be more creatures in front of me than there were before. My head swims, and I'm not sure if it's a reaction to the blow or the certainty I'm about to die.

'Keep fighting, you ninny,' a familiar voice yells in my ear as Verona pushes

Grossman out of the way. 'Where's your sword?'

I glance at the ground and duck one of Grossman's swings as I bend to pick up the useless item.

There's a groan, and Grossman stumbles back, a sword sticking out of his shoulder. Blood stains his shirt red, and the smell of warm iron hits me, sending my head swimming, and it's all I can do to remain on my feet.

Ed'rathe roars, and the earth shakes. Grossman loses his balance and collapses, and I scan the area as Gregor and several other students close in on the rebels.

'It's over,' Gregor shouts. 'Drop your weapons.'

Most of the enemy does as he commands, but a few around Giles stand back to back, ready to fight till the end.

'You,! What are you doing here?' Giles snarls, pushing through his followers as his daughter moves to stand beside Gregor.

'I know you won't understand, Father, but I'm doing what's right,' Verona says.

'You're besotted with him, and he's turned your head.' Spittle flies from Giles's mouth as his eyes spin wildly. 'Can't you see this madness between you and him is what we are trying to stop?'

He's lost it, and he's going to do something stupid. At that exact moment, Giles leaps forward, sword aimed at Gregor's heart.

What happens next is so fast, it's a blur of arms and weapons. Then Giles falls to the ground, a sword in his side. Verona drops to her knees, tears streaming down her face, her hands empty.

'Dad.' Her voice is full of pain and regret.

Behind her, Gregor clutches his stomach and blood seeps through his fingers. He stares at his wound as if he can't believe it's there before collapsing silently behind her.

I'm so transfixed by the scene, I almost don't hear Mandor say, 'Snake, it's safe. We can take it from here, Ed'rathe.'

I do feel cold air as Ed'rathe shuffles away. *Do you want to come with me?*

I survey the devastation and shudder as Verona's scream of anguish when she sees Gregor on the ground cuts me to the core. *No, Ed'rathe, I think I am needed here now, unless the Dragon Queen still wants something from me.*

I will be above, watching. Should she need you, I will find you.

'Prisoners are being held in the refectory,' Mandor says, his voice cutting through the murmurs echoing in the courtyard.

Ed'rathe launches into the sky, and I reach down and pull Grossman to his feet. He groans in pain, but he will live. I'm not so sure about Giles and

Gregor. Effie and Genie are tending to them, but their wounds are serious.

'Wait. Wait,' Grossman says.

I pause. 'What?'

'Your princess still owes me,' he pleads.

Anger washes over me, and he winces as I squeeze his arm. He's going to ask me to let him go. He's going to get away with this. 'You want me to release you, don't you?'

His head drops. 'No, I have done some bad things, and I must pay for what I did… helped do. I have a wife and children in the World Above. It is them I worry about. I did it for the gold, to take care of them. Please, make sure they stay safe.'

I don't know what disgusts me more—the thought that creatures would support Bernais and the council because they endorse their racist beliefs or that someone could support them for money alone.

Either way, Grossman's family should not have to suffer for his actions. And Pris does owe him for letting us go from Wistman's Woods.

'I'll do what I can,' I say, pulling him after the others.

We mourn the loss,
The Worlds all weep,
Her memory safe,
The dragons will keep.

I repeat the words under my breath, and beside me Irene stiffens.

'What?' I ask over my shoulder, unwilling to take my eyes off the enemy even though no one is moving.

'A Dragon Bonded is dead,' Irene says, 'That's the dragon lament for one they consider to be of their own.'

Queen Ariana is with the ancestors, Am'ratha sends.

No! I didn't know her well, but she was my great-aunt, and the World Below will miss her. And it couldn't happen at a worse time. Or perhaps it isn't as bad as it might have been. The Queen hadn't signed the agreement, and many on our side saw her as part of the problem.

However, I bet there are some followers of Bernais who are excited about this because now they have a chance to claim the throne.

The clash of sword meeting sword rings out in the silence, then it is all on again. Aeron, Irene, and I carry on fighting in our small circle. Irene's wound hinders her, but she is still better at this than I am.

Minutes or perhaps hours later, a shout goes up, and everyone turns towards the palace as if drawn by an invisible force. I can just make out a figure on the balcony. 'Mum?'

Aeron bellows, 'Long live Queen Cecily!'

Others follow suit, followed by gasps and murmurs as creatures on both sides realise what this means; Queen Ariana is dead and Queen Cecily now sits on the throne. Seconds later a thundering fills the air as figures pour around the palace like a wave.

The centurion royal guard are finally joining the fight. My spirits soar as I see the fear on the mercenary soldiers' faces. They look like they want to run, but there is nowhere to go.

As the fighting begins again, a shout rings through the square. Somewhere above me, a dragon I know lands on the building directly across from the palace. Two figures descend—Adina and her son, Bernais. He waves, and our opponents cheer—even the mercenaries are shouting their support. Then again, being under a curse, they probably have no say in the matter.

Suddenly the fighting becomes more intense as dragons take to the sky above us, ready to protect their bonded creatures.

Get to a safe place, and I will pick you up.

Am'ratha's voice distracts me, and I take a nick to my forearm.

No. I am staying here.

You are now heir to the throne, and I cannot protect you in amongst that.

As if in concert with Am'ratha, Irene commands Aeron to get the heir to the throne out of the square. Before I can protest, Aeron picks me up and throws me over his shoulder. He slices his way through the crowd, and I do my best to protect his back from my ungainly position.

We almost make it. Struggling through the edge of the fighting a sword comes out of nowhere and slices across Aaron's back, finding exposed flesh where the minotaur's armour has moved as I fought.

Aeron staggers a few steps into a side street, then drops to the ground. I roll to the side and pull my legs out from under his bulky form. 'Aeron!' I scramble back to his side, rip at my shirt, and apply pressure to the wound. Blood seeps through the fabric as panic surges inside me.

Am'ratha, come find me. Aeron is down.

THE WINDOW IS cool as I lean my forehead against it. I itch to be down there helping my friends fight. A hand squeezes my shoulder as if in sympathy, but I do not take my eyes from the scene below.

'We are too old and not warrior enough to launch ourselves into that,' Jasper says.

'I know, and we have an important job to do here,' I respond wearily.

'Or not.' Drow's voice comes from behind us as he stares at the map, a paper plane message in his hand.

We rejoin him at the table, and I study the map. Nothing is different. What has changed for Drow?

'What's going on?' I ask as a dragon shadow appears over the palace and the site of the battle in front.

'I believe this is the endgame,' Drow says.

As if his words are portents, the library door crashes open, and King Maddox appears. Although he is moving fast, his face is ashen and his eyes dull.

'Come quick, we must go and protect Cecily and Malachai,' he commands.

'But the map...,' I say lamely.

'Go. I can keep the map updated,' Jasper says.

Drow doesn't need to be told twice, but I pause. 'Ed'ruven can't take all of us.'

Maddox grabs my hand and starts dragging me out of the room. 'Then it is a good thing the Dragon Queen sent along Ed'rima, my brother's Dragon Bonded. As you a Dragon Friend, he will allow you to ride him.'

My heart almost stops in my chest. I have not had much luck riding dragons, and that was with someone else on back with me. My mouth is dry as Maddox pushes open the door to the roof, and I see the silver dragon lounging beside the midnight black Ed'ruven.

King Maddox and Drow are already seated when I take my first steps towards the dragon who has offered to take me to the palace.

Hello, Dragon Friend. I have heard much about you, and I am honoured to escort you to the palace.

He stays down as I tentatively climb onto his back.

It is my honour entirely, I tell him even though I am quaking in my boots.

The dragon chortles. *Do not be afraid. I will use magic to ensure you stay safe. There will be no… accidents.*

Thank you.

Even though I trust his words, I grip the scale in front of me tightly as we fly over the city. He descends to the main palace balcony and uses magic to place me safely by the doors. When my feet touch the ground, my shoulders sag with relief.

Thank you, my friend.

As he and Ed'ruven take to the skies, I look across the marketplace below and at the dragon perching on the roof of the building opposite. A quick 'far-see' spell shows me Bernais, Adina, and Magnus Baaronson watching the proceedings.

As if in response to our arrival, Adina and Bernais climb onto Am'nera's back. As the dragon takes to the sky, Am'rena appears from nowhere, screeching a warning, determined to protect her new Queen.

I do not get to watch the battle play out because King Maddox again grabs my hand and pulls me into a crowded room. There is Cecily, surrounded by people all yabbering at her. Before I can intervene and rescue her, the door opposite opens, and Malachai strides in, followed by Elias, who overtakes the King Consort and commands, 'Quiet. QUIET!'

Miraculously the crowd parts to let him through. He takes Cecily's arm and leads her to the throne to the right of the balcony doors.

'The throne is not just a sign of office. It also makes sure petitioners cannot surround you,' I hear him tell the Queen as he helps her sit. 'Now, one at a time, please.'

Elias spies us by the window and motions us forward. 'Make way for the Queen's advisors,' he orders, and the creatures part to make way for us.

Before we can take a single step, a shout rings out from behind me. 'How dare you sit on my throne.' Fury and disdain drip from the words.

Everyone's attention shifts to the balcony. I can see nothing through the throng of taller creatures, but I know that voice—Bernais Baaronson. How did he get by Am'rena?

'Make way for the true King,' a woman's voice bellows.

Adina is with him. Of course Am'rena could do nothing that might hurt the Dragon Bonded.

The creatures who had previously crowded around Queen Cecily draw back to the edge of the room, leaving Bernais and Adina to continue confronting Cecily and Elias. In a split second, Maddox and Malachai take their place in front of the throne, brandishing their swords.

Surprisingly, there are a couple of courtiers lining up with Bernais. Had the palace harboured traitors all along, or are these courtiers merely bending with the prevailing wind? They don't have their swords out, so they're clearly not that committed to Bernais's cause.

'Now, now,' Adina is saying, 'there is no need to fight. Cecily, come down from there and let Bernais take his rightful place.'

The princess is speaking as though to a child. I cannot believe she thinks this will work.

'Really, Aunt Adina, this is not a fight between cousins. This is a matter of state, and the line of succession is a matter of public record. I may not have been crowned, but I am Queen.' Cecily's voice is confident as she embraces the role of ruler.

'You have no right to the Crown. You gave it up when you chose that dark elf over your people, cousin,' Bernais responds, clearly trying to goad Cecily.

'Interesting that you choose that as your bone of contention, not that I left the World Below,' Cecily says. 'Can you not see that the era of elven dominance is drawing to a close, and no amount of bloodshed will prevent it?'

'It is you who are wrong,' Bernais says, lunging forward just as Adina moves, arm outstretched.

'No, Bernais,' she says, but she is too late. He pushes past her, and in his fury, his sword slices through her clothing, drawing blood.

The room freezes as Adina clutches her wound, her eyes wide on her son. She sways, then falls to the floor as if in slow motion. Bernais does not pause or hesitate. He screams and carries his attack forward, facing the two dark elves he so despises alone.

As Bernais leaves his mother behind, a figure detaches itself from the handful of courtiers to help Adina. It is Ginth fo Drefin, Snake's mother. Drow steps forward to help her escort Adina to a couch as a servant leaves to find someone to tend to the elf princess's wounds.

Back in the centre of the room, King Maddox is forcing Bernais away from the throne. 'I will not let a Baaronson make me cower this time.'

King Maddox's face is a mask of anger, and each clash of swords pushes Bernais back a step.

Bernais is a picture of righteous fury. 'How dare you think you have the right to decide who sits on our throne.' Disdain is threaded through each word as he spits them out. 'When I am King, we will return to the old ways, and abominations such as you will be banished from the land.'

Gasps fill the room, and the creatures who had stood behind Bernais use the distraction of the fight to melt back into the crowd.

'You don't get it, do you?' Maddox counters. 'The time of Seelie Elves setting the rules is over.'

As if the goddess hears his words and acts, Bernais slips on the blood on the floor and falls to one knee.

'I will never accept that,' Bernais chokes out as he tries to regain his feet.

Before he can rise, Maddox has his sword pointed at the elf's throat. 'Give me an excuse, any excuse, to finish this,' he says with a sneer.

Bernais locks eyes with the King of the Unseelie Court. 'Do it,' he dares him.

A ripple of fear runs through the courtiers. Most of them want to see Bernais defeated, but few of them are prepared to witness his cold-blooded murder.

'Maddox, no.' Cecily pushes past Malachai. 'He must stand trial for his actions. It is the only way we can start healing.'

For a moment I think he's going to ignore her. Then he nods. 'Spoken like a true Queen, sister.'

Malachai steps forward and takes Bernais's weapon, and King Maddox moves his sword a little away. 'Someone get a guard to take this creature to the dungeons.'

I'm so engrossed in the scene that my heart nearly leaps from my chest when I feel cold steel at my throat.

'I think not. Not if you want this sprite to continue breathing.'

AFTER THE HEAT OF BATTLE

THE SOUND OF that voice sends terror through to my very soul. The pain of my transformation knots my joints, and I sweat as if my body is attempting to return to its natural state but cannot.

'Step away from my son and allow him to bring my wife to me.'

The voice is as commanding as ever, and it turns my insides to water. Fury at his plans being thwarted rolls off him in waves.

Cecily sends me a compassionate look, and I know what she is going to say before the words leave her lips. 'You know I cannot do that, Uncle. It is time to stop fighting and to work together to heal our world's wounds.'

Magnus's grip tightens, and I cringe as a sticky substance dribbles under my shirt collar. *My blood?*

'Isn't this poetic, sprite! I finally get to finish what I started. It will give me great pleasure to sever your life force.'

'No! Please, Uncle Magnus. I don't want my first act as Queen to be prosecuting you for murder.' There is real distress in Cecily's voice, but there is also determination.

'Then don't. Stop this nonsense and throw your support behind Bernais.'

Cecily holds out her hand towards her uncle. 'No matter how much I don't want to see Percival hurt, I can't. It's not what Ariana would want. It's not what I want. And, more importantly, it's not what most creatures want. It is time for us to all work together to mend the rifts between us for the good of our world.'

'Never. We will not accept the dilution of our race or see our land devolve into chaos. If you will not join us, Cecily, then you leave me no choice.'

The blade pushes more firmly against my throat, and I send up a silent goodbye. This is my end, and rather than sending off my father's spirit, I will join him soon. While I'm not happy at the thought, I am grateful that I at least repaired things with Nisha before this moment came.

The sharp edge of the knife cuts into my skin, and I tense, then my body is shoved forward, and I am falling to the ground. My knees crack against the polished stone, my hands landing in a pool of blood, and I do a body check. Where is it coming from?

I turn my head and find myself staring into Magnus's lifeless eyes. Blood oozes from a slash across his throat, and I sag with relief. As I haul myself to my feet, I am helped by King Maddox, who has a satisfied grin on his face.

'You know, I have wanted to do that since I arrived in the World Below. He treated me as less than when I first arrived here—me, a prince of my people.'

'Arrest him! He murdered my father,' Bernais is calling to the guards who have finally arrived.

This is where I see Cecily, who I have known since she was a child, come fully into her new position.

'Halt.'

The guards pause mid-way to King Maddox.

'Bernais is a traitor. He is to be taken to the dungeons to await trial.'

The Guard Captain motions for two of her creatures to take Bernais into custody.

'What about Governor Baaronson's attacker?'

'Magnus threatened Percival's life. King Maddox saved him and ended a threat to us all.' Cecily's eyes rake the room, daring anyone to refute her claims.

Only Adina moves. On uncertain feet, clutching at her side, she crosses the floor and kneels beside her husband. The room holds its breath as we prepare for her grief.

'How typical of you, Magnus,' Adina snarls, surprising us all. 'You make yourself the centre of attention, follow it up with a grand gesture, then leave it for me to clean up your mess and take the heat. Well, I won't do it.'

We're all stunned by the disdain and anger in her voice. Then, before anyone can react, she grabs Magnus's knife and plunges it into her stomach.

The entire room draws in a breath in shock as Bernais grief is displayed for all to hear. 'Mother, no!'

'Is there a healer in the room?' Queen Cecily calls as the guards move to the two figures on the floor.

They are quick, but not quick enough. The lifeless body of Princess Adina rests beside her husband, her eyes locked on the son she risked everything for.

The world stops again as another Dragon Bonded dies.

THE WORLD BETWEEN

THE SECOND SHOCK wave occurs as I leave the refectory, the last of the prisoners finally under guard. My intention had been to head to the control room, as I had just received an update from Ed'rathe.

We mourn the loss,
The Worlds all weep,
Her memory safe,
The dragons will keep.

I collapse against the cold, hard wall as the words ring in my head.
Ed'rathe? What's happening?
Everyone in the square is staring at the palace. Am'nera and Am'ratha are missing.
No. It can't have been Pris. Please don't let it have been Pris.
The witch sisters join me in the hallway.
'Another death of a bonded princess?' Euphemia asks.
I nod, unable to trust my voice.
Noble One, the Dragon Queen calls you back.
What? No! I have to find Pris.
Eleanora rubs my arm. 'Snake, what is it? You've gone white as a sheet. Is it Pris?'
I shake my head. 'I don't know, nor does Ed'rathe. The Dragon Queen wants me.'
'Then you must go,' Eleanora says decisively.
'But… Pris?'
I can't do it. I can't leave when I don't know what's happened to her.
'Who ever has died, you cannot do much about it now,' Eugenia says. 'Go to the Dragon Queen, and we will do what we can to find Pris.'
Shouts from the courtyard tell me Ed'rathe has likely landed. Euphemia gives me a gentle shove. 'Go. We have things covered here.'
As Ed'rathe flies over the city, my heart is breaking, and I can't breathe. There are still some minor skirmishes, but the fighting has mostly stopped. I search for Pris, and I think I see Am'ratha in a corner of the palace square, but we are so high, I'm not sure which dragon it is.
We travel to the World Between by conventional flight, and it takes forever. I just want to finish this and go back to the World Below to find Pris. Even though I know I have to accept the possibility of losing her one way or the other once this is over, her death is the worst of the two options.

By the time we reach the landing space, tears stream from my eyes. My sense of loss is so strong, I can't bear it. It is all I can do to pull myself together as Ed'rathe leads me into the audience chamber.

The dragons gathered in the cavern are sombre. With two Dragon Bonded dead, the court is in mourning, or so Ed'rathe tells me. He also warns me that today is not the day to test the Dragon Queen's patience.

Bearing that in mind, I bow before the monarch, and I wait for her to speak even though every fibre of my being wants to be gone from here.

It is done, Noble One. The fate of the World Between has been decided.

Really?

Queen Ariana was successful in her quest to restore magic, giving her body to the flow in the end. Cecily will be brought before me and confirmed as Queen in her place. Her commitment to cleansing the flow will return to a biannual event—midsummer and midwinter. She will be joined by King Maddox. In return, I will restore his court.

If all is well, then why am I here? I should be out looking for Pris. I don't even know if she's okay.

Ed'rathe drops his head and nudges me, reminding me that I have perhaps been a bit too bold.

In spite of your bad manners, I have an offer for you. I would like you to be my envoy to the new Queen, and, perhaps more importantly, to the new council she will form.

I'm confused both by the request and the urgency. Couldn't this have waited? However, mindful of Ed'rathe's advice, I choose my next words carefully.

While I am honoured, do you really need a creature to speak with the Queen? You can talk directly to her through her dragon.

Ed'rathe shifts beside me, reminding me not to go too far.

In the past that is what I have done, but my words are only for the ruler. If I have a creature speak for me, then everyone hears and can take dragon-kind's wishes into account when they make decisions.

I tilt my head to the side, my fears for Pris momentarily eclipsed. That is actually an important distinction, given the changes that are likely to happen in the World Below.

Ahh, and you need me to agree now because Queen Cecily will be listening closely to her advisors even as we speak.

See, I knew you were the right creature for the job.

I am honoured, but this is not the future I had planned. Once this was over, I intended to return to studying magic.

I appreciate your concerns. You would not need to spend all your time at court.

You would only be required to attend council sessions, giving you time to continue your studies.

That is more appealing.

And, as an incentive, I would allow you to bond fully with Ed'rathe.

Really? I place a hand on the dragon's flank. He has given up so much to remain with me. This would be my way to pay him back for not bonding with Pris's dad.

Perhaps I could study magic at the university in the World Below? Drow would be able to help me sort that out. It would also be an opportunity for me to spend more time with my family.

What about my mother? She would be alone in the World Above. Then again, I would have to move away to attend university there—would this be any different?

Life is difficult as an adult when you have to balance so many competing interests, the Dragon Queen says, interrupting my tumbling thoughts. *And you have been through so much. What say we start on a trial basis?*

But what about Ed'rathe? It would be unfair to keep him waiting about his position while we find out if this will work.

I think that as this is a new initiative, I could allow the full bonding to take place as a reward for your service to creature and dragon-kind.

I laugh. *And I am more likely to take the job if I am bonded to my friend.*

The Dragon Queen bares her teeth in what I hope is a smile and not a sign that she is about to eat me. *I see we understand each other. Now, Ed'rathe, perhaps it is time to cement your formal bond before Snake Fieth changes his mind.*

A shiver of pleasure comes down the bond from Ed'rathe as he bows his head. *As you command, Your Majesty.*

I follow him from the audience cavern, excited about the possibilities the future offers, pleased to have cemented my friendship with Ed'rathe, but unable to fully appreciate it because of my gnawing worry about Pris.

'DO YOU HAVE to push so hard?' Aeron groans.

'Do you want to die?' I snap back. 'Medic,' I yell at the top of my lungs.

'What's that supposed to do?' Aeron mutters. 'You already called your dragon, I presume.'

'What makes you say that?'

He looks over my shoulder into the square. I half turn and find Am'ratha peeking around the corner.

'I thought you said you couldn't land.'

It seems when a dragon wants to land somewhere, creatures move out of their way.

'I'll bet they do,' I say, frantically looking round for someone to help me get Aeron on Am'ratha's back.

'Can you help me get him up?' I ask her.

Aeron grabs my wrist. 'Are you trying to kill me?'

'I thought you said your wound wasn't too bad.'

'I meant I am not dead yet, but I will be if you try to get me onto her.'

'What should I do, then?' I ask, anger rising. 'I can't let you stay here either.'

I have contacted Princess Petunia via Am'ralla. She is sending a healer as soon as she can find a witch to open a portal.

'Thank you. And thank you for protecting us while we wait,' I tell Am'ratha.

Princess, I have not been protecting you. Most of the fighting has stopped. Did you not feel the change in the air?

'I heard another Dragon Bonded was lost, but I've been too busy taking care of Aeron to worry about who it was and what it meant for the war.'

A ruler has been named.

Hold on, a Dragon Bonded lost, and a ruler named? My panic comes back full force. 'Am'ratha, is my mother all right? And Snake? Is he Dragon Bonded yet?'

I am sorry, Princess. Dragons are mourning, the Dragon Queen is busy, and no one will answer me.

When we were fighting, I had been frightened for my life, but now I'm frantic. Is Mum okay? Has Snake survived the battle? Is Bernais now King?

I search around desperately, trying to find someone to ask or to look after Aeron while I find out what is going on. No, I can't leave him. He is only like this because he was trying to protect me.

Am'ratha, I need you—

The air a few meters away crackles and seems to shimmer, almost vibrating and a loud *pop* follows it.

A portal opens up across the street, and Nisha steps through, followed by a couple of dwarves.

'Princess, I can take over from here,' the sprite tells me as she makes her way to my side.

Able to be relieved of my duties, I suddenly have no desire to go. I can't leave Aeron, and I am not really sure I want to know the outcome of today's battles. If Bernais is King, perhaps I will be better off at the hospital.

Beneath my palm, Aeron's breathing is becoming shallow. Nisha gently nudges my hand aside. 'Let me help him, Princess.'

I push to my feet, and a dwarf leads me away so Nisha can deal with his wound.

'He has lost a lot of blood. Where is that stretcher?'

The other dwarf lays down the stretcher beside the Minotaur, and I can't help the thought that Aeron will break that in a heartbeat. Then again, this is the realm of magic. They levitate Aeron onto the stretcher and start moving him to the portal.

I go to follow, but Nisha places a restraining hand on my arm.

'No, Princess. If you come, he will worry more about you than himself. He needs time to heal, and you have responsibilities here.'

I want so much to argue with her, but she is right.

'But he will be alone.' I can't bear the thought of that.

Nisha's lips curve into a knowing smile. 'Princess Irene arrived just as I was leaving. I am most certain he will not be alone.'

I hesitate. They both took care of me. Shouldn't I be there for them? No, I would only be in the way. Nisha squeezes my arm, then follows the others through the portal.

Princess, I believe we should go to the palace.

If Bernais is King, then is this over—or are our forces regrouping? If we won, where am I meant to be? Irene or Aeron would know. Or Percival.

We should go to the palace, she repeats.

'Do you have any more information?'

I believe everything will become clear once we are there.

With no strong alternative coming to mind, I decide to trust Am'ratha. 'Okay.'

I pick up my sword, and for the first time I take in the blood covering my hands and sleeves—Aeron's blood. 'Please be all right.' I freeze, not seeing anything but the stains.

Princess? Pris? We should go.

I sheath my sword, then use a little of what I know of magic to remove what blood I can. It's not the best, but it no longer appears as if I've been ruthlessly slaying creatures with my bare hands.

Am'ratha rises gently, then banks around, giving me a bird's-eye view of the square. Creatures have dropped where they stood, all facing the palace. Some have wounds being tended to by their fellows, and every now and then, a portal appears to transport the more badly wounded to the hospital.

Creatures in pairs are carrying soldiers to the edge of the marketplace. At first I think it is to make transportation to the hospital easier. Then I work out that they are the bodies of the dead. There are so many of them. Tears well in my eyes as I think of all the souls lost today.

Am'ratha hovers over a balcony at the front of the palace, then lands. I wipe away the tears before slipping down her foreleg.

I will wait on the roof, she tells me.

I'm so tired and hollow inside and worried about what I might inside. How nice it would be to ask her to come in with me so I don't have to face what is waiting for me alone. Instead, I say, 'Thank you for staying close and being there when I needed you.'

She inclines her head in acknowledgement, and I step through the doors into what appears to be a large reception room. To my right, there is a throne, and in front of it is something on the floor covered by what looks to be a large curtain. I shudder at the crimson blood soaking through the material—there are bodies under there.

A centaur who would rival Fairburn in stature and magnetism is talking to two human guards by the open door across from me. They have hold of a prisoner. It takes a moment for me to register that the creature they are holding is Bernais.

'Take me into custody if you must, but my parents deserve justice,' he is saying to the guards.

I glance back at the bodies. Are those his parents under there? I almost sag with relief. Adina was Dragon Bonded. My mother must still be alive.

I'm brought back to the present by the sound of voices in the room to my left. The guard by the door is so preoccupied with the drama going on, I am able to slip by them and stand in the shadows by the door as I assess the lie of the land. This room is smaller and cosier, studded with groups of chairs and couches. Standing by the fireplace, my mother is talking to a majestic female centaur.

'All the mercenaries you rounded up are to be taken back to the World Above, and they are to have their memories of this place wiped. You will need to take a healing witch with you. See if you can find Eugenia. It would be best if it were she, as they will be her responsibility to check on later.'

'Yes, Your Majesty.'

Although I'm used to seeing my mother take control of things, hearing her called Your Majesty is a whole new level of weird.

'And what about the governors' guards?' the centaur asks.

'As we have discussed, regional governors will no longer be able to keep standing armies. The current guards are to be offered places in a to-be-formed Council Guard. The alternative is banishment.'

The Royal Guard salutes and leaves. Seconds later the door she left through opens to admit Elias, who is followed in by Snake. He's alive and unhurt.

THE WORLD BETWEEN

I'm sure I'm grinning stupidly as I receive the second lot of good news this evening. However, this is not how I wanted Snake to be introduced to my parents. I take a step forward as the guard says, 'Your Majesty, may I present Snake Fieth, ambassador for the Dragon Queen.'

What? Snake is still ambassador? When did that happen? Does that mean he's staying?

From the back of the room, I watch him bow to my mother.

'Am'rena told me of your appointment, and that you have been brought up to speed on where we are. We welcome you as a representative from the World Between. I am sure you will be a great asset to the new council and to me in the meantime.'

Snake grins, and my heart melts. 'I'm not sure how this is going to work, but I am told my first duty is to escort you to the Dragon Court for you to affirm your commitment to maintaining the flow of magic.'

'Of course. Once we have things stabilised here, it will be my priority.'

The adrenalin leaves my body as the realisation that this is finally over hits me. My father, King Maddox, Glinth, and Drow join Mum and Snake, and I suddenly feel on the outside looking in. They have all moved on and accepted the changes this war has brought about. My head is spinning and I need time to think…, to regroup.

I quietly escape the room and head back to the balcony. As I watch the chaos below slowly return to order, I can't believe this whole adventure is really over. Someone moves in beside me, and I stiffen, wiping away the tears gathering in my eyes.

Percival clears his throat, a sound I know well, and I relax.

'I nearly died today,' he says.

'Me too. Wait, you were supposed to be at the command post.'

'I was, but I flew alone on a dragon to get here.'

The laugh escapes, and I can't stop giggling. It's good to be alive. I drop an arm around Percival's shoulders and give him a hug. 'I'm pleased you survived that trauma. Wait, how did you get that cut on your throat?'

'It is nothing. A story for another day.'

I study my friend, and the light I had started to let in blinks out. 'Percival, what is it?'

'Drow and I sent a small group of creatures to rescue the prisoners in the hospital, and we haven't heard back from them. I am afraid they are dead.'

'Oh, Percival.' I hug him again, picturing the bodies piling up around the market square in my mind.

'I can't believe I sent them to die.'

The reality that we both sent creatures to their death sobers me. My part in this will never leave me. 'So much about this is messed up, Percival. I believe we did what we had to.'

He is silent.

'And that doesn't make any of this any easier,' I say.

We stand together, watching the sun set over the battleground below us, so lost in our thoughts, neither of us hears someone approach from behind.

'Excuse me, Percival.'

We both jump at the noise, then turn as one.

'Alyce, have you any news?' Percival asks, and the hope in his voice brings tears to my eyes.

'The prisoners and their rescuers remained holed up in the hospital building throughout the fighting. They are all being taken to the hospital in Melliores. Would you like me to take you there?'

Percival looks towards the room where the new leaders of the World Below are making plans, then back at Alyce.

'Percival, I am sure the witches and Nisha have things under control in Melliores. Perhaps you could go and tell Mother and Drow the good news that the last of our people have been accounted for.'

'And what about you?' he asks.

I finally allow myself to smile. 'I have some other creatures I need to hug.'

COUNTING THE DEAD

WHY EVERYONE GETS excited about riding dragons is beyond me. What is wrong with a horse and carriage? Or, better still, why doesn't someone invent a type of car like they have in the World Above? Now that magic is fixed, it should be possible. I think I should suggest it to someone— maybe Mandor.

'Percival, can you quit wriggling? You'll have us both off in a minute,' Snake hisses in my ear.

As if I would let him fall.

'You did once,' Snake reminds Ed'rathe.

How was I to know he would turn into a cat? The dragon's tone is sulky.

'I have forgiven you, Ed'rathe, and I trust you to keep me safe. It is just that this is not a sprite's natural habitat.'

See, Snake?

It is like riding with children. My only consolation is that none of the other riders with us appear any happier about this trip to the World Between.

In front of us, Cecily has Mandor on her dragon. He is upset that the Dragon Queen has cast a spell preventing unauthorised portals being opened into the World Between. When he muttered something to Snake about bringing it up today, Cecily mentioned something about the World Below regulating portals too. He went quiet after that.

El'ruven is tucked in behind us. After Queen Ariana's death, he took over as leader of the bonded ones and is taking his new duty of care seriously. Never one who enjoyed additional passengers, he even deigned to take Drow with Maddox without too much grumbling. Drow had initially refused to come, saying he was not officially a councillor. Cecily insisted he did to ensure any dragon requirements are enshrined in our new constitution.

I heave a sigh of relief as we touch down in front of the Dragon Queen's audience chamber. After a little preening, our procession enters with Queen Cecily and King Maddox at the head. As a mark of the occasion, the Dragon Queen is standing on all fours as she awaits us. I rather wish she had stayed lying down, as she is even more formidable when upright.

The Dragon Queen adjusts her glamour as we approach. Even so, she radiates an almost crippling amount of power.

Welcome Queen Cecily, King Maddox. And welcome to your guests.

'Thank you for allowing them to accompany us, Your Highness,' Queen Cecily says. 'I believe Ambassador Fieth informed you of the proposed changes in the World Below, and from now on the creature responsible for maintaining magic will need to be agreed to by the ruling council.'

The gaze the Queen sends our way is intense. *Do you mean to say that in the future that it will not be a King or Queen?*

'Your Majesty, we propose that any creature with magical abilities can be considered for the role in the future,' Cecily suggests.

Mmm. You would still require my endorsement—

'Of course, Your Majesty. In fact, our intention is for both courts to work more closely with you to ensure a growth in magic in all the realms.'

Then I guess this is the way it will be. And where is Princess Priscilla today?

'She begs your forgiveness, but she is spending some time with friends and family who were injured in the recent war.'

I guess that is acceptable. Come forward, Queen Cecily and King Maddox.

The two rulers take a step forward.

Do you both swear to maintain the flow of magic between the worlds?

'I do,' Cecily says.

King Maddox hesitates.

Is there a problem?

'No, Your Majesty. I do so swear. But I am wondering why you would take my word for it when I so recently let you and Queen Ariana down.'

Yes, well, you can thank El'ruven for that. He explained the pressure you were under, and he believes you have learnt your lesson.

'I have, Your Majesty. And thank you for trusting me.'

I do not trust you. I trust El'ruven. He has vouched for you and your commitment to the Unseelie Court. It is for this reason, and as a deathbed boon to Queen Ariana, that I will bring the court back into time. Do not let either of them down.

I smother a grin. The Dragon Queen is a canny creature. Perhaps the one creature alive who Maddox cares about more than himself is his bonded dragon. He would not lightly do anything that would hurt El'ruven—not even if it were only to hurt his reputation and standing in the Court of the World Between.

'I will not, Your Majesty.'

The official swearing over, the Dragon Queen lowers herself onto her rock and eyes the two monarchs. *What will happen in the World Below now?*

It is Queen Cecily who answers. 'Elias is finalising details for the state day of mourning for the casualties of war tomorrow and the funeral of Queen Ariana two days later. Two days after that, my coronation and the signing of our new constitution. Then the real work will begin.'

You have a busy time ahead. And what about you, King Maddox? Will there be changes in your court?

'I believe it might be time to shake things up a little, but nothing so drastic as in the World Below. I currently have no heir, and I have been thinking of holding an election.'

I catch Drow's eye. He shakes his head. He had no idea King Maddox was planning this either.

Then we had best set about retrieving your court.

'We have a few days yet, Your Majesty. I would like to see Cecily safely on the throne before I leave for the World Above.'

Of course. Thank you all for your time today, and may all our realms prosper.

And with those words, we are dismissed.

Percival, please stay.

The others continue to file out, and I appreciate the Dragon Queen's words are for me alone.

'Your Majesty?' I ask, stepping forward from the shadows.

I think it is time.

'Time for—'

The rest of my words are stolen from me as every cell in my body explodes in pain. Heat whips up my spine, burning through my veins and spreading out to every limb. The torment goes on until I think I can bear it no longer, then it suddenly stops, and I fall to the ground. Through my exhaustion I experience a bliss that has been a memory for too long. I am me again.

Thank you.

You are welcome, Dragon Friend.

I LEAN BACK against Am'ratha and watch Aeron and Irene choose their weapons.

'Are you sure you should be doing this?' I say as they test bows and choose their arrows.

'How else are we to find out who is the best archer?' Aeron asks.

'One arrow each at ten, then twenty, then thirty paces,' Irene says, ignoring me altogether.

I try again. 'Aeron, you still have stitches in your side, and Nisha will have your guts if you burst them.'

Following Irene's lead, the Minotaur tests the string of his crossbow and tries to hide his wince of pain.

They are going to do this regardless of what you say, Am'ratha sends, her tone amused.

I sigh. 'I just wish they would both rest a while and allow themselves to recover.'

It is not in their natures. They both need to be doing something.

'I know how they feel.'

Shading my eyes, I watch Irene line up and pull back her bow. The shot she releases flies smoothly through the air and lands dead centre in the bull's-eye.

'Nice.'

'Your foot was not behind the line,' Aeron complains.

'Rubbish, you're just worried you can't do better,' my aunt counters.

'And we are not going to find out today.' Nisha's voice comes from behind Am'ratha.

I scramble to my feet in time to see the sprite striding towards the Minotaur. Instead of his usual bravado, Aeron kicks a hoof through the dirt, and he reminds me of a child caught doing something they know they shouldn't.

'I did not use my medical and magical skills to heal you only to have you undo my good work,' Nisha lectures, and Aeron's head drops.

'I'm sorry, Nisha. I got carried away in the moment. It won't happen again.'

'And as for you—' Nisha turns to Irene. 'If you are encouraging this foolishness, then you are ready to be discharged. Princess Priscilla, perhaps you would be good enough to escort the princess back to the palace with you?'

I place a hand on Am'ratha's side. *Are you okay with that?*

I do not want to court Nisha's displeasure, do you?

I chuckle under my breath. *No.* 'We are happy to escort Irene to the palace.'

'Excellent. Thank you, Princess. Aeron, if you will accompany me, I will check your wound. If it is healing well, then there is plenty to busy yourself with in the hospital where I can keep an eye on you.'

As Nisha leads the Minotaur away, he glances back over his shoulder and mouths, 'See you soon for the rematch.'

Irene laughs. 'Name the time,' she tells him.

'You shouldn't encourage him,' I say to Irene as she joins us.

'As if that would stop him getting into trouble,' she says gruffly, but there is real affection in her voice.

'True. Do you have anything you need to get before we leave?'

Irene shakes her head. 'Mum took my armour away when she visited, and I am wearing the only clothes I have here. I'm sure I can sort myself out when we get to the palace.'

'Okay,' I say. 'You know your mother is in her old suite of rooms, and she is ready for you to join her.'

Irene's face twists into a grimace.

'What's wrong?' I ask.

'Is it ungrateful to say I feel like I've gone out and forged my own path, and now I'm returning home to Mum, and it just doesn't feel right?'

I bark out a laugh. 'I couldn't have put it better myself. I mean, it's nice to be back with family and to be safe, but I can't return to the way things were.'

Irene is nodding as I speak. 'And you can't because you are not the same.'

'Exactly. And, even worse, my parents haven't even noticed the change.'

'So, my wise and thoughtful niece, what do we do about this?' Irene's tone is playful, but her question strikes a chord.

I lean my cheek against Am'ratha's scales and draw strength and resolve from the contact. 'I think we should make a pact. We will not fall back into our old lives. Instead, we will seek out new challenges.'

Irene stares into the distance, and I'm worrying I read this situation all wrong when a smile forms on her face. 'You are wise beyond your years, Pris. And I have an idea where I can make a difference. We need to get back so I can talk to King Maddox.'

'I'm pleased for you. Now all I need to do is find my niche,' I say as I climb up to position myself behind Am'ratha's neck.

As Irene joins me, Am'ratha says, *You are in a new world. You need time to find your role. It will come.*

The confidence I sense through our bond gives me hope that like Snake and Irene, I, too, will find my place in the magical worlds.

THE STATE DAY of mourning is the first time I've had to myself since the end of the war. During the day, I've had one meeting after another, and at night, I'm often called to the World Between to update the Queen and receive my instructions. I've barely had a moment to breathe, let alone spend any time with Pris, and the time we're apart is making me more and more desperate to see her.

Some nights I fall exhausted into bed in the room I've been assigned at the palace. Others I sleep in a room in the royal quarters in the World Between, only to be woken before dawn so I can be flown back to the palace. Thank goodness the palace brownies have taken me under their wing and kept me in clean clothes, otherwise I would have spent the whole time in the same outfit.

Now I finally have a day off, and the Fieth has called a Cruinniú Teaghlaigh—some sort of family meeting I have to go to. I tried to wrangle an invite for Pris because we'd organised a picnic together. I'm still waiting to hear back from my grandparents, so I take that as a no. Pris is having breakfast with her parents, and I have to resort to cancelling with a note.

At a loose end, I decide to walk, but I still arrive at the family home on the outskirts of the Capitol early enough to spend time with my mother—another creature I have spent little time with lately. Mum, Heart, and Mender are staying in the guest suite, and they are all in the small sitting room when I am shown in. Taking in their formal dress, I ask, 'Are you all going to the gathering?'

'Ginth is family, so we are apparently family by extension,' Mender says. 'So it would be rude not to.'

'And how does dad feel about your going?' The words are out before I have a chance to appreciate how abrupt the question is.

Heart claps me on the back. 'Not subtle at all, Snake.'

'Sorry, Mum, it's just that….'

'I know, Snake. Now that you've found I wasn't exactly truthful about the past, you're wondering about your dad and me and perhaps what my plans are?'

I lean back in the chair, making as if I don't mind if she doesn't answer, but in reality, I'm still struggling with the secrets Mum kept about her mixed heritage and what really happened with my father. Then again, if I've learnt anything over the past few months, it's that life doesn't go to plan and we all have our secrets. And maybe also that we don't have the right to know everything about our parents.

'Well, I'm staying in the World Below for a while. I want to spend some time with Dad and his family. He's going back to the village to take over the music shop from Mender, and I will be returning with them.'

'Oh.' I don't know what to say. It's irrational, but I feel abandoned even though I would have been leaving home myself this year. Then again, she will be closer than she would have been if she returned to the World Above. 'What will you do all day?'

She taps the side of her nose. 'I have something lined up. 'Mum laughs and leans over and ruffles my hair. 'You look like I just said I was abandoning you forever to do something nefarious. But it's just for a while, and I promise you I won't be doing anything illegal—there will be no more Bad Fairies turning up on my doorstep. Besides, you have a dragon. You can come and check up on me any time.'

'And I hope you do,' Mender interrupts.

'This is a big thing for me, Snake. I had a lot of time to think when I was a prisoner. It's time I stopped blaming everyone else for the horrid things in my life and start taking control. I can do that best if I spend some time finding out who I really am.'

'I get that, sort of,' I say.

'And Princess Petunia has promised that when I'm ready, she will arrange an introduction to my mother's family. When I meet them, do you want to come with me?

I'd almost forgotten I had another set of grandparents out there somewhere. 'That might be nice,' I tell her, not sure if it will be. Pris didn't have much fun meeting all of her family.

'And as for your father and me, we're friends. If there is more than that, well… we'll see with time.'

The door opens, and a young gnome pops a head in. 'Sorry about the tea, Ginth, but the Fieth's called everyone to the main room,' she says.

I bite back a sigh. I can't even get a decent cup of tea before going to yet another meeting.

My young relation leads us through corridors cut into a living tree. As I did last time I was here, I run my hand over the wood and believe I can almost feel my ancestors embrace me.

In the main room, I find a space beside my uncle Earth and his wife, Glisth. They are the only members of my Fieth family who have always been there for me. Earth hugs me, and Glisth passes me a steaming cup of coffee and a hefty slice of banana cake. She shows her love through food, and for once, I am grateful for it.

I have time to eat most of the cake before the Fieth calls the room to order.

There must be about fifty or more gnomes over the age of thirteen here. I had no idea the immediate family was so large.

When we are silent, the Fieth rises to his feet. 'Before we head out into the garden to the children and the feast we have prepared for this day, I have an announcement. This war we fought has shown me I am too old and too tired to run this family. Chroma and I are retiring to the Wyld Woods to live the rest of our days in peace.'

The Fieth holds up his hand to forestall any comments. 'Save your words for later. I will hear you all out. We have a house with many bedrooms picked out. Ginth is coming with us to help us set up and to spend some time with her extended family. After a month or so, I am sure we would love to have visitors, but not before then.'

The room is so silent, you could hear a pin drop.

Beside my grandfather, my father hauls himself to his feet. 'I have a big shadow to fill, but I am happy the first task he set me is a happy one. Let the feasting begin.'

I wait for everyone else to leave before asking Earth, 'Are you and Dad going to stand for the new council? I know Queen Cecily asked Dad to represent the gnomes on the interim one.'

Earth shakes his head. 'Glisth and I are happy in Mawnan. We will return home after the coronation and carry on supporting the creatures in the World Above as best we can.'

'What about Dad?'

Earth glances up, then takes Glisth's hand. 'You'd best ask him, lad. Come, my darling. Let us go and eat before there is nothing left but pickings.'

I stand up to let them past before turning to my father.

'Goodness, son, you have grown since we last saw each other. Trouble seems to agree with you.'

In spite of the warmth radiating from him and the love I find in his eyes, I still feel awkward around my father. 'It has been a difficult time,' I say.

'And it will not be any easier in the months to come.'

'So, are you going to take the position on the interim council?' I ask. It will be odd working with my father, but it might also give us an opportunity to get to know each other better.

'No, son, I am not. The time of the Fieths supporting the monarchy is over. It is time we look to the needs of our own race.'

I have to admit, I'm a little disappointed. 'But can't you do that on the council?'

'Drow is making sure gnomes will have their say, and we will definitely be well represented—I have been speaking with Mender about that. Maybe it is time for the gnomes in the Wyld Woods to stand up.'

'But what will you do?'

'I will be learning the family business and maybe looking at some changes. Some of our less… aboveboard activities no longer seem appropriate in light of Queen Cecily's intentions.'

'You mean her declaration that any gnome who wishes can be unbound?'

'Exactly. I am putting the Fieth resources at the disposal of the council to identify gnomes and organise the transition.'

'Won't that mean we will simply be elves?' I ask.

'I thought so, too, but apparently not. Even though our magic will be unbound, genetically we will still be different, and we have developed our own distinct culture, so we will still be a separate race,' my father explains.

'Good. I really don't see myself as an elf,' I say, and I mean it. When I first found out I had elf blood in my veins, I didn't know how to take it. I believed I didn't fit in anywhere. However, when Queen Cecily made her announcement, it clarified my thinking. I am a gnome and proud of it.

My father rests a hand on my shoulder. 'You have a room here, and I would like you to move back home and spend time with your family when you're not working at the palace.'

The offer is heartfelt, and I'm surprisingly pleased by it. Part of me wants to accept, but I have already made other plans.

'Drow has introduced me to Professor Xander—he specialises in the study of magic at the university—and he has accepted me as a part-time student. Drow also organised a shared suite for me in the dorms there so I will have more time to study'

Sadness passes across my father's eyes, but he pastes a smile on his face.

'I am pleased for you and proud of you, son. You will still have your room here should you need it.'

'Thank you. I am sure there will be weekends where I will want to escape duties and study and just be a gnome.'

'And you will be more than welcome.' He drapes his arm around me and says, 'Come, they can't actually start the feast until I'm there.'

'NOT ONLY DID you keep a whole other world from me, but when I finally turned up here after leading an army to rescue you, you were so busy ruling the realm, you didn't even think to ask if I was alive or dead.'

I've been avoiding this conversation with my parents ever since we reunited because I wasn't sure how to approach it, and my parents have clearly been waiting for me to raise the subject.

So, I've decided on a jokey approach, but I don't quite hit the right note. Instead, I sound kinda hurt and angry. I think Mum senses this isn't easy, because there's no lecture for being childish. Instead, she hands me the strawberry jam I can't quite reach, then takes a sip of her coffee before responding.

'We *had* planned a holiday to Scotland after your graduation, and we were going to stay with Mum and Dad at Urquhart Castle. The idea was to ease you in gently by introducing you to my family first.'

'We thought Maddox and the Unseelie Court might be a bit much for your introduction to the magical world,' my father explains dryly.

I'm not ready to let them off the hook yet. 'Did you really tell Uncle Maddox I would join the court when I was older?'

He stops buttering his toast and glances up, surprise clear in his widening eyes. 'No, of course not. I did say that when your mother and I had to retire from the World Above at the end of a human's natural life, we would likely go to the Unseelie Court because I was not welcome in the World Below.'

'Oh.'

'And before you ask again,' my mother says, 'Am'rena was in constant contact with Am'ratha. I had asked her to help protect you.'

They have an answer for everything, but I'm still angry with them.

Mum places a hand over mine where it rests on the table. 'We tried to protect you from the worst aspects of the World Below long after you were capable of facing them, and for that, I am sorry. I'm also sorry that we were not the ones to introduce you to our extended family. And even more sorry that this meant so many of them kept things from you when telling you would have been a better choice.'

Dad leans around Mum. 'Yes, so much would have been easier for you if they had taken it as our wishes in normal circumstances rather than a royal edict to be obeyed even in extreme situations.'

Their eyes show genuine sorrow, and I can't hold them responsible for what others have done, no matter how much I want to.

'There's still something else bugging you, isn't there?' Mum asks, releasing my hand and turning so her attention is fully on me. 'You have seen how busy things are around here. If we don't deal with it now, I'm not sure when we'll have time together again as a family.'

She is right. Best to get everything into the open. 'I feel like a spare wheel.

You guys have all been so busy, and I haven't been doing anything.

Mum's brows draw together. 'You've had a tough few months while we lazed in luxury. Your father and I thought you would enjoy the break and a chance to catch up with Susan.'

'But I've hardly even seen her. She is busy with Irene and Uncle Maddox setting up the embassy for the Unseelie Court.'

'And to visit Aeron at the hospital,' my dad adds.

'He's healing well, and is already up and about, helping the orderlies out.'

'And spending time with Verona Coronas. I hear she isn't in a good way,' he finishes.

'She can't bear to be here now without Gregor, so has been spending time with Eleanora and her daughter, making plans for creature support in London. Everyone is busy.' I know I sound like a spoilt child, but I am not built for doing nothing.

'So what you telling me is that you're bored,' my mother says, a touch of impatience in her voice.

'Yes, I am, but it's not just that,' I add quickly when I see her frown deepen. 'I've spent weeks championing change in the World Below, only to find that now I have achieved it, I'm no longer needed.'

'Perhaps it's time,' Dad says.

'Time for what?'

'Time for you to return home and begin university as planned,' he says.

I stare at my parents in disbelief. 'You're kidding, right? I can't simply go back and pretend none of this ever happened.'

'We thought you would want a bit of normalcy after this?' Mum says.

Dad follows with 'This isn't anything to do with young Snake, is it?'

My glare hardens. My parents are treating me like the Pris they left behind. She would have wanted home comforts and would have been swayed by her friend, but I am no longer that person. How I wish Percival and Snake were here. They see me as I am, and that always gives me confidence.

My mother's voice breaks into my tumultuous thoughts. 'How do you see things moving forward?'

I shake my head. 'What?'

'I want to know what you would want to do if you could choose anything.' she says.

I want to spend time with Snake, really getting to know him and finding out if what I feel is real. I don't say this, though. Not only would my practical parents wonder what had got into me, but my whole life can't be about what Snake wants. So I take a breath and wait for the answer to come to me.

'I am heir to the throne, which I believe you are turning into a constitutional monarchy.'

'For starters,' Mum responds.

'There is a lot I need to learn about this world, given I didn't grow up here.'

She nods. 'That is also true.'

'So, I think I should stay.'

'Doing what?' my father intervenes. 'You know long term we won't countenance you sitting around all day.'

As if I had even considered that an option.

'What are you going to be doing?' I ask him, sure he would never be a King Consort who spends his time accompanying Mum and making sure she was okay.

'I'm going to work with your uncle and a professor at the university, Xander, contacting the other magical realms and reopening lines of communication that were broken when the elves took over the World Below.'

'You're planning something bigger, though,' I say, suddenly interested.

He grins. 'Professor Xander has a special interest in magic, and we want to see if we can improve magic in our realm and rekindle magic in the World Above. We want to learn from other communities where magic still flourishes both in the creature and human realms.'

Dad's eyes sparkle with excitement, and I'm energised by his enthusiasm. 'Oh, that sounds huge.'

'It is.'

I know I only have to ask, and Dad would include me in his project in a heartbeat. It's amazing, but it's really not my thing.

Mum leans forward. 'You were going to study law. Can we find you something around that?'

'Isn't Drow Fieth leading the group drafting the constitution and reviewing the laws to see which ones will need to be changed?' Dad asks.

Mum chews her bottom lip. 'He is, but Pris is nowhere ready to work on redrafting laws.'

Dad shifts in his seat, suddenly excited about something. 'Drow has a team working for him on the legal side. He doesn't need anyone else for that. But I overheard him and the Chancellor of the University discussing his teaching a new class on constitutional law. He might want someone to help him co-ordinate his two roles until the university term starts—a PA, so to speak.'

Now I'm interested. Drow is a legal mastermind. Even being around him doing menial work for a while would teach me so much.

'I could go and talk to him,' I say.

My father beams. 'I know you're all grown up and saved our bacon, but I didn't like the idea of you being so far away in the World Above.'

I grin. My dad comes across all tough, but he's a marshmallow at heart.

'What about you and your young man?' Mum asks, and my bubble of joy bursts.

'I'm not sure he's my young man anymore. We haven't really spoken since the day of the battle. Every time we try to catch up, he gets called away.'

'These things have a way of sorting themselves out for the better,' Mum says, and that cryptic comment tears at my heart.

We have not been apart for long, but we have not spent enough time together for Mum and Dad to understand how the past few months have changed me. I am no longer their little girl, and what I feel for Snake is no teen crush.

So, I will work with Drow for the moment, if he will have me, until I find what I want to do. And I will not leave my future with Snake to chance. And, in time, Mum and Dad will come to know the adult me.

WHERE TO FROM HERE?

BEING DROW'S ASSISTANT is a mixed blessing. I'm learning so much, but he is ultra-organised and wants things done just so. Like right now, he has me reorganising the papers in his files in the correct order in front of the whole interim council.

I understand that he wants to lay his hand on any document at a moment's notice, but this proceeding is a formality. On the top of every individual's file is their signed confession and their agreement to their punishment, so they're hardly likely to object to anything now.

When I'd mentioned this to Drow a couple of minutes ago, I'd earned a withering glare that then had me worried that he regretted bringing me on board.

'If we always do things the right way every time, we do not have to guess whether or not they will be correct this time,' he had told me.

I hand him back the files just as the conspirators enter the room. They arrange themselves around the lower end of the oval table, facing the members of the interim council. There are a few specialists and assistants like myself and Drow sitting around the walls. When the room falls silent, my mother begins.

'You have all signed confessions attesting to your treasonous actions. And, in consultation with your representatives, we have agreed that there will be no public trials.'

When I'd heard this, I was beyond surprised, especially as Bernais Baaronson was more than happy to live his life in the spotlight. However, Grossman Greene, the elven councillors, and the other governors had persuaded their leader to agree to a private hearing and sentencing.

'In a perfect world,' my mother continues, pulling me back into the room, 'I could trust that, now the line of succession is in place, you will work with us for the good of the worlds.'

Bernais leans forward in his seat, his eyes challenging my mother, but his tone is even when he speaks. 'You will pull our land apart with these changes. The very heart of elven society is here in this room. Elves are the strongest magic users and have been protecting our people for years.'

'I believe you are wrong in your thinking, Bernais. Your view of the world does not acknowledge the contribution all creatures make to our community,' my mother responds.

Tensing, I await an outburst from the creature who has dictated the course of my life with his bigotry and hatred of other creatures.

Instead of railing against my mother, he slumps back in his seat. 'You won the war, and, as history shows, the victor is always right and the looser is always evil.'

Mum runs a hand through her hair, signalling to those who know her well that she is uncomfortable. 'I wish life were that black and white, cousin, but it is lived in the grey. There are many, some of whom are around this table, who would have liked nothing better than for all of you to be executed publicly for the damage you have brought to our realm.'

Some of the accused gasp, and a few mutter objections. However, Mum holds up her hand before any of the traitors can protest. 'Others of us choose to believe that you were trying to fix some very real problems in the World Below, just perhaps not in the way your fellow creatures appreciated. It is for this reason we have agreed on the following sentence for your treasonous actions.'

This is Drow's cue. He stands up and reads from the signed declaration. 'For your actions against creature-kind, each of you will lose your title and rank. You will be magically bound to your lands for a period of fifty years. Your families will go unpunished, except that because you have lost your titles, you cannot pass them on to your heirs.'

'Fifty years is a long time,' one of the advocates says.

'Not long enough,' Snake mutters under his breath.

'Perhaps,' Drow says, 'but the council deems that by then, the coming changes in the World Below will have been around for long enough that any trouble you stir up will fall on deaf ears.' He takes his seat, and Mum continues.

'The council removed your titles from the rolls. If you attempt to break the spell keeping you on your lands, then you will be banished from this world and your lands sold. The gold will be deposited so you can use it to fund your life elsewhere.'

'This all seems so civilised,' Grossman says, before quickly adding, 'Not that I'm complaining. But it would have been easier to execute us?'

I know the answer to this because I'd asked Drow the same question. This was before I understood that he considered himself my mentor and, as such, I would never get another answer out of him again.

'You already know why,' he'd said.

'Is this some kind of a test?'

'Perhaps.'

It had taken a while, but I finally came up with something from my history classes at school. 'Because they would be martyrs. And, as martyrs, they could be a rallying point for their followers.'

'Very good,' Drow had said, and I'd beamed with pride.

However, this was not the answer my mother gave to Grossman. Her response was more positive.

'We all want what is best for the World Below, and the new government does not wish to punish those who offer alternative points of view. For our new council to work, we must welcome questions and opposition. Therefore, your sentence is not for treason but for promoting hate and violence against other creatures, hence the lighter sentence. This sends a message that, while we appreciate differing opinions, we strongly oppose violence.

Grossman Green nods at my mother, then turns to Snake. 'Thank you,' he mouths, and I wonder what that is about.

As Bernais and his followers are led from the room, I lean forward and whisper to Snake, 'If you're free, perhaps we could get some lunch somewhere private.'

He grins at me. 'As it happens—'

'Drow would like to go over the details of the interim governing document— he prefers we don't call it a constitution—before we all formally sign it tomorrow,' my mother interrupts.

I shoot a withering look at my mentor, who does not appear the least apologetic. 'You do not have to stay for this if you have something better to do,' he says.

'But *I* do,' Snake mutters.

I sigh and sit back in my chair as servers bring in food and beverages so we can work through lunch, Snake leans over and rubs my leg in sympathy. Sometimes helping to right the world can be so frustrating.

RUNNING A FINGER around under the high collar of my suit jacket, I groan inwardly—I can't believe I'm dressed like a stuffed turkey again. Drow assures me I look the part of an ambassador in the long brocade jacket over a white linen shirt and slim fitting trousers, but the whole thing is itchy and uncomfortable. I guess the coronation of a queen will not happen every day, but today I'm even more aware that by remaining here, I'm giving up jeans and T-shirts for the foreseeable future.

Although I could have taken a position on the dais as a member of the interim council and representative of the Dragon Queen, I chose to stand with my father—the Fieth and titular head of the gnomes. We have a front-row view, but at least no one is staring at us.

Along the back of the dais, the Royal Guard has arranged itself. It is odd not to see Fairburn there. Rumour has it, the death of his Queen devastated him, and after her funeral, he retired to Aeron's property to mourn.

Speaking of Aeron, he stands among the guards. It seems he has decided to stay in the Capitol and continue to guard Pris. When I catch his eye, he sends me a hip-level finger wave. Georgio glares it him. Aeron grins back, not scared of the newly appointed Guard Captain in the least. A trumpet sounds, and Aeron immediately stands at attention—he'd never let Pris down by fooling about.

The Royal family walk in procession from the back of the room, led by the Queen and King Consort. Princess Petunia follows them with an elf I assume is her husband, Duke Anatola. Theirs was an arranged marriage, but the story goes that after he arrived from the mountains of Russia, they were soon besotted with each other.

Escorting Princess Irene is her brother, Prince Wilfred. The two look so alike, they could almost be twins. Next in line is King Maddox, proudly walking beside Pris, his head held high as he escorts her to the dais. She is so beautiful, she takes my breath away. Although she'll no doubt hate being dressed for the occasion as much as I do, she looks every bit the princess in her deep purple Edwardian-style dress and her hair piled on top of her head.

As she passes by, I catch a glimpse of her footwear and grin. Underneath her dress, she is wearing the World Below version of a trainer. As I applaud her personal style, the ache inside me grows. I worry she is now too far out of my reach. Maybe it's a blessing we have spent little time alone together because she couldn't tell me it's over, which grants me extra time to emotionally prepare for the hurt that's bound to come. My father drops an arm over my shoulders, and I'm grateful for his silent support.

I am so focused on Pris, I almost miss Elias's entrance. He had been Chancellor for so long, it is easy to forget he is a prince. He is accompanied by a stunning elven woman and two elven girls around my age. The girls are wearing simple outfits, and their facial expressions show their displeasure at being on display.

Once the royal party is in place, the interim council files in from a side door. Percival sends me a meaningful stare, and I grin back. This is a World Below celebration, and the Dragon Queen agreed with me that as a representative of the World Between, I should take a back seat.

When everyone is on the dais, Queen Cecily steps forward and stands in front of the throne. Elias and Percival take the trappings of office from servants, then join her. Elias places the crown on her head, and Percival hands her the staff of justice.

Then Elias says something that I am sure is meaningful, and so does Queen Cecily, but my eyes are all for Pris, and I don't hear a word of it. In fact I don't hear anything until Pris steps forward.

'I formally introduce my daughter, Princess Priscilla, heir to the throne.'

Pris takes her place to the right of the throne. Then Princess Petunia steps forward.

'I formally and irrevocably renounce my place in the succession of the throne of the World Below and my allegiance to the Seelie Court. Although a part of my heart will always remain here, I do this to support my husband, the Keeper of the Pathway for the Unseelie Court.'

'Know that you and your husband will always be welcome in the Seelie Court, Aunt.'

Princess—no, just plain Petunia now—returns to her place by her husband.

Princess Irene now steps forward. 'I formally and irrevocably renounce my place in the throne's succession of the World Below, and my allegiance to the Seelie Court. I grew up in the Unseelie Court and hope to best serve both our worlds in my role as an ambassador for them here in the World Below.'

The ex-princess joins her mother.

'I now formally introduce my brother, Prince Wilfred and my cousin, Prince Elias, second and third in line to the throne, respectively.'

The two princes join Pris.

'And finally, I formally introduce you to my cousins, Princesses Ember and Eloise. They are the last of the line of royal blood and will be fourth and fifth in the line of succession.'

'Who are they?' I whisper to my father.

'Elias's twin daughters. They have always preferred a life away from court, so I cannot imagine they are enjoying this.'

The newly crowned Queen takes her seat on the throne, and there ends the formal announcements. Although the council had wanted Queen Cecily to renounce the Baaronson family line verbally and declare they have been removed forever from the line of succession, she had decided that declaring who was included in the line was enough for this gathering. The formal disinheritance was a matter of written record and would have to do.

A priest of the goddess enters and formally blesses the royal family, then wishes Queen Cecily a long and prosperous rule. Once he has cleared the stage, Queen Cecily stands up. The room is silent. This is the first time most of those here have heard her speak, and there is much riding on her words, as she wants to begin bringing the creatures of the World Below together.

'This is odd for all of us,' she starts, and there is a ripple of displeasure round the room.

'This is not how a Queen speaks to her subjects,' I hear the woman behind me whisper.

In my head, I tell her that this opening is the point. Queen Cecily aims to be a ruler like no other.

'I believed I had hundreds of years before I would be called to the throne, and many of you thought I would never be here at all.'

The room falls silent again.

'I come to this position after a civil war—however brief—that has torn not only our realm but families apart—mine included. My job will be to rebuild our world so it is better able to weather the storms of progress in the future. To do that we must ensure every adult creature has a say in how that is done. I will not be ruling with absolute authority, guided by a council. I will chair a council of elected representatives who will make decisions on your behalf.'

Despite the rumours, the surprised looks in the room confirm that the idea is unsettling to many. And if they find that confronting, the next part about creature equality is going to blow their minds.

A loud *crash*! echoes through the cavernous space.

Every head turns to the back of the room—to the source of the interruption. A tall, imperious, supercilious figure moves into the aisle between the seats and saunters towards the dais. From the corner of my eye, I clock the guards moving closer to the royal family while still others leave the dais. The identity of the intruder has my hackles rising.

The strutting peacock stops when he recognises me. 'I see you didn't make the cut, Snake. What a shame. Guess that leaves the way open for me.'

He turns his attention to Queen Cecily and says, 'Hello, Mother-in-Law.'

No one moves. The audacity of this unknown elf has them all frozen in place.

Queen Cecily raises a disdainful eyebrow. 'Do I know you?'

'You have not yet had the pleasure, but I am here to rectify that. I am Lord Dinian, Heir to the Unseelie Court, and betrothed of Princess Priscilla.'

A growl rises from the pit of my stomach, and it is all I can do not to leap over my father and wring the neck of that duplicitous creep. Where had he come from? And how did he get in here? I might not kill him, but I can't just stand here and let him preen.

As I slowly rise to my feet, I glance at Pris. Her lips are curled with distaste, and her fists are clenched as though she'd like nothing better than to punch that smug look from Dinian's face. She can't do anything from where she is, but I can.

'Dinian, I thought you would have grown a spine by now, but you've obviously been hiding while the rest of us have been fighting for what we believe in.'

'My court is the *Unseelie Court.* I saw no reason to get involved in your little squabble.'

Ugh, he's so... so...

King Maddox steps forward. 'Dinian, this is not the time or the place. Let us retire where we can discuss things in private.'

Dinian pulls out a gun and points it at Pris. 'No, Maddox. I will not listen to your honeyed words again. I. Am. Owed. Her.'

I launch myself forward, placing my body between Pris and that gun, then stare at the weapon and freeze. I didn't think this through. I have no plan.

Mandor appears from nowhere, and before the elf can use the weapon he's pointing, the witch opens a portal. Dinian half turns at the noise, and Aeron moves with a blur of speed. He pushes Dinian through the opening, which Mandor snaps shut behind him.

In the meantime the guards have bustled the royal party from the dais. It seems the formal part of the proceedings are over. Not exactly the ending we expected, but Queen Cecily still has a chance to win over hearts and minds at the reception. And I might get some time with Pris—once I manage to get my pounding heart under control.

Unfortunately, Pris, Aeron, Mandor, and Maddox are not in the reception rooms when we arrive. I join Irene and Petunia, introducing them to my father. As Drow enters, I scan the room again for Pris. Irene leans in and says, 'She won't be coming. She has gone with the others to sort out young Dinian.'

Yet another opportunity gone. Although my head is starting to tell me we're not meant to be, my heart refuses to move on.

THE WORLD BETWEEN

STANDING BETWEEN ELEANORA and Nisha, I watch the great and the good of creature society enter the ballroom. As a sprite, I stand tall and proud to be part of this moment in our history even though I think our inclusion is long overdue. There are a few brownies, sprites, pixies, and gnomes here, but too few compared to elves, witches, goblins, and dwarves. This will change. I will see to that—I promised the grove I would.

Ed'rima had dropped me at the grove after our audience with the Dragon Queen. She insisted I needed time to recover, although my thoughts were of singing my father's spirit to rest—and of course testing my ability to be at one with the forest.

It was odd being in the grove without Nisha, who still had work to do in the Capitol, but the gap her presence left was more than filled by the grove itself—my home sang to me for the first time in hundreds of years. Tears form in my eyes even now as I remember the joy rushing through me.

The elders soon swept my plans aside. 'We are pleased you are back with us and able to commune.'

'Thank you,' I had said. 'I hope to bring Nisha back and settle here once the new government is in place.'

'And you would be welcome, but we want you to consider a different option. You have been in the world for some time now and know how it works, yet you also know what it means to be a sprite. We would like you to put yourself forward for election to the new council.'

My first thought had been to reject their request, but my brother Emrys had taken me aside. 'Our father foresaw this, and the spirits of the grove sense it is right. Please, think about it.'

Nisha's hand on my arm draws me from my thoughts. 'Surely you should do something other than stand here daydreaming.'

'Perhaps, but let us simply enjoy being here for a while before I do my duty and greet the members of the court.'

She smiles at me, and my heart leaps. My time in the grove was nothing compared to last night. Ed'rima had come and taken me back to the palace so I could prepare for today. When I entered the rooms I had been allocated, I found Nisha had transformed the bedroom into a grove away from home.

She had removed my bed and replaced it with trees. All right, the trees are in pots, and the moss around the base will require a lot of upkeep and will probably have to be changed frequently, but it is a grove. And in that grove, I can sleep in sprite form and recharge my energy.

Last night, bathed in candlelight and connected with the trees, Nisha and I had finally cemented our bond—and it was life altering. Being fully bonded is a transformation like no other. It is not that we became one, but that we became three. There is Nisha, there is me, and there is us. When we choose, we open the connection our bond created and share our essence, and we are one.

The memory brings a smile to my lips until Nisha digs me in the ribs and whispers, 'If you are going to think inappropriate thoughts, then perhaps it is time we mingled.'

Eleanora chokes back a laugh, but she schools her face as Queen Cecily heads our way, leading the two newly anointed Princesses of the Royal Blood.

'Eleanora, Percival, and Nisha, may I present Princess Ember and Princess Eloise.'

'Please,' Princess Ember says, colour infusing her cheeks, 'just Ember will do.'

'It is a pleasure to meet you, Princess Eloise and… Ember,' I smile kindly at the princess. She reminds me a little of Pris when I first met her.

As we form a group, the two princesses position themselves near Nisha.

Queen Cecily starts, 'The twins are studying healing at the university and asked especially to be introduced to you, Nisha.'

It is my bonded mate's turn to colour. She is not used to being the centre of attention and though she no longer shies away from it, nor does she court it.

Princess Ember steps closer. 'We have been told that you might have time on your hands now that your patients have been moved to the hospital in the Capitol. So… Eloise and I thought you might consider teaching a semester class in sprite healing techniques. We have already spoken to the Head of Faculty, and he is quite excited by the idea.'

Nisha takes my hand and through our bond asks, *What do you think, Percival? Should I do this?*

Not used to having her in my head, I'm also not sure I am in a position to advise her. She loves the grove, but from the way she helped during the war, it is clear she has so much to offer the wider world. Perhaps this would be good for her.

You would make a wonderful teacher, but it is up to you. We think there will not be full elections for perhaps ten or so months, so I will be in the Capitol longer than a semester.

Nisha nods at me, but still chooses her words carefully before answering, 'I would be honoured to take up such a role, but I have other commitments. I am training two students in the grove, and I cannot leave them for that long.'

'I would be happy to sponsor them for entry into the university. That way they could continue to study,' Queen Cecily says.

A ghost of a smile hovers at the edge of Nisha's mouth, telling me that this is only part of her plan.

'That is very generous of you, Your Majesty, but I am afraid I could not ask such young sprites to spend so much time away from the grove. The Capitol is not a healthy place for our kind to live.'

Queen Cecily taps her lips in thought. 'I believe you have transformed your quarters into a sort of grove.'

'That is merely a stop gap, Your Highness. For sprites to feel welcome and at home in the Capitol, we really need our own grove here. It would also help me better teach the healing practices of our kind.'

Queen Cecily smiles, appreciating how deftly Nisha has handled the situation.

'Cousin Cecily, this is such a great idea. Ember and I would love to help Healer Nisha establish a grove in the Capitol,' Princess Eloise gushes.

Now Queen Cecily is grinning. 'I am going to like having you around, Nisha, although I sense I am going to have to watch myself. I will discuss this with the interim council, but I am sure we will be able to accommodate your request. The Capitol should have a place for all creatures to feel at home and supported.'

As Queen Cecily leads her cousins away, I lean close to Nisha and say, 'I'm not sure I am the best one of the two of us to be sitting on the interim council. You are a much better politician'

Nisha smiles a shy smile. 'I think the creatures of the Capitol should watch out for both of us. Together we will ensure sprites are seen in this new world we are making.'

BEGINNINGS AND ENDINGS

EUGENIA'S SECOND-STORY apartment overlooks a leafy square in the Witch's district. Normally, it is more of an office cum dormitory. Tonight it is alight with candles, and a large circular dining table laden with food fills the room. The wine has been flowing, as has the conversation as the three witch sisters, Drow, Heart, Mandor, Nisha, and myself eat, drink, and celebrate our being together.

As Drow and Genie clear away the last course, I study the usually spartan room, noting little changes here and there. I am sure that painting on the wall used to be in Ellie's bedroom in Wimbledon. And that armchair by the window definitely was not here last time I visited.

'Ellie?'

'Mmm?' my friend responds, not taking her eyes from the pie Drow is carrying into the room.

'Have you something you wish to tell me?'

A cheeky grin transforms Ellie's face as she turns towards me. 'Perhaps.'

'Is it something about your staying in the World Below?' I guess.

She barks out a laugh. 'You are too observant, old friend. Yes, I am staying.'

'But what about your role as the Witch of Wimbledon? Who will look after creatures in London?' Eleanora has been The Witch of Wimbledon for so long, I cannot see anyone else ever filling her kitchen.

'Mae has been training for years. She is ready,' Ellie says.

'Won't she be busy, what with the shop and—'

'And filling your pocket with cake?' Ellie teases.

It is true, I had set up a small portal back to a room in Ellie's house accessed via my trouser pocket. Mae is good enough to ensure it is always stocked with cake and tea. However, that was not what I meant.

'And your grandson,' I say a little tartly.

'Mae is going to be working with Verona. Unbeknown to me, the two have been talking about setting up a creature way station in London for years. The health food shop in Wimbledon will be a contact point, and Verona wants to turn the elven house in Grosvenor Square into a kind of hostel,' Ellie explains.

I suddenly feel very old. 'It seems the younger generation have it all in hand.'

'They do. And that frees me up for some new challenges.' Ellie passes me a plate filled with apple pie and ice-cream.

I place the dessert in front of me, sneak a quick glance Mandor's way, then ask, 'And do those plans include anyone else?'

Ellie eats some pie before answering, her face thoughtful. 'Possibly, or yes, and depending on why you're asking. I will work with Cecily and Mandor to find places for the ex-wizards who do not want to return to the order.'

I raise an eyebrow. 'I thought the order would disband because the new constitution allows any creature to study and use higher magic.'

Ellie shakes her head. 'No, some like the quiet of the Wizard Order, and some are not happy that the study and use of higher magic outside of the order will have to be licensed. So, a few are returning and taking their vows.'

'And I take it from your new role, not all of them want to study higher magic with Mandor to get a licence?'

'No, not all of them, especially the younger ex-wizards born into the order. We want to find a place for all of them. In fact, one of them, Alyce, is going to the World Above with Genie, isn't she?' Ellie turns to her sister.

Genie looks up from her dessert, swallows her mouthful, and says, 'What? Alyce? Yes, I am pleased she is coming with me to train as the new Hag in the Bog, as Pris once called me.'

Effie joins the conversation. 'And you'll find one for me too, won't you?'

I do not believe what I am hearing. 'You are all retiring? But you are in the prime of your lives.'

Effie barks out a laugh. 'Retiring from our roles in the World Above, but we're not going out to pasture yet. When I've trained a replacement, I will work with Petunia setting up a community where human magic workers can live in peace. Loch Ness is so remote—it's a perfect place for them to gather. Maddox has agreed to support us as part of his efforts to improve the creation of magic in the World Above.'

'So you won't return to the World Below?' I ask.

Effie's eyes drift to Drow, then back to me. 'There is nothing here for me. At least not now that Drow and Elias have rekindled their friendship.'

My eyes widen, and Effie's mouth twists into a sad smile. How long has she known?

'Oh, Effie…,'

'I have always known his heart lay elsewhere, just not where until recently. So, although I may visit sometimes, I will pledge myself to the Unseelie Court,' Effie says.

'And what will you do when you retire?' I ask Genie to give Effie some space.

My witch friend beams. 'I am going to do what I always wanted to. I am going home to help Mamma tend to magic in the Wyld Woods.'

'And keep an eye on Bernais,' Drow adds.

Genie nods. 'Yes, that too.'

There is a lull in the proceedings, and Mandor chooses that moment to push back his chair and stand up. 'Who knew when we fought the blight and challenged the council that we would end up here, hundreds of years later, having finally achieved what we once set out to do? I toast us, my friends, and I toast the World Below—may we in the World Below finally be as one.'

We raise our glasses and drink, and I can't help but think that this really is the end of something. It's a beginning, too, but it is the end of our youthful dreams as we step up and take on the mantel of community elders.

As if we all sense the mood has changed, the evening winds up. Nisha and I say our goodbyes, and, feeling a little melancholy, I suggest we walk home via the university.

As we enter the courtyard, the ancient oaks whisper to me. A welcoming hum fills my ears, and tears fill my eyes as I send soothing greetings back. As always I feel sad that the song of the trees in the Capitol is but a shadow of the music their counterparts make in the grove.

A long time ago, in what seems to be another lifetime, I came here and listened to the song of the oaks, and it almost broke my heart. When I had attempted to commune with the trees, it had almost crushed my spirit. I place my hand against the trunk of the closest tree, letting it know I am here and it is loved. I smile as the tree returns my affection.

Nisha appears oblivious to the ancient oaks and our shared emotions as she studies the buildings surrounding us. 'I never studied here like you, yet I will begin teaching students next week,' she says, amazement and excitement glinting in her eyes.

'You are a great healer, but I am sure you are an even better teacher.'

She turns to me. 'I want to teach, Percival. In my bones, I feel this is right for me. If I stay after this semester to teach and help sprites who want a future in the Capitol, will that work for you? Will it work for the life we wish to build?'

She has had a calling, and she is asking if I will support her. Part of me desperately wants to go home to the grove, to make up for lost time with my family and to find a role there. However, the elders and the grove wish a different path for me.

'If you want to be here, Nisha, then we will be here.'

'You will stand for council?'

'I will.'

'And together we will make a difference for sprite-kind.'

The song of the trees is thrumming through me now, as if agreeing with our decision. I take Nisha's hand and place it beside mine on the wood. She closes her eyes and we become one as we change and merge with the trees. Moving from tree to tree, we begin the process of healing.

AFTER CLOSING THE leather straps on the bag containing the clothing and supplies my father and mother had thoughtfully provided for me, I lean the neck of the guitar Brynn allowed me to keep on top of it before turning to my father.

'I guess that's it, then.'

'I hope you left something here just in case you want to stay the occasional night,' Dad says, clearly trying to keep the tone casual, but he is unable to hide the hope in his eyes.

I smile. 'Of course. Everyone has made it clear that Sunday dinners are an open invitation, and I'm sure I'll need something decent to eat if most of my meals are coming from the university canteen.'

Dad's brows draw into a frown. 'You don't have to eat there. I have opened an account for you. There's enough in there to cover fees and some spending money too.'

I flush and fiddle with the straps on my bag. My father has been trying for years to find ways to support my mother and me, so I know this means a lot to him. I give him this moment and keep the fact the dragons are paying me a salary to myself.

'Thank you,' I say. 'It'll take a weight off my mind. Professor Xander suggested I apply for the position of his research assistant to cover fees, but

I was wondering how I was going to fit that in with my duties at court.'

My father beams, and I'm pleased I kept my mouth shut.

A face appears over my father's shoulder. Dad steps aside, and Drow enters. 'The carriage is downstairs, if you're ready.'

I nod briefly, but I'm not. Over the past couple of months, I have done so much, grown up so much, but this is too like leaving home for the first time. My palms are sweaty, and I'm suddenly finding it hard to breathe.

As if sensing my unease, Dad picks up the guitar, leaving the bag for me, and leads the way downstairs. Drow follows, catching us up at the door. I'm almost relieved to find Earth and Glisth standing outside, waiting for us.

'I always imagined this day would happen in the World Above,' Earth says, wiping a tear from his eye.

Glisth draws me into a hug, then hands me a paper bag. I catch a whiff of chocolate, and my stomach rumbles appreciatively. 'A little something to tide you over until Sunday.'

Drow places my luggage in the horse-drawn carriage and follows it inside.

'Bye, Dad.' I give him a quick hug, then get inside before I lose my nerve.

Dad leans his head in through the window. 'We are here if you need us.'

Drow snorts. 'He will have me close by should he run into trouble.'

Dad and I exchange a knowing glance. For all his best intentions, Drow is often too caught up in his own world to remember where he is, let alone care for someone else.

The ride to the university is short. In fact, I could easily have walked it except Drow had rented a carriage to take his books and offered me a lift. As he had been so good about arranging rooms for me at the last minute, I felt I had to accept.

I regret my decision as soon as we arrive. The few students mingling in the courtyard stop what they are doing and watch our progress. They follow the carriage to the main entrance to see what is going on. So much for staying under the radar here.

Oblivious to the stir we're causing, Drow sweeps through the vestibule, then up a flight of stairs, and I follow in his wake. 'These rooms belong to those with places sponsored by the Crown,' Drow tells me. 'Nisha's trainees will have the suite beside yours.' He points at a door as we pass before stopping at the next one and opening it. 'You know, this is the very same suite Eleanora and Percival had when they attended the university.

'Cool,' I say, stepping inside. 'I so want Percival's room.'

Opposite me are two sets of windows overlooking the courtyard with a small dining table set between them. To the left is a sofa and two armchairs in front of a fireplace. On the far side of the fireplace is a door, and there is another directly opposite.

'His was on the right,' Drow tells me. 'And it looks like your roommate is not here yet, so the room is all yours.'

I cross the room and open the door to peek inside. As I do, a porter arrives with my bags and bundles past Drow.

'It looks like you're set, Snake, and I had best go and settle in. I need to be ready for classes starting tomorrow, and I still have so much to do. Do you want me to come back and take you to the dining room for dinner?'

'Will you be eating there?'

'Goodness no. I will dine in my rooms.'

'Then I will be fine.'

Drow seems reluctant to leave. 'I am sure your roommate should arrive soon. I expected them to be here already. They are cutting it a bit fine.'

'Drow, go. I'll be okay.'

My uncle turns somewhat reluctantly. 'I will.. um, check on you later?'

'All right,' I say as he shuts the door behind him.

Returning to my room, I look out the small window into the courtyard. It is strangely comforting that Percival probably stood here and did the same thing.

I unpack my belongings and set up my desk, and the bell still hasn't rung for dinner. I pick up the guitar, strum a few chords, tune it, then strum again. Before I know it, I'm playing the Extreme song 'More Than Words'— a song I associate with Pris.

Alone in this room, I indulge my sense of loss and allow myself to mourn the closeness we once had and are never likely to have again. I let myself have this quiet moment to admit how much I miss her.

I'M RUNNING SO late. My meeting with Mum and Dad took longer than I'd anticipated, but I wanted to get things sorted today. It had taken a while, but they finally agreed in principle to my setting up a legal-aid clinic for the creator creatures who can't afford lawyers, provided I get Drow to supervise it.

The idea had come to me as I listened to yet another creature gush over Drow and Percival and how they had changed the law on behalf of creator creatures centuries ago. It saddened me to think little had changed for them since then. It turns out finding my calling in the World Below was as simple as listening and applying a World Above solution.

As I push open the door, the sounds of a song drift my way. I close my eyes and allow a little hope to enter my heart. Hope that I haven't left it too late. Hope that he still plays this song for me.

I wait for the music to finish, then drop my bag on the floor. Before I can make it across the room, the door to the right opens.

'Hi, I'm….'

'Snake Fieth, pleased to meet you. I'm Priscilla Crown, but you can call me Pris.'

He runs his hand through his hair, which is a little long—just the way I like it—and smiles tentatively. 'I know who you are. I thought you were my roommate.'

His eyes drift to the bag on the floor, then widen a little as they return to me.

'Hope you don't mind. I pulled some strings with Drow. You know Percival—'

'And Eleanora used to share here.'

'I bags Perc—' I peer past him through to the bedroom. 'You already have, haven't you. Now I'm stuck with Eleanora's room. She's probably booby-trapped it especially for me. I knew I should have gotten here sooner.'

Snake is silent. He just stands there staring at me. Am I too late? He's changed his mind these past few days. I tried to find time to talk with him, to let him know what I'm thinking, but it was like the universe was always working against us, keeping us apart.

'You pulled strings with Drow?' His voice is quiet and even, and it's maddening because it gives nothing away.

'Yes. He's sponsoring me to study creature law here. He and Mum thought it would be useful in case I become Queen—if they can't find some way to get me out of it before then.'

Is it that? The whole royal thing again? Dammit, if I don't want to do it, how can I expect Snake to take it on? Maybe I can convince him it won't impact us. I step towards him. He doesn't move away, but he looks… bemused.

'So, you're staying in the World Below? I thought….'

Blast all of this, it's too much like a trite romance novel. Will they, won't they? This could go on forever, and I won't wait that long.

'I thought you said you chose me. Then you turned up as the Dragon Queen's representative to the council, and I thought you had decided on a different path. Then my mother reminded me of how difficult it is to turn the Queen of Dragons down and said that I should give you a chance to explain. Then things got away from us, and there never seemed to be any time to talk. And I was aware that I never said the words back to you and that you probably thought I didn't care. And my whole future was up in the air, and my family thought I might want to go back home, but I knew you would be staying, and, well….'

Goddess, I'm blabbering like a fool. I suck in air and try to calm my racing heart. 'I heard you were going to be staying in these rooms, and I pulled some strings, and here I am.'

'Tell him the words, Pris,' says a voice from the other side of the door.

'Aeron, you said you'd wait in your room across the hall until I called you,' I groan in exasperation.

Snake stares at the door, a smile tugging at the corner of his lips. 'Aeron's here?'

'Yeah, Mum insisted I have a guard, and he volunteered.'

'He'll blend right in,' Snake jokes.

I smile, the tension leaving me a little. 'He wanted to stay in the Capitol. Something to do with an ex-princess he's sweet on.'

'That's private,' comes a shout through the door.

'If you don't want to hear me talking about you, you should have done what we agreed in the first place.'

Seconds later, a door slams, and I laugh. Not that Aeron's absence makes this whole situation easy. It's just so much harder with an audience.

I turn back to Snake, trying to read his expression, worrying I've said too much. I'll wait for him to make the next move.

He does, sort of. He takes a couple of steps and picks up my bag and carries it towards the other bedroom door, and I follow. As we pass the window, I make out the figures of two dragons perched on top of the opposite building. Really, is nothing private?

Snake opens the door and says, 'We'd best check for booby traps.'

I flick my hand in a go-away motion, knowing full well the dragons can see me with their extra keen eyes.

I follow Snake into a spartan room containing only a plain wooden bed, chest of drawers, desk, chair, and wardrobe. I have nothing with me to make it more homely, but I guess we all have to start somewhere.

'Dinner will be soon. I'll let you get unpacked.'

Snake moves to pass me, and I grab his arm, spinning him around to face me. If he wants to be friends, I will work with that, but I have to at least try for more. Aeron is right, I have to say the words.

'Snake, I choose us. I. Choose. Us.'

Time freezes, and I am not sure which way this will go. A moan rises from inside Snake, and I don't know exactly how it happens, but I'm in his arms and pulled tightly against his chest. As his lips press to mine, I have one thought—I am home.

WE SHOULD GIVE them privacy now, Ed'rathe.

You should teach the princess better shielding. Every dragon in the realms will know they fully bonded today.

Come, it is time to return home. They will call us of they need us.

Am'ratha takes to the sky. With one last glance at the embracing couple, her brother joins her.

THE END

THE
WORLD
BELOW

ACKNOWLEDGEMENTS

THE WORLD BELOW has been a wild ride. Starting with the USA Today Bestselling Realm of Darkness Box-set containing The World Below, through to the mammoth last book in the series, The World Between. I've fallen in love with the characters in this world, and I shall miss them terribly, although I already have plans for some of them….

I couldn't have done this without an amazing support team, starting with Creating Ink, and especially Sali Benbow-Powers who helped me realise my vision. Then there's the team at Hot Tree Editing, and McKinley Hellennes Krantz for improving my storytelling and making it sparkle.

I have also been so lucky with the creative input from; anabazel, who drew the original covers, Kim at Kila Designs, who created the omnibus covers and the internals for the printed editions, and Selina Fenech who added her special edges flourish on the hardcover edition. You have all made my words appear stunning.

As always, my love and thanks to my moral support, Jim, and my son, Sam for putting up with me when I hide away to finish a book. Without them I wouldn't eat, and I'd miss every deadline. And to Trouble and Lola for keeping me company when I write, and for instructing me in the ways of animals.

Finally, thank you for reading my musings. The love for this series has overwhelmed me. I especially want to thank those readers who tracked me down at events for the latest instalment—you make writing worthwhile. If you've enjoyed these books, please leave a review on your favourite book site.

ABOUT THE AUTHOR

VIVIENNE HAS BEEN writing books since she was fifteen years old, but only friends and family were allowed to read them. Forced to give up work because of family commitments she was encouraged by friends and family to finally put some of her writing out there for others to read.

In the real world after leaving university with a BA in History and Politics she worked as a Personnel Officer, an Office Manager, a Project Manager, a DBA and IT Manager then as a Business and Data Analyst, adding an MSC in Information Systems along the way. In her world she continued to write.

Born in Invercargill (New Zealand), she has lived in; Dunedin (New Zealand), London (England), Petersfield (England) and currently lives with her husband and son, their dog Trouble and kitten Lola in Sydney (Australia).

If you are interested in her future releases, or simply want to find out more about her books, you can find Vivienne at **www.viviennelfraser.com.au** or on Facebook at **www.facebook.com/vivienneleefraser**